The L and the
FOUND

Also by Cat Clarke

ENTANGLED

TORN

UNDONE

A KISS IN THE DARK

The LOST and the FOUND

CAT CLARKE

Quercus

First published in Great Britain in 2015 by

Quercus Publishing Ltd
Carmelite House
50 Victoria Embankment
London EC4Y 0DZ

An Hachette UK company

A CIP catalogue record for this book is available
from the British Library

PB 978 1 84866 395 4
EBOOK 978 1 84866 825 6

10 9 8 7 6 5 4 3 2 1

Typeset by Nigel Hazle

Printed and bound in Great Britain by Clays Ltd, St Ives plc

For Julia Churchill

Chapter 1

She knows. She definitely knows.

I'm not sure *how* she knows. I'm not stupid enough to keep a diary, and I'm not one of those weirdos who's all Mum's-my-best-friend-and-we-tell-each-other-everything. Perhaps it's some kind of sixth sense, unique to mothers?

It's there in her eyes every time she looks at me. The problem is, I can't tell how she feels about it. Why can't that show up in her eyes too? Is she angry? Disappointed? Disapproving? Resigned? A little bit proud?

'How's Martha's mum getting on at work? Have they announced the redundancies yet?'

It's a trap. Classic. Of course there's no way I'm falling for it. I shrug. 'Dunno. She came in pretty late last night. I think she went out for drinks after her evening class.' I sip my tea, cool as you like.

'Martha says she's been pretty stressed about it though.'

Mum nods. She knows when she's beaten. 'It must be tough.'

'They're loaded though, aren't they? Martha's dad earns enough for both of them. I don't know why she bothers working in the first place.'

This was the wrong thing to say. I wouldn't normally be so careless, but I'm exhausted. Mum's big time into feminism and equal opportunities and not relying on men. Funny thing is, I agree with her, but I'd never tell *her* that. Arguing is much more fun. Mum's not biting today though. She's obviously got other things on her mind.

'Are you OK, Mum?' I try not to ask more than three times a day, but it's a habit. One that I learned at a very early age. When she retreated into herself, into that hellish world inside her head, sometimes it was the only way I could get her to talk to me. I never believed the answer though, which was usually the same, no matter what sort of day it was: 'I'm fine, love.'

There's no deviation from the script today, which is oddly reassuring. I was half expecting her to come out with something like 'No, I'm not OK, thanks for asking. My daughter lied to me about where she was

2

last night so that she could go and lose her virginity to Thomas Bolt in the back of a van.'

There's a newspaper lying face down on the kitchen table. I hadn't noticed it before, because I was too busy trying to work out how I feel about losing my virginity to Thomas Bolt in the back of a van.

All I can see is the sports page: some team beat some other team and some guy scored more points than he'd ever scored before. But I know the kind of thing I'll see if I flip the newspaper over. That's why Mum is giving me all these weird looks. That's why she put the newspaper down as soon as I came into the kitchen; she doesn't want me to see it.

In a normal house — in Martha's house and Thomas's house and houses all over the country — a newspaper is just that: some paper with news in it. Wars and politics and prize-winning giant marrows. In our house — our anything-but-normal house — a newspaper is often an unexploded bomb.

I don't let on that I've noticed the paper. Mum gets up to wash the dishes, her shoulders slumped with the unbearable weight she carries with her every day. While her back is turned I slide the paper over and on to my lap. Unexploded bomb or not, I need to know.

It's always bad. Even when it looks like it's good, it turns out to be bad. That's actually worse: getting your hopes up only to have them dropped from a great height and splattered on the pavement. It's hardest for Mum; that's what everyone always says. And I suppose they're right, but it's hard for Dad too. And it's not exactly a walk in the park for me either. But Dad's got Michel and I've got Thomas; Mum has no one.

I pray that this won't send her into full-on tortoise mode. Last time she didn't leave her bedroom for a week. I brought her meals on a tray but she barely ate a thing. She wouldn't talk to me and she wouldn't answer the phone. When Dad came round to see her I listened at the door. 'You have to snap out of this, Olivia. For Faith's sake. She needs you.' He was wrong about that. I was coping perfectly well, even though the timing was hardly ideal – right in the middle of my exams. I don't *need* her, not like when I was little. It'd just be nice if she talked to me about it once in a while. I wish she knew that there are other options besides 'complete and utter breakdown' and 'plastic smile, everything's fine'. There's a middle ground, waiting to be found.

I turn the paper over. It's bad.

'I KILLED LAUREL LOGAN!'

An involuntary noise escapes from my mouth and Mum turns around. She whips the paper out of my hands and crumples it up. She stuffs it into the bin even though the bin needs emptying. Some of the headline's huge black letters are still visible because the lid won't shut. Mum sees me staring at it and swears and stuffs the paper as deep as it will go. The bin lid swings back and forth.

She sits down and takes my hand. Her hand is cold – her hands are always cold. I often wonder if they used to be warm. *Before.* 'I was going to talk to you about that.' Lie. 'I've already talked to the police and it's nothing. The man's a lunatic. They would lock him up for this if he wasn't already serving two life sentences.' She sighs. 'It's just more irresponsible journalism – it even says inside that there's no way he could have done it. But that wouldn't sell papers, would it?'

There are tears in my eyes and I'm not even sure why. This happens on a regular basis – these stories in the papers or on TV or online. It's been happening my whole life, so you'd think I would be immune to it by now. And I usually *am* immune, but for some reason today I've decided to be pathetic.

Mum doesn't like it when I cry. I'm sure that's true of all mothers about their daughters, but there's something about when Mum says, 'Oh, darling, *please* don't cry,' that always makes me think it's more about her than me. As if it just makes things harder for her. So I try not to cry when she's around, because there's nothing worse than being upset and then being made to feel guilty for being upset.

When she's sure I've got the tears under control, Mum tells me all about this guy who claims to have killed my sister. He killed his whole family ten years ago and is safely locked up in a high-security prison. Recently he's decided his favourite thing to do is to make up lies about murdering people, as if the ones he *actually* killed aren't quite enough for him. Mum does a good impression of pretending it doesn't bother her, but I can see through her.

Even if I didn't know from experience, I'd know from that interview she did last year. I think she forgets that I read it, or maybe she forgets that she talked all about how awful and heartbreaking it is for her when these news stories appear.

Dad claims he never reads the interviews Mum gives. It's difficult for him, having stuff about their marriage splashed across newspapers he despises. But he can't say anything, because he knows we need the money. Plus, there's always the chance someone who knows something about Laurel will see one of these stories and call the police. Whenever anyone asks Dad's opinion about Mum's 'media activities', he always says the same thing: Let's hope the ends justify the means.

'What time is Michel picking you up?' There's always something slightly off about the way she says Michel — a slight wrinkling of the nostrils. Or that could just be my imagination.

I check the time on my phone. 'He's coming at ten.'

'But you've only been home for an hour!' There's silence for a moment or two and then Mum coughs and I know she's about to say something awkward. 'I've been thinking . . .' It's never good when parents *think*, is it? 'It might be nice for the two us to spend a whole weekend together sometimes. We could do whatever you like — we could even go away somewhere. A city break to Prague or Paris?'

'Um . . .' A text from Martha flashes up on my phone and I angle the screen away from Mum to read it. It just says: *Well? SPILL. x*

I have no idea what to say to Mum. She knows full well what the deal is: I spend Saturdays and Sundays with Dad and Michel. It's been that way for six years. It wasn't decided by a court or anything; Mum and Dad arranged everything between them. It was a remarkably amicable divorce — that's what they always tell people.

I don't want to argue with her this morning. I don't want to tell her that I can't imagine anything worse than wandering round Prague or Paris or any other city beginning with 'P' with her. Because we both know full well how it would turn out. She would pretend to be enthusiastic, dragging me round all the tourist sights. She would smile and make me pose for pictures in front of the Eiffel Tower or whatever, but she'd never let me take a photo of her. And the reason she wouldn't let me is that then there would be photographic evidence of her unhappiness. She would smile and you'd see her teeth, which might make someone else think that it was a real, proper smile. But I would look at her eyes and see that there was something dead there.

There are photos of Mum in the newspapers all the time and none of them ever show her smiling; she's careful never to smile when there are photographers around. She says they'll criticize her for it and she's probably right. (*What's she got to smile about? How can a mother smile with her daughter still missing?*) So she doesn't smile . . . and they criticize her anyway, calling her 'cold' and 'hard'. It's lose/lose.

So I tell Mum I'll think about it – spending the weekend with her – and say maybe we could talk to Dad and Michel about it in a month or two. She nods but I can tell she's disappointed by my reaction. I feel guilty. Guilt is never far away in this house. It lurks under the floorboards and behind the walls. You can hear it whispering late at night if you listen closely. I'd hoped that we'd left it behind in the old house when we moved, but Mum must have packed it up carefully, wrapping it in bubble wrap and putting it in a box, labelling it in fat black marker pen and putting it in the removal lorry along with everything else. The guilt will follow us wherever we go.

I get up and give Mum a hug. She's tense for a second, then she relaxes and hugs me back. She's so very thin. So sharp and pinched and angular. She used to be slightly overweight; she looked much better like that. I wish I could remember that version of my mother, but all I've got is photos. My favourite is one of the three of us baking a cake together – Mum, Laurel and me. Mum's wearing a pink apron and her cheeks are rosy and she's laughing – *really* laughing. I'm standing on a chair so that I can reach the worktop. I have a streak of flour across my nose and I'm sticking out my tongue at the person taking the photo (Dad? I can't remember). Laurel is stirring the mixture in the bowl, her brow furrowed in concentration. For some reason Laurel's wearing a feather boa and I'm wearing a tiara – obviously appropriate baking attire for a six-year-old and a four-year-old.

The phone rings and Mum gives me a kiss on the cheek before she goes to answer it. Her lips are dry and chapped.

'Hello? Speaking.' She tucks the phone between her shoulder and her ear and starts to wipe the crumbs from the kitchen counter.

I nip upstairs to pack my bag for going to Dad's. I don't need much – I keep some clothes and toiletries there. It can be annoying sometimes; I'm always leaving my favourite jacket at Mum's when I go round to Dad's and vice versa. Still, it's worth the inconvenience just to escape for a couple of days a week. I feel different when I'm at Dad and Michel's flat – it's easier to breathe somehow. But perhaps that's just the air conditioning.

Mum's standing with her back to me when I come back into the kitchen. She's still holding the phone in one hand even though she must have ended the call. 'Mum?'

She ignores me.

'Mum? Are you OK?'

The 'I'm fine, love' that I'm expecting doesn't come. She's deviated from the script.

She still won't turn round so I have to shuffle

around the side of the kitchen table and position myself right in front of her. She's paler than she was when I left her. A single tear is trickling down her left cheek and she does nothing to halt its progress. I watch as it negotiates the contour of her jaw and continues down her neck.

She finally looks at me and there's something different in her eyes. I have no idea what it is but it scares me.

Mum clears her throat. She starts to speak and then stops herself. I can't decide if I want to hear what she has to say, but it looks like I don't have a choice in the matter.

'That was the police.'

No. Please God, no. Not today. The call she's been dreading every single day for thirteen years. It can't be today.

Mum sways a little as if she's about to faint so I help her over to the table. She slumps into a chair and the phone clatters on to the tabletop. She takes my hands in hers and I crouch down in front of her.

'Tell me, Mum. *Please.*'

She clears her throat again. 'A girl has been found. At Stanley Street.' Stanley Street is where we were living when it happened. 'They think it's . . . Laurel.' She squeezes my hands so hard it hurts. 'They

11

want me to go down to the police station straightaway to . . . identify her.'

My legs buckle beneath me and it's a good job I'm so close to the floor already. 'Oh, Mum, I'm so sorry. I can't . . . Oh God.'

And that's when Mum smiles. 'Oh no, Faith! I didn't mean . . . goodness, I should have thought!' She lets go of my hands and reaches out to touch my cheek. 'They think it's her . . . they're almost certain . . . Faith? She's alive. Laurel's alive!'

Chapter 2

I don't believe it. I won't allow myself to believe it. Mum's trying to stay calm too, but I can see it in her face — something I haven't seen for years: hope. She thinks it's different this time, which means the police must think it's different this time. They wouldn't have called her otherwise. They think this is *it*. After hundreds, maybe even thousands, of crank calls and false sightings and psychics claiming Laurel was living with goat-herds in the mountains of Uzbekistan.

But it makes no sense. Her turning up in the front garden of our old house after *thirteen* years? I picture a six-year-old girl, shiny blonde hair. She's wearing a brand-new dress for the first time. The dress is white with multicoloured polka dots on it. There's a tiny Ribena stain on the front, but you'd never know because it just looks like another polka dot. The girl is smiling and she's missing one of her front teeth. She's cradling a teddy bear in her arms like it's a baby. The only thing slightly spoiling this perfect photo is a nasty scab on the girl's right cheek. Perhaps it looks like the sort of scab that a child might end up with if they'd been chased around the living room by their little sister and they'd tripped and fallen and hit their cheek on the corner of the coffee table.

If you saw that little girl, you'd probably think she was the cutest little girl you'd ever seen. Chances are, you *have* seen her. The photo of blonde-haired, gap-toothed, polka-dot dressed, teddy-bear cradling Laurel Logan has surely been printed in almost every newspaper in the world (probably even the *Uzbekistan Times*, now that I think about it). You'll have seen the polka-dot ribbons that people used to wear, or the ones they tied to trees all along Stanley Street. I think it was Mum's idea, that polka-dot campaign. Anyway, two hours after Mum took that photo, Laurel was gone.

I was also in the original photo: four years old, cute in the way that all four-year-olds are, but nothing special. Not like her. Frizzy brown hair, beady little eyes, hand-me-down clothes. I was playing in a sandpit in the background, slightly out of focus. That's how it's been my whole life: in the background, slightly out of focus. You hardly ever see that version of the photo — the one where I haven't been cropped out.

Laurel would be nineteen years old now. An adult. My brain struggles with that concept. Of course we've all seen the age-progressed photos. The last one was four years ago: Laurel Logan at fifteen. None of the images ever look quite right though. You can see that they've taken that photo — *the* photo — and done some computer wizardry, but the results are always weird in some way. They never end up looking quite like a real person.

I'm looking at Mum and she's looking at me and she's still holding back. There's some small part of her that doesn't believe it can be Laurel. That won't allow her to fully believe that the nightmare could finally be over. She's had her hopes raised and dashed so many times before.

I realize she's shaking and I take hold of her hand to steady it. 'Are they sure? How do they *know*?'

'I have to phone your father. Natalie said she'd call him but I thought it would be best if I did it. Do you think he'll be at home or should I try his mobile first?' She looked at her watch, too big for her wrist. 'Michel's probably on his way round here by now anyway. You should still go . . . I'm not leaving you here by yourself . . . I'll call as soon as I know more . . .'

'Mum! Stop! Just stop talking for a second. How do they know it's . . . her?' For some reason I can't seem to say her name.

'Remember she hurt herself the day she was . . . Natalie says she has a scar on her cheek! After all these years . . .' She shakes her head in disbelief as she squeezes my hand tightly. 'And there's something else. She's got Barnaby!'

It's her. My sister has come home.

There were lots of photos of Barnaby in the newspapers too, at first. I don't remember, of course, but I've done enough research that I could probably write a book about what happened. Mum and Dad gave Laurel a teddy bear for Christmas – six months before she was taken. I got a bear too. I lost mine years ago.

Mum and Dad took us to one of those shops where you can customize your cuddly toys. Apparently Laurel took ages, making sure her bear was just the way she wanted it. You can record a voice message that will play every time you squeeze the toy's tummy. Laurel was too shy to do it herself, so Mum and Dad did it for her. Her bear said: HAPPY CHRISTMAS, LAUREL! LOTS OF LOVE FROM MUMMY AND

DADDY!' I recorded my own message, babbling some nonsense about a teddy bear's picnic.

Laurel's bear was brown and extra fluffy. He was dressed in blue dungarees with a red-and-white striped T-shirt and a blue hat with his name embroidered on it. Laurel didn't have to think long about the name — she said 'Barnaby' as soon as they asked her.

Barnaby the Bear is unique. Even if there happened to be another bear with the same dungarees and T-shirt and hat and embroidery, there is only one bear in the whole wide world that has a message from my parents recorded on it. And when Laurel was taken, Barnaby was too.

It was a tiny crumb of comfort to my parents, I think. Knowing that wherever she was, Laurel wasn't alone. She loved that bear. She carried him everywhere and told him all her secrets. Depending on her mood, she would sometimes insist that he had his own chair at the dinner table. I can picture that, if I close my eyes and really try. But I'm sure the details are wrong. Like all of my memories of Laurel, this one is second-hand. It doesn't even count as a memory, does it?

Sometimes I lie in bed at night and try to clear my head of everything. I empty my brain bit by bit — Mum and Dad and Michel and school and Thomas and Martha and what I had for dinner. I let all of it leak out of my ears on to the pillow, leaving nothing but blankness. Then I wait for her. For a real memory — one that's mine and only mine and not something I've read in the newspaper or on the Internet or something that my grandparents told me.

Sometimes it works. I can see her laughing and I know it's really her — it's not from one of the three home-video clips that the whole world has seen, or from any of the other videos I used to watch over and over again until I mouthed the words coming out of Laurel's mouth when she had her first pony ride and was scared she was going to fall off. This laugh is different — it's just for me. Secret laughter between sisters. And she has two clips in her hair — they're shaped like stars and they shimmer in the sunlight.

That's it. That's all I have: a laugh and a couple of hair clips. That's all I was left with for thirteen years. But now she's back.

Chapter 3

Mum comes back into the kitchen after phoning Dad. She's been crying a lot – her face is red and blotchy. Clearly she didn't want me to hear that conversation. I'm not sure why.

Then it hits me. 'Is she hurt?' I can't believe I didn't think to ask before.

'What?' Mum's distracted, trying to find her car keys. They're on the shelf in the hall, exactly the same place they always are.

'Is she hurt? Is there something . . . wrong with her?' It's a perfectly reasonable question.

'No! The police said she's in remarkably good health, considering . . .'

I wait, but Mum doesn't finish her sentence. She's too busy trying to sort out her make-up in the hall mirror.

'Mum? I'm . . . I'm scared.' She turns to me and I

can tell straightaway that she doesn't get it. 'Scared? Whatever for? There's nothing to be *scared* of, Faith. This is . . . well, it's a miracle, isn't it?' She pulls a face at the mirror and adds a slick of lipstick to her chapped lips. 'There.' I stare at her as she stares at her reflection. 'Do you think she'll recognize me?' she asks, in the smallest voice imaginable.

The doorbell rings. There are a few possible answers to Mum's question, but only one that's honest. I go and stand behind her and our eyes meet in the mirror. I tuck a few strands of hair behind her ear. 'Of course she will, Mum.' Honesty isn't always the best policy.

Her face lights up and she turns to hug me tightly. 'My baby's coming home,' she whispers. The mean, twisted little voice in my head – the one I have to silence every single day – whispers something so pathetic and selfish that it makes me want to hug Mum extra hard and never let her go: *What about me? I'm your baby too.*

Michel already knows; Dad must have called him in the car. He says 'I can't believe it' at least three times in as many minutes. While Mum's filling him in on the rest of the details, he keeps on glancing over at me.

Mum seems to have forgotten her feelings about

Michel. She hugs him, the first time I've ever seen her do that. Michel's as surprised as I am when she launches herself at him. She babbles away, barely pausing for breath. She's usually painfully polite – but distant – towards Michel, and I hate her for it. Especially because he never has a bad word to say about her. He just shrugs it off like he doesn't mind one little bit. Sometimes I wish I could be more like him ('be a little more *French*,' he says).

Michel tells Mum that we'll wait at the flat for news. We were supposed to be going to a new exhibition at the art gallery, but he says we can go next week or the week after.

'Maybe the three of you can go, when Laurel's back with us?' Mum says this as if it's a normal thing to say.

Michel moves his head and you can tell Mum interprets it as a nod, but it wasn't one. 'You'd better get going, Olivia. John will be there soon.' That was exactly the right thing to say to get Mum out of the house – she won't want Dad to get there first.

The goodbyes are awkward. Mum seems to have remembered that hugging Michel is not the kind of thing she does, and she doesn't seem to know what to say to me. The moment is too big, so she settles for kissing me on the cheek and telling me she loves me.

'I love you too, Mum. I hope . . .' Now it's my turn to leave a sentence hanging in the air. Mum just nods as if she knows exactly what I wanted to say. But she doesn't.

I hope it's really, truly, definitely her. I hope she recognizes you after thirteen years even though I have my doubts. I hope you don't die in a terrible car crash on the way to the police station. I hope things are going to change around here but not *too* much. I hope you don't forget all about me once you've got your perfect daughter back.

Maybe the sentence *was* finished after all: I hope.

Michel drives carefully – both hands on the steering wheel, checking his mirrors all the time. I always feel safer in his car than I do in Dad's. 'How are you doing, *ma chérie?*' Michel knows that I like it when he speaks French, so he indulges me once in a while.

I close my eyes and listen to the traffic. How *am* I doing? An hour and a half ago I had a pretty good idea how this weekend was going to play out: the exhibition with Michel; meeting up with Dad for a pub lunch; baking in the afternoon; takeaway and film tonight; an early start on Sunday morning and off to the food market with Michel, where he miraculously transforms into the most French person you could ever imagine (wearing a beret, for crying out loud), ramping up the accent and charming all the women into buying our (admittedly amazing) macarons; back home on Sunday evening to slump in front of the TV with Mum.

The routine of the weekend is comforting to me. Michel and Dad's flat feels like *home*. I'd have asked to move in there full-time if I hadn't known it would break Mum's heart. Plus I'm pretty sure Dad wouldn't be all that keen on having me around all the time. Being a weekend dad suits him perfectly, I think.

I was eleven years old when my parents got divorced. Apparently most kids are upset when their parents split up, but I wasn't. I don't remember crying at all. Not even when Dad drove away with his car packed full of his belongings. Mum still finds it strange that I didn't react how a normal kid would (should) react. You'd think she'd be relieved that I wasn't upset. Surely it showed that I was remarkably well-adjusted for my age, understanding and accepting that my parents could never be happy together after what had happened to Laurel.

Dad's bisexual – always has been, as far as I know. Mum knew that he was bi when they met at university and fell 'head over heels in love with each other'. The only reason I know this is because she talked about it in an interview a few years ago. Dad was *not* happy about that. She was on a mission though — a mission to set the record straight. So many awful things had been written about them both — and about Dad in particular ('LAUREL'S DAD IN GAY ROMP!') — that she wanted to tell the truth. The papers always say he's gay — they never bother to get it right. And back then they said that he pretended to be straight and lured my mother into marrying him because he was desperate to have children. For a while the media were obsessed with the fact that Laurel was adopted. They wanted to know WHY.

I was a miracle baby. Something to do with a very low sperm count (gross) on Dad's side and something wrong with Mum's ovaries. The chances of them conceiving naturally were minuscule. Technically I shouldn't even exist. I often wondered how they *really* felt about that. Mum usually sticks to the whole 'miracle baby' spiel, saying how blessed she and Dad felt to have two beautiful daughters. I've never asked her for the real story because I know she'd never tell me the truth.

So for a few years the papers liked to make my father out to be some kind of depraved sex fiend. The 'gay romp' headline came after he was photographed coming out of the front door of Michel's apartment building three months after they started dating. Not exactly the news story of the century.

It was hard on Michel, but he doesn't like to talk about it. I have no idea why he got involved with my dad in the first place. Surely any sane person would run a mile from someone with that much baggage. But Michel is a Good Person. The best person I know, probably. He's a vet; I think it's probably a prerequisite that you have to be nice to be a vet. You have to be caring and sympathetic and not mind being puked on by a parrot.

Dad's OK too, but I'll never understand what Michel sees in him. Michel is very, very good-looking. He has good skin and messy black hair and permanent stubble. If he was a couple of inches taller and a lot more vain he could have probably been a model. Dad's not ugly or anything – he just looks very *English*. He looks like you'd expect a man called John to look. Boring hair, regular enough features, pale skin, slightly too thin, shoulders permanently hunched.

'Faith? Are you OK?' Michel asks again.

I still don't have an answer so I decide to go down a different route. 'I had sex with Thomas last night.'

Chapter 4

I have my very own spot on the sofa at Michel and Dad's flat. They've got one of those huge corner sofas, and my spot is right in the corner where I can look out of the window and see the canal. I always try to sit in corners when I can. I didn't even realize until Michel pointed it out to me one day. Then Dad laughed and said it was true, and that I'd been doing it since I was a little girl. He stopped laughing when I said that maybe I didn't like having my back to the room because photographers have a nasty habit of popping up from nowhere and snapping away. I like to see them coming, at least.

Michel's made us both a cup of tea and I'm sitting in my usual spot; the sun is streaming through the windows and Tonks the cat is curled up on my lap. (Michel is a massive Harry Potter fan; Dad barely even knows who Harry Potter is.)

'So . . . you and Thomas . . . ?'

'Yeah, me and Thomas.'

'That's big news! How are you feeling about it all?'

I shrug. 'I don't know. Good, I think. It was . . . nice.'

'Wow. That bad? You mean the earth didn't move and angels didn't sing and there were no fireworks?' I shake my head. 'Well, that's exactly how your first time is supposed to be — average at best. God, I remember my first—'

I stick my fingers in my ears. 'La la la I'm not listening!' I only take my fingers out when I'm sure that he's stopped talking. 'I don't want to hear about you having sex, because that makes me think about Dad having sex and that's just . . .' I shudder and make a gagging sound.

Michel smiles at me. 'Oh, right, so I have to sit here and listen to you, but you don't want to hear about the time when Jean-Luc waited for me in the changing rooms after football practice and —'

I throw a pillow at Michel's head and laugh so hard that Tonks leaps from my lap and stalks off without a backward glance. It feels so good to laugh with Michel, even though I know he's only trying to distract me from thinking about what's happening at the police station.

27

'Seriously though, are you OK about all this?'

'OK about what? Losing my virginity or Laurel?'

Michel shrugs and smiles. 'Both, I guess.'

'I'm OK.' I nod as if to reassure myself. 'Yeah, I'm OK. I think I love Thomas and I think he loves me, and we've been together *forever*, so there really wasn't any reason *not* to have sex. And I think I'm going to like it. We just need to practise a bit more . . . and find somewhere a bit better than the back of his van.'

'Romantic,' Michel deadpans.

'As for Laurel . . . well, I'm happy, of course.'

Michel shuffles over to sit right next to me. 'You don't have to pretend with me. You know that, don't you?'

I *do* know that. I've always been honest with him. I don't know what it is about Michel but I've trusted him almost since the day we met. I can tell him *anything* and he would never even dream of telling Dad. I close my eyes and take a deep breath. 'I'm scared, Michel.'

'What are you afraid of?'

'You know that thing they say – be careful what you wish for? I've wished for this my whole life, it seems. I've dreamed of this day, but I suppose I never really thought it would happen. I mean, at the time I

28

thought I believed it would happen . . . It's only now that I realize I was so sure she was gone forever. Does that make sense?'

Michel nods.

'I've been in her shadow ever since she was taken. You know how much I've hated that everything is *always* about Laurel. And that I couldn't have a normal childhood like everyone else. But now that she's back, it's all going to be different, isn't it? And maybe . . . I don't know . . . maybe I'll realize I was sort of OK with being in her shadow after all.'

Michel puts his arm around my shoulders and I lean my head against his. 'It's OK, you know? Whatever you're feeling is OK. There's no right way to feel about this. It's hardly a normal situation, is it?'

Normal. I've always been jealous of normal. Boring too. I'd have been perfectly happy with the most boring, normal childhood you can imagine – like Martha's. Nothing remotely interesting has ever happened to anyone in Martha's family and she doesn't even realize how lucky she is.

Michel's phone rings and it's Dad calling from the police station. Michel looks at me guiltily and I can tell we're both thinking the same thing: he really should have called me first. Michel's end of the conversation mostly consists of 'yes', 'OK' and 'I see'; it's not particularly enlightening. I leave the room to look for Tonks and find her under the duvet in my room. I scratch her head until she forgives me for spooking her.

Eventually Michel comes in and hands me the phone. He leaves the room to give me some privacy and I immediately wish he'd stayed.

'Faith? It's her . . . It's really her.' Dad's crying down the phone – I've never heard him cry like this, huge gulping sobs. 'The teddy bear . . . you remember that bear of hers?' He doesn't wait for me to answer. 'Well, somehow they got the sound chip to work! They played us the recording! Can you believe it?' Again he doesn't wait for me to speak. 'She's . . . oh my God, Faith . . . it's really *her*! Laurel's come home!'

I say, 'That's great, Dad,' and it sounds like he's just told me his football team has won the league. My reaction is *all* wrong, so I try again. 'It's amazing.' A little better, but not much.

Dad clears his throat. 'She's been asking for you. She *remembers*. Isn't that wonderful? Just wait till you see her, Faith. She's a beautiful young woman . . . just like you.' It couldn't be more obvious that the 'just like you' is an afterthought.

'She's really asking for me?'

'Yes! She wanted to know if you're still obsessed with building sandcastles!' Dad chuckles.

I was building a sandcastle in the sandpit when she was taken.

'We showed her a picture of you, Faith. She couldn't believe how grown-up you are!'

This is all very nice, but there's something he's not telling me. 'Where has she been? What happened to her?'

I hear muffled voices. Dad must have put his hand over the phone. I wonder if Mum's been listening in this whole time. 'We'll talk about that when I get home, love. All that matters is that Laurel's back — safe and sound.'

Dad tells me that Laurel will be staying in a hotel for the next few days. Mum will stay with her, but he'll come home. The police need to talk to Laurel and she needs to get checked out by a doctor and a psychologist and various other people. There's a specialist counsellor on her way up from London.

I'm not allowed to tell anyone yet — not even Thomas and Martha. (*Of course* I'm going to tell Thomas and Martha.) Apparently there's going to be a press conference tomorrow afternoon. I wonder how they can possibly have all this planned out already.

'You can meet her tomorrow, love. How does that sound? Seeing your big sister?' Dad's using his coaxing voice – the one that makes me feel like a child.

How does that sound? Utterly terrifying.

'I can't wait,' I say.

Chapter 5

Michel manages to convince me that making macarons will make me feel better about everything. For the past couple of years the two of us have spent every Saturday afternoon in the kitchen together. Dad's usually watching football or out on one of his bike rides.

It started off as a bit of a laugh. My pathetic efforts would often end up in the bin and Michel would take his perfect macarons into the veterinary practice and share them with his colleagues (after we'd eaten our fill, of course). It was Dad who suggested we start selling them at the local farmers' market. We weren't sure that people would go for it, but on the first day we sold out within an hour. That's when we discovered that the French accent was definitely an asset. It was my idea that Michel should play up the whole French thing. Who wouldn't want to buy authentic French macarons made by an authentic Frenchman who just happens to be very, very handsome?

Thomas texts when Michel and I are having our customary pre-macaron-making cup of tea. He wants to know why I haven't been in touch all day. He's worried I might be upset about what happened yesterday. I text back: *Upset after all the sex, you mean?* Thomas doesn't like to talk about sex. I don't have to worry about him bragging in the boys' changing rooms. Not that he'd ever be in the boys' changing rooms — he's not exactly the sporty type. Thomas likes to think of himself as a tortured artist. He sketches and writes poetry and drinks far more coffee than can possibly be good for him.

I reply to Martha while I'm at it. I bet she's been waiting patiently all day, trying not to check her phone every two minutes: *Last night was good! Ta again for covering for me. Speak later? I have news (not sex-related).*

Martha texts back first: *WHAT NEWS?*

Thomas: *I miss you.* I roll my eyes at that; I can't help it. Thomas does not do text banter, no matter how hard I try to lure him into it.

I'll tell them both about Laurel tonight. They deserve to know. They're the ones who stood by me when bullshit stories appeared in the papers, when girls at school were harassing me, when Mum was having another one of her mini-breakdowns.

Today's macarons are a spectacular failure on my part. Michel's are fine though, so he makes another couple of batches (one batch of raspberry and one of salted caramel – my favourite). He realizes that I'm missing my macaron mojo and tells me we don't have to go to the market tomorrow, that it's totally up to me. He can go on his own or stay home – whatever I'd prefer. I don't think it's possible for me to love him any more than I do at this exact moment. I tell him I want to go to the market. I don't tell him the reason why: this might be the last time that we get to do this – just the two of us. Maybe Laurel will want to come next week, and maybe she'll be miraculously brilliant at baking and her macarons will have perfect shiny tops every time.

Dad arrives home early evening; he looks worn out. He hugs Michel for the longest time, then he hugs me for the second-longest time. They say a few words to each other in French – speaking quickly so that I can't even try to understand.

We sit down on the sofa and Dad talks. Laurel is slightly malnourished, with a serious vitamin-D deficiency from lack of sunlight, but she's physically OK otherwise. First impressions are that she's in better psychological shape than anyone could have expected. But at the same time, she's clearly traumatized; she lashed out at a policeman trying to take a cheek swab for DNA testing. It took an hour for Mum to calm her down but she wouldn't let anyone else near her. Apparently everyone was very understanding about it. After all, says Dad, Laurel has been through a terrible ordeal.

Dad doesn't go into much detail, other than to say that she was taken by a very sick man who kept her locked up in a basement. A lot of people had suspected that was the case. Mum always maintained that maybe she was taken by a couple who were desperate to have a little girl – and maybe they were raising her as if she was their own, and taking the best care of her. Nobody dared to disagree with her whenever she mentioned this theory of hers. They tended to nod and smile awkwardly.

'Did she escape?' I like the idea of Laurel escaping, being daring and brave. Fighting back.

Dad shakes his head. 'He let her go.'

'*Why?*'

'We don't know.'

'Why would you go to the trouble of keeping

someone locked up for all that time, only to let them go all of a sudden?'

'I'm just glad he did.'

I am too. Of course I am. 'Did the police catch him?'

Another shake of the head. 'No. We don't even know where she was being held. The guy blindfolded her, drove her to Stanley Street and left her in the garden. By all accounts, the couple living there got a bit of a shock when she knocked on the door. The police are doing everything they can to find the man, obviously. And Laurel's trying her best, but it's hard for her. She can't really remember how long they drove for. And she can't tell us much about where she's been kept all these years – the bastard was clever about it.' Dad *never* swears in front of me.

'So this psycho's still out there? What if he comes back?'

'The police think he'll lay low – go into hiding. But they're not taking any chances. They'll be watching us, OK? There's no need for you to worry about that.'

I sit back and try to process this information. The police have *no* idea who this man is. How is that even possible? I try to picture the sort of man who would do something like this. A man who would keep a girl locked in a basement for all those years. 'He abused her, didn't he?'

Dad looks at Michel, and Michel nods, and it makes me so angry that my father can't make a decision by himself for once. 'Yes. He bcat her too.' Dad's jaw is tight. 'The abuse was . . . systematic.'

I close my eyes to blink away the tears.

'I'm not saying this to upset you, Faith. But you need to be prepared. What she's been through . . .' He shakes his head and breathes out slowly. Then he sits up straighter and pats me on the leg. 'But the most important thing is that she's safe now. We can be a family again.' I think he's forgetting that we can't exactly go back to being the sort of family we were thirteen years ago.

Dad says we need to give Laurel time to heal, and that she'll be getting the best help available – therapy and counselling and whatever she needs.

Mum and Dad have arranged for me to go and see her tomorrow morning. It looks like I won't be going to the market with Michel after all. There's no point in arguing – they wouldn't understand.

It doesn't seem to have occurred to my parents that I might have slightly conflicted feelings about seeing my sister for the first time in thirteen years. That I might be nervous – even scared.

Chapter 6

Michel tells Dad he should go and lie down for a bit and Dad gives me another hug. 'I can't believe it's over. I didn't think . . .' He shakes his head and murmurs something about a miracle before he trudges off to his bedroom.

Michel's going to pick up the takeaway. He asks me to go with him but I say I'd rather be alone for a few minutes.

'It's a lot to take in, isn't it?' His brown eyes are full of warmth and understanding.

I nod. 'Are you not . . . worried?'

'Worried about what?'

'I don't know . . . that Mum and Dad might get back together?' I'm not saying it to be mean, I'm really not.

Michel smiles. 'What are you trying to do? Make me paranoid? I'm not worried at all. Why? You think I should be?'

'I don't know! Dad's acting all weird.'

'Of course he's acting weird! It's been a pretty weird sort of day, don't you think?'

'Did they tell her that they're not together? Does she know about you?' I can't believe I didn't think to ask earlier.

Michel picks up his leather jacket – I think it must be older than I am. 'She knows. Your mum wanted to wait for a few days before telling her, but John insisted.'

'And?'

'And . . . nothing! She was totally fine with it. So you don't need to worry your pretty little head about it!' He moves to ruffle my hair, which he only ever does to annoy me.

I try to put myself in her shoes. Coming back to your family after all that time. You'd want things to be the same as when you left, wouldn't you? But a lot can change in thirteen years. Your mother can wither away to nothingness and your dad can get together with a lovely Frenchman and your little sister can stop building sandcastles and start building a wall around herself instead.

I go to my room as soon as Michel leaves, closing the door so Dad can't hear. I call Thomas first. He's annoyed that I've hardly been in touch all day, so I tell him immediately.

'Are you serious? This is a joke, isn't it?' He's never really understood my sense of humour. The fact that he thinks there's even the remotest possibility that I would joke about something like this is baffling to me.

I say nothing.

'Oh shit. You *are* serious. Oh my God. What happened? Where has she . . . ? Is she . . . ?'

I tell him everything I know, finding it vaguely reassuring that he asks a lot of the same questions as I did. It makes me feel like less of a freak. And when he asks how I'm feeling about it all, I feel a surge of love for him.

I know I did the right thing, having sex with him last night. Because I hadn't been sure about it at all. I was scared. I'd never have admitted that to him or to Martha. Luckily, losing my virginity turned out to be very unscary. It was mostly sweet and awkward and a little bit hilarious (for me anyway – when Thomas got a cramp in his leg). I don't know why people make such a big deal about it.

Thomas is a very good listener. He never interrupts and hardly ever disagrees. He is, to all intents and purposes, a good boyfriend. Even if I will never

41

understand any of his poems. And he writes *a lot* of poems.

I tell Thomas that I might not be able to see him outside of school for the next few days. I have no idea how things are going to go with Laurel. Is she just going to come home and move into her room straightaway? Because she *does* have a room in our house – Mum insisted when we moved. At least she didn't insist on decorating it like Laurel's room in Stanley Street – all pink and sparkly. It just looks like a nice guest room, with a few of Laurel's possessions dotted around. Mum felt so guilty about moving. She hated the idea that everything wouldn't be exactly the same when Laurel came home. (It was always 'when', never 'if'.) The only reason she eventually agreed to the move was to release more money for the fund to find Laurel.

Thomas tells me to take as much time as I need and says that I should call him any time I need to talk. He tells me he loves me and I tell him I love him too and I hang up, feeling sane for the first time in hours.

Martha says, 'I can't believe it.' Over and over again. I give her a quick rundown of everything I know, which isn't all that much now that I think about it, and she says 'I can't believe it' a few more times. She asks when I'm going to meet Laurel, and it makes me realize that I won't be *meeting* her, because you can only meet a total stranger, can't you? But meeting feels like exactly the right word in this case.

I hang up after promising to call Martha tomorrow. She didn't ask how I'm feeling. Why would she? Laurel's abduction has dominated (and ruined) my whole life, and now she's back. Problem solved.

We eat our takeaway (sushi) and Dad doesn't stop talking about Laurel. We have coffee and I eat six macarons and Dad doesn't stop talking about Laurel. We try to watch a film, but Dad keeps on mentioning Laurel so we give up after half an hour. He apologizes, but that doesn't stop him talking about Laurel. He spends the rest of the night phoning family and friends – presumably the ones Mum hasn't already called – to tell them the good news, and to swear them to secrecy about it. Not one of them asks about me.

I say I'm going to get an early night and Dad nods enthusiastically. 'Good idea, love. Big day tomorrow.' He hugs me and says he can't wait to see 'my two girls together, side by side'. Michel hugs me and tells me he loves me. I wonder when he'll get to meet Laurel – there's been no mention of him coming with us tomorrow.

the lost and the found

When I go to close the blinds in my bedroom I realize that I can see where she's staying. The neon blue 'H' of Hilton peeks out from behind a high-rise office building. Laurel is in there somewhere, with my mother. *Our* mother.

Chapter 7

A persistent buzzing rouses me from sleep. The entryphone. By the sounds of it, someone really, really wants to come in. I stumble through from the bedroom to find Dad taking the phone off the hook and Michel hovering nearby, looking worried. Before I can ask what's going on, the phone starts ringing. Then Dad's mobile, which is charging on the kitchen worktop.

'Journalists,' Dad says. 'Didn't take them long, did it? Not much point having press conference now.' He looks more resigned than upset.

I look at the clock on the kitchen wall. It's not even eight o'clock. Michel yawns as he fills up the coffee machine with water. I hear my phone ringing from the bedroom and go to get it. I'm vaguely aware of Dad trailing behind me, saying, 'They wouldn't dare . . .'

I don't recognize the number. Dad says, 'Faith, don't,' but I do.

'Hello?'

'Am I speaking to Faith Logan?'

'Who's this?'

'This is Jeanette Hayes. Can I ask how you're feeling this morning?'

Jeanette Hayes. Only *slightly* more popular than Satan in our family. Mum and Dad got along OK with some of the reporters over the years – one or two have even become friends – but Jeanette Hayes is most definitely not one of them. It started a couple of months after Laurel went missing. The campaign to find her was in full swing, and the story was still mentioned in one paper or another almost every day. Jeanette Hayes decided that the amount of attention Laurel's case was getting was unfair. She wrote this big article about all the other children who had gone missing recently – and there were more than you might expect. The headline was: 'THE FORGOTTEN CHILDREN'. Hayes had this theory that Laurel's case was getting all the attention because she was pretty and blonde and middle class, and that my parents had 'connections' to the media. She even went so far as to say that vital police resources were being taken up by the hunt for Laurel when they could have been put to better use elsewhere.

All that would have been bad enough, but she wrote another story a week later saying Laurel was probably dead and it was high time the whole country 'got real' about it. Neither of these stories made her very popular. Other journalists were falling over themselves to disagree with her, to call her 'unfeeling' and 'heartless', and to say that the reason she didn't understand was that she wasn't a mother herself. She even got death threats. It didn't seem to bother her though, because she went right ahead and wrote a book all about it. I used to look at it in the library when Mum's attention was elsewhere.

The book was full of photos and stories of other missing children. In some cases Hayes had interviewed their families, asking how they felt about their child's plight being sidelined to a tiny column on page 12 when Laurel Logan was still splashed all across the front page. ('What's so special about *her*?' said a father from Peckham, London.) The rest of the book was a bit of a hatchet job on my family. She hadn't even tried to talk to Mum or Dad to find out the truth.

There was a black-and-white photo of Jeanette Hayes inside the back cover of the book. She was staring at the camera in a challenging sort of way. She looked like a serious journalist, I thought. But that was probably just the glasses perched on the end of her nose. I used to stare at that photo, wondering why she hated us so much. Wondering why she didn't want Laurel to come home to us.

I clear my throat and Hayes repeats the question. How am I feeling this morning?

'I'm more interested in how *you're* feeling this morning.'

'I'm sorry, I don't quite understand. I'm looking for a quote – something short and snappy but heartfelt; you know the sort of thing.'

'And I'm looking for a quote from *you*. Something about how you were wrong about Laurel and wrong to write all that stuff about my family . . . you know the sort of thing.'

Dad's gesturing to me to hang up the phone. Reporters have never been allowed to talk to me, or even print a picture with me in without blurring out my face. The one or two times they tried, they found themselves on the receiving end of a hefty lawsuit. That was another thing Hayes criticized my parents about – their 'litigious nature'.

'OK, I see what you're saying.' She doesn't sound angry. 'I was wrong about Laurel. And I'm obviously *delighted* I was wrong . . .' I smile, triumphant. 'But I stand by everything I wrote about the police and your parents.'

Bitch. I want to say something clever – something that will cut her deeply. I want her to know how much pain she's caused my family – as if the pain of losing Laurel wasn't enough – and I want her to feel bad about it. But Dad saves me the trouble by grabbing the phone from my hand and shouting expletives before hanging up and throwing it on the bed in disgust. 'There. See if they'll print *that*.'

I've never heard my father say some of those words. It's kind of cool.

'It was her, wasn't it?' he asks softly.

I nod.

He puts his arm around me. 'We're not going to let them ruin today, OK? This is *our* day.'

I nod again. 'I'm going to take a shower.'

What do you wear to meet the sister you thought was dead? My wardrobe here only has a few things in it so my options are limited. I settle for grey jeans, Converse and a black T-shirt; I want to look like me.

Michel tells me I look great, which can't be true because I've hardly slept. He manages to keep a cheerful sort of chatter going all through breakfast, ignoring Dad's phone buzzing every few minutes. I wish he was coming with us.

In the lift Dad tells me to keep my head down in the

49

car. When the car pulls out of the car park, the flashes go off and photographers crowd around, shouting and jostling each other and risking getting run over just to get a picture of us. I stare at the dashboard, where the plastic nodding dog I gave Dad for Christmas a few years ago is nodding away as if he approves of this madness.

Dad manages not to run over anyone's toes – he must be feeling charitable. And then we've left them behind and we're on our way to the hotel. I keep checking in the mirrors in case any photographers are following us on motorbikes, but it looks like we're in the clear.

Dad drums his fingers on the steering wheel until I ask him to stop. He apologizes and I apologize and he asks why I'm apologizing. Then we both laugh nervously.

'Are you OK, love? You look a bit green around the gills.'

I look up at the sky, grey and heavy; I wouldn't be surprised if it started snowing. 'I hope she likes me.'

Dad barks out a laugh. '*Like* you? She's going to LOVE you! She's your sister!' And weirdly enough, this does make me feel better.

There are no photographers waiting outside the hotel or hanging around the lobby, which is something to be grateful for. A red-haired woman in a too-tight black suit hurries over to us as soon as we enter. Her gold badge identifies her as Gillian Crook, Assistant Manager. She is very keen for us to know how very, very happy she is for us and how honoured she is to have 'Little Laurel' staying here. She shakes Dad's hand for far too long, then she hugs me, which is awkward because I make no effort to hug her back. I don't tend to go around hugging random hotel assistant managers.

Gillian Crook starts crying because it's all too much for her, thinking about Little Laurel being reunited with her family here in her hotel (of all places!). She reckons it's a story she'll tell her grandchildren one day (not that she's even married yet!) and I feel sorry for those hypothetical grandchildren. Dad and I nod as politely as we can and try to leave her behind, but she says there's someone we have to talk to before heading upstairs.

Gillian leads us over to the bar, empty except for a woman tapping away on a laptop. She stands when she hears us approach. She's around thirty years old, shoulder-length curly brown hair, with the type of face you forget as soon as you turn away. Her name is Maggie Dimmock. She's the counsellor who flew up from London last night. Maggie is a specialist in 'family reunification', which is a real thing and not something someone made up yesterday because no one has a clue how to deal with a situation like this.

We sit down with her and Gillian Crook hovers nearby until Maggie gives her an even more pointed look than she did the first three times. Maggie tells us her qualifications as if she's trying to prove something. Apparently she flew over to Switzerland last year to deal with a case 'remarkably similar to this one'. Except it wasn't all that similar at all, really, because the Swiss girl had only been gone for two years. You know your perspective is pretty messed up when you think two years is hardly any time at all for a girl to be away from her family.

Maggie Dimmock has already spent a couple of hours with Laurel, which doesn't seem fair when I haven't even seen her yet. Maggie says she's a remarkable young woman and Dad nods along with everything she says. She'll be having sessions with Laurel every day for the next week or so, as well as sessions with the four of us together. It's all about creating a 'smooth transition'. She says that we can't expect everything to be hunky-dory straightaway. She sounds like a kids' TV presenter, full of enthusiasm and good intentions. I feel sorry for her.

Maggie talks some more, but I've stopped

listening; I just want to see my sister. I want to get this over with. The nerves are too much to bear.

Dad and I take the lift to the top floor. Apparently the hotel insisted that Laurel stay in the presidential suite. No doubt they're hoping for some good publicity out of this.

There's one more obstacle between us and Laurel – Sergeant Dawkins, our family liaison officer, is waiting outside the room. I've known Sergeant Dawkins (Natalie) for years. I like her, but I just want to get inside that room. Still, I let her hug me, because she's been through this whole thing with us from the start. This is a big day for her too.

'She's so looking forward to seeing you, Faith.' I wish people would stop saying that.

Sergeant Dawkins takes Dad to one side and they whisper. There's always something they don't want me to know or don't think I can handle. I'm so used to it happening that it barely even registers any more.

And then Dad's knocking on the door and Mum answers it so fast I'm sure she must have been standing right there all along and Dad's hand is on my shoulder almost but not quite pushing me into the room. And I'm standing in front of my sister.

I have a sister now.

Chapter 8

She bursts into tears, this new sister of mine. She runs over from the window and she hugs me tightly and I stagger back a couple of steps but she doesn't let go. Mum and Dad hang back for a second or two; they have the biggest smiles on their faces. I've never seen them smile like that before. They can't resist for long and they soon pile in so that I'm right in the middle of this big, laughing, crying, disbelieving family hug. There's a wholeness, a completeness, a certain symmetry to it. It amazes me.

After a while we disentangle ourselves and step back and just look. Mum and Dad are looking from Laurel to me and back again. Laurel is staring at me as if she can't quite believe I'm real, and I'm staring at her because I can't believe how beautiful she is even though I always knew she'd be beautiful. I had a picture in my head of what she would look like, and it never quite matched the age-progressed pictures the police came up with, but it was actually pretty close to the girl standing in front of me.

She's a couple of inches taller than me – about five foot seven. Her hair is a little longer than shoulder length; it looks like she cut it herself. Her eyes are very blue. She's not wearing any make-up and her skin is slightly greasy and sallow but her beauty still astounds me. The scar looks a little like a silvery white teardrop on her cheekbone.

She's skinny – the hoodie and jeans she's wearing are hanging off her. That's when I realize that the clothes she's wearing are mine. There's nothing I can say about that without it sounding petty and wrong. I want to make a joke about it – because it's such a classic sisterly sort of thing (*Muuuuum, she's borrowed my jeans without asking AGAIN!*) but this probably isn't the right time. I don't mind that she's wearing my clothes, but it would have been nice if Mum had bothered to ask me. Knowing her, she's already got some big shopping spree planned for Laurel. She's always wanted a daughter to go shopping with, and I have never been that daughter.

'You're so grown-up!' Laurel smiles through her tears.

Dad's got his phone out of his pocket. He wants to take a photo. Laurel and I stand in front of the sofa and she puts her arm around my shoulder and we smile for the camera. We have to keep smiling a little too long while Dad presses the wrong button and accidentally starts recording a video of us, but he manages to get it right eventually.

'Right,' Mum says, 'we're going to go out and get some coffee and leave you girls to it.'

I'm panicking slightly at the thought of being left alone with Laurel, but at the same time I know it will be easier without Mum and Dad here, watching everything, trying to record it for posterity. They dispense more hugs before they leave. It looks like we're going to be a huggy sort of family from now on.

Laurel curls up in one corner of the sofa, tucking her bare feet beneath her. I sit on the armchair next to the sofa. I haven't had a chance to look around the presidential suite, but it's obviously bigger than my house.

Laurel notices me looking around. 'It's too big.'

'What?'

She fiddles with her cuffs of her (my) hoodie. 'I wish it was smaller. I'm used to . . .'

Oh God. She's been locked up in a basement for thirteen years. It stands to reason that big spaces would freak her out. 'You should say something. Tell

Mum. They'll sort out a smaller room for you, no problem.'

Laurel shakes her head. 'Mum really likes it.'

It is unbelievably odd to hear someone else calling my mother 'Mum'. And I can't get my head around the fact that I am sitting in this ridiculously opulent hotel room, talking to my sister.

'This is weird, isn't it?' Sometimes it's just best to get these things out in the open and acknowledge the awkwardness before someone else does.

Laurel smiles. 'It's definitely weird.'

We sit in silence for a moment or two. Laurel stares at the door and I wonder if she's trying to work out when Mum and Dad will be back. Maybe she'd have preferred it if they'd stayed. They seem to know the right things to say and do; clearly I do not.

'I'm glad you're back.' It's a banal thing to say, but it's important that I say it out loud. It's important that she hears it. Laurel smiles again. Her teeth are perfect. 'Your teeth are perfect.'

'Um . . . thanks?' She's looking at me as if that was a weird thing to say, probably because it *was* a weird thing to say.

'Sorry . . . I was just . . . it's just that I was thinking that you haven't been to the dentist and here's me going every six months or something and having fillings and braces and . . . OK I'm going to stop talking now. Sorry.' What is *wrong* with me?

Laurel doesn't look at me like I'm crazy. She doesn't look at me at all. 'I brushed my teeth for five minutes, three times a day. Mouthwash and flossing too. It was one of his rules.'

Oh God. 'I'm sorry. I didn't mean to . . .'

'It's OK. I'm going to have to get used to talking about it, aren't I? I only brushed my teeth for a couple of minutes last night. Same this morning. And I haven't flossed.' Finally a ghost of a smile appears on her face and I breathe again. 'You don't need to worry, you know. I can talk about it. About . . . him.'

If the things that had happened to her had happened to me I don't think I'd ever ever talk about them again, I think. 'I can't even begin to imagine what you've been through.' Yet more banality.

'Good. You shouldn't have to.' She goes to bite her nails and then stops herself, tucking her hands inside the sleeves of the hoodie. I wonder if that was another one of his rules. 'Anyway, I want to hear about you. I've got some catching up to do, haven't I? How about you tell me every single thing you've done in the last thirteen years?' She laughs at the alarmed look on my face. 'I'm kidding! Sort of.'

'Um . . . where do you want me to start?'

'I'm sorry. I didn't mean to put you on the spot.'
She stares off into space again and I'm not sure where
she's gone but I'm almost certain I should be glad that
I can't follow her there. 'You know . . . no matter
how bad things got, I was always glad he took me and
not you. Whenever I was scared or couldn't sleep I
thought about you.'

I've read articles asking that question: why her
and not me? Most people seem to think it came down
to age and/or hair colour. I was four years old with
brown hair; Laurel was six years old with blonde hair.

I used to have recurring nightmares of a man
standing over the two of us. The sun was always behind
him so his face was in shadow. He would lead Laurel
away by the hand and I would go back to playing in the
sand. Sometimes I would run after them and ask for
an ice cream and the man would take my hand and the
three of us would walk down the road together.

'Have you still got that nightlight?'

I have no idea what she's talking about and she can
tell from the look on my face.

'The penguin one? With the red hat and scarf? You
had this weird name for it, but I can't seem to . . .'

All of a sudden I can picture it, crystal clear. 'Egg!'
Laurel nods vigorously, eyes bright, and we both laugh
at the miracle of a shared memory.

How could I have forgotten about Egg? For years I couldn't get to sleep without that penguin's tummy glowing from the corner of the room. Egg was the only thing protecting me from the monster under the bed and the monster in the wardrobe. And then he was the only thing protecting me from the monster in the front garden – the one who led little girls away by the hand and made their families sad.

Laurel tells me that she used to think about Egg when she couldn't sleep, when she felt suffocated by the darkness around her. She would try to picture him in her mind, focusing on every little detail. 'Sometimes it felt like I could actually *see* him – but only if I concentrated really, really hard. Those were the best times. I was able to go to sleep then. But sometimes I couldn't quite remember the exact shade of red of his hat, or the shape of his beak didn't feel right.'

I nod as if I understand. And I do understand, in a theoretical sort of way. But I'll never truly understand what she's been through, will I? Even if she was to tell me every single thing that happened to her, I will never really *know*. I'll never know what it's like to be locked in a pitch-black basement, scared and alone – or even worse: scared and *not* alone.

Chapter 9

Laurel is disappointed that I have no idea what happened to the nightlight, so I tell her we'll look for it when she comes home. 'Home,' she says. 'I like the sound of that.'

She asks me about school and it all sounds amazing and interesting to her because she can barely even remember going. I ask her if she can read, then I apologize because it seems like an insensitive question. Laurel doesn't mind though. She learned to read and write. She learned pretty much all the same subjects I did. I ask how that's possible, not bothering to hide my scepticism.

'He taught me.'

'Like . . . proper lessons?'

She nods. 'He hated ignorance. He said there was no excuse for it.'

'So you had textbooks and everything?'

'Some. Mostly he had his own handwritten notes. A coloured folder for each subject.'

It's too bizarre to get my head around. The idea of this monster – this psychopath – teaching her maths and grammar and science. He brought her novels to read too – but only if she was good. She didn't go into detail about what being 'good' entailed. A couple of years ago he taught her how to use a computer, saying everyone needed to be able to use computers in the modern world. He wired up an old desktop one for her. It wasn't connected to the Internet – obviously.

We talk and talk and gradually I begin to build up a picture of her life for the past thirteen years and she begins to build up a picture of mine. We swap information, filling in the gaps, asking questions and answering them. I steer clear of anything that I think might upset her though, which means a lot of my questions aren't the ones I really want to ask.

Laurel finds it fascinating that I have a boyfriend. She asks lots of questions about Thomas and I try my best to answer them. She even asks if Thomas and I have had sex. There's an awkward silence before I tell her the truth. She asks me if I liked it and I say I sort of did. Then she goes quiet and I say maybe we should talk about something else.

She shakes her head fiercely and says, 'I *hate* it. I

never want to do it again. It's disgusting.' She looks so intense and angry and I want to kill the man who made her feel like this. No – I want to hurt him, inflict the worst sort of pain and *then* kill him. What he did to her doesn't count as sex. He attacked and violated a little girl in the most horrifying way possible. She *must* see the difference.

'What was he like? The . . . man. It's OK if you don't want to talk about it.'

Laurel leans forward and grabs a sheet of paper that was face down on the coffee table. She hands it to me without comment.

It's a drawing of a man's face. It's hard to tell how old he is – somewhere between forty and fifty perhaps. His eyes are slightly too far apart, which is supposed to make a person look more trustworthy. His face is utterly nondescript, apart from the nose, which is big and hooked, with weirdly distracting nostrils. His hair is short and spiky. 'This is him?' Laurel nods. I am looking at the man who took my sister.

'It's not quite finished. The police artist is coming back later to work on it before the press conference. The nose isn't quite right yet.' She stares at the picture and I have the strongest urge to scrunch up the paper, to set fire to it and watch his face blacken and burn.

'What's his name?'

A faint smile appears on Laurel's face. 'At first I called him Smith. He was hardly going to tell me his real name, was he?'

Smith. Probably the most common name in the country. 'At first?'

Laurel tilts her head questioningly.

'You said at first you called him Smith. What did you call him after that?'

She looks away and keeps her eyes averted from mine as she tells me the name she called him – the name he made her use even though she knew it was wrong.

'Daddy.'

My parents choose that exact moment to come back. They've brought drinks and food. When I look at the clock I see that Laurel and I have been talking for more than two hours. When I look out of the window I see that it's snowing, thick and fast.

I manage to get rid of the appalled look on my face while Mum and Dad take their wet coats and scarves off. They both try to hide it, but they're looking at us closely to see how things are going. Laurel and I smile to show them that things are going just fine, thank you very much. I bet Mum wanted to come back ages ago but Dad made her wait, to give us more time.

Daddy. The thought of her saying it to that man sickens me. I hope she hasn't told my parents. *Our* parents.

Dad starts pulling sandwiches out of a plastic bag. 'Prawn mayonnaise?' Laurel says, 'Eurgh!' and I make a gagging noise, then we both laugh. Dad rolls his eyes and says, 'I suppose I'll be having that one then,' but you can tell he's delighted that we're *bonding*.

Laurel and I both reach for the BLT baguette and she insists that I have it and I insist that *she* has it. In the end it all comes down to who's more stubborn, so of course I win. I end up with ham and cheese; it's dry and hard to swallow. I want to ask Laurel what kind of food she's been eating, because whatever it was, she clearly wasn't eating enough of it. She makes short work of the baguette and devours a packet of crisps too. I realize that all three of us – me, Mum and Dad – are watching her eat. Laurel doesn't seem to notice, or if she does, she doesn't seem to care.

There's a slightly awkward moment at lunch when Mum says something about this being our first family meal together in thirteen years. She apologizes that it's not something more special and says she'll cook something soon – a roast dinner, perhaps? – so that we can sit down as a family at long last.

Laurel says that would be really nice and Dad requests roast beef and Yorkshire puddings. Mum blushes (I have no idea why).

'Will Michel be invited too?' I can't help myself. Someone needs to remind them that things are different now.

For a second the only sound is that of Laurel tearing into a second packet of crisps. She says, 'I hope so. I can't wait to meet him,' and Dad smiles gratefully because he knows as well as I do that Laurel has just averted an argument.

Mum says, 'Of course Michel will be there,' as if that was the plan all along. As if she hadn't completely forgotten his existence for a minute there. She's a bit quieter after that, which makes me feel guilty, but I won't allow Michel to be sidelined. He's as much a part of this screwed-up family as the rest of us. And unlike the rest of us, he actually *chose* to join it.

A bunch of people turn up after lunch and it's chaos. They're trying to organize this press conference, even though everyone's fully aware that the press already have the story. It's on the Internet, of course. #LaurelLogan is trending on Twitter. When I check my phone I see that lots of people have messaged me.

Only a few of these people are actually my friends. Martha and Thomas have both texted and I text back to say everything's fine. Martha texts again immediately: *What's it like having a brand-new big sister?* A stranger might think she's being insensitive, but this is just the way Martha and I communicate with each other. I think for a second, looking over to where Laurel is talking to a senior-looking policeman. I wonder why he has to wear a uniform if he's so senior. Perhaps he thinks the uniform adds gravitas. There's another, much younger, policeman standing behind the first one. He has the beginnings of a black eye, which makes me wonder if he's the one Laurel supposedly lashed out at yesterday. I must remember to ask Dad later.

Whatever it is they're talking about, Laurel doesn't look happy. She shakes her head a number of times during the conversation. Eventually Mum puts her arm around Laurel and leads her off to the bathroom. What was all that about?

When they finally come out of the bathroom, Laurel sees me watching and aims a shy little wave in my direction. She even manages a smile.

Everyone told her that it would be better if she stayed away from the press conference. They said it would be overwhelming for her, but she's adamant that she wants to be there. She even wants to read a statement. 'I won't let him win,' she whispered to me. I felt something suspiciously close to pride.

I text Martha back: *I think I'm going to like it.*

Chapter 10

I watch the press conference — alone — on the massive TV in Laurel's bedroom. They didn't want me down there any more than I wanted to be there.

It's surreal, watching my family (*now new and improved, with added Laurel!*) walk into the ballroom fifteen floors below. Laurel's flanked by Mum and Dad; Mum's crying already. I can't help comparing it to the press conference they held when she went missing; I must have watched it a hundred times on YouTube. Dad spoke straight into the camera, talking to whoever had taken Laurel. 'She belongs with us. Faith keeps asking where her big sister has gone. Please, if you're listening, do the right thing. Bring our daughter back to us. Bring Laurel home.' That was the moment when Dad really broke down. He'd managed to keep it together up until then, but you could tell it was there, bubbling under the surface. He slumped back into his chair and Mum took his hand and squeezed it tightly, as if she was trying to force some of her strength into him. But by that point she was sobbing too.

This press conference is very different. It's rowdier, for one thing. Journalists start shouting questions the minute my family walk in. The camera flashes go crazy. The senior-looking policeman reads a statement, after pausing to take a pair of glasses from his breast pocket. Another policeman reads another statement and shows the cameras a new picture of 'Smith'. This one's been done on computer, I think. It's a bit different from the one I saw – the face is narrower, the nostrils larger. Both policemen say that while they're delighted that Laurel is home, they will not rest until the 'perpetrator of this sickening crime' is brought to justice. They used that line at the press conference when Laurel was taken – not these policemen, but ones just like them.

Policeman Number Two says officers are knocking on doors and asking questions *as we speak*. Laurel was able to give them some very useful information about her captor. (Really? That's news to me.) It's only a matter of time, apparently.

The police ask if there are any questions, and of course there are. Most of them are aimed at Laurel and Mum and Dad so the policemen ignore those. But they do answer a couple.

'How can you be sure that Laurel is safe now? Why would he just let her go?'

'We are as sure as we can be that Laurel's ordeal is over, and we will be doing everything in our power to keep her safe. As to why she was released? I think, today of all days, we should just be grateful that she's back home with her family. There will be plenty of time for those questions in the coming days and weeks.'

'Were there any sightings of the suspect leaving Laurel in the garden yesterday?'

'Not that we're aware of, but officers will be going door to door in Stanley Street, speaking to every resident.'

'Did the police fail Laurel?'

An almost inaudible sigh from Policeman Number One. 'We did everything we could to find Laurel Logan, mounting the biggest search the county has ever seen. But sadly, tragically, it wasn't enough . . . Now, Bernard Ness would like to say a few words before I hand over to the Logans.' He doesn't quite manage to hide the disdain in his voice.

Bernard Ness is our local MP. God knows what he's doing there. Bernard Ness is not a fat man, but he walks as if he is. He huffs and puffs his way up to the microphone and I become transfixed by his nose. It's bulbous and red, much like the rest of his face. His sideburns are damp with sweat.

He was also present at the press conference thirteen years ago, slightly less red, less bulbous, milling around in the background. This time he's right there up onstage with my family. It quickly becomes clear that Bernard Ness is here for two reasons: he likes the sound of his own voice; and he's desperate to associate himself with a good-news story (and let's face it – this is the best good-news story there's been in a long, long time). Maybe he thinks it will help people forget the financial scandal he was involved in last month.

Bernard says that thirteen years ago 'our community' was shocked and devastated and a few more words that all amount to the same thing. The crime against 'Little Laurel Logan' threatened to tear 'our community' apart, but in the end it brought us closer together. 'We' never gave up hope, apparently.

He talks for far too long, but no one tries to shut him up. Laurel and Mum and Dad listen politely in the background. Laurel's face is perfectly expressionless. Finally Ness starts winding down. He ends his pointless speech by turning towards Laurel, pausing for effect, then saying, 'Welcome home, Laurel.' Laurel nods; she doesn't smile.

Dad's up next. The first thing he says is, 'I'm going to keep this short,' and I love him for it. In the background Bernard Ness nods as though this isn't a dig at him. Dad talks about how happy we all are to have Laurel home, and thanks everyone who never gave up searching and hoping and believing she would come back. He thanks the police and says (emphatically) that they should not be held responsible for what 'that man' did to his daughter. Then he does something weird. He addresses Laurel's captor directly. 'Whoever you are, wherever you are, I want you to know that we *will* find you, and you will be held accountable for your crimes.' He lets that hang for a beat or two before taking a steadying breath. His hands grip the sides of the lectern. 'But for now, today, I want to thank you.' There are no gasps from the crowd or anything, but you can tell people are shocked. I certainly am. 'Thank you for bringing our daughter back to us.'

Dad sits down and no one seems to know what should happen next. The policemen exchange glances, and Mum looks at Dad, and Dad looks at Laurel, and Bernard Ness looks at the photographers (of course). Laurel stands up and walks over to the lectern.

Laurel looks out at the crowd in front of her and it seems like she's looking at each and every face and camera. She doesn't flinch under the constant flashing. 'My name is Laurel Logan.' She clears her throat and takes a shaky breath. I can't believe how brave she is, doing this. 'My name is Laurel Logan, and I'd like to take this opportunity to thank some people.' She echoes what Dad said – thanking the police and the public – but she also mentions the press. 'Thank you for keeping my story alive – thank you for never forgetting.' It's a little odd, but I bet the journalists down there are lapping it up. I'm sure Dad doesn't approve, after everything he's been through with that lot, but I reckon Laurel's earned the right to say whatever she wants.

Laurel stares into the camera and it feels like she's looking at me. It must feel the same way to everyone who's watching – our friends and family, Thomas and Martha, people up and down the country and all over the world. The camera moves in closer on Laurel's face so that you can't see anyone else. They didn't do anything about her hair before the press conference and it still doesn't look like she's wearing make-up – maybe just a bit of powder. She looks like a girl who has been through some seriously bad stuff.

'Yesterday my nightmare came to an end. I don't

think I ever believed it would happen. I hoped for it and prayed for it every single night, and when things got really bad –' she pauses and blinks hard to stop herself from crying – 'well, I hoped and prayed even harder. Yesterday my prayers were answered.' She bows her head for a moment before looking at the camera again. 'I don't have the words to express what I'm feeling right now. To know that I have a mother, a father and a sister. To know they never stopped looking for me. Never stopped caring. And they've told me that *you* never stopped caring either. They told me that total strangers from all over the world have sent cards and letters – even money. They told me that the police worked tirelessly to try to find me, and that my story has hardly been out of the newspapers – all this time. I can't tell you how much this means to me. To know that I wasn't forgotten.' Another bow of her head. I bet half the people in that room have tears in their eyes.

Laurel finishes by thanking everyone. She doesn't mention Smith. She says she's looking forward to getting to know her family again – especially her little sister, Faith. She smiles when she says my name, and the camera flashes start up again. I realize I'm smiling too.

As soon as she stops talking and moves away from

the lectern, the journalists start shouting questions. You might think they'd have a little bit more respect – and sensitivity – today, but you would be wrong. It's hard to distinguish individual questions, but most of them seem to start with some variation of 'How do you feel . . . ?'

A man takes Laurel's place. He was one of the ones milling around the suite earlier. He makes calming motions with his hands; he looks like he's directing traffic. It takes a long time for the shouting to die down, and when it does you can hear a woman's voice shouting out one final question: 'Laurel! Laurel! Have you been shopping yet?' I swear at the TV while laughter ripples around the room downstairs. Even Mum and Dad smile; Laurel does not.

The press conference is over and a man and a woman with perfect hair sit in a futuristic-looking TV studio and talk about how brave Laurel is. They use the word 'remarkable' a lot and they say that they hope the media will leave our family to heal in peace, which is ironic because one of their correspondents has been known to shout questions through our letter box.

The shiny news presenters decide that the moral of the story is that we should never give up hope, no matter how bad things seem. They seem very pleased with themselves for having found a greater meaning in Laurel's story.

Martha texts: *That was surreal.*

Yes, it was.

Chapter 11

Mum stands back to admire her handiwork. 'There. What do you think?'

The room looks much better than it did a week ago. It looks cosy and comfortable and welcoming. Mum asked Laurel what colours she liked and whether there was anything special she wanted in her room. Laurel said she didn't mind. Her only request was that the bed faced the door; Mum didn't need to ask why.

It took hours of rummaging through boxes in the attic (not to mention a traumatic spider-in-hair incident), but eventually I found what I was looking for. I plug it in to the socket next to the door and switch it on. Egg the Penguin is the finishing touch. Laurel's room is ready for her. My sister is coming home.

*

Someone (Maggie the Counsellor, perhaps?) had decided that Laurel shouldn't come home right away. She needed some time to adjust to life in the outside world. Mum wasn't too happy about that, but Dad convinced her to go along with it. 'It's only one more week, love.' He was right: one week was nothing compared to thirteen years. The two of them took turns staying in the extra bedroom in Laurel's suite.

Laurel's been talking to the police almost every day, repeating her story over and over again to different police officers. Mum told me that Dad lost his temper with them on Wednesday because they kept on asking the same questions and Laurel freaked out when they tried to do the cheek swab again. They got a policewoman to try this time; the reaction was less violent, but the result was the same. Laurel locked herself in the bathroom until the woman went away. Laurel refused to tell my (our) parents what the problem was, but I guess it must have triggered some bad memories or something. Dad reckons they really need to leave her alone now. (*'She's got enough to deal with without the police hounding her all the bloody time. And what do they need a DNA test for anyway?!'*)

Laurel's been talking to a psychologist too. About the abuse, I think, but I haven't asked. We've had two family sessions with Maggie Dimmock — one in the hotel and one in what used to be our favourite Italian restaurant. That second one was a big deal; Laurel isn't used to going outside. She has *been* outside. Once a week the man would blindfold her and put her in his van and drive her to a forest. The police were obviously keen to learn as much as they could about that forest, even showing Laurel pictures of different kinds of trees in case they could narrow it down that way. But Laurel thought the trees were probably pines, which are just about as common as you can get. She wasn't even sure how far the forest was from where she was being held. She tried to count the seconds and minutes she spent in the van, but Smith wasn't stupid — the journey would take anywhere between one hour and three hours, but they would always end up at the same place. He would let Laurel out and tell her to exercise. She only tried to run away once; he made sure she didn't try ever again.

So that was Laurel's only experience of the outside world — for thirteen years. Just walking down the street was a huge achievement for her. We took it slowly and tried to ignore the journalists and photographers shadowing our every move. The police made sure they kept their distance.

I walked with Laurel, a little way behind Mum

and Dad. Maggie was behind us, not really dressed for the weather, her shoulders hunched against the cold wind. Laurel couldn't stop staring at everything — the cars, the shops, the people. She grabbed my hand when an ambulance screamed past, siren blaring. I murmured words of reassurance and squeezed her hand. I tried to imagine what this must be like for her, but of course I could never know. She didn't let go of my hand until we were safely inside the restaurant, which was empty. Maggie must have called ahead to make sure.

Laurel was baffled by the menu — confused by being able to choose what to eat. 'Can I have *anything* I want?'

'Anything,' Mum and Dad said in unison.

Mum suggested spaghetti. 'It used to be your favourite.'

Laurel loved it. She made a complete mess of eating it, and I did the same with mine so she wouldn't feel self-conscious.

It didn't really feel like a counselling session, but maybe Maggie was just really good at her job. Sometimes she'd throw a question out there and we'd remember why we were here. She asked if there was anything we were worried about. I shook my head, even though there were lots of things I was worried about.

We talked about how things would work when Laurel came home. Mum and Dad had obviously talked about this beforehand. They'd decided that Laurel and I would stay at his place on the weekends. I wondered if Mum had put up a fight about that. Laurel and I would have to share a room.

'You don't mind, do you, love?' asked Dad as he snapped a breadstick in half.

I shook my head.

Laurel cleared her throat. 'I don't mind sleeping on the sofa.' She looked down at her empty plate.

'No, really, it's fine. It'll be fun.' I smiled at Laurel; I wanted her to believe me.

Maggie seemed pleased with how things were going, but she warned us that there might be 'bumps in the road ahead' and we shouldn't put pressure on ourselves for things to be normal straightaway. 'The important thing is that you keep talking – and listening – to each other. Communication is the key.' She said that any one of us could call her if we had anything we needed to talk through, and that we would keep on going for sessions with one of her colleagues who lives locally.

Dad ordered a bottle of champagne (ignoring the disapproving look from Mum) and poured five glasses. Laurel had never had alcohol before. She grimaced at the first sip but quite liked it by the fourth. Mum told her to go easy.

Laurel giggled and downed the rest of her glass.

I had to go back to school on Thursday, even though Dad was taking the whole week off work. It wasn't fair. Mum and Laurel were going shopping for clothes then on to the hairdresser. It seemed like something the three of us might have done together – if you ignore the fact that I hate shopping.

School was predictably insane, but at least I had Thomas and Martha there. It was the first time I'd seen either of them since Laurel came back; it was the first time I'd seen Thomas since I had sex with him in his van. We'd texted a bit though and he knew I was coming in.

He was already in the common room when I arrived half an hour before registration. He was sitting on the floor with his back against a radiator dappled with peeling paint. He was reading a book and eating an apple. Thomas always eats the whole apple – seeds, core, everything except the stem. The first time he did it in front of me I told him it was disgusting; he lectured me about the 'frankly appalling' levels of food wastage in the world.

I sat down next to him, sliding my back down

the radiator, probably peeling off some more paint in the process. I started to speak but he held up a finger to silence me. I was used to this: Thomas never stops reading until he's reached the end of a paragraph. Finally he put his book down and kissed me. Unsurprisingly he tasted like apples.

He put his arm around me and I leaned my head against his. 'Crazy week, huh?' he whispered.

'The craziest.' I closed my eyes. For the first time in days I felt like myself again.

'I'm here if you want to talk about things, OK? But it's fine if you don't. Whatever you need.' He kissed my forehead and I remembered why I liked – loved – him.

The common-room door opened and a group of girls piled in. They clocked me straightaway. I knew what was going to happen and I wanted to avoid it at all costs. I stood up and turned my back to them, pretending to look for something in my bag. 'Thomas, let's go,' I whispered.

Thomas was too slow getting his stuff together.

'Faith! Oh my God, Faith! Oh. My. God!'

I could stay facing the wall, but it wouldn't do any good. Laney Finch would wait all day if she had to. I turned around slowly, as if facing a firing squad.

Before I knew what was happening, Laney Finch had flung herself at me. I stumbled back against the radiator, hitting my elbow on the corner. Her arms were around me and it felt like she had too many of them – I was being hugged by a Laney squid. My arms stayed rigidly by my sides.

The hug went on far too long. Over Laney's shoulder I could see her friends hanging back, whispering and staring. At least two of them looked like they might want to hug me too. There were tears in their eyes and they held their hands to their chests as if the emotion was just too much for them.

Laney pulled back but still had my arms firmly in her grip. She was crying, of course. 'I can't believe it, Faith. It's just TOO amazing for words. It's a miracle, isn't it? I totally think this qualifies as a miracle, don't you? I prayed, you know. Every night. I told you that, didn't I?'

Laney had indeed told me that she prayed every night for my sister. It was her opening line the day she decided we should be best friends. That was five years ago. Laney Finch likes to think that she feels things more deeply than the average person. Of course, this is total bullshit. She has no more empathy than anyone else – it's all talk. She's the type of person who sees a natural disaster in some faraway country on the news and cries about it. (*Oh, those poor people . . . Imagine what they must be going through . . . It breaks my heart.*) Five minutes later she's on the phone to one of her pathetic friends, moaning about how unfair it is that her parents won't buy her a new MacBook Air for her birthday.

From the day she arrived at school Laney Finch tried to latch on to me; I was determined to be unlatchable. She never seemed to get the message though. Every time there was a story about Laurel in the papers, Laney Finch popped up, shooting sympathetic looks across the canteen or asking intrusive questions. I only lost my temper with her once: when she said she knew exactly how I felt because her cat had gone missing and hadn't been seen for a week. I didn't punch her in the face, which was what she deserved. I *did* tell her to fuck off, which seemed to shock her just as much.

I was determined to at least *try* to be nice this time so I mumbled, 'Thanks,' and tried to extricate myself from her grip. Thomas was no help at all – he was busy putting his book back in his bag oh so carefully, so he didn't damage the cover.

Laney let go of my arms and daintily dabbed at her eyes. I wondered if she wore waterproof mascara every day so that she was fully prepared for her regular crying stints. 'It's such wonderful news, Faith. I haven't stopped smiling since I heard so I can't even begin to imagine how you must be feeling.' She shook her head and smiled, as if that proved that she had *literally* not stopped smiling for the past five days. I waited. She smiled some more. I said I'd better get going, even though there was nowhere I had to be for at least twenty minutes. I turned to take Thomas's hand but Laney somehow managed to manoeuvre herself in between us. 'So . . . what's Laurel like? I bet she's really . . . God, I don't even know . . .'

Laney likes to *know* things – especially things that other people *don't* know. Gossip is oxygen to her – without it, she'll, like, literally, you know, die or something.

'She's fine. Thank you.' I gave Thomas a look that very obviously said, 'GET ME OUT OF HERE!' but for some reason he didn't seem to understand it.

Laney leaned close to me and I could smell toothpaste on her breath. 'Why do you think he let her go? It's weird, isn't it?' she whispered, eyes wide.

'Oh, do fuck off, Laney.' Martha's timing was impeccable.

Laney flinched and turned to face Martha. 'Excuse me, but this is a *private conversation*.'

Martha stood next to me and smiled sweetly. 'I

don't think so. In fact, I don't think it counts as a conversation at all when you just talk *at* someone. So why don't you leave Faith alone and go and cry over some Cambodian orphans or endangered pygmy elephants? Or endangered Cambodian pygmy elephants who also happen to be orphans.'

Laney was too shocked to speak. Her mouth opened and closed again.

Martha crossed her arms, looking like a burly bouncer. Martha is tall. Sturdy. Intimidating if you look at her in the right light. 'Go. Away.'

Laney looked to me for help, eyes pleading. 'I was just trying to . . . I really do care, you know.'

I nodded.

Laney fled, her gaggle of friends enveloping her, sweeping her away and shooting us dirty looks at the same time.

Martha waved at them before turning to me. 'You're welcome.'

'Thank you.'

We hugged. It's quite nice having your own personal bodyguard.

Martha and Thomas stuck to me like superglue for the rest of the week. If one of them wasn't with me, the other one was. Laney wasn't the only one who wanted to talk to me; the teachers were at it too. At least I'd missed the special assembly they held on Monday.

It should have been nice and I shouldn't have minded the attention. But it wasn't nice and I did mind. I just want to be left alone. It's bad enough having photographers and camera crews stationed outside our house night and day – and a police car down the street – without being scrutinized at school too. Hopefully things will get back to normal soon. Whatever normal is.

Chapter 12

'Laurel! Laurel! How does it feel to be coming home? Laurel! Can you tell us . . . ?'

The front door closes, muffling the shouts from the garden. The curtains are already closed, but you can still see the flashes from the cameras. I wonder why they're still snapping away – there's nothing to see now that she's safely inside.

Dad locks the door and leans against it. 'So much for them giving us some privacy,' he says. He was interviewed on Sky News last night – *on the eve of Laurel's homecoming* – and he'd asked for exactly that: privacy. Unfortunately it seems that's the one thing the media is unable (unwilling) to give.

Mum's clasping her hands together and looking anxiously at Laurel, who is standing rooted to the spot, looking around the room, taking it all in. A teddy bear is nestled in the crook of her arm. It's battered and worn and I can smell it from here. It also seems to be missing one arm. Barnaby has been through more than your average bear.

I bet the photographers got a shot of Laurel clutching the bear. That will be *the* photo – the one that will be on the Internet in a matter of minutes, on the news in a few hours, on the front page of the papers tomorrow morning. Maybe they'll print the old photo of Barnaby the Bear next to the new one. Maybe they'll use the word 'poignant' a lot and draw ridiculous parallels between the bear and Laurel.

The noise from outside dies down. Laurel (and Barnaby) and I sit on the sofa and Dad takes the chair next to the fire. Mum makes tea. I notice Laurel staring at the mantelpiece – there's a picture of her, aged five, right in the middle. There's a picture of me around the same age, just off to one side. There are no pictures of my parents. In the old house, we used to have a photo of the two of them on their wedding day on the mantelpiece. They look young and kind of drunk, both of them raising glasses of champagne to the camera. I wonder what happened to that picture.

Mum wanted to put up a 'welcome home' banner but I managed to convince her it would be tacky. It's the kind of thing you do when your daughter's come back from her gap year in Nicaragua or from a

91

stay in hospital, not when she's been kidnapped and repeatedly raped by a psychopath.

Laurel likes tea. Smith brought her tea when she was feeling sad. He said, 'The world always looks brighter when you've got a mug of tea in your hand'. Mum was horrified when she heard that; she says almost exactly the same thing. When she was with him, Laurel always drank out of the same bright yellow mug, with a smiley face on it, until she dropped it one day. It smashed on the concrete floor. Smith slapped her so hard she fell and cut her hand on one of the broken shards of mug. He stitched up the wound himself, doing such a good job that you can barely even see the scar on her palm. The police wondered if that meant that Smith might have been medically trained, but Laurel said she didn't think so. He had several huge medical books that he used to refer to whenever she was ill.

Mum comes back in with the tray and hands round the mugs. Laurel's is red, with her name on it. Her face lights up when she sees it, then she looks to Mum for an explanation. Mum nods in my direction.

'I . . . I thought you should have your own mug. It's the same as mine.' I hold mine up as proof. My mug has a chip on it and the 'I' in Faith is starting to wear off.

Laurel looks at her mug as if it's something precious

and miraculous. Then she looks at me in pretty much the same way. 'Thank you, Faith. That's . . .' her voice catches, 'really kind of you.'

I shrug. 'It's no big deal.' But I'm really pleased she likes it. Everyone should have their own mug; it makes tea taste so much better.

After tea, we all head upstairs to show Laurel her room. Mum clears her throat as she steps back to let Laurel go first. 'I'm so sorry we moved house, Laurel . . . I always wanted you to come home to your own bedroom . . . That's how it was supposed to be.' She doesn't look at Dad, and he doesn't look at her.

Laurel doesn't seem to notice the awkwardness though. 'I don't mind at all. *This* is home. Wherever you are.' She couldn't have said anything more perfect. Mum's eyes glisten with tears.

'Well, what do you think?' I wish Mum didn't sound so needy. The room is nothing compared to the presidential suite — for one thing it has a single bed instead of a super-king-size one — but it's a whole lot better than where she was before. With *him*. A camp bed and a dirty sleeping bag. A bare light bulb. Mice.

Laurel spots him immediately. 'You found him!'

I shrug again. I seem to be doing a lot of shrugging these days. 'I thought you might like to have him.'

'I can't believe it! He looks exactly like . . . he

looks the same!' She shakes her head and kneels down to inspect the nightlight; she touches his head with a certain reverence. She looks up at me, eyes shining with unshed tears. 'Is it really OK if I keep him? I don't like the dark.'

I nod. 'Of course it's OK!'

Mum crouches down next to Laurel. 'You can leave your door open at night, if you like. That way you'll get the light from the landing too.'

Dad says, 'Why don't we leave the girls to it? Faith can show Laurel everything she needs. I'll bring up the bags in a bit.'

Laurel sits on the bed, moving her hand back and forth across the duvet cover. Her other hand still clutches Barnaby. 'It's nice. This room, I mean.'

I sit down next to her. 'Mum was worried you'd hate it. She says we can redecorate anytime you want.'

'Why would I hate it? It's perfect . . . a room of my own.'

She sets Barnaby the Bear down on the chair in the corner. I want to tell her that he could really do with a bath, but it doesn't seem like the right thing to say.

Mum's thought of everything. Toiletries and pyjamas and a hairbrush. There's even some brand-new make-up on the dressing table. Laurel touches everything, as if to make sure it's all solid and real and isn't going to be taken away from her at any second. She spends a long time looking at a tube of foundation, and it hits me: she won't know how to use make-up. I explain what everything is and tell her I'll show her how to use it all. 'Not that you need make-up. You're beautiful without it.' I feel my cheeks flush.

'I'm not beautiful,' she says flatly.

'You are.'

Laurel shakes her head and moves from the dressing table to the bedside table. There's a mobile phone – an old one of mine, with a new SIM card. 'Is this for me?' I nod, and she picks it up. I show her how it works, and scroll through the numbers I've already added to her contacts: me, Mum, Dad. I probably should have added Maggie Dimmock too.

'See? You can call me anytime.'

Laurel presses a button and my phone buzzes in my jeans pocket. I take out my phone and say hello. She says hello into her phone and we both laugh.

'Where's your bedroom?' she asks.

'Right next door. Want to see?'

My room has a lot of stuff in it. More stuff than a room this size should probably have. Mum's always trying to get me to throw things out or give them to charity, but I like it this way. There's something comforting about it. I don't like getting rid of stuff; I don't like throwing memories away.

'Wow,' says Laurel.

'Sorry it's such a mess.'

She shakes her head and turns around, trying to take it all in. There are pictures all over the walls – photos I've taken, pictures cut out from magazines. You can barely see the walls underneath. I realize there are no photos of Laurel and I wish I'd thought to put one up before she came home.

On the desk there are three rows of little toys from Happy Meals and Kinder Eggs. They're lined up like little soldiers. There's a stack of shoe boxes on the floor next to the desk. Laurel doesn't investigate, but I wonder what she'd make of a box full of sugar sachets and cubes. For a while it was a bit of an obsession of mine. I only stopped collecting them last year.

Laurel asks me about some of the pictures on the walls, which means I end up talking about my favourite films and bands. It's easy to forget that she has no frame of reference for most of the things I talk about. She doesn't seem to mind that I keep on having to go off at tangents, that I keep having to explain more and more things before I go back to telling her what I wanted to tell her in the first place. She just takes it all in. She seems to concentrate hard on what I'm saying. She really listens; I like that.

Laurel has seen *some* films. Occasionally Smith would bring an old TV and video player and hook them up in the basement. (Who has *videos* in this day and age?) Laurel reckons this only happened once a month, or even less often than that. There was no rhyme or reason to it – it didn't seem to be a reward for good behaviour. The films she watched were all really old – *Mary Poppins* and *The Sound of Music* and one called *One of Our Dinosaurs Is Missing* that she particularly liked.

'Is this your boyfriend?' Laurel points to a photo next to my bed. It's the last thing I see before I turn off the light at night.

'Yeah, that's Thomas.'

'He's very good-looking.' Thomas *is* good-looking, but not in an obvious way. He *looks* like he writes poetry. His hair is too long, and he's pale and interesting rather than tanned and chiselled. There's something gentle about his features – a softness that I like. When he first turned up at school, you could tell none of the boys were threatened; there's nothing remotely alpha male about Thomas. But something strange happened within days: girls were drawn to him. Some of the most popular girls in my year started trailing after him, offering to show him around the school and help him 'settle in'. He saw straight through them, politely declining their advances, preferring to spend time alone. Then he started following me around.

I didn't even notice at first; Thomas is very good at skulking. But then I realized that I was seeing him *all* the time – in the corridors, in the library, in the courtyard. I mentioned it to Martha one day and she rolled her eyes at me. '*Finally*. I was wondering when you were going to notice.' She was the one who encouraged me to talk to him, although 'Why the hell are you stalking me?' probably wasn't quite what she had in mind.

Thomas was startled when I confronted him in the library, but he didn't try to deny it. He said, 'I think you're interesting.'

'Look, if there's something you want to ask about my sister, just come right out and ask it.' It happened all the time – people staring and whispering. It got to a point where I almost preferred the ones who were brazen enough to actually talk to me about it – like Laney Finch.

Thomas just stared at me.

'Well? I have better things to do than stand here being gawped at, so if you don't mind, I'm just going to go.' I wasn't usually quite so rude, but something about his face riled me.

'Why would I want to ask about your sister?'

I crossed my arms and waited.

He closed his notebook and waited too. Eventually he broke the stalemate by asking a question I'd never been asked before: 'Who's your sister?'

I think it was those three words that did it for me. I'm not saying I fell head over heels in love with him as soon as he said them, but they unlocked something inside me. They made it possible for me to not hate him, to start sort of liking him, to start really liking him, and finally, after a few months, to maybe sort of almost love him. None of that would have been possible if he hadn't asked me that question.

Thomas has lived in more countries than most people have been to on holiday – he's an army kid. He moved here when his parents retired a couple of years ago. He doesn't like to talk about the army thing – it doesn't exactly mesh with his strictly pacifist views.

When I realized Thomas wasn't joking, I told him who my sister was. He nodded vaguely. 'Oh yeah, I think I've heard of her.' He said this in exactly the same way I do when I tell him I've heard of this poem or that book, when the truth is I have no idea what he's talking about.

I stayed and talked to him until the bell went. Two weeks later, he asked me out. I kissed him for the first time one week after that. I've never told him that I wouldn't even have considered going out with him if he'd asked me about Laurel.

Laurel sits down on my bed and asks me more questions about Thomas. She asks why I like him. (She doesn't say 'love'.) Why, out of all the boys at school, Thomas is the one I chose to be my boyfriend. It makes me smile, her saying that. As if all the boys in school are clamouring to go out with me. I don't tell Laurel the truth: that the reason I chose him to be my boyfriend was because he was the one person who never – not even once – asked about her.

Chapter 13

Mum didn't ask Laurel if this was OK – she went right ahead and organized it, only telling her this morning. I wonder what Laurel would have said if she *had* been consulted. It's overwhelming even for me, so God knows what it must be like for her.

I have never seen so many members of my family in the same room before. Laurel sits in the middle of the sofa and everyone else forms a ring around her. There have been lots of tears; there has been quite a bit of champagne. (These two facts may or may not be linked.)

The only person missing is my grandmother. Dad's mother lives in the south of France; she's very frail. Her husband died when I was five years old, almost exactly a year after Laurel was taken. I don't remember him. Mum's parents are here though; Gran keeps fussing over Laurel, brushing imaginary bits of fluff from her T-shirt just for an excuse to touch her.

Mum's sister, Eleanor, has had six glasses of champagne. (I've been counting.) Mum and Eleanor look really similar, but when they stand next to each other it's obvious that one of them has been through some awful shit and the worst thing that's happened to the other one was missing out on a Marc Jacobs coat in the January sales. Maybe that's a little unfair. Mum always says she couldn't have got through those first weeks and months without her sister. Eleanor dropped everything and moved into our house, spending most of her time looking after me.

At one point in the afternoon, Dad's brother, Hugh, thinks it's appropriate to ask Laurel about the offers she's had. 'Might as well get something out of all this, eh?' He nods emphatically and doesn't seem to notice the suddenly uncomfortable atmosphere. His wife, Sally, elbows him. 'Hugh!' And Hugh says, 'What? What did I say?'

Dad glares at Hugh until Hugh turns his concentration to the crudités, taking a long time to decide between a carrot stick and a radish. No one's going to tell him that the offers have been pouring in. TV interviews, newspaper interviews, magazine features, photo shoots (a fashion designer with a ridiculous name that I can never remember saw Laurel at the press conference and is convinced that she's his new muse. He wants to design a whole collection – 'Lost & Found' – inspired by her. Laurel is baffled by it all. 'Why do all these people care about me?' Of course, they *don't* care. They're only interested in money, just like everyone else. Everyone wants a piece of Little Laurel Logan.

I think she'll end up accepting some of the offers. Dad's warned her that she needs to be careful, that she needs to get advice and talk to her psychologist before she does anything. He's worried about the repercussions of her doing anything other than hiding out at home. He thinks she's too fragile. But this morning I overheard Mum talking to Dad in the kitchen. 'It's hard . . . the money would come in handy. I mean, what's she going to do now? Go and get a job? Go to university? She needs some financial security, John.' Dad's voice was quieter, so I couldn't hear what he said.

Dad stayed over last night. He wanted to be here for Laurel's first night at home. 'What about Michel?' I asked, when Dad wheeled in his little case and put it in the corner of the living room yesterday morning.

Dad looked blank. 'What *about* Michel?'

'Shouldn't he be here? He's part of this family too, *remember*.'

'I'm perfectly aware of that, thank you very much.' I stared at him. 'Your mother thought it would be nice if the four of us were here tonight, together.'

'I bet she did. She hates him.' Mum was at the supermarket, stocking up on supplies for the party she hadn't bothered to tell anyone about.

'She doesn't *hate* him. It's more complicated than that.' Parents always say things like this, trying to make out that you couldn't possibly understand the complexities of their relationships.

'He should be here.' I wasn't willing to let it go.

'It's not up to me. Her house, her rules.' That made it sound like he wanted Michel to be here, at least. That my mother was being unreasonable, trying to recreate a perfect, simple family that hadn't existed in thirteen years.

'I hope he's OK.'

'Why wouldn't he be?'

I shrugged. 'It can't be easy for him . . . Laurel coming back.' Dad looked genuinely confused by this, so I elaborated. 'Maybe he's worried you're going to leave him, go back to Mum.' There. I'd said it. It had been on my mind all week. Most kids I know would be thrilled at the idea of their parents getting back together. Not me.

Dad laughed. 'What? Are you . . . ? You're serious, aren't you? Oh, Faith . . .' He put his arm around me, pulling me close. 'That's never going to happen. Your mother knows that. Michel knows that. I *love* him.' It made me squirm a bit, Dad saying that. But it reassured me too.

I texted Michel last night, just to check on him. He texted back to say he was watching the Alien movies back to back, making the most of having the flat to himself. He asked how things were going with Laurel. *Great*, I said.

Mum cooked a roast dinner. She really went overboard — it was like Christmas. We discovered that Laurel loves peas but doesn't like Brussels sprouts. She had two helpings of roast potatoes. She's starting to put on a little weight. You can see the difference already; she looks a tiny bit healthier every day.

No one was quite sure what to do after dinner. We sat in the living room, drinking tea. Laurel sat in my usual spot on the sofa but I didn't mind. It was me who suggested watching TV. That's what normal families do on a Saturday night, after all. Dad handed Laurel the remote control and she flicked through channel after channel. I presume she must have done the same in the hotel room, but she still had this look of amazement on her face at all the choices on offer. She couldn't decide between a film featuring a giant killer shark and a documentary about earthquakes. She looked to me for help and I mouthed the word 'shark' and nodded hard. She nodded back, grinning, and for the first time I felt something. We were *sisters*. We had a bond. It was new and as fragile as a strand of spider web blowing in the wind, but it was there, glinting in the sunlight if you saw it from the right angle.

Then we saw Laurel on the TV. She flicked right past the channel before she realized what she was seeing, then flicked right back again. Mum tried to get her to change the channel, but it was no good. I wouldn't change the channel if I saw myself on TV either. It's human nature, isn't it? If you walk past an open door and hear your name, you're going to stop and listen to what's being said.

It was a studio setting and there was a huge screen with a picture of Laurel, a photo from the press conference. I'm almost sure it was that moment when she smiled when she mentioned me. The caption under the photo was: *Laurel Logan — What's next?* Two men in suits were sitting there, talking about my sister.

One of them was supposedly a psychologist, an expert in post-traumatic stress. He wore the kind of geeky glasses a person wears when they're perfectly secure in the knowledge that they're not actually a geek. He kept on using the word 'damaged'. When he said it the second time, Mum said, 'I think that's enough,' but Laurel said she wanted to hear it.

'The hard truth is that it will be difficult for Laurel to live a normal life. The details we're starting to hear about what she's been through . . .' He shook his head in disbelief, trying to convey just how awful those details were without actually mentioning any of them.

The presenter (shiny black hair, jutting chin) leaned forward in his chair. 'But surely this is the result we've all been waiting for?' He made my sister's homecoming sound like a football match. In fact, I think I recognized him from a TV show *about* football. So what the hell was he doing sitting at a serious desk for serious people, asking questions about my sister? 'This is fairy-tale stuff – happily ever after . . . isn't it?' He sat back in his chair. He was pleased with that line, you could tell.

'Of course, it's wonderful news that Laurel's been reunited with her family. No one's going to argue with that. All I'm trying to say is that things are rarely that simple. A girl who has been through years and years of abuse does not just slot back into the family unit as if nothing happened.' Dr Geeky Glasses touched the corner of his glasses. I bet they were brand new, bought especially for his appearance on this pointless TV show.

Mr Shiny Hair Football Pundit thanked Dr Geeky Glasses before turning back to the camera. 'Well, that was a fascinating perspective on this story, which is, let's face it, the story the whole nation is talking about.'

The TV screen went dark; Laurel had switched it off. Mum put her hand on Laurel's knee. 'Just ignore it, darling. They don't know what they're talking about. They don't know *you*.'

My parents and I are used to that sort of thing happening. You're going about your day, maybe listening to the radio, or browsing for a magazine in the newsagents, or looking for something to watch on TV. Then BAM! You hear her name or see her face, and your day is ruined. Laurel's not used to it though; she was really upset.

She started to cry. 'Everything's going to be OK, isn't it? *I'm* going to be OK? I'm home now. This is *home*.'

Dad looked like his heart might break in two.

Mum had tears in her eyes. 'That's right, love. You're home now. Everything's going to be fine, I promise.' And she gathered Laurel up in a hug and rocked her like she was a baby.

I went to make more tea.

Chapter 14

The party's been going on for too long now, and I suddenly realize I haven't seen Michel in a while. He was clearly uncomfortable from the second he arrived. He's never met Mum's family before, and he was nervous about meeting Laurel. She was great though; she gave him the biggest hug and said she was looking forward to getting to know him. She even asked if he could teach her some French.

Aunt Eleanor's been a little bit *too* welcoming, trying to flirt with him whenever Mum and Dad aren't looking.

I find Michel in the kitchen, cracking eggs into a bowl. 'What are you doing, hiding in here?'

'I'm not hiding!' I gave him a sceptical look. 'OK, I'm hiding. But have you tasted that dip your mum bought? *Dégoûtant!* She asked me to whip something up.' More like she wanted to keep him out of the way so she can play happy families. I'm almost certain Michel knows this too, but he's better off in the kitchen anyway.

I check I closed the door behind me. 'So . . . what do you think of Laurel?'

Michel starts whisking the eggs. 'She's lovely. I don't know why I was so nervous!'

'Because you want her to like you. I was the same.'

'Do you think she will? Like me?' He avoids eye contact, concentrating on whisking.

'*Everybody* likes you, Michel.'

'Everybody except your grandparents.' He's not wrong there. I've caught them staring at him a couple of times. God knows what Mum's told them about him.

I nudge him with my elbow. 'But Aunt Eleanor seems to like you . . . *a lot.*'

'She terrifies me,' Michel whispers.

'Just make sure she doesn't get you alone. You're lucky I found you first.'

We joke around about Eleanor clambering over the kitchen counter to get to him. Michel's pouring a thin stream of olive oil into the bowl when he asks me how I'm doing. 'It's a big change, yes? Was everything OK at school?'

Mum and Dad didn't bother to ask. I grimace. 'It was fine . . . I suppose. The usual gawkers and fakes. Nothing I can't handle.'

'Give it time. They'll have to stop eventually.'

I shrug. 'Martha's making mincemeat out of them.'

Michel laughs. 'I *bet* she is. That girl can be pretty scary when she puts her mind to it.' He's not wrong about that. 'You know, I'm really looking forward to next Saturday.'

The plan is for Laurel and I to stay at Michel and Dad's place next weekend. Mum tried to say it was too soon, but Dad said, 'Too soon for *what*? Our flat is their home too, remember?' I was proud of him for saying that, for standing up to her. Anyway, Laurel's looking forward to it. She asked if we could have a midnight feast; she'd read about them in Enid Blyton books. I didn't tell her that midnight feasts are for little kids. I said *of course* we could have a midnight feast – ginger beer and all.

Dad comes into the kitchen and slips his arm around Michel's waist. 'What are you two up to?' Michel holds out a teaspoon of aioli for Dad to taste. 'More salt, I think.'

Michel rolls his eyes. 'You *always* say more salt. It's not good for you!'

Dad sticks his tongue out. 'But it makes everything

taste SO delicious. Faith agrees with me, don't you, Faith?'

I hold up my hands and back away. 'Don't look at me! I'm not getting involved in your little domestic.'

Dad laughs and shakes his head. 'OK, Mich, you win. Serve your bland, tasteless aioli and be done with it.' Another eye roll from Michel, but he does reach for the salt.

'Laurel was asking where you'd disappeared to, Faith. I think she could do with some back-up. It's probably all a bit much for her – too many people.'

I tell Dad that I'd thought it was a terrible idea, having everyone here all at once. Dad shrugged. 'I know, love. But once your mum gets an idea in her head, there's no stopping her. And I suppose at least this way Laurel gets it over with all in one go.'

Mum sticks her head round the door. 'Time for photos!'

Oh God.

Laurel poses for pictures with *everyone*. Almost every single permutation is allowed for – Laurel with Gran, Laurel with Gramps, Laurel with Gran *and* Gramps. It takes a very long time. Everyone wants an extra shot taken on *their* camera or phone. Michel watches from the doorway while everyone takes pictures of Mum,

Dad, Laurel and me. At least Mum and Dad aren't standing next to each other; Laurel and I form a buffer zone between them.

Mum insists on having a photo of Laurel and me. We stand in front of the fireplace, a couple of inches apart from each other at first. Mum and Dad both take some pictures; Mum has tears in her eyes. Again.

I hate having my photo taken — always have, always will. But I understand that my parents need this, and that their need is more important than my awkwardness. Everyone's watching (apart from Eleanor, pouring the last dregs from the last bottle of champagne into her glass).

I sling my arm over Laurel's shoulder and pull her closer to me. She puts her arm around my waist and we lean our heads together. I smile a real, proper, beaming smile, not even caring about the gap in my teeth.

Two sisters, reunited at last.

Chapter 15

Laurel turns out to be a natural at making macarons. She really enjoys it, too. I was worried it would spoil things, having someone else there. I've always felt like this time with Michel is sort of sacred somehow, but it's actually nice having her with us. Michel turns up the music on the iPod dock — we always listen to cheesy nineties French pop. I know a lot of the words by heart, even though I don't necessarily know what they mean. We get a little production line going, with Michel at the end, piping the mixture on to the baking trays.

Dad was reluctant to go out, which probably should have offended me. He never minded leaving us when it was just Michel and me. But I can't really blame him, can I? He's missed out on thirteen years of Laurel's life; he's got a lot of catching up to do. It's natural that he'd want to spend every possible moment with her. Mum's been the same, even though you can see she's trying desperately not to smother her. She keeps saying that Laurel needs her space, but it's as if she's saying it to remind herself rather than anyone else.

Laurel's only been home for three weeks. Four weeks since she came back to us. The time has gone so fast.

Things have been a bit more normal since the media circus packed up their cameras and microphones and left. There was no reason for them to stay; there were only so many times they could show footage of Laurel leaving the house. Mum hated having them there, practically camped out in our front garden. It didn't seem to bother Laurel though. I caught her waving to them from my bedroom window one night. I warned her not to, that it was always best to ignore them. After that I didn't catch her at it again, but I know she still did it because I saw some footage on TV one day.

The police car is still there, parked a few doors down and across the street. The officers inside must be bored out of their minds. They certainly look that way whenever I walk past.

Laurel is gradually learning how the world works. Sometimes it's easy to forget that she's not a normal nineteen-year-old girl who's had a normal, average, *boring* sort of life. Sometimes she acts exactly like

116

you'd expect a nineteen-year-old girl to act. But then something will happen, or she'll ask a question or do something weird, and you'll remember. Like the time she insisted that Barnaby the Bear had a seat at the table for dinner. Mum acted like that was a perfectly normal request. Luckily Barnaby was clean by that point; Laurel had given him a bath in the sink.

I've been trying to teach her as much as I can, because I hate the idea of her being out *there* — in the big wide world — without knowing how to deal with the stuff life throws at you. The counselling sessions are helping her too. She's still seeing the psychologist twice a week, and she likes her new counsellor, Penny. Penny takes her out on trips; Laurel's favourite was the zoo. The trip to the cinema wasn't so successful. Laurel had a panic attack ten minutes into the film. No one knows what triggered it. They weren't watching some torture-filled horror flick or a psychological thriller or anything like that — the latest Pixar movie had seemed like a safe choice. Laurel wouldn't talk about it afterwards. When she doesn't want to talk about something, she closes her mouth tight, lips pursed. Her chin dimples up and she looks like a little girl. Penny told us not to push her. She said there are bound to be lots of things Laurel isn't able to deal with yet. We have to give her time.

I don't think it helps that the police won't leave us alone. There are always more questions they want to ask or something that needs clarifying. It feels like a setback every time they come round. It's hard for us to act like a normal family with the constant reminders that we're not one. Mum completely lost her shit with Sergeant Dawkins and another police officer the other day after they arrived unannounced.

Sergeant Dawkins said they really had to get the DNA swab over and done with. She reassured Laurel that it wasn't going to hurt and it would only take a second, but Laurel was having none of it. She backed away from them as if she thought they were going to pounce on her any second. Mum asked them whether it was really necessary; Sergeant Dawkins said it *was* necessary. That's when Laurel started freaking out again – crying and clutching at her hair. 'No no no no no,' she muttered under her breath, shaking her head the whole time.

Mum tried to calm her down, to reassure her that everything was OK, but it was no good. Mum told me to take Laurel upstairs. As soon as we got to her room, she crawled under the dressing table. That was the first time I saw the den she'd created. You couldn't tell when the stool was in front of the table, but there were a couple of cushions and a blanket down there.

It was a tiny space, barely big enough for a child, let alone a grown woman.

Laurel somehow managed to fold her limbs into the space, then she pulled the blanket up to her chin. The blanket was mine; I hadn't even realized it was missing. I kneeled down in front of Laurel and asked if she was OK. She didn't answer. No matter what I said, she wouldn't answer. She stared into space. I crossed my legs and sat right in front of her. 'It's OK, Laurel. There's nothing to be scared of any more. You're safe now. I'm going to stay right here.' I babbled some more, talking about what we were going to have for dinner (baked potatoes), the essay I had to write for English (*Twelfth Night*), anything I could think of to bring her back. Eventually her hand snaked out from under the blanket, reaching out for mine. 'I won't leave you, Laurel,' I said. She squeezed my hand and looked at me. There were tears in her eyes. 'Thank you,' she whispered.

It was the first time Laurel had eaten a baked potato. I made sure it was perfect – plenty of salt, plenty of butter, far too much cheese. She loved it. Mum was still ranting about the police (*How dare they? Why can't they leave her alone after all she's been through? Why don't they just get on with* catching *that monster?*), but Laurel seemed much better. I'd managed to coax her out from her little den and she'd folded the blanket and put the stool back in front of the dressing table. She was fine by the time Mum came upstairs to check on her. I haven't told Mum about the den; it would only upset her.

Dad comes home just as we're filling the last couple of macarons. He clearly didn't want to stay away a minute longer than he had to. Laurel gives him a little plate with three macarons. She says she saved the best ones for him. (This is a lie. She tried to give them to Tonks, and Michel had to explain that Tonks should only have cat food, because she's on a special diet for some weird kidney problem.) Dad smiles widely and eats the macarons, saying they're excellent. He winks at me. 'Look out, Faith, you've got some competition! Macaron mastery must run in the family.' We all laugh. No one says that our cooking skills can't possibly run in the family, because Laurel was adopted. And Dad keeps quiet about the fact that he hates macarons. He's never tried any of the ones I've made.

Laurel and I stay up late, talking. She gets the bed, I get the inflatable mattress. We tossed a coin to see who sleeps where. There's barely enough floor space for the mattress; it fits snugly between the wardrobe and the bed. It was strange at first, sleeping so close to this person I don't really know that well. When I stay at Martha's I always sleep in the spare room, and she's never slept over at my house. I'm not really sure why.

Laurel lies on her left side, peeking out from under the duvet. I lie on my right side, trying to pretend the mattress is as comfortable as the bed (*my* bed). She likes to talk after we've turned out the lights. It's not exactly dark; Dad bought another nightlight so Laurel wouldn't have to bring Egg with her every weekend. Laurel likes me to tell her stories – but they have to be *true* stories. She never tires of me talking about my childhood or about school or about Thomas.

She was nervous about meeting him. She didn't say so, but I could tell. She kept on checking her hair in the mirror and fidgeting. I'd arranged for Thomas and Martha to come over for pizza and a movie. That seemed like the best way of getting the introductions over and done with. I just wanted all of the most important people in my life to know each other and to get along. I even convinced Mum to go out for the evening; she arranged to meet a friend in town for cocktails. She's never done that before, as far as I know. Maybe this is part of what constitutes 'normal' for her, but if so, it's a normal that hasn't existed for the last thirteen years.

Martha and Thomas arrived at the same time. The introductions were a little awkward, but we all laughed at the strangeness of the situation. Thomas was driving, so he was on soft drinks. Martha, Laurel and I had wine. Mum said we should stick to one bottle, so of course we ended up having two. Laurel downed her first glass with remarkable speed, but she slowed down after that. Martha was really shy at first, which is not like her at all. Only Thomas seemed to be at ease straightaway. He was polite and charming and even offered to pay for the pizza. I was about to take him up on the offer when Laurel pulled a couple of twenty-pound notes from her pocket. Mum had given her the cash before she left. I ignored the niggling feeling that it was odd that Mum hadn't given the money to me. Was this how things were going to be from now on? Laurel is the oldest, after all. She insisted on being the one to phone up for the pizza; she'd never done that before. There was a pause and then she said her name. I winced and looked over at Martha – she knew the score. Thomas was too busy flicking through the channels on the TV to notice. Laurel said 'yes' in answer to a question that was almost definitely something along the lines of 'Laurel Logan? *The* Laurel Logan?' I went to grab the phone from her but she waved me away. Her face lit up. 'Thank you. That's very kind. Yes . . . Yes. It's wonderful to be back. I really appreciate that.' There was another pause as she listened, then she laughed. 'Thank you! Have a good evening, Phil. Bye . . . Yes . . . I will do. Bye!' She pressed the button to end the call and then turned to us, triumphant. 'He said he'd throw in some free garlic bread and a bottle of Sprite.'

'Why?' I asked.

Laurel shrugged and said, 'I don't know. He saw me on TV. He said I was pretty.'

I wasn't about to lecture Laurel about the dubiousness of getting freebies from strangers who've seen you on TV and 'feel a connection with you'. (That's what they always say – all the strangers who stop us on the street or who've sent cards and letters and presents. They all feel this mysterious 'connection'.) Anyway, Thomas was pleased about the Sprite. He raised his glass in Laurel's direction. 'Cheers, Laurel!'

My sister smiled at him and I tried to ignore the pointed look that Martha was aiming in my direction. When the pizzas arrived, Laurel insisted on going to the door. I'm not sure 'giving money to the pizza delivery guy' counts as one of the essential life skills her counsellor is always going on about.

There were a couple of awkward moments when we were trying to choose a film to watch. Thomas scrolled through all the options on Netflix and Laurel kept on suggesting this film or that film, even though she had no idea what they were about. And that was the problem. You'd be surprised by how many films include abduction or a sinister psychopath or sexual abuse or some kind of family trauma. I kept having to say no to Laurel's suggestions, which made it look like I was being difficult. Thomas was getting annoyed. He handed me the remote control. 'Why don't *you* choose then?!' So I did. A romantic comedy that none of us had seen. Thomas despises romantic comedies. He despises most films, in fact. Unless they're four hours long and subtitled. He kept on taking the piss out of the one we watched, which was fine because it was dire. It didn't matter though, because Laurel loved it. She cried at the end, and then laughed at herself for crying.

Laurel thanked me when Martha and Thomas had gone home.

'What for?' I nibbled on a leftover pizza crust.

She looked so serious. 'Letting me into your world.'

I wasn't quite sure what she meant by that. She saw my confusion and started again. 'I mean, I really appreciate you letting me spend time with you and your friends. It can't be easy for you . . . having a brand-new sister appear out of nowhere, turning your life upside down.' She looked shy all of a sudden, embarrassed by what she was saying.

I put the pizza crust down and shook my head. 'You've got it all wrong.'

'What do you mean?'

'My life *was* upside down. Before. You've . . .' Was I really going to say this? It was a line so cheesy it wouldn't have been out of place in the film we'd just watched. I looked at Laurel and her face was so open and honest and expectant. 'You've turned my life the right way up again.'

Laurel's smile made me glad I'd said it.

Sometimes it's OK to be cheesy.

Chapter 16

It starts almost as soon as we arrive at the market. It's the first time Laurel's come with us. The last two Sundays she's stayed home with Dad. Maureen runs the stall next to us, selling fancy vinegars – strawberry balsamic is her latest obsession. She's really friendly, always cheerful no matter how bad the weather is or how few customers there are.

'Got another little helper today, Michael?' She never calls him Michel; he never bothers correcting her.

Michel nods and says good morning. He's forgotten his beret so he's looking slightly less French than usual; his ears are already turning red from the cold. Maureen stops lining up bottles of vinegar and comes over to our stall, where Laurel is busy laying out the plastic tablecloth (red and white checked, of course). 'Hi! I'm Maureen, but you can call me Mo. Nice to meet . . . Oh my God!' She turns to look at Michel. 'Is this . . . ?' Then she turns back to Laurel. 'Are you . . . ?'

Michel stops unloading the car and walks over to Maureen. 'Yes, but could you keep it to yourself?'

Maureen snorts. 'Keep it to myself? You do know she's probably one of the most famous people in the whole bloody country right now, don't you?'

Laurel is watching this little exchange, yet to say a word. Sometimes I wish I could read her mind.

Maureen asks if she can give Laurel a hug. I'd have said no, but Laurel nods. 'You poor, poor girl,' murmurs Maureen, holding her close. I turn away, grabbing my beret from the dashboard.

It's a disaster from the start. The first customer recognizes Laurel, even though she's at the back of the stall wearing my beret, with a scarf covering half of her face. No one knew who we were before. We were just Faith and Michel, purveyors of the finest macarons this side of Paris. I was not Little Laurel Logan's sister and he was not Little Laurel Logan's almost sort of stepfather. Maureen keeps shaking her head in wonder, even while she's serving her own customers. She called Michel a dark horse for not telling her about Laurel.

By half past ten there's a crowd of people around

our stall. No one is buying macarons. One woman pushes to the front. She wants her daughter to have her photo taken with Laurel. The daughter (maybe ten years old, stuffing her face with Quavers) doesn't seem bothered either way. Laurel takes her hat off and hands it to me. She goes round to the front of the stall and stands next to the girl. The smile on her face seems to be genuine, but how *can* it be? The woman doesn't even thank her.

More and more people ask to have their picture taken with my sister, as if she's some contestant from a TV talent show. It doesn't matter to them that she's a teenager emerging from an awful ordeal: she's *famous*. They'll be able to go home and tell their families over lunch. They'll say that she's thinner than she looks on TV or prettier or taller or nicer. They'll say that you'd never guess what she'd been through, if you didn't know. They'll say her sister wasn't very friendly, and nowhere near as pretty, and what on earth does she have to be so grumpy about? Shouldn't she be happy that her sister is back?

Michel tries his best to deal with the situation, but when the crowd swells to thirty people or more he knows he's fighting a losing battle. 'I think I should take Laurel home. What do you think?'

I nod and tell him I'll look after the stall until

he gets back. I hear someone shouting a question at Laurel: 'Laurel! Aren't you afraid he's still out there somewhere?' Someone else — an older woman, it sounds like — says, 'Oh my goodness, she's right. He could be watching right now!' It's as if some kind of madness has crept over these people. Maybe when they left their houses this morning they were normal, reasonable people who had an idea of the kinds of things it's appropriate to say, but now they're rude and obnoxious and have no qualms about scaring a girl they don't know.

I pull Laurel away from them. She actually apologizes. 'I'm *so* sorry. I have to go now.'

People are still taking photos when I open the car door and practically push her inside. No doubt they'll be posting them on Twitter and Instagram in a matter of minutes. Michel asks if I'm going to be OK and promises he'll be back as soon as he can. It takes him ages to reverse the car through the crowds, because more and more people stop to see what the fuss is all about.

As soon as they're gone, the crowd starts to dissipate. A too-tanned woman in her twenties approaches the front of the stall and asks if she can ask me a question. 'I'm not talking about Laurel so you can just piss off, OK?'

But it turns out she only wanted to ask if I'd recommend the salted caramel over the chocolate and passion fruit. I apologize profusely and end up giving her one of each so she can choose.

Maureen brings me a cup of tea and says she'll mind the stall for a few minutes if I want to get away for a bit. She's a nice person really. There's just something about Laurel – about her story – that seems to turn people into idiots. I shouldn't blame them; it's not their fault.

I go and sit on the steps in front of the church, sipping my tea even though it's still far too hot. I hope Laurel's OK; she didn't *seem* traumatized by the experience. My heart is still thumping from the stress of it all. Somehow, despite being locked in a basement for most of her life, my sister is more comfortable around people than I am. It doesn't quite seem fair.

Dad's furious when he finds out. Laurel cries because she thinks she's done something wrong so Dad has to reassure her that it's other people he's angry with, not her. He calls them parasites.

Laurel feels bad about how things turned out.

'It's not your fault,' Michel and I say at the same time.

Laurel looks down at her lap; her hair falls in front of her face. 'It *is* though, isn't it? If it wasn't for me, none of that would have happened. I should have . . . I don't know. I should have told them to go away instead of posing for pictures.'

I kneel down in front of her, trying to get her to look at me. 'Hey . . . listen to me. You did the right thing. You *have* to be nice to them. I can just see the headlines if you weren't – "LAUREL LOGAN SWORE AT MY MUM"!' Laurel's mouth twitches into a smile. 'But you know what's really cool? *I* don't have to be nice to them. I can say whatever the hell I want because no one's ever going to write a headline about me. So if that kind of thing happens again, I'll sort it, OK?'

Laurel looks up. 'It was scary . . . all those people.' This surprises me; she seemed to take it all in her stride. Maybe Laurel's better at hiding her feelings than I thought. Maybe that's something you learn, dealing with a psychopath on a daily basis for all that time.

'How dare they? How bloody *dare* they?' Dad goes off on one again, wittering on about invasion of privacy. Michel ushers him over to the kitchen, suggesting a cup of tea might be a good idea.

I get up from the floor and sit next to Laurel on the sofa. She thanks me.

'You're going to have to stop thanking me, you know.'

'Why?' She looks worried, as if she's just committed some sort of dreadful faux pas.

I smile to let her know that there's nothing to worry about. 'You don't need to thank me for every little thing. We're family. We look out for each other.'

'That sounds good to me.' She bites her lip and tucks a few strands of hair behind her ear. I'm slowly – too slowly – starting to learn some of the signs. Some of the little tics that belong to her. The lip-biting and hair-tucking mean she's unsure about something. (Or maybe they just mean she's got chapped lips and is fed up of her hair falling in front of her face.) She looks to check Dad and Michel aren't listening, then whispers, 'I'm sorry I haven't been here to look out for *you*.' A knotty lump sprouts in my throat. 'That's what big sisters are supposed to do, isn't it? They're supposed to *be* there. And I wasn't.'

'You're here now and that's all that matters.' This is a lie. It all matters – every little bit of it. But the truth is there's nothing we can do to change the past. I surprise myself by making a silent vow to be the best sister possible – to do everything in my power to make up for those lost years. It's the least that I can do, really.

Chapter 17

Silent vows are ridiculous. You shouldn't have to keep a promise you only made inside your head. It shouldn't count if you didn't actually say it out loud. But for some reason I feel like I have to keep my promise to Laurel, which is why I find myself in a TV studio, in front of an audience of giddy middle-aged women, sitting on an overstuffed sofa next to Mum and Dad. Laurel gets her own chair, right next to Cynthia Day. It is my worst nightmare, fully realized.

Dad didn't want to do it either, even though he and Mum had appeared on *The Cynthia Day Show* twelve years ago to try to drum up publicity for Laurel's case, which was waning as the first anniversary approached.

We're doing this for Laurel. I just have to keep reminding myself of that, with every banal, pointless question Cynthia asks, trying to extract tears from us. That's her speciality: making people cry, then showing how much she empathizes with them by crying too. For some bizarre reason (and completely unbeknown to me, otherwise I'd have done something about it), Laurel has been watching *The Cynthia Day Show* religiously for the past month or so. A producer got in touch with Mum straight after Laurel came home, asking if Laurel would go on the show. She said no, but she must have told Laurel about it, which was probably why Laurel started watching. When the producer got in touch a month later, offering an obscene amount of money for the whole family to appear on the show, Laurel really, really wanted to do it. So we sat down as a family to discuss the pros and cons, which was a waste of time as the only thing that really mattered to any of us was what Laurel wanted. Her eyes were bright and brimming with excitement as she talked about wanting to see a real, live TV studio, and wanting to meet Cynthia (*She's SO nice!*). The decision was made. The money would go straight into a bank account for Laurel.

Thomas was appalled. He couldn't fathom why I would agree to be a part of something like this. He only stopped going on about it when I snapped at him, telling him he had no idea what I was going through. He clammed up, barely spoke for the rest of the day. Martha was more supportive, which was reassuring because I feel like I've barely seen her recently. We've still been hanging out together at school, but I've been spending so much time with Laurel that Martha's fallen by the wayside a bit. I haven't been round to her house since Laurel came back, and she's invited me at least four times. Martha understands though – she gets it. And she's been round to our house a couple of times, so it's not like I've been neglecting her.

It's too hot under these lights. I'm sweating. No one else seems bothered by the heat. Mum and Dad have been on TV loads of times, so this is nothing new to them. They didn't even seem nervous. And Laurel was just excited to be here. When we came on set earlier she pointed out a picture that had been drawn by a kid the week before. Laurel told me all about it. 'It was amazing! You should have seen it, Faith. He was only little – maybe five or six. And he sat on the floor and drew a portrait of Cynthia while she interviewed his parents. It only took him a few minutes, and then Cynthia cried when she saw it and said she would treasure it forever and the little boy just shrugged and said she should probably sell it. Oh my goodness, it was so funny. The people in the audience were going crazy!' Laurel realized I wasn't reacting to this story with as much enthusiasm as she was expecting and asked me if I was OK. I told her I was nervous. When

Mum and Dad had asked, I said I was fine. For some reason I don't mind admitting weakness to Laurel. She put her arm around me and said there was no need to be nervous. 'Cynthia is so nice. There was this woman on the show yesterday, and she'd started this charity that . . .' I tuned out.

The wardrobe lady tutted when she saw me. 'No, no, no, that won't do at all.' The clothes that Mum and Dad and Laurel were wearing were all fine, apparently, but mine were not. I'd wanted to be comfortable, so I'd opted for one of my favourite jumpers – a black V-neck. There's nothing wrong with the jumper, but the wardrobe lady said it 'wouldn't do me any favours on camera'. I asked what she meant, but she wouldn't elaborate. That's how I've ended up wearing an orange top with purple stripes on the sleeves. When Laurel saw me in it she said I looked nice, so I didn't kick up a fuss.

Cynthia Day came into the dressing room half an hour before the show started. The first thing I noticed was the smell that wafted into the room with her – the most cloying perfume you could imagine, heavy and unbearably floral. The second thing I noticed was her gravity-defying hair. Bouffant and *then* some. It doesn't move when she moves her head – not even a little bit. Laurel whispered, 'Oh my God, it's really her,' under her breath while Cynthia was saying hello to Mum and Dad. 'It's OK, remember she's just a normal person,' I whispered back.

'She's a *famous* person.'

'So are you,' I reminded her.

Then Cynthia turned her attention to us and she clapped her hands together. 'Laurel! I can't tell you what an *honour* it is that you agreed to come on my little show.' She kissed Laurel on both cheeks and turned to me. 'And this must be Faith. Thank you so much for being here.' She didn't kiss me and I was glad because the choking perfume was even worse close up. Cynthia perched on the edge of a table and told us what to expect. She said there was no need to be nervous, that the questions wouldn't be anything we hadn't heard a million times before. 'Just tell your story. That's all my audience wants to hear.' And then she was gone. Unfortunately the stench of perfume remained.

The audience is ninety-five per cent women. They lean forward in their seats, straining to get closer to Laurel. They nod when she speaks and turn to each other and smile in a sad, sympathetic sort of way. Laurel's doing brilliantly. She takes her time answering Cynthia's questions, thinking before she speaks. She looks over at Mum and Dad and me every so often as if to check that she's doing OK; Mum and Dad nod encouragingly.

Cynthia introduces some footage on the big screen behind her. 'As you all know, we are very lucky to have had the Logans on our little show before. I just want to take a moment to remind you of what they've been through. Twelve years ago, Olivia and John sat on this very sofa . . .' she smiles and corrects herself, 'well, not this *actual* sofa. This sofa is brand new — I chose it myself . . . do you like it?' The audience clap, showing their approval for Cynthia's choice of furnishings. 'Anyway, where was I?' This is one of Cynthia's tricks — acting ditzy. I reckon she thinks it puts people at ease.

The footage shows Mum and Dad on a sofa very much like the one we're sitting on now. Cynthia's interior-decorating tastes clearly haven't changed in over a decade. I've seen this interview before in one of my YouTube forays. I only watched it once though, because it wasn't very interesting. My parents looked sad and worn out. There had been no new developments in the case. They talked about how it felt to have been without Laurel for a whole year. Mum said she couldn't put it into words, and Cynthia nodded even though you could tell that she really, really wanted Mum to at least *try*.

The clip finishes with Cynthia talking straight to camera. 'Laurel, if you're watching this . . . your parents love you very much, sweetheart.' That was just weird – the idea that Laurel would be watching. I think she probably said that on the spur of the moment, unlike everything else, which seemed to be so carefully orchestrated. It made her look stupid.

The screen goes blank and Cynthia says nothing for a moment or two, letting everyone stare at my parents and marvel at how different they look today. Then she makes a joke about how fat she was back then and everyone laughs. It's true. She was almost double the size she is now. The hair hasn't changed a bit though.

'So, Laurel, how does it feel being back with your family?'

Laurel shakes her head, beaming widely. 'It feels like a miracle.' The audience loves that. They clap and whoop and cheer. Everybody loves a happy ending.

Cynthia smiles and waits for Laurel to elaborate. Laurel takes a deep breath and looks over at us. 'I used to dream about it. About seeing my family again. Those dreams were *so* real. And then I would wake up in total darkness . . . in that basement, and it felt like my heart was breaking. It happened all the time at first – the dreams. But over the years, they happened less and less until I just . . . stopped dreaming.' She bows her head and there's total silence in the studio, until someone in the audience sneezes and ruins the moment completely. Laurel looks up at Cynthia again. 'All I know is that seeing them again, after all this time, well, it's even better than those dreams I had. Knowing that they never forgot me, knowing that they never gave up hope . . . it's . . .' she shrugs and holds up her hands, 'a miracle! Sorry, I'm repeating myself. I'm not so good with words. Sorry.' She might be blushing, but it's impossible to tell under all the make-up she's wearing.

Cynthia puts a hand on Laurel's knee. Her nail varnish is burgundy and she has rings on almost every finger. A huge diamond adorns her ring finger. (She's just got engaged to a man half her age; it will be her third marriage.) 'I think we can all agree that you're doing just fine, Laurel.'

Laurel smiles. 'Thank you. Can I just say . . . I'm such a big fan of your show. I watch every day. Sometimes even twice!'

The audience makes an 'Awwww' sound; it's as if each person has been programmed to react in exactly the same way. 'Well, that is very lovely to hear.' Cynthia keeps her hand on Laurel's knee. 'And can *I* just say . . . I'm such a big fan of yours!' She laughs and looks at the audience, who are lapping this up.

Cynthia asks some more questions, varying the tone between light and dark. A question about clothes (*I love your top. You must be having so much fun, going shopping, doing the usual things girls love to do?*) is swiftly followed by one about Laurel's captor (*If you could say something to him right now — anything at all — what would that be?*). I can feel Mum tense up beside me. I don't think the police would be too happy about it; what if Laurel's answer provokes him in some way? What if he decides to come back and take her from us again? I've been having nightmares about that. I haven't told anyone. I dream about Laurel and me in the front garden of the Stanley Street house, but this time we're all grown-up. We're sitting on a polka-dot picnic blanket, eating BLT baguettes. A man opens the front gate and it creaks on its hinges. He stands over us and holds out his hand to Laurel. She looks up at him and she's not scared. I look up at him too, but for some reason his face is blurred, like Vaseline smeared on glass. Laurel takes his hand and stands up and walks away. The gate creaks again. I start to cry but I'm not sure why. I think I've lost something. I usually wake up the moment I realize what's happened — when the horror engulfs me.

Laurel's answer to Cynthia's stupid question about Smith isn't so bad after all. 'I have nothing to say to him.' She has a neutral expression on her face and her voice has a neutral tone. It's perfectly judged.

Cynthia nods, as if this was the answer she was expecting. 'I bet you don't.' A hush descends on the room and Cynthia shakes her head slowly, trying to convey sympathy for Laurel and disgust for her captor, all at once. 'I just *bet* you don't.'

Cynthia turns towards the camera. 'Now we're going to take a short break, but don't go anywhere. When we come back, we'll be talking to Olivia and John about their ordeal, and let's not forget Faith, reunited with her big sister at long last. See you in three!'

Chapter 18

Cynthia tells us we're doing great. 'This is *gold*,' she says. I presume someone has switched the microphones off, because Cynthia burps. Not a full-on belch – it's slightly more ladylike than that. She smiles and apologizes. She leans towards us and confides, 'Cauliflower always gives me gas, but do I ever learn? No, I do not!' I find this far too funny, because apparently being on live TV reduces my sense of humour to that of an eight-year-old boy. Cynthia looks at me as if *I'm* the odd one for laughing so hard.

Dad asks how I'm feeling and I tell him I'm OK. I'm not, of course. I'm unbelievably nervous. Cynthia's going to talk to me, and I'm going to be expected to say words that make sense, maybe even stitch some of them together into whole sentences. I really, really need the toilet, but there's not a whole lot I can do about that now.

I keep thinking about Martha, sitting at home watching me humiliate myself. And Thomas, *not* watching. I can't believe he said he wasn't going to watch. Part of me is glad, relieved that he won't see me wearing this disgusting top and smiling and simpering at Cynthia Day. But I'm also a little bit hurt. He should *want* to watch; it's not every day your girlfriend appears on the third biggest chat show in the country. He should have said he wanted to watch, and I should have told him not to. *That's* how it should have worked.

I wonder if Penny's watching too. We talked about it at our last family counselling session. She lets Laurel go on and on about this stupid show, wasting our time when we should be talking about other things. Anyway, Penny didn't come right out and say that she thought it was a terrible idea, but I bet she disapproves. She's just too busy listening and nodding and oozing empathy all over the place to say how she really feels.

A girl wearing black rushes onstage – a make-up ninja. She powders my face and runs off just in time for the countdown to the end of the adverts. No one else's face needs powdering, because no one else is sweating as much as I am.

Cynthia talks to Mum and Dad next. She talks to

them as if they're still together, making no reference to the fact that Dad doesn't live with us. There's no mention of Michel, or Dad's 'lifestyle', as some of the papers insist on calling it. She asks what it's like having Laurel back home, and they say it's wonderful. At one point Mum cries and Dad hands her a handkerchief.

An image pops up on the screen behind Cynthia and she turns to look at it. It's the last age-progressed image of Laurel; the one that was supposed to show what she might look like age fifteen. I watch as the people in the audience stare up at the picture, then stare at Laurel, then back at the picture again. Then I do the same. It's not as bad as I thought, actually. But the girl in the picture has a bland, regular sort of face. It's the kind of face that's easy to forget. Laurel does not have a forgettable face. There's something about her face that makes you keep looking. It's the eyes, I think. Of course, it doesn't help that the picture on the screen is in black and white, while the real Laurel is full colour, not to mention 3D.

Cynthia comments on the image, saying it didn't do Laurel justice, but that the police had done the best they could. She asks Dad how he feels about the police, knowing that they weren't able to find

Laurel and don't seem to be able to find her captor despite receiving 'literally hundreds of calls from the public'.

Dad is at his diplomatic best, saying, 'Olivia and I are grateful for all the hard work they've put in — and continue to put in — every single day.' Cynthia tries to get him to say something juicy, tries to put words in his mouth (those words being 'police incompetence') but he's a pro at this.

Finally Cynthia turns to me. I wonder what would happen if I vomited right now. Would it be best to just puke on the floor in front of me, or should I try puking over the back of the sofa? Would they cut to an advert break?

I'm concentrating so hard on not vomiting that I only start listening towards the end of Cynthia's question, which doesn't appear to be an actual question. '. . . *such* an appropriate name. That's what we all clung to, wasn't it? *Faith*.'

I don't roll my eyes even though I really, really want to. She's not the first person to talk about my name like that. People thinks it's so poetic; I think they're fools.

'So tell me, Faith, what's it been like for *you*?' She smiles encouragingly.

All eyes are on me; I preferred it when all eyes

were on Laurel. 'Good . . . it's been good.' Oh God. Could I possibly sound *more* stupid?

Cynthia laughs, but not in a mean way. She turns to the audience. 'Well, I suppose that just about sums it up! Now, Faith, I have a big sister of my own — hello, Diane, if you're watching! — and if there's one thing I know for sure it's that I couldn't cope without her. What does it feel like, having your big sister back after all this time?'

I look over at Laurel. She's sitting back in her armchair, looking perfectly at home. She winks, but no one else can see because her face is angled away from the cameras and the audience. It puts me at ease, that wink. It says, 'This is all bullshit, but let's play along'. I start to relax.

'It's the best thing that's ever happened to me.' While Cynthia's saying, 'Bless!' and the audience are going, 'Awwww' and Dad's patting my leg, I examine that statement from all possible angles, picking it up with tweezers and looking at it under a microscope. I come to the conclusion that it's actually the truth. Having Laurel back *is* the best thing that's ever happened to me. This surprises me more than it should.

Laurel's grinning at me and I grin right back at her. Cynthia asks me what it was like growing up 'in the shadow of this terrible crime'. She says it can't have been easy for me. A couple of months ago I'd have jumped at the chance to tell *my* side of the story for a change, to moan about how awful it's been, how no one could ever understand what it was like. Today I shrug. 'It was nothing compared to what my sister went through. Mum and Dad did their best to protect me from it all, to try to make sure that I had a happy childhood.'

Cynthia pounces. 'And did you?'

I glance at Mum, then Dad. 'I did.'

I half expect Mum to call me a liar, which would certainly make for interesting viewing. Instead I hear her catch her breath. She's crying again. Cynthia's not going to miss an opportunity like that. 'Olivia, are you OK? Can you tell us why that makes you so emotional?'

Mum breathes deeply, trying to pull herself together. 'It . . . means a lot, to hear that. We tried so hard to make sure Faith had a normal childhood, but it was hard. And sometimes I think . . . I think we failed her.'

I turn to look at her and reach past Dad to take her hand in mine. 'You didn't.' And suddenly Mum and I are standing up and hugging, and it's the oddest thing to be hugging your mother in front of a studio audience, knowing that millions of people are watching all over the country. It's even odder not to feel embarrassed about it.

Cynthia appears to wipe away a tear; she's loving this. She asks me a few more questions, and it's really not that bad if you just focus on what she's asking and forget about the rest. I end up almost enjoying myself. It's quite nice having someone absolutely focused on you, asking about your feelings and opinions. It makes you feel like you *matter*.

Cynthia turns to Laurel. 'And what's it like for you, getting to know your baby sister again? Is she different to how you expected her to be?'

Laurel takes a moment to think. I probably should have done more of that – weighing up what I was going to say instead of just blurting out the first thing that came to mind. 'In some ways, Faith's exactly how I expected her to be. I used to lie awake at night and think about what she would be doing and how she would look. It got harder, as the years passed. But she was always here.' Laurel taps her temple. 'I never let go of her.' There's a perfect pause and Cynthia nods her approval. 'But Faith's also different to how I expected her to be. I could never have hoped for her to be so supportive and kind and loving towards someone she can barely even remember. Having a sister like that is . . . Well, I feel like the luckiest girl in the world.' Cheers and clapping from the audience. 'She's teaching me so much – it feels like she's the older sister and I'm the younger one!'

Laurel looks at me when she says, 'I just wish everyone was lucky enough to have a sister like Faith.'

Chapter 19

My English teacher, Mrs Truss, asks me to stay behind after class. I'm sure she's going to complain about the essay I handed in last week — the one I'd rushed so I could teach Laurel how to make spaghetti carbonara. Instead, she asks me what Cynthia Day is *really* like. She empathizes with her because she's been married three times too. Mrs Truss thinks that it might be third time lucky — for her and for Cynthia.

Laney Finch finds me at lunchtime; she *always* finds me. She's alone this time. She tells me how beautiful my sister is (*like,* really *beautiful*), and how brave she was to go on *The Cynthia Day Show.* 'If I'd been through something like that, I think I'd want to hide away forever.' I nod instead of telling her how offensive she's being. As an afterthought, Laney says, 'You were really good . . . It was nice to see you looking so happy. And I *loved* your top. Where's it from?'

Martha was less kind. She called me when we were driving back from the TV studio. 'What's with the personality transplant? Did they give you some happy pills or something? Is that one of Cynthia's little tricks?' Martha took my silence as a sign to continue taking the piss. 'And that top? Jesus Christ, I'm not sure my eyes will ever recover.'

I didn't mind Martha mocking me; after the madness of the previous few hours, it was refreshingly normal. I couldn't say too much in the car though. Mum and Dad were thrilled with how it had all gone. 'Better than I expected,' Dad had said when they took off his microphone. Laurel had barely said a word since we'd got into the car. Mum and Dad didn't seem to notice, but I nudged her and mouthed, 'Are you OK?' while Mum was busy talking about Cynthia. Laurel nodded and whispered that she was just tired. She spent the rest of the journey staring out of the window.

We picked up some Thai food on the way home, calling in the order from the car when we were half an hour away. I asked Laurel if she wanted to make the call, but she shook her head. I wasn't worried – not exactly. It had been a lot to process – all that attention, all those crazy women in the audience with their damp eyes and scrunched-up tissues.

As soon as Dad left, I went up to my room to call Michel. I couldn't imagine what it must be like to watch the person you love on national TV, acting like you don't exist. He sounded exhausted. I can always tell when Michel is tired because he sounds more French. It's the only time he ever struggles to find the English word he's after, and it frustrates the hell out of him. He prides himself on his perfect English.

I asked him what he thought of the show; he'd taken the afternoon off work to watch it. But it turned out there had been an emergency at the surgery – a Rhodesian Ridgeback had eaten a shoe (brown leather brogue) and Michel had been called in for the surgery. So Michel had missed the show; I was glad. He asked how it went and he said he was proud of me. 'For what?' I asked.

'For going on that awful show in the first place. You didn't have to do that. No one would have blamed you.' He was wrong about that; Mum would have blamed me.

We talked for a little while, about the Rhodesian Ridgeback (doing well, expected to make a full recovery) and the cooking show we both watch (not doing so well after a format change for the new series). It was nice to talk about something that didn't involve Laurel. I heard Michel say hi to Dad when he arrived home, but he didn't hang up until he was quite sure that there was nothing more I wanted to say. He asked whether he should watch *The Cynthia Day Show* online and I told him not to bother. I hoped curiosity wouldn't get the better of him.

Curiosity gets the better of *me*, and I watch the whole show again a couple of days later. It's strange, how different it is from the way I remember. It's all a bit soft-focus, for one thing. Cynthia probably insists on that so her wrinkles don't show up on camera. It's excruciatingly embarrassing, watching myself – and even worse hearing myself speak. I almost don't recognize that girl wearing the orange top and sitting up too straight. At least you can't tell I was sweating profusely, thanks to the make-up ninja. Laurel comes across really well, although she looks at the camera a lot instead of looking at Cynthia. It feels like she's talking directly to the viewer sometimes. I can just imagine people up and down the country, sipping cups of tea and eating chocolate digestives, watching my sister. It's no wonder people feel like they know her.

Since Laurel came home, people have been sending emails and cards and presents. Mum set up a PO box years ago, so luckily most stuff goes straight there. But some people always manage to find out our address.

It's not exactly hard to figure out after watching all the outside broadcasts filmed on our doorstep. Google Street View is the stalker's friend. Not that these are stalkers; they're just people who sometimes come across that way. Laurel's had seven marriage proposals since she came back. What kind of weirdo sends a letter or email asking to marry some girl they've never met before? Three of them sent photos. One of the guys was buck naked.

Mum doesn't tell Laurel about the crazies. She goes through every bit of correspondence before it gets anywhere near Laurel. Lots of people are still sending teddy bears, forgetting that Laurel is a grown woman now. At least Barnaby has lots of new friends.

Many of the letters say the exact same words: 'I feel like I know you.' I would never dream of writing to a stranger and saying something like that. Laurel doesn't seem to find it as odd as I do. She says it's nice that people are so thoughtful. Mum says that the people who write these letters usually have some reason to write them – some tragedy or misfortune in their own lives that leads them to project their feelings on to Laurel. I'm not convinced.

Laurel has replied to some of the letters – just a short note to thank them. Mum bought her a hundred thank-you cards and she's already written thirty or so.

It will take her forever at this rate, so last night we went on the laptop. I helped Laurel to set up a template of a basic thank-you letter that she can amend as she sees fit; then she can print them off in the study and sign them. She wasn't convinced at first. 'Wouldn't people prefer to have a handwritten card? It seems more . . . personal.' She came round to my way of thinking when I pointed out exactly how many letters she had to reply to, and the fact that she could copy and paste the template into emails too. We set up two email accounts – one for her to reply to all the emails that were pouring in every day, and a personal one. Mum's going to start forwarding her the messages that aren't weird or offensive or upsetting or perverted, and she'll keep intercepting the post from the PO box. Hopefully the deluge will die down soon. Interest will wane; it always does.

I like helping her with this sort of thing; it's nice to feel useful. Laurel *needs* me; no one has ever needed me before. Thomas never says that he needs me. He never says, *I can't live without you*, or, *I would die if you left me*, or any of those devastatingly romantic/downright weird things people in love are supposed to say. But then I suppose I never say that sort of thing to him either.

Laurel doesn't know what to do with her personal

email account. She has no one to email. 'You will,' I told her. She smiled, but I could tell she didn't believe me. I was brushing my teeth last night when I realized she was standing in the doorway, watching me. 'How do you get friends?'

I spat out the toothpaste foam and watched it as it trickled down the plughole. 'What do you mean?'

She was wearing her pyjamas – an old T-shirt of mine that she'd taken a liking to and a pair of red checked pyjama bottoms. Her face was scrubbed free of make-up and her hair was twisted into a messy ponytail. She looks better without make-up; I think it makes her look too old. She's a better colour already – she was pale as a ghost when she came back. I bet she tans really well in summer. She straightened the towels hanging from the rail. Mum's always doing that too. Like mother, like daughter. 'How do you become friends with someone? How do you even find people to be friends with in the first place?'

I splashed cold water on my face, giving myself time to think. Laurel has a lot of questions about a lot of things and I try to answer each one as best I can. I only lost my patience with her once, when I really needed the loo and she was asking me to explain something about the Internet and search engines. I snapped at her – nothing too bad; I just asked if she could give the constant questions a rest for *one* minute. She took a step back, bumping into the banister, and for an awful second I imagined her plummeting over the side and breaking her neck on the stairs. I apologized straightaway, but the stricken look was slow to leave her face. The trouble was, I was still bursting for the loo, so I told her to wait outside the bathroom. When I came out, she was gone. I found her sitting on the floor behind the door in her bedroom. I apologized again but she said nothing. She only started talking to me when I said that Thomas would be a better person to ask about computer stuff. I think he must have been a proper computer geek before he decided that being into poetry and philosophy was probably cooler. (If not cooler, certainly more likely to attract girls – not that he would ever admit that was one of the deciding factors.) She asked me if I would ask him to help her. Then she apologized for asking questions all the time. That made me feel lower than low so I apologized to *her* and she apologized to me again and we eventually laughed and agreed to stop apologizing. Now I try to answer every single one of her questions, whether my bladder is about to explode or not.

How *do* you become friends with someone? It's not something I've ever been particularly good at. It was OK when I was little, before I realized that kids usually only wanted to talk to me because of Laurel. I had plenty of friends up until the age of eight or nine. That's when things changed. That's when girls started whispering about me and boys started teasing me. That's when some of the girls in my class started playing a game at break time. One of them would pretend to be Laurel, playing innocently in the front garden (a patch of grass in the courtyard, well away from any patrolling teachers). One of them would be 'The Shadow', who had to try to get to her by dodging past the other girls (who were supposed to be The Detectives). They asked me to play once; I said no.

Martha was the first real friend I ever had. She wasn't interested in Laurel, which was enough to make me interested in her. She made me laugh. I didn't realize how important laughter was until I was friends with Martha. My childhood hadn't exactly been brimming with the stuff.

Laurel was waiting for an answer.

'I suppose you usually make friends at school. You find someone who likes the same things you do and you talk to them.' Laurel had only had one year of school before she was snatched from us. 'And I suppose it works the same way when you leave school. I don't know . . . maybe you have a hobby and you meet up with other people with the same hobby. Or you can meet people on the Internet. There's a girl at school who met her best friend *and* her boyfriend on an online forum for her favourite band.' Then I had to explain about Internet forums. I didn't tell Laurel that there are a lot of forums about *her*. They used to be all about the abduction and solving 'the crime that shocked the nation', but they've diversified since she came home. I found one the other day that was all about the clothes she wears. People post photos of her and then comment on 'the style choices of lovely Laurel Logan'. It no longer surprises me that people have nothing better to do with their lives.

'I'd like to have friends.' Laurel didn't say this in a self-pitying way. She said it in exactly the same way I would say I'd like to have a biscuit with my cup of tea.

'You *do* have friends. You have me.'

She shook her head. 'That's different.'

'You have Thomas and Martha.'

'They're *your* friends.'

'They're *our* friends now.'

Laurel wasn't sure about that; she wasn't sure they liked her. Of course they liked her, I said. I promised Laurel she would have plenty of friends. It would just take a bit of time, that's all. And she would have to be careful about who she trusted, because some people would want to be friends with her because she's Laurel

Logan – The Girl Who Came Home. It will take a while before she can spot them though – the ones who are interested for all the wrong reasons. But I'll be there, watching. I won't let anyone take advantage of her.

Chapter 20

Thomas and Laurel are sitting at the kitchen table, shoulders almost touching. He's explaining something exceptionally boring about the Internet while he taps away on my laptop. Laurel is hanging on his every word, nodding and asking questions. Thomas is loving it; boys seem to really like *knowing* things.

I made them both a cup of tea and even put out a plate of biscuits (Chocolate Hobnobs). That was two hours ago. Since then I've read the magazine section of the Sunday paper, two chapters of the new Stephen King book and an article about Laurel on my phone. The article raves about her 'performance' on *The Cynthia Day Show*. I don't like how the journalist calls it a performance – 'appearance' is surely the right word.

I can't seem to settle. It's weird not being at Dad and Michel's. They've gone to France for a long weekend. A couple of days in Paris before they go to visit my grandmother in Nice. I think it will be good for them to get away for a bit. Hopefully Dad will stop neglecting Michel. He seems to be over here all the time these days. Whenever I ask where Michel is, Dad says he's at work or out with friends. According to Dad, Michel is perfectly fine, busy getting on with his life. And according to Michel, that's actually the case. He says he doesn't mind, that he understands that Dad wants to spend as much time as possible with Laurel.

Martha texts and asks if I want to meet her in town. I'm about to say that I can't make it but then I change my mind and tell her I'll meet her in Caffè Nero in half an hour. Thomas looks panicked when I announce that I'm leaving them to it. 'But . . . but . . . I thought we were going to . . .' He can't finish this sentence, because he can't very well say that I'd hinted we would have some 'alone time' after he'd helped Laurel with computer stuff.

We haven't had sex again – not since the night before Laurel was found at Stanley Street. We haven't even been on a date. He's been really patient; he understands that Laurel's my priority right now. But I'm well aware that his patience has its limits. We do need to be alone together soon.

Definitely before his birthday. Definitely *not* in his van.

I'm grabbing my coat from the hall cupboard when it suddenly hits me that maybe Laurel doesn't want to be left alone with Thomas. She's only met him a couple of times – he's little more than a stranger to her. I kick myself for not thinking this through. 'Laurel? Can you come here for a second?'

She pops her head round the living-room door.

'Are you . . . ? I can stay if you like. I don't have to go out. I didn't think . . .'

Confusion clouds her features for a moment before she nods in understanding. 'No, you should go. It's fine. Really. I'll be fine.' I watch her closely, searching for any hint of a lie. 'You don't need to wrap me up in cotton wool, you know!' She smiles.

'I know. I'm sorry. I just thought . . . you haven't been alone with a—'

'*Don't.*' The word comes out harsh and flat, but she does her best to soften it with a hand on my arm. 'Faith, I said it was fine, OK?' She looks over her shoulder, then turns back to me and whispers, 'I like him. I trust him.'

'Why?'

She smiles as if that's a stupid question. 'Because you do.'

*

I told Laurel to text me if she wants me to come home. She rolled her eyes and said, 'Yes, *Mum*!' Then she hugged me and told me to have fun with Martha.

But it doesn't turn out to be very much fun at all. It starts to go wrong almost straightaway, when Martha tells me that the girl serving the coffee recognized me from *The Cynthia Day Show* and asked her if it would be OK to ask for my autograph.

'Bullshit! You're lying.' I risk a glance at the girl in question. She's rearranging the muffins on the top shelf of the cabinet.

'Don't stare! She'll know we're talking about her!'

I ignore Martha. The girl doesn't look over – not even once. 'You're hilarious, Martha. Really.'

'I'm not lying! She wanted to know if I'd met Laurel. I told her to mind her own business . . . *after* she'd made the coffee. I didn't want to risk a serving of saliva in my latte. Look, you're just going to have to face facts: you're famous now.' She sips her drink but fails to hide the sly smile on her face. Normally I don't mind Martha taking the piss out of me, but I'm not in the mood for it right now.

Things take a turn for the worse when I tell her I've left Laurel and Thomas at home together. She doesn't say anything, but she raises her eyebrows and widens her eyes.

'*What?*' I ask.

Martha tears off a piece of blueberry muffin and pops it into her mouth. Then she gestures that she can't talk because her mouth is full. I wait, impatiently, before repeating the question.

'Nothing!' All wide-eyed innocence.

I wait her out.

'It's nothing . . . honestly. I was just thinking that if *I* had a boyfriend, and if I had a sister who looked like Laurel . . . well, I probably wouldn't . . .'

Martha has never had a boyfriend. 'Probably wouldn't what?'

She shrugs and takes a sip of coffee. I don't think she has any idea of how infuriating she's being. 'I probably wouldn't want to leave them alone together.'

I knew that was what she was going to say, but that doesn't make it any easier to hear. It's not the words themselves, but the fact that Martha's the one saying them. It's the kind of stupid thing I wouldn't be surprised to hear spouting from Laney Finch's mouth. '*What?*'

'You *asked*! I was just being honest.' She's looking at me as if *I'm* the unreasonable one. Then she tries to backtrack. 'It was a stupid thing to say. I'm sorry. I wasn't thinking. Of course it's fine to—'

'What the hell is *wrong* with you? As if Thomas is going to pounce on my sister, after everything she's been through! *God*, Martha.' I realize too late that I'm speaking far too loudly. People are staring – including the girl behind the counter.

Martha seems taken aback by my reaction. 'That's not what I was . . . Look, can we just talk about something else. This is silly.'

'You're the one who started it.'

Normally she'd say something sarcastic – that I have the argumentative skills of a five-year-old perhaps – but today she just apologizes. I accept her apology and we try to move on.

It's the strangest thing, but I can't think of anything to say. I'm still furious about what she said. The thought of anything happening between Thomas and Laurel is too ridiculous for words, so I should have just been able to laugh it off. But for some reason it's lodged in my brain like a splinter. I look across the table at Martha, who's looking back at me, waiting. What do we usually talk about? I can't even remember. I can't remember how to have a conversation that isn't about Laurel.

'Um . . . how's it going with your mum's job?'

One look at Martha's face confirms that this was the wrong thing to ask. She puts her mug down. 'She got made redundant last month.'

'Last *month*?! Why didn't you tell me?'

'I don't know. I tried, but you were so busy with Laurel and everything. I told you she had that meeting with her boss, remember?'

'No, you didn't.' Did she? Maybe she did. The day before Laurel came home. A text message.

'Look, I'm not going to argue with you, Faith. You've had a lot to deal with recently. I *get* that. I don't blame you.'

Why does Martha saying that she doesn't blame me give me the distinct impression that she *does*? 'I'm sorry.' An apology seems like the best way to defuse the situation.

Martha downs the last of her drink. 'It's OK. Thomas was really nice about it.'

It feels like ice water, trickling through my veins. People always say that anger is hot, but for me it's so cold that it burns. 'You talked to Thomas about it?' My words are clipped, my mouth barely able to open enough to force them out.

She shrugs and it seems like the sole intention of that shrug is to infuriate me. 'Well, *yeah*. I had to talk to *some*one.'

'And I suppose that someone had to be my boyfriend?'

Another shrug. Martha looks up at the wall next to us, suddenly interested in the blander than bland art.

I grab my phone and put it in my bag. 'I have to go.'

Martha looks at me and for a second I think she's going to apologize, but instead she says, 'Since when have you been bothered about me talking to Thomas? Why are you being so weird, Faith?'

I stand up and look down at Martha. Her hair is a mess. She really should think about at least running a brush through it once in a while. Maybe then she might be able to get a boyfriend of her own instead of trying to borrow mine. I want to tell her to fuck off. I want to tell her that she has no idea what I've been going through, and that I *do* care about what's going on in her life, and I *do* care about her mum losing her job.

In the end, all I say is, 'I'll see you at school.'

'Fine.' She gets her phone out and pretends to look at something.

I walk out of the coffee shop with as much dignity as I can muster. It was hardly a screaming row. There were no tears, there was no swearing, there were no real insults to speak of, but it was still the first argument Martha and I have ever had. Why did it have to happen now, when things are going so well with Laurel?

Chapter 21

I'm not jealous about Martha talking to Thomas. I'm not. I've always liked the fact that they get on OK. It makes things easier for me. But the thought of her confiding in him doesn't sit well. That's not meant to happen. They are supposed to talk about books and films and people at school – not things that actually *matter*.

It doesn't take long for me to realize that my feelings have more to do with guilt than jealousy. I've hardly spent any time with Martha since Laurel came back. I seem to have forgotten that other people have things going on in their lives too – that the whole world does not in fact revolve around Laurel and me. Of course I should have remembered to ask Martha about her mum; I knew how worried she was about it.

Maybe Martha shouldn't have said that stupid thing about leaving Laurel and Thomas alone together, but she didn't mean anything by it. I should have just brushed it off. That's what you do with your best friend, isn't it? You forgive them for making mistakes. When did I forget how to do that?

A worrying thought nudges at the edge of my brain. It won't go away no matter how hard I try to ignore it. That whole conversation with Martha was all wrong – like we'd forgotten how to be friends. Like *I'd* forgotten how to be a best friend. It's the same with Thomas too. I feel as if I've forgotten how to be his girlfriend.

I've forgotten how to be anything other than a sister.

I text Martha from the bus: *I'm sorry I've been a crappy friend. Let's not fight. We're really not very good at it.*

She doesn't text back straightaway and I don't blame her for leaving me hanging. I'd probably do the same. I'm just getting off at my stop when she finally texts: *I'm sorry too. Should have told you about Mum. Still besties?*

That makes me smile. Martha would never ever use the word 'besties' in normal conversation – unless she was taking the piss out of someone.

Still BFFs, I text back.

She has the last word: *Squeeee!!!!*

The squeeee might have been sarcastic as hell, but the sentiment is still there. We're OK.

The news vans left weeks ago. This story is over as far as they're concerned – all neatly wrapped up, with a polka-dot bow on top. Of course, I know better than to believe they're gone for good – they'll be back as soon as anything happens. They'll be back when the police catch that monster. They *will* catch him; he can't hide forever.

In the meantime the neighbours are happy to have their parking spaces back and I'm happy to be able to walk down my own street and not have to worry about what my hair looks like or whether I'm wearing the same top I had on yesterday.

There's laughter coming from the living room. I expect to find Thomas and Laurel where I left them – sitting at the dining-room table – but they're lounging on the sofa. The laptop and mugs of tea have been abandoned, the biscuits left untouched. Four bottles of beer sit on the coffee table alongside a gaping bag of Doritos. There's a film on the TV. I can't place it at first, but then one of the actors says something in French and I realize it's *Three Colours: Red* – Thomas's favourite film.

I stand in the doorway for a couple of seconds before Thomas looks up. 'Hi! You're back early.' He sits up straight as if I've just told him off for slouching, when I have, in fact, said nothing.

Laurel pats the space next to her on the sofa – the space between her and Thomas – and says I should sit down. She asks if I had a nice time with Martha and if I would like a beer and if I've seen this film before. Clearly Thomas forgot to mention that we went to see it together on one of our first dates.

'I need a cup of tea. Do either of you want anything?'

Laurel takes a great big swig from her beer bottle. 'I'm fine with this, thanks.'

Thomas shakes his head. He's watching me closely, trying to work out how I'm feeling. I turn my back to him and head into the kitchen. He joins me a minute later, just as I'm switching on the kettle to boil. He closes the door behind him. 'Hey,' he says as he leans against the counter.

'Hey,' I say.

'Are you annoyed?'

'Why would I be annoyed?' I take my mug from the cupboard above the kettle and open up the ceramic jar labelled 'COFFEE', which is where we keep the tea bags. I broke the jar labelled 'TEA' a couple of years ago, smashing it into hundreds of pieces on the kitchen floor. On purpose.

Thomas shrugs and I feel my shoulders tense up. If one more person shrugs at me today I will not be held responsible for my actions. 'I don't know. You just seem . . . annoyed.'

'Well, I'm not.'

'OK,' he says, in that sarcastic whatever-you-say tone. 'How's Martha?'

I turn away from him and open up the fridge. The milk carton is almost empty. We always used to have plenty of milk, but Mum hasn't adjusted how much she buys now that there's an extra person in the house. I pour the last dregs into my mug, even though it's not enough for a decent cup of tea.

'Faith? I asked you a question.' Thomas hates being ignored. He thinks everything he has to say is of the utmost importance and should be listened to with a bowed head and a serious expression on your face.

'I've got a question for you. Why didn't you tell me about Martha's mum losing her job?'

He wasn't expecting that. 'What are you talking about?'

'It's a perfectly straightforward question.' I take a teaspoon from the drawer – the one that doesn't match the rest of the set. I always used to use it to eat my boiled egg and soldiers because I felt sorry for it; I thought it must be lonely, being the odd one out among the rest of the cutlery. 'Martha told you about her mum. You didn't bother to tell me. I'm asking you why.'

'I don't know. I thought you knew.'

'Well, I *didn't* know.' The kettle has boiled. I pour the water into the mug too fast and it splashes on to the countertop. Thomas grabs a tea towel and wipes up the water. I dunk the tea bag and press it against the side of the mug, making sure the colour is as close to perfect as I can get it under the circumstances.

Finally the tea is made and there's nothing else for me to occupy myself with. 'Faith? What's the matter?' Thomas's voice is gentle and coaxing. 'Are you annoyed about Laurel and me watching *Red*? Is that it?'

I *am* annoyed about that. That film has always been our thing – mine and Thomas's. We must have watched it at least eight times. 'I'm not annoyed about that . . . You shouldn't be giving her beer though.'

Thomas moves closer to me and puts his hand on the back of my neck. His fingers start to work their magic. I've almost forgotten what it feels like to have him touch me. 'She's nineteen years old, Faith. I think you forget that sometimes. Besides, it was her idea.'

I move away, out of reach. 'Did you at least show her all the computer stuff she wanted to know?'

Thomas nods. 'Yeah, she picked it up really quickly. She's a natural.' Thomas looks at the door as if to check it hasn't suddenly turned transparent in the last couple of minutes. 'Can I have a kiss?'

I really don't want to kiss him. I want to go sit in a quiet room with my mug of tea and not talk to another human being until tomorrow at the very earliest. 'OK,' I say.

He smiles and I can tell he's relieved. Everything must be fine if I'm happy to kiss him. He leans in towards me and the smell of cheesy Doritos assaults my nostrils. I count to ten – slowly – while we're kissing. I don't want to pull away too soon. After all, this is the most action he's had in weeks.

We watch the rest of the film. I sit in between Laurel and Thomas on the sofa – Laurel insists on it. She wants another beer but I say that she probably shouldn't so she doesn't.

The sofa seems too small.

Chapter 22

It was a blip, that's all. One bad day. I must have got out of the wrong side of bed or something. Everything is fine at school the next day. Martha, Thomas and I have lunch together and Thomas monopolizes the conversation, talking about a Peruvian poet who's just died. Sometimes I think he scours the Internet searching for the most obscure people he can find to make himself look knowledgeable, but this time Martha's heard of her too. I nod along with them, just pleased that things seem to be back to normal and no one's talking about yesterday's weirdness.

I can't quite rid myself of the nagging idea that Martha and Thomas might have talked to each other last night, comparing notes. If they have, there's not a lot I can do about it. I should be glad that my boyfriend and my best friend get on so well. I *am* glad.

*

Things can start to get back to normal now that Laurel has settled in. Soon she won't need me so much, and some time after *that* she won't need me at all. And that will be a good thing. That's what we're all working towards – normality. We're getting there, slowly but surely. The other night Laurel and I disagreed about what to watch on TV. It was nothing serious, and I let her have her way in the end, but I noticed Mum watching us closely the whole time. She didn't look annoyed like you might have expected, and she didn't tell me to give the remote control to Laurel and be done with it. She was smiling.

'What are you grinning at?' I snapped at her.

That only made her smile more. 'Nothing.' She tried to wipe the grin from her face and concentrate on the television.

'Tell us!' said Laurel.

The two of us stared at our mother until she relented. 'It's just . . . it makes me so happy to see you two bickering like that. It's just like me and your Auntie Eleanor when we were your age.'

'So?' I asked.

The smile slipped from her face. 'Well, I never thought this would . . . I mean, I always hoped . . . It's just so nice to see you being sisters. It's all I've ever wanted.' Then she dissolved into tears, but she said it was OK, they were happy tears. Laurel and I looked at each other and smiled. I handed her the remote control and she turned off the TV. I moved over to the sofa so I was sitting next to Mum, then I hugged her. Laurel hugged her too. Mum had one arm around Laurel and one arm around me and we stayed like that for a long time. The sofa felt the right size again.

I know something is up the second I get home from school. Mum and Dad and Laurel are sitting at the dining table. Dad wasn't supposed to be arriving until later. Mum invited him and Michel round for dinner (because I nagged her until she agreed to it just to shut me up). As far as I'm concerned, this will be our first *real* family dinner.

I look at the faces around the table, searching for clues. Mum and Laurel look fine; Dad doesn't look too happy. I dump my bag on the sofa then sit down on the spare chair. We only have four. I'll have to bring one through from the kitchen before Michel arrives.

I ask what's going on. Then I get the strangest flashback to the moment when Mum and Dad told me they were splitting up. They sat me down at the same dining table, in a different house, and spoke to me in soft, sympathetic voices. (*We still care about each other, very much. And we love you just the same as we always have. There's really no need for you to worry.*)

Mum tells me that nothing bad has happened, and Dad raises his eyebrows as if he's not so sure about that. Laurel winks at me, which reassures me more than Mum's words ever could. I wait for someone to tell me what the hell is going on here.

Mum looks at Dad, but he shakes his head and puts his hands up. 'I'm having nothing to do with it.'

Mum purses her lips. Then she turns to me. 'Laurel and I had a meeting this morning.' It's the first I've heard of any meeting. 'With a publisher. They've got a proposal for us.'

'What kind of proposal?' I ask, even though there's only one kind of proposal it could possibly be.

'A book deal. They're prepared to pay a *significant* amount of money.'

'They want you to write a book?' I ask Laurel.

Laurel opens her mouth to speak, but Mum gets in there first. 'They want *us* to write it.' She places her hand on top of mine. 'As a family.'

'Well that's weird.'

'The editor said it will be the first book of its kind. "Groundbreaking" was the word she used.' It doesn't escape me that Mum used the word 'will' instead of 'would', as if this is already a done deal. From the look on Dad's face, it hasn't escaped him either. 'Of course, the lion's share of the book would be about Laurel, but they want to hear the *whole* story – what it's been like for each of us. They've already found the perfect ghostwriter for the project. They're hoping to publish in time for Christmas.'

'Why would anyone want a book about us – about Laurel – for Christmas? No offence, Laurel.' Laurel is sitting quietly, just watching.

'My point exactly,' Dad says triumphantly.

Mum rolls her eyes. 'You two are so cynical. It's the perfect book for Christmas – it's a story of hope, isn't it?'

'Anyway,' says Dad, 'it's a decision we have to make as a family. I've already made my feelings on the matter quite clear. I think the public has probably had just about enough of us by now. It's time to move on.' He looks at Laurel, but her face is curiously blank. 'But I've agreed to abide by your decision.' He looks from me to Laurel and back again.

That is so typical of Dad, taking the easy way out.

'Well, Faith, what do you think?' Mum's eyes are wide and hopeful even though she knows (she *must* know, surely?) what I'm going to say.

'I think it's a terrible idea.' I can practically see the thought bubble coming out of Dad's head: *That's my girl*.

Mum sneaks a glance at Laurel before focusing back on me. 'But why? Don't you think it would be good to set the record straight? To tell our side of the story?'

'You've been telling *your* side of the story for years.' This sounds worse out loud than it did in my head. I try again. 'I just don't see the point of this. Of keeping on talking about what happened. It's in the past now.'

There's silence around the table. I stare at the empty mug in front of Laurel – the one with my name on it. I'm not sure why, but she seems to prefer it to the one I bought for her.

'Faith has a point, Olivia.'

'Yes, I know she has a point. *Thanks*, John, for stating the bloody obvious . . . as usual.'

Dad holds his hands up as if he's being held at gunpoint. 'Whoa there! There's no need for this to turn nasty.'

Mum sighs and sits back in her chair. 'We have to think about Laurel's future. The kind of money they're talking about could set her up for life.' I wish they wouldn't talk about Laurel as if she wasn't here.

But it's almost as if she *isn't* here. She isn't reacting to anything anyone says. She doesn't seem bothered by Mum and Dad arguing, which makes me think they were probably arguing before I got here. 'And you'd get a share of the money too, Faith . . .'

I hadn't thought of that. For some reason I assumed it would all go to Laurel. I wonder how much . . . No. No amount of money is worth that kind of invasion of privacy. I stand up; Mum tells me to sit down. I ignore her. 'I just want to live a normal life without everyone knowing our business. You three can do what you want, but there's no way I'm getting involved in this.'

I grab my bag from the sofa and walk out of the room. Mum and Dad both call me back but I ignore them. Upstairs, I slam my bedroom door then flop down on the bed.

Is it always going to be like this? Why can't people just leave us alone? Everyone seems to want their pound of flesh, and Mum seems perfectly willing to carve it up for them and serve it lightly sautéed with a side of Béarnaise sauce.

I keep waiting for someone to knock at the door. Dad, maybe, coming to say that he's proud of me for taking a stand against all this bullshit. Mum, coming to apologize and say that she's had a change of heart and realized that the idea of us all writing a book together is truly, truly terrible. Or Laurel. I have no idea what she would say. But no one comes, so after a while I pick up a book and start reading. Time passes, slowly.

Chapter 23

I clear my throat. 'Can you pass the salt, please?'

Mum doesn't move, even though the salt shaker is closest to her. Michel reaches across the table, almost catching his shirt sleeve on the candle flame. He grabs the salt and puts it down in front of me. '*Merci*,' I say, under my breath.

Poor Michel. He has no idea what he's walked into. Unless Dad called him to warn him. No one's mentioned the book deal since I stormed out of the conversation. It's not the elephant in the room – it's bigger than that. A blue whale, floundering and gasping for air.

There are lots of awkward silences. Michel does his best to fill them, but it's a losing battle. He's already complimented Mum on the food – slow-roasted shoulder of lamb – five times.

Dad's on his third glass of wine already. Mum says

it would be nice if he left some for other people. He ignores her and pours himself some more. The glass is so full that he has to lift it to his mouth excruciatingly slowly so he doesn't spill a drop on the pristine tablecloth.

Laurel has barely touched her food. Mum's noticed – she keeps on glancing at Laurel's plate. Laurel moves the food around with her knife and fork, as if that's fooling anyone.

'Is everything OK, love? Are you not hungry? I can make you something else if you'd prefer?' Mum's always fussing over Laurel. She can't leave her in peace.

'No, it's really good, thanks.' Laurel eats a tiny bit of potato, which seems to make Mum feel better. She stops watching Laurel like a hawk and concentrates on her own plate for a couple of minutes.

Michel starts telling us about a man who came into the surgery with baby turtles in his coat pockets. Laurel smiles politely and I even manage to laugh. Dad drinks more wine.

We're having pudding – chocolate mousse served in little espresso cups – when Mum finally crumbles. (I wish we were having crumble – Mum does a really good one.) 'Look, we're going to have to sort this out. Zara – that's the editor, she's really lovely by the way – wants an answer tomorrow.'

Michel doesn't ask what Mum's talking about, so Dad must have given him the lowdown after all. Everyone looks at me.

'What are you all looking at me for? I've told you what *I* think. Write the book without me – no one would give a toss about what I have to say anyway.'

Mum dabs at her mouth with her napkin. 'I think you're being remarkably selfish.'

Dad leans forward. 'Now hang on a minute, Olivia. That's not fair. Faith's entitled to her opinion on the matter. Some of us are just . . . more private than others.'

'Well, some of us have more *reason* to be private than others,' Mum snaps back, tossing her napkin on to the table.

'What's that supposed to mean?' Dad's face is red and I can't tell if it's because he's angry or drunk or both.

'You know full well what it means.'

'How *dare* you? After everything I've been through with the press . . .' He shakes his head in disgust.

Things are getting out of hand. Someone needs to step in and say something. I thought Michel might be the man for the job but he's always so careful around Mum.

I try to think of something to say to defuse the

situation. 'Have either of you bothered to ask Laurel what *she* wants to do?'

Mum's lips twitch into a half-smile and that's when I know I've made a mistake. She wants to do it; Laurel wants us to write the fucking book.

'Laurel? Why don't you tell Faith what you told us earlier?'

Laurel takes a sip of water. She hasn't touched her glass of wine; I'm surprised Dad hasn't poured it into his own (now empty) glass. Laurel's hands are in her lap. She almost looks like she could be praying, if it wasn't for the fact that her eyes are open. The chocolate mousse in front of her has a single spoonful carved out of it. Laurel's mouth is clamped shut as if she's worried someone will force another spoonful into her mouth if she opens it even a little bit.

'Laurel?'

'Leave the girl alone, Olivia!'

'Can you please stop fighting?' Laurel says, her voice little more than a whisper. Everyone hears though.

Mum and Dad both apologize and Michel shoots me a look that I can't decipher. Laurel looks at me too.

'It's OK,' I say. 'You can tell me the truth.'

'I want to write the book. I want us *all* to write the book.' I half expect Mum to high-five her and run a victory lap round the dining table. But I'm pretty sure my mother has never high-fived anyone in her entire life, and she doesn't 'do' running.

'Why?' It's a simple question, but I'm almost certain Mum never bothered to ask it.

Laurel stares up at the light above the table – the one that looks like it's made up of three flying saucers from the 1970s. The one Mum's been meaning to replace ever since we moved in. The last time I mentioned it, she said it was 'growing on her'. Like a fungus.

The silence goes on for too long; it's as if Laurel's gone into some kind of trance, staring at that ugly light. 'Laurel?' I reach across the table to touch her hand and something flashes across her face. I'd have missed it if I'd blinked. Perhaps Mum, Dad and Michel were blinking, all at the exact same moment. I take my hand away and start to doubt myself immediately, because what possible reason could there be for her to have that look on her face? All I did was touch her. Surely that didn't warrant a look of pure revulsion?

A flashback. That's the only explanation that makes any sense. Laurel's counsellor, Penny, told us that flashbacks were more than likely. That they can happen at any time, without any warning. She said there were bound to be things that Laurel had gone through that she might have buried in the recesses of her mind to protect herself. Those things might stay buried forever, or they might just lurk there, waiting to jump out at her when she least expected it.

'Well?' Mum nudges me with her foot under the table.

'Sorry . . . what?'

'The least you can do is listen to what Laurel has to say.' I'm not even sure Mum realizes what a bitch she's being.

I look at Laurel and wait. There's no hint of revulsion on her face now. It's hard to imagine the twisting grimace I saw — thought I saw? — only seconds ago. Now her expression is warm and kind and open. 'I think . . . I think it would help us heal. As a family.'

I say nothing.

Now it's Laurel's turn to reach across the table and take my hand in hers. 'I think it would give us closure.' *Closure.* That's what you get for watching *The Cynthia Day Show* every day. Cynthia's always spouting that kind of psychobabble nonsense; her audience laps it up like kittens.

Laurel squeezes my hand. 'It would be a project that we can all do *together* — as a family.' She looks over at Mum and they share a sad little smile, like they're both thinking of all the things we've missed out on doing *as a family*.

But why does it have to be a *book*? Why can't we do something that normal families do, like go to Alton Towers? Or IKEA.

Martha would be horrified if I agree to this. Thomas too. Laney Finch would be delighted – and that's putting it mildly. I don't even need to look at Michel to know that he thinks this is a terrible idea, but he won't say anything because Dad's in an impossible situation here. Dad would do anything for Laurel – anything at all. Because he's spent so many years not being able to do a single thing for her.

Laurel lets go of my hand. 'I'll understand if you don't want to do it, Faith. We *all* will.' Mum nods in agreement, because that's what Laurel wants her to do. 'It's up to you.'

One last try. 'But can't you do it *without* me?'

Laurel shakes her head. 'I wouldn't want to. You can say no, Faith. We don't have to do it. We can forget all about it,' she says. I believe her. Mum might hold it against me until the end of time, but Laurel wouldn't.

In the end, it all comes down to one thing: my sister. Laurel's future *with* thousands and thousands of pounds in a savings account, or Laurel's future *without* thousands and thousands of pounds in a savings account. Maybe I'm wrong. Maybe she would be able to get a regular job like a regular person. Maybe she can go to university and study law and end up being some hotshot corporate lawyer in London. Maybe she can live a normal life and lock up the memories of what happened to her and store them away somewhere in her brain, never to be found again. But maybe she can't. And if she can't live a normal life, she's going to need money. Lots of it.

Mum's the only one who seems genuinely shocked when I say, 'Let's do it. Let's write the book.' Shocked, but happy. Laurel rushes round from her side of the table and hugs me. 'Thank you,' she whispers.

Dad's not surprised at all. He knows I feel the same way he does: Laurel is our priority now. Her needs come first.

Chapter 24

Michel volunteers to do the washing-up and asks me to dry the dishes. Mum, Dad and Laurel stay in the living room.

'You didn't have to do that, you know,' Michel says quietly as he hands me the wine glass he's just washed.

'I did.' I wipe the glass with a tea towel, careful to get rid of every last drop of water before placing it on the worktop.

'No, you really didn't. It's your life too.' I want him to stop talking. 'They shouldn't have pressured you into it.'

'They didn't pressure me into anything. I'd already made up my mind to do it.' I have no idea why I'm lying to him, especially since it's abundantly clear that he knows I'm lying to him.

He stops washing dishes and turns to look at me.

I carry on drying because I can't face looking at him. 'I'm worried about you, Faith.'

'Worried? Why would you be worried about me?'

He's silent for a moment. Either he's choosing his words carefully, or he can't think of the exact English words to convey what he's thinking. 'You're not being yourself.'

My grip tightens on the stem of a wine glass. I wonder if I could shatter it if I grip hard enough. 'I don't know what you're talking about.'

'I know you don't,' says Michel. He sounds tired.

I'm about to ask him what the hell he's on about when Mum walks in, asking whether I've seen the posh biscuits she bought at Waitrose last week.

'I haven't seen them.' Laurel and I polished off the whole lot on Tuesday night. 'Actually, Mum, I've got a bit of a headache. I might just go to bed, if that's OK? I'll sort out the rest of the dishes in the morning.'

Mum comes over and touches my forehead with the back of her hand. I didn't say anything about having a temperature so I'm not sure what she's hoping to achieve. She prescribes a pint of water and two ibuprofen.

Michel tells me he hopes I feel better soon. I thank him and leave the kitchen. I don't hug him goodbye like I always do.

Dad and Laurel are sitting on the sofa, talking quietly. I tell them I'm not feeling so good and give each of them a hug. Laurel's worried. She asks if she can bring me anything, then she asks Dad if he thinks we should call a doctor. Dad laughs and tells her not to be silly, and I can tell she doesn't like being called silly but she doesn't say so. I reassure her that I'll be fine, I'm just tired. I don't think she believes me, but she says goodnight, and that she'll come up to check on me in a little while.

She doesn't come though. I lie in bed, listening. I hear Dad and Michel leaving after half an hour or so. I listen to their footsteps on the gravel outside. Michel will be the one to drive them home – he's *always* the one to drive them home. He says he doesn't mind not drinking, which is just as well because Dad would definitely mind.

I'll apologize to Michel tomorrow, even though I'm not quite sure what I'll be apologizing for. He was only looking out for me when he said I didn't have to be involved in this ridiculous book idea. I know that. He's always the one to look out for me. But what was that nonsense about me not being myself? Where the hell did *that* come from?

It's not true. I *am* being myself. I'm always myself, because what else is there to be? The weirdest thing

196

is that, these past few weeks, I've felt more like 'me' than I ever have before. Not that I go around thinking about how 'me' I'm being. But since Laurel came home I've been feeling more settled somehow, despite all the upheaval. It's as if I can breathe again – great big gulps of air – after a lifetime of feeling slightly suffocated.

Less than an hour after Michel and Dad leave, I hear footsteps on the stairs. Mum's footsteps. I know that, because she always steps over the creaky stair, third from the top, when she thinks I'm asleep. The footsteps come closer and stop outside my bedroom door. I clutch the edge of the duvet and my whole body tenses up. There's something creepy about someone standing listening on the other side of a closed door, even if it is your mother.

Perhaps she wants to apologize. I'd like to think she feels bad for pressuring me about the book deal. But I suspect she hasn't even given it a second thought. I don't necessarily think it's a case of her putting Laurel's needs before my own. It's more like she's putting *her* needs before mine – and Dad's. She's always been more comfortable with the publicity side of things than he has. And she's always claimed that it's because she would do anything in her power to get Laurel back. Since she couldn't go and knock down every door in the country or search every abandoned warehouse or travel around the world looking for clues, it was her only option. Making sure as many people as possible knew about Laurel Logan, and making sure they never forgot her. That was her mission, her obsession.

On my unkinder days – and I've had a lot of those – I used to wonder if maybe my mother enjoyed the attention a little bit. She seemed so comfortable being in the limelight – going on talk shows and speaking in front of huge crowds – that sometimes it was hard to think otherwise. Dad went on the talk shows too, and read out all of the official family statements, but there was always a sense of reluctance about it. He gritted his teeth and did what had to be done – for Laurel. He hated all of it. And, like me, he probably thought those days were over. He probably thought that we could go back to being a normal family. Maybe not quite the normal family we were thirteen years ago, but a slightly different version, with Michel included.

The Cynthia Day Show was one thing, but this book deal is a whole different ball game. This will be big news. This will make sure the spotlight remains firmly fixed on the Logan family for months and months – maybe even years. What was I *thinking*?

Certain sections of the press will have a field day with this. It won't be the first time that we've been accused of courting attention, but this will be different. Back then, there was always a reason, and no one could really argue with that reason without being vilified themselves – just ask Jeanette Hayes. My parents were desperate to get their daughter back. Who couldn't relate to that? But now Little Laurel Logan is back home where she belongs. Of course people will still be interested in her – in hearing about how she's doing. People want their 'happily ever after'. But the danger is that they'll soon tire of the story, that we'll be seen to be milking the situation for all its worth. And before you know it, journalists will be digging around for nasty stories about Laurel or Mum or Dad . . . or me.

People will buy the book – I have no doubt about that. But that doesn't mean we should write it. We don't have an obligation to satisfy anyone's curiosity – the most morbid curiosity you could ever imagine. I've agreed to it now though; there's no going back. I just have focus on the fact that Laurel will be set up for life – or at least for the next few years. And she'll get to tell her own story, in her own words (well, a ghostwriter's words). If she's happy to talk about it – for everyone to know what that monster did to her – then she has the right to be heard. It's not the choice I would make, in her situation. But Maggie and Penny have both said that it's good for Laurel to talk about her experiences, and that the real danger is in her bottling things up inside.

I lie in bed and wait for Laurel to come and check on me like she promised. I stare at the glowing red numbers on my alarm clock and count the seconds in each minute, trying to catch the exact moment the numbers change. I never get it right though. The sixty seconds I count out in my head are always faster than the real sixty seconds.

She must be staying up to watch TV. I don't mind that she's forgotten to come and see me. It's not as if I need her to tuck me up in bed in order for me to get to sleep. But for some reason I *can't* sleep. My brain is too busy, flitting from one topic to the next and back again, like a hyperactive housefly. I'm dreading telling Martha and Thomas about the book. Martha will mock me mercilessly, but I've had years of practice dealing with that. It's Thomas I'm more worried about. His favourite insult is 'sell-out', and he uses it a lot. He stopped liking his favourite band as soon as they became popular. (*Their new material is far too commercial.*) We argue about it sometimes, but it's more bickering than properly arguing. I maintain that he only likes obscure bands that no one's heard of because he likes to be the one who 'discovered' them, even though that's total bullshit. He likes to be able to say that he saw them play in some sweaty little back room of a club *long* before they were famous and playing huge arenas. The trouble is, the bands he likes always seem to end up being popular, which clearly means that when it comes down to it, the music he's into is little more than the lowest common denominator.

Thomas will be disappointed in me. Even if he doesn't say it (and he probably *will* say it), I'll know it's true. I can hardly blame him though – I'm a little bit disappointed in myself. But I'm just going to have to get over that, because I'd rather be disappointed in myself – and have Thomas disappointed in me – than let Laurel down. If Thomas can't understand that, then maybe he's not the right person for me. As soon as I start thinking that, a jagged ball of anxiety lodges itself in my chest. It's nothing new; it magically appears almost every time I really let myself think about my relationship with Thomas these days. To be honest, I was having doubts even before Laurel came back. But I always stomped on those doubts, grinding them down to dust under my shoe.

The truth is that I had sex with Thomas in an effort to convince myself that we should stay together. The logic is more than flawed, but it made sense to me at the time. I haven't even talked to Martha about it. It's not that I think she wouldn't understand, more that

I'm not sure I can put how I feel into words. I don't know if it's normal to feel like you love someone one day and then feel like you hate them the next. Actually, that's not even how it is. It's more of a minute-to-minute thing. Thomas can be really, really kind and sweet. I like him the most when we're laughing about something silly – not *at* someone. But then he'll say something so insufferably pompous that I'll want to slap him. Sometimes I imagine actually doing it. Of course, I never, ever would, but it's fun to picture the look on his face.

It can't be normal to have these feelings about the person you're supposed to be in love with. Or maybe it *is* normal, and being in love is a global conspiracy in which everyone vows to keep quiet about the fact that it's actually a bit rubbish.

I'm not sure what would have happened if Laurel hadn't come back. Would Thomas and I still be together? Is having a boyfriend you're not entirely sure about better than having no boyfriend at all?

Chapter 25

At 1.32 I realize that there's no way I'm getting to sleep. I'm thinking hot chocolate is the way to go. If Laurel hasn't fallen asleep on the sofa I'll make one for her too. I put on my dressing gown and creep downstairs, careful to avoid the creaky stair.

The lights are off in the living room; the TV is off too. Laurel's not on the sofa. A strip of light under the kitchen door confirms her whereabouts. Maybe she's read my mind and has already got the milk heating on the hob. I like the idea that we might have some kind of psychic connection.

I open the kitchen door and Laurel jumps in her chair. She knocks over the glass that was on the table next to her and water goes everywhere. 'Shit! Faith! I was just . . .'

I rush over to the sink and grab the kitchen roll. 'Sorry, I didn't mean to scare you!' That's when I notice what's on the table: a photo album. Luckily the photos are protected by plastic, so the water hasn't done any damage.

'Why did you sneak up on me like that?' Laurel grabs some kitchen roll from me and starts dabbing at the photo album while I concentrate on the water on the table.

'I didn't mean to! I just came down for some hot chocolate.' Laurel is breathing hard, her face is even paler than usual. Something's not right here. 'Laurel? Are you OK?'

She shakes her head and closes her eyes for a second, trying to compose herself before she speaks. 'I'm sorry. I didn't mean to freak out. It just . . . it reminded me of *him*.' Oh God. 'I . . . I never knew when to expect him.'

'I'm so sorry, Laurel.' I don't like it when she mentions him. I try my hardest to forget that he's still out there, because it scares me. He could be anywhere. The police have assured us that it's highly unlikely he'll be anywhere within a hundred miles of us, that he'll be lying low, given that he's now the most wanted man in the country. That seems to be good enough for Mum and Dad and Laurel, but it's nowhere near good enough for me. A couple of police officers parked down the street wouldn't be able to stop him – not if he really wanted to get Laurel back. I've been having nightmares about him creeping into our house and taking her back.

Laurel walks over to the kitchen window and her shoulders start to shake. Mum must have forgotten to pull the blinds down, so I can see Laurel's reflection in the window. Her hands are up to her face, as if we're playing a game of hide-and-seek. I hate it when it's dark outside and light inside and you can't see if someone's lurking in the shadows. Whoever is out there can see you, but you can't see them. There's a security light above the back door, but it's been broken for nearly a year.

I go over and put my hand on Laurel's shoulder. She flinches slightly and it breaks my heart. I rub her back and tell her everything's going to be OK. In between sobs, Laurel apologizes for overreacting. I tell her there's no such thing as overreacting, after everything she's been through. She turns to me and I go to wipe away her tears, but her eyes are dry. She sniffs and wipes her nose with her sleeve and takes a long, juddery breath.

'Do you want a hot chocolate? It always makes me feel better.' It's true. It's been my comfort drink since I was little. I used to have three cups a day until Mum decided I was getting too fat. She didn't exactly *say* I was getting fat, but I knew she was thinking it. She stopped buying crisps and Coke and suggested I take up a new hobby . . . some kind of sport, perhaps? I was ten years old. She must be happy now that she's got the skinny daughter back, even if she's only skinny because she's been practically starved for the past thirteen years.

'No, thanks. I think I'll just go to bed. Would you . . . ? Oh God, this is going to sound so silly . . .' Laurel shakes her head. 'No, it's OK actually. I'll just . . .'

'What is it, Laurel?' I ask gently.

She stares at a spot on the wall, avoiding eye contact. 'Would you mind staying with me until I fall asleep?' She says this quickly, running the words together.

'Of course I will.'

Laurel doesn't look at the table as she walks past it; I do. There are two photos on each open page of the album. Four photographs, all taken at Christmas. A sleepy, pyjamaed eight-year-old me standing beside the Christmas tree. Me opening my presents, sitting cross-legged in a scrunchy sea of wrapping paper. Dad carving the turkey, looking proud of himself even though Mum was the one who did all the cooking. An awkwardly posed family picture: Mum, Dad, me (wearing an orange paper hat), Gran and Gramps, Auntie Eleanor.

'What were you doing with those? Looking for tips on how to have the worst haircut in the whole history of human existence?'

Laurel doesn't laugh. 'I think your hair looks cute in those pictures.'

'Why were you looking at them?' It makes me sad to think of her sitting down here all by herself, poring over photos of things she missed out on. The photos give a false impression though. Everyone looks happy (even me, with my disastrous hair), but that's because no one took pictures of Mum sobbing in the kitchen or Dad staring into space instead of watching the Christmas film I insisted we watch together every year. Laurel would never know any of that from looking at these photos. These photos make it look like we didn't miss her at all, like everyone just got on with their lives and couldn't care less about her.

'Mum was showing me them earlier.'

I nod and close the album. I turn off the light and we go upstairs. I wait in Laurel's room while she gets changed in the bathroom and listen to the water running as she brushes her teeth. She never gets changed in front of me. Mum's the only one of us who's seen what marks that monster might have left on my sister's body.

Laurel gets into bed and I perch on the stool in front of her dressing table. We talk for a little bit, then I turn out the light and wait for her to fall asleep. It's at least fifteen minutes before I hear the change in her breathing and I creep out of her room and into my own.

It's a long time before sleep comes for me. I keep replaying the scene in the kitchen. Laurel lied to me. She looked me in the eyes and lied. Mum didn't show her that photo album, I know that for a fact. Because Mum didn't know where it was.

Two days before Laurel came home I took the photo album from the bookshelf next to the fireplace. I sat in bed staring at the photos, trying to make sense of everything that I was feeling. Thinking about the past and wondering about the future. The next morning I didn't take the album back downstairs. I wanted to keep it close to me so I put it in one of my bedside drawers – the bottom one. It lay there on top of a couple of old swimming certificates, a pair of Mickey Mouse ears and a 'book' I'd written (and illustrated) when I was eight years old.

Mum stopped rooting around in my room years ago. She wouldn't dare go through my stuff. There's only one explanation: Laurel has been snooping in here. I know it. And she must *know* that I know it. So why didn't she just say she found the photo album while she was looking for something in my room? I'd probably have believed her. Even if I hadn't believed her, I wouldn't have been annoyed. There are a couple of things in there that I wouldn't be too happy if Mum found, but I've got nothing to hide from Laurel.

There shouldn't be any secrets between sisters.

Chapter 26

I expect her to put up a bit of a fight when Laurel suggests it, but Mum doesn't bat an eyelid. Penny must have talked to her beforehand, laying the groundwork. 'I think it's a great idea. Faith and I can come and meet you for a late lunch and we could go shopping afterwards – just us girls.' Mum's been in a good mood since we signed the contract for the book deal. The publisher paid the first chunk of money a couple of days ago: we are now officially rolling in it.

So Laurel is going into town by herself for the very first time today. She's already showered and dressed by the time I come downstairs. It's the first Monday of half-term. I usually sleep in really late during the holidays, but for some reason this morning I woke up at seven thirty – exactly the same time my alarm is set for me to get up for school. Laurel makes me a cup of tea and we sit together at the kitchen table.

'Wrong mug,' I say, stifling a yawn.

'What?' Laurel seems edgy this morning, distracted.

I hold the mug up for her to see her name. 'Oh. Do you want to swap?'

'Nah. How are you feeling about this morning?'

'Fine,' she says. But she's drumming her fingers on the table.

'You don't have to do this if you're not ready, you know. I can come with you.' I take a sip of tea. Laurel makes good tea.

Her eyes widen. 'No.' It's too loud, that word. Too forceful, given that I was only offering to be nice. 'No,' she says, more softly this time. 'Thanks, but I'm ready. I should have done it weeks ago. You and Mum must be sick of the sight of me.'

'That's not true.'

Laurel shrugs. 'I need to be more independent.'

She's right, I suppose. And maybe she's feeling stifled, hardly ever being alone. It hasn't occurred to me before, that maybe it's hard for her to have people around *all* the time. With Smith she was left alone for hours on end — sometimes even days. She's used to her own company. Maybe she even prefers it that way.

'Don't forget to take your phone.' I sound like

Mum, which makes me cringe. 'Text if you need me or if you just feel like some company.'

Laurel takes two big gulps of tea, then winces because the tea's too hot for gulping. 'Thanks. I'll be fine though. Really.'

'And you're sure you know how to get to the sushi place?'

She says nothing. Instead she stands up and takes something out of the pocket of her jeans, unfolding it carefully for me to see. I drew the map last night, only getting it absolutely right on my fourth attempt.

'Sorry. I know you're perfectly capable of finding your own way around.'

'Really?! Is that why you felt the need to mark which side of the road I should walk on?' She laughs.

'It's only cos there's a building site there at the moment and the pavement's closed . . . I didn't want you getting run over.' I sound ridiculous. I *am* ridiculous. Laurel is nineteen years old. 'Sorry.'

'It's OK! You don't have to keep apologizing! It's nice that you care.'

'What are you planning on doing this morning anyway?'

Laurel takes her mug over to the sink and squeezes some washing-up liquid into it. She turns the tap on too fast and a spray of water shoots up from the sink, drenching her. 'Shit! Shit shit shit shit!' She slams the mug down on the worktop so hard I'm worried she might have cracked it.

I get up and help her, dabbing at her shirt with a clean tea towel. 'It's OK, it'll dry in a few minutes.'

'Are you sure? Maybe I should change my top.' She looks at her watch; Mum bought her the same one I have. I swear sometimes she forgets that Laurel and I aren't actually twins. 'Yeah, I'm going to change.'

I explain that there's really no need. She can just keep her jacket buttoned up till the shirt is dry. Laurel doesn't seem convinced but I manage to persuade her. I make her check that she's got enough change for the bus, then she's out the door.

Mum comes downstairs a couple of minutes later and asks where Laurel is. 'But nothing's open at this time! Why didn't you tell her?'

I should have known this would somehow be *my* fault, despite the fact that Laurel is a grown woman. I say as much to Mum and she apologizes. The apology wrong-foots me; normally we'd be gearing up for a proper argument right about now.

'She'll be fine,' Mum says distractedly as she opens the fridge. 'She'll be absolutely fine.'

'Of course she will.'

'There's really nothing to worry about.'

'No, there really isn't.'

'OK then! Breakfast . . . Did you finish the milk again?'

Now it's time for an argument. *You're so selfish, you never think of others, if only you could be a little more thoughtful sometimes.* I don't even bother to hide the smile on my face. There's something profoundly reassuring about hearing the same old spiel. There's no point telling her it was Laurel who used the last of the milk to drown her Weetabix. I'm happy to take the blame, so the argument sort of fizzles out before it's even started.

While she's waiting for her toast to pop up Mum tells me that she's got a surprise for Laurel and me. I ask what it is and she says I'll have to wait and see. I tell her she's infuriating, and what's the point of telling me there's a surprise if she's not going to tell me what it is. She should have just kept her mouth shut in the first place. So she gives in and tells me: she's treating us both to a shopping spree. A thousand pounds each to spend this afternoon, from her share of the book-deal money.

Mum looks so pleased with herself that I don't tell her it's a crazy amount of money to fritter away in one afternoon. She's arranged for us to meet a personal shopper at the fanciest department store in town – the one where you have to run a gauntlet past terrifying women intent on giving you a makeover or spritzing you with perfume that would give Cynthia Day's a run for its money. She asks me if I think Laurel will be happy about it and I say that I'm sure she will be. 'It's every girl's dream, isn't it?' she says, sounding hopeful.

I bet she hasn't told Dad, because I'm pretty sure he wouldn't approve. He'd be thinking about how it might look if the story gets into the papers – us cashing in on what happened to Laurel. A photo of Laurel emerging from the shop, laden with bags emblazoned with designer logos. Jeanette Hayes would have a field day.

I suppose we'll just have to hope the photographers stay away – that no one in the store calls them to tip them off about Laurel's presence. And that none of the sales assistants or other shoppers think to snap a picture of Laurel on their phone. Perhaps we'll be lucky.

I don't want to spoil this for Mum; she looks so happy. The physical changes in her are almost as noticeable as those in Laurel. Before Laurel came home, there was something pinched and angular about Mum's face. Her eyes had this haunted, sometimes vacant, quality. The angles are still there, but it's as if they've been softened somehow – someone has smudged those hard lines, rounded off the corners. Her eyes are starting to look like the eyes of a normal person with a normal life. I'm not the only one to notice. The *Daily Mail* website printed two pictures of her, side by side, last week. Before and after. Complete with commentary from three different beauty experts. One of them was certain that Mum has 'had some work done' and suggested she'd be better off using a different shade of blusher.

I spend the rest of the morning in my bedroom. It's easier to stop myself saying something mean to her that way. I scroll through the usual suspects – the websites most likely to have mentions of Laurel. I've got it down to a fine art now – no more than twenty minutes. There's nothing interesting today – there hasn't been much for the past couple of weeks. I know I should stop checking, that it might seem a little obsessive, but I can't help myself. Besides, no one else has to know. Mum's stopped reading the papers altogether, which is why she has no idea about that stupid *Daily Mail* feature.

I'm always careful to delete my Internet history so that Laurel can't see what I've been looking at. For some reason it feels like a betrayal – reading what people are saying about her and not telling her. But that hasn't stopped me.

It seems like Laurel is on my laptop all the time since her little tutorial with Thomas. I don't mind, but she doesn't seem to realize that I need it for schoolwork. She never uses Mum's desktop, even though Mum's hardly ever on it. I have a brainwave and Google to see if the department store has an electronics department. With a thousand pounds to spend, Laurel can buy a much better computer than mine. Or maybe I should buy one and give her my old one. It's not like I'll find any clothes there that I would ever actually wear. I just have to get Mum to agree to it, because I'm pretty sure that's not what she had in mind when she planned this little shopping spree.

When Mum calls from downstairs I realize I've lost track of time down the Internet rabbit hole and I won't even be able to have a shower before we leave. A few extra sprays of deodorant will have to do.

'We have to go NOW!'

'All right, all right, I'm *coming*!'

'I don't want your sister arriving at the restaurant before us. I TOLD you to be ready by twelve thirty!'

I ignore her and chuck my phone into my bag. A quick look out the window, then I put an umbrella in too. I'm heading out of the door when I realize I haven't deleted my history. Best to do it now, just in case I forget later.

I do it as fast as I can, ignoring Mum's increasingly annoyed shouts.

I stop when I get to the first site I looked at this morning. The next link on the list isn't one of mine. I'm not sure what makes me click on it, particularly when it sounds like Mum's head is about to explode if I keep her waiting any longer. But I do.

It's a map of Blaxford, a town about an hour away. I've never been, but I recognize the name. One of Aunt Eleanor's ex-boyfriends lived there. She described the town as like something out of a Ken Loach film. I've never seen a Ken Loach film so I had no idea what she was talking about until Mum told her not to be such an insufferable snob.

It must have been Laurel; Mum never touches my laptop. But why would Laurel be looking up a map of Blaxford of all places? I check the next link. Another map, the city centre this time. That makes more sense. Still, I wouldn't have bothered drawing her a map if I knew she'd already looked at a proper one.

I clear the history, deleting all of the links. I close the lid of the laptop, then shove the computer under my pillow. Laurel will have to ask if she wants to use it in future. I don't mind sharing, but maybe it's time I stopped making allowances for her. She needs to learn that she can't always have her own way, that people won't always be falling over themselves to make things easy for her. The sooner she realizes that, the better.

Chapter 27

Laurel steps in front of the mirror and examines herself from every possible angle. Mum has tears in her eyes; the personal shopper has pound signs in hers. You'd think she was trying on a wedding dress, the fuss they're making. The dress is nice, there's no denying it. It's red and short but not too short and the fabric clings in all the right places but in a classy sort of way. Still, it's not worth five hundred quid. No dress is worth that much.

'Doesn't she look *wonderful*, Faith?'

I smile and nod. She *does* look amazing. Mum suggests she takes her hair down, so she shakes it out of the ponytail and it's almost like a slow-motion shot from an advert.

'Oh *yes*!' says the personal shopper.

Laurel giggles and twirls around. The Laurels in the mirror giggle and twirl too.

'It's too much,' Laurel says when she's stopped twirling. 'I can't . . .'

'You can and you must!' says Mum emphatically, as if we're talking about something really important here. My suggestion that Laurel buy a laptop with her money didn't exactly go down well. I should have known. Mum said that today isn't about buying things we *need* – it's about having fun, apparently. She said there would be plenty of time – and money – for boring things like computers.

The personal shopper (who seems to think that Laurel looks amazing in everything, even the things that really don't suit her) says that she sold the exact same dress – in the same size! – to a footballer's girlfriend at the weekend. Mum asks which one, the personal shopper says a name and Mum pretends to know who she's talking about.

The dress is wrapped up in tissue paper and carefully placed in a shiny black bag with ribbons for handles. Laurel hugs Mum and thanks her. Then Mum turns to me. 'It's your turn now, Faith!'

The personal shopper looks about as happy as I do at the prospect; Laurel clearly makes a better mannequin than me.

*

We spent a fortune at the sushi place, piling up the plates. Laurel was a bit dubious about raw fish to start off with, but she soon got over her squeamishness. She loved the conveyor belt, just like I thought she would. That was the main reason I'd suggested we go there for lunch. She couldn't stop staring as the dishes went by. 'And we can just take *whatever* we want?' she said shaking her head in disbelief.

I kept on expecting Mum to ask the question, but she kept on not asking the question. In the end I had to do it. 'So . . . Laurel . . . what did you get up to this morning?'

'Nothing much. I just wandered around.' She took the last slice of miso aubergine – the one that I'd had my eye on.

'For *four* hours?'

She shrugged. 'I went to a cafe too.'

'Which one?'

Mum gave me a sharp look but I pretended not to notice.

'I can't remember. Starbucks? Or Costa, maybe?'

'They all look the same, don't they?' Mum says helpfully.

'So you didn't go to Blaxford then?'

'Why on earth would Laurel go there?!' Mum

laughed as if it was the most absurd idea in the world.

Laurel's brow furrowed in confusion. 'Where?'

Mum told her about Eleanor's ex-boyfriend *(such a good-looking man)* and that he tried to get Eleanor to move in with him and his three kids in their tiny flat but Eleanor said no and broke up with him. 'She said she just couldn't see herself living in a place like that, but I think it was more about the children, really. Three kids under ten? Not exactly Eleanor's cup of tea and *that's* an understatement. I mean, she likes children, she really does. But she's never wanted any of her own.' A pause for a long, wistful look at Laurel, barely a glance in my direction. 'She doesn't know what she's missing out on. I think it affected her quite deeply – what happened to you.' She squeezed Laurel's hand. 'She saw what it did to me, losing you like that.' Laurel put her arm around Mum's shoulders and it made me wish that I was the one sitting next to Mum.

Laurel had arrived at exactly the same time as us in the end, so Mum's worrying about being late had been completely unnecessary. There had been one booth free next to the conveyor belt. I slid in to one side (with my back to the door, knowing that Laurel would want to sit facing it), Laurel scooched into the booth on the other side, leaving Mum with a choice. Which one of her daughters would she choose to sit next to? No contest.

Mum insists that I at least buy something, and in return I insist that we go to a different shop. The personal shopper makes a (very) half-hearted effort at stopping us: 'I'm sure we can find something you'll like!' Mum thanks her and stage-whispers, 'Oh you know what they're like at that age! No appreciation for the finer things in life.' I don't even mind because at least she's agreed that we can finally leave this awful place teeming with awful women buying awful clothes.

We go to Gap, and yes, it's boring, but at least the clothes are normal here. I buy a pair of grey jeans exactly the same as the ones I'm wearing, ignoring Mum's suggestion to look at the other colours they have. Laurel decides to buy the same jeans as me, and suddenly Mum's saying, 'You can't go wrong with grey, can you? Classic.' The sales assistant clearly recognizes Laurel but is trying her best to act like she doesn't. It's exactly how Martha and I acted when we saw someone off *The X-Factor* in Pizza Express last summer.

We stop for coffee at around four thirty – an independent coffee shop, at Mum's insistence. We end up in another booth and yet again Mum sits next to

Laurel. They're talking about clothes and I'm bored out of my mind. Laurel tries to convince Mum to buy something – to treat herself to a new coat or handbag.

'No, no, I don't need anything.'

Laurel elbows Mum gently and says, 'You deserve to be spoiled too, you know! You're so busy looking after the rest of us that you forget to look after yourself. What do you think, Faith?' She looks at me in that chummy, conspiratorial way that usually makes me feel happy.

'Yeah, I suppose so.' I don't have the energy to fake enthusiasm. I have a killer headache and my feet are sore and I'm starting to feel like an outsider in my own family.

Mum says, 'I think *someone* got out of the wrong side of bed this morning.'

'What are you talking about?'

'Nothing! No need to be so touchy!' Mum laughs and takes a sip of her coffee. 'Now, where shall we go next? I've nearly run out of that conditioner I like, so I was thinking we could pop into Boots, if you don't mind. Maybe you could get some nail varnish to match your new dress, Laurel?'

'Sounds good to me!'

Laurel always says the right thing. She never seems to be grumpy or tired.

*

Mum can't find the conditioner so she sends me off to ask someone if the line has been discontinued. I have no idea why she doesn't just ask someone herself. Maybe she's testing me, trying to push me until I snap. I interrupt a couple of sales assistants barely older than me and one of them shoots me a hate-filled look before she turns her back to stack some shelves. The other one is helpful, but has more to say about hair products than I would ever want to hear. All I want to know is whether they have Mum's conditioner or not, but she's busy telling me about limited editions and argan oil.

While the sales assistant is wittering on I catch sight of Laurel at one of the make-up counters. The orange-faced woman behind the counter is busy giving an old lady a makeover. I watch Laurel watching them. A flicker of movement catches my eye and I lower my gaze to Laurel's hand. It glides over the counter, over the shiny tubs and bottles and compacts. Her fingers curl around something – mascara or eyeliner perhaps? – and she drops it in the bag from the department store. Then she does it again, watching the two women behind the counter the whole time.

The sales assistant finishes her spiel by suggesting we try another branch of Boots and I thank her. She wanders off but I stand stock still, staring at Laurel.

She picks up something else, but this time she doesn't drop it in the bag. She twists the cap off and draws on the back of her hand, testing the colour. Finally she turns away from the counter and sees me. She smiles and waves.

I turn my back on her and go to find Mum to tell her the bad news about her conditioner. She sighs and says, 'Back to the drawing board,' and goes to choose another one. I'm tempted to tell her what I saw. What would she think about her darling daughter shoplifting? She probably wouldn't believe me, but the proof is right there in Laurel's bag.

I'm going to tell her. 'Mum?'

'Yes, darling?' she says distractedly.

I'm trying to decide the tone I should adopt — shocked? Sympathetic? Shocked *yet* sympathetic? — when I realize it's too late. You can always tell when someone's standing right behind you. 'Mum? Will you come and help me choose a nail varnish? I think I've narrowed it down to two — one of them is a slightly better colour match but the other one says it lasts for seven days.' Laurel's voice is the very essence of breezy.

Mum looks up and her face breaks into this huge smile. 'Oh, they tell such LIES! Maybe one day they'll invent a nail varnish that doesn't chip as soon

227

as you look at it, but until then we'll just have to make do.'

Laurel and Mum walk off arm in arm and I trail behind them. They spend at least ten minutes choosing between colours that look identical to me. From time to time they ask my opinion and I say whatever they want to hear. Eventually Laurel makes a decision and the two of them go to the checkouts and queue up and pay. *Laurel* pays. I watch as she takes a twenty-pound note out of her purse and gives it to the guy on the till.

I hold my breath as we're leaving the shop, fully expecting the alarm to go off. It doesn't.

Chapter 28

Cheese on toast for dinner, made by Laurel. Mum compliments her on grilling the cheese just right.

After dinner Mum goes upstairs to call Eleanor. Laurel and I sit in front of the TV. Laurel's recorded *The Cynthia Day Show*; today it's about a woman who was badly burned in a house fire. Her husband started the fire on purpose. Cynthia Day has just announced that she's sending the woman and her kids to Disney World and everyone in the studio is crying. I glance over at Laurel; she's not crying.

'I saw you.'

'Saw me what?' She doesn't bother to look at me.

'Stealing.'

Now she looks at me. 'What are you talking about?' She looks genuinely baffled.

'I saw you stealing that make-up in Boots.'

She laughs and I want to smack her in the face. How dare she laugh at me?

'Why would I do something like that?'

'I was going to ask you the same question. You know you could have bought those things if you really wanted them.'

'I didn't steal anything.' She folds her arms across her chest and turns her attention back to the TV.

Mum comes back downstairs and we spend the rest of the evening watching rubbish TV shows – all Laurel's choices of course.

I'm getting ready for bed and replaying my conversation with Laurel in my head. She was very convincing – not even a hint of guilt or embarrassment. Could I have been mistaken about what I saw? Maybe Laurel picked up the make-up and put it right back down again but I was in such a weird mood and so desperate to see something to tarnish the image of the golden child that my eyes tricked me into believing that I'd seen her stealing.

The fact that I'm even attempting to second-guess myself about something like this is revealing. I'm not delusional. I know what I saw. I just can't make sense of it, that's all.

My phone buzzes with a text message. It's probably

Martha. I was supposed to text to tell her all about the big shopping trip. She'd thought it was ridiculous too, wasting all that money. And she'd actually been quite understanding about the book deal, when I'd explained it all to her. Thomas had been a dick about it, but nothing worse than expected.

The message isn't from Martha or from Thomas — the only two people who ever message me. It's from Laurel: *Can you come here?*

That's weird. Why didn't she just knock on the wall like she usually does? I take my time getting changed and brushing my hair before I go next door.

Laurel's room is dark, the only light coming from Egg the Penguin. I flick the switch next to the door, flooding the room with brightness. At first I think she must be in the bathroom, but then I catch sight of her head. She's sitting on the floor on the other side of the bed, wedged into the small space between the bed and the wall. I thought she'd stopped doing that. I've been checking the space underneath the dressing table every few days, to see if she's still using it as a hideaway.

'Laurel? Are you OK?'

'They're on the bed.' Her voice has a dull, mechanical quality.

A tube of liquid eyeliner and a lipstick. I perch on

the edge of the bed to examine them. The eyeliner is electric blue and the lipstick is an unappealing shade of purple.

'I'm sorry.'

'Why did you do it?'

No answer.

I get off the bed and kneel in front of her. She won't look at me. Her hair hangs down over her face so I can't see her expression. 'Laurel? You can talk to me, you know. I'm not going to tell anyone.' I'm feeling more charitable now that she's admitted it.

'I don't know why I did it.'

I wait for her to come up with something better and eventually she looks up, pushing her hair behind her ears. 'It's the *truth*!'

It doesn't make sense. People don't just steal things for no reason; they steal things because they can't afford to buy them. 'I don't think the colours will go with your new dress.' When in doubt, try to lighten the mood.

A trace of a smile flickers across her face. 'I can't explain it . . . It was . . . I don't know. I wanted to see if I *could* do it. I didn't think I'd get away with it, and I wanted to see what would happen. Does that make any sense at all?'

I shrug, because it doesn't. 'You know if you'd

have been caught it would be all over the newspapers, don't you?'

She nods. 'Maybe that's what I was hoping for.'

'Why would you want that?' I'm starting to realize there's more to my sister than meets the eye.

Laurel stares into space, focusing on a spot on the wall. 'Because maybe then they'd see that I'm . . . normal. That I'm a regular person who makes mistakes sometimes. I'm not someone to look up to. Little kids shouldn't be asking for my autograph or wanting to get their pictures taken with me. It's not right.'

I thought she loved all that stuff – she certainly does a good job of smiling and *looking* like she's enjoying herself. 'You don't need to do those things, Laurel. No one's forcing you.'

'I want to take it back. The make-up. I'll go tomorrow.'

'You can't! They'd probably catch you sneaking it back on to the shelves and think you're stealing!'

'Well, I'll just tell them what I did. Talk to one of the sales assistants.' She looks like a little girl determined to get her way, jaw jutting, eyes defiant.

'No. You won't. Look, let's just forget all about it. Pretend it never happened. I understand why you did it, but there's no need for anyone else to find out about it.' The lie is instinctive; I still don't understand why she did it — not really. 'It would only upset Mum.' That's the truth.

'I could explain—'

'No. She wouldn't get it. Trust me on this.'

Laurel asks if I'm sure, and if there's anything she can do to make amends. There are no amends to be made, I tell her. I'm pretty sure Boots aren't going to go under because someone nicked twenty quid's worth of make-up. In that little-girl voice she sometimes adopts, she asks if I'm angry with her.

'Of course not,' I say.

'Are you sure? It's just . . . the last few days I've had the feeling that . . .' she shrugs, and I don't want her to finish this sentence, 'that maybe you resent me a little bit.'

My mouth opens to issue a denial. My mouth shuts again. When I finally speak, I tell the truth. 'You're right.' The look on Laurel's face just about breaks my heart, so I rush ahead. 'No, no, it's nothing you've done! Honestly, it's *my* issue, not yours. I think I maybe got a little bit used to getting my own way . . . while you were gone. And now you're back and I suppose it's just taking me a little longer to adjust than I thought.'

She nods slowly. 'It must be hard for you.'

I feel ashamed, hearing her say those words, seeing

her looking at me with sympathetic eyes. It must be hard for *me*? Compared to everything she's been through? I start to cry, and she comforts me, which makes me feel even more ashamed. I am the worst person in the world.

Chapter 29

It was Laurel's idea, to get up early and make breakfast for Mum. She asked me what Mum would like and I said bacon and eggs, served with toast cut into triangles and served on the toast rack. In truth, Mum would probably prefer something a bit healthier, but the only fruit we have in the house are three tasteless apples and a speckled banana.

I teach Laurel how to fry an egg, and how to get the bacon just the right side of crispy. She prepares a tray, complete with one of the napkins that we only use at Christmas. We make a pot of tea and pour a glass of orange juice, then Laurel carries the tray up the stairs. I knock on Mum's door and we go in. She's sprawled across the bed like a starfish, which always makes me wonder how she ever used to manage to share a bed with Dad. It takes her a few seconds to wake up, but she finally sits up and props a pillow behind her. Her sleepy smile makes me feel good inside.

'What's all this?' she says as Laurel places the tray on her lap.

'We made you breakfast!' Laurel says proudly.

'Yes, I can see that! But what have I done to deserve the royal treatment?'

Laurel looks to me for an answer, but I don't really have one. 'We just thought it would be nice.'

Mum takes a slice of toast from the rack and munches on the corner. 'Mmm, I could get used to this.'

Laurel and I perch on either side of Mum and we talk while she eats her breakfast. Mum says it's the best breakfast she's ever had, and that's including the one she had the morning after she got married, when she and Dad stayed in a very expensive hotel. 'My two girls,' she says. There's so much love in her eyes that it almost hurts to look at her. The shame from last night bubbles up in my throat again, threatening to spill out of my mouth and on to the duvet cover.

Laurel starts quizzing Mum about her wedding, and I learn things that I never knew before. Dad was so nervous he threw up in the bushes outside the church; he had to ask around for chewing gum so that he didn't have vomit breath for the 'You may kiss the bride' moment. Mum had a blazing row with Gran the night before the wedding, but she can't remember what it was about now. The first dance was some terrible song from the eighties, which Mum insisted on having even though Dad hated it.

Mum doesn't seem to mind talking about it, which surprises me. I'd have thought she'd be keen to forget all about the day she married my dad. I say something to that effect, but Mum shakes her head. 'I could never regret marrying your father.'

'Why?' Laurel asks. By this point she's lying on the bed next to Mum.

Mum gives Laurel a look as if to say, 'It's obvious, isn't it?' but it's not obvious to us.

'Because of you two, of course!'

The three of us smile at each other, and I wonder if I'm the only one thinking that if she hadn't married Dad, Mum would have been spared thirteen years of unhappiness – the kind of unhappiness that few people ever have to endure in their lives. I quickly come to the conclusion that, yes, I am definitely the only one thinking that.

Thomas's patience has finally run out; it's hardly surprising. He hasn't come right out and said that we need to have sex again soon or he will break up with me, but I bet that's what he's thinking. I'm amazed he's waited this long, to be honest. He's not like other boys our age – or rather, he *is* like other boys our age, but he would rather die than admit it.

I want to do it again too. Just to see. The truth is, I haven't really missed him. I've been happy just to see him at school, mostly. And I'm sure that can't be right. I'm sure I'm supposed to miss him, to be pining for him, aching for the touch of his skin on mine. So this is an experiment – to test my feelings for him once and for all.

When Mum announced that she was going away for a spa day (and night) with Eleanor, the plan popped into my head straightaway, as if it had been lurking in the wings just waiting for the right circumstances to present themselves. This time, the sex will be happening in the proper place – in a bed – just to see if that makes any difference. Laurel and I are going to start watching a new box set that Martha told her about. Then I will say that I'm tired and want to have an early night. I'll make sure that Laurel goes to bed at the same time, which shouldn't be too hard. Things have been really good for the last couple of days. We've been going out of our way to be nice – both of us falling over ourselves to make sure the other one is happy.

As soon as I'm in my room, I'll text Thomas to let him know that the coast is clear. Or maybe I'll get him to wait half an hour – or even an hour – to make sure that Laurel is asleep. He will text when he's outside, I'll creep downstairs to let him in, the two of us will creep back upstairs and get down to business. We'll have to be quiet – definitely no laughing this time. As soon as the sex is over, he'll have to leave. I can't risk us falling asleep and him still being there when Laurel gets up tomorrow.

Of course, I could just *tell* Laurel. She would probably be fine about it. It might even bring us closer together, hatching a plan, keeping a secret from Mum. But it doesn't feel right. The idea of her in the next room, knowing what Thomas and I are doing. Even if she agreed to sleep in Mum's room so she wouldn't accidentally hear anything, it still wouldn't feel right.

I haven't told Martha either. I have a good excuse though: she's down in London staying with some family friends. But that's not the real reason I haven't told her. She would ask too many questions and I'd probably end up telling her how unsure I am about Thomas. A few months ago that would have been fine and we could have talked about it and she would have understood. But now she actually properly *likes* him, rather than thinking he's a bit of a pretentious wannabe. I bet she would stay friends with Thomas if I broke up with him, and I bet I wouldn't be as cool about that as I would have to pretend to be.

Chapter 30

I end up resorting to underhand tactics to make sure Laurel doesn't want to stay up late. We open a bottle of wine and I make sure she drinks most of it. She still can't take her drink – she was falling asleep on the sofa halfway through the third episode of the box set.

The plan goes smoothly and I text Thomas just after eleven. His reply arrives with lightning speed; he's clearly raring to go.

I was going to change into my pyjamas but they would definitely spoil the mood, and it's not as if I have any sexy lingerie hiding at the back of my chest of drawers. So I decided to keep my clothes on – for now.

Thomas leans in to kiss me as soon as I open the front door. He tastes savoury, but not in a bad way. Still, it means he hasn't brushed his teeth in the last few hours. I brushed mine till my gums bled. He grins. 'Is she asleep?'

I nod. I listened outside Laurel's door for long enough to hear the snuffly breathing sound she makes when she sleeps. Thomas and I creep upstairs. He mutters something about the van being a much simpler option and I shush him. I follow him into my bedroom and shut the door.

The lighting is low – I put my bedside light on the floor just in case Thomas decides he wants to do this with the lights on. I didn't bother to change the sheets because Mum changed them two days ago and, besides, Thomas isn't exactly fastidious when it comes to personal hygiene.

It's only the third time Thomas has been in my bedroom. Mum always insists that we stay downstairs when she's around – and up until recently she's almost always been around. He doesn't waste any time, launching himself at me and kissing me hard. Too hard – our mouths slam together and for a moment I think I might have chipped a tooth. I tell him to slow down, that there's no rush.

'Easy for you to say,' he murmurs, in between kisses on my neck.

I pull away. 'What's that supposed to mean?' I

ask, forgetting that we're supposed to be keeping the noise down. I repeat the question in a whisper when Thomas doesn't answer.

'Nothing,' he whispers, pulling me into his arms again. 'I just . . . I've been looking forward to this.'

It's such an innocent thing to say that it makes me smile. Thomas seems to have this ability to say the right words to turn things around. He doesn't always find the right words at first, but he gets there in the end.

There's a brief moment of worry when Thomas thinks he's forgotten to bring condoms; I start to wonder if maybe God (I don't believe in God) just doesn't want us to have sex again. That he's putting too many obstacles in our way. It's a SIGN. But then Thomas remembers that he put the condoms in his jacket pocket because his jeans were in the wash.

He pulls his T-shirt over his head to reveal his skinny, hairless chest. He's not self-conscious about his body at all, unlike me. He pulls down his jeans and stands in front of me, with his socks and pants still on. He looks at me and waits. 'Well, aren't you going to . . . ?' He gestures to my clothes.

I take off my top slowly. Reluctantly. All of a sudden I'm not sure that this is the best idea in the entire world. It doesn't seem fair on Thomas to be doing this with him when I can't seem to make up my mind about how I feel about him. But then he comes closer to me, and he tells me I'm beautiful. I look in his eyes and I believe him. I'm sure about his feelings for *me*, and shouldn't that count for something?

I lean into him and tuck my head into that space between his head and his shoulder – the space that I always thought was custom-made just for me. He holds me tight and tells me that we don't have to do anything if I don't want to. 'I can just hold you for a little while.' I can't see his face to check, but it feels like the truth. He really *wouldn't* mind. And that's when I realize that I do care about him. I *want* to do this.

I kiss him fiercely to get the message across, then I push him towards the bed.

It hurts more this time, which doesn't seem fair. I close my eyes and try not to feel. It will be over soon. I wonder if Mum is having a nice time at the spa with Eleanor. If I know Eleanor, it will be more champagne and massages than wheatgrass juice and Bikram yoga. Then I wonder if it's normal to think about what your Mum is up to while you're having sex with your boyfriend. Probably not.

Thomas's breathing is getting faster and noisier in my left ear. Hopefully it won't be long now. I'm completely silent, unlike the last time. I run my fingers up and down his spine and it reminds me of the bumpy back of a dinosaur I saw in the Natural History Museum on a school trip to London. How old was I then? Eleven? Twelve? No, definitely eleven.

I don't know what makes me open my eyes. I didn't hear anything. But I look over to the door and it's open – just a few centimetres. I'm sure I closed it behind us.

She's there, watching. A scream rises in my throat but lodges there like a thorn before it can escape from my mouth. My body jolts in shock and I gasp, but Thomas is too close to coming to notice.

My gaze catches hers and she doesn't even flinch at being caught. I expect the door to slam shut, but it doesn't. I don't know what to do. I want to look away, but I can't. Any second now.

Thomas's orgasm seems to take an age. Then he lies perfectly still on top of me and the whole weight of him is on me and I feel like I'm being crushed even though he hardly weighs anything at all – certainly less than I do.

Eventually he raises himself up on his arms and kisses me; his face has a fine sheen of sweat and a couple of red blotches have appeared on his cheeks. I look back towards the door. It's closed. She's gone.

I let Thomas lie next to me for a few minutes. He asks me what I'm thinking. Nothing, I say. He asks me if I'm happy. I say yes. He gets dressed and tells me he loves me. He leaves.

I lie in bed, naked. I clutch the duvet with my fingers and pull it right up to my neck. I'm acutely aware of her presence next door, just as she must be aware of mine. I feel hot with embarrassment, cold with confusion. Why didn't I push him off me the second I noticed her? Why didn't I tell him, afterwards?

What the hell was she *thinking*, spying on us like that? What am I going to say to her? Should I go and talk to her now?

I don't move. I watch the door and hope and pray that it doesn't open again.

Chapter 31

I get up early after a fretful night. If I slept, I don't remember. I get dressed in jeans and a hoodie, careful not to make a sound. I open my bedroom door and stand and listen. I hear cars passing outside, the gurgling from the radiator on the landing, a dog barking. No sounds from Laurel's room.

I don't risk brushing my teeth because the noise from the pipes will almost certainly wake her. I go downstairs and out of the front door. I end up in a cafe, rushing to use the toilet before I join the queue at the counter.

I sit in a corner, facing the door. I drink two cups of dreadful, swill-coloured tea and check the time on my phone every couple of minutes. I can't stay away forever; Mum will be back at lunchtime.

Just before nine I get a text from Martha asking if I want to do something this afternoon. She doesn't specify what that something might be, so it's probably nothing, but we'd be doing nothing together at least. I reply and say I'll go round to her house at three. Anything to get out of the house.

Another text arrives, from Laurel this time. She wants to know where I am; she's made breakfast. I reply and say I'll be home soon, that I just went out to buy some milk. She texts again: *OK, I'll put the kettle on! xxx*

I forget the milk, but Laurel doesn't say anything when I walk into the kitchen empty-handed. There's plenty in the fridge though – Mum stocked up before she went, buying enough groceries for us to endure a three-month siege even though she was only going to be gone for twenty-four hours.

Laurel's trying her hand at scrambled eggs today. 'I figured they would be the easiest to do on my own.' She smiles warmly. Her hair is tied up in a ponytail. She hasn't showered yet either.

I look in the pot that she's stirring; the eggs have been seriously scrambled. The toast pops up from the toaster and Laurel asks me to butter it. She's put our matching mugs out on the worktop. I touch the kettle – just boiled.

I concentrate hard on the task at hand. The

scraping sound of the knife on the toast scratches at my nerves; I wonder which one of us is going to be the first to crack. Someone has to bring up the subject, and I don't think it should be me. Laurel pours hot water into the mugs and finishes making the tea.

We sit down at the table – she's already put out the cutlery, and even a couple of sheets of kitchen roll to use as napkins. The eggs are rubbery and weirdly crusty in places. I don't want to eat them, but I don't want to hurt Laurel's feelings. Cooking is one of the things she seems to really enjoy. I blame Michel – he keeps going on about her being a natural and saying maybe she should look into a career that involves food. Dad always shuts down this kind of talk; he thinks she has no chance of having a normal job like that.

I eat a corner of toast with the tiniest bit of egg I can get away with. I realize that Laurel's looking at me, eyebrows raised in expectation. 'Delicious,' I say, talking with my mouth full because Mum's not around to moan about it.

'Liar. But that's OK, they'll be better next time.'

We eat in silence for a couple of minutes. The toast is hard to choke down, so I start eating more eggs to aid in the process.

'So . . . did you sleep well?' she asks.

That's when I realize how we're going to play this.

In true Logan style, we are not going to talk about it. We are going to bury it, hope that a cement mixer comes along and pours concrete over the issue so that it will never see the light again.

'Fine, thank you,' I say with a smile. 'How about you?'

'Like a baby,' she says. 'That's a weird saying, isn't it? Slept like a baby. Babies are always crying.'

I smile again and agree that it is a weird saying. Then I ask Laurel about her plans for the day.

All the time we're talking I'm wondering what she's really thinking. She knows that I saw her, so she must be scared that I'm going to say something – accuse her of spying on Thomas and me. She saw me notice her. There was eye contact – *prolonged* eye contact. But I suddenly remember something Martha once said about her mum's eyesight, that she can't see more than a few inches in front of her face without her glasses. I rack my brain to remember if Laurel's had an eye test since she's been back. I'm not sure. Being kept in a basement for all those years would surely have an effect on your eyesight. How could it not? So maybe – just maybe – Laurel *doesn't* realize that I caught her watching us. And I'm not sure whether that's a good thing or not. Perhaps she's blind as a bat and no one's bothered to check? Maybe there's a chance her eyesight is so bad she didn't even realize what Thomas and I were doing. (Nice try – *of course* she knew what we were doing.)

It's a relief, in a way. Not to have to talk about it. Not to have to stutter and stumble over my words as I try to explain why I'd been so secretive about Thomas coming over. I'd have to beg her not to tell Mum too. Mum would not be happy to find out that Thomas and I are having sex. It doesn't matter to her that it's legal, or that we're in a serious, long-term relationship, or that we're using protection. What matters to her is that she doesn't like Thomas and never will. If she found out, she'd never leave Laurel and me alone in the house again. I'm sure that Laurel would agree to keep it secret from Mum, but now I can't ask. She won't tell her, I'm almost certain of that. Because if she did then she'd have to admit that she was watching us, and that would just be awkward.

It's better this way, brushing it under the carpet, pretending nothing odd – nothing excruciatingly, embarrassingly weird – has happened. Now I just have to try to erase the memory from my head. If only it was that easy. I have a funny feeling I will never be able to forget the shock of seeing her standing there, watching. Judging.

*

Mum comes home sporting a pair of sunglasses, accompanied by a vaguely winey vapour. 'Never again,' she says. 'She's a bad influence on me, you know.'

Laurel says she'll make Mum a sandwich, but Mum winces at the mention of food. 'Thanks, love, maybe later. I think I'll have a little lie-down first. Anyway, did you two have fun last night?'

'We had a lovely time, thanks. A really nice girly night,' says Laurel. I'm almost sure – not enough to bet fifty quid but sure enough to risk a tenner – that she puts a slight emphasis on the word 'girly'. And if I'm right, then Laurel is toying with me. Perhaps it amuses her to see me squirm.

Mum trudges towards the stairs with her overnight bag, taking careful steps as if she's on a boat in a storm. Laurel catches my eye and shakes her head, smiling. This is supposed to translate as something like, 'Parents, huh?' or, 'What is she *like*?' I'm supposed to return the look in kind, or maybe roll my eyes and laugh. Instead I ignore it completely. My eyes pass over her as if she's not even there.

Mum stops on the third stair. 'Oh, I nearly forgot! How could I forget?!' I refrain from remarking on the obvious correlation between alcohol consumption and memory loss. 'You'll never guess who called me last night! Well, she called but I didn't answer because

I was . . . anyway, she left a voicemail, and when I listened to it this morning I could hardly believe it. Talk about a blast from the past!'

'Who was it?' I hate guessing games.

'Dana Fairlie!' Mum looks at me expectantly. I have no idea who Dana Fairlie is, which is quite obvious from the confused look on my face. 'The Fairlies? Number 24?' Nope. Not a clue.

Mum heaves a big sigh as if I'm being deliberately awkward. She comes back down the stairs. 'Laurel, you remember little Bryony? The two of you used to be inseparable. Always in and out of each other's houses, making mischief.'

Laurel nods, vaguely at first and then more decisively. 'Yeah. Yes. I remember.'

It turns out that the Fairlies used to live a couple of doors down from us in Stanley Street. They had two daughters around the same age as Laurel and me, so they became friends with Mum and Dad. They emigrated to Australia a month before Laurel was taken. I remember now, but the memory is of a photograph I saw a long time ago. Laurel and another girl. Two little blonde girls, as alike as sisters (*real* sisters). Their hair in matching pigtails, heads together, faces tilted at an angle, big smiles. I remember what I thought when I saw that picture. Why couldn't the other little girl have been taken away instead of my sister? And now I know why: because she was thousands and thousands of miles away. Safe, on the other side of the world.

'Anyway, they're *back*! Well they're not *back* back, but they're here for a month or so. Kirsty wants to go to university over here – just think of that, little Kirsty, all grown-up and off to university! It's hard to believe . . .'

In typical Mum fashion, she's arranged for us all to meet up tomorrow without bothering to check with us first. I mean, it's one thing to do that to Laurel – she never has any plans – but I actually *have* a life. I agree to it though, because I'm curious to see these people who could have so easily been us. Say the paperwork for the emigration hadn't come through yet, or Mr or Mrs Fairlie had to stay in the country for an extra month to finish off some big project at work, they would have still been on Stanley Street that day when our lives fell apart. Bryony and Kirsty could have been playing in their front garden, and maybe Laurel and I would have been inside because one of us wasn't feeling very well. We would be snuggled together on the sofa watching a Disney film when the shadow passed our house. Bryony Fairlie's face would be on the front page of every newspaper and my parents would feel terrible about it, and do everything they could to help the

Fairlies through their ordeal, taking care of Kirsty and making lasagnes that Mrs Fairlie could reheat after yet another press conference. Mum and Dad would join the search party and put up posters saying 'HAVE YOU SEEN THIS GIRL?' and rack their brains in case they might have noticed something that day. A car that didn't belong on the street or a man acting suspiciously. And all the while, as Mum hugged Mrs Fairlie and told her everything was going to be OK, and Dad exchanged grim looks with Mr Fairlie, they would be thinking the same thought. Over and over again. *Thank God it wasn't one of* our *daughters. Thank God.*

Chapter 32

Every surface in Martha's kitchen is covered with jars. There are two huge pots bubbling away on the stove, and Martha's mum is dipping a metal thermometer into one of them. She looks happier than the last time I saw her. Being unemployed seems to suit her.

Martha drags me away from the kitchen and upstairs to her room. 'The jam making is completely out of control! She reckons she can make a business out of it, even though I told her it's a stupid idea.'

I shrug. It seems like an OK idea to me. Customers at the farmers' market think nothing of spending £4.95 on a jar of artisan jam. But I let Martha rant and moan, because that's what best friends do.

I almost tell her about what happened last night, but it's all too complicated. Plus, I don't want Martha thinking I'm weird. She wouldn't understand why I didn't confront Laurel for spying on Thomas and me. I don't even tell Martha about the shoplifting, but I do talk about Laurel. I tell Martha about the dress and she agrees that it's an obscene amount of money to spend on one item of clothing. I moan about the book deal and the fact that I have to go and meet the ghostwriter next week. They've decided that I should be the first one to be interviewed, probably because I have the least to say. At least I got to choose the meeting place; the editor (Zara Double-Barrelled) told Mum it should be somewhere I feel comfortable. Mum said I should do it at home, thinking I would be reassured by her presence. I suggested a cafe-bar near the canal – where it's highly unlikely I'll see anyone I know.

It starts with the dress and the book deal and before I know it I'm telling Martha (almost) every little thing that Laurel's done to annoy me over the past couple of weeks. 'She's just always *there*, you know?' Because that's what it really comes down to: Laurel is around *all* the time. Unless you count her twice-weekly visits to the psychologist and random sessions with Penny. But other than that, there's no respite, no escape.

'So having a big sister isn't all it's cracked up to be then?' Martha says with a smirk.

And there it is again: the guilt. It's always there too, shadowing me, just like Laurel. I feel like I have to be grateful *all* the time, that any negative feelings – no matter how small – are not allowed. Sometimes, late at night when sleep eludes me, I worry that something awful will happen to Laurel. That she'll get run over by a car or choke to death on a fishbone or drown in the bath, all because of me. Because I haven't been grateful enough to have her back. I worry that Laurel is going to be taken away again just to punish me.

I tell Martha that I didn't mean it, that I do like having a big sister, honestly. She laughs and says, 'It's OK, you know. You don't have to pretend with me.' She leans over and squeezes my knee. 'This is a *safe* place,' she says, with a fake sympathetic expression on her face.

I know she's taking the piss but I'm so grateful I could cry. Just knowing that she doesn't mind listening to me whine, and that she doesn't think I'm a terrible person, makes me feel a whole lot better.

I tell Martha about the Fairlies and how weird it's going to be. Martha reassures me that however weird it is for me, it's going to be ten times weirder for Laurel. Everyone will be focused on her anyway; they always are.

*

'What are you going to wear to the party?' Martha's sitting at her desk with her back to me. She always sits up straight, like a character in a costume drama. People her height usually slouch.

'What party?' I'm sitting on the floor with my back against the bed, deleting old messages from my phone. It's been a bit of a waste of an afternoon. We could have at least gone to the cinema, but Martha said there was nothing she wanted to see. Still, it's been good to get away from home for a few hours. God knows how I'll get through the rest of the week with my sanity intact.

'Thomas's party.' She doesn't turn and look at me, and I'm not sure whether it's because she's worried about my reaction or because she doesn't realize that I have no idea what she's talking about.

'I'll say it again: What. Party?'

Now she turns, unable to ignore my frostiness. She looks confused. 'His surprise party? For his eighteenth? How can you not . . . ? Hasn't his mum . . . ? She said she was going to get in touch with you last week.'

There are so many things wrong with what Martha's saying that I really don't know where to start. First of all, Thomas hates parties *and* surprises.

260

Put the two together and you pretty much have his worst nightmare. Second of all, how come Martha knows about this before I do? Last, but by no means least, what the hell was she doing talking to Thomas's mother?

Martha rushes to explain, trying to get the words out as quickly as possible – the words that will remove the look on my face. 'Oh . . . wow . . . OK, I was sure she'd have talked to you by now. Anyway, I can fill you in. So, she's planning a surprise party next week. She's already invited all the family. She knows that it's not really Thomas's thing at all, but she said this was her last chance to throw a party for "her little baby", and he hasn't let her do much to celebrate his birthday for the past couple of years so she decided just to go for it. I did say it might not be the best idea, but she thinks he'll probably secretly love the attention. She said that he might pretend to be all cool and intellectual but underneath he's just a little boy whose favourite food is jelly and ice cream. Did you know that? I thought his favourite food was sashimi.' Finally she pauses to check how she's doing. Is the look on my face still unimpressed, or has it morphed into something friendlier?

It has not. 'When were you talking to his mum?'

Martha shrugs. 'Last week? Or maybe the week

before. I can't remember exactly.' She's going to have to do better than that, and she knows it. 'I needed to borrow a textbook. Thomas went upstairs to get it and she cornered me in the kitchen.' Thomas's house is nowhere near Martha's. In order for her to get there, she would have to get a bus that passes right by the end of my street. There are no textbooks that Martha would need to borrow from Thomas that she wouldn't be able to borrow from me. 'You were out,' she says, answering a question I didn't ask.

'He didn't mention it.'

'Why would he? Anyway, what are you going to wear? Mrs Bolt said "smart/casual", whatever that means. Do you think it means we can't wear jeans?'

She's making a decent effort to distract me, or rather, she would be if we were the sort of girls who have conversations about clothes. The fact that we're *not* the sort of girls who have conversations about clothes makes me realize that she hadn't been able to find a better entry point into a conversation about the party, and that she was therefore fully aware that I knew nothing about it. My head hurts.

I do a good job, I think, of acting like I don't mind about Martha having cosy little chats with

Mrs Bolt – the kind of chats that Mrs Bolt has never shown any interest in having with me. Martha watches me closcly for signs that I'm pissed off, but after my initial failure to hide my feelings, I'm back on track.

A surprise party for Thomas's eighteenth is a terrible, terrible idea. He will hate every minute. He will hate the presents people give him – the presents that prove that they don't know him at all. He will hate the music, having his photograph taken, blowing out the candles on his cake (which, Martha informs me, will be in the shape of a pile of books). It will be funny to watch him squirm. In a way I'm glad his mum didn't talk to me about it, because I probably would have managed to talk her out of it. I wouldn't miss this for the world.

I ask Martha who's invited. Thomas has a few friends at school, but no one really close. Mrs Bolt will be getting in touch with them over the next couple of days, leaving it until the last minute so they don't 'ruin the surprise'. It seems to me that leaving it so late is much more likely to mean that they won't be able to come. It's not as if people will have cleared their social calendars just in case there's an outside chance they'll get an invite to the coming of age of Thomas Edwin Bolt. (I take the piss out of Thomas about his middle name on a regular basis. Not that Thomas is much better; why can't he just be Tom like a normal person?)

While we're talking I get a text message from a number I don't recognize. Speak of the devil. Thomas's mum has finally bothered to inform me about the impending celebration. She doesn't even apologize for leaving it so late. The message answers the next question I was about to ask Martha: the venue. The Bolts have hired a room above a pub near their house. Another text arrives before I've finished reading the first: *Don't forget to invite your sister!*

'She wants me to bring Laurel.'

'So?'

I sigh. If I have to explain this to Martha, it means she doesn't get it. 'I'm just surprised, that's all.'

Martha shrugs. 'You know . . . it might be a good thing, Laurel coming to the party. It's the perfect opportunity for her to make some friends, don't you think?'

There's a chance Martha could be right. As long as there are some half-decent people there, there's bound to be someone Laurel can hang out with. I think Thomas mentioned something about a cousin who's studying at Oxford; she might be a good place to start. It's times like this that I'm grateful to have a friend like Martha – someone who sees things slightly differently. I smile. 'You're a genius.'

Martha sighs dramatically and flops down on to the bed behind me. 'I *know*. A brain like mine is *such* a burden. You have *no* idea.'

Chapter 33

Laurel's *really* happy about being invited to the party, and I can tell from the look on Mum's face that she's happy about it too. Mum probably thinks that this is a *beginning*, that maybe Laurel can start to live something close to a normal life after all. I swear them both to secrecy, explaining that Thomas knows nothing about the party.

Laurel looks at me with wide eyes. 'I don't know how you manage not to say anything to him! I could *never* keep a secret like that.'

I don't tell them that I've only just found out about it myself, and I haven't talked to Thomas, so keeping the secret has been easy as pie so far. I should have known about this weeks ago and been fully involved in planning it. That's what people would expect – and what Mum and Laurel clearly think – so I'm not going to tell them any different.

'Thomas doesn't really strike me as the type of person who'd like a surprise party,' Mum says coolly, sipping her wine. She's clearly decided that hair of the dog is the only way to deal with her hangover.

'He's not,' I say. They both look at me, waiting for me to continue. 'That's what makes it such a brilliant idea!' I laugh, and Mum laughs too and says I'm terrible.

Laurel's face is blank and I realize this is one of those everyday human interactions that seem to baffle her. She can't understand why I would be so gleeful about something that Thomas will hate. I try to explain, but it doesn't do any good. Laurel narrows her eyes and looks thoughtful. 'Do you mean you think he'll actually secretly enjoy it? He'll just be pretending to hate it?'

A quick glance at Mum, who nods almost imperceptibly. 'Yes, that's exactly what I mean.'

Laurel seems nervous about meeting up with the Fairlies. While we're waiting for Mum to get ready, she keeps on getting up and staring at herself in the mirror above the fireplace. For reasons known only to herself, she's decided to wear her hair in pigtails today. Mum raised her eyebrows when she saw her, but said nothing.

I ask Laurel if she's OK and she nods and smiles and says of course she is. I don't believe her. It's understandable that she's anxious, I suppose. I'm a little nervous too, but Mum's really excited. Yesterday's hangover is a distant memory and the prospect of lunch out with 'her girls' seems to make her happy. She eventually comes downstairs wearing far too much make-up. There's no point in saying anything though – it would only upset her. I can understand her wanting to look her best to see a friend she hasn't seen for years. I just wish that she would understand that she doesn't need to wear that much make-up these days. Now that the trauma of Laurel's disappearance is starting to erase itself from her face, she doesn't need to wear a mask any more.

I spy them from the other side of the restaurant. They're in a big curved booth that reminds me of a clamshell; I wish they'd sat at one of the normal tables instead.

None of us have been to this restaurant before; I have no idea why Mum chose it. On the way over to the booth I look at the other customers and notice that they're mostly well dressed, a lot of women with bags from posh shops. So *that's* why Mum chose this place: she's trying to impress.

The Fairlies file out of the booth and Mrs Fairlie hugs Mum. 'Olivia! It's so wonderful to see you!' She hugs me next, which surprises me. Most people notice Laurel first. 'Little Faith! Oh my goodness! Look at you!' I never understand what that means: *Look at you*. It's the kind of thing you say when someone has a new haircut. It's neither positive nor negative, but people tend to take it positively. They hear what they want to hear, rather than what's actually been said.

Over Mrs Fairlie's shoulder I see the two girls. Bryony and Kirsty. They're both smiling shyly and looking about as awkward as I feel. Then Mum hugs them too and we all keep getting in each other's way in our efforts to greet everyone.

Mrs Fairlie hugs Laurel for the longest. That's to be expected, I guess. Bryony embraces me next. It's a loose sort of hug – the kind where you barely touch the other person. Kirsty and I sort of wave at each other from a couple of feet away, while Bryony and Laurel hug.

Eventually we go to sit down. Mum and Mrs Fairlie make sure that Bryony and Laurel are sitting next to each other.

'Well,' says Mrs Fairlie, 'long time no see!' Her accent is odd – mostly English with a slight upward lilt at the end of each sentence. Bryony and Kirsty have full-on Australian accents. It suits them. They *look* Australian: tanned and blonde and beautiful.

The waiter comes along and Mum orders a bottle of champagne before anyone else can say anything. 'Kirsty's allowed to drink, isn't she, Dana?' Mrs Fairlie looks slightly taken aback – she's probably wondering who's going to pay for the champagne – but she confirms that yes, Kirsty is allowed a glass of wine once in a while.

As soon as the champagne has been poured, Mum raises her glass. After a moment's hesitation we all do the same. 'To old friends!' We all clink glasses and take a sip. Then there's a pause before Mum launches into a barrage of questions about the Fairlies' 'life Down Under', as she calls it. I see what she's doing: trying to divert the focus from Laurel and pretend that this is just your standard reunion with old neighbours.

Before long Mrs Fairlie and Mum are deeply involved in a discussion about the benefits of the Australian outdoor way of life (*We eat outside eight months of the year!*). Laurel and Bryony are talking quietly on the other side of the booth. I can't hear what they're talking about because Mum and Mrs Fairlie are being so loud.

Kirsty keeps staring at Laurel, as if she can't quite believe Laurel is real. I mostly concentrate on my plate – a beetroot salad with three different varieties of beetroot. The food is really good actually.

'So . . .' Kirsty has a mouthful of food but she's clearly not going to let that stop her from speaking, 'what's it like, having her back? It must be *weird*!'

I want to hate Kirsty for being so blunt, but I can't. She's one of the only people to recognize the strangeness of the situation. I only wish she'd said it louder so Mum could hear that there are other ways of looking at Laurel's return – it's not all smiles and hugs and rainbows.

'Yeah, it is. It's good though.'

She snorts loudly and Mrs Fairlie looks over, disapproval etched on her face. Kirsty ignores the look. 'You don't sound so sure!'

'I *am* sure . . . but you know what it's like having a sister.'

Kirsty looks across the table at her sister and I look across the table at mine. Their heads are close together as if they're sharing secrets. Kirsty takes a big gulp of champagne, checks her mother isn't looking, grabs the bottle and fills her glass to the brim. 'Do I *ever*? I always wanted a brother, you know? Someone who'd shove me or smack me if we had an argument, rather than give me the silent treatment for three days.'

'Bryony seems nice though?' I whisper, subconsciously mimicking the inflections in Kirsty's voice.

Another snort from Kirsty. 'Yeah, that's what everyone thinks. They have no idea what a raving *bitch* she can be – especially when she's on her period. Fucking nightmare!'

Mum must have heard the swearing, because she turns her attention to us. 'What are you two gossiping about?'

'I was just telling Kirsty about us going on *The Cynthia Day Show*.' The lie trips off my tongue.

'Oh my goodness, is that woman not dead yet?!' says Mrs Fairlie. 'I used to watch that show when I was at uni! I can't believe it's still running . . . Who watches that garbage?'

Thankfully Laurel doesn't seem to hear Mrs Fairlie badmouthing her favourite TV show. Mum doesn't seem offended even though Mrs Fairlie has essentially lumped us in with the garbage. Mum tells her that *The Cynthia Day Show* has actually got a lot better in recent years. 'It's less about teen pregnancy and paternity tests and more about human-interest stories.' She can tell herself that all she wants, but it still won't be true. Laurel told me that yesterday's show featured a woman who wasn't sure of the identity of the father of the baby she was carrying, but she was 'ninety per cent sure it was either her fiancé or his twin brother'.

Kirsty keeps asking me questions about Laurel, but I don't really mind, because the questions are different to the ones people usually ask. She's actually interested in what it's like for me and how it's changed *my* life. At one point she admits that she used to wish *her* sister would disappear, but then she sees the look on my face – or rather the absence of the look she wanted to see – and apologizes. I'm surprised to find that I quite like Kirsty. Maybe if the Fairlies hadn't moved to Australia we would have been friends.

The waiter brings the dessert menus and Mum and Mrs Fairlie both say something along the lines of 'Oh no, I *shouldn't*', before ordering deconstructed sticky-toffee pudding and raspberry crème brûlée respectively. I don't order anything; I do my best to ignore the approving look from Mum. Kirsty orders the same as her mum, and then everyone turns to Laurel and Bryony.

Laurel smiles and says she's not hungry. The

smile is a bad photocopy of a real one, blurred and smudged. It's not as simple as they say – that you can tell a fake smile because it never reaches the eyes. No, Laurel's better than that. But there's a strained quality, as if she's working the muscles in her face so hard they might go into spasm any second now. It's in her voice too – slightly too loud, slightly too chirpy. She is *not* happy. I'm sure I'm the only one who notices; the Fairlies don't know her well enough, and Mum has a tendency only to see what she wants to see.

The interesting thing is that Bryony doesn't look too happy either. She says she doesn't want any pudding, and Mrs Fairlie nudges her and says, 'But sticky toffee pudding is your favourite!'

Bryony scowls and says, 'I *said* I didn't want anything.' Then she looks up at the waiter (who is being remarkably patient, waiting to take our coffee order) and asks him where the toilet is.

'I'll go with you,' Laurel says quickly, and you can tell Bryony isn't too thrilled about that, but she doesn't say anything.

Laurel and Bryony head off in the direction the waiter pointed and Mum and Mrs Fairlie look at each other and smile. 'Like two peas in a pod, those two,' says Mum.

'Taking a pee together!' says Mrs Fairlie, laughing at her own terrible joke.

'God, you're *so* embarrassing,' says Kirsty, rolling her eyes.

Chapter 34

'That was lovely. Wasn't that lovely?' Mum turns to look at me. The bus is packed with commuters and shoppers. There was one double seat available – for Mum and Laurel, of course – so I'm sitting behind them, next to a skinny bloke wearing jeans, a denim shirt *and* a denim jacket. He keeps looking at me out of the corner of his eye.

'Yeah, it was nice.' I want Mum to stop turning round. I don't want Triple Denim listening in to our conversation and having the chance to work out who Laurel is.

Mum turns to Laurel next. 'Such a nice family. I was so upset when they moved away!'

Laurel says all the right things – how much she enjoyed the lunch, and how wonderful it was to see Bryony. I can only see the side of her face as she talks to Mum, but it's her voice that's the real giveaway. Too polished, too shiny.

When Bryony and Laurel came back from the toilet the other three were engaged in a pointless debate about the sexuality of some middle-aged actor Mum's always fancied. No one else noticed the awkwardness between the two girls, or the fact that instead of talking to each other, they spent the rest of the meal focusing on Mum and Mrs Fairlie's conversation. Bryony was sitting as far away from Laurel as she could possibly get, perched right on the edge of the bench seat. Mum and Mrs Fairlie were probably too distracted by the puddings – they both kept on making 'ooh' and 'mmm' sounds with each spoonful.

I caught Laurel's eye, arching my eyebrows in a silent question. *Is everything OK?*

Her response was half a nod – a brief raising of the chin. *Everything's fine.*

The goodbye hugs were less awkward than the hellos. Kirsty suggested we exchange numbers, given that she's going to be at uni over here next year. There were tears in Mrs Fairlie's eyes. 'This has been *so* special . . . I'm so glad everything turned out OK.' She glanced at Laurel, but Laurel was busy staring out of the window. Mum and Mrs Fairlie vowed to keep in touch and Mum said we might even go to Australia on holiday sometime in the next couple of years. She neglected to mention who was included in that 'we'. There had been no mention of Dad during the meal, I was pretty sure of that.

I seemed to be the only one who noticed that Bryony and Laurel didn't really say goodbye to each other.

As soon as we get home Laurel announces that she has a headache. 'Too much champagne?' Mum enquires with a gentle laugh.

'I only had one glass!' Laurel's voice is brittle.

'I know, I know. I was only teasing. Why don't you go upstairs for a lie-down? There's paracetamol in the bathroom cabinet if you need it.'

Laurel's halfway up the stairs when I call up to her. 'I'll bring you up a glass of water if you like?' I get an approving look from Mum for that.

Laurel says there's no need, that she can swallow the pills dry, but I insist.

She's sitting on her bed when I come in. I ask her if she wants me to get the painkillers for her. No thanks, she says.

'You don't really have a headache, do you?'

'No.'

I sit down next to her on the bed. 'What's the matter?' I don't say that I noticed the awkwardness at lunch; it's better if people don't know that you can read them so easily.

'Nothing. I'm just tired, I think.' I'm about to quiz her further about Bryony and what was said, but she says, 'The nightmares have been bad the last few nights.'

'I'm sorry.' There's not much else I can say. My nightmares are bad enough. They're horrible at the time, but the horror recedes as soon as I wake up. Laurel's nightmares are different, obviously. She's lived inside a nightmare for most of her life. I'm not sure if she'll ever be able to truly escape.

I'm dying to find out what happened with Bryony, but I can't ask Laurel while she's sitting there looking so desolate.

I've started to notice a pattern, if you can count something happening three or four time as a pattern. There are times when someone – usually me – asks Laurel a question or says something to her, and out of nowhere she'll mention Smith or something that happened to her in that basement. It's almost as if she feels the need to remind you (me) about what she's been through. As if there are some things she doesn't want to talk about, and shouldn't *have* to talk about, solely because of what that man did to her. The strange thing is, the questions that spark this reaction rarely have anything whatsoever to do with what happened to her. I try to remind myself that any little thing could trigger a memory for her. But I can't get rid of the niggling feeling that sometimes she uses her ordeal as a sort of Get Out of Jail Free card when she wants to shut down a conversation.

Chapter 35

The ghostwriter is late; I was twenty minutes early. I chose a couple of sofas next to the window in the corner, putting my coat and bag next to me so she would have to sit opposite me. Mum arranged to meet a friend for lunch in town so she could give me a lift. She invited Laurel too, but Laurel said she wanted to stay home. 'I hope you're going to do something other than watch TV?' Mum said, and it was the first truly Mum-like thing I've heard her say to Laurel. It was nagging, pure and simple, and I was very, very happy to hear it. Laurel didn't seem to mind either. She promised she'd only watch one episode, then she would make a start on dinner. She's going to have a go at making pasta from scratch, which she's been keen to try ever since she saw some fake Cockney TV chef making it in his fake apartment.

'Are you sure you're going to be OK on your

own?' Mum asked. 'Don't answer the door to anyone you don't know, remember.'

'I'll be *fine*. Stop worrying and go and have some fun!' She hugged Mum, then turned to me. 'Thank you for doing this.'

'For doing what?' But I know what she's talking about. Of course I do.

'The book. It means a lot to me. You know that, don't you?' I nod. 'I hope it won't be too painful for you to talk with the writer. All those memories . . .'

'I'll be *fine* . . . as long as I have a decent dinner to come home to! By the way, there's regular pasta in the cupboard if it all goes horribly wrong.'

Mum waited till she heard Laurel locking the door behind us before getting in the car.

I feel pretty good about things. The last couple of days have been nice. I've spent most of my time hanging out with Laurel and Mum and everything has been normal, even though it's a new kind of normal. Thomas and I went for a walk yesterday and it was nice even though the weather was dreadful. We huddled under his umbrella and talked – really, properly *talked* for the first time in ages. We talked about things that had nothing to do with my sister.

I thought I would be more nervous about meeting

with the ghostwriter. I *am* nervous — of course I am, it's a weird thing to have to do — but I'm glad I'm doing it. Laurel is so grateful; I like her being grateful. And the money will come in handy, even though Mum says I can't get my hands on my share until I'm eighteen. She's put my money in a special savings account, but at least she's increased my allowance. Laurel's getting a much (MUCH) bigger share of the money from the publisher, and she has access to hers now. It makes sense — it is *her* story. Martha asked me if it bothered me — Laurel getting so much more cash than me — and I said it didn't. She called me a liar. I knew she could never understand. Laurel needs this money; I don't.

A woman walks into the bar and cranes her neck to look around. I don't wave just in case she's not who I'm waiting for. In my head, the ghostwriter is short and thin and mousy, rounded shoulders and rounded glasses. She's the kind of woman who fades into the background. I realize my mistake as soon as this woman starts striding in my direction. She covers the distance in remarkably few steps.

'You must be Faith. Kay Docherty. Lovely to meet you.' She holds out a hand and I shake it. She must be at least six foot tall — even taller than Martha. White-blonde hair in a severe bob with an equally severe fringe. She's dressed in lots of complicated layers in varying shades of grey, finishing off the look with a pair of black leather Converse.

'Nice to meet you,' I say as she starts unwinding a very long scarf.

She takes one look at my bag and coat before picking them up and putting them on the other sofa along with her coat and scarf. She doesn't even ask if I mind. She takes out a notepad, pen and a tiny recording device and lays them out on the table, then she sits down and grabs the cocktail menu. She flicks through it, then puts it down again.

She beckons the waitress over and says, 'Bombay Sapphire, tonic, three ice cubes and a wedge of lime, please.' The waitress doesn't seem to think this request is anything out of the ordinary. She looks at me and I'm tempted to ask for the same, even though I've never tried gin and tonic, but I don't want to risk being asked for ID so I just order a Coke. A drink might help loosen me up a bit, but I can just imagine it ending up in the book – *Laurel's ordeal drove me to drink*.

I have to turn in my seat to face Kay and she does the same. She places the tape recorder between us, switches it on and tells me to ignore it. Easier said than done. She explains a little bit about how it's going to work, that I can just tell the story in my own words or she can ask questions to prompt me. We'll probably need a couple of sessions like this, depending on how much I have to say. Then she'll go away and write it up and send it to me for approval.

'So you write it like you're pretending to be me?' It feels dishonest somehow. That people will read this book and think they're reading *our* words.

'Sort of. I like to think of it as something like channelling your spirit.'

She laughs at the sceptical look on my face. 'OK, OK, that sounds like bollocks. But it's actually not far off. Last year I was working with a very famous footballer – not mentioning any names! It was a fascinating project, trying to work out how *he* would write the story, trying to nail his voice . . . It's about capturing the essence of a person – the essence of their story. Anyway, you don't need to worry about all that now.'

'Wouldn't you rather write your own story?'

The waitress arrives with our drinks and sets them down on little black napkins. My Coke has three ice cubes and a wedge of lime, just like Kay's drink. The waitress glances at the recording device on the sofa, then she looks from me to Kay and back again, trying to work out what might be going on here. Maybe she thinks that Kay is famous and I've won a competition to interview her for my school newspaper. The waitress asks if we would like anything else and goes on to list the available bar snacks. She's clearly just dragging things out, waiting to see if we'll give anything away, but we both say, 'No, thanks,' so she has to go away.

'My own story? You know, in all the years I've been doing this, no one has ever asked me that question. No one whose book I've worked on, anyway.' She can't have been doing this job for *that* long; she looks quite young. 'I'm afraid my story wouldn't sell many copies . . . there's nothing much to tell.'

For some reason I'm interested in Kay Docherty. I ask her if she's ever written any novels, and she claims not to have the imagination for it. 'No, it's real lives that interest me.'

'But isn't it annoying to do all that work on a book and have someone else take the credit for it?' I would hate it.

She shrugs and shakes her head. 'Not at all. It's . . . rewarding, helping people to tell their stories. Plus, the money is *insane!*' She leans back and laughs, then she shakes her head and frowns. 'Nice try, Faith.' She smiles as if she's got the measure of me.

'What do you mean?' I take a sip of my Coke.

'Asking me all these questions, trying to distract me. We're here to talk about *you*, not me. So . . . why don't we start at the beginning. What — if anything — do you remember about life *before* Laurel was taken?' She leans closer to me and cocks her head to one side.

I look at the recording device, then back at Kay. She nods encouragingly. I start to talk.

I'm hesitant at first, stumbling over my words, forgetting things or not saying them the right way, then having to go back and correct them. Kay is patient and tells me not to worry, that there's no need to apologize if there's something I can't remember. She asks about Mum and Dad and their relationship, which I try to gloss over as quickly as possible. I'll leave that to *them* to explain. Kay asks me about the day Laurel went missing, about any memories I have of the man who took her. She asks a lot of questions about how I felt at various times, asking me to describe my emotions in as much detail as I can.

I start to relax. Kay orders me another Coke, after enquiring whether I would like anything stronger. She asks for some wasabi peas too. I've never tried them before. They're vile, but for some reason I keep popping another one into my mouth every couple of minutes.

After an hour or so I realize I'm actually enjoying myself, even though most of the stuff I'm talking about isn't exactly cheery. But Kay is really nice. She doesn't mind when I go off-topic and start talking about something that has little or nothing to do with Laurel. It almost feels like a normal conversation – like we're friends just catching up on each other's lives.

Kay is very sympathetic about everything I've been through. She asks if I ever felt neglected or ignored by my parents, in the aftermath of Laurel's disappearance. I tell her the truth: yes. All the time.

She asks whether it was hard for me to make friends and I tell her the truth: it was.

I'm honest about everything, which surprises me. I'm used to editing my thoughts and feelings when I talk to people – particularly when talking to strangers. It feels good, to talk about this stuff with someone I've never met before. Therapeutic, almost.

I try not to think about the fact that there might be some things that Mum and Dad will wish I'd been slightly less honest about. But I can always ask Kay to take those bits out when she sends me the rough draft to read through. Besides, it's not as if I've said anything particularly earth-shattering. Laurel's the one with the real story. People will probably skip my chapters to get straight to hers; I know I would.

I surreptitiously check the time while reaching for

another wasabi pea. Mum will be waiting outside.

Maybe I wasn't so surreptitious with the watch-checking after all, because Kay says, 'Well, I think that's about it for today. I know how tiring it can be, dredging up all these memories.' She downs the rest of her gin. 'You've done really well. There's some good stuff here,' she says, tapping the recording device. 'I think one more session should do it. Whenever you're ready, there's no rush.'

She gives me her card and tells me to call her to set up our next meeting. She goes up to the bar to settle the bill – the publisher is paying, apparently.

We put on our coats and Kay air-kisses me and thanks me again. I have this strange urge to tell her that we should stay here and carry on with the interview. I could call Mum and tell her I'll meet her at home. Instead I tell her that I was actually a bit reluctant to go ahead with the book, and that I'd been a bit nervous, not knowing what to expect.

'You're a natural storyteller, you know,' Kay says as we walk towards the door.

I laugh and feel a blush creeping up my checks. 'No, I'm not. You're just good at asking questions.'

Kay shakes her head and holds the door open for me. 'Well, that may be true, but you've got a gift, young lady. Trust me.'

*

A natural storyteller? The words keep popping into my head while Mum is quizzing me about how it went. What did Kay mean by that? Was it a compliment? Or was it a roundabout way of calling me a liar? I can't decide. I'm going to have to ask her next time I see her.

I should be relieved that there's only one more session. But I can't help feeling offended, if that's even the right word. Kay thinks that after sitting down with her for another couple of hours I'll have nothing more to say. After five hours of talking to me, she will have the measure of me. The sum total of all that is interesting in the life of Faith Logan, aged 17½.

Of course Kay will spend days and days talking to Laurel, finding out every minute detail about her time in captivity and how she feels now that she's home. This is *The Laurel Show* and my role is nothing more than a bit part.

'You seem quiet, love.' Mum glances over at me. We're stuck in a traffic jam. I always start to feel claustrophobic after being in the car with Mum for more than a few minutes. There's no escape if she decides to start an argument.

'I'm just tired. I don't think I've ever talked so much in my life.' This is the truth. I'm much more likely to be sitting in a corner, watching and listening. I thought I preferred things that way, but I'm starting to wonder if maybe that isn't the real me. Perhaps the real me — the me I would have been if my life hadn't been completely overshadowed by Laurel's abduction — *likes* being the centre of attention. Perhaps she likes having people hang off her every word.

'I wonder how your sister's getting on with the pasta,' says Mum.

I'd forgotten all about that. I'd forgotten all about Laurel, in fact. Even though I've been talking about her all afternoon.

Chapter 36

We hear the laughter coming from the kitchen as soon as Mum opens the front door. The kitchen door is closed. Mum and I exchange a look. Laurel's laugh is loud; the other laugh is quieter, and deeper. I recognize it immediately.

Mum takes off her coat and hangs it on one of the pegs next to the front door. I head straight through to the kitchen, opening the door with such force that it bangs against the wall. Mum *hates* it when I do that.

The scene in front of me can only be described as chaos. There is flour *everywhere*. Broken eggshells litter the worktop. Laurel is kneading a big lump of dough; Thomas is standing next to her, holding a glass bowl. He has flour on his nose. Thomas freezes when the door slams open, but Laurel doesn't even blink. 'You're back! How did it go?' She carries on kneading as if this is a perfectly normal situation.

'It went OK, thanks,' I say coolly.

Laurel smiles and says, 'I'm so glad! Hey, can you pass me some more flour?'

I get the open bag from the table, she lifts the lump of dough and I scatter some flour on the worktop. I don't tell her that I think adding more flour is a mistake, that the TV chef she's so fond of always warns you not to use too much.

Thomas looks very uncomfortable with the situation. He seems to not want to let go of the bowl, which is probably a good thing, because I have a sudden urge to smash it over his head. 'Hi,' he says, 'We were just . . .'

'Hello, Thomas. I didn't realize you were coming round this afternoon.' Mum comes into the room and stands next to me. 'Oh my . . .' She's a bit of a neat freak, especially when it comes to the kitchen.

Laurel pre-empts Mum's dismay. 'It's OK, it's OK! I'll clear it up in a minute! I just need to leave the dough to prove . . . or rest or whatever it's called.'

'I didn't say a word,' Mum says with a smile.

'But you were going to!' Laurel laughs.

Laurel is babbling away about making pasta not being as easy as it looks and something about egg yolks. Mum gets a cloth out of the cupboard under the sink and gets started on the clean-up operation, even though Laurel tells her she has it under control. Thomas finally puts down the bowl. I think he's deciding whether to come over and kiss me, or hug me at least. Instead he asks if anyone would like a cup of tea. Mum and Laurel say yes please, I say no.

Mum keeps glancing over at me. She can tell I'm not exactly thrilled with the situation, but she would never say anything in front of Laurel. Thomas is watching me like you might watch a poisonous snake that's escaped from its cage and is slithering its way towards a group of unsuspecting children. It's amazing that Laurel doesn't sense the atmosphere in the room. So amazing, in fact, that it makes me wonder if she *does* sense it, but is choosing to ignore it.

Laurel places the dough in the bowl and wraps cling film over the top. 'Thomas was just saying he thought we were *brilliant* on *The Cynthia Day Show*. Isn't that nice of him to say?' This just gets better and better. Either Thomas lied to me about not watching it, or he lied to Laurel just now. The answer is clear from the look on his face and the fact that he's concentrating so hard on the tea bag he's dunking. Why didn't he just admit that he'd watched it? That's just plain weird.

'I'm just going to the loo,' I say, and walk out of the room before anyone can say anything else to piss me off.

I go up to my bedroom. I sit on the bed. Thomas joins me a couple of minutes later, bringing two mugs. 'I thought you might have changed your mind about the tea.'

'I haven't.'

He puts both mugs down on the bedside table. He's given me the one with Laurel's name on it. 'Is everything OK? You seem annoyed. Are you annoyed?' He sits down next to me and takes my hand in his. I don't snatch my hand away. That's something, at least.

'Why would I be annoyed?'

'Is it the Cynthia Day thing? I'm sorry I lied. I didn't want to make you more nervous about it.' I don't want to look at him. I'm doing such a good job of *not* looking at him. But I can't work out if he's telling the truth. I risk a glance and he maintains eye contact, nodding ever so slightly as if that's going to convince me.

Silence seems like the best policy. I count to twenty-seven in my head before Thomas speaks again. 'She texted me, asked me to come over to help with the pasta.'

'Because you're so *renowned* for your cooking skills?'

'Well, um . . . I suppose no one mentioned to her that I'm useless in the kitchen. I told her as much, but she sounded stressed. She really wanted to cook you something nice for tonight. I think she feels bad about you being pressured to do this book.'

He thinks he's saying the right things, but with every word he utters I feel myself getting more and more wound up. 'I wasn't pressured into doing anything. I can make my own decisions, you know. But it's nice to know that you two talk about me when I'm not there.'

'We don't! It's not like that.' He lets go of my hand. 'God, I should have *known* you'd be like this. I can't seem to do anything right these days.'

'What's that supposed to mean?'

'Nothing,' he mumbles. 'Forget I said anything.'

'No. Tell me what you're talking about.'

He sighs and stands up. 'I think I should go. I don't want to fight with you.'

'We're not fighting.' I'm not sure why I say this. Perhaps because I really want it to be true.

He almost smiles. 'I'm sorry if you're annoyed that I came over when you weren't here, but I wanted to see you after your meeting with the writer. I was worried about you.' He reaches out and touches my cheek and I find myself leaning in to his hand.

Everything Thomas is saying sounds reasonable enough, and every feeling I've had since I got home suddenly seems petty and small and paranoid. I look up at Thomas and he's looking at me with so much patience and understanding that I feel ashamed of myself. I'm fed up with feeling ashamed of myself. 'I'm sorry.' I think Thomas is as surprised as I am to hear me say those words. He crouches down in front of me and tells me that he loves me. 'I know,' I say.

'Now are you sure I can't tempt you with that tea? I made it just the way you like it.' He arches his eyebrows and looks at me expectantly.

'No one makes it just the way I like it except me . . . but I will sample your pitiful attempt.' Thomas laughs and says that I'm incorrigible. I like the way the word sounds when he says it.

We sit side by side on the bed, drinking our tea. 'Not bad at all,' I say, even though it's a lie. The tea is too strong and too cold, but Thomas can only be blamed for one of those things.

'We're OK, aren't we?' I ask, after downing the last dregs from my (Laurel's) mug.

'Of course we are,' says Thomas. 'I'm really looking forward to my birthday, you know.'

'Me too.' A romantic meal. Just the two of us, sitting at a table bathed in soft lighting, gazing into each other's eyes, eating fancy French food. That's what Thomas is expecting anyway. The restaurant he thinks we're going to is next door to the pub we're *actually* going to. Thomas's mother roped me in as the bait to get Thomas to where he needs to be for the big SURPRISE! moment. The poor boy has no idea what's in store for him.

Chapter 37

She's done a good job with the pasta, I have to admit. Mum and I both have second helpings. Laurel doesn't eat much, taking ages to twirl the fettucine around her fork only to let it fall back on to her plate. 'Not hungry, love?'

Laurel shrugs. 'It's not as good as the pasta you get from the shop, is it? What's the point of going to all that effort if it's not better than the ready-made stuff?' She seems genuinely upset about it.

'Ah, welcome to my world!' says Mum with relish. 'That's why you'll never find me making my own pastry . . . Life's too short.' She doesn't seem to realize how upset Laurel is, so I give her a nudge while Laurel is staring forlornly at her plate. She clears her throat. 'Honestly, love, this is delicious. The best meal I've had in ages. And it is better than the shop-bought stuff . . . because it's made with *love*.'

I manage not to laugh at Mum's cheesy line, which is just as well, because it's made Laurel smile. 'Really? You're not just saying that? You promise?'

Mum smiles indulgently. 'Really. Honestly. Truly. I *promise*.' She looks to me for back-up and I nod enthusiastically, which is all that I can do, given that my mouth is full of pasta.

Mum puts her spoon and fork down. 'It's amazing how far you've come in such a short time, Laurel,' she says, and I can tell she's about to get all emotional again. You'd think she'd be over all that by now, but no, these little scenes are still happening on a daily basis. 'I'm so proud of you.' It's not that I roll my eyes or pretend to gag or anything obvious like that, but Mum must sense my irritation because then she says, 'I'm proud of *both* of you.' We all clink our water glasses together. And Laurel finally starts eating her dinner.

Later, Laurel and Mum are downstairs watching some rubbish on TV. I have to get started on research for a history essay. That's the reason I go upstairs. There's nothing on my mind apart from wondering if I remembered to take the right book out of the school library last week. I'm almost sure I *did*, but now that I think about it . . .

Laurel's bedroom door is open and the bedside light and main light are both switched on. Mum obviously hasn't given her the lecture about saving electricity yet. Or maybe she never will, given that Laurel has spent so much of her life in darkness.

I could kid myself that something caught my eye in Laurel's room, that *that's* the reason I find myself in there, looking around. But nothing caught my eye. I don't have an excuse. If she came upstairs right now and saw me, I'd be able to think of something. Looking for my laptop? That would do. Except we both know full well that she doesn't have my laptop – I've been hiding it in a different place every day, just in case. She hasn't asked to borrow it, so I guess the novelty of using it must have worn off.

The nightlight is still there, but not switched on. Laurel's one concession to saving the environment perhaps. The room is tidy. Laurel has yet to accumulate the little possessions that make a room look like it belongs to someone. Most of the gifts people send her get sent straight on to the children's hospital. That was her idea, one that made Mum positively glow with pride. I didn't point out that most of the gifts are teddy bears and other cuddly toys, so it would be weird for her to keep them. When are people going to start remembering that Little Laurel Logan is a nineteen-year-old woman now? It's as if the entire country – my family included – has a mental block about it. She's kept a couple of cuddly toys though. One Winnie the Pooh and a random reindeer.

There's only one teddy bear that means anything to Laurel – Barnaby. I look over to Laurel's bed, neatly made, pink and purple cushions lying at a perfect angle in front of the plumped-up pillows. No sign of Barnaby. He's usually there, isn't he? Nestled in between the two cushions, tucked in under the duvet. I go over for a closer look, careful to step softly so Laurel and Mum don't hear that I'm in here. I pull back the duvet, but he's not there. He's not stuck between the pillows or behind the cushions. I put everything back just the way I found it – or as close to it as I can get.

I kneel down and look under the bed, just in case Barnaby has taken a tumble and is awaiting rescue. He's nowhere to be seen. This is odd. I briefly wonder if Laurel might have taken him downstairs with her. For the first week or so after she came home, she often carried him around with her, sitting him down next to her on the sofa. I could tell it broke Mum's heart, seeing her clutching that scruffy old bear.

Barnaby has disappeared. I have no idea why this bothers me so much. I stand back and look at the room, trying to work out where he could be hiding. The wardrobe is the only option. This definitely counts as snooping. If Laurel catches me looking in there, the only option I have is to say that I want to borrow an item of clothing, which I haven't done once the whole time she's been back.

The wardrobe is a mess. Now her tidiness makes sense – everything has been crammed in here. I smile, reassured that Laurel isn't so perfect after all. There's only one clothes hanger in use; the red dress lording it over all the other clothes. T-shirts and tops and jumpers and jeans are all higgledy-piggledy on the shelves. The ones on the bottom of the piles are folded neatly, the ones on the top are not. In the space underneath the hangers, there is a heaped pile of shoes. A shiny shoe box sits in the corner. A quick peek inside confirms my suspicions: a pair of very expensive red shoes. They match the dress perfectly. Mum and Laurel must have been on another shopping trip without bothering to tell me. Not that I blame them – I was clearly spoiling their fun the last time.

I wrap the shoes back up in the black tissue paper and put the lid back on the box. The lid won't go on properly – one of the corners is being stubborn – so I go to pick up the box. That's when I see the leg. A brown furry leg with a bald patch just above the paw.

Barnaby the Bear has suffered the same fate as the

Wicked Witch of the West, except he's been subjected to Death by Designer Shoes instead of Death by Tornado-Dumped House. I pick up the box to survey the damage. Actually Barnaby hasn't been completely flattened by the shoe box, and he still has three out of four limbs intact. But that doesn't stop the sight of him from hurting my heart. His head is at an unnatural angle, as if his neck has been broken; he looks *wrong*.

Why is he stuffed into the bottom of the wardrobe like this? Laurel *loves* that bear. He's her prize possession – one of the only things that truly belongs to her. But he didn't toddle into the wardrobe on his own, lift up the shoebox and snuggle under it. Mum wouldn't have done this – no way. So Laurel must have put him here.

I know what I'm about to do is stupid. And I know it means Laurel will know that I've been in her room, rooting around in the bottom of her wardrobe. But it feels like I have no other option; I can't stand to leave him where I found him.

I put Barnaby the Bear back where he belongs, tucked up in Laurel's bed, snug between the cushions. 'There,' I whisper to the battered bear. 'That's better, isn't it?' For the first time I start to wonder if there might be something wrong with me, because it feels like maybe my brain isn't working quite as it should.

But it's pointless, thinking that way. I'm fine. *I'm* not the one with the problem.

I switch off the bedside light and the main light.

Laurel will know for sure that I've been in here. The question is: what is she going to do about it?

Chapter 38

Nothing. That's what Laurel does about it. I hide out in my room for the rest of the evening, with a brief trip downstairs to say goodnight. So I don't see Laurel until the next morning. I'm sitting on the sofa flicking through the Argos catalogue when she comes downstairs. It's one of my favourite things to do when I'm anxious. I have no idea why staring at pages and pages of terrible jewellery and cheap furniture soothes me, but it does.

'Morning,' she says.

I'm slow to look up from the catalogue, busy marvelling at the price of an outdoor trampoline. 'Morning.' When I finally do look up I see Laurel smiling down at me. Already dressed, with her jacket and bag in her arms too. There's a short silence – a moment when either of us could mention Barnaby or the fact that I've been through her stuff. A look passes between us, neither friendly nor unfriendly, and then it's over and she's putting on her jacket. 'Where are you off to?' I ask.

'Nowhere special.' She picks up her bag and puts it on her shoulder.

'I've heard it's really good there.'

A brief, baffled look before she gets the joke. 'Ha,' she says.

'Fancy some company?' I don't want to go with her, wherever she's going, but I do want to see what she says.

'No, thanks. Not today. Penny says it's time I started being more independent. Anyway, I'd better get going.' She turns away and heads towards the door.

'What's the rush? Is Nowhere Special open this early?'

She doesn't even bother with a 'ha' this time. She doesn't even turn around. 'I'm not rushing. I'm just ready to go, that's all. See you later, OK?'

I say goodbye but the door is already closed.

I jump up from the sofa and the Argos catalogue falls on my foot. I hobble over to the window and watch Laurel walk down the street. I'm ready to duck down out of sight in case she suddenly turns around, but she doesn't. I press my nose up against the window and lean as far as I can so that I can watch her for as long as possible. She walks with her shoulders straight – with an easy confidence I've never even attempted let alone mastered.

As soon as Laurel's out of sight I rush to the front door and open it. The ground is wet and the damp starts soaking through the soles of my slippers the second I step outside. I peer around the hedge, not caring how suspicious I look. I'm just in time to see Laurel reach the end of our road. If she turns left, she'll be going to the bus stop where you take the bus to the city centre. I seem to spend half my life waiting at that bus stop.

Laurel turns right. Unless she's going to the crematorium (which seems highly unlikely), she's probably catching a bus in the opposite direction, away from town. Why would she be going that way? The only time I ever go to that bus stop is when I'm going to Thomas's house and he refuses to come and pick me up.

A light drizzle begins to fall as I stand on our front path in my pyjamas. The postman is walking down the street towards me, back bent under the weight of the postbag. He says a cheery 'Morning' as he hands me two letters and a postcard (both addressed to Laurel). 'Morning,' I echo. He doesn't comment on my clothes or look at me as if I'm crazy; I guess he must see all sorts of odd things, doing a job like that.

The drizzle turns into proper rain and I realize I should probably get inside. My legs want to go the other way though – they want to follow Laurel, to check if she's waiting at the bus stop and maybe even to wait and see if she gets on the number 67, which stops five minutes away from Thomas's house. I stand rooted to the spot for a few seconds before my brain finally wins the battle. My brain knows that there's no way Laurel's going to Thomas's house. She doesn't even know his address. Unless he told her.

I go upstairs to get my phone, texting Thomas to see what he's up to this morning. I ask if he wants to meet up. His reply arrives about an hour later: *Can't this morning. Sorry. Mum wants to go shopping for my bday present. Tonight?*

Thomas's mum wants to buy him a watch for his birthday, but she knows she wouldn't be able to choose the perfect one by herself. Thomas already told me this. They're even going to get it engraved. So there's no reason to think he's lying. I text back to say I'm suddenly not feeling very well so I'd better stay home tonight. He says he hopes I feel better soon.

Laurel must have gone somewhere else. Maybe she's just planning to hop on a bus and see where she ends up. That's exactly the kind of weird thing she would do.

I decide to put it out of my mind completely. I will not allow myself to turn into a paranoid wreck. I tell myself that I don't care where Laurel has gone – it's none of my business. Anyway, I'm only a third of the way through the Argos catalogue.

When I eventually go to get dressed, I pop my head into Laurel's room. The bed is neatly made, cushions in place.

Barnaby the Bear is not there. He's not in the wardrobe either.

Chapter 39

The week has been drama-free. I haven't mentioned Barnaby. Laurel and I had a good weekend at Dad and Michel's. Since being mobbed at the farmers' market, Laurel has stayed home. Business is booming, probably because people feel that they can't come up and ask questions about Laurel without buying something. Michel is happy to take their money, but he never tells them anything about Laurel.

The only awkward moment was when Dad sat Laurel down to tell her that the DNA test the police keep going on about has been scheduled for a week on Thursday. They can't put it off any longer, apparently. He'd tried his best to convince them it wasn't necessary, that Laurel had been through enough. But they wouldn't budge. At least they've agreed that Mum can be the one to do the cheek swab, to minimize Laurel's distress.

Laurel asked why they needed to do the test and

Dad said that Sergeant Dawkins had told him they needed to double-check something in their files. She'd left three messages on his phone about it, so it must be pretty important. Dad told Laurel that there was nothing to be afraid of. She looked like she was about to puke. Dad put his arm around her and asked if it was OK with her. She said nothing for the longest time.

I decided to chip in. 'You should do it, Laurel. Get it over with. I'll be with you, if you want.'

Laurel looked over at me, sitting in my corner with Tonks on my lap. I nodded encouragingly, and after a second's hesitation she nodded back. She turned to Dad and said, 'OK.'

Thomas has been quiet this week. Martha and I have been teasing him about getting old. I asked him how the shopping trip with his Mum went. 'Fine,' he said.

'So you found a watch?'

'Yeah,' he said, before changing the subject. Maybe he was pouting because his mum hadn't bought him the vintage one he wanted. Or maybe he was starting to realize that he should have asked for money instead, like a normal person.

On the day of his birthday, I get to school early and tie a helium balloon to the radiator where we normally sit in the common room. The balloon is tacky as anything — silver and heart-shaped, with multicoloured letters saying 'BIRTHDAY BOY'. I have his present in my bag, along with a home-made card. I haven't decided whether I'll give them to him at school or at the party. Either way, I'd prefer it if Thomas and I were alone. No one else would think the present was particularly impressive, but I know Thomas will like it. I bought it months ago, long before I started wondering if I still wanted him to be my boyfriend. I remember being so pleased with myself at the time — so smug that I'd found the perfect present for him even though he's impossible to buy for.

Martha arrives a couple of minutes before Thomas. She eyes the balloon with approval and suggests that we start singing 'Happy Birthday' as soon as Thomas walks through the door. I'm tempted — just to see his reaction — but he's got enough public humiliation in store for him tonight.

We sit with our backs against the radiator and watch the door until Thomas comes in, head down, earphones in, completely oblivious to everything around him. He doesn't look up until he's right in front of us. He smiles when he notices the balloon bobbing away. 'Aw, you guys! You shouldn't have!' he says in an overly enthusiastic voice. Then he gives us a withering look. 'I suppose this was your idea,' he says, looking at Martha.

'No, no, I couldn't possibly take the credit for this little delight,' Martha says as she rummages around in her bag. 'But I can, however, take ALL the credit for this!' She produces a huge envelope with a flourish. Inside is the ugliest card I've ever seen, complete with an equally ugly saucer-sized badge saying '18 TODAY!!!'

'Happy Birthday, Mr Bolt,' says Martha, standing up and giving him an awkward hug.

I stand too, feeling almost shy all of a sudden. 'Happy birthday,' I say.

'Don't I get a birthday kiss?' This surprises me. Thomas isn't normally one for PDAs. I give him a quick kiss on the lips.

'You know, Thomas, you look different somehow . . . more manly, I think.' Martha grabs his upper arm and squeezes it. 'Nope, my mistake. Still the same old noodle arms.' For a second I think Thomas is going to be really annoyed, even though he's not particularly sensitive about his body, but he just laughs and says he prefers to think of them as 'sinewy'.

He fiddles with the badge and I can't believe he's going to wear it. He twists the pin on the back so that it's pointing outwards. Then he looks at me. 'May I?'

'You may.'

The sound of the balloon popping makes everyone in the common room jump and turn round to see where the noise came from. Laney Finch clutches her hand to her chest and leans on one of her friends to steady herself. One of the boys standing next to the coffee machine shouts the word 'DICK!' in our direction, probably embarrassed because he jumped so high his head almost hit the ceiling. Thomas gives the boy a little salute; the boy responds with a raised middle finger.

I decide to give Thomas his present at lunchtime – there's no way I can wait until tonight. We arrange to meet at a little deli around the corner from school. I arrive before him and order our paninis. The guy behind the counter knows our order off by heart. Thomas doesn't like him, probably because he's really handsome and is always very friendly to me while having a tendency to ignore Thomas.

The guy puts the food down on the table at the exact moment the door opens and Thomas walks in. 'Shame . . . I thought I was going to have to join you.' He winks at me and stands back to let Thomas sit down. I smile politely and wonder whether it's weird that I don't know the deli guy's name.

Thomas takes a huge bite of his sandwich and the

melted cheese forms oozy strings from his mouth to the panini. It makes me feel slightly nauseous, watching him. I nibble on the edge of my sandwich and try not to look. In between bites, Thomas tells me about his morning. One of his favourite things to do is to embarrass teachers by showing off his superior knowledge on certain subjects; his current number-one target is his English teacher. I used to think it was funny, but today it just seems childish. I smile and laugh in all the right places though – it is his birthday after all. He demolishes his sandwich in record time, despite the fact that he's hardly stopped talking since he arrived.

'Are you not eating that?' He looks at my sandwich like a hungry hyena.

I push the plate towards him. 'Go for it.'

'I probably shouldn't . . . I don't want to spoil my appetite for this slap-up meal tonight.' He puts his hand on his stomach, which is as smooth and flat as anyone could wish for. Little does Thomas know, the most he'll be getting to eat tonight is some Scotch eggs and mini sandwiches.

'That's *hours* away! You should eat it.' He doesn't take much convincing.

I take the present and card out of my bag when Thomas has finished eating. At first he says he wants to wait till tonight, that he'd rather open his present in the restaurant than here. Again it doesn't take much to convince him. The card makes him smile. On the front there's a drawing of us walking hand-in-hand through a forest. There are wolves and monsters lurking in the shadows of the crooked trees. It took me seven attempts before I was happy with the drawing, and then I had to trace it on to the card. I've never gone to that much effort for *anyone* before. 'I didn't know you could draw! You're really good, you know? This is . . . *really* cool. Creepy, but cool.'

Inside the card I've written the kind of thing that a girlfriend writes to her boyfriend on his eighteenth birthday. Thomas leans over the table to kiss me. He calls me a dark horse.

The present is next. He tears into the wrapping paper like a kid on Christmas Day. When he sees what it is, he smiles and says, 'Wow!' and thanks me profusely, but I can tell something isn't right. He says 'wow' far too many times. 'Wow' is not a very Thomas-like thing to say. It's a first edition of a book by some poet I'd never heard of before I met Thomas – in mint condition even though it's nearly forty years old. It's the *perfect* gift – for Thomas at least. If someone gave it to me I'd probably use it to prop a door open.

Thomas leans over and kisses me again, for longer

this time. 'It's perfect. *Thank* you,' he whispers in my ear. I wonder if maybe I was being paranoid and maybe he *does* love it after all. Perhaps he was so keen to show just how much he loved it that he accidentally went overboard on the enthusiasm and ended up sounding like Laney Finch. But now I feel strange and unsure, and disappointed that the moment didn't go the way I wanted it to go. What is *wrong* with me?

Chapter 40

'You're not skiving off school, are you?' Kay sips her gin and tonic, raising an eyebrow to make it abundantly clear that she wouldn't care if I *was*.

'Nope, free period.'

She was waiting for me this time. Same spot on the sofa, same drink in front of her. For some reason I find myself telling her that it's my boyfriend's birthday today. I tell her about the poetry book and the surprise party, and the fact that Thomas's mum seems to prefer Martha to me. Kay's amused smile makes me stop talking. 'Sorry, we should probably be talking about Laurel, shouldn't we? Um . . . what else do you need to know?'

Kay switches on the recording device. 'Well, why don't we pick up where we left off? Tell me about the first time you saw Laurel again after all those years . . . it was in a hotel room, wasn't it?'

I talk about what it was like seeing this young woman in front of me and trying to reconcile that with the picture of the little girl I had in my head. I talk about when Mum and Dad left us alone, and how it didn't feel like being left alone with a stranger. I talk about how surreal it was, sitting in that suite watching the press conference going on downstairs.

Then it's on to Laurel's first days back home with us. I can tell Kay is happy with how it's going. She asks if I'd like something to drink and I say I'll have what she's having.

I've never had gin and tonic before. It's horrible.

Kay leans back and crosses her legs. 'So, Faith, it can't *all* have been sweetness and light since Laurel came home . . . For all intents and purposes you'd lived the previous thirteen years as an only child. It can't have been easy to have a sister thrust into your life all of a sudden.' She sees the confused look on my face and adopts a chummy voice that I find off-putting. 'I know what it's like – my sister and I used to fight like cat and dog, especially when we were teenagers. Remind me to tell you one day about the time we both fancied the same boy.' I know what she's playing at. She thinks I'm stupid. She thinks she'll get something interesting out of me if she acts like my friend. She probably doesn't even have a sister.

I don't know why she's bothering. Even if she did manage to get me to say something juicy, there's no way I'd approve it to go in the book. Maybe she's just nosy or maybe she's looking for a story she can sell to the newspapers on the sly. Or perhaps I'm just being paranoid and she's just genuinely interested and thinks that a little bit of grit would be a good addition to the story – to make it less sugary, more real.

I take a sip of my drink and shake my head. 'No . . . it's been wonderful. We get on so well, it's as if we've never been apart. Anyway, I've never felt like an only child. Even when Laurel wasn't around, she was there.' I pause and wonder if what I want to say next would be going too far. Kay seems like the sort of person who can detect bullshit a mile away, unlike Cynthia Day. I decide to go for it anyway. I touch my hand to the middle of my chest and say, 'She was always *here*.'

Kay doesn't laugh or raise her eyebrows, and she doesn't call me a liar. She just nods thoughtfully then asks me another question, this time about press intrusion. It's the perfect opportunity for me to get my revenge on Jeanette Hayes, to tell the world exactly what we think of her. But instead I say that we've been so grateful that people have respected our privacy and given us the time and space to get to know each other again.

Kay leans forward. 'So you're not bothered about what people are saying on Twitter?'

I shake my head. 'I never go on there any more. I've got better things to do.' This isn't me. I don't know where this stuff is coming from, but I do know one thing: Mum will be happy. It will be worth it, telling these lies and half-truths, if it makes her happy.

It would almost be funny to see the look on Kay's face if I told her the truth – all of it. If I told her that Laurel gets away with murder – that she can wrap my parents around her little finger without even trying. I could tell her about the shoplifting, about her weird little trips off by herself and, best of all, that she spied on me and my boyfriend having sex. Now *that* would be a story people would want to hear. But it doesn't fit with the image they have of Little Laurel Logan, so maybe they wouldn't want to hear it after all. Maybe Laurel would call me a liar and everyone would believe her, because put us side by side and I can't think of a single person who would take my word over hers.

Kay asks if there's anything else I'd like to say before we wrap up. 'Anything at *all*?' She does a decent job of concealing her disappointment when I say I have nothing more to add.

It's Laurel's turn in a couple of weeks. They've scheduled in three whole-day sessions to start off with. 'I'm a bit nervous actually,' Kay says quietly, as if she's letting me in on some big secret. 'I've never worked on a project quite like this before. Nothing quite so . . . harrowing.'

Does she want me to comfort her, when all she has to do is listen to what Laurel went through? That's not going to happen. I just stare at her until she starts talking again. 'Well, I think that's us done. Thank you so much for your time. I'll let you know when I have something for you to read. I'll probably work on Laurel's sections first though, so it might be some time.'

That's fine with me. I'm in no hurry to read my words filtered through another person's brain. We say our goodbyes. Unlike last time, today I'm glad it's over. I'm glad I don't have to talk about Laurel any more.

Chapter 41

I didn't leave myself enough time to get ready. I'd wanted to wash my hair, but it takes ages to dry. I'll just have to hope that no one notices it's on the edge of being greasy. I always think of it as 'on the turn', the way Gran describes milk that's a few days old.

At least I don't need to stress about what to wear, because I already laid out my clothes this morning. Black jeans, boots, a red top. Nothing too fancy. When I go downstairs, Laurel's watching TV. 'You look nice,' she says. She couldn't have picked a blander word, but I thank her anyway. She asks what time she should get there, and I swear I must have blocked out that she was coming to the party. I have no idea how my brain managed to do that. It's fine though – I won't have to babysit her. She'll have people crowded round her, hanging on her every word, as per usual.

I tell her she should probably turn up around nine

o'clock. She looks surprised and says, 'That's a bit late, isn't it?'

I shake my head and say most people probably won't be arriving until then. This is a lie, obviously. It's not that I don't want her there, it's that I'd like a bit of time before she arrives and hogs all the attention.

Laurel says she's nervous and I tell her there's nothing to worry about. There's no time to give her any more reassurance than that. I can tell she has more to say, that she would like me to stay and talk for a while, but I'm going to be late as it is. 'I'll see you later. You know where you're going, right?'

Mum's dropping her off. She'll be fine.

The bus arrives five minutes late and I spend the whole journey willing it to go faster. I tell myself that I was perfectly nice to Laurel. She can stand on her own two feet now – she doesn't need me to prop her up. Besides, the party will be pretty tame. It's not as if it's some raucous house party with sex and drugs and random strangers. This will be good for her.

Martha's already there when I arrive, moving chairs around under the strict direction of Mrs Bolt. Thomas's dad is standing on a chair trying to hang one end of a banner from a light fitting. It looks like he might fall and break his neck any second. That would probably ruin the mood a bit.

Mrs Bolt spies me lurking in the doorway and beckons me over. Thomas's mum doesn't look like the sort of person who's spent most of her adult life in the army. I was surprised, the first time I met her. Thomas teased me about it, asking me what I'd been expecting. I didn't answer, but the truth was I'd imagined short hair, stocky build, maybe some camouflage. I definitely wasn't expecting her to look like she could have had a decent shot at a modelling career. Tall, very slim, long blonde hair, nice clothes. At least Thomas's dad conformed to my (admittedly ridiculous and stereotyped) expectations. He looks hard as nails.

Mrs Bolt gives me a dry peck on the cheek and asks how I am. Before I can answer she's already lost interest, so I just mumble that I'm fine, thanks. She looks beautiful tonight. Elegant is the word. She intimidates the hell out of me; I never know what to say to her. I'm sure that she hates me, no matter what Thomas says. She shoos me away to help Martha with the chairs.

Martha has a fine sheen of sweat on her forehead from shifting all that furniture. She's dressed even more casually than I am — faded jeans and a fitted black shirt. Martha doesn't seem to need my help, which is good, because I got sweaty enough rushing from the bus. I look around for something else to do, but it seems like everything's just about ready. I am officially surplus to requirements.

Thomas's mum makes sure the wine glasses are lined up properly on the table in the corner, then she picks up one of the glasses and holds it up against the light. She looks over and sees me watching, so I go and ask if there's anything else I can do to help. Mrs Bolt looks around the room, and it reminds me of Terminator, as if she has a computer in her head, analysing every tiny detail in front of her. 'No, I think we're just about ready. Thank you.' The 'thank you' was definitely an afterthought. She looks at me, eyes narrowed. 'You haven't told him, have you? You haven't ruined the surprise?'

'No!' I probably should have toned down the indignation a little bit.

She's doing that Terminator thing again, trying to work out if I'm lying. 'Good.' She turns her back on me without another word and heads over to where Thomas's dad is testing some fairy lights he's strung up over one of those awful stuffed reindeer heads.

There's no doubt about it: Thomas's mother is a straight-up bitch.

*

People start arriving, most of whom I don't recognize. I've hardly met any of Thomas's family, which is weird when you think about it, because he's met *all* of mine. I sit in a corner with Martha, and we try to guess who everyone is. At last a couple of people from school arrive and one of them swipes a couple of bottles of wine and some glasses from the table and brings them over to our booth. I'm pretty sure Mrs Bolt wouldn't be too happy about that – she's probably got a strict two-glasses-of-wine-per-person policy.

Five minutes before Thomas is due at the restaurant, I go over to Mrs Bolt – because I don't want her coming over to us – and say that I'm going to head outside. She claps her hands together and shouts to everyone to be quiet, then she tells them what to do. 'Right, off you go!' she says impatiently, practically pushing me out of the room.

I stand in the doorway of the restaurant and look at the menu. I sort of wish we *were* going in there, spending the evening alone together. Maybe that's exactly what we need – to do something different, something special, and reconnect after the weird couple of months we've had. I wonder what Mrs Bolt would do if we just didn't turn up.

'Hey, you.' Thomas has snuck up behind me.

'Hey.' I turn to kiss him and I'm so shocked that I

can't speak for a second. He looks good – *really* good. He's slicked back his hair so I can actually see his face for a change. His clothes look brand new – even the shoes. He looks exactly how you should look when you're going to a fancy restaurant for dinner – he's even wearing a tie. 'You scrub up *well*,' I say, standing back to have a proper look.

He's embarrassed to have me staring at him, so he pulls me close and kisses me. 'Seriously,' I whisper in his ear, 'you look great.'

'You're just saying that because you're hoping to get lucky tonight . . .'

He tells me that I look beautiful and it sounds like he really means it. It's easy to remember why I fell for him when it's like this.

'Shall we go inside?' He puts his hand on my shoulder to usher me in but I don't move. 'What's the matter? You must be freezing out here . . . Why didn't you bring a coat?'

I have a decision to make. When it comes down to it, it's not even difficult. 'OK, promise you won't be annoyed . . . ?'

Instead of saying what he'd usually say – that he has no intention of doing any such thing until he knows what I'm talking about – he just says, 'I promise,' and smiles.

I tell him about the surprise party. I tell him everything. His shoulders slump with every detail. 'Oh,' he says. 'Right. OK.'

'And you have to make sure you act surprised when we walk in, because otherwise your mum will know I told you and she'll probably put me in front of a firing squad or something. I'm sorry. I know this is your worst nightmare. I'm so sorry.'

He looks gutted – a little boy who's just been told that Christmas is cancelled. 'So we were never going in there then?'

'Nope. But we *can* go. I'll phone tomorrow and book a table, OK? My treat. This was such a terrible idea . . . I should have said something to your parents. I should have stopped this. Forgive me? Please?'

He closes his eyes for a second and I wonder if he's going to dump me on the spot. I wouldn't blame him. A couple of weeks ago I'd have probably been relieved, but something's changed. The knowledge is inside me – it's been there all along but I wouldn't allow myself to see it. Things have been too confusing, with Laurel being back. I lost focus on what's important in *my* life. I do love him. He may not be perfect, and he drives me crazy on a regular basis, but I *love* him. And if he dumps me now, right here outside this restaurant, I will only have myself to blame.

330

Thomas straightens his shoulders, and maybe it's because it's his eighteenth birthday or maybe it's because I'm being ridiculous, but I'd swear that he really does look like a *man*. A proper grown-up man who makes proper grown-up decisions. He puts his hands on my shoulders and takes a deep breath. 'OK, let's do this thing.'

'You mean . . . ?'

'I *don't* blame you. I know what my mother's like when she's got an idea in her head. She's a force of nature. *Hurricanes* get out of her way when she's on a mission. So here's the plan: we will go inside and I will do my absolute best to act surprised, and if that's not working out for me I'll just hug you so that no one can see my face. We will eat dodgy party food and drink more than we should and I will do my best to introduce you to my extended family — if I can remember their names. I will even dance with you, if that's what it takes to prove to everyone that I'm having a good time.'

I'm somewhat taken aback by all of this. Especially the bit about dancing. I have never seen him dance — I can't even imagine him dancing. I'm tempted to say, 'Who are you and what the hell have you done with my boyfriend?' but that would be a bad idea. Instead I go for 'But you won't be, will you? Having fun, I mean. I'm so sorry I let this happen.'

'Hey,' he says softly, 'stop that. Anyway, who says I won't have fun? Maybe a surprise party complete with everyone I've ever met in my entire life is *exactly* the way I wanted to spend my eighteenth?'

'You're kidding, right?'

Thomas puts his arm around me and we walk towards the entrance to the pub. 'Of course . . . but as long as you're with me, I can get through anything.'

I push him up against the wall and kiss him. 'I love you, Thomas Bolt.'

He looks amused as he tells me that he loves me too.

Through the door and up the stairs and I hold the door open for Thomas and we enter the darkened room and SURPRISE!

Chapter 42

Thomas is good at this. Really good. No one seems to have any clue that he knew about the party. He keeps on shaking his head in disbelief and playfully punching his dad's shoulder. As soon as the whole 'surprise' bit was over, he hugged his mum and wagged a finger at me to tell me off. Everyone laughed at that. Mrs Bolt rewarded me with an approving nod.

As the drinks flow and the music gets louder, I start to see a whole new side to Thomas. He's confident and at ease as he introduces me to various members of his family. He keeps a hand on the small of my back, and it reassures me. The weight of it, the warmth of it. Because I am far from confident and at ease. There are too many people and the room is too hot and it's hard to breathe. But it gets better. And I'm pretty sure it's no coincidence that the getting better correlates with Thomas topping up my wine glass. He drinks steadily too; clearly that's his strategy for surviving the party.

An hour or so in, we are far from sober. Not drunk, exactly. Not stumbling or falling over or laughing uncontrollably. Just that perfect level where it's easy to talk to strangers and every song you hear reminds you of some happy memory or other. Where smiling is your default state, rather than something you have to think about.

A song comes on and Thomas and I exchange a look. He starts laughing first, but I'm not far behind. The song was playing on the stereo in his van the night we first had sex. He'd commented on it that night – 'how apt' – because the lyrics are filthy. Mrs Bolt must have delegated the choice of music this evening to one of her minions.

Thomas holds out his hand to me and bows. 'Who do you think you are? Mr Darcy?' I say. He laughs even though it wasn't particularly funny. I take his hand and we head on to the dance floor. No one else is dancing yet. I catch Martha's eye – she's still at the same table with the kids from school. I can tell she's surprised. She knows I hate being the centre of attention. But as soon as Thomas and I start dancing, I forget about the fact that people are looking at us. I don't care what

I look like, or the fact that I'm sweating, or that my limbs are flailing all over the place.

People join us on the dance floor after only a minute or so, as if they were just waiting for someone to be brave enough to be the first ones up here. It feels good to be brave for once. Martha's still watching so I beckon her over. She shakes her head, which is exactly what I would expect her to do. So I grab Thomas's arm and we make our way over to her table and I proceed to drag Martha from her seat. 'Wait, wait, WAIT!' she says, wriggling out of my grasp. Then she downs her glass of wine, pours another and downs that too and says, '*Now* I can dance.'

Martha takes a while to loosen up. She's self-conscious at first – half-heartedly moving from side to side, trying to look like she's enjoying herself. But before long she's properly dancing, and after ten minutes or so Thomas and Martha are engaged in some kind of dance battle with rules that only they seem to understand.

I'd never have believed it could be so much fun, dancing with them. It feels like something we should have done a long time ago.

When Mr and Mrs Bolt make their way on to the dance floor, I take it as my cue for a loo break. I check to see if Martha wants to come with me, but Thomas's dad is already twirling her around all over the place and she doesn't seem to be minding one bit.

Getting to the toilets is a bit of a mission. You have to go downstairs and through the main room of the pub, which is packed full of people watching a football match. I recognize a couple of men from the party hovering at the bottom of the stairs. They probably know full well how Mrs Bolt will react if she catches them loitering down here. After I pee, a quick look in the mirror confirms that my make-up is just about OK. Anyway, I left my bag upstairs so there's not a whole lot I can do about it right now.

A woman comes out of one of the stalls, washes her hands, then starts putting on some lipstick. Her face contorts in the mirror and I look away. Not before she catches me though. 'It's Faith, isn't it?' She must be one of the only people Thomas hasn't introduced me to, but it's obvious she's related to Mrs Bolt.

I nod and say, 'Hi,' before heading over to the hand dryers. Should I have offered to shake her hand? Is that something people *do* in pub toilets?

'SORRY, I FORGOT MY MANNERS! I'M DAWN! THOMAS'S AUNT!' she shouts, unwilling to wait the extra few seconds for the hand dryer to stop.

'NICE TO MEET YOU!' And of course the dryer stops in the middle of me shouting, making me look like the kind of lunatic who shouts random things in pub toilets.

'Keep me company for a minute, will you, love? I've been sweating like a pig on a sunbed up there! This new powder I've got is supposed to work miracles, but even J.C. himself would have trouble sorting out *this* face.' It takes a moment or two for me to realize she's talking about Jesus. I watch as she powders her face and it *does* seem to do the trick. I'm sure she'd let me borrow it if I asked, but there is no chance of me doing that.

It takes me approximately five seconds to realize that Thomas's aunt is one of those people who can have an entire conversation by themselves, with little or no input from the person they're supposedly talking to.

Dawn talks about how she's been *dying* to meet me, but she hardly ever gets to visit because she lives so far away. She tells me all about the farm where she lives and how far it is from the nearest village, and the fact that she insists on going into town at least once a week. Within a couple of minutes I know more about Thomas's aunt than I do about some members of my own family. I'm hoping for someone else to come into the toilets and distract her so I can make my escape, but the door remains firmly shut. A loud roar erupts from outside and I briefly wonder if I can feign an interest in football, but then Dawn is suddenly saying something that interests me. 'It's so funny how things turn out, isn't it? Who would have thought that you two would end up together? God works in mysterious ways, doesn't He?' I have no idea what she's talking about. 'It was the tenth anniversary that did it, you know.'

'Tenth anniversary of what?'

Dawn looks at me like I'm stupid. 'Laurel going missing! All those programmes and articles. You couldn't avoid the story if you tried . . . not that you'd want to try, but you know what I mean. He read all the books, you know – about all sorts of awful unsolved crimes, not just about your sister. Serial killers and that sort of thing.' She shudders at the thought.

I stare at my reflection in the mirror and see myself starting to understand.

'It only lasted a few months, but Cath was a little worried all the same. Such a morbid thing for a young lad to be interested in!' Dawn shakes her head and giggles. 'Sometimes you just have to let these things run their course. If there's one thing I know about teenagers, it's that they go through phases. My Kevin dyed his hair bright blue when he was fifteen and I didn't say a word. Sure enough, three weeks later, he was sick of it and asked me to take him to my salon to get it dyed back! With Thomas it was poetry, wasn't it? He got keen on that and the whole crime thing sort of fell by the wayside. He loves his poems, that boy. I like limericks, myself.'

I try to smile but the muscles in my face seem reluctant to cooperate.

'Laurel's coming tonight, isn't she?' Dawn looks at her wrist; there's a tan line where her watch would be. 'I thought she'd be here by now. Everyone's dying to meet her!' Dawn moves closer to me and I worry that she's going in for a hug. Instead she brushes her knuckle on my cheek; it's oddly intimate. 'Now come on, enough chatting; let's get back to the party!'

She links her arm through mine and leads me towards the door. When we're snaking our way through the crowd of drinkers at the bar, I tell her I have to make a phone call so I'll see her upstairs. 'Don't be long – I think they're bringing out the cake soon!'

I stand outside in the cold.

My relationship is based on a lie. It would never have even started – would have been dead in the water – if Thomas had told the truth. I'd honestly believed that he was the *one* person who wasn't interested in my sister. But *of course* he was. Just like all the others.

One question fights its way to the top, clambering over all the others crowding my brain. Was Thomas only interested in me because of my sister? Is *that* why he pursued me?

I'm not even sure I want to know the answer.

Chapter 43

I can't stay outside forever and I can't just go home; my bag is upstairs.

Laurel should be here soon. I shouldn't blame her for this. Maybe I should even thank her? If it wasn't for her, maybe Thomas would never have even spoken to me. I would still be waiting for someone – anyone – to take an interest in me. I would still be a virgin.

I need to talk to him. I need to know the truth – about all of it. Because even if he only wanted to get to know me to find out more about my sister, that can't be the reason he stayed with me. It *can't* be. What we have now, what I felt when I was dancing with him a few minutes ago, that's real. It's real and it's mine, and it has nothing to do with my sister.

I expect to hear the music pumping as I trudge up the stairs, but there's silence. Everyone's gathering around a spot in the centre of the room. Thomas is standing next to a trolley with an enormous cake on it. Mrs Bolt is standing next to him, her arm around his shoulders. Thomas's dad is taking a photo of the cake. I can't help thinking that Mrs Bolt did this on purpose – wheeling out the birthday cake when I was out of the room.

Thomas is looking around, scanning faces. His eyes settle on me and he smiles and waves me over. People turn and shuffle out of the way to let me pass. I stand next to him while everyone sings 'Happy Birthday'. Thomas reaches for my hand and squeezes it twice. Two squeezes means: Are you OK? I squeeze back twice, meaning: I'm fine.

The cake must have cost a fortune. I recognize most of the titles on the spines of the cake books – they're Thomas's favourites. There are eighteen candles on top of the cake. I count them while I sing (mime).

When the singing stops, everybody cheers. Mrs Bolt leans forward and says, 'Go on then. Blow out the candles. Don't forget to make a wish!'

Thomas turns to look at me and I have the strangest feeling – the kind of feeling someone like Laney Finch would call a premonition. I can picture Thomas and I standing in a different room, in front of a different cake. This cake is white and tiered. The image is gone before I can get a grip on it, but it leaves my heart beating fast and my head spinning.

A hush descends on the room as Thomas leans over, preparing to blow out the candles. I catch Martha's eye and she mimes a yawn and I love her for that. Mrs Bolt hisses, 'What are you waiting for?!' and Thomas takes a deep breath, ready to blow out all the candles in one puff.

The silence is making me uneasy – it's as if people think Thomas is trying to defuse a bomb instead of blow out some candles on an overpriced cake that probably won't even taste good.

The silence stretches out as Thomas exhales, moving his head to catch every single flame. A door opens. Doors open and close all the time, and people barely even notice. No one apart from Thomas noticed my entrance a couple of minutes ago. *Everyone* notices this entrance. Heads turn, and I swear there are even a couple of gasps.

It's my sister, of course. Choosing the worst possible time to arrive – or the best, depending on your point of view.

She's wearing the red dress.

Laurel looks like a film star who took a wrong turning on her way to the red carpet. Red shoes, a little black clutch that I recognize as Mum's. Her hair flows over her shoulders, shiny and glossy. Nicely judged make-up.

Laurel stops in the doorway. People stare.

Someone – I don't know who, but Dawn would be my first guess – starts clapping. A couple more people follow suit, and then the whole room is filled with applause. Martha's clapping too – traitor. The last people to join in are Mrs Bolt and Thomas. At least he has the sense to look at me in bafflement before he puts his hands together.

Laurel looks as confused as I feel. Why are these people *clapping* for her? It's not *her* birthday. She spots me and hurries over, head down, a shy smile on her face. A couple of people pat her back as she passes them. 'Hi! Sorry I'm late . . . and sorry about that . . . I don't know why they . . .' She turns to Thomas. 'Anyway! Happy birthday! I'm not interrupting anything, am I?'

Thomas gestures to the blown-out candles, tendrils of smoke wisping upward. 'Not at all. Would you like some cake?'

I stand back as Thomas introduces Laurel to his mother. Mrs Bolt embraces my sister warmly. It's weird. You'd think she wouldn't want her here, if she'd been so worried about Thomas's 'interest' in

Laurel's story. But it seems the lure of my sister is irresistible to her too.

Laurel asks me to hold her bag while she helps Thomas cut the cake. Surely that should be my job?

Some people are still staring, but most of them have returned to the serious business of drinking. Laurel seems perfectly at ease, despite the fact that she's seriously overdressed. Mrs Bolt compliments her on the dress (of course) and asks her where it's from. Laurel says she can't remember, which is an odd lie for her to tell.

Laurel and Thomas hand round little plates, each with a slice of book cake and a tiny fork. The napkins have books on them too. Clearly the one thing Mrs Bolt knows about her son is that he likes to read.

'You look like you need a drink.' Martha appears with a glass of red wine.

'Haven't you got anything stronger?' I ask, after a couple of huge gulps.

'Nope. You have to pay for spirits. So . . . Your sister looks . . .' Martha does this weird grimace, making it look as if the bottom left side of her mouth has been caught by a fish-hook. I look at her expectantly, waiting for the end of the sentence. If Martha says the wrong thing, this will be a very short conversation. '. . . kind of ridiculous.'

I burst out laughing, narrowly avoiding spraying red wine in Martha's face. 'Come on,' she says. 'Have you tried the chicken satay skewers? I've had seven.'

There's one satay skewer left and I manage to nab it just as someone else is reaching for the platter. I'm wondering whether to tell Martha about Thomas. She might tell me to break up with him. And I'm not sure how I'd feel if she told me to do that. Maybe I'd be better off telling her tomorrow. I need to figure out how *I* want to handle the situation first. I don't want to do anything I'll regret.

My plan for the rest of the evening emerges before I've put the satay skewer in one of the little jam jars that have been placed on the table for that express purpose. Mrs Bolt really has thought of everything. Military precision, I guess. The plan: get drunk enough not to care that my boyfriend may or may not only be going out with me because of my 'famous' sister. Forget all about it, just for a couple more hours. Try to spend as little time as possible with the aforementioned boyfriend and sister, because spending time in their presence will make the not caring somewhat difficult, and the forgetting even harder.

After about twenty minutes, Thomas and Laurel make their way over to us with two plates of cake. Thomas hands one of the plates to Martha and she thanks him. Laurel tries to hand me a plate, but I say I'm not hungry.

'But you have to have some birthday cake! Isn't it bad luck if you don't?' Laurel waves the plate under my nose.

'No. It's really not.'

'It's really good, you know,' says Thomas.

'I said I'm not hungry.' I at least make an effort to keep the edge out of my voice.

Thomas kisses me on the cheek and says he'll save me some for later. 'You might need it to soak up some of that alcohol,' he says with a laugh.

Martha comes to the rescue, wading into the awkward silence. 'Laurel! That dress is so . . .' Tacky. I want her to say tacky. Or over-the-top. Or even inappropriate. But Martha doesn't even get the chance to finish her sentence because Laurel says, 'Thanks!'

One of Thomas's uncles interrupts this little scene with a request for a second slice of cake. 'Duty calls,' Thomas says apologetically. 'Laurel, if you want to stay with Faith, I can take care of this.' But then the uncle sticks out his hand to her and says, 'Laurel Logan, it is *such* a pleasure to meet you.' She turns away to talk to him. No wonder it's taking the two of them so long to distribute the cake – everyone wants the chance to talk to Laurel. She didn't need to dress up like that to get people to notice her; all she had to do was step through the door.

I sit in a corner with Martha and drink. I drink so much that even she tells me it might be a good idea to slow down a bit. 'But we're supposed to be *celebrating*!' There's no hint of a smile on my face when I say this. Martha asks me what's up. 'Is it Laurel?'

I clink my glass against Martha's, so hard that some wine sloshes on the table.

'Do you want to talk about it?'

'No,' I say, adding, 'thanks,' as an afterthought.

Martha shrugs; she knows better than to push it.

'Mind if I join you ladies?' Martha and I look up to see a guy a couple of years older than us, shaved head, stubbled jaw. He's wearing a tight T-shirt with a scooped neckline, as if he has cleavage to show off. He looks, in short, like someone Martha and I would never talk to (and also, coincidentally, like someone who would never talk to us).

I gesture to the spare seat next to me. 'Go ahead.' I ignore the glare that Martha's sure to be giving me and turn to face the guy. 'Are you a cousin then?'

'I *am* a cousin, as it happens. Most people are, aren't

they?' He smiles. He thinks he's being charming and amusing. 'I'm Steve. It's a pleasure to meet you.' I will let him sit next to me and try his best to be charming and amusing, because I need the distraction. The more I look at him, the more distracting he becomes. I just wish he'd stop talking.

Chapter 44

Martha is not happy, especially when she discovers that Steve is essentially a gatecrasher. He was downstairs watching the football and came upstairs 'for a slash'. Martha wrinkles her nose in disgust at that little nugget of information. 'The toilets are *down*stairs. Obviously.'

Steve laughs. 'Well, I know that *now*, don't I?'

'So hadn't you better go then? We wouldn't want you having an accident, would we?' Normally Martha's snideness would make me laugh, but now it just seems rude.

'Thank you for your concern about the state of my bladder. I appreciate it, I really do. But I went for a piss and came back up here, so we're all good. The football was dull *as*, anyway. I'd much rather spend my time talking to beautiful ladies.' The way he says 'ladies' is almost too much for me. *Laydeeez*. 'So whose party is this anyway?'

'Her *boy*friend's,' Martha supplies, helpfully.

'Boyfriend, eh? Fair enough. Which one is he then, this boyfriend of yours? If I had a girlfriend like you, I wouldn't leave you alone for a *second*. You never know who's going to swoop in, do you?'

'I'm perfectly capable of looking after myself, thank you very much. I don't need him to protect me.' I sound prim and awful, but Steve doesn't seem to care.

He lifts his head and gives me a look – *the* look, you might call it – and says, 'I'd swoop in on you any day of the week, and twice on Sunday!'

'What does that even *mean*?' Martha's had enough now. I'm glad, because I'd quite like her to go away. 'I'm going to the loo.' It's as if she read my mind. 'Will you be OK?' she asks me as she stands up.

'Of course she will!' Steve says, patting my knee. 'I'll look after her.' I don't look at him to check, but I'm willing to bet he accompanies this with a wink. Martha's facial expression seems to suggest as much anyway.

I learn a lot about Steve in the next few minutes. He's twenty-one years old, studying tourism at the local college. He's the youngest of three brothers. He likes drinking, clubbing and girls, mostly. He asks me what clubs I go to, and seems disappointed when

I say, 'None.' He says we should go clubbing together sometime – 'As friends . . . I wouldn't want to step on anyone's toes!' – and asks for my number.

I surprise myself by giving it to him. That's probably when I realize I am drunk. Properly drunk, not just halfway there. 'So can I call you then? Your boyfriend won't mind?' His hand is on my thigh. His hand is heavier than Thomas's. Meatier, somehow.

'Am I supposed to believe that you'd care if he *did* mind?'

'You got me there.' Steve laughs. I like his laugh; it's genuine. Real.

I know I should tell him to move his hand, especially when I catch Dawn staring at me. But I don't. I tell myself that if he moves his hand higher up, *then* I'll say something. It's perfectly OK to touch someone's leg – it's friendly. Reassuring. It doesn't have to be sexual, does it? Anyway, it's not as if I'm touching *him*. I'm just sitting here, minding my own business, drinking more than is good for me.

'Seriously though, which one is he? No, wait, let me guess . . . Is it *that* guy?'

'No.'

'That one? The one with the nose?'

'Well, you're getting closer. My boyfriend does indeed have a nose.'

Steve makes several more guesses and I say no each time. He even makes me stand up and crane my neck to see guys on the other side of the room. At least that solves the hand-on-leg problem.

'You're having a laugh, aren't you? You don't have a boyfriend, do you? Your friend just said that to try and get rid of me.' We sit down and he moves his chair even closer to mine.

Steve is talking but I'm not listening. I'm looking round the room. But I'm not looking for Thomas; I'm looking for the flash of red. I'm looking for the telltale crowd of adoring fans, but I don't see it. I spy Martha, back with the kids from school. She's obviously decided to leave me to make my own mistakes. I thought friends were supposed to stop you from doing things you'll regret, instead of scarpering at the first hint of trouble.

'So what do you say? You up for it?' Steve whispers, and I realize he's sitting so close he's practically on my lap.

'Up for what?' As if it's not completely obvious.

'Getting out of here . . . You can come back to mine.'

I laugh, and at first Steve laughs along with me, but after a couple of seconds he realizes my laugh isn't the flirtatious, conspiratorial one he was expecting. It is not a nice sort of laugh at all. I stand up, a little unsteadily this time. 'There is no way I would ever, *ever* do that. I mean . . . *ever*.' His face is a picture.

I walk away without another word, without bumping into anyone (although there are a couple of near misses). I say hi to Dawn as I pass by and she pretends not to hear me.

I feel a little bit sick. Whether that's down to the alcohol or having acted completely out of character, I can't say. I should probably go to the loo in case I really do need to throw up. But there's something I need to do first.

Thomas is nowhere to be seen. My sister is nowhere to be seen. I stopped believing in coincidences a long time ago.

It's funny, really. When you read about these things or see them on TV, it's always this huge shock. This big dramatic reveal to end the chapter or just before the credits roll. The girl or the woman – it's hardly ever a man – never seems to *know*. It's like Dad's always saying about those boring old war movies he loves so much: as soon as a character says something like 'I'm getting married next month' or 'My wife is having a baby – due any day now', you know they're dead meat. So I suppose in this case it would be something like 'My boyfriend and I are sooooo happy together' or 'Tonight I realized I really do love him after all'.

Dead meat. Except I'm not dying. But when I see them together, my heart certainly feels like a lump of dead meat, nestled inside my ribcage.

I knew. As I checked downstairs and outside and in the toilets, I *knew*. When I finally went to open that door – the one marked 'PRIVATE' – I knew what I would find on the other side. I didn't need to see them together; it would only make things harder for me. But I wanted them to know that I knew.

There are chairs stacked up haphazardly against the walls. A strip light on the ceiling bathes the room in a sickly yellow glow. She is standing with her back to the door. He is standing too. He has one hand on her back. I can't see what her hands are doing, which is just as well, I suppose.

Thomas looks over Laurel's shoulder and sees me standing there. 'Wait! It's not . . .' I stare at him. He doesn't finish his sentence, thank God. *It's not what you think.* One of the oldest clichés in the book.

Laurel turns around and the expression on her face isn't what I expect. It's not shock or embarrassment or shame or even surprise. It's impossible to read, notable only for its nothingness. She doesn't say a word.

Thomas moves away from Laurel, like he's afraid she might lunge at him again. Because that's what must have happened. There is no question in my mind about who is more to blame here. Of course, there's still enough blame to go round for Thomas to have his fair share. But this was her fault; she *made* this happen. 'Faith, I can explain! Can we talk about this? Please?' Thomas begs.

'No. We can't.'

'What are you saying?'

'I'm saying that I never want to talk to you again.' I'm amazed that I'm not crying. I am made of steel and ice.

'Faith, *please*! Don't do this. You're making a mistake. We were just . . .' His words trail off into nothing. He takes a couple of steps towards me and I step back. His eyes are pleading, but I am made of steel and ice.

'I mean it. Don't call me, don't come round to the house, don't talk to me at school. We're finished.' Just like that. My first relationship, over. Steel. Ice.

Thomas looks pissed off. He actually has the nerve to be annoyed at me. 'You're making a big mistake.'

'The only mistake I made was going out with you

in the first place. You know full well I wouldn't have gone anywhere near you if I'd known you were only interested in finding out more about my sister.'

That shocks them both; I almost smile. 'What are you talking about?' he says.

'I had a nice little chat with your aunt earlier. She told me all about it. Your "true crime" phase or whatever. Who do you think you are? Sherlock Fucking Holmes?'

'What is she talking about?' Laurel asks Thomas, but he just shakes his head.

'Oh, did he forget to mention it to you as well? So, it turns out that Thomas here got a little bit *too* interested in your story. Read all the books, watched all the TV shows. Probably had a fucking scrapbook for all I know.'

'Is this true?' Her expression is still unreadable, her voice almost bored.

Thomas is squirming now. 'It's not as bad as it sounds . . . honestly.'

I laugh. 'And this –' I gesture with my hand – 'is not as bad as it looks, I suppose? You two deserve each other. Really. I hope you'll be very happy together.'

I open the door to leave, but close it again because there's something else I have to say. I look at Laurel, still red-carpet fresh, out of place in this dingy little storage room. I know I shouldn't say this. I know it's wrong, even after everything she's done. But I want to see her flinch. I want to see her feel *something*.

She stares at me, waiting. And I think maybe she knows what's coming. I clear my throat, which has chosen this exact moment to close up, as if it's trying to stop me from saying what I'm about to say.

I take one last look at Thomas (pathetic, tearful) before my gaze alights on her.

'I wish you'd never come back.'

Chapter 45

She doesn't flinch. There's no hint of pain in her eyes. The first reaction is a slight tightening around the jaw. And maybe I'm imagining it – I must be, surely – because it almost looks like she nods.

'Faith!' Thomas is horrified.

I ignore him and address her. 'I think it would be best if you stay at Mum's tonight. I'm sure Thomas will make sure you get home safely.'

'What will I tell her? She'll know something's wrong,' says Laurel.

'I don't care what you tell her. You could tell her you threw yourself at my boyfriend . . .' The tears arrive now, seconds before I was going to make my escape. 'Or . . . or just make something up. You're good at that.' I spit out these last words, hoping the venom in my voice will distract them from the tears spilling down my cheeks.

Thomas wants to put his arms around me. He wants to comfort me, I can tell. This must not happen. I must stay strong. 'You know something, Thomas?' There's hope in his face. He thinks that as long as I'm still here, talking, there's a chance things will be OK. He's wrong. I look at Laurel, who opens her mouth to speak (to apologize?). I get there first. 'You don't know how lucky you are — being an only child. Having siblings isn't all it's cracked up to be.' A thought strikes me — a terrible thought, but no worse than what I've already said. One last shot at hurting her the way she's hurt me.

'Then again,' I say, swiping at the tears on my face, 'it's not as if you're my real sister anyway. Not by *blood*. If Mum and Dad had known how much pain you'd cause, I bet they never would have adopted you.'

I don't wait to see her reaction — or his. I leave the room and head back to the party. I manage to get my coat and bag without bumping into Martha or Steve, then I leave. I walk to Dad and Michel's place even though it takes nearly an hour. Martha texts to ask where I am. I tell her I'm not feeling very well — a lie that also happens to be the truth. She's annoyed at me for bailing without saying anything, but I tell her I puked and that mollifies her somewhat.

*

Dad's already in bed when I arrive. Michel is on the sofa, reading. Tonks is curled up next to him. I tell Michel the same lie I told Martha.

'Too much to drink?'

I nod and head to the kitchen to grab a pint of water.

'Where's your sister?' Michel follows me and leans against the counter, Tonks winding her way around his legs.

'She decided to stay at Mum's.'

'Why?'

'How should I know? I'm not her keeper.' Sullen, childish.

'OK, OK. Sorry I asked!' He's wearing old trackie bottoms and a France rugby shirt. His feet are bare. His face is kind, attentive, worried. 'Do you want to talk about it?'

I gulp down the water. God, I'm tempted to tell him everything. Every little thing I've been feeling and every not so little thing she's done. Michel would say all the right things. He wouldn't blame me for the terrible things I said to her. He would understand where they came from – that dark, bitter place inside of me. The place I'm usually so careful to keep hidden from the world.

I know I would feel better for talking to him.

And that he might make me see that there's a way for Thomas and me to work through this. To get past the fact that he kissed my sister, and the fact that he lied to me all this time about not really knowing about her story. And Michel would put Laurel and me in a room together and force us to talk. Maybe she would explain why she did what she did. And perhaps I would understand and we would hug and agree to forget all about it, because sisters shouldn't let a boy come between them. Of course I would have to apologize too. I'd have to say that I didn't mean those things I said. That I *am* glad she came home. That the fact that we're not actually related by blood means nothing to me. She's my sister – always has been, always will be.

I look at Michel, and the temptation to break down is so strong that I can barely stand it. I close my eyes, down the rest of the water, then say, 'There's nothing to talk about. Thanks though. And if you could forget to tell Dad about the puking, I'd really appreciate it.'

'Your secret's safe with me, *ma chérie*.'

'You're a poet and don't even know it.'

His eyebrows knit in confusion and I have to explain yet another bit of weird British humour. It feels normal, doing this. Michel and me staying up late after Dad's gone to bed, talking about anything and everything. That's how things used to be – *before*.

Before Laurel. And with that thought the moment — the tiny crumb of comfort of talking to Michel — is swept away.

I hug him goodnight, and if he notices that I hold on a little too tight and for a little too long, he doesn't say anything. I leave him in the kitchen, crouching down to pick up Tonks. 'You sleep well, OK? You'll feel better in the morning.'

I'm pretty sure he's wrong about that.

Chapter 46

I sleep surprisingly well and wake up at half past six. I'm not too hungover, which is pretty miraculous under the circumstances. There's a text from Martha waiting on my phone. It takes me a while to decipher it (autocorrect gone wild, drunken fingers) – the gist is that she might have kissed that guy Steve. It's so like Martha to say she *might* have done something that she blatantly *has* done. It's *unlike* Martha to kiss a random guy, particularly one like Steve. I'm not sure how I feel about this.

Thomas has left three voicemails; I delete them without listening.

There are no messages of any kind from Laurel. I don't know what to make of that. Is she sorry? Is she upset about what happened? Then that niggling question: is she even at home? When I close my eyes it's all too easy to picture the two of them together, in the back of his van. Thomas wouldn't do that to me, I'm almost sure of that. But I can't say the same about her.

Has Laurel been after him the whole time? Was that why she spied on us having sex? It doesn't seem to add up, especially not when you consider everything that's happened to her. For the first time, I consider the idea that maybe I got it wrong – that it wasn't what it looked like. After all, what had I seen, really? The two of them standing close together, his hand on her back. The angle had meant that I couldn't actually see if their mouths were touching. He could have been checking to see if she had something in her eye. They could have been whispering, exchanging secrets so sensitive they had to leave the party to find somewhere more private and, even then, they needed to be whispered in case there were any recording devices in the immediate vicinity.

There are possibilities *other* than kissing. That's what I try to tell myself as I shower and dress and put on the bare minimum of make-up. I add a couple more ideas to the list: a huge spot had suddenly erupted on Thomas's nose and Laurel was helping him apply some concealer so it wouldn't show up in the photos; Thomas had lost his voice from trying to shout above the music upstairs so Laurel had to stand really close in order to hear his hoarse whispers. They're beyond flimsy though, these 'possibilities' of mine. They are the preposterous imaginings of someone who doesn't want to accept the truth.

I rush to leave the flat before Michel and Dad get up. I leave a note on the kitchen counter. It's much easier to lie on paper than in person. Having said that, the lie I do tell is more than a little lame: a school project, spending the day in the library.

I wander the streets, but my feet start to hurt, so I actually do go to the library in the end. It calms me, walking among the shelves, picking up books and putting them down again. Then I accidentally end up in the poetry section, which makes me think of Thomas and spoils things a bit.

My legs take me up the stairs and past seven rows of shelves to the part of the library I know the best. Over the years I've spent a lot of time sitting cross-legged on the floor, reading as fast as I can, worrying that Mum will realize I'm not in the children's library downstairs. She never caught me though, not once.

The three books are all there, present and correct. I thought someone might have borrowed them, what with all the press recently. But these days people can get all the information they need on the Internet, can't they? And these books are out of date now; the story they tell is incomplete.

Little Girl, Lost. Schmaltzy, over the top, written by a tabloid journalist who'd never even bothered to speak to my parents.

TAKEN! The REAL story of Laurel Logan. Another tabloid journalist, this one convinced that Laurel had been sold into slavery and/or prostitution. He spent months travelling around Europe trying to find her, and made bold claims that he'd arrived at some brothel in Eastern Europe mere *hours* after Laurel had been moved by 'gangland bosses' who knew that he was 'hot on their heels'. (The police had followed up, of course. Lies, all lies.)

And then there's Jeanette Hayes. The book that my mother wouldn't allow in the house. She wouldn't have been happy about me reading any of these books, but if she'd caught me reading the Hayes one she'd have gone apeshit. Mum always said that Hayes had some kind of vendetta against us. She refused to even say her name. In our house, Jeanette Hayes has always been known as 'that woman'.

I hate her for what she did to our family. I've been *conditioned* to hate her. I mean, Mum always *tried* not to talk about things like that when I was in the room, but she failed often and badly. Maybe that's not quite fair; as a child I developed a habit of listening at doors before I entered rooms and after I left them. I heard many, many things that weren't meant for my ears, but I never felt guilty about it. I saw it as my right.

I sit down on the floor and cross my legs. The Jeanette Hayes book isn't as worn as the others; it's a new, updated edition that I haven't seen before. I check the date and see that it was published last year. I must have read the old version of the book four or five times. I would mark my place by folding over the corner of the page and continue where I left off the next time I was in the library. Mum and I didn't come to the library every week so it could take me a long time to finish reading it. Back then I was looking for clues – reasons why this woman hated my family. I couldn't understand why she didn't care about Laurel, why she was the lone voice of dissent when everyone else was saying that everything possible must be done to find my sister.

Hayes argued that kids went missing every day, that there was no good reason for the police and the media to focus on 'Little Laurel Logan' when there were all these other kids being ignored. The word that kept cropping up was 'injustice'. She seemed to be saying that just because Laurel was white and blonde and pretty and middle class, no one should care. But it wasn't Laurel's fault that the media latched on to her story. Why should she be punished just because people were more interested in her than the other missing children Hayes talked about?

I read the introduction once again. I know the words so well I could almost recite them by heart. And the strangest thing is that today I can almost see what Hayes was getting at. It wasn't fair. Of course it wasn't. Every missing child should be a priority. Who knows how many of these kids could have been found if even a tenth of the manpower and money and resources that were invested in the search for Laurel had been spent looking for them? It's a horrible, horrible thing to think about. That's why Jeanette Hayes got so much flack for it, I suppose. The hate mail and the death threats were because people didn't *want* to think about it. They didn't want to see the truth of it – the awful truth that they skipped over a one-paragraph news story about a missing black kid from a council estate in London without even blinking. They would carry on sipping their coffee or tea or orange juice without taking even a second to worry about the fate of that child. And if, by some miracle, they *did* think about it, they would assume that the kid had run away or been snatched by their deadbeat dad (because even in a tiny paragraph the journalist had somehow managed to find space to mention that the kid had three siblings, all with different fathers).

It's despicable. And I'm despicable for not realizing that sooner. Even though I pored over Hayes's book for hours and hours, I often skim-read the parts about the other missing children. I didn't care about them. I only cared about Laurel. But at least I have an excuse – two excuses really: I was young, and Laurel was my *sister*. Still, I never thought to check the Internet to see what became of any of the other kids. For all I know, half of them are back with their families now. For all I know, some of them are dead.

I slam the book shut. I can't read any more. The thing I'm trying really hard not to think about is whether my little Jeanette Hayes epiphany is because this is the first time I've read her words since Laurel came home (possible), or whether it's because I'm reading them *today*. If I'd looked at the book a few days after Laurel came home, I'd probably still be calling Jeanette Hayes 'that woman' and hating her, because that was what's expected in our family. Which leaves me with an uncomfortable explanation for my change of heart. I agree with Hayes now, this morning, today, that too much attention was paid to 'Little Laurel Logan', because now, this morning, today, I hate not-so-little Laurel Logan. And even though I said those words in anger last night — not even believing them myself — I realize now that they were true.

I *do* wish she'd never come home.

Chapter 47

I should talk to Laurel. I know that's the sensible thing to do. We have to fix this, if not for our sake, then for Mum and Dad's. The two of us have to find a way to live together, even though she's exactly the opposite of the kind of person I want to live with.

With Thomas, it's easy. I can cut him out of my life like a malignant tumour. Of course I'll still see him at school, but I can tune him out, pretend his existence means nothing to me until it means nothing to me. Martha will be on my side, no question about that. Soon he will be nothing more than one of the 'Others', as Martha used to call everyone at school who wasn't us. Thomas will cease to be Us and will become Them.

Laurel is family though, and family's different. *Blood is thicker than water.* Even though we're not *actually* related by blood. I can't cut her out; all I can do is learn to live with her, try to minimize the damage she does.

I text her: *We should talk.*

I carry on reading Jeanette Hayes's book while I wait for a reply. This time I read some of the stories about the other kids. Each one represents a family destroyed. A family like mine, but different. We are the lucky ones. Our missing jigsaw piece was found and returned to us. Who knows what these families are still going through?

Half an hour later there's still no reply from Laurel, but I'm not giving up that easily. Perhaps she's scared to talk to me, worried I'll tell Mum and Dad. She has no way of knowing that's the last thing I'd do – that it would be excruciatingly embarrassing to admit that my sister stole my boyfriend. (*Has* she, though? Has she stolen him? Is he gone for good? There's no way of knowing unless I talk to him.)

I send another text: *We'll be OK, you know.*

I nearly didn't hit 'send' on that one, because I doubt it's the truth. And if *I'm* doubting it, then Laurel probably is too.

I read more stories, more families torn apart, more parents bitter that their little boy or girl was considered less important than my sister. I wonder what it was like for Hayes, actually sitting down with these people, witnessing their grief first-hand.

My phone buzzes with a text. Finally. But it's not from Laurel. It's from Kirsty Fairlie: *Hey. Am in town. Fancy a coffee? Flying out tomorrow.*

We've been texting a bit since we all had lunch together. The Fairlies have been doing the rounds, looking at universities and staying with various relatives. I type a reply: *Can't today, I'm ill. Sorry!*

I'm about to send the message when I change my mind. I can't just stay here all day, can I? Plus I'm starving. And Kirsty is nice, if a little loud. It might take my mind off things. So I text her back and we arrange to meet in a coffee shop that's about twenty minutes away from the library. I put the Hayes book back on the shelf, ignoring the temptation to shove it in my bag. Then I rearrange the shelf so that the book is standing in front of the others, with the cover facing out. Other people should read this book; it's important.

Kirsty's already there, tucking into a slice of Victoria sponge. I order the same and ask for a slice of carrot cake too. Kirsty gives me a look as if to say 'Greedy bitch!' and I mutter something about having forgotten to have lunch. Then she orders some carrot cake too and says, 'Well, I had my lunch but it was bloody revolting. Jeez, the food in this country is rank. Why can't you people even make a proper sandwich?'

Usually I'd feel the urge to defend my country, maybe say something snide, like she should go back to Australia if the food here is so terrible. (*Chuck another prawn on the barbie.*) But I just nod and agree with her, because she's not wrong.

We talk about our plans for uni, a subject that we didn't get round to at lunch because that was all Laurel this and Laurel that. It turns out that there are a couple of the same universities on our lists. She asks which one is my top choice, and I say, 'Whichever is furthest away.' It doesn't come out quite right though; I'd meant it to sound like a joke, like something anyone might say when they're talking about escaping from their family. But from the way Kirsty is looking at me, I can tell she caught the bitterness in my voice. I try to make light of it and say something about not wanting Mum to turn up on my doorstep every weekend, but Kirsty leans towards me, looking concerned. Her hair brushes over the top of her Victoria sponge, but I don't say anything. 'Are you OK? You seem a little . . . I don't know.'

A sip of tea buys time. A second sip buys more. 'I'm fine. Just tired. Late night.' Two-word sentences, stripped bare of emotion.

'Are you sure?' God, she's as bad as Michel. I hate people being nice to me when I'm trying not to cry. Hate it.

This time the 'I'm fine' dies on my lips and is swiftly replaced by 'Not really'. And the desire to talk is just too overwhelming. It's like when I talked to Kay, but better because I know nothing is being recorded.

I don't tell Kirsty everything of course. Just the high(low)lights. I don't tell her about Laurel walking in on me and Thomas having sex, because nobody needs to hear that. I do tell her about the book deal and how I'm only doing it for Laurel's sake and how does she repay me? By kissing my boyfriend.

'Holy shit!' Kirsty says, sitting back in her chair. 'That is fucked *up*.' And I swear I could kiss her right now. It's such a relief to be talking to someone who isn't Laurel or Thomas or even Martha, and to have her say exactly what I've been thinking: it *is* fucked up. 'What did you do to them?' Her eyes are wide, and her expression is sort of gleeful, but I don't really mind.

'What do you mean?'

'Well, I can tell you something for nothing . . . if it had been my sister and my boyfriend, I'd have given *her* a good slap and kicked *him* in the nads. At the very least there would have been a drink chucked in someone's face.'

'Um . . . I didn't really *do* anything. Just . . . you know . . . said some stuff.'

Kirsty's disappointed. 'Like what?'

I'm too embarrassed to say. 'Just . . . *stuff.*'

'Aw, mate, you didn't *cry*, did you?'

I nod.

She shakes her head sadly. 'Ah well, can't be helped. No use crying over spilt tears. You dumped him on the spot though, right? Tell me you did *that* at least?'

I nod again. Someone seems to have pressed my mute button.

'Thank fuck for that. *Bastard.*'

I clear my throat. 'I'm more angry with her than him.' It feels shameful to admit this, as if it's a betrayal of my sex.

'I don't blame you. He's just some guy, right? Like, I'm sure you love – loved, past tense, thank you very much – him and everything, but he's just a bloke. She's your *sister*. Nothing should come between you two. Blood is—'

'Don't say it. Please, don't say it.'

Kirsty sits back, shoves some more cake in her mouth. I'm grateful for the pause in her ferocity, however brief it might be. It turns out to be very brief, because she starts talking again before she's swallowed her second bite of her second slice of cake. 'I can't believe it. I mean, you'd have thought . . .'

'Thought what?'

She looks down, carving off a mountainous slice of cake with her fork. 'Nothing . . . It's just . . . I dunno. You'd have thought getting with a guy would be the last thing on her mind, after all that . . . y'know.'

I nod again. Kirsty might be a little over the top, but she definitely talks sense. She narrows her eyes, thinking hard. 'Unless she just wanted to . . . I don't know, *experiment* or something? Like to see if it was OK, kissing a guy who wasn't going to torture her and rape her or whatever?' She winces, reaches out to touch my hand. 'Sorry, that was . . . Sorry.'

I turn that thought over in my mind. *An experiment.* I suppose if you were going to conduct such an experiment, Thomas would be a good option. And for Laurel, the only option. She doesn't know any other boys our age. Boys *my* age, actually. Thomas is nineteen months younger than Laurel.

It's an interesting theory; the more I think about it, the more I like it. If Laurel just wanted to kiss a boy to see whether she could do it without freaking out or having flashbacks or something, it would still be wrong. I mean, you can't just go round kissing other people's boyfriends like that. But at least it wouldn't be *as* wrong. I realize I'm desperate to find a way for this to be OK. I don't *want* to hate my sister. I would love to have a decent reason to not hate her.

'Maybe that's it . . .' I take another bite of cake and for the first time it doesn't feel like it wants to lodge itself in my oesophagus.

'Of course, she could just be a massive slut,' she says with a sly grin.

'Kirsty!' I have to act shocked – I can't *not*.

'Sorry! I forgot you're not supposed to say anything bad about people like her. *Victims*. It must be pretty cool actually. She gets a free pass to be a total dick for the rest of her life, doesn't she?'

I know I should say something to defend my sister. Kirsty is practically a stranger to me; there should be no question about where my loyalty lies. But it's so nice to talk to someone who doesn't think Laurel is a bloody saint for a change. It's a breath of fresh air in the fetid stink that my life has become.

'Anyway, at least your sister has half a brain – even if she was schooled by a psycho rapist. Bryony is as dumb as a brick. You should hear some of the stuff she comes out with sometimes. You know she used to think baked beans were made of pasta? And for a whole year when we were kids I managed to convince her that unicorns were real – not that it took a lot of convincing.'

I laugh, but admit that I used to get confused between dragons and dinosaurs when I was little. 'Do you think we'd have been friends if your family hadn't moved to Australia?' As soon as the question is out of my mouth, I regret it. It's an odd, needy sort of question. A pointless one too. What ifs are the worst.

Kirsty looks up at the wall above my head. She takes her time, really thinking about it. 'Yes. I think we would . . . and then *I* could have kicked your boyfriend in the nads for you last night.' Her smile is rapidly replaced by a frown. 'But it would have been weird for Bryony, I reckon. We'd have had to let her hang out with us because *her* friend would be . . . gone. God, it's freaky even thinking about it.'

'Did Bryony say anything about that lunch? I thought things between them were a little . . . weird.'

Kirsty shrugs. 'It's not exactly a normal situation, is it? I think Bry was just freaked out. I suppose she was a bit quiet for a couple of days afterwards – withdrawn, you know? I just enjoyed the peace – made a nice change. Oh man, you're gonna love this . . . it's priceless! You know, she actually asked me if I thought Laurel might have been brainwashed! As if that's a thing that actually happens in real life and not just in shitty movies.' She laughs. 'Honestly I find it hard to believe we're related sometimes. I reckon she must have been dropped on her head right after she was born. Slipped right out of the nurse's hands like a greased eel.'

'*Brainwashed?* Why would she say that?'

Kirsty's eyes bug out and she makes a Scooby-Doo noise. 'I dunno . . . Well, she said something about Laurel not seeming to remember stuff. Like, things they did together when they were little, you know? Playing with dolls and stuff. Apparently they had this secret language? That must have been Laurel's doing, cos English is more than enough for Bry to cope with. So anyway, Bry started talking to your sister in this bullshit made-up language and your sister just looked at her like she was a fucking nutcase. So of course that *must* mean she was brainwashed.'

Something niggles at the back of my brain, like a raised hand at the back of the classroom trying to attract attention. But Kirsty is so full-on that the hand has to be ignored. 'I didn't know anything about a secret language.'

Kirsty laughs. 'Um . . . why would you? It was secret. That's kind of the whole point! Poor Bry was so disappointed though, you know? It was almost like

Laurel didn't remember her at *all*. And Bry prides herself on being memorable. I mean, she is, I guess, but for all the wrong reasons. I set her straight though. Laurel's been through a lot of shit, you know? Shit we can't even begin to imagine. So it kind of makes sense that there's stuff she doesn't remember . . . from before. There's only so much a person's brain can deal with, right?'

The hand at the back of the classroom appears again, but I can't think straight. 'I think I have to go now.'

Kirsty looks taken aback. 'Um . . . OK. Is it something I said?'

'No, not at all. I just . . . there's somewhere I have to be. I forgot.'

I can tell she's pissed off even though she tries to hide it. 'Listen, thanks so much for meeting up with me. I feel a lot better about everything.'

She looks at me like *Really?*

We agree to stay in touch. I say that it would be cool if we ended up at the same university and I actually mean it. I thank her again, then rush out of the door, leaving a half-drunk cup of tea, a whole slice of carrot cake and a slightly baffled Australian girl.

Chapter 48

I close the front door behind me as quietly as possible, and I listen. Nothing. Maybe Mum and Laurel have taken the opportunity to go on another one of their little mother–daughter outings. Mum probably didn't even question why Laurel came back here last night instead of staying with me at Dad's. I bet she wishes it was like this every weekend. Just the two of them.

The plan isn't really a plan as such. It's more a vague idea of a rough sketch of a half-remembered dream of a plan. Something isn't right, that much is obvious. I need to look in her room.

I creep up the stairs. Somehow it doesn't really feel like my home any more. I don't seem to belong here quite like I used to.

Laurel's door is closed, and I don't think anything of it at first, because she's been keeping it closed recently.

I open the door.

The wardrobe is open, clothes strewn on the bed and floor. A huge rucksack – an old one of Dad's – lies on the bed. Unless Laurel is hiding under the bed, she's not here.

I hurry towards my room. My hand is on the door handle (my door is closed too – why didn't I notice that before?) when the door opens from the inside and Laurel is standing there in front of me. 'Hi!' she says. Too loud. Forced. 'I thought you were—'

'What are you doing in my room?' I ask as she tries to squeeze past me.

'I was just looking for . . . something.' She couldn't look more suspicious if she tried.

'What's that behind your back?'

'Nothing. I . . . Nothing.'

'Show me.'

For a second I think she might try to barge past me, but I think we both know that I could take her in a fight.

'Listen, it's not what you think.'

'*Show* me.'

She holds out her hand. Five twenty-pound notes, six ten-pound notes, three fivers and a few pound coins. I only know this because it's exactly how much there was in the little tin next to my alarm clock.

'Give me that!' I reach for it but she puts her hand behind her back again.

'I need it.'

'Need it for what?'

She looks scared. Why is she scared of me? 'I can't . . . Look, I have to go. She'll be back soon. You have to let me go.' Then she does barge past me and I don't stop her. I just follow her back into her room and watch as she stuffs the money into the side pocket of the rucksack and starts shoving clothes inside.

'What's going on? Is this because of last night?' I take a deep breath and prepare to be the bigger person. 'You don't have to worry about it. I'm not going to tell Mum and Dad.' She carries on packing, but I know she's listening. 'Thomas wasn't right for me anyway. We'd have broken up sometime . . . You just helped it happen sooner rather than later. Hell, I should probably *thank* you!'

She stops for a moment. She's holding the red dress, the fabric all scrunched up between her clenched fists. She throws it back in the wardrobe. 'I'm sorry,' she says. And I know she's not apologizing about her treatment of the dress.

'It's OK.' I touch her arm and her shoulders slump. 'You don't have to run off, you know. People make mistakes.' I look around the room. 'Do you want me to help you sort this out before Mum gets back? Where is she anyway?'

'I asked her to get me some cough medicine from the chemist. I needed to get her out of the house.' Laurel sounds tired, numb. That makes two of us.

I'm wondering whether I should hug her – whether I can bear to hug her after what she did to me – when she takes a deep breath and starts packing again. 'Laurel! Stop! What are you doing? I told you, everything's going to be fine!'

She's shaking her head and muttering under her breath. '*I'm not* . . . I'm not . . .' She starts to cry softly.

I grab her shoulders and turn her to face me. 'Laurel! Please! You have to stop this. It's insane.'

She looks into my eyes, and I look into hers. I see something there, and I'm not even sure what it is but it stops me dead.

She opens her mouth to speak, and I know what she's going to say. I finally pay attention to the hand at the back of the classroom. 'You're not . . .'

'I'm not Laurel.'

Chapter 49

She's not. I know she's not. I've no idea how it's possible that I know this, but I do. Have I always known, on some level? Or was it a gradual thing? An accumulation of tiny things that don't add up to my sister.

She's not Laurel.

I'm gripping her shoulders so tightly that she has to wrench herself out of my grasp. She cowers away from me, as if she's expecting me to hit her. The tears are really flowing now, and these sobs are coming out of her – great big gasping sobs like there's not enough air in all the world for her to be able to catch her breath. 'I'm sorry I'm so sorry I didn't mean to I mean I did but I'm sorry.' Her hands are balled into fists and she seems smaller than she did a minute ago; a little girl, lost.

She's not Laurel. I look at her and wonder how I ever could have believed she was my sister.

Relief. That's what I feel first, I think. It's hard to pinpoint each feeling though. There are so many and they're so noisy, and they're all bumping into each other because so many of them are contradictory. But I am glad this girl is not my sister.

Then it hits me. If this girl is not Laurel, then Laurel is still missing. The nightmare of the past thirteen years continues. It's bad enough knowing the real Laurel is still out there somewhere — alive or dead — and no one's been looking for her because we thought she was home. But the thing that is unimaginable to me is that someone's going to have to tell my parents. It will have to be me. This will shatter them into a thousand tiny pieces and I don't think anyone or anything will be able to put them back together again.

A stranger is in front of me, staring at me like I'm a landmine she's just stepped on. We're both frozen, each of us waiting for the other to say something.

'Who are you?'

She shakes her head. 'It doesn't matter, does it? I'm not her.'

My sister is still out there, and nobody knows except me. And this girl, whoever she is. I wait. Her eyes keep darting between the rucksack and the clock by the bed. She keeps clasping and unclasping her hands. For the first time I feel fear. I don't know what this girl is capable of. I know nothing about her, except that somehow — how? — she managed to fool us all. What if this Not Laurel girl wants to hurt me? She could have a weapon in that rucksack, for all I know. But I suppose I can't really believe that, or I would be running down the stairs and out the front door right now.

I take my phone out of my jeans pocket and hold it in front of me. 'Tell me who you are or I'm phoning Mum right now.' My mum, I should have said. She's mine; not hers.

'Don't do that! Please. I'm begging you.' Her face is red and blotchy from crying, but deathly pale underneath.

I touch the screen, bring up my contacts. Scroll down to find Mum.

'Sadie. My name is Sadie, OK? Now please, put the phone away!' I should call Mum, get her to come home right away and deal with this madness. But I can't do it to her, not yet. I need to find out the truth first.

Sadie. It's quite a pretty name, familiar somehow. A phone chimes with an incoming text and I know it's not mine because I keep mine on silent. The girl flinches and starts rummaging underneath the clothes on the bed until she finds her phone. 'Shit. *Shit.* I have to go. Now. Mum's on her way back.' My eyes bore holes straight into her brain. 'Your mum, I mean.'

'You're not going anywhere.'

'I have to! You don't understand!'

The landmine finally explodes. 'You're right. I *don't* understand. How the hell am I supposed to understand some stranger coming into our family and pretending to be my long-lost sister? Pretending to have been *abused*! What kind of person even does that? Is it about the money? Is that it? Or the fame? Did you like being on television, telling all those lies? Were you laughing at us? Was this funny to you?' By the end of this little speech, the girl is backed up against the open wardrobe and I am shouting in her face. One more step and she'll be inside the wardrobe. I could shut her in there, find something to wedge the door closed and wait until Mum gets back.

The girl is breathing hard; I am too. The seconds are ticking away.

'Do you really want to know the truth?' the girl asks quietly.

I nod.

'Then come with me.'

'Are you out of your mind?! I'm not going anywhere with you!' I nearly add that she could be some psycho

390

killer for all I know, but she seems to read my mind because she says, 'I'm not going to hurt you.'

I shake my head, but I step back and she moves past me to finish packing the rucksack.

I stand in silence as she buckles up the top, then checks to see if she's forgotten anything. The bag doesn't look heavy; clearly she wants to travel light. She puts on her jacket, then shoulders the rucksack.

I want to know the truth. I need to. But this is madness.

She sees me wavering, this girl called Sadie. 'You'd better decide right now, because I'm going – with or without you.'

'What about Mum? If she comes back to find you gone, she'll freak out. Probably call the police in two seconds flat.'

She comes up with a plan. She'll leave a note for Mum, saying that she's decided to stay at Dad's tonight. I'll text Dad and tell him I'll be home late. Dad will never know that 'Laurel' is supposed to be at his place, and Mum won't know that she never turned up there. Until it's too late.

'I don't think this is a good idea,' I say, making one last attempt at being sensible.

Not-Laurel/Sadie stands in front of me, too close. *Family* close. 'I'll make you a deal. If you come with me right now, I'll do whatever you say. After. If you still want me to come back with you, I'll do it. I swear.' She's careful to maintain eye contact as I examine her face looking for the truth. I would probably believe her if I didn't already know that this girl is the best liar I've ever met. But it almost doesn't matter if she's telling the truth or not. If she's lying, I'll deal with the fallout afterwards. My need to know the truth – why she would do something like this, go to such extreme lengths to steal my sister's identity – outweighs everything else.

'OK, let's go.'

Chapter 50

We're ready in five minutes. While she was writing the note to Mum I briefly wondered whether I should take a knife from the kitchen. Just in case, you know. But the thought of actually using it – actually stabbing it into someone's flesh, even if that someone was trying to hurt me – was so absurd that I dismissed it immediately.

Sadie pauses before closing the front door. She looks at the hallway and stairs with such intensity that I wouldn't be surprised to see the wallpaper start to melt. There's nothing much to see: shoes in a neat little row against the wall, a hessian bag and a couple of coats hanging from pegs by the door, a pile of envelopes on the bottom stair. I watch as she gulps hard and clenches her jaw. I know what it's like, trying to swallow your feelings so they won't overwhelm you.

We turn right at the end of the road and wait at the

bus stop. 'So this is where you've been disappearing off to?'

She looks like she's about to disagree, to tell another lie, but I think we both realize the time for lying has passed. 'Just once.'

'Are you going to tell me where we're going?'

'It's better if I show you.'

The bus pulls up and we get on and Sadie hurries to the back with her head down, clearly worried that someone will recognize her. Unlikely though – she's got her hair hidden under a black beanie and she's not wearing any make-up. She looks like a normal girl today. One you wouldn't even notice unless she did something to attract your attention. The only person to look up at us as we walk down the aisle is a boy around our age, but it's the disinterested, unfocused gaze of someone whose mind is elsewhere. He's busy talking on the phone. 'Mate, awwww, mate! You would not believe what happened last night with Fat Jim! Maaaate . . . for real, man, I'm not even joking!'

Sadie breathes a sigh of relief when we reach the last row but one. She sits next to the window and puts the rucksack on her lap; I'm tempted to sit across the aisle, but that would risk someone else getting on and sitting next to Sadie.

It feels wrong sitting so close to her, our thighs

touching. I've sat this close to her loads of times over the past couple of months, but we were sisters then.

I can't even begin to imagine where we're going, but that doesn't stop me trying. A high-rise flat on one of those rundown estates? One of those buildings where there is a lift but it stinks of piss and it's always broken. I've never been to a place like that before, but I've seen them on TV. I can picture the two of us walking down a corridor and standing in front of a door and the door opening and a woman standing there. I look from this woman to the girl standing next to me and back again and I can't believe I ever thought the girl was my sister.

The woman – the mother, the real mother – was probably in on it. Maybe it was even her idea. She was flicking through the newspaper one day and noticed that Sadie looked a bit like the age-progressed photos of that missing girl – the one there was all that fuss about. Money – that was the motive, surely. But you'd have to be mad to think you could get away with something like this. It would only be a matter of time before someone from Sadie's real life recognized her and phoned the police. It suddenly dawns on me that *this* is why Sadie kicked up such a fuss about the DNA test. The game would have been well and truly up as soon as the results came in. Looking back, it seems ridiculous that none of us were suspicious about that. We were so desperate to believe that Laurel had come home to us that logic and common sense were forgotten.

I stare out of the window. My sister is still out there somewhere. She needs me and I am off on some wild goose chase with this unstable girl. For all I know, Laurel's time could be running out and I am wasting it. All this time the police haven't been looking for her, thinking her case was all tied up neatly with a ribbon. So maybe an extra couple of hours won't make a difference, but I've read enough about these cases to know that it can be – and often is – crucial.

I won't give up on you. I will find you. I will. I say the words over and over in my head.

It's strange. It's never occurred to me before that the search for my sister was something I could be involved in. It was always something for other people to do, and if I was lucky I might overhear something about it. I must have heard the phrase 'The police are doing everything they can' a thousand times during the course of my childhood. I was a kid; there was nothing I could do to help. But I'm not a kid any more. There *must* be something I can do now. I'm not stupid enough to think that anything I could do would be a match for the teams of detectives who have worked on Laurel's case over the years. But maybe I could give some interviews, go on TV and do an appeal. Something. I could visit the countries that have had the strongest leads in the past. *Talk* to people.

Someone, somewhere, knows where Laurel is. It's just a matter of finding that someone – and getting through to them. It's time I stopped being so passive.

'You should text your dad.'

She remembered this time. That he's my father, not hers. I text him. Cinema with Martha is my cover story. He texts back straightaway, asking me to pick up some of those chocolate stars you can buy at the concession stand. He's addicted to those things.

'Are we nearly there?' I don't turn to look at her when I speak, so I feel rather than see the shrug of her shoulders.

'Where are we going?' I know she's not going to answer. There's a stillness to her now. I can't seem to stop fidgeting and looking around, but she is a statue next to me. If there was even the remotest chance she would tell me, I would ask what she's thinking.

*

The journey is interminable. One of those bus routes that stops at every little back-end-of-beyond place you can think of. The bus is almost empty by the time Sadie reaches across to press the 'stop' button. I look out of the window for clues, still half-expecting to see the imaginary high-rise building where Sadie's imaginary mother is waiting for us. But all I can see is trees. I have no idea where we are. I probably should have paid more attention.

We stand on the road and wait until the bus has turned the corner. There's a short row of terraced houses on the other side of the street. They look like they don't belong here, because here seems to be the middle of nowhere.

Sadie starts walking away from the houses, in the direction the bus came from. I have no choice but to follow. I stay a step or two behind so I can keep an eye on her. It will be getting dark before too long.

A couple of cars pass as we walk. Sadie keeps her head down, but I look at the drivers, half hoping that one of them will stop and ask if everything's OK. But why would they? We are just two girls out for a late-afternoon stroll in the sunshine. They have no reason to notice us in the first place, let alone stop and talk to us.

After about half an hour we come to a patch of

woods. At first glance it looks exactly the same as every other patch of woods we've passed. It's the countryside — it all looks the same to mc. Then I notice that there's a track running into this particular stretch of woods. There's a gate, with a sign saying 'KEEP OUT'. It's hidden; you wouldn't even notice it if you were driving past.

'What is this place?' My voice sounds too loud out here. The only sounds I can hear are our feet on the road and the occasional flurry of birdsong.

Sadie turns to look at me, as if she's expecting some kind of reaction to the sight in front of us. There's something not right here. Something not right with her.

'We're here.'

Chapter 51

Instead of opening the gate, Sadie walks around it. It's not attached to a fence or a wall or anything. It can stop vehicles, but not us. She walks off down the track, but I hesitate. We are literally in the middle of nowhere. Anything could happen; I could scream for help and no one would hear.

I've come this far though. I might as well see this through. Plus I'm not exactly wild about the idea of being left out here on my own. I edge my way around the side of the gate, trying to avoid stepping in the muddy ditch.

The track curves gently through the woods. It's gloomy in here, the treetops tightly knit overhead. I think of Little Red Riding Hood and suddenly I can't remember the end of that story. Did she escape? Did she kill the wolf with her bare hands? Or did she curl up in a corner and wait for him to eat her up?

Finally there's a house in front of us. I'm not sure what kind of place I was expecting to find, but it definitely wasn't this. The house is ugly and grey and squat, with a flat roof and peeling paint around the windows. It's best for everyone that it's hidden in the woods, a house this ugly. That's when I realize I was half expecting something from a fairy tale. A little white cottage with a thatched roof with smoke puffing out of the chimney. This place looks more like a military installation than a home.

The weirdest thing is the garden, which *does* look like something out of a fairy tale. There's even a white picket fence around it. There's an ornamental rock garden and ceramic pots of herbs, and ivy climbing up the wall next to the front door. It's as if this ugly building has landed here in a tornado, crushing the little old lady's house that belongs here to smithereens. If I look closely I might see a pair of old-lady shoes peeking out where the wall meets the ground.

On closer inspection, the garden looks a bit neglected. Weeds are starting to take over. The little square patch of grass is overgrown: it clearly hasn't seen a lawnmower in a long time.

Sadie watches me as I take it all in. 'What is this

place?' I ask for the second time.

'Home.' She laughs but it sounds all wrong.

She doesn't knock on the door or ring the doorbell (not that I can see a doorbell). She doesn't take out a key either. She just puts her hand on the doorknob and turns it. She walks in, leaving the door open behind her.

The first thing that hits me is the smell. It seems to coat the inside of my nose and throat. It's thick and cloying and deeply unpleasant. I stop worrying about someone else being here, because this house is empty. You can just feel it. I leave the door open in the vague hope that some air will start to circulate.

The inside of the house doesn't match the outside, just like the outside doesn't match the garden. A dusky pink carpet runs through all the rooms, with various hideous rugs placed on it at regular intervals. Green patterned wallpaper. There is a lot of furniture, some of it antique, some of it from the seventies by the look of it. Every surface has ornaments on it – little crystal animals or jugs in the shape of squat little men or dainty little teacups and saucers. I spy an ancient-looking TV in a corner.

There's a hulking bookcase opposite the front door. The books are an odd mixture of true crime and romance, black spines stark among the pinks and peaches and purples. The bottom shelves are filled with textbooks and reference books.

None of the rooms have doors, not even the bedroom or the bathroom. It doesn't even look like the doors have been removed – the house must have been built this way to someone's (a *weird* someone's) specifications. I peek into the bathroom – more dusky pink carpet. Pink toilet, sink and bath too. Lots of bottles and jars lining the windowsill. Old-lady beauty products to match the old-lady decor.

The bedroom has an enormous bed with a flowery bedspread and too many pillows and cushions. In the corner there's a much smaller bed – almost small enough to be a child's. Next to this bed there are three bottles of pills and a leather-bound bible. Instead of proper bedlinen there's a pancake-flat pillow and a filthy sleeping bag – a discarded cocoon. On the floor next to the bed lies a laptop, its once shiny casing smeared with fingerprints.

The bigger bed has been made neatly, all the corners tucked in. On the bedside table there is a cup. The cup has something dark green and mottled and foul in it. There's a framed photograph of an old woman and a younger man. She's sitting ramrod straight in a comfy chair. She is smiling (or grimacing, it's hard to tell) and her cheeks are rosy with too much blusher. A bright blue handbag sits on the floor on her left-hand side. The man kneels on her right. He is small and pale, with big round eyes. There's something nocturnal about him. His face is bland, almost but not quite good-looking. He isn't smiling.

'What are you doing?' Sadie has crept up behind me, scaring the life out of me. Her voice is dull, toneless, her facial expression hard to read.

'I was just . . . looking around.' I indicate the photo on the bedside table. 'Do they . . . ? This place is so . . .'

'Weird?'

I nod. 'And what is that smell? It smells like . . .' I have no idea what it smells like. Nothing good, that's all I know.

She turns around and at first I think she's ignoring my questions, but then it's clear that I'm expected to follow her. She heads into the living room and stands in front of the overstuffed sofa.

My view is obscured at first; the smell is stronger than ever. I cough, trying to clear the metallic tang from my throat. Sadie steps aside and that's when I see it.

The stain is big. The size of a pillow or a medium-sized dog or a jumper. It's remarkably even around the edges, as if someone has carefully poured a pot of paint on to the carpet.

The stain is dark. Black? It could be oil or treacle or balsamic vinegar.

It's none of those things though. It's blood.

Some things you just *know*, without having to be told. It doesn't stop me asking though. 'What . . . ? Whose . . . ? That's blood. Isn't it? What happened here?'

Sadie is staring at the stain with a strange, almost dreamy look on her face. 'Smith.'

Chapter 52

I don't understand. I take a step backwards, knocking the backs of my calves on the sofa. I feel dizzy all of a sudden. The stench of blood is thicker and heavier and it feels like it's suffocating me. I want to sit down but I can't sit down here. Not in this place.

'I don't . . . But you made that stuff up. About Smith and the basement and . . .'

I follow her gaze to a door in the hallway. I didn't notice it before. The only door in the house, apart from the one we came in. There's nothing particularly noteworthy about this door, but Sadie is staring at it with a look so intense that it burns. I walk over to the door, a little unsteadily. My legs feel like they belong to someone else.

The door has a lock with a key in it. It's a Yale lock, big and sturdy. I turn the key and open the door.

I look back at Sadie, still rooted to the spot next to the stain on the carpet. She nods at me.

I think I'm starting to understand.

In front of me there are stairs leading downward. The stairs are rough concrete. There is a bare light bulb overhead, with a cord hanging next to the door. At the bottom of the cord there is a doll's head. The cord is tied around her hair. The doll's eyes are closed, as if she's sleeping. Or dead. I don't want to touch the head, so I grab the cord just above the doll and pull. The light comes on, illuminating the rest of the stairs.

I want Sadie to come with me, but something tells me I can't ask her.

I count the stairs. Seventeen. One for each year of my life.

At the bottom of the stairs there is another door, identical to the first. Another lock with another key. I unlock this door and push it. Darkness beyond.

I fumble around on the wall inside, searching for a light switch. I could use the light from my phone, but I'm too scared to go inside unless I can see every corner. You never know what could be lying in wait in the darkness. I look around me and realize there's a light switch at the bottom of the stairs, outside the door, almost too high for me to reach. There is no good reason to have a light switch that high up. I manage to flick it with the very tips of my fingers.

I step into the room. I know this place.

The camp bed against the opposite wall. The small stainless-steel sink with a red bucket next to it. The bookshelf – again, almost too high for me to reach – with different-coloured folders lined up neatly. Labels on the spines with neat black writing. Maths. English. Science.

There's a rickety chair and a Formica-topped table against the left-hand wall. On the table sits an ancient desktop computer. The keyboard in front of it is missing three of its keys.

There's a pile of what look like old clothes and blankets in one corner.

Then I look up. Above the door there is a tiny video camera, pointing at the camp bed.

This is not a room. It's a cell.

Chapter 53

The walls seem to close in on me. I've been standing here less than a minute, and the door is wide open behind me. If someone was to lock me in here and turn out the light, how long would it be before I lost my mind?

I turn and go back up the stairs as quickly as I can, not bothering to turn out the lights or close the doors. The front door is open. She's sitting on the steps. I sit down next to her.

'How long?' I ask, staring at a patch of pink heather clinging to a rock.

'Fifteen years.'

'You killed him.' Not quite a question, not quite a statement.

She nods.

'And then . . . ?'

'I had nowhere to go.'

So she came to us. She needed a family. We fitted the bill. I can't get my head around it. It's too much, too crazy.

Sadie looks at me and I look at her, even though I don't want to. 'I'm sorry,' she says.

I can't say that it's OK or that I forgive her. Because it's not OK and I do not forgive her. She tricked us all. Lied to us.

'So all that stuff about Smith . . . the things he did . . .'

'All true.'

I wait. The sky is red. If I concentrate hard enough on the pretty garden in front of me, maybe the house of horrors behind me will cease to exist.

Sadie starts to talk. Slowly, haltingly at first. Then faster and faster as if she's racing to get the words out before darkness falls.

She is twenty-three years old now. She was eight years old when she was taken. It happened in a shopping centre, lots of people around. She can't remember much about her life before. 'There were men,' she says. 'Bad men.'

I ask about her family. Her *real* family. She tracked them down. It was the first thing she did when she escaped. Her mother is dead. Overdose.

'What about your dad?' I ask. 'Don't have a dad,' she says.

I ask about Smith. 'Is he the one in the picture?'

She nods.

'So you lied to the police about what he looked like?'

She nods again. 'I couldn't have them finding out who he really was.'

I think about this for a moment. If she had accurately described Smith, there would have been a good chance someone out there would have recognized him. Even if he did live like a recluse out here, someone would surely have been able to identify him. Then the police would have come here. Found the bloodstain on the carpet. 'Where is he . . . did you bury him?'

'Back there.' She gestures with her head, nodding towards a path leading round the side of the house.

I try to picture her dragging his body through the house and out the front door. The head, thunking on the steps we're sitting on. She must have wrapped the body in a sheet or something. There were no signs of blood on the carpet other than the stain next to the sofa.

I want to ask how she did it. What it was like to kill a man. Was it quick?

It's as if she reads my mind. 'I only hit him once. I

didn't mean to. I just wanted to knock him out. Give myself a chance to run. His back was turned. He was crying. I think he expected me to comfort him. I picked up the iron without thinking. It was just sitting there next to the fireplace. I'd never even noticed it before. It belonged to his mother, I think. Probably an antique.' She pauses and a ghost of a smile plays across her lips. 'Caved in his skull. Didn't know my own strength.'

What do you say to someone who is essentially confessing to a murder? But does this even count as murder? I don't think it's self-defence. Still, it's hard to imagine a jury convicting her, after everything she's been through.

I ask her if she ever tried to escape before. 'A couple of times,' she tells me. 'Mostly in the first year or two.'

'And after that?'

Sadie shrugs. 'I stopped trying. I got used to it. Got used to *him*. He took care of me.' She sees the horrified look on my face. 'I know how fucked up it sounds. You don't need to tell me.'

'I'm sorry.'

'No one can ever understand what it was like. No one except . . . me.'

Something isn't quite adding up. Lots of things,

in fact. 'Why didn't you just go to the police? After you . . . After he was dead.'

'I didn't know *what* to do. I was alone. For the first time in my whole life there was no one telling me what to do. I ate when I wanted and slept when I wanted and went on the computer and walked in the woods. It was . . . peaceful. It was only when the food started to run out that I realized I couldn't stay.'

This is the bit that doesn't make any sense. The missing piece of the puzzle. Everything else I can sort of understand – or at least try. But how did she come up with the idea to pretend to be my sister? I wait for her to explain but she says nothing.

It's almost fully dark now. I'm not looking forward to walking back to the main road. 'I can call Dad, you know. He could come and get us.' I stop and think for a second. Yes. This could work. 'We can explain everything. I know it won't be easy and of course they'll be upset . . .' Understatement of the century, but I keep going. 'But they'll . . . I think they'll understand. In time. And I'm sure we can find someone – a family member or whatever – to take care of you. You must have grandparents or aunts or something. And they will have been looking for you, just like we've been looking for Laurel. Just think what it will be like, when you turn up after all these years.' I know exactly what it will be like. A miracle. And for them, the miracle will actually be real.

'Faith,' she says, but I carry on gabbling about how everything will be OK and people should really know that this Smith guy is dead. Right now the police are wasting valuable manpower looking for a guy who doesn't even exist when they should be looking for my sister. I keep talking, hoping that something I say will get through to her. I know I could just call Dad anyway – I don't need her permission – but suddenly it seems important that Sadie is OK with it.

'FAITH! Stop! Just . . . stop.' Sadie gets up and starts pacing. Gravel crunches underneath her feet. She brings her hands up to her face and mutters something. When she removes her hands there are tears in her eyes. She's biting her lip so hard that it's started to bleed.

I stand up and put my hand on her shoulder, trying to reassure her. But she flinches at my touch. She backs away from me. 'I need to . . . I didn't want to . . . There's something you need to see. I'm sorry.'

I follow Sadie around the side of the house. Her shoulders are hunched and she's sobbing. I don't know what to say to her. I don't know what's going on here.

There's no back garden. The trees are so close that the branches brush against the windows. I have to get my phone out and use the screen to light my way. Sadie doesn't seem to have any problem seeing where she's going though. She's used to the dark.

We walk past a mound of earth, about six foot long. She doesn't stop. She doesn't look down as we pass. She doesn't say anything at all to give me an idea of what is underneath that mound. She doesn't have to. I wonder what the body looks like. Decaying flesh, sunken eyeballs. Worms and insects.

Finally Sadie stops in a small clearing. The moonlight shines overhead. It might be a nice spot for a picnic, in the daytime.

'I'm sorry,' she says again. Why does she keep saying that?

Then I see. I *see*.

Another mound of earth, about the same size as the one we passed. Someone has placed lots of tiny stones around it, forming a border. A crooked wooden cross sticks up from the earth. There's something leaning against the cross. I move closer to see what it is.

A teddy bear, missing one arm.

I stare at the mound of earth.

I fall to my knees in front of my sister's grave.

Chapter 54

ONE MONTH LATER

My sister has been dead for just over four months. I have been mourning her for one month. Apart from Sadie, I am the only person in the world who knows that Laurel Logan is dead. I intend to keep it that way.

These are the facts as Sadie told them to me that night. I have no way of knowing if she lied to me about any of it. I have no choice but to trust her version of events. Any questions I might want to ask must remain unanswered: she is gone.

Sadie was the first girl the monster took. She was not the last. Something drove him to take my sister. Another little blonde girl, younger this time.

Sadie hated my sister. She was jealous of her. Little girls like attention, that's what she told me. Sadie used to pinch Laurel and pull her hair. Once, after about two years together, Sadie pushed Laurel into a wall. Laurel lost a tooth. Smith punished Sadie; she didn't say how.

My sister didn't hate Sadie. She clung to her whenever she got the chance. 'Will you be my new sister?' she asked, as the two of them lay in the darkness. My sister slept on the camp bed, Sadie now relegated to the floor.

Every night, Laurel talked about her family. She talked for hours and hours, in between fits of tears. At first Sadie stuck her fingers in her ears and told Laurel to be quiet. But eventually she came to like Laurel's stories. She looked forward to them. She didn't have any stories of her own; most of *her* memories were unhappy ones.

Sadie built up a picture in her head – of me and Mum and Dad and our home. Laurel told her about a nightlight called Egg, about playing in the sandpit with her little sister. She said that Sadie could borrow Barnaby the Bear if she ever felt like she needed a hug.

They lived together for thirteen years, spending almost every minute of every day together. Except for the times when the monster took Laurel upstairs.

Eventually Sadie stopped hating Laurel. Time and Laurel's goodness wore her down. Laurel let Sadie sleep next to her on the camp bed, the two girls often falling sleep in each other's arms.

Laurel never gave up hope. She knew we would be looking for her. When the monster told her that we didn't care about her, that we were glad she was gone, she shook her head, mouth clamped stubbornly shut. She knew we loved her. That comforts me, when I'm lying awake in bed at night, wondering whether I've done the right thing. Her belief in us was unshakeable, right to the end.

I asked Sadie what Laurel was like. 'She had a good heart,' she said simply. I pressed her for more details. 'There was . . . It was like she had a light inside her. Something pure and good that I never had.' The age-progressed photos didn't do her justice. Sadie said the two of them looked similar, at first glance. Laurel was more fragile though. She was weaker than Sadie. She got ill a lot. And of course she never saw a doctor.

They were happy sometimes. When the monster left them alone. He would leave them alone for twenty-four hours or more on a regular basis. On those days they would be hungry, but they never minded that. They were safe at least.

They made up stories together. They pretended they were princesses, locked up in the dungeon by an evil ogre. Laurel made up a story about Sadie coming to live with our family. She said they would share a room, like sisters. That was Sadie's favourite story.

I asked about the scar on Sadie's cheek – the one that matched the scab that Laurel had when she was taken. She didn't want to tell me at first, but eventually I got it out of her. Laurel had been ill for over a month – headaches and vomiting. Smith was getting frustrated, so he took Sadie upstairs. He cut her hair and dressed her up in my sister's clothes. But that wasn't good enough: he wanted his Laurel substitute to look exactly like her. He cut her cheek with a kitchen knife and said, 'There, that's better.' She didn't say what happened next.

I forced myself to ask more questions I wasn't sure I wanted to hear the answers to. I asked if Laurel had been scared. I asked if she remembered us – remembered *me* – after all those years away from us. I asked how she died.

The answers:

Sometimes. But she never got used to the darkness.

She never forgot us. Never stopped talking about us.

The last question was the only one Sadie couldn't answer. I didn't believe her at first, I was sure she was lying to protect me. She insisted she was telling the truth. 'One morning she just didn't wake up,' she said, eyes pleading, begging me to believe her.

I couldn't accept it. 'People don't just die,' I said. But of course they do. People die every day. Old people and middle-aged people and young people and babies. And who knows what kind of health problems Laurel might have had, living the way she did? Maybe if she'd had access to proper medical care she would still be alive, but it's pointless to think that way.

My sister was an hour away from home when she died. She'd been an hour away from us for thirteen years, and we'd had no idea.

The monster was inconsolable. He kept on saying, 'I loved her,' over and over again, clutching my sister's body in his arms. He blamed Sadie. He shook her and shouted at her to tell him what she'd done. She cowered in the corner under her filthy blankets. She didn't cry. She was in shock.

Smith made Sadie dig the hole to bury my sister. She was the one who arranged the smooth little pebbles around the mound of earth. She found the sticks to make the cross. Smith wanted to bury Barnaby the Bear with Laurel, but Sadie begged him to let her keep the bear. He wouldn't listen. He said Laurel needed Barnaby 'to help her sleep well'. But he left Sadie alone to fill in the grave. He left her out there all by herself, to shovel soil on top of my sister's body. Sadie took the bear from the grave and hid him under some leaves.

It's strange, that I forgot all about Barnaby. That should have been the first thing I thought of when Sadie told me she wasn't Laurel. I should have realized there had to be a connection between the two of them, but I didn't. Sometimes I wonder if a part of me knew the truth, somehow, even then. But that can't be true, can it?

Sadie killed the monster three days after Laurel died. 'I should have done it sooner. We could have got away,' she said. I told her she needed to stop thinking like that. I told her I didn't blame her. I said the words 'I forgive you' repeatedly, until she listened.

The plan emerged in my mind almost fully formed, minutes after seeing my sister's grave. It sprang from one thought: that I never, ever wanted my parents to feel what I was feeling. They would never recover.

It was getting late. The last bus back to town was in less than an hour. It wasn't easy to convince Sadie to come back with me. She wanted to stay at the house, figure out her next move. 'I'm not leaving you here,' I said. 'That is not an option.' I told her the plan. We would get the bus home. I'd tell Dad that I'd invited

Laurel to the cinema at the last minute and she'd decided it'd be easier to stay at his place rather than going back to Mum's.

Sadie backed away from me and I was scared she was going to bolt into the woods. I wouldn't let that happen though. I would chase her down and drag her back with me, if that's what it took. But it didn't come to that. I talked her round, made her see sense. I managed to make her understand that she didn't stand a chance without my help.

We didn't say a word to each other on the bus back to Dad's house.

It took us four days. We could have done with more time, but the police were coming to do the DNA test on Thursday. She had to be gone by then. I pretended to be ill and stayed home from school. Mum didn't even question it, especially once Sadie/Laurel agreed to stay home and look after me. Mum was going to be busy all week – she was planning some big charity dinner or something.

Money wasn't a problem. Sadie had her share from the book deal, and I had a decent amount in my savings. I withdrew the lot and gave it to her. She didn't want to take my money, not at first. But I knew she'd need every penny she could get. She wouldn't be able to go abroad, which made things more difficult.

That left two problems. Problem one: the fact that she was one of the most recognizable people in the country. Problem two: my parents.

The first problem was solved easily enough. At least I assume it was solved, because I've been checking the Internet every day since she left, half expecting to see that someone's spotted her. A pair of scissors and some brown hair dye in the dead of night. But even with short brown hair, she was still too easy to recognize. She let me shave her head. The effect was startling. She looked like a skinny, beautiful boy.

The problem of my parents was trickier. They'd only just got their daughter back. Were they really going to just sit back and accept losing her again?

I wrote the letter and Sadie copied it in her own handwriting, under strict instructions not to change a single word. It was vital that the letter did its job. Sadie kept asking me if I thought it would work. 'Of course it will work,' I said, even though I couldn't possibly know. It took me two hours to get it right, to strike the right balance. It was horrible, writing that letter. I just had to keep telling myself that I was doing the right thing – that I was doing this to protect them.

*

I said goodbye to Sadie just before five o'clock in the morning the Wednesday after Thomas's party. We were in my bedroom and she'd just done a final check of her rucksack. We'd gone over it again and again, making sure she had everything she needed. There was one last thing I wanted to give her.

'What's this?' It was wrapped in a T-shirt of mine that I knew she loved. 'Egg!' The penguin nightlight. The one Laurel had talked about so much that Sadie had been able to describe it down to the tiniest detail. 'I can't take this. Or this,' she said, holding out the nightlight and the T-shirt.

'I want you to have them.' She shook her head, but I was ready for that. 'Mum would expect Laurel to take the nightlight with her. So you might as well take it so I don't have to chuck it in the bin.'

Sadie gave me this look, like she knew exactly what I was playing at, but she nodded and wrapped the penguin in the T-shirt and managed to fit him in a side pocket of the rucksack. 'Thank you,' she whispered. And it seemed like she wasn't really thanking me for the nightlight or the T-shirt. It was a *bigger* thank you than that; weightier somehow.

'Right,' she said, 'I'd better get going.'

'OK. OK,' I said, and I suddenly felt panicky. There was no way this plan was ever going to work, so why were we even trying? It was madness. What if we'd forgotten something? 'Are you sure you've got everything? And the map? You know where you're going? We can go through it again if you like. We've got plenty of time before Mum gets up.'

Sadie put a hand on my arm. 'It's OK, I know what I'm doing. Everything will be fine.'

There were so many questions I hadn't thought to ask about Laurel, and this was my last chance. But if I started down that route, I'd probably never stop. The more Sadie told me, the more I wanted to know. I would *never* know enough about my sister, about how she lived. And how she died.

There was one question I could ask though. Something I needed to know before she left. A selfish question. Silly, really, given everything that's happened since. But I asked it anyway, as Sadie was shouldering the rucksack, testing the weight. 'Why did you kiss Thomas?'

Sadie stopped and stared at the wall for a second, as if the answer might be written there. But then she looked at me. 'I needed you to hate me.' I clearly had no idea what she was talking about, so she elaborated. 'I knew I needed to leave before the police came over.

425

But I couldn't make myself actually do it. I . . . I like it here. A lot. I thought it would be easier if you pushed me away. I was right.' She smiled ruefully. 'You should probably know that he didn't kiss me back.'

I thought about that for a second. It made a weird sort of sense. But there was something niggling me, like a sharp little stone in my shoe. 'How did you know I was going to walk in and see you two?'

She gave me this strange look, like she knew I'd caught her out. 'OK, maybe there were two reasons. I wanted to see what it felt like. With someone . . . someone who wasn't Smith.'

There was nothing I could say to that. Not one single thing.

I'm not sure who initiated the hug. Maybe me, maybe her. Or maybe we both had the same idea at the same time. It didn't feel strange to be hugging her. It didn't feel like hugging a stranger. And when it came down to it, I really didn't want to let go. She was the first to pull away.

'I'm sorry. About everything. I never meant to hurt anyone, I hope you know that.' There were tears in her eyes. In mine too.

I nodded. 'You . . . You take care, OK?'

'I will.'

She walked over to the door, then turned. We

looked at each other in silence for a moment or two. If everything went to plan, I would never see her again. She smiled sadly, and it made me wish for things I could never explain, even to myself. She spoke softly. 'You know something? I liked being your sister, even for a little while.'

She closed the door behind her. I listened for her footsteps on the stairs, but I heard nothing. I went over to the window and watched her walk down the street. She didn't look back.

'I liked being your sister too,' I whispered.

Chapter 55

If saying goodbye to Sadie was hard, watching my mum read the letter was worse. I thought she would never stop crying. 'Did you know about this?' she said, holding my shoulders and shaking me. I didn't break. 'No, I swear. I had no idea.' Mum phoned Dad and he arrived within twenty minutes, face still creased from sleep. He didn't cry. He was too stunned, I think.

I watched as they read the letter again, heads close together. I had to remember to ask to read it myself. I wasn't supposed to know every word by heart.

Dear Mum, Dad and Faith,
I have to go away for a while. I'm sorry. I know this
won't be easy for you to understand, but I need you to
know that it's the right thing for me. It's what I want.
I need some time to find out who I am, and what I

want to do with my life. I need to be alone. I'm sorry I can't explain it better than that.

Please don't blame yourselves. Coming home to you was better than I could have ever dreamed. You are the best family in the world. I am so lucky to have you in my life.

I'm excited about the future. About going to new places and making new friends. Meeting people who have never heard of Laurel Logan. A fresh start. I want to see if I can stand on my own two feet. I'm sure you can understand that.

Please, PLEASE don't come looking for me. I beg you. I need to do this, and I need to do it without your help.

I'm not sure how long I'll be gone for. But I will come back to you, one day. I love you all.

Laurel

Reading it again, over the shoulder of my sobbing mother and frozen father, it didn't seem good enough. Not even close. I should have said more, really laid it on thick. It was too short, too stilted.

I'm not sure my acting was up to much. I didn't even manage to cry.

'How could she do this to us? I don't understand.' Mum fell into Dad's arms. He murmured words of comfort. I took the letter, stared at it just for something to do.

Mum pulled away. 'I can't lose her again, John. I . . . I just can't. We need to phone the police. She can't have gone far. Let me find that . . . Where's that number again?' She opened the kitchen drawer where all the takeaway menus and random scraps of paper are stored.

'Stop,' said Dad, but Mum didn't listen so he had to go over and close the drawer and take her hands in his. '*Stop*. We have to . . .' He swallowed hard. 'I don't like it any more than you do, but we have to let her do this. She's nineteen, Olivia. She's an *adult*. This isn't about us. It's about what's best for Laurel.'

'And you think what's best for her is being out there all by herself?' Mum shouted. Her face was red and wet with tears that she didn't even bother to wipe away. 'Anything could happen!'

'You mean something worse than what's already happened?' Dad said quietly.

That's what did it, I think. She didn't come round to the idea right away, but she at least started to listen. I put the kettle on, trying to ignore the mug with Laurel's name on it when I opened the kitchen cupboard.

We sat round the kitchen table, talking things

through. Mum had the idea of calling Laurel and begging her to come home. Dad didn't object. Mum was the only one who was surprised when we heard the phone ringing from upstairs.

Three hours later, my parents had both agreed to abide by Laurel's wishes. 'We owe it to her,' said Dad. 'She'll come back when she's ready. And we'll be here waiting, ready to welcome her back with open arms. That's all we can do.' He didn't sound convincing – or convinced – but it was a start.

I was the first one to mention the press. Sadie and I had talked about it. Even if Mum and Dad decided not to look for her, the media would be all over it in a matter of days. There would be no escape. So we decided that it would be best to pre-empt the problem. Release a statement saying Laurel was abroad, maybe seeking long-term treatment for some medical problem or other. And that's exactly what we did.

The story died down much quicker than I expected. Without her here, there were no photos to accompany the articles. People aren't as interested when there aren't any pictures. Yesterday I did my usual trawl of the Internet, looking for any new mentions of Laurel Logan. For the first time, there was nothing. Not even a single random conspiracy-theory blog post. I sat back and smiled. We'd done it.

*

Things haven't been easy, especially with Mum. She barely left the house for the first couple of weeks. She's been letting the phone ring, saying she doesn't want to speak to anyone. The book editor, Zara, has left seven messages for her already. Who knows what's going to happen about the book deal. Perhaps we'll have to pay the money back, or maybe they'll still want to publish the book, even though 'Laurel' is gone.

Mum kept on asking me what she did wrong; she still doesn't really accept my answer of 'nothing'. I think she'll be OK though, in time. She's going out for drinks with her friend Sita tonight. That's got to be a good sign, right?

Dad seems to be coping better. He's really busy at work; he says it helps keep his mind off things.

We had dinner together on Sunday – Mum, Dad, Michel and me. It was Mum's idea. She thinks we should do it every week. I think she's hoping that doing lots of family things together will make Laurel come home sooner, as if she'll somehow *know*, wherever she is.

Dad and Michel came round early. Dad read the papers, while Mum fussed around in the kitchen, worrying that she hadn't bought a big enough piece of beef. Michel insisted on peeling the potatoes. 'You go and put your feet up, Olivia,' he said. Mum smiled and thanked him, and both the smile and the thanks were genuine – for the first time ever, I think. I was about to go and sit down too, but Michel asked me to stick around and keep him company.

I hadn't been alone with him since she left. I've been avoiding Martha too, as best I can. The urge to talk – to tell someone the truth – has been so strong at times that it's almost overwhelmed me.

I see Thomas at school. He hasn't tried to speak to me, not even once. I thought he might have tried harder to fight for our relationship, but it seems like he's given up. I can't help thinking it's a bit odd, especially if Sadie told the truth about him doing nothing wrong. The weird thing is, I don't miss him. Not even a little bit. We should never have even been together in the first place; it feels right, being alone.

'So how are you doing? It's been a crazy couple of months, *hein*?' said Michel, rinsing the potatoes under the tap.

'I'm OK.' Keep it simple. First rule of lying.

'Really? You don't look OK. You look like you haven't slept in a month.'

I laughed and elbowed him. 'Jeez, thanks, Michel! You know you should never, ever tell a girl she looks tired, don't you?'

Michel didn't laugh. He didn't even look at me. He just started peeling the potatoes, while I stood next to him, ready to cut them into perfect roastie-sized chunks. After a while he spoke, so quietly I had to lean in to hear him. 'There's something I want you to know. I hope you know it already, but I'm going to say it anyway. There are some things in life that are too big to deal with on your own. You might think you can cope by yourself, but a thing like that can . . . eat away at you. It can poison you. A burden like that, it's too heavy for one person. So if there's ever anything you wanted to talk to me about – *anything* – you need to know that I'm here. You can trust me.'

I listened and watched his profile as he concentrated on the potatoes. What was he talking about? He couldn't possibly know. Sadie and I had been so careful. 'Um . . . thanks. Everything's fine though. Really.'

Then he turned to me. His eyes locked on mine. He started talking in a faux-casual voice as if this was a perfectly normal conversation after all. 'Did you know that cuckoos don't have nests of their own?' I shook my head, thinking he had well and truly lost the plot. 'They lay their eggs in another bird's nest and then leave. The other bird has no idea, because the eggs are camouflaged to look the same as *its* eggs. So it ends

434

up caring for the cuckoo's eggs along with its own. The poor bird is none the wiser, even after the eggs hatch.'

My heart was slamming in my chest, my mouth bone dry. He knew. Somehow, he *knew*. I looked towards the door; it was still shut. 'What are you . . . I don't understand. What are you saying?'

Michel shrugged in that impossible French way of his. 'Nothing. I'm saying nothing. It's just interesting, that's all. Some people, they think that this makes the cuckoo evil.'

'What do you think?'

Another Gallic shrug. 'Me? I think it's a survivor. What's that phrase? *La fin justifie les moyens.* The end . . .'

'Justifies the means,' I finished the sentence for him.

So Michel knows the truth — part of it at least. There's no way he could possibly know what really happened to Laurel; maybe he suspects that she died years ago. I should probably be panicking that he might say something to Dad, but I'm not. I think if he was going to do that, he would have done it already. Maybe he has his reasons for staying quiet, just like I do.

I've slept better since that night, which surely can't be a coincidence. Maybe Michel was right about sharing the burden. Still, I have no intention of ever actually talking to him about it. Because he must never be allowed to know the whole story.

I made a promise, one that I intend to keep for the rest of my life.

The phone rang this morning, just as I was leaving the house. A flash of hot panic when I heard Mum say, 'Hi, Natalie.' I slammed the front door shut so Mum would think I'd left. I stayed in the hall. I needed to hear this. Why was Sergeant Dawkins calling Mum? Maybe there had been another sighting of 'Smith'; there have been a lot of those recently. I bet there's some poor guy out there who looks *exactly* like the description Sadie gave to the police. I hope he doesn't get arrested.

I crept closer to the living room door. 'Any news?' There was a pause as Mum listened. 'But there must be something! Someone must have seen her, surely! She can't have just disappeared off the face of the planet.'

I closed my eyes and leaned against the wall. Took a deep breath. I should have known. It was too good to be true that she would just accept Laurel disappearing again. That she wouldn't try to find her. Fuck.

*

I get on a bus going in the opposite direction to school. I spend the whole journey hoping and praying that Sadie is better at hiding than the police are at seeking.

I walk down the country lanes in the rain. I forgot to bring an umbrella.

Barnaby the Bear is sodden. I pick him up and hold him close.

I kneel on the ground next to the grave and I talk. I thought it might feel silly, doing this, but it feels like the most natural thing in the world. I tell Laurel about Mum and Dad and Michel. I only talk about the good things, the happy things – the things I would want someone to tell me if I'd been away from my family for years and years.

I tell her I'm sorry. I tell her we did everything we could to find her. I tell her we never gave up hope.

I tell her I'm not sure I've done the right thing. I ask her what she would have done in my position, and I actually stop and listen as if I'm expecting an answer.

I tell her I'm proud of her, for being so brave for all those years when she must have been so very, very scared. I'm proud of her for befriending Sadie, for being there for her when no one else was.

I tell her that I love her.

There's nothing left to say after that. I'll be back —
in a week or a month. Whenever the urge to tell
someone gets too much for me, I'll come here and
talk to my sister. She's the only one who understands.
That's one thing I'm absolutely sure about. Some
people might find it hard to accept why I've done what
I've done. They might think it's unforgivable, that my
parents deserve to know what happened to Laurel.

But my sister and I know the truth.

We know that sometimes you have to do whatever
it takes to protect your family.

Imagine you're playing in the sandpit in the front
garden on a warm summer's day. You're showing your
little sister how to build a sandcastle. Your mum is
inside, in the kitchen perhaps. You can hear your dad
mowing the lawn in the back garden. A man stops to
talk to you. He seems nice. He looks up and down the
street, then opens the gate and walks towards you.
The man takes your sister by the hand, he says he's
taking her to get an ice cream. What do you do? You
tuck your teddy bear under your arm, then push your
sister away — so hard it makes her cry. You say, 'No! *I*
want an ice cream! Faith can stay here.' And you walk
away with the man, quickly. You don't look back.

You do whatever it takes.

Excerpt from The Forgotten Children, *by Jeanette Hayes (New and Updated Edition, 2014)*

. . . Sarah Braithwaite, known to her family as Sadie, was last seen on 7 April 2000. The police were convinced she was snatched by her father, notorious local criminal Eddie Gibbons. Sarah's mother Gail never believed that version of events. Sadie's disappearance was only reported to the police after a week. For seven whole days and nights, no one was aware that anything was amiss. It was only when a neighbour visited, finding Gail Braithwaite unconscious in a pool of her own vomit, that the alarm was finally raised.

Gail Braithwaite was unable to help the police with their enquiries. A drug-and-alcohol addict of many years, she was not a credible witness, to say the very least. The police investigation into the disappearance of Sarah Braithwaite was closed within a month; the investigation into Laurel

439

Logan's disappearance is still ongoing, twelve long years after she went missing. The fact that the two little girls lived less than an hour away from each other only serves to highlight this terrible contrast.

UPDATE: I visit Gail again, fourteen years after Sadie's disappearance, ten years after I last saw her. The town of Blaxford may have changed little since my last visit, but the woman who greets me at the door could not look more different to the one I interviewed all those years ago. Today, she may look slightly older than her forty-three years, but Gail Braithwaite is healthy and, to some extent, happy. 'Sober for eight years,' she says proudly.

'I think about Sadie every day, you know. She's the first thing I think about when I wake up in the morning, and the last thing I think about before I go to sleep at night.'

As we're talking, a little face peeks out from behind a door. 'This is Selina,' Gail says proudly. The little girl is shy at first, but before long she's sitting on her mother's knee, bouncing up and down and pretending to ride a horse. The resemblance to Sadie is striking, and I say so.

Before Gail can say anything, the little girl pipes up. 'Sadie! Sadie! Sadie!'

Gail smiles sadly. 'We talk about Sadie a lot. I think it's important that Selina knows all about her big sister. So that she's not confused when Sadie comes home to us.'

Selina's face shines with hope as she looks up, unaware of the living hell her mother has endured. 'Sadie come home?'

Tears glisten in Gail's eyes as she looks at the photo of her missing daughter, in pride of place in the middle of the mantelpiece. 'One day, sweetheart. Maybe one day.'

Acknowledgements

Sincerest thanks to Julia Churchill, Roisin Heycock, Niamh Mulvey, Lauren Woosey, Talya Baker, Glenn Tavennec, the Sisterhood, YA Thinkers, UKYA bloggers, Gillian Robertson, Sarah Stewart, Lauren James, Cate James, Ciara Daly, Robert Clarke and Caro Clarke.

Cat Clarke was born in Zambia and brought up in Scotland and Yorkshire, which has given her an accent that tends to confuse people. Cat lives in Edinburgh with four unruly pets and an unruly French wife. Her first novel, *Entangled*, won the Redbridge Teenage Book Award and was longlisted for the Branford Boase Award. *Undone* won the Lancashire Book of the Year Award.

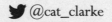 @cat_clarke

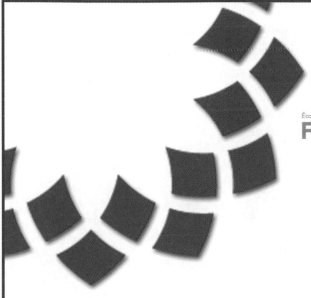

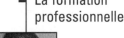

Table des matières

100 carrières de la santé et des services sociaux

Comment va la santé? **24**

La santé est de loin l'un des secteurs les plus prometteurs en matière d'emploi au Québec. Dans ce vaste domaine, rares sont les formations qui n'ont pas la cote auprès des employeurs. Radiographie d'un secteur d'emploi qui tient la forme.

Infiltrez le réseau! **30**

Le réseau de la santé et des services sociaux offre des milieux de travail diversifiés. Découvrez les particularités de chacun.

Ai-je le profil? **36**

Côtoyer chaque jour la maladie et la détresse humaine tout en restant serein n'est pas donné à tout le monde. Avez-vous les qualités et les aptitudes nécessaires?

u un métier **d'avenir?**

Ces programmes offrent des perspectives d'emploi intéressantes dans toutes les régions du Québec !

- Archives médicales *(411.A0)*
- Assistance aux bénéficiaires en établissement de santé *(5081)*
- Assistance familiale et sociale aux personnes à domicile *(5045)*
- Assistance technique en pharmacie *(5141)*
- Santé, assistance et soins infirmiers *(5287)*
- Soins infirmiers *(180.B0)*
- Technique d'analyses biomédicales *(140.B0)*
- Technique d'éducation à l'enfance *(322.A0)*
- Technique d'électrophysiologie médicale *(140.A0)*
- Technique d'hygiène dentaire *(111.A0)*
- Technique d'inhalothérapie *(141.A0)*
- Technique de médecine nucléaire *(142.B0)*
- Technique de radiodiagnostic *(142.A0)*
- Technique de radio-oncologie *(142.C0)*

Renseigne-toi sur les programmes de formation du ministère de l'Éducation dans les secteurs Santé et Services sociaux. Tu peux consulter les sites Internet suivants.

www.meq.gouv.qc.ca
www.inforoutefpt.org
www.avenirensante.com
et imt.emploiquebec.net

Éducation
Québec

avenirensante.com

Le site de référence sur les carrières du réseau de la santé et des services sociaux

Que tu aspires à des études secondaires, collégiales ou universitaires, des opportunités de carrières dans des milieux diversifiés s'offrent à toi...

soins de santé | services sociaux | technologie | recherche | enseignement | gestion

Quarante-cinq titres d'emploi

Les établissements d'enseignement et leurs programmes de formation

Des témoignages vidéo

Des références utiles

Des liens vers les sites d'Emploi-Québec et de Santé Montréal

Tu es de ceux et celles qui ont à cœur de soulager et de soigner les gens ?
Le réseau de la santé et des services sociaux offre des perspectives d'emplois de qualité et des conditions de travail avantageuses.
Renseigne-toi sur avenirensante.com

Santé et Services sociaux
Québec

Avec la participation de :
Ministère de l'Éducation
Ministère de l'Emploi, de la Solidarité sociale et de la Famille

Index

Des professions et des témoignages
> **Par niveau de formation**

Voici la liste des professions traitées sous forme de témoignages et figurant de la page 42 à la page 152.

Formation professionnelle

Formation collégiale

Index

Des professions et des témoignages (suite)
> Par niveau de formation

Formation universitaire

Index

Des professions et des témoignages (suite)
> Par niveau de formation

Études médicales

Index

Des professions et des témoignages
> Par milieu de travail

Voici les professions classées selon le milieu de travail où travaillent les professionnels interviewés. Ces témoignages figurent de la page 42 à la page 152.

Index

Des professions et des témoignages (suite)
❯ Par milieu de travail

Index

Des professions et des témoignages (suite)

> Par milieu de travail

Une carrière chez HÉMA-QUÉBEC

Vous devrlez y penser!

HÉMA-QUÉBEC a pour mission :

- **De fournir avec efficience des composants, des substituts sanguins et des tissus humains sécuritaires, de qualité optimale et en quantité suffisante pour répondre aux besoins de la population québécoise.**

- **D'offrir et de développer une expertise, des services et des produits spécialisés et novateurs dans les domaines de la médecine transfusionnelle et de la greffe de tissus humains.**

LES POSTES EN FORTE DEMANDE

- **Infirmier(ère)**
- **Assistant(e) technique de collecte**
- **Technicien(ne) de laboratoire**

- **Commis service à la clientèle - Gardien(ne)**
- **Assistant(e) technique de laboratoire**

INFORMEZ-VOUS SUR NOS AUTRES SECTEURS D'EMPLOIS

audits • assurance qualité • sang de cordon • tissus humains • formation • services-conseils aux donneurs • moelle osseuse • recherche et développement • communications • technologies de l'information • ressources humaines • transports • affaires juridiques • comptabilité • achats

Pour en savoir davantage et pour postuler, consultez notre site Internet :

www.hema-quebec.qc.ca

Une grande
mission
une grande
é**🌢**uipe
HÉMA-QUÉBEC

Santé !

L'UQAM est fière d'annoncer la création de l'Institut
Santé et société. Cet institut réunit quelque 150
professeurs issus de différents domaines.
Ceux-ci poursuivent leurs recherches sur des sujets
touchant les aspects biologiques, psychologiques,
économiques et sociaux de la santé.

Grâce à son approche interdisciplinaire, l'Institut
Santé et société pourra apporter des solutions
novatrices à des problématiques complexes comme
le suicide, l'itinérance, la violence, les troubles
anxieux ou le cancer.

L'Institut souhaite accroître le mieux-être de la
population, notamment par des programmes de
recherche axés sur la prévention, généralement
menés en partenariat avec le milieu.

Information
(514) 987-3000, poste 2250
www.iss.uqam.ca

UQÀM
Prenez position

Comment interpréter l'information

100 carrières de la santé et des services sociaux

Le groupe de recherche Ma Carrière, division de Jobboom et chef de file dans la création de contenus portant sur l'emploi, la carrière et la formation, est fier de présenter ce guide d'exploration des carrières de la santé et des services sociaux.

100 carrières de la santé et des services sociaux se veut d'abord un outil permettant de faire un premier survol des possibilités de carrière dans le domaine, une sorte de «bougie d'allumage» pour tous ceux qui s'intéressent à ce secteur d'activité offrant d'excellentes perspectives d'emploi.

Nous tenons à remercier de leur précieuse collaboration les nombreuses personnes jointes au cours de cette recherche, plus précisément les responsables des services de placement dans les centres de formation professionnelle, les cégeps et les universités, les personnes-ressources dans plusieurs associations et ordres professionnels – un merci particulier à la Fédération des médecins résidents du Québec (FMRQ) qui nous a recommandé plusieurs médecins spécialistes –, de même que les nombreux professionnels de la santé et des services sociaux qui ont bien voulu nous accorder de leur temps. Tous nous ont permis d'enrichir nos recherches, notre réflexion et l'information que nous publions dans ce guide.

Attention **Le contenu de ce guide n'entend pas couvrir TOUTES les professions pratiquées dans le réseau de la santé et des services sociaux, celles-ci étant fort nombreuses et diversifiées. L'ouvrage vise plutôt à illustrer la plupart des professions liées aux principaux programmes d'études offerts dans le réseau public de l'éducation et à fournir quelques pistes sur les cheminements scolaires et professionnels qui mènent à ces postes (voir les encadrés «Mon parcours» dans les témoignages).**

▶ Notre démarche de recherche et de rédaction

Au printemps 2003, l'équipe du Groupe de recherche Ma Carrière a établi la liste des principaux programmes d'études liés à la santé et aux services sociaux offerts dans le réseau public de l'éducation aux trois niveaux d'enseignement (formation professionnelle, collégiale et universitaire). Les professions illustrées dans ce guide sont celles qui sont généralement pratiquées par les diplômés de ces programmes. Pour compléter notre sélection, nous avons aussi jugé pertinent d'ajouter quelques professions périphériques au domaine de la santé et des services sociaux.

Nous avons ensuite fait appel aux services de placement dans les centres de formation professionnelle, les cégeps et les universités, de même qu'à plusieurs associations et ordres professionnels pour obtenir des coordonnées de diplômés ou de professionnels œuvrant dans le domaine de la santé et des services sociaux sur le marché du travail.

Les recommandations reçues ont parfois été abondantes et nous avons dû faire un choix parmi l'ensemble. Nos critères de sélection ont été les suivants : diversité des milieux de travail représentés; ratio équilibré d'hommes et de femmes; représentativité de l'ensemble des régions du Québec. Nous avons aussi tenté de privilégier des professionnels récemment diplômés qui cumulent aujourd'hui quelques années d'expérience sur le marché du travail (entre trois et cinq ans). Cependant, certains professionnels présentés possèdent une plus longue expérience, notamment ceux qui ont poursuivi des études universitaires de deuxième cycle.

▶ À propos de l'information contenue dans les témoignages

Ces brefs portraits permettent au lecteur de se familiariser avec le rôle des professionnels de la santé et des services sociaux, de découvrir leurs motivations à œuvrer dans ce domaine et les principales étapes de leur cheminement scolaire et professionnel.

Ces contenus reflètent l'opinion et l'expérience du professionnel interviewé et ne représentent pas nécessairement toutes les facettes d'une même profession. En ce sens, la rubrique «Des milieux de travail potentiels» démontre bien qu'il est possible d'œuvrer dans d'autres milieux que celui illustré dans le témoignage. Les tâches et les responsabilités des professionnels peuvent alors varier.

• Répertoire des principales formations (page 159)

Ce répertoire regroupe les principales formations liées à la santé et aux services sociaux offertes aux niveaux professionnel, collégial et universitaire au Québec et permettant de pratiquer les professions illustrées dans ce guide. L'information était à jour en septembre 2003. L'offre des programmes peut avoir été modifiée depuis. Contactez les établissements qui vous intéressent pour vérifier l'offre de leurs programmes.

• Répertoire des principales associations et des ordres professionnels (page 162)

Ce répertoire regroupe les principales associations et les ordres professionnels québécois liés aux professions illustrées dans ce guide. Pour constituer cette liste, nous nous sommes basés sur les ordres et associations répertoriés dans le site aveniriensante.com produit par le ministère de la Santé et des Services sociaux du Québec. Nous l'avons ensuite étoffée grâce à notre propre recherche. Notez que nous avons cherché à répertorier les grandes associations provinciales et que nous n'avons pas nécessairement inclus les associations régionales ou canadiennes. Ce répertoire contient aussi les coordonnées de quelques organismes clés du domaine de la santé et des services sociaux (ministère, etc.). L'information était à jour en septembre 2003. ■ 09/03

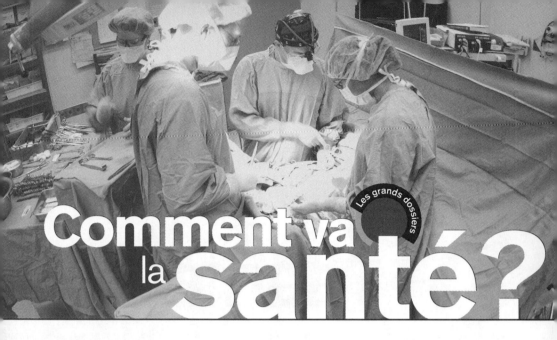

Comment va la santé?

Ce n'est un secret pour personne : la santé est, de loin, l'un des secteurs les plus prometteurs en matière d'emploi dans la province. Dans ce vaste domaine, rares sont les formations qui n'ont pas la cote. Au ministère de la Santé et des Services sociaux du Québec comme dans les établissements du réseau, tout est mis en œuvre pour recruter des professionnels.

Par Guylaine Boucher

Le ministère de la Santé et des Services sociaux (MSSS) estime que de 11 000 à 20 000 postes par année seront à pourvoir dans le réseau d'ici à 2011. En 2003 seulement, plus de 11 000 personnes ont été embauchées. Sur ce nombre, environ 3 000 ont été recrutées pour pourvoir des postes devenus vacants à la suite de départs à la retraite.

Selon Robert Tremblay, directeur de la recherche, de la planification et du développement de la main-d'œuvre au MSSS, plusieurs éléments expliquent l'actuelle demande de main-d'œuvre, en commençant par le vieillissement. Non seulement le personnel en place vieillit-il, ce qui entraîne de nombreux départs à la retraite, mais la population avance en âge elle aussi, et requiert de plus en plus de soins. «Plus de 2 000 personnes ont pris leur retraite en 2002. Le nombre de départs devrait augmenter progressivement, pour atteindre 8 000 personnes par année en 2009. Et c'est sans compter le fait que l'accroissement de la demande de services exigera la création de nouveaux postes, particulièrement dans les soins directs aux patients, notamment pour les infirmières, infirmières auxiliaires et préposés aux bénéficiaires», précise M. Tremblay.

Bien que touchant la quasi-totalité des secteurs, les besoins de main-d'œuvre sont particulièrement criants dans certaines professions. C'est le cas notamment pour les infirmières, infirmières auxiliaires, orthophonistes, ergothérapeutes, physiothérapeutes, pharmaciens, inhalothérapeutes, techniciens en radio-oncologie et techniciens en radiodiagnostic. Pour ces professions, M. Tremblay parle carrément de pénurie de

Les besoins de main-d'œuvre sont particulièrement criants dans certaines professions. C'est le cas notamment pour les infirmières, infirmières auxiliaires, orthophonistes, ergothérapeutes, physiothérapeutes, pharmaciens, inhalothérapeutes, techniciens en radio-oncologie et techniciens en radiodiagnostic.

main-d'œuvre. À titre d'exemple, en 2003, en soins infirmiers, tous niveaux d'enseignement confondus, l'Ordre des infirmières et infirmiers du Québec parlait d'un manque de 1 200 travailleurs.

La situation n'est guère plus reluisante en matière d'effectif médical. Au MSSS, le directeur de la main-d'œuvre médicale, Daniel Poirier, estime à 800 le nombre de médecins omnipraticiens manquants. Certaines régions écopent davantage que d'autres. C'est le cas notamment du Bas-Saint-Laurent, du Saguenay–Lac-Saint-Jean, de l'Outaouais, de l'Abitibi-Témiscamingue, de la Côte-Nord et de la Mauricie.

Chef du service des affaires médicales à la Régie régionale de la Côte-Nord et présidente du Comité inter-régional des effectifs médicaux en régions désignées, Danielle Murray évalue que 40 médecins manquent à l'appel dans sa région immédiate. «Les plans d'effectifs – N.D.L.R. : la planification de la main-d'œuvre en fonction des besoins estimés – sont actuellement incomplets dans la majorité des établissements de santé de la Côte-Nord. Globalement, pour les établissements, si on exclut les médecins qui font seulement de la pratique privée, on a 96 médecins alors que le plan en prévoit 135.»

Le manque de professionnels se fait aussi sentir dans les différentes spécialités de la médecine. À la Fédération des médecins spécialistes du Québec, on estime qu'il y a une pénurie d'environ 1 000 médecins spécialistes dans la province. L'ensemble des 35 spécialités sont touchées, mais 9 champs de pratique semblent être boudés par les étudiants en médecine : la radio-oncologie, la médecine nucléaire, l'anesthésiologie, la cardiologie, la chirurgie, la néphrologie, la psychiatrie, la médecine d'urgence et l'anatomopathologie.

Même les gestionnaires se font rares, selon Nicole Brodeur, présidente-directrice générale du Centre de référence des directeurs généraux et des cadres. D'ici à 2010, il faudra en fait remplacer un peu plus de 5 300 cadres, soit l'équivalent de 300 à 500 postes par an. Ces postes sont majoritairement de niveau intermédiaire : coordination, encadrement clinique, etc. (voir le texte *La gestion du système de santé* en page 148). ▶

▶ Dans les établissements d'enseignement

Témoins privilégiés de l'évolution du marché de l'emploi, les différents établissements d'enseignement qui offrent des programmes de formation en santé ont vu la demande de diplômés s'intensifier au cours des dernières années. À la Commission scolaire du Fleuve-et-des-Lacs à Trois-Pistoles, dans le Bas-Saint-Laurent, où deux formations en lien avec le domaine sont offertes, soit *Assistance aux bénéficiaires en établissement de santé* et *Assistance familiale et sociale aux personnes à domicile*, la conseillère pédagogique en formation professionnelle, Johanne Tremblay, qualifie le placement de «très bon». En fait, sur 18 personnes ayant terminé leur formation en assistance aux bénéficiaires en mai 2003, seulement deux étaient encore sans emploi en septembre de la même année.

Le scénario se répète du côté des formations collégiales. Par exemple, au Cégep de Trois-Rivières où l'on offre trois programmes en santé dont *Hygiène dentaire*, *Techniques de diététique* et *Soins infirmiers*, on a peine à répondre à la demande dans certains cas. «Au cours de la dernière année, en hygiène dentaire, nous avons reçu 68 offres d'emploi pour seulement 12 candidats. C'est plus d'une offre d'emploi par semaine. En soins infirmiers, 65 % de la centaine d'élèves se sont placés en une journée, soit lors de la journée carrière que nous avons organisée en janvier», explique Maryse Paquette, responsable du Service de placement.

Au niveau universitaire, les diplômés ont la cote. À l'Université du Québec en Outaouais, la conseillère en emploi Chantal Bilodeau confirme voir les sortants en soins infirmiers de son établissement se trouver un emploi avant même d'avoir terminé leur baccalauréat. «Les employeurs viennent les chercher sur les bancs de l'école, avant même qu'ils aient fini. Depuis que les étudiants peuvent faire de l'externat en deuxième année, les employeurs leur offrent un travail à temps partiel et les embauchent officiellement lorsqu'ils reçoivent leur diplôme. C'est assez exceptionnel.»

Peu importe le niveau d'enseignement concerné, les emplois émanent majoritairement du secteur public : CLSC, centres hospitaliers, etc., mais aussi dans une bonne proportion du secteur privé : entreprises de maintien à ▶

→ À chaque région ses besoins

Pour chacune des régions du Québec, voici des professionnels de la santé pour lesquels les perspectives d'emploi sont «favorables» et «très favorables» selon Emploi-Québec.

Abitibi-Témiscamingue

- Audiologistes et orthophonistes
- Ergothérapeutes
- Infirmiers
- Infirmiers auxiliaires
- Inhalothérapeutes
- Médecins généralistes et spécialistes
- Pharmaciens
- Physiothérapeutes
- Psychologues
- Techniciens de laboratoire médical
- Travailleurs sociaux

Bas-Saint-Laurent

- Ambulanciers
- Ergothérapeutes
- Infirmiers
- Infirmiers auxiliaires
- Inhalothérapeutes
- Médecins généralistes et spécialistes
- Pharmaciens
- Psychologues
- Technologues en radiologie
- Techniciens de laboratoire médical
- Travailleurs sociaux et communautaires

Capitale-Nationale

- Dentistes
- Ergothérapeutes
- Infirmiers
- Infirmiers auxiliaires
- Inhalothérapeutes
- Médecins généralistes et spécialistes
- Pharmaciens
- Physiothérapeutes
- Technologues en radiologie
- Technologues en santé animale

Centre-du-Québec

- Ambulanciers
- Dentistes
- Ergothérapeutes
- Hygiénistes dentaires
- Infirmiers
- Infirmiers auxiliaires
- Médecins généralistes et spécialistes
- Pharmaciens
- Techniciens de laboratoire médical
- Vétérinaires

Chaudière-Appalaches

- Ambulanciers
- Dentistes
- Ergothérapeutes
- Infirmiers
- Infirmiers auxiliaires
- Inhalothérapeutes
- Médecins généralistes et spécialistes
- Pharmaciens
- Physiothérapeutes
- Techniciens de laboratoire médical
- Technologues en radiologie
- Vétérinaires

Côte-Nord

- Dentistes
- Infirmiers
- Infirmiers auxiliaires
- Médecins généralistes et spécialistes
- Pharmaciens
- Techniciens de laboratoire médical

Estrie
- Ambulanciers
- Assistants dentaires
- Dentistes
- Infirmiers
- Infirmiers auxiliaires
- Inhalothérapeutes
- Médecins généralistes et spécialistes
- Pharmaciens
- Physiothérapeutes
- Psychologues
- Sages-femmes
- Techniciens de laboratoire médical
- Techniciens en radiologie
- Technologues de laboratoire médical et assistants en pathologie
- Travailleurs sociaux

Gaspésie–Îles-de-la-Madeleine
- Ambulanciers
- Infirmiers
- Infirmiers auxiliaires
- Médecins généralistes et spécialistes
- Pharmaciens
- Techniciens de laboratoire médical
- Technologues en radiologie
- Travailleurs sociaux

Lanaudière
- Ambulanciers
- Assistants dentaires
- Dentistes
- Ergothérapeutes
- Hygiénistes dentaires
- Infirmiers
- Infirmiers auxiliaires
- Inhalothérapeutes
- Médecins généralistes et spécialistes
- Pharmaciens
- Physiothérapeutes
- Psychologues
- Techniciens de laboratoire médical
- Technologues de laboratoire médical et assistants en pathologie
- Technologues en radiologie
- Travailleurs sociaux

Laurentides
- Ambulanciers
- Assistants dentaires
- Dentistes
- Diététistes et nutritionnistes
- Ergothérapeutes
- Hygiénistes dentaires
- Infirmiers
- Infirmiers auxiliaires
- Inhalothérapeutes
- Médecins généralistes et spécialistes
- Opticiens
- Optométristes
- Pharmaciens
- Physiothérapeutes
- Psychologues
- Techniciens de laboratoire médical
- Technologues en radiologie
- Travailleurs sociaux

Laval
- Ambulanciers
- Assistants dentaires
- Dentistes
- Diététistes et nutritionnistes
- Ergothérapeutes
- Hygiénistes et thérapeutes dentaires
- Infirmiers
- Infirmiers auxiliaires
- Médecins généralistes et spécialistes
- Optométristes
- Opticiens
- Pharmaciens
- Physiothérapeutes
- Techniciens de laboratoire médical
- Technologues de laboratoire médical et assistants en pathologie
- Technologues en radiologie
- Technologues en santé animale

Mauricie
- Ergothérapeutes
- Infirmiers
- Infirmiers auxiliaires
- Inhalothérapeutes
- Médecins généralistes et spécialistes
- Pharmaciens
- Physiothérapeutes
- Technologues en radiologie

Montérégie
- Ambulanciers
- Assistants dentaires
- Audiologistes et orthophonistes
- Dentistes
- Ergothérapeutes
- Hygiénistes dentaires
- Infirmiers
- Infirmiers auxiliaires
- Inhalothérapeutes
- Médecins généralistes et spécialistes
- Opticiens
- Optométristes
- Pharmaciens
- Physiothérapeutes
- Techniciens dentaires et travailleurs à l'établi dans les laboratoires dentaires
- Techniciens de laboratoire
- Technologues de laboratoire médical et assistants en pathologie
- Technologues en radiologie
- Technologues en santé animale
- Vétérinaires

Montréal
- Ambulanciers
- Assistants dentaires
- Audiologistes et orthophonistes
- Dentistes
- Diététistes et nutrionnistes
- Ergothérapeutes
- Hygiénistes dentaires
- Infirmiers
- Infirmiers auxiliaires
- Inhalothérapeutes
- Médecins généralistes et spécialistes

- Optométristes
- Pharmaciens
- Physiothérapeutes
- Psychologues
- Sages-femmes
- Techniciens de laboratoire médical
- Technologues de laboratoire médical et assistants en pathologie
- Technologues en radiologie
- Travailleurs sociaux

Nord-du-Québec
- Dentistes
- Infirmiers
- Infirmiers auxiliaires
- Médecins généralistes et spécialistes
- Pharmaciens
- Techniciens de laboratoire médical

Outaouais
- Ambulanciers
- Assistants dentaires
- Dentistes
- Diététistes et nutritionnistes
- Ergothérapeutes
- Infirmiers
- Infirmiers auxiliaires
- Inhalothérapeutes
- Médecins généralistes et spécialistes
- Pharmaciens
- Physiothérapeutes
- Techniciens de laboratoire médical
- Technologues de laboratoire médical et assistants en pathologie
- Technologues en radiologie

Saguenay–Lac-Saint-Jean
- Ambulanciers
- Infirmiers
- Infirmiers auxiliaires
- Inhalothérapeutes
- Médecins généralistes et spécialistes
- Pharmaciens
- Physiothérapeutes
- Techniciens de laboratoire
- Technologues en radiologie

Source : *Perspectives professionnelles 2002-2006*, Emploi-Québec.

domicile, cliniques médicales privées, etc. Elles proviennent aussi d'un peu partout au Québec. Résultat, beaucoup de diplômés n'ont pas à déménager pour se trouver du travail. À Trois-Pistoles par exemple, Johanne Tremblay estime que «90 % des sortants trouvent un emploi dans la région même et n'ont pas besoin d'aller vers les grands centres». En Mauricie, la situation est moins tranchée. Aussi, selon Maryse Paquette, «en 2003, 56 % des diplômés en soins infirmiers et 60 % des sortants en diététique se sont placés dans la région. Les pourcentages évoluent parce que les gens sont portés à être plus mobiles pour aller chercher des meilleures conditions de travail.»

En matière de conditions de travail, les spécialistes du placement sont d'ailleurs unanimes : si les emplois sont nombreux pour les jeunes diplômés, beaucoup restent tout de même à temps partiel, de nuit ou même occasionnels. Cela se vérifie dans la plupart des établissements, et particulièrement dans le milieu hospitalier. «Plusieurs des postes offerts, même après l'obtention du diplôme, ne sont pas des postes réguliers», explique Chantal Bilodeau. Une analyse partagée par Johanne Tremblay. «Tant et aussi longtemps que les diplômés n'ont pas acquis une certaine expérience, ils doivent prendre les horaires de soir, de nuit et de fin de semaine. Dans certains cas, il faut quelques années avant que ça change, plusieurs doivent en fait attendre que d'autres nouveaux employés arrivent.»

La surcharge de travail, les nombreuses heures supplémentaires, le travail de nuit, à temps partiel ou en disponibilité en convainquent plusieurs d'aller pratiquer à l'extérieur du Québec. En Outaouais, en raison de la proximité avec l'Ontario, c'est un choix naturel pour beaucoup de professionnels de la santé. Les difficultés de rétention de personnel qui en découlent augmentent encore davantage les besoins de main-d'œuvre.

> **En matière de conditions de travail, les spécialistes du placement sont d'ailleurs unanimes : si les emplois sont nombreux pour les jeunes diplômés, beaucoup restent tout de même à temps partiel, de nuit ou même occasionnels.**

Freiner l'hémorragie

Malgré tout, au MSSS, on se montre optimiste. «Il y a plusieurs façons de faire face aux problèmes actuels, explique Robert Tremblay. La première est d'augmenter les admissions dans les programmes de formation. Il est encore trop tôt pour en mesurer l'impact véritable. Nous accordons aussi désormais beaucoup d'importance à la promotion des professions de la santé. Nous sommes présents dans tous les salons de l'emploi.»

Beaucoup d'énergie a également été consacrée à la réorganisation du travail. «Il n'y a aucune raison pour que des infirmières donnent des bains ou fassent des lits : tout cela peut être accompli par d'autres, des préposés aux bénéficiaires par exemple. Nous faisons en sorte que chacun se concentre sur ce pour quoi il a été formé», explique M. Tremblay.

En médecine, Daniel Poirier rappelle que cette réorganisation du travail se concrétisera dans les groupes de médecine familiale. «Dans ces nouvelles organisations, beaucoup de tâches habituellement effectuées par les médecins (la pesée, la prise de tension artérielle, etc.) seront confiées à des infirmières. Cela réduira leur charge de travail, leur permettant ainsi de voir davantage de patients. En bout de ligne, on pourrait même constater que l'on a besoin de moins de médecins qu'on le croyait.»

Selon Robert Tremblay, l'amélioration des différents milieux de travail est aussi l'une des pistes privilégiées pour favoriser la rétention de la main-d'œuvre. «Nous n'avons pas la réputation d'être de bons employeurs. Nous travaillons très fort pour changer cette réalité. Les établissements du réseau public ont déjà fait beaucoup. Ils se penchent notamment sur la conciliation travail-famille ainsi que sur une meilleure gestion des horaires. Peu à peu, les choses changent. Pendant des années, nous avons eu des surplus de main-d'œuvre. Aujourd'hui, il faut apprendre à vivre avec une situation toute différente.» ■

Vivre une expérience humaine et professionnelle stimulante à la Baie James

Êtes-vous attiré par le dépaysement, des contacts culturels enrichissants, des activités plein air, un environnement sain, un rythme de vie différent ? Êtes-vous prêt pour un rôle professionnel élargi, l'approche multidisciplinaire, une pratique plus humaine ? Dire oui, c'est choisir un environnement sain tout autant qu'une orientation de carrière. Voilà certes un défi à votre mesure !

Le Conseil Cri de la santé et des services sociaux de la Baie James planifie, organise, développe et dispense les services sociaux de santé aux 16 000 cris et non-cris résidant dans les neuf communautés de l'immense territoire cri. Membre du réseau du MSSS comme région 18, il regroupe les missions d'une régie régionale et dispense ses services par le biais d'un centre hospitalier, de deux CLSC, de huit points de service, d'un centre de services sociaux, d'un centre de réadaptation, de deux foyers de groupe, d'un service de santé publique, d'un centre administratif et de quatre autres points de services pour les patients cris à l'extérieur de la région. Il administre aussi les programmes suivants : santé mentale, diabète, soins à domicile, alcool et drogues.

Cette organisation dynamique est en plein développement et donc en constant recrutement pour des assignations permanentes, long ou court terme, de professionnels et de techniciens dont entre autre : infirmiers, médecins, pharmaciens, dentistes, nutritionnistes, physionthérapeutes, ergothérapeutes, travailleurs sociaux, techniciens dentaires, en laboratoire, en radiologie, archivistes.

Les conditions salariales sont très avantageuses incluant primes, logement meublé fourni, frais de déménagement, d'entreposage et de sorties défrayés.

Envoyez-nous sans plus tarder votre candidature à l'adresse suivante :

C.C.S.S.S.B.J., Service des ressources humaines
Case postale 250, Chisasibi (Québec) J0M 1E0
Télécopieur : (819) 855-2680
Courriel : info@conseilcri-baiejames.ca

Conseil Cri de la santé et des services sociaux de la Baie James

Infiltrez
le réseau!

Pour quiconque s'intéresse
au secteur de la santé et des
services sociaux, le Québec
offre des milieux de travail
diversifiés : secteurs public
ou privé, ou encore organismes
sans but lucratif, il suffit d'y
regarder de plus près!

Par Guylaine Boucher

Le secteur public

C'est dans le secteur public que l'on retrouve au Québec la plus grande variété d'emplois en santé et services sociaux. À lui seul, le réseau public regroupe en effet un peu plus de 230 000 employés[1]. Ces derniers œuvrent dans cinq grandes catégories d'établissements : les centres hospitaliers (CH), les centres locaux de services communautaires (CLSC), les centres d'hébergement et de soins de longue durée (CHSLD), les centres jeunesse (CJ) et les centres de réadaptation (CR). Au total, 349 établissements publics sont actifs dans la province[2].

La quasi-totalité des métiers liés à la santé peuvent mener à un emploi dans un centre hospitalier, que ce soit aux urgences, dans les différentes unités de soins ou encore en salle d'opération.

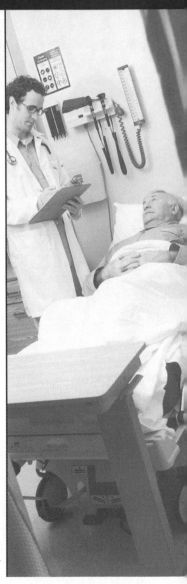

Accessibles à l'ensemble de la population, les **centres hospitaliers** offrent des soins médicaux de base ou spécialisés, allant du simple point de suture à l'intervention chirurgicale complexe, comme la transplantation d'organe. Les maladies liées à la santé mentale telles que la schizophrénie, la dépression, l'anorexie, etc., peuvent aussi être traitées en centre hospitalier.

Un champ d'action aussi large requiert la contribution d'un grand nombre de professionnels. En fait, la quasi-totalité des métiers liés à la santé peuvent mener à un emploi dans un centre hospitalier, que ce soit aux urgences, dans les différentes unités de soins ou encore en salle d'opération. On y retrouve également les professionnels des services sociaux, notamment des psychologues et des travailleurs sociaux.

Les services offerts dans les **CLSC** diffèrent d'un établissement à l'autre, mais tous sont cependant tenus de dispenser des soins médicaux de base, de même que certains services à caractère social : consultation psychologique, accompagnement parental, etc. C'est aussi à eux qu'incombe la responsabilité des services de soins à domicile et le service de consultation téléphonique Info-Santé. Les CLSC peuvent intervenir auprès des individus de tout âge.

Pour mener à bien leur mission, ils ont recours à un vaste éventail de professionnels. Ainsi, outre les médecins et les infirmières, les CLSC comptent dans leurs rangs bon nombre de travailleurs sociaux, psychologues, techniciens en travail social ou aides domestiques.

Contrairement aux CLSC, les **CHSLD** desservent uniquement la population adulte. Ils ont la responsabilité d'offrir des services médicaux, psychologiques et d'hébergement aux adultes qui, pour des raisons de santé physique ou mentale, ne peuvent plus demeurer chez eux. Ils les accueillent pour des périodes allant de quelques semaines à quelques années. La majorité de la clientèle de ces établissements est âgée de plus de 65 ans, mais un adulte, souffrant par exemple du SIDA et requérant des soins continus, pourrait aussi avoir recours à leurs services.

▶

En raison des nombreuses compressions qu'a connues le réseau de la santé et des services sociaux, plusieurs établissements ayant des missions différentes se sont regroupés. En région éloignée par exemple, l'ensemble des services sont la plupart du temps offerts par un seul établissement, alors appelé centre de santé.

Cette catégorie d'établissement emploie beaucoup de personnel médical, en majorité des infirmières, des infirmières auxiliaires et des préposés aux bénéficiaires. Des médecins omnipraticiens y œuvrent également à temps partiel. On peut parfois y retrouver des pharmaciens, des ergothérapeutes, des physiothérapeutes ou des techniciens en réadaptation physique. Plus rarement, certains centres d'hébergement peuvent aussi embaucher des récréologues, des techniciens en loisirs, des psychologues ou des travailleurs sociaux.

De leur côté, les **centres jeunesse** entrent en scène lorsqu'une situation d'abus ou de mauvais traitement nécessite le retrait d'un enfant de sa famille. Ils gèrent donc un imposant réseau de familles d'accueil. Ils agissent également auprès des personnes condamnées en vertu de la Loi sur les jeunes contrevenants. La médiation familiale, l'adoption et la recherche d'antécédents biologiques (lorsqu'un enfant adopté souhaite retrouver ses parents biologiques) sont également de leur ressort. Des spécialistes de la relation d'aide, tels que les travailleurs sociaux, les psychologues, les criminologues, les techniciens en travail social, en éducation spécialisée et en délinquance, représentent donc la majorité des employés des centres jeunesse. D'autres professionnels peuvent aussi être mis à contribution. C'est le cas des médecins omnipraticiens, des pédopsychiatres et, dans certains cas, des avocats qui voient à la bonne application de la Loi sur les jeunes contrevenants. Fait à noter, une bonne partie du travail des employés des centres jeunesse se fait directement sur le terrain, soit auprès des familles aux prises avec des problèmes. La clientèle des centres jeunesse est âgée de 0 à 18 ans. Leur intervention s'étend aussi à l'entourage de leurs jeunes clients.

Finalement, le réseau public compte aussi sur plusieurs **centres de réadaptation**. Ils se divisent en trois grands groupes : les centres de réadaptation en déficience physique (CRDP), les centres de réadaptation en déficience intellectuelle (CRDI) et les centres de réadaptation pour personnes alcooliques et autres toxicomanes (CRPAT).

Jobboom remercie particulièrement la Fédération des médecins résidents du Québec pour sa collaboration à la recherche des témoignages de médecins résidents présentés dans ce guide.

La Fédération des médecins résidents du Québec

Il existe 21 centres de réadaptation en déficience physique[3], 23 centres de réadaptation en déficience intellectuelle[4], et 20 établissements œuvrent auprès des personnes alcooliques et autres toxicomanes[5]. Ils ont tous pour mission d'offrir des services d'adaptation, de réadaptation et d'intégration. En déficience physique, c'est dans ces centres qu'une personne récemment handicapée apprendra, par exemple, à marcher avec sa nouvelle prothèse, à se mouvoir de son fauteuil roulant à son lit, etc.

Les centres de réadaptation en déficience intellectuelle offrent pour leur part des services de stimulation précoce pour les enfants, d'intégration en garderie, à l'école, au travail et dans les loisirs. ▶

Environ 1 000 cliniques médicales privées et près d'une trentaine de laboratoires médicaux privés sont en activité au Québec.

▶ Quant aux centres de réadaptation pour personnes alcooliques et autres toxicomanes, ils offrent des services d'hébergement, de désintoxication, de consultation psychologique et d'intervention sociale.

Parce qu'on y travaille sur tous les aspects de la personne, les centres de réadaptation emploient tant du personnel médical que des professionnels de la relation d'aide. En réadaptation physique, ergothérapeutes, physiothérapeutes, techniciens en réadaptation physique et prothésistes côtoient donc les travailleurs sociaux, psychologues et techniciens en éducation spécialisée. Les centres de réadaptation en alcoolisme et toxicomanie emploient pour leur part à la fois des professionnels des relations d'aide, des médecins et des infirmières. Seuls les centres de réadaptation en déficience intellectuelle comptent presque exclusivement sur des spécialistes de la relation d'aide.

Par ailleurs, il faut savoir qu'en raison des nombreuses compressions qu'a connues le réseau de la santé et des services sociaux, plusieurs établissements ayant des missions différentes se sont regroupés. En région éloignée par exemple, l'ensemble des services sont la plupart du temps offerts par un seul établissement, alors appelé centre de santé.

(→) Le secteur privé

L'entreprise privée offre également des possibilités d'emploi intéressantes. En 2003, l'Association des résidences et CHSLD privés du Québec comptait par exemple 484 résidences membres[6]. Il s'agit surtout d'établissements conçus pour les personnes âgées autonomes ou en légère perte d'autonomie qui offrent des services d'hébergement, mais aussi certains services médicaux de base.

Environ 1 000 cliniques médicales privées[7] et près d'une trentaine de laboratoires médicaux privés sont aussi en activité au Québec[8]. Les services vont des simples consultations médicales aux examens plus pointus, tels que les mammographies ou les échographies.

Il est difficile de connaître le nombre d'emplois générés par le réseau privé. En revanche, on sait que les CHSLD privés embauchent plus de 7 000 employés[9], notamment des techniciens de laboratoire, des infirmières, des infirmières auxiliaires et des préposés aux bénéficiaires.

(→) Les organismes sans but lucratif

Au cours des dernières années, plus d'une centaine d'entreprises d'économie sociale spécialisées en aide domestique ont vu le jour. Elles se spécialisent notamment dans la préparation des repas, les soins corporels, l'accompagnement et l'aide aux achats. Le Regroupement des entreprises en économie sociale et aide domestique estime que ces entreprises donnent un emploi à plus de 5 000 travailleurs, surtout des gens ayant une formation en assistance familiale et sociale aux personnes à domicile[10]. ■

1. *Effectif cadre et syndiqué du réseau sociosanitaire,* Info-Sérhum, Bulletin d'information concernant les ressources humaines et institutionnelles du système de sociosanitaire québécois, ministère de la Santé et des Services sociaux, avril 2003.
2. *Idem.*
3. Entrevue, Association des établissements de réadaptation physique du Québec.
4. Site Internet, Fédération québécoise des centres de réadaptation en déficience intellectuelle.
5. Site Internet, Fédération québécoise des centres de réadaptation pour personnes alcooliques et autres toxicomanes.
6. Entrevue, Association des résidences et CHSLD privés du Québec.
7. Entrevue, MSSS.
8. Entrevue, Laboratoire de santé publique du Québec.
9. Site Internet, Association des établissements privés conventionnés.
10. FOURNIER, Jacques. *Nouveau portrait des entreprises d'économie sociale en aide domestique*, Regroupement québécois des intervenants et intervenantes en action communautaire en CLSC et en Centres de santé, 2003.

Ai-je le profil?

C'est bien connu, les emplois ne manquent pas en santé. Par-delà les taux de placement intéressants, certaines qualités et aptitudes sont cependant nécessaires pour faire le travail. Côtoyer chaque jour la maladie et la détresse humaine tout en restant serein n'est effectivement pas donné à tout le monde… Portrait-robot des travailleurs de la santé.

Par Guylaine Boucher

À 49 ans, Lise Danis fait figure de vétéran dans le réseau de la santé et des services sociaux. Infirmière auxiliaire, elle travaille en centre hospitalier depuis bientôt 30 ans. «J'ai vécu la stabilité des années 1970, l'abondance des ressources humaines dans les années 1980 et le manque de personnel des années 1990. La pratique est plus difficile aujourd'hui qu'auparavant parce qu'on doit prendre en charge un nombre plus élevé de patients, mais je ne voudrais pas changer de métier pour autant. J'ai choisi de devenir infirmière auxiliaire parce que je voulais aider les gens. Quand je rentre chez moi après le travail et que je peux me dire que j'ai fait du bien à six, sept ou dix personnes dans ma journée, je suis comblée.»

→ Relation d'aide : un petit côté «sauveur»

De l'avis de Martine Lemonde, conseillère d'orientation au sein de la firme Brisson Legris et Associés, l'histoire de Lise Danis illustre bien le profil type des travailleurs de la santé. «Peu importe le poste qu'ils occupent, ceux qui œuvrent en soins de santé aiment généralement **être près des gens** et avoir le sentiment de pouvoir les aider. Ils ont aussi souvent un **grand intérêt pour les sciences** et tout ce qui concerne le corps ou le comportement humain. Ils cherchent à **comprendre des phénomènes complexes** et à savoir pourquoi ils surviennent. Ce sont aussi, en général, des gens **curieux**.»

Évidemment, selon les fonctions occupées dans le réseau de la santé et des services sociaux, certaines qualités particulières sont nécessaires. Ainsi, les personnes qui travaillent en relation d'aide, que ce soit à titre de psychologue, travailleur social ou intervenant communautaire, doivent faire preuve de **calme**, d'**empathie**, de **rigueur** et d'un excellent **sens de l'écoute**.

La **capacité de prendre ses distances** par rapport aux difficultés vécues par les patients est aussi essentielle, selon Michelle Arcand, psychologue et auteure de plusieurs livres sur le travail en relation d'aide. «Les personnes qui optent pour ce type de profession ont toutes un petit côté "sauveur". Ce sont, la plupart du temps, des gens très responsables et généreux. Par contre, s'ils souhaitent pouvoir faire ce travail longtemps, ils doivent apprendre à se ménager un peu, à mettre de la distance entre eux et leurs clients.»

→ Personnel soignant : en première ligne

Les qualités humaines considérées comme essentielles pour les professionnels des services sociaux sont aussi de rigueur pour le personnel soignant. Préposés aux bénéficiaires, infirmières, infirmières auxiliaires, médecins, tous doivent faire preuve d'**écoute** et de beaucoup de **patience**. «Quand nous devons prendre soin de douze personnes à la fois et que l'une d'entre elles refuse un traitement, on doit garder son calme, expliquer pourquoi les soins sont nécessaires, que cela ne fera pas mal, etc. Rassurer les gens fait partie de notre tâche. Si on est impatient et nerveux, cela ne marchera pas», explique Lise Danis. ▶

Êtes-vous fait
pour le secteur de la santé?

1. Je m'intéresse à la santé mais je me sens plus à l'aise de travailler avec des données, des faits et des chiffres que d'être directement en contact avec des patients.
Oui ☐ Non ☐

2. J'ai une bonne dextérité manuelle.
Oui ☐ Non ☐

3. Le fonctionnement du corps humain me fascine.
Oui ☐ Non ☐

4. J'aime communiquer avec les gens.
Oui ☐ Non ☐

5. Je m'intéresse aux politiques gouvernementales et à la gestion des organisations publiques.
Oui ☐ Non ☐

6. Je suis rigoureux(se), précis(e) et méthodique..
Oui ☐ Non ☐

7. Je suis doté(e) d'un bon sens de l'observation, d'une grande capacité d'analyse et de sens critique.
Oui ☐ Non ☐

8. Je peux vivre au quotidien en ayant à prendre des décisions et en ayant à poser des gestes qui ont des implications de vie ou de mort.
Oui ☐ Non ☐

9. Je m'intéresse davantage au fonctionnement psychologique qu'à la mécanique du corps humain.
Oui ☐ Non ☐

10. Je préfère réaliser des tâches que je connais bien que de constamment me retrouver face à des situations inconnues.
Oui ☐ Non ☐

11. J'ai une excellente capacité d'écoute.
Oui ☐ Non ☐

12. Je suis capable d'accomplir des tâches selon des directives déjà établies.
Oui ☐ Non ☐

13. J'aime travailler avec mes mains et manipuler des instruments.
Oui ☐ Non ☐

14. J'ai du plaisir à planifier des activités, diriger, contrôler et organiser les tâches.
Oui ☐ Non ☐

15. Je préfère travailler avec de l'équipement de bureau que des instruments médicaux.
Oui ☐ Non ☐

Trouvez le ou les secteurs de la santé correspondant aux énoncés ci-dessus en consultant le tableau qui suit. Si vous avez répondu «oui» à la majorité des énoncés rattachés à un secteur, vous y découvrirez peut-être une carrière qui vous convient!

Attention : il est fort probable que les énoncés auxquels vous aurez répondu «oui» soient liés aux professions de plus d'un secteur. N'hésitez pas à explorer les carrières de la santé qui correspondent à chacun d'eux.

Secteur	Énoncés correspondants
Soins	2-3-4-6-7-8-13
Emploi technique ou de soutien	2-3-4-6-10-12-13
Relation d'aide	4-7-9-11-15
Recherche	1-2-6-7-13
Gestion	1-5-10-14-15

QUELQUES PROFESSIONS EN LIEN AVEC CHACUN DES SECTEURS :

Soins : acupuncteur, chiropraticien, ergothérapeute, kinésiologue, infirmière, omnipraticien, orthophoniste, pédiatre, physiothérapeute, sage-femme, technicien en réadaptation physique, etc.

Emploi technique ou de soutien : archiviste médical, assistant technique en pharmacie, auxiliaire familial et social, préposé aux bénéficiaires, secrétaire médicale, technicien en électrophysiologie médicale, technicien en inhalothérapie, technologue en médecine nucléaire, technologue en radio-oncologie, etc.

Relation d'aide : psychologue, technicien en éducation spécialisée, technicien en travail social, travailleur social, etc.

Recherche : anatomiste, biologiste médical, généticien, immunologue, microbiologiste, pharmacologue, neurophysiologiste, virologiste, etc.

Gestion : chef des services financiers, contrôleur général, directeur administratif, directeur de la planification des services sociaux, directeur des soins infirmiers, directeur général d'un centre hospitalier, infirmière-chef, etc.

ÉVALUATION ET GESTION DE CARRIÈRE
Brisson Legris & Associés
CONSEILLERS D'ORIENTATION

La rigueur et l'esprit d'analyse sont indissociables du métier de chercheur.

▶ Parce qu'il lui faut manipuler beaucoup d'appareils de précision, faire des injections, etc., le personnel en charge des soins doit aussi, selon Martine Lemonde, «pouvoir compter sur une excellente **dextérité manuelle**». Une bonne **résistance physique** n'est pas non plus à négliger, compte tenu des longues heures de travail.

Souvent employés d'organismes offrant des services 24 heures sur 24, il est possible que les professionnels des services sociaux et des soins de santé connaissent des **horaires de travail irréguliers**. En situation de crise, quand par exemple un enfant victime de mauvais traitement est signalé à la Direction de la protection de la jeunesse et qu'il doit être sorti de son environnement rapidement, leur journée se termine seulement lorsque le problème est résolu et que l'on a trouvé une famille pour accueillir l'enfant, du moins temporairement.

→ **Gestion : prévoir l'imprévisible**

Les gestionnaires du réseau de la santé et des services sociaux ont généralement des horaires plus réguliers, bien que les urgences soient toujours possibles.

Leur travail étant davantage axé sur les tâches administratives, le profil «aidant» est cette fois moins marqué. «La **capacité de s'adapter**, la **créativité** et le **sens de l'initiative** sont des aptitudes sur lesquelles on insiste beaucoup désormais lors de l'embauche de gestionnaires. Dans un contexte de pénurie de ressources, il faut savoir faire preuve d'**imagination**», explique Nicole Brodeur, présidente-directrice générale du Centre de référence des directeurs généraux et des cadres.

Au ministère de la Santé et des Services sociaux, la Direction générale des politiques de main-d'œuvre insiste aussi sur le **leadership**, le **sens de la communication** et la **capacité de planification**. Rien de plus normal, si l'on considère que c'est généralement le directeur général d'un établissement et ses gestionnaires qui travailleront à développer des nouveaux services, à les organiser et à mobiliser le personnel nécessaire, même dans les périodes plus difficiles.

→ **Recherche médicale : patience et curiosité**

Parce qu'ils ne sont ni intervenants ni gestionnaires, les chercheurs en santé sont souvent considérés comme du personnel à part. Pourtant, les qualités et aptitudes indispensables à leurs tâches ne sont pas très éloignées de celles exigées pour le personnel de la santé en général. La **patience** est, là encore, primordiale. Développer de nouveaux médicaments, déchiffrer un gène ou analyser différentes substances peut en effet prendre beaucoup de temps et nécessiter de nombreux essais avant de parvenir au résultat recherché. Pour les mêmes raisons, la **persévérance** est essentielle, tout comme la **curiosité**. Enfin, la rigueur et l'esprit d'analyse sont indissociables du métier de chercheur. ■

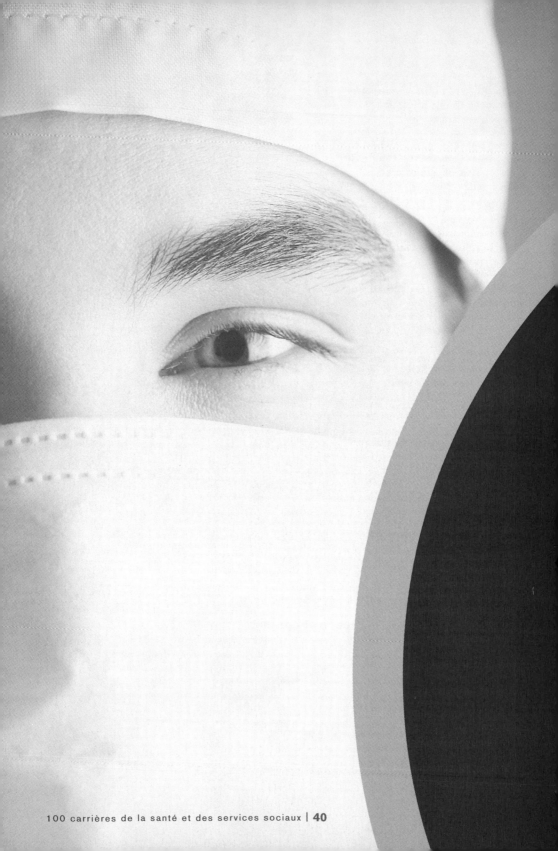

Des professions
et des
témoignages

Œuvrer dans le domaine de la santé et des services sociaux permet d'évoluer dans des milieux de travail variés, auprès d'une clientèle diversifiée. Cliniques privées, laboratoires médicaux, centres hospitaliers, centres d'hébergement et de soins de longue durée, CLSC, etc., sont autant d'avenues à explorer, selon ses goûts et ses aspirations.

En ce qui concerne la formation requise, là encore, les possibilités sont nombreuses : diplôme d'études profession-nelles (DEP), diplôme d'études collégiales (DEC), bacca-lauréat ou doctorat en médecine suivi d'études spécialisées pour devenir médecin spécialiste.

Quelle que soit la voie qu'ils ont choisie, les professionnels de la santé estiment qu'il s'agit d'un milieu de travail stimulant offrant des carrières où les défis ne manquent pas.

Au fil des pages qui suivent, découvrez les témoignages de 100 d'entre eux. Ils nous parlent de leurs tâches quotidiennes et de leur motivation au travail. Ils livrent aussi des conseils à la relève et partagent avec elle les principales étapes de leur parcours scolaire et professionnel.

Page 42 à 152

Assistante dentaire
❯ en clinique privée

mon travail

Assistante dentaire au Centre dentaire Michel Perrier à Granby, Josée Davignon est en quelque sorte le bras droit du dentiste. Toujours à ses côtés, elle tente d'anticiper ses gestes et lui passe les instruments, tout en veillant au bien-être du patient. Elle explique aussi à ce dernier les plans de traitement prévus : orthodontie, traitement de canal, couronnes, etc., «traduisant» pour le client les termes techniques employés par le dentiste.

Entre deux rendez-vous, Josée ne chôme pas car elle doit désinfecter les salles opératoires et stériliser les instruments.

Des milieux de travail potentiels

- ❯ Cabinets privés de dentistes
- ❯ Cabinets privés de denturologistes
- ❯ Centres hospitaliers
- ❯ Cliniques dentaires (privées et publiques)
- ❯ Fabricants de produits dentaires
- ❯ Laboratoires dentaires

ma motivation

«Au quotidien, ce que j'aime le plus, c'est le contact avec le patient, souligne Josée. Prenons l'exemple de quelqu'un qui nous arrive avec une bouche partiellement édentée ou gâtée. On lui fait des implants et des couronnes et il voit l'aspect de ses dents s'améliorer au fil des rendez-vous. C'est valorisant pour lui, mais ça l'est aussi pour nous!»

Quatre dentistes et trois hygiénistes travaillent au Centre dentaire Michel Perrier. C'est un défi pour Josée, qui doit s'adapter aux différentes personnalités. «Il est important d'être polyvalent et de se plier au style de chacun. Mais ça permet aussi d'éviter de tomber dans la routine.»

Les cliniques dentaires utilisent généralement de l'équipement extrêmement sophistiqué. «Dans notre domaine, la technologie évolue sans cesse. On est continuellement en formation, ce qui est très motivant. En plus d'assister à des cours, je dois aussi rester à jour, fouiller dans les livres ou appeler le fabricant pour m'assurer que j'utilise l'appareil comme il faut. C'est un défi quotidien.»

mon conseil

La première règle de l'assistante dentaire, c'est évidemment d'avoir le sourire. «Il y a tant de gens qui craignent les visites chez le dentiste... Faire preuve d'entregent et sourire, ça les rassure et ça brise les barrières.» Il est également nécessaire d'être rapide, souligne Josée. «Après avoir reconduit le patient à la porte, il faut libérer et désinfecter la salle rapidement. Les pauses, on ne connaît pas! Même les heures de lunch peuvent être escamotées s'il y a des retards dans l'horaire.» 05/03

mon parcours

C'est la mère d'une amie, elle-même assistante dentaire, qui a transmis à Josée la piqûre du métier. «J'allais souvent à son cabinet et j'aimais beaucoup l'ambiance qui y régnait. Avant de choisir ma formation, j'ai passé trois mois en milieu de travail avec elle pour être certaine de ne pas me tromper.» Elle terminait alors une formation en sciences humaines au cégep. Qu'importe : son diplôme d'études collégiales (DEC) en poche, elle s'est inscrite au Centre professionnel 24-juin de Sherbrooke, où elle a obtenu son diplôme d'études professionnelles (DEP) en assistance dentaire. Elle travaille pour le Centre dentaire Michel Perrier depuis près de quatre ans.

Les mots en caractères **gras** sont définis à la page 153.

Assistante technique en pharmacie
> en pharmacie

mon travail

Sylvie Champagne est assistante technique à la Pharmacie Jean Coutu à Charny. «J'accueille les clients et je prends leur ordonnance pour l'entrer ensuite dans l'ordinateur et mettre leur dossier à jour.»

Elle prépare aussi les médicaments : elle peut notamment compter les comprimés, préparer des antibiotiques liquides ou des mélanges de crème. «Quand j'ai terminé, tout ce que le pharmacien a à faire est de vérifier mon travail, de s'assurer que les doses sont exactes et de donner les conseils au client.»

En examinant le dossier du patient, elle vérifiera qu'il n'y a pas d'interaction entre l'ordonnance et d'autres médicaments qu'il pourrait déjà prendre. Le cas échéant, elle en avisera le pharmacien. «Même si je ne prodigue pas de conseils, mon travail comporte une grande part de responsabilités», dit-elle.

Le régime d'assurance-médicaments n'a plus de secret pour elle. Heureusement, car c'est encore du chinois pour plusieurs clients! «Je l'explique 300 fois par jour! C'est normal, il y a eu plusieurs réformes depuis son entrée en vigueur.»

Des milieux de travail potentiels

> Centres d'hébergement et de soins de longue durée
> Centres hospitaliers
> Pharmacies communautaires
> Pharmacies d'établissements de santé

ma motivation

Il y a quelques années, Sylvie travaillait dans une pharmacie d'hôpital et traitait uniquement avec des infirmières et des médecins. «Aujourd'hui, j'apprécie beaucoup de travailler directement avec les clients. J'ai l'impression de pouvoir contribuer à alléger leurs souffrances.»

Pour elle, chaque patient est un nouveau défi. «Il arrive que certains soient mécontents, qu'ils se plaignent du coût des médicaments. Mais à l'inverse, d'autres sont satisfaits et nous remercient. C'est grâce à eux qu'on aime notre travail.»

Une pharmacie de la taille de celle où travaille Sylvie prépare entre 400 et 500 ordonnances par jour. «Ça roule vite, et il faut une bonne entente dans l'équipe pour travailler efficacement.»

mon conseil

Attentif, méticuleux, ordonné : si vous n'avez pas ces qualités, ne songez pas à faire ce métier, affirme Sylvie Champagne. «Il faut avoir une méthode de travail et être précis. Ça se comprend, on travaille avec des médicaments. Les erreurs peuvent avoir de lourdes conséquences.»

La formation n'est pas obligatoire pour occuper un poste d'assistant technique en pharmacie, mais Sylvie la recommande vivement. «Le salaire est meilleur si vous êtes formé, mais surtout, vous aurez appris la composition de certains médicaments et les rudiments du fonctionnement des assurances-médicaments.» 05/03

mon parcours

Sylvie a obtenu en 1998 son diplôme d'études professionnelles (DEP) en assistance technique en pharmacie au Centre de formation professionnelle du Fierbourg. Peu de temps après, elle décrochait un poste dans une pharmacie. «Je n'ai pas arrêté de travailler depuis. J'ai œuvré pour diverses bannières de pharmacies, puis dans une pharmacie d'hôpital, et enfin chez Jean Coutu.»

Les mots en caractères **gras** sont définis à la page 153.

Auxiliaire familiale et sociale
> **en CLSC**

mon travail

Les courses, la lessive, la popote : pour le commun des mortels, ce sont là des corvées, mais pour certaines personnes, il s'agit carrément de tâches insurmontables. Christine Arseneault, du Centre local de services communautaires (CLSC) du Grand Chicoutimi, a pour rôle de leur faciliter la vie.

Des milieux de travail potentiels

> Centres locaux de services communautaires (CLSC)

> Domicile des bénéficiaires dans le cadre des services offerts par les CLSC

> Organismes privés ou publics offrant des services de maintien à domicile

«J'aide des personnes et des familles en difficulté qui ont besoin de soutien dans diverses tâches du quotidien», explique-t-elle. Sa clientèle est surtout constituée de gens malades, âgés, handicapés (physiquement ou intellectuellement) ou ayant des problèmes d'ordre social.

«Je vais les visiter, voir comment ils vont. Selon les besoins, je prépare leur nourriture, je fais leur entretien ménager, je les aide à faire leur toilette ou je les accompagne chez le médecin ou à la banque. Mais surtout, je les écoute et leur apporte du soutien!»

ma motivation

«Quand je suis dans une résidence, avec du mobilier non adapté aux besoins particuliers des personnes que j'aide (sauf pour le bain), je suis seule pour trouver les solutions, raconte Christine. C'est quand j'arrive sur place que je sais ce qui m'attend. Car, contrairement au milieu hospitalier où tout est standardisé, il n'y a pas deux cuisines pareilles, pas deux où on range la farine au même endroit. Toute ma débrouillardise est sollicitée, et ça, j'aime ça!

«J'ai même eu à aider une personne à organiser son déménagement, poursuit-elle. Ça veut dire l'aider à visiter des logements, à établir le budget, à préparer des boîtes, etc. Mais ce que je fais, je le fais toujours avec les personnes, jamais à leur place.»

Au bout du compte, c'est l'aspect humain qui tient le plus à cœur à Christine. «Quand je vais préparer à manger pour quelqu'un, je peux y passer deux ou trois heures. En plus de lui rendre service, je l'écoute, je lui tiens compagnie. C'est particulièrement gratifiant comme travail.»

mon conseil

«Bien qu'on ne soigne pas, il faut avoir une connaissance de base des maladies les plus courantes, comme le diabète ou l'emphysème, affirme Christine. C'est essentiel pour savoir ce que l'on doit observer chez ceux qu'on va visiter et pour avoir le bon réflexe.» Par exemple, une personne qui éprouve de la difficulté à respirer peut souffrir de simples allergies, mais aussi de problèmes plus sérieux. «Si je sais qu'elle fait de l'emphysème, j'ai conscience que ça peut être très grave et que je dois réagir.» Ce travail exige beaucoup de patience, de débrouillardise, de jugement et d'équilibre psychologique. «Il faut vraiment aimer aider les autres, les respecter, et être discret en tout temps.» 06/03

mon parcours

Christine était technicienne dans un laboratoire dentaire quand elle a commencé à éprouver des ennuis de santé à cause des produits chimiques. À 40 ans, elle a donc quitté son emploi et réorienté sa carrière. C'est à L'Oasis de Chicoutimi qu'elle a obtenu un diplôme d'études professionnelles (DEP) en assistance familiale et sociale aux personnes à domicile. Fraîchement diplômée, elle affirme aujourd'hui adorer son nouveau travail.

Les mots en caractères **gras** sont définis à la page 153.

Infirmière auxiliaire
> en milieu hospitalier

mon travail

Vous souvenez-vous de la dernière grippe qui vous a cloué au lit? Rien que marcher vers la salle de bains vous semblait plus épuisant qu'un trek en montagne. Imaginez alors ce que ressentent les personnes hospitalisées. Dans leur situation, savoir que quelqu'un est là pour veiller sur elles est pour le moins reposant. «Dès qu'on entre dans leurs chambres, les patients sont contents de nous voir», clame Julie Inkel, infirmière auxiliaire à l'Hôpital Charles-LeMoyne, de Longueuil. Nous ne faisons pas seulement partie de l'équipe de santé, nous sommes aussi des confidents, des oreilles attentives.» Lors de chaque visite, Julie mesure la tension artérielle du patient, prend sa température et son pouls, change ses pansements, l'aide à s'habiller ou à se laver, en plus de s'assurer qu'il prend ses médicaments. Elle surveille également tout changement dans sa condition pour informer les autres membres de l'équipe, comme les infirmières et les médecins.

Des milieux de travail potentiels

> Centres d'hébergement et de soins de longue durée
> Centres hospitaliers
> Centres psychiatriques
> Cliniques médicales
> Centres locaux de services communautaires (CLSC)
> Domicile des bénéficiaires dans le cadre des services offerts par les CLSC

ma motivation

«Nous avons un contact privilégié avec les patients; parce que nous sommes moins intimidants pour eux qu'un médecin, ils se confient davantage à nous. En fin de traitement, certains nous offrent des cadeaux, des cartes de remerciement.»

Selon ses observations, les gens croient à tort que les infirmiers auxiliaires travaillent uniquement dans les centres d'hébergement de soins de longue durée. «Ce métier nous permet de toucher à toutes sortes de domaines et de clientèles, ce qui est très stimulant. Les tâches varient selon qu'on travaille, par exemple, en chirurgie ou en orthopédie.

«Présentement, je suis affectée en psychiatrie, et ma description de tâches inclut davantage de relation d'aide. C'est très valorisant. Lorsque je travaillais auprès des nouvelles mamans, c'était différent. Je donnais davantage de conseils, par exemple sur l'allaitement.»

mon conseil

Bien réagir aux situations d'urgence et gérer efficacement son stress est primordial, selon Julie. Car à toute heure, un patient peut voir sa condition physique se détériorer très rapidement. «Personnellement, je pratique divers sports pour garder la forme. C'est bon pour contrer le stress, mais aussi pour affronter les longues journées debout.» 04/03

mon parcours

Après son diplôme d'études professionnelles (DEP) en santé, assistance et soins infirmiers au Centre de formation professionnelle Pierre-Dupuy (rebaptisé l'École des métiers des Faubourgs de Montréal), Julie a fait ses premières armes à la Résidence De Longueuil, un centre d'accueil privé. Par la suite, elle a été embauchée à l'Hôpital Charles-LeMoyne, où elle a d'abord travaillé auprès des femmes enceintes, des nouvelles mamans, des poupons et des jeunes enfants. Puis, elle a fait partie de l'**équipe volante** affectée à l'ensemble des unités de soins de l'Hôpital, jusqu'à ce que l'unité de psychiatrie la prenne sous son aile.

Les mots en caractères **gras** sont définis à la page 153.

Préposée aux bénéficiaires
❱ en centre d'hébergement et de soins de longue durée

mon travail

Cynthia Legault est préposée aux bénéficiaires au Centre d'hébergement et de soins de longue durée (CHSLD) Les Eskers, à Amos. Elle prodigue à ses patients, des personnes âgées en perte d'autonomie, tous les soins dont ils ont besoin en matière de confort, d'hygiène, d'alimentation ou de déplacement.

«Je m'occupe d'abord de leur toilette et leur donne un bain ou une douche. Ensuite je les habille et les fais manger. Puisqu'il s'agit de personnes à la mobilité réduite, je dois moi-même les changer de position pendant que j'effectue ces tâches. Je suis aussi chargée de donner certains traitements, appliquer des onguents par exemple.»

Cynthia ne voit pas uniquement au bien-être physique des bénéficiaires. «Ils veulent aussi parler, se confier, avoir de la compagnie. Ce n'est pas toujours facile de trouver le temps pour s'acquitter de toutes ces tâches...»

Des milieux de travail potentiels

- ❱ Centres hospitaliers
- ❱ Centres d'hébergement et de soins de longue durée
- ❱ Centres de réadaptation
- ❱ Centres psychiatriques

ma motivation

Cynthia apprécie la compagnie des personnes âgées. «J'aime les aider, leur rendre service et voir leurs visages s'éclairer d'un sourire. C'est valorisant de sentir qu'un petit geste, une attention ou de l'écoute de notre part peut leur apporter un peu de joie.»

Elle avoue toutefois qu'il n'est pas toujours facile de côtoyer quotidiennement la souffrance. «J'ai fini par me forger une carapace. Cela me permet de garder une certaine distance émotionnelle.»

En évoluant avec des personnes en perte d'autonomie, Cynthia a dû aussi relever un défi personnel : apprendre la patience. «On aimerait parfois aller plus vite, mais il faut respecter le rythme de chacun. J'ai dû m'adapter à cette réalité et mettre un frein à mes élans!»

mon conseil

«Il n'est pas toujours facile de travailler dans un milieu où les gens souffrent physiquement et quelquefois moralement. Plusieurs bénéficiaires se sentent seuls, isolés. Le préposé doit apprendre à garder son optimisme.»

Selon Cynthia, avant d'opter pour ce métier, on devrait s'informer sur le milieu de travail dans lequel on devra évoluer. Elle estime en effet que ce dernier ne conviendra pas nécessairement aux personnes trop sensibles.

mon parcours

Après avoir décroché son diplôme d'études professionnelles (DEP) en assistance aux bénéficiaires en établissement de santé au Centre de formation Harricana à Amos, Cynthia n'a mis que deux jours à dénicher son emploi actuel.

«J'avais réalisé mon stage au CHSLD Les Eskers, et dès que j'ai obtenu mon diplôme, on m'a offert un poste. Je n'ai même pas eu à envoyer de curriculum vitæ ou à chercher un travail. Cela fait maintenant cinq ans que j'œuvre dans cet établissement.»

Il faut aussi être à l'aise au sein d'une équipe de travail, car plusieurs intervenants œuvrent auprès des bénéficiaires : médecins, infirmières, etc. «Mais cela ne doit pas nous empêcher de donner notre opinion au sujet de l'état de santé des patients. Nous les connaissons bien et sommes proches d'eux.» 09/03

Les mots en caractères **gras** sont définis à la page 153.

Secrétaire médicale
❯ en CLSC

mon travail

Danielle Vaillancourt est secrétaire médicale au Centre local de services communautaires (CLSC) du Marigot, à Laval. Elle travaille au Service de maintien à domicile et s'occupe d'une clientèle qui demande beaucoup d'encadrement, notamment des patients atteints du sida ou des personnes présentant des déficiences intellectuelles.

Elle passe une grande partie de ses journées au téléphone. «Je parle avec les patients et je résume ensuite leurs besoins aux médecins...» Il peut s'agir, par exemple, d'un renouvellement d'ordonnance ou d'une demande de consultation. Et à l'inverse, elle transmet aussi les demandes des médecins aux patients, entre autres lorsqu'il y a des résultats de tests à communiquer. «Mais, souvent, mon rôle consiste simplement à écouter et à réconforter un patient qui appelle parce qu'il s'inquiète de son état.

«C'est sûr que le travail est différent dans une clinique privée, où la prise de rendez-vous et la facturation prennent plus d'importance, poursuit-elle. Au Service de maintien à domicile, j'ai un contact serré avec la clientèle puisque je le côtoie régulièrement.»

Des milieux de travail potentiels

- ❯ Cabinets privés de chirurgiens
- ❯ Cabinets privés de dentistes
- ❯ Cabinets privés de médecins
- ❯ Centres hospitaliers
- ❯ Centres locaux de services communautaires (CLSC)

ma motivation

Naturellement empathique, dotée d'une grande capacité d'écoute, Danielle se dit motivée par le fait de soulager les patients. «J'aime la relation d'aide. C'est d'ailleurs ce qui m'a attirée dans ce métier : j'aime être utile, apporter du réconfort. Mais il serait faux de dire que j'ai toujours le sourire. Quand les patients m'appellent, c'est souvent parce qu'ils ne vont pas bien. Mon défi est de contribuer à faire en sorte qu'ils se portent mieux.

«Côtoyer les médecins est tout aussi stimulant, ajoute la secrétaire médicale. Ils sont présents, accessibles; je peux parler avec eux. J'aime beaucoup ce contact.»

mon conseil

«La principale qualité d'une secrétaire médicale est la discrétion, affirme Danielle. On gère des données confidentielles et on sait plein de choses sur des gens. C'est très important de ne pas dévoiler ces renseignements.» Évidemment, ce travail exige beaucoup de patience et de capacité d'écoute. «Quand on parle au téléphone avec un patient en phase terminale ou avec un toxicomane, il faut savoir quoi dire, jusqu'où aller.»

Enfin, avoir une bonne attitude est essentiel. «Dans ce métier, le savoir-être est aussi important que le savoir-faire.» 09/03

mon parcours

Danielle a étudié en sciences humaines au Cégep de Rosemont avant de se tourner vers le secrétariat. «Comme secrétaire, j'ai toujours travaillé dans le domaine de la santé, en assistance médicale internationale, puis dans une clinique privée.» C'est après s'être retrouvée sans emploi qu'elle s'est inscrite à une formation d'un an en secrétariat médical offerte par le Centre d'emploi de Saint-Eustache, il y a une dizaine d'années. Après un stage de quelques mois au CLSC de Saint-Eustache, elle a obtenu son emploi actuel.

Les mots en caractères **gras** sont définis à la page 153.

Acupunctrice
❯ en clinique privée

mon travail

Parmi les moyens d'intervention thérapeutique de la médecine traditionnelle chinoise, l'acupuncture est sans doute la plus connue. Pour les acupuncteurs, une maladie est un déséquilibre de l'énergie.

«Avec les aiguilles, on rétablit l'équilibre de la circulation énergétique», explique Nancy Deschênes, acupunctrice à la Clinique médicale Chemin Saint-Jean, à La Prairie.

La technique de base consiste à introduire des aiguilles métalliques très fines dans des points précis du corps, afin de diriger adéquatement l'énergie vitale. Il existe 365 points, situés sur les **méridiens**.

«Les chercheurs ont remarqué qu'à la suite d'un traitement, le corps sécrète plus d'endorphine, la circulation sanguine augmente localement et les muscles sont plus détendus, précise Nancy. Comme l'endorphine est une sorte de morphine naturelle, cela pourrait expliquer scientifiquement l'efficacité de l'acupuncture pour contrer la douleur, l'anxiété, etc.»

Des milieux de travail potentiels

❯ Cabinets privés

ma motivation

En acupuncture, on évalue les patients de façon globale. «Si quelqu'un vient me voir pour un mal de cou, je vais considérer la douleur mais aussi prendre en compte sa santé en général», note Nancy. Elle apprécie cette façon de faire qui lui paraît plus complète.

En outre, le fait de rencontrer les malades sur une longue période – en moyenne, un traitement peut durer de 6 à 10 semaines, à raison d'une fois par semaine – permet également d'établir un lien de confiance avec eux.

Nancy ne voit pas le jour où elle aura fini d'apprendre dans son domaine. «Il y a les enseignements chinois, mais les Vietnamiens, les Coréens et les Japonais ont eux aussi développé leurs propres techniques.»

mon conseil

Dans ce métier, avoir l'esprit ouvert est essentiel, estime Nancy. «L'acupuncture n'est pas une science exacte, il faut être capable d'accepter que l'on pratique une médecine qui n'est pas du tout précise. On a beaucoup de marge de manœuvre dans nos protocoles de traitement. Le résultat peut sembler mystérieux. On doit accepter des choses qui ne sont pas toujours compréhensibles pour nous, Occidentaux», souligne Nancy. 05/03

mon parcours

Après une formation collégiale en sciences humaines au Cégep Édouard-Montpetit, Nancy s'est inscrite à l'Université de Montréal. Elle y a fait deux années d'études, l'une en linguistique, l'autre en sociologie. Mais l'acupuncture a piqué sa curiosité, et c'est au Cégep de Rosemont qu'elle a par la suite obtenu son diplôme d'études collégiales (DEC) en acupuncture. Nancy est membre de l'Ordre des acupuncteurs du Québec. Elle a aussi fait une mineure en psychologie. En ajoutant ce diplôme à ses deux autres années universitaires, elle a ainsi pu décrocher un baccalauréat.

Les mots en caractères **gras** sont définis à la page 153.

Archiviste médicale
❯ en milieu hospitalier

mon travail

Un patient entre à l'urgence. Un médecin établit un diagnostic et décide d'une intervention chirurgicale. Le patient est opéré, puis récupère, prend des médicaments et reçoit son congé. Toutes ces étapes produisent de la paperasse, constituant un dossier qui aboutit entre les mains de l'archiviste médicale.

«Chaque jour, les infirmières prennent des notes, les médecins rédigent des ordonnances, et tout se retrouve au dossier. Plus un séjour à l'hôpital se prolonge et plus le dossier s'épaissit», explique France Côté, archiviste médicale au Centre hospitalier Pierre-Le-Gardeur de Repentigny.

Le travail de base de l'archiviste consiste à coder en chiffres : à chaque symptôme, maladie, médicament, etc., correspond un code qui sera inscrit au dossier. Elle est également chargée d'analyser les dossiers pour s'assurer qu'ils sont complets.

Les archivistes peuvent aussi gérer la divulgation d'informations, par exemple entre les hôpitaux où une personne a été traitée. «Je suis la gardienne de la confidentialité, précise France. Le patient doit donner son consentement avant que nous puissions fournir l'accès aux renseignements contenus dans son dossier.»

ma motivation

«J'ai toujours été attirée par la médecine et par ce qui touche à la gestion des documents, confie France. C'est sûr qu'il y a moins de papier de nos jours, car les dossiers sont de plus en plus numérisés. Mais cela demeure quand même intéressant de suivre l'évolution d'un patient.»

La codification et l'analyse des dossiers sont des tâches routinières. Pour briser cette monotonie, France participe aux travaux de deux comités de recherche médicale, sur la **bioéthique** et la **traumatologie**. Elle est d'ailleurs responsable du «registre de trauma», c'est-à-dire des statistiques sur les patients accidentés soignés à l'Hôpital Pierre-Le-Gardeur. Elle apprécie beaucoup cet aspect de son travail, qui permet de varier ses tâches.

mon conseil

«Quand on commence dans le métier, on fait beaucoup de codification. C'est seulement avec les années qu'on nous confie davantage de responsabilités, comme la participation à des comités de recherche», remarque France. Ses camarades de classe ont parfois déchanté une fois sur le terrain, les tâches quotidiennes ne coïncidant pas avec l'idée qu'ils s'étaient fait de la profession. Il faut aussi savoir que les contacts avec les patients sont rares, sauf quand ils se déplacent eux-mêmes aux archives d'un hôpital pour obtenir une information sur leur dossier. 05/03

mon parcours

Âgée de 50 ans, France a longtemps œuvré dans le secteur de l'agriculture. Forcée d'interrompre ses études dans sa jeunesse, elle s'était promis de retourner sur les bancs de l'école, plus particulièrement dans le domaine de la santé. Entre 1995 et 1998, elle a suivi les cours du soir en archives médicales au Collège de l'Assomption, où elle a eu son diplôme d'études collégiales (DEC). Il lui a fallu ensuite quelques mois pour obtenir un poste à l'Hôpital Royal-Victoria à Montréal, puis à Pierre-Le-Gardeur.

Les mots en caractères **gras** sont définis à la page 153.

Audioprothésiste
❯ en clinique privée

formation collégiale

mon travail

«Les gens arrivent à moi avec un problème d'audition et repartent avec un outil pour améliorer leur communication et leur qualité de vie», explique avec fierté Dominique Landry, audioprothésiste.

Quand Dominique reçoit un patient à sa clinique privée, elle prend d'abord connaissance de l'**audiogramme**, réalisé par l'**audiologiste**, et du certificat médical émis par l'**oto-rhino-laryngologiste** (ORL). Puis elle discute avec le patient de ses difficultés auditives au quotidien et choisit le type d'**aide auditive** qui lui convient le mieux. Elle examine ensuite ses oreilles et prend leur empreinte au moyen d'une pâte en silicone. Les empreintes sont expédiées chez un manufacturier, qui fabriquera la prothèse requise.

Une fois l'appareil auditif reçu à la clinique, Dominique le prépare ou le programme (s'il s'agit d'un modèle à commande numérique) et l'ajuste aux oreilles du patient, auquel elle donnera enfin des instructions et des conseils pour bien utiliser la prothèse auditive. Si son travail s'effectue surtout auprès de personnes malentendantes, Dominique intervient aussi dans le domaine de la prévention, en procurant des protecteurs auditifs personnalisés à des travailleurs exposés au bruit.

Des milieux de travail potentiels

❯ Cliniques privées
❯ Fabricants de prothèses auditives

ma motivation

L'audioprothésiste apprécie particulièrement la relation d'aide qu'elle crée avec chaque patient. Pour déterminer quel appareil auditif répond le mieux aux besoins d'une personne, elle doit considérer non seulement la sévérité de sa surdité, mais aussi ses activités et sa dextérité (on ne recommande pas un appareil compliqué à manipuler à une personne ayant des problèmes de motricité fine). Le choix ainsi posé est déterminant pour le confort du patient et la qualité de son gain auditif.

Pour elle, l'un des plus grands plaisirs du métier est sa pratique avec les enfants. Son plus jeune patient n'avait que 18 mois. «Avec les enfants, bien choisir et ajuster l'appareil ne va pas de soi. Le jeune patient ne peut répondre aux questions. Et il faut aussi faire un travail de psychologie avec les parents, qui doivent faire un deuil face à la déficience auditive de leur enfant.»

mon conseil

La technologie évolue rapidement dans ce secteur. Par exemple, il existe maintenant des appareils auditifs programmables à commande numérique. Dominique estime donc qu'il est important de lire et de suivre des formations continues afin de bien connaître l'évolution des appareils auditifs ainsi que les différentes méthodes d'appareillage. Par ailleurs, le métier suppose que l'on aime le contact avec les aînés, qui constituent la plus grande partie de la clientèle. 06/03

mon parcours

Déjà, au secondaire, Dominique savait que le domaine de la santé l'intéressait. Au bout de deux ans en techniques d'inhalothérapie au Cégep de Rosemont, elle a décidé de bifurquer vers le programme d'audioprothèse avant de décrocher son diplôme d'études collégiales (DEC) dans cette discipline. Elle a exercé à Montréal dans une clinique privée à titre de salariée avant de retourner dans son Sept-Îles natal pour ouvrir sa propre pratique.

Les mots en caractères **gras** sont définis à la page 153.

Cytologiste
> **en milieu hospitalier**

mon travail

Pour dépister le cancer du col de l'utérus, le médecin prélève des cellules dans le col lors de l'examen gynécologique et les dépose sur une lame de verre en vue de l'analyse en laboratoire.

Cindy Chartrand, cytologiste au Centre hospitalier régional de Lanaudière, reçoit ces spécimens et procède aux examens des échantillons. «Les cliniques nous font parvenir des lames sur lesquelles ont été étalées des sécrétions. Par différentes techniques de coloration, nous préparons les spécimens qui devront être étudiés au microscope. Après analyse des prélèvements, toute anomalie est signalée aux pathologistes avec qui nous travaillons en étroite collaboration.»

La majorité des cytologistes travaillent au sein des centres hospitaliers. Les centres privés de dépistage du cancer, les centres de recherche et les universités embauchent également ces spécialistes.

Des milieux de travail potentiels

> Centres de recherche
> Centres hospitaliers
> Établissements d'enseignement
> Laboratoires privés

ma motivation

«J'adore regarder dans l'œil du microscope et utiliser mon discernement pour reconnaître les bonnes cellules et les mauvaises», explique Cindy. Dans le doute, elle consulte les ouvrages de référence et partage ensuite le résultat de ses recherches avec ses collègues cytologistes. «J'aurais pu être technicienne de laboratoire médical, mais le contact étroit et constant avec le public qu'exigent les prélèvements de sang et d'urine, combiné à un horaire de travail irrégulier ne me tentaient pas. Je préfère nettement travailler dans un laboratoire avec des machines et regarder dans les microscopes. L'horaire est aussi beaucoup plus régulier et me convient davantage.»

Et pour contrer le côté monotone des tâches, le personnel travaille en alternance. «Une semaine sur quatre, on est chargé de la coloration de spécimens. Durant les trois autres, on est au microscope.»

mon conseil

Ceux qui optent pour cette carrière doivent avoir un intérêt marqué pour la biologie, en particulier pour l'étude des cellules du corps humain. «Il faut parfaitement bien maîtriser la théorie pour être en mesure de porter un jugement approprié dans la pratique.» Cindy encourage les personnes ordonnées et minutieuses à opter pour ce métier. «Mais il est préférable d'avoir une nature patiente, car on doit rester longtemps assis au microscope à examiner des échantillons», souligne-t-elle. 05/03

mon parcours

Après son diplôme d'études collégiales (DEC) en technique d'analyses biomédicales au Collège de Saint-Jérôme, Cindy a obtenu une attestation d'études collégiales (AEC) au Collège de Rosemont en cytotechnologie. «On apprend d'abord la théorie sur le système génital féminin, puis on passe aux travaux pratiques pour apprendre à distinguer les cellules normales des cellules anormales.» À la fin de sa formation, Cindy a effectué un stage à l'Hôpital Notre-Dame et a ensuite rapidement décroché son emploi actuel.

Les mots en caractères **gras** sont définis à la page 153.

Dans un grand hôpital

près de chez vous...

... une carrière stimulante vous attend !

L'Hôpital Charles LeMoyne, affilié à l'Université de Sherbrooke, est un centre régional de soins de courte durée offrant à sa clientèle une gamme complète de soins de services hospitaliers et ambulatoires généraux, spécialisés et ultra spécialisés, et ce, en santé physique, en santé mentale et en réadaptation.

QU'EST-CE QUE L'HÔPITAL CHARLES LEMOYNE ?

Avec près de 400 lits, 2700 employés, 300 médecins, plus de 300 000 visites d'usagers par année et un budget fonctionnel de 150 millions de dollars, l'établissement est l'un des 10 plus grands centres hospitaliers du Québec. Il a un mandat de centre de référence pour l'ensemble de la Montérégie.

L'Hôpital Charles LeMoyne a développé des créneaux d'excellence en dialyse rénale, en oncologie, en traumatologie, en réadaptation ainsi qu'en enseignement et en recherche. Grâce à l'expertise de son personnel et à son équipement de pointe, il a été désigné comme l'un des quatre centres tertiaires de traumatologie au Québec. De plus, on y retrouve un pavillon spécialement dédié à la réadaptation.

LA SITUATION GÉOGRAPHIQUE

L'Hôpital Charles LeMoyne est situé sur la Rive-Sud, près de Montréal, à quelques minutes de la station de métro Longueuil. L'établissement se trouve sur le boulevard Taschereau, l'une des plus importantes artères commerciales du Québec.

Vous recherchez un milieu de travail dynamique et professionnel ?
L'Hôpital Charles LeMoyne a besoin de personnes qualifiées pour occuper différents postes :

- INFIRMIER(ÈRE)S DIPLÔMÉ(E)S
- CANDIDAT(E)S À L'EXERCICE DE LA PROFESSION D'INFIRMIER(ÈRE)
- EXTERNES EN SOINS INFIRMIERS
- INFIRMIER(ÈRE)S AUXILIAIRES
- PRÉPOSÉ(E)S AUX BÉNÉFICIAIRES

- ORTHOPHONISTES
- PHARMACIEN(NE)S
- PHYSIOTHÉRAPEUTES
- ERGOTHÉRAPEUTES
- INHALOTHÉRAPEUTES

- TECHNICIEN(NE)S EN RADIOLOGIE
- ÉDUCATEUR(TRICE)S
- TRAVAILLEUR(EUSE)S SOCIAUX(ALES)
- PERSONNEL DE BUREAU

Hôpital Charles LeMoyne
Centre affilié universitaire
et régional de la Montérégie

UNIVERSITÉ DE
SHERBROOKE

Direction des ressources humaines, HÔPITAL CHARLES LEMOYNE
Télécopieur : 450-466-5745
Courriel : recrutement.chcl@rrsss.16.gouv.qc.ca
Site Internet : www.hclm.qc.ca

Denturologiste
❯ en clinique privée

mon travail

Josée Bouthillier est propriétaire de sa propre clinique de denturologie. Elle rencontre les clients et évalue leurs besoins en matière de prothèses dentaires. «Je procède à un examen buccal et je fais remplir un questionnaire médical pour savoir si la personne souffre de problèmes digestifs, de poids ou de maux de tête, par exemple. Ces troubles peuvent en effet être causés par une prothèse inadéquate.»

Josée conseille alors au client la sorte de prothèse qui répondrait à ses besoins. Puis elle passe à l'étape de fabrication. «Je prends d'abord les empreintes de la gencive et j'en fais un moule. À partir de là, je fabrique la prothèse avec de l'acrylique, et j'y insère les fausses dents. Ensuite, je procède à la cuisson, ce qui permet aux dents de rester en place. Enfin le client essaie la prothèse, et on procède aux ajustements si nécessaire. Pour compléter toutes ces étapes, il faut compter environ cinq visites.»

ma motivation

Josée confie qu'elle a en elle un côté artistique qui est comblé par son métier. En effet, créer une prothèse dentaire relève aussi de l'art!

«Je ne connais pas la routine, car il n'y a pas deux bouches semblables. Chaque cas est unique. Il y a souvent des défis intéressants à relever, par exemple une personne qui a eu un accident et dont la dentition est très abîmée. Il n'est pas facile de créer une prothèse adaptée aux besoins de chacun. Il faut changer les règles de l'art et savoir s'adapter. C'est très stimulant.

«On doit aussi se plier aux demandes des clients et faire preuve de diplomatie», poursuit-elle. En effet, certains peuvent avoir des demandes difficiles à réaliser ou qui ne conviennent tout simplement pas à leur bouche. Il faut le leur faire comprendre sans froisser les susceptibilités.»

mon conseil

Josée estime que pour faire sa place au soleil dans ce métier, il faut être fonceur. «Au début, ce n'est pas facile de monter sa clientèle. Comme une prothèse dure au moins cinq ans et que la plupart des personnes étirent cette période jusqu'à dix ans, il faut avoir une bonne quantité de clients pour réussir à vivre convenablement.»

Josée précise également qu'il est très important de se tenir à jour. D'ailleurs, l'Ordre des denturologistes du Québec suggère à ses membres de suivre régulièrement de la formation continue. 07/03

mon parcours

Après avoir obtenu un diplôme d'études collégiales (DEC) en techniques de denturologie au Cégep Édouard-Montpetit, Josée a travaillé dans une clinique privée. Puis, désireuse d'avoir son propre cabinet, elle a contacté plusieurs denturologistes qui approchaient de l'âge de la retraite. «C'est ainsi que j'ai pu racheter une clinique et sa clientèle. C'est un très grand avantage, car je n'ai pas eu à monter toute une banque de clients. Quand on part de zéro, cela peut prendre au moins de quatre à cinq ans.»

Des milieux de travail potentiels

- ❯ Cabinets d'autres professionnels de la santé
- ❯ Cabinets de denturologistes
- ❯ Cabinets de dentistes

Les mots en caractères **gras** sont définis à la page 153.

Hygiéniste dentaire

> en clinique privée

mon travail

Une visite chez le dentiste équivaut à une visite chez l'hygiéniste dentaire, car l'un ne va pas sans l'autre. «L'hygiéniste prend des radiographies des dents et procède au détartrage, communément appelé nettoyage des dents. Il y a aussi tout l'aspect de la prévention et de l'éducation, car on explique aux patients comment ils pourraient améliorer leur santé buccale», précise Martine Daneault, hygiéniste dentaire pratiquant à la Clinique dentaire BPST à Sainte-Foy.

Les dentistes délèguent aussi aux hygiénistes un certain nombre de tâches. Les fonctions de ces derniers varient donc d'un environnement de travail à l'autre. Pour sa part, Martine peut mesurer les poches parodontales, c'est-à-dire la perte d'os autour des dents. D'autres pourraient effectuer l'insertion des **obturations** (plombages) dans les dents ou encore réaliser des travaux en laboratoire, comme couler un modèle en plâtre.

Des milieux de travail potentiels

> Cabinets de dentistes

> Centres hospitaliers

> Centres locaux de services communautaires (CLSC)

> Cliniques d'orthodontie ou de parodontie

ma motivation

L'hygiéniste a tout le loisir de s'entretenir avec le patient, d'apaiser ses craintes et d'établir avec lui une relation de confiance. «J'aime le contact avec la clientèle. On revoit les mêmes personnes régulièrement et on peut ainsi suivre des changements dans leur vie. Par exemple, une patiente qui était enceinte revient en nous racontant qu'elle a accouché d'un petit garçon et nous demande des conseils d'hygiène pour son poupon.

«En cabinet privé, plus le dentiste nous confie de tâches, plus c'est intéressant», souligne Martine. Son rêve : travailler dans un CLSC avec les enfants. «J'adore le contact avec les jeunes. Ce serait une évolution intéressante dans ma carrière, car un hygiéniste dentaire œuvrant en CLSC va dans les écoles et fait de la prévention, de l'éducation et du dépistage.»

mon conseil

Aux personnes intéressées, Martine recommande de réaliser un court stage d'observation en milieu de travail. «Pour avoir une idée plus juste de cette profession et voir comment ça se passe réellement, on peut demander à son dentiste ou à son hygiéniste de l'accompagner une demi-journée en clinique.»

Bien que Martine juge que sa formation a été d'une grande qualité, «la réalité du marché du travail réserve toujours des surprises... des bonnes et des moins bonnes. À ce chapitre, en clinique privée, on doit prendre ses vacances en même temps que le dentiste.» Par ailleurs, Martine estime que sa profession est très valorisante, car elle permet d'améliorer la santé buccodentaire des gens ainsi que leur santé globale. 08/03

mon parcours

Martine a obtenu un diplôme d'études collégiales (DEC) en techniques d'hygiène dentaire au Cégep de Saint-Hyacinthe. Par la suite, elle n'a pas eu de difficulté à dénicher son emploi actuel dans cette clinique de Sainte-Foy.

Les mots en caractères **gras** sont définis à la page 153.

Infirmier
> en milieu hospitalier

mon travail

Infirmier du programme de **soins de longue durée** de l'Hôpital Notre-Dame de la Merci à Montréal, Daniel Desjardins distribue les médicaments aux patients, fait les pansements et, à l'occasion, administre les soins de base, par exemple les soins d'hygiène corporelle. Il voit aussi aux traitements spéciaux, comme la **dialyse**.

En tant que chef d'équipe et assistant chef d'unité, il planifie le travail d'un groupe d'employés composé de ses collègues infirmiers, de préposés aux bénéficiaires et de commis.

Cette équipe suit de près les patients dont elle est responsable. «Nous élaborons des plans de soins, explique Daniel. Par exemple, pour une personne qui a mal aux jambes, on peut en venir à la conclusion, après avoir étudié son cas, qu'il lui serait bénéfique de recevoir des soins d'un physiothérapeute ou d'un ergothérapeute.»

ma motivation

Daniel, qui aime le travail physique et le contact avec le public, se sent bien dans le milieu hospitalier. Toutefois, son poste aux soins de longue durée le confronte à une réalité particulière du métier. «Contrairement au personnel infirmier qui s'occupe d'une clientèle régulière, je ne peux pas vraiment espérer une guérison de mes patients. Mon objectif premier est donc de les soulager. Certains ont passé les 30 dernières années de leur vie à l'hôpital. C'est bien différent des gens qui y entrent pour subir une opération.»

Daniel apprécie également la confiance que les médecins lui accordent quand ils lui demandent son avis au sujet de certains patients. «J'ai l'impression de faire le lien entre les patients et ceux qui prennent les décisions quant aux traitements. C'est stimulant et valorisant.»

mon conseil

Infirmier depuis maintenant 11 ans, Daniel avoue qu'il a énormément appris «sur le tas». «C'est un milieu qui bouge beaucoup. Il faut donc s'adapter rapidement. Par exemple, certains médicaments que j'administrais à mes débuts n'existent plus aujourd'hui, tandis que de nouveaux ont fait leur apparition sur le marché. La façon de faire les pansements a aussi changé.» La capacité de prendre des décisions tout seul est également à cultiver, mais cela ne s'apprend pas forcément sur les bancs de l'école. 08/03

Des milieux de travail potentiels

> Centres d'hébergement et de soins de longue durée
> Centres hospitaliers
> Centres locaux de services communautaires (CLSC)
> Cliniques privées
> Service Info-santé

mon parcours

Avant d'être infirmier, Daniel a été préposé aux bénéficiaires pendant sept ans à l'Hôpital de Gatineau. Après avoir étudié la sociologie à l'Université d'Ottawa et le travail social à l'Université du Québec à Hull, il a finalement décidé d'entreprendre un diplôme d'études collégiales (DEC) en soins infirmiers au Collège de l'Outaouais. «Mon expérience en tant que préposé aux bénéficiaires m'a apporté une belle base pour le travail que je fais aujourd'hui», conclut-il.

Les mots en caractères **gras** sont définis à la page 153.

Inhalothérapeute

> **en milieu hospitalier**

mon travail

Quiconque éprouve de grandes difficultés à respirer remet sa vie entre les mains de l'inhalothérapeute, un spécialiste de l'aide respiratoire. Cette profession est largement mécanisée, puisque la respiration de certains patients – sous anesthésie, notamment – est entièrement contrôlée par des appareils.

Fannie Clément est inhalothérapeute au Centre hospitalier de l'Université Laval (CHUL). «L'inhalothérapie est présente partout dans l'hôpital : au bloc opératoire pour assister l'anesthésiologiste, pour toutes les opérations de surveillance du patient lorsqu'il est endormi, aux soins intensifs, à l'unité néonatale pour les grands prématurés, etc. C'est vraiment interdisciplinaire. On travaille avec les infirmières et les médecins.»

Des milieux de travail potentiels

> Centres d'hébergement et de soins de longue durée
> Centres hospitaliers
> Centres locaux de services communautaires (CLSC)
> Domicile des patients

ma motivation

Fannie apprécie particulièrement la polyvalence de cette profession. «L'inhalothérapeute peut travailler dans plusieurs départements d'un hôpital, dans les laboratoires de diagnostic pulmonaire, les cliniques du sommeil, etc. On en retrouve aussi dans les CLSC, dans le cadre du service à domicile des malades chroniques qui ne peuvent respirer par eux-mêmes.»

Un inhalothérapeute peut également faire partie d'une équipe de recherche médicale (avec des médecins, des spécialistes de la santé publique, etc.) ou encore faire de l'enseignement.

«Hormis la multidisciplinarité que permet mon métier, ce qui me motive le plus est le contact avec le patient, insiste Fannie. Quand une personne s'apprête à passer sur la table d'opération, elle se sent vulnérable, sa nervosité est palpable. Alors il faut savoir créer un contact avec elle, la rassurer et lui apporter un peu de réconfort.»

Sans oublier les situations d'urgence, par exemple lors d'un arrêt cardiorespiratoire, où la survie du patient est une question de minutes. Dans ces cas, il faut savoir garder son sang-froid et ne pas perdre ses moyens, malgré le stress.

mon conseil

Si l'on se destine au métier d'inhalothérapeute, il faut être à l'aise dans le milieu hospitalier, car c'est le principal employeur. De plus, il faut savoir travailler en équipe, car on est perpétuellement en contact avec d'autres professionnels de la santé. Enfin, l'autre enjeu majeur est de se tenir à jour. «La formation continue n'est pas obligatoire, mais dans les faits, dès qu'un nouveau modèle de respirateur entre à l'hôpital, on est tous formés pour apprendre à l'utiliser. Il y a toujours de nouvelles technologies, de nouvelles études scientifiques. Il faut suivre!»

05/03

mon parcours

Dès l'obtention de son diplôme d'études collégiales (DEC) en techniques d'inhalothérapie au Cégep de Sainte-Foy, Fannie a été engagée par le CHUL. Elle y œuvre depuis trois ans. Pendant les deux premières années de sa carrière, elle a également fait des remplacements à l'Hôpital Laval de Québec et à l'Hôtel-Dieu de Lévis.

Les mots en caractères **gras** sont définis à la page 153.

Opticienne d'ordonnance
❯ dans une lunetterie

mon travail

Mélanie Bolduc, opticienne à la Lunetterie New Look à Saint-Jérôme, est responsable de toutes les étapes de la production de lunettes ou de lentilles cornéennes, à l'exception du travail de laboratoire.

Elle s'occupe de tout, depuis l'ordonnance de l'optométriste jusqu'à la livraison du produit. «Je reçois l'ordonnance, je guide le client dans son choix de monture, je prends les mesures de son visage et je commande les lunettes au laboratoire. Quand elles me sont retournées, je vérifie que l'ordonnance a bien été respectée, que la monture s'ajuste parfaitement au client et qu'il est à l'aise avec ses lunettes.»

En plus de la variété que lui offre son travail, Mélanie apprécie l'équipe qui l'entoure, composée d'autres opticiens, de conseillères pour le choix des montures et d'un optométriste.

Des milieux de travail potentiels

❯ Laboratoires privés
❯ Lunetteries

ma motivation

C'est probablement le sens de l'esthétique et le souci du détail de Mélanie qui l'ont conduite vers ce métier. Mais ce qu'elle apprécie le plus, c'est de pouvoir satisfaire la clientèle : «Il y a des moments magiques; tout à coup, le client s'exclame qu'il voit bien et que ses lunettes sont enfin confortables. Là, j'ai le sentiment de l'avoir bien conseillé et je suis fière de moi.»

Mélanie affirme que son travail lui a apporté la confiance en elle-même et l'estime de soi. «Avant, j'étais très gênée. Mais au fur et à mesure que j'ai développé ma pratique du métier, j'ai acquis de l'aisance.»

Avec l'optométriste, elle doit aussi résoudre des problèmes particuliers, par exemple un client insatisfait de la vision que lui procure sa nouvelle paire de lunettes, pourtant conforme à l'ordonnance. «Il faut se creuser la tête pour trouver des solutions!»

mon conseil

Mélanie a appris à ne pas prendre toutes les responsabilités sur ses épaules, malgré la pression de la clientèle. Par exemple, si le laboratoire accuse un retard, ce n'est pas sa faute.

«Il faut être très patient et savoir garder son calme. Développer la capacité de deviner ce que veut le client et d'aller au-devant de ses attentes est également un atout appréciable.» En outre, la manipulation des verres et des lentilles exige de la précision et de la dextérité. 05/03

mon parcours

Après une année en sciences humaines et plusieurs visites de milieux de travail, Mélanie a opté pour la technique d'orthèses visuelles offerte au Collège Édouard-Montpetit, le seul à donner ce programme au Québec. Les excellentes perspectives d'emploi et l'accueil reçu au département quand elle a visité les lieux l'ont fortement motivée. Elle a obtenu un emploi dès la fin de ses études, il y a cinq ans, et a travaillé pour deux bureaux d'opticiens, dont Lunetterie New Look, son employeur actuel.

Les mots en caractères **gras** sont définis à la page 153.

Orthésiste-prothésiste

❯ en laboratoire privé

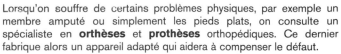

mon travail

Lorsqu'on souffre de certains problèmes physiques, par exemple un membre amputé ou simplement les pieds plats, on consulte un spécialiste en **orthèses** et **prothèses** orthopédiques. Ce dernier fabrique alors un appareil adapté qui aidera à compenser le défaut.

Des milieux de travail potentiels

❯ Centres de réadaptation

❯ Laboratoires privés d'orthèses et de prothèses

Philippe Durocher, orthésiste-prothésiste dans un laboratoire privé, rencontre d'abord le client pour faire une évaluation. «Dans le cas de pieds plats, je commence par réaliser un examen biomécanique qui permet de vérifier l'alignement des membres grâce à des appareils de mesure. Puis, je réalise une empreinte du pied dans du plâtre ou de la mousse, qui me permettra de faire un moule sur lequel je fabriquerai l'orthèse.»

La deuxième partie du travail de Philippe consiste à préparer l'orthèse proprement dite. «Au laboratoire, nous avons un établi, un four et différents outils pour travailler les matériaux. Pour un pied plat, je dois faire un appareil qui créera une arche au pied afin d'améliorer la démarche de la personne.» Enfin, Philippe rencontre à nouveau le client pour qu'il essaye la prothèse et procède à des ajustements si nécessaire.

ma motivation

Philippe aime son métier, car deux de ses passions y sont réunies : le travail manuel et la relation d'aide. «C'est un peu comme faire de la sculpture ou de la poterie. Je dois concevoir et fabriquer de mes mains un objet qui soit à la fois utile, pratique, efficace, confortable et esthétique. De plus, j'éprouve une grande satisfaction lorsque la personne se sent à l'aise avec son appareil. Le bien-être du client, c'est capital pour moi.»

mon conseil

Il n'est pas toujours évident de porter un appareil correcteur. «Lorsque la personne est lourdement handicapée, par exemple quand il y a eu amputation d'un bras ou d'une jambe, le port de l'appareil peut être difficile à accepter. Il faut alors l'aider à s'y adapter.»

Être à l'aise dans les relations d'aide et faire preuve d'empathie sont donc des attitudes indispensables pour l'orthésiste-prothésiste.

Ce travail demande aussi beaucoup de créativité. Chaque personne représentant un défi différent, on doit être ingénieux et inventif pour trouver des solutions adaptées aux besoins de chacun.

«Il est également nécessaire d'être habile de ses mains, car on manipule toutes sortes d'outils et de matériaux.» 05/03

mon parcours

Après le cégep, Philippe a étudié un an en administration à l'université. «J'étais insatisfait, je trouvais ça trop abstrait. L'un de mes amis étudiait en techniques d'orthèses et de prothèses orthopédiques, et cela m'a tout de suite intéressé.» Philippe a obtenu son diplôme d'études collégiales (DEC) dans ce domaine au Collège Montmorency, seul établissement au Québec à offrir cette formation. Par la suite, il a rapidement décroché son poste actuel.

Les mots en caractères **gras** sont définis à la page 153.

Technicien ambulancier
❯ en coopérative

mon travail

Quand il reçoit un appel d'urgence, Dominic Chaput passe en mode alerte. Déclenchant sirène et gyrophares, l'employé de la Coopérative des techniciens ambulanciers du Québec métropolitain (CTAQM) n'a qu'une chose en tête : intervenir à temps. «Lors d'un arrêt cardio-respiratoire, par exemple, il peut y avoir des dommages irréparables au cerveau dans les quatre à six minutes qui suivent, explique-t-il. Et si le cœur est en **fibrillation**, les chances de survie de la personne diminuent de 10 % chaque minute.» À son arrivée sur les lieux de l'incident, Dominic évalue l'état de la victime, détermine les moyens d'intervention appropriés, prodigue les soins d'urgence, jauge si une conduite à l'hôpital est nécessaire en plus d'interroger l'infortuné ou son entourage. Les renseignements qu'il recueille, comme la nature des symptômes, les antécédents médicaux et les circonstances de l'accident, seront utiles au personnel qui prendra le relais à l'hôpital.

Les techniciens ambulanciers sont autorisés à poser de plus en plus d'actes médicaux susceptibles de sauver des vies, précise-t-il. «Fin 2002, j'ai reçu une formation qui me permet d'administrer des médicaments contre les crises d'allergies graves, l'hypoglycémie, le diabète, les troubles cardiaques et les difficultés respiratoires comme l'asthme.»

ma motivation

Attiré par les soins de santé – il a été patrouilleur de ski alpin pendant six ans –, Dominic a trouvé sa vocation dans cette profession qui bouge. Les situations inattendues le stimulent. «Lorsqu'on porte secours à un accidenté de la route, la voiture peut être dans un ravin, anéantie, dans une fâcheuse position. Il faut alors faire preuve de débrouillardise pour sortir la victime du pétrin. Tout ne s'apprend pas sur les bancs de l'école.»

Le technicien se réjouit en outre de l'élargissement du champ d'action de sa profession, en ce qui a trait aux actes médicaux. «Il y a un agréable vent de changement actuellement.»

mon conseil

Quelqu'un qui choisirait cette profession pour l'attrait du camion, des gyrophares et de la sirène ferait fausse route, selon Dominic. «On s'y habitue vite! Il faut opter pour ce métier parce qu'on aime les gens et leur prodiguer des soins. Il y a autant de soutien psychologique que de manipulations techniques.» Par ailleurs, Dominic prévient les futurs techniciens ambulanciers qu'au moment de postuler un emploi, ils auront probablement à démontrer leur savoir-faire dans le cadre de simulations. Autant s'y préparer, croit-il. «Au cégep, on se réunissait un petit groupe les week-ends. On imaginait toutes sortes de cas fictifs. En entrevue, les employeurs ont vu la différence.» 05/03

mon parcours

Dominic a obtenu une attestation d'études collégiales (AEC) en techniques ambulancières au Cégep de Sainte-Foy. Pour se perfectionner, il a aussi suivi un cours d'appoint en arythmie cardiaque donné par le même établissement. Son diplôme en poche, Dominic a été embauché par son employeur actuel. Pendant deux ans, il a également été professeur en techniques ambulancières au Cégep de Sainte-Foy.

Des milieux de travail potentiels

- ❯ Coopératives
- ❯ Entreprises privées offrant des services ambulanciers
- ❯ Urgences-santé (organisme sans but lucratif relevant du ministère de la Santé et des Services sociaux du Québec)

Les mots en caractères **gras** sont définis à la page 153.

Technicien de laboratoire
❯ dans un organisme public

mon travail

Samuel Caron est technicien de laboratoire à Héma-Québec, l'organisme responsable de fournir les produits sanguins aux hôpitaux québécois. Au quotidien, il analyse les dons de sang afin d'identifier les différents **groupes sanguins**.

«Contrairement à ce qu'on peut penser, il existe beaucoup plus de groupes sanguins que les traditionnels A, B et O. Dans mes analyses, je dois repérer les plus rares afin de répondre aux besoins des hôpitaux qui nous adressent des demandes particulières.» Ainsi, lorsque Samuel découvre un groupe sanguin exceptionnel, il congèle le sang, qui pourra servir à une transfusion jusqu'à dix ans plus tard.

«Ce genre de travail se fait surtout à Héma-Québec ou dans les laboratoires des banques de sang», précise Samuel. Un technicien de laboratoire peut aussi exercer, par exemple, dans un département de biochimie, pour mesurer le sucre ou le cholestérol dans le sang; ou encore dans un département de micro-biologie, afin de détecter des microbes, des bactéries ou des virus dans différents types de prélèvements.

ma motivation

Pour Samuel, l'analyse en laboratoire est un travail stimulant qui permet d'apprendre continuellement. «Il y a toujours de nouvelles connaissances, de nouveaux tests à apprendre. C'est un milieu dynamique où les gens qui sont curieux intellectuellement trouvent constamment une source de motivation.»

Bien que son travail ait lieu loin des chambres d'hôpital, Samuel sait qu'il contribue à sauver des vies. «Il arrive, par exemple, que des médecins demandent des tests ou du sang de façon urgente. Parfois, je peux être appelé à décongeler du sang très vite alors qu'un patient avec un groupe sanguin particulièrement rare doit subir une transfusion. Ce n'est pas tout le monde qui apprécie ce genre de défi, mais moi, j'aime beaucoup travailler dans des situations stressantes.»

mon conseil

Samuel est catégorique : le technicien de laboratoire doit posséder une bonne méthodologie de travail pour être efficace en situation d'urgence. La discipline et la minutie sont aussi essentielles dans le métier. «Évidemment, la curiosité intellectuelle et scientifique est primordiale, car on doit aimer apprendre et aller toujours plus loin dans nos recherches.»

Samuel a d'ailleurs effectué un certificat en biotechnologie pour se perfectionner. «Ce certificat n'est pas obligatoire pour obtenir un poste de technicien de laboratoire, mais il apporte des connaissances qui ouvrent davantage d'horizons sur la recherche et le développement.» 06/03

mon parcours

Après avoir obtenu son diplôme d'études collégiales (DEC) en technologie d'analyses biomédicales au Collège de Shawinigan, Samuel a été engagé en disponibilité à l'hôpital où il avait fait son stage. Il est ensuite retourné aux études, à l'Université Laval, pour décrocher un certificat en biotechnologie. Puis, il a travaillé comme technicien dans un laboratoire privé de Québec avant de passer chez Héma-Québec.

Les mots en caractères **gras** sont définis à la page 153.

TECHNOLOGUES en RADIOLOGIE

PROFESSION D'AVENIR

➠ **Radiodiagnostic**
➠ **Médecine nucléaire**
➠ **Radio-oncologie**

 Ordre des
Technologues en
Radiologie du
Québec

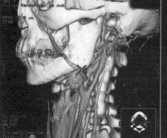
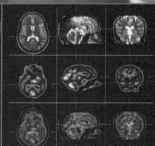

Technicienne dentaire
> **en laboratoire privé**

mon travail

«J'ai toujours aimé aller chez le dentiste! raconte Julie Jacob. Je voulais devenir hygiéniste dentaire, mais la perspective de travailler dans la bouche des gens ne me plaisait guère... Pour moi, le travail de technicienne dentaire est donc vraiment idéal.» Employée au Laboratoire dentaire Julien & St-Jean, Julie fabrique et répare différents types de **prothèses dentaires**. Sa spécialité, c'est la conception et la confection de prothèses amovibles (que le patient peut enlever lui-même) en métal et en acrylique (partiels et dentiers).

Julie travaille à partir des empreintes des dents d'un patient et d'indications écrites, qui lui parviennent d'un dentiste ou encore d'un médecin, d'un prosthodontiste, d'un orthodontiste ou d'un denturologiste. Elle crée d'abord un modèle de la bouche, puis elle fabrique la prothèse par divers procédés (moulage, coulée, pressage, polissage, etc.). Ce travail d'orfèvre s'effectue sous un bon éclairage, en position assise, à l'aide de toute une panoplie d'outils manuels et électriques. La technicienne utilise également une grande variété de matériaux, comme la pierre artificielle, les cires dentaires, l'acrylique, la céramique, les résines composites, différents alliages de métaux et même l'or.

Des milieux de travail potentiels

> Cabinets privés de dentistes

> Laboratoires de fabrication de prothèses

ma motivation

«Je sais que la personne pour qui je fais mon travail va retrouver le sourire, et ça, c'est ma plus belle motivation!» explique Julie. Mais pour parvenir à ce résultat, elle doit faire preuve de beaucoup de minutie. «Si je ne fais pas une prothèse parfaitement adaptée aux besoins du patient, elle peut engendrer plus de problèmes qu'elle n'en résout. Par exemple, une prothèse mal adaptée peut pousser sur les autres dents, les rendre mobiles ou plus vulnérables à la carie.

«L'art du technicien, c'est vraiment de trouver l'équilibre entre les aspects fonctionnel, esthétique et budgétaire, poursuit Julie. Il y a plusieurs sortes de matériaux et leurs prix varient selon leur qualité et leurs caractéristiques.» La technicienne se fait donc un devoir de bien connaître les différentes matières premières.

mon conseil

La fabrication de prothèses dentaires n'a pas lieu en vase clos, prévient Julie. «Ça prend une bonne communication entre le patient, le dentiste et le technicien dentaire, car c'est un travail d'équipe.» L'exercice du métier demande aussi un œil artistique. «Je m'efforce d'imiter la nature le plus possible, sinon ça paraît tout de suite que c'est du faux!» Comme le domaine évolue rapidement, il importe de maintenir ses connaissances à jour, ajoute-t-elle. «Il existe maintenant des logiciels qui permettent la modélisation de prothèses. 06/03

mon parcours

Julie a obtenu son diplôme d'études collégiales (DEC) en techniques dentaires du Collège Édouard-Montpetit, le seul à offrir cette formation au Québec. Elle a décroché son premier emploi en demandant à un propriétaire de laboratoire l'autorisation d'y faire ses travaux scolaires. C'est après avoir travaillé huit ans à temps partiel pour cet établissement qu'elle a obtenu son poste actuel. Elle termine en ce moment un baccalauréat en enseignement en formation professionnelle à l'Université du Québec à Montréal, en vue de transmettre son savoir-faire.

Les mots en caractères **gras** sont définis à la page 153.

Technicienne d'intervention en loisir
> en résidence pour personnes âgées

mon travail

Quand Marie-Eve Leblond est dans les parages, les résidants du Manoir St-Amand, à Québec, n'ont pas le temps de s'ennuyer. Son rôle? Divertir ce groupe d'aînés autonomes et semi-autonomes et, du coup, améliorer leur qualité de vie.

Concrètement, elle organise et dirige pour eux des activités de loisirs : cafés-causeries, jeux de devinettes, etc. Quand il y a des anniversaires à souligner, c'est elle qui y voit. Elle a même déjà fait venir des animaux de l'Institut de zoothérapie du Québec, le temps d'une journée. «L'idée m'est venue en voyant un résidant, habituellement marabout, sourire en flattant le chien d'un visiteur», raconte-t-elle. Au besoin, elle agit comme personne-ressource, par exemple pour aider à mettre sur pied un comité de résidants. Sa journée type commence peu après midi. En arrivant, elle salue les résidants un par un, dans la salle à manger. Ensuite, elle va cogner à la porte de ceux qui pourraient oublier le bingo qu'elle anime dès 14 h. Le reste de l'après-midi, elle planifie d'autres activités, par exemple une sortie aux quilles le lendemain.

Des milieux de travail potentiels

> Centres d'hébergement et de soins de longue durée

> Centres hospitaliers

> Centres locaux de services communautaires (CLSC)

ma motivation

«Mon travail, c'est d'établir des relations avec les gens, de leur faire sentir que je suis là pour eux. Quand je vois une personne âgée sourire durant une de mes activités, je sais que j'ai atteint mon but!» confie Marie-Eve.

Pour y parvenir, elle doit souvent faire preuve de patience. «Il peut arriver que des participants ne comprennent pas les consignes. Il faut donc que je répète et que je reformule pour me faire comprendre, pour que tous puissent tirer plus de satisfaction de l'activité.» Tout en prenant le temps d'être à l'écoute, Marie-Eve tient à rester elle-même; si un jour elle est triste, elle ne le cache pas. «Si on met un masque, les gens le sentent.» Elle attache aussi une grande importance à ce qu'elle appelle la congruence, qu'elle illustre ainsi : «Quand je demande aux autres de ne pas se couper la parole, je ne dois pas la leur couper! Être cohérent, c'est agir en lien avec ce que l'on dit et ce que l'on est. C'est aussi se connaître suffisamment pour savoir où sont nos limites et en tenir compte.»

mon conseil

Un diplômé en techniques d'intervention en loisir comme Marie-Eve peut travailler auprès de diverses clientèles (personnes handicapées, délinquants ou **mésadaptés socio-affectifs**, par exemple), et dans différents contextes (écoles, bases de plein air, municipalités, etc.). «Les tâches varient selon le milieu», indique Marie-Eve, qui conseille aux intéressés d'explorer les différentes possibilités, en variant les stages et les expériences de travail, pour déterminer ce qui leur convient le mieux. 07/03

mon parcours

Marie-Eve voulait être psychologue, mais elle a dû revoir son choix, faute d'avoir de bonnes notes au secondaire. Inscrite en techniques de tourisme au Cégep de Matane, elle a abandonné après un an. «Je n'y trouvais pas la satisfaction de faire du bien aux gens.» Elle s'est donc dirigée vers le programme *Techniques d'intervention en loisir*, au Cégep de Rivière-du-Loup. En cours de stage, lors d'une visite au Salon des aînés de sa région, elle a rencontré la directrice administrative du Manoir St-Amand, qui lui a offert son poste actuel. Bingo!

Les mots en caractères **gras** sont définis à la page 153.

Technicienne en diététique
> **en milieu hospitalier**

mon travail

À l'Hôpital de Montréal pour enfants, les jeunes patients ne mangent pas tous la même chose. Selon sa maladie, chacun se voit prescrire par une diététicienne les aliments qui lui conviennent. La technicienne en diététique, elle, s'assure que ces directives sont respectées.

Car au quotidien, ce sont les patients qui font leur menu. Ils savent généralement ce qu'ils peuvent manger, mais une technicienne comme Marie-Claude Tranquille vérifie qu'ils font les bons choix. Chaque jour, elle révise donc une trentaine de menus afin d'ajuster les quantités et de varier les types d'aliments en fonction de l'état de chaque patient.

Son évaluation terminée, Marie-Claude rédige des rapports détaillés qui comprennent les instructions aux cuisiniers de l'hôpital. Elle y inclut non seulement les différents menus, mais aussi la quantité précise de chaque aliment ainsi que son mode de cuisson. «Tous ces détails peuvent avoir une incidence sur la santé des patients», souligne-t-elle.

ma motivation

Marie-Claude aime transmettre son savoir en expliquant aux patients ce qu'ils doivent manger et pourquoi. Mais comme ce sont des enfants, elle doit souvent les convaincre d'avaler des carottes plutôt que des frites, entre autres. Pour y arriver, elle use de tact et tente de les séduire en faisant valoir les bienfaits de tel ou tel aliment sur leur santé. Et quand un patient lui fait une «demande spéciale», parce qu'il a soudain une rage de chocolat par exemple, elle prend plaisir à essayer de le satisfaire, en vérifiant si X grammes de l'aliment convoité peuvent nuire sa santé.

Par ailleurs, l'évolution des connaissances et des tendances en matière de nutrition la tient en haleine. «Il y a constamment des scientifiques qui découvrent qu'un aliment est meilleur qu'un autre. Je me tiens à jour en suivant chaque année une formation à la Société des technologues en nutrition du Québec et en lisant des articles spécialisés.»

mon conseil

Quand on est responsable de l'alimentation des patients, l'erreur n'est pas permise, soutient Marie-Claude. La minutie est donc une qualité particulièrement importante. Par ailleurs, la technicienne prévient qu'il faut faire preuve de persévérance pour exercer en milieu hospitalier. Avant de se voir offrir un poste stable et permanent, on doit travailler en disponibilité et selon des horaires variables, de jour comme de nuit. Mieux vaut accepter de rentrer le plus souvent possible, autrement, on risque de ne plus être rappelé. 06/03

Des milieux de travail potentiels

> Cafétérias commerciales et institutionnelles
> Centres d'hébergement et de soins de longue durée
> Centres hospitaliers
> Industries alimentaires

mon parcours

Marie-Claude a obtenu un diplôme d'études collégiales (DEC) en techniques de diététique au Collège de Maisonneuve. Avant de travailler à l'Hôpital de Montréal pour enfants, elle a été en disponibilité comme technicienne en diététique dans deux centres d'accueil et dans un centre de réadaptation.

Les mots en caractères **gras** sont définis à la page 153.

Technicienne en éducation spécialisée
> en CLSC

mon travail

Quand l'infirmière du Centre local de services communautaires (CLSC) Sainte-Rose se doute qu'un patient vit des problèmes de pauvreté ou de drogue, par exemple, elle refile ses coordonnées à Lyne Desjardins, éducatrice spécialisée, qui prendra le temps d'appeler la personne en question pour lui offrir une relation d'aide.

«Une relation d'aide consiste à écouter l'autre, à tenter de comprendre son problème et ses besoins, puis à l'accompagner dans la recherche et l'atteinte de son objectif», explique Lyne. Par exemple, on peut avoir pour objectif d'apprendre à dire non à un conjoint joueur compulsif qui demande sans cesse de l'argent. «Il faut y aller très délicatement, car ces gens-là n'ont pas nécessairement appelé au CLSC en disant "j'ai besoin d'aide".» Lyne anime également des ateliers destinés aux parents, dont deux qui portent sur le développement moteur et affectif des petits de 1 à 24 mois et un autre axé sur l'acquisition des habiletés sociales des bambins de 2 à 4 ans.

ma motivation

Fascinée par le comportement humain, Lyne a découvert que chaque individu donne à ses actions un sens qui lui est propre, unique, «...donc il y a toujours quelque chose à apprendre. Cela me motive beaucoup.» Avec le temps, elle a appris qu'il valait mieux tenter de comprendre les autres que de les juger. «Quand je travaillais aux Centres jeunesse de Montréal, je côtoyais des gens qui, de père en fils, vivaient de l'aide sociale. Ils n'étaient pas heureux de cela, ni fiers d'eux-mêmes, mais ils n'avaient pas ce qu'il fallait pour s'en sortir, ne serait-ce qu'une capacité à s'exprimer suffisante pour rencontrer un employeur potentiel.»

Pour elle, le cheminement personnel est indissociable du travail de relation d'aide. «Comment être sensible à la souffrance et aux besoins des autres si on ne s'est jamais arrêté aux siens? Un des pièges du métier, si on n'a pas appris à se connaître soi-même, sera de vouloir régler les problèmes des autres, de se les approprier.»

mon conseil

Le métier exige de savoir gérer ses émotions, pour ne pas se laisser envahir par la détresse ou l'agressivité de ceux que l'on tente d'aider, mais demande aussi de la générosité. «Si une crise familiale éclate à 20 h 30, on ne peut pas s'en aller en disant "j'ai fini ma journée, désolée".» Lyne conseille aux intéressés d'essayer différents milieux de travail pour déterminer ceux où ils se sentent le plus à l'aise : les techniques d'intervention varient beaucoup d'un employeur à l'autre. «Et il ne faut pas avoir peur de demander du soutien psychologique, à ses pairs ou à un psychologue, ajoute-t-elle, parce que ce travail peut être très insécurisant.» 07/03

Des milieux de travail potentiels

> Centres de réadaptation
> Centres hospitaliers
> Centres jeunesse

mon parcours

Pendant ses études collégiales en éducation spécialisée au Cégep de Saint-Jérôme, Lyne a fait deux stages : l'un dans une école primaire et l'autre dans un centre de réadaptation pour adolescentes. Elle a ensuite travaillé sept ans au Centre Rosalie-Jetté, auprès de mères en difficulté, puis trois ans pour le compte de la Direction de la protection de la jeunesse (DPJ), avant d'obtenir son poste actuel au CLSC.

Les mots en caractères **gras** sont définis à la page 153.

Technicienne en électrophysiologie médicale
❯ en milieu hospitalier

mon travail

Josée Chaumont souhaitait œuvrer dans le domaine médical, mais elle ne voulait pas faire d'études universitaires. La lecture d'une monographie sur la technique en électrophysiologie médicale ayant piqué sa curiosité, elle demande à effectuer un stage d'observation d'une journée dans un hôpital et est séduite par ce qu'elle découvre.

Certains organes, comme le cerveau et le cœur, génèrent de l'activité électrique. Un médecin qui soupçonne son patient d'éprouver un problème lié à l'un de ces organes peut faire tester cette activité. C'est là qu'entre en scène le technicien en électrophysiologie médicale, un spécialiste formé pour administrer les tests qui permettront de savoir si l'activité électrique est normale.

«C'est difficile d'expliquer en quoi consiste mon travail, car ce n'est pas concret», confie Josée, technicienne en électrophysiologie médicale au Centre hospitalier universitaire de Sherbrooke. En résumé, elle pose sur le patient des fils reliés à des appareils qui permettront de mesurer l'activité électrique du cœur (électrocardiogramme) ou celle du cerveau (électroencéphalogramme).

Des milieux de travail potentiels

- ❯ Centres hospitaliers
- ❯ Cliniques médicales
- ❯ Fabricants d'appareils ou d'accessoires d'électrophysiologie médicale
- ❯ Laboratoires de recherche

ma motivation

Elle apprécie tout particulièrement la polyvalence qu'exige son métier. Selon les journées, Josée évolue en effet en cardiologie ou en neurologie, deux spécialités dont les tests sont complètement différents. «Un électrocardiogramme dure cinq minutes alors qu'un électroencéphalogramme peut exiger jusqu'à une heure et demie.» Elle a également suivi une formation complémentaire lui permettant de vérifier le fonctionnement des stimulateurs cardiaques, ce qui ajoute à la diversité de ses tâches.

Sa plus grande satisfaction? «C'est quand je détecte quelque chose – une anomalie dans l'activité électrique – qu'on ne voit pas souvent. Ça aiguise l'esprit, cela m'oblige à rester en alerte et à retourner dans mes livres pour chercher de quoi il s'agit.»

mon conseil

La lecture d'une monographie de la technique en électrophysiologie médicale peut se révéler aride. «Le mieux est de se rendre dans un hôpital pour voir concrètement en quoi consiste ce métier», conseille Josée. Avant d'opter pour ce choix de carrière, il faut également s'assurer que l'on peut faire preuve d'empathie tout en gardant une certaine distance émotionnelle, afin de ne pas trop se laisser toucher par ce que vivent les patients. «Il faut aussi avoir beaucoup de patience : nous ne sommes pas autorisés à divulguer les résultats des tests; ce sont les médecins qui s'en chargent. Mais il y a des malades qui insistent, et nous devons garder notre calme.» 05/03

mon parcours

Josée a obtenu un diplôme d'études collégiales (DEC) en techniques d'électrophysiologie médicale au Cégep Ahuntsic, le seul établissement à offrir cette formation au Québec. Dès la fin de sa première année d'études, elle a été employée comme préposée en électrophysiologie médicale dans un hôpital, ce qui lui a permis d'acquérir de l'expérience.

Les mots en caractères **gras** sont définis à la page 153.

Technicien en génie biomédical
> **en milieu hospitalier**

formation collégiale

mon travail

Brian Cyr est technicien en génie biomédical à l'Hôpital Saint-Luc, du Centre hospitalier universitaire de Montréal. Il entretient et répare les appareils des départements d'**hémodialyse** et des différents laboratoires.

Il peut s'occuper, par exemple, des générateurs d'hémodialyse – machines qui nettoient le sang des personnes souffrant de maladies des reins – ou des **centrifugeuses** qui séparent les globules rouges du plasma.

Téléavertisseur à la ceinture, coffre d'outils à la main, Brian est constamment en disponibilité. Une fois devant la machine, il détermine quel est le problème, puis procède à la réparation, ce qui peut prendre quelques minutes ou quelques jours. Si la tâche se révèle trop complexe, Brian fait directement appel aux techniciens de l'entreprise ayant conçu l'appareil.

Des milieux de travail potentiels

> Centres hospitaliers
> Fournisseurs d'équipements médicaux

ma motivation

Passionné des machines, Brian a un réel plaisir à comprendre comment elles fonctionnent. «Je m'occupe d'une soixantaine d'appareils différents et il arrive que certains d'entre eux me soient totalement inconnus. C'est donc un défi de cerner leur principe de fonctionnement. Il arrive que je sois découragé devant l'ampleur du problème, mais lorsque je finis par trouver la solution, je trouve cela très valorisant», explique-t-il.

Pouvoir, à sa façon, contribuer à la guérison des patients est une autre source de motivation. «Certains malades ne pourraient vivre sans ces appareils. C'est le cas du générateur d'hémodialyse par exemple, qui assure la survie de personnes dont les reins fonctionnent à moins de 10 % de leur capacité.»

Sans compter que Brian est souvent considéré comme un «sauveur» lorsqu'un appareil tombe en panne. «Le personnel médical ainsi que les patients s'affolent un peu parce que cela interrompt le traitement. Mais une fois la machine remise en marche, les gens me remercient.»

mon conseil

Ce n'est que depuis septembre 1999 que le certificat *Technologies biomédicales : instrumentation électronique* est offert à l'École Polytechnique aux aspirants techniciens. Brian, qui a appris sur le tas, conseille fortement aux jeunes de s'inscrire à ce programme. «Cela leur permettra de mieux connaître le milieu biomédical et d'avoir une formation à la fine pointe de la technologie», conclut-il. 05/03

mon parcours

Brian est titulaire d'un diplôme d'études professionnelles en électromécanique de systèmes automatisés (DEP) du Centre de formation professionnelle Pierre-Dupuy (rebaptisé l'École des métiers des Faubourgs de Montréal), et d'un diplôme d'études collégiales (DEC) en électronique, option télécommunications, de l'Institut Teccart. Cette formation l'a amené à travailler chez Vidéotron comme technicien en installation, puis chez Nortel comme technicien en électronique, avant d'occuper son emploi actuel.

Les mots en caractères **gras** sont définis à la page 153.

Technicienne en thanatologie

> dans un salon funéraire

mon travail

Le thanatologue est le professionnel responsable de l'embaumement des défunts. Si sa tâche peut sembler très technique, elle requiert aussi une bonne dose de sens artistique puisqu'il doit faire en sorte que la personne exposée retrouve une apparence la plus naturelle possible. «Il faut parfois aller jusqu'à refaire des parties du visage à la cire, par exemple dans des cas d'accidents de la route ou de meurtres, remettre des cheveux quand quelqu'un a subi une opération à la tête, refaire une moustache, etc.», explique Nancy Lazure, thanatologue chez Alfred Dallaire.

Mais la tâche de Nancy ne s'arrête pas là, puisqu'elle doit également recevoir les familles en deuil, savoir les conseiller sur les arrangements funéraires possibles en tenant compte de leurs besoins et de leurs moyens financiers. Enfin, elle accueille les visiteurs lors de l'exposition et veille à ce que tout se déroule bien.

Des milieux de travail potentiels

> Cimetières
> Crématoriums
> Entreprises funéraires

ma motivation

C'est toute petite que Nancy a découvert son intérêt pour les personnes défuntes. «Mon école primaire était située en face d'un salon funéraire et j'étais fascinée par les corbillards que je voyais passer. J'étais peut-être la seule à l'être!»

Si c'est la profession de coroner qui l'intéressait initialement, car elle voulait effectuer des autopsies, les études universitaires requises pour l'exercer étaient trop longues à son goût. Elle a donc opté pour la thanatologie, qui demande une technique collégiale.

Nancy apprécie tout particulièrement de pouvoir faire une différence dans le souvenir que les proches d'un défunt garderont de lui. «Quand on me dit que la personne décédée a l'air naturel, qu'elle est belle, surtout quand il s'agit de quelqu'un que la maladie avait beaucoup changé et amaigri, je sais que j'ai fait un bon travail.»

mon conseil

Côtoyer des morts peut impressionner et déranger, de sorte que «beaucoup laissent tomber dès la deuxième année d'études, au moment où s'effectue le premier contact», avertit Nancy. Il pourrait donc être sage de tenter d'effectuer un stage d'observation dans une maison funéraire avant d'envisager d'embrasser la profession.

Il faut également s'assurer que le sang et les aiguilles ne nous font pas peur et que l'on possède une certaine force physique. «Même si nous avons des appareils à notre disposition pour nous aider, un corps c'est lourd à déplacer. De plus, on doit avoir la force psychologique nécessaire pour faire face à des personnes en deuil; certaines sont agressives, d'autres pleurent ou ont des fous rires. C'est loin d'être facile.» 05/03

mon parcours

Nancy a obtenu un diplôme d'études collégiales (DEC) en techniques de thanatologie du Collège de Rosemont, le seul établissement à donner le programme au Québec. Elle a eu la chance de se voir offrir un emploi dès la fin de son premier stage pratique pendant ses études, de sorte qu'elle a pu terminer sa dernière année de formation tout en travaillant à temps plein dans le domaine.

Les mots en caractères **gras** sont définis à la page 153.

Technicienne en travail social
> **en organisme communautaire**

mon travail

Dominique Brisson est à la tête de L'Entretoise du Témiscamingue, un organisme communautaire qui reçoit une clientèle adulte avec des problèmes sévères de santé mentale (**schizophrénie**, **paranoïa**, **maniaco-dépression**, etc.). «Je coordonne la comptabilité, la gestion financière (qui comprend la préparation des demandes de subventions et la recherche de financement) et la gestion tout court (organisation d'activités, suivi des employés, etc.). Je fais tout ça avec la collaboration d'une petite équipe de six personnes. Je consacre 60 % de ma journée à traiter les dossiers administratifs, et le reste aux interventions directes avec la clientèle», raconte Dominique.

Ces interventions sont très diversifiées, précise-t-elle. «Je peux accompagner une personne pour remplir sa demande d'aide sociale ou encore apprendre à quelqu'un à faire l'épicerie. On s'adapte aux besoins des gens, que ce soit pour de l'écoute, de l'information, des activités éducatives, etc.»

Des milieux de travail potentiels

> Centres jeunesse
> Centres locaux de services communautaires (CLSC)

ma motivation

«J'aime être avec les gens, déclare Dominique. Je me réserve des moments dans ma journée pour être avec l'équipe et la clientèle, pour échanger avec eux. Je ne pourrais pas les représenter et défendre leur point de vue (auprès des organismes qui subventionnent, par exemple) si je ne les connaissais pas.

«La clientèle de L'Entretoise est surtout constituée de gens ayant été hospitalisés pendant de très longues périodes. Plusieurs n'ont jamais appris à accomplir les tâches du quotidien dans un logement. Certains sont paralysés à la simple idée de passer un coup de téléphone. Leur redonner confiance est un défi quotidien pour moi!»

Elle et son équipe prennent donc le temps qu'il faut pour soutenir et guider les différents individus dans leur évolution. «Chaque personne a son propre rythme et peut prendre des semaines, des mois ou des années à progresser. Notre travail, c'est de les aider à réintégrer la société, de leur faire sentir qu'ils sont des citoyens et de les amener à devenir assez autonomes pour habiter en logement.»

mon conseil

«Dans un petit organisme communautaire, les employés se doivent d'être polyvalents», souligne la coordonnatrice. Selon elle, cumuler des expériences d'emploi ou d'engagement social variées favorise l'accès au marché du travail. C'est d'ailleurs ce qu'elle a fait. «J'ai monté un système d'urgence pour un centre d'aide à la famille, j'ai travaillé pour un service téléphonique de prévention du suicide, j'ai animé des groupes d'entraide. Ça m'a beaucoup aidée à me faire connaître.» 06/03

mon parcours

Dominique a obtenu son diplôme d'études collégiales (DEC) en techniques de travail social au Cégep de l'Abitibi-Témiscamingue. Elle a tenu à faire chacun de ses quatre stages avec des clientèles différentes (adolescents, personnes âgées, etc.), ce qui l'a amenée à confirmer son intérêt pour le domaine de la santé mentale.

Les mots en caractères **gras** sont définis à la page 153.

Technologue en médecine nucléaire

mon travail

Au service du Centre hospitalier de l'Université de Montréal (CHUM), au pavillon Notre-Dame, Marie-Claude Carrier prend des photos très spéciales appelées «scintigraphies». «En médecine nucléaire, les rayons "sortent" littéralement des patients grâce aux substances radioactives fixées sur l'organe ou le tissu à examiner. Les images sont captées par une caméra, puis visualisées sur un écran d'ordinateur et ensuite reproduites sur papier», explique-t-elle.

Les scintigraphies renseignent sur la forme des organes – au même titre que les radiographies –, mais aussi sur leur fonctionnement.

Tous les matins, Marie-Claude prépare donc les produits radioactifs qu'elle administrera aux patients, par injection, inhalation ou en comprimés. Puis, elle leur explique le déroulement de l'examen et vérifie le fonctionnement des caméras. La technologue doit aussi s'assurer de la bonne qualité des clichés avant de les montrer au radiologiste. Ce dernier les interprétera, puis transmettra son rapport au médecin traitant qui, lui, posera le diagnostic.

Des milieux de travail potentiels

❯ Centres hospitaliers

ma motivation

Marie-Claude ne connaît pas la routine. Bien sûr, les mêmes ordonnances de scintigraphie reviennent fréquemment; mais elle apprécie son milieu de travail qui lui permet de faire passer différents types d'examens, sans la limiter à une spécialité particulière (scintigraphie osseuse, cardiaque ou pulmonaire, par exemple).

Les bonnes nouvelles pour un patient font partie de ses plaisirs. «Quand je vois qu'un traitement contre le cancer a été efficace, alors j'éprouve une grande satisfaction, même si ce n'est pas moi qui lui annonce le résultat.» En fait, les relations humaines occupent une place importante dans la journée de travail de Marie-Claude. Car derrière la caméra se trouve un patient souvent anxieux, toujours inquiet. «Il faut savoir rassurer les gens et bien expliquer l'examen. Même si c'est un domaine technique, les relations humaines sont très importantes.»

mon conseil

Marie-Claude estime avoir acquis beaucoup de maturité et d'empathie depuis qu'elle occupe cet emploi. «Être en contact avec des malades, déplacer des patients souffrants, c'est parfois difficile. Mais sur le plan humain, ça apporte beaucoup.»

Elle ajoute que le travail en équipe avec les autres technologues fait partie du quotidien, et que le goût des sciences reste un préalable pour étudier dans ce domaine.
05/03

mon parcours

Marie-Claude a d'abord fait une année en sciences humaines au cégep. Puis, elle a travaillé dans le domaine de la restauration pendant deux ans. Elle a ensuite amorcé ses études collégiales en technologie de médecine nucléaire au Collège Ahuntsic, le seul à offrir ce programme au Québec. Immédiatement après son stage au CHUM, elle y a été engagée, son diplôme de technologue en médecine nucléaire en poche. Elle occupe cet emploi depuis deux ans.

Les mots en caractères **gras** sont définis à la page 153.

Technologue en radiodiagnostic
> en milieu hospitalier

mon travail

Pneumonie, fracture, accident de la route... Quel que soit le problème des patients qui se présentent le soir à l'urgence de l'Hôtel-Dieu de Montmagny, Véronique D'Auteuil voit à effectuer les radiographies nécessaires. Elle commence par consulter leur dossier pour s'enquérir de l'examen prescrit par le médecin. Elle installe ensuite le malade et procède à la radiographie demandée.

Véronique quitte parfois son département pour se rendre au bloc opératoire afin d'assister les chirurgiens dans leurs interventions. Ainsi, à l'aide d'un appareil de **fluoroscopie**, elle peut guider les mouvements d'un orthopédiste qui s'apprête à poser une vis sur l'os d'un patient, par exemple. Elle peut aussi se rendre directement au chevet de malades trop affaiblis pour se déplacer, et leur faire subir des examens à l'aide d'un appareil mobile.

ma motivation

Véronique n'aimait pas les hôpitaux. C'est donc étonnant qu'elle ait choisi cette profession. «J'ai toujours été fascinée par l'anatomie et la biologie et j'aime le contact humain. C'est ce qui m'a finalement poussée dans cette voie. Mon emploi me permet d'explorer toutes ces facettes. J'adore aider les gens, participer à leur guérison et veiller à leur confort. Et même si le contact que j'ai avec les patients est assez bref, il est généralement très agréable.»

Véronique aime travailler en équipe dans un environnement qui évolue sans cesse. «Je suis toujours en contact avec les médecins et les infirmières. La guérison d'un patient résulte d'un travail d'équipe, et j'apprécie beaucoup cette dynamique. De plus, ma profession est loin d'être routinière. Chaque cas est unique et demande des examens qui diffèrent d'une fois à l'autre.»

mon conseil

Selon Véronique, la théorie apprise à l'école est plutôt rose face à la réalité de la profession. «En cours, on apprend l'abc du radiodiagnostic, sur des patients dits "normaux". Sur le terrain, c'est différent, car on peut traiter des individus qui saignent abondamment, dont les os sont déformés ou brisés, qui souffrent énormément. On doit s'adapter et trouver des façons de faire. Et c'est sans compter les horaires de travail irréguliers : on peut œuvrer le jour, le soir, la nuit, les fins de semaine et les jours fériés. Il est indispensable de se questionner sur les répercussions possibles de ce type d'horaire sur sa vie privée et familiale, avant d'opter pour cette voie. Je crois que suivre des stages en milieu de travail pendant ses études permet également de se faire une idée réaliste de la profession», précise Véronique. 05/03

Des milieux de travail potentiels

> Centres hospitaliers
> Centres locaux de services communautaires (CLSC)
> Cliniques privées

mon parcours

Dès qu'elle a obtenu son diplôme d'études collégiales (DEC) en technologie de radiodiagnostic au Cégep de Rimouski, Véronique a décroché son emploi actuel à l'Hôtel-Dieu de Montmagny. Elle a également suivi un programme en **scanographie** à l'Ordre des technologues en radiologie du Québec afin de se spécialiser dans ce domaine.

Les mots en caractères **gras** sont définis à la page 153.

Technologue en radio-oncologie
❯ en milieu hospitalier

mon travail

Au département de radio-oncologie de l'Hôtel-Dieu de Québec, Mathieu Bergeron accompagne les personnes atteintes de cancer dans leur traitement de **radiothérapie**, un procédé thérapeutique de radiation locale. Tant du point de vue technologique qu'humain, il s'assure de mettre tout en œuvre pour les aider à guérir.

Il planifie d'abord le traitement qui sera réalisé à l'aide d'appareils d'imagerie médicale (radiographie et scanographie). Il détermine ensuite la quantité, la durée et l'emplacement du traitement. Puis, il installe le patient et prépare l'appareil selon les paramètres établis. Pendant le traitement, il quitte la salle pour ne pas s'exposer aux radiations et prend place dans une pièce adjacente d'où il fera fonctionner les appareils à distance. Il s'assure toutefois que le patient reste dans la même position, qu'il est à l'aise et que la machine fonctionne adéquatement. Finalement, Mathieu fait le suivi des différents effets secondaires causés par les traitements et envoie les patients à des médecins ou des diététistes afin de réduire au maximum ces inconvénients.

Des milieux de travail potentiels

❯ Cabinets privés de chirurgiens

❯ Cabinets privés de dentistes

❯ Cabinets privés de médecins

❯ Centres hospitaliers

ma motivation

Comme un traitement de radiothérapie se déroule en moyenne cinq jours par semaine pendant quatre à cinq semaines, Mathieu a le temps de nouer des liens avec les patients. «Il y a une relation, un apprivoisement qui se crée au fur et à mesure des rencontres. Je deviens un confident, un accompagnateur, mais aussi un agent de motivation dans les mauvais jours. Pour moi, c'est un privilège d'être témoin de l'évolution d'un patient et de son cheminement face à la maladie. Ce sont aussi des gens qui nous donnent de grandes leçons de vie et nous ramènent à l'essentiel», raconte Mathieu.

Très stimulé par sa profession, il estime qu'il est porteur de polyvalence. «Je touche à l'anatomie, à la physique, à la biologie. C'est aussi très intéressant de voir l'évolution des appareils et des techniques de traitement. Il faut toujours rester à la fine pointe des progrès technologiques dans ce domaine.»

mon conseil

Face à la détresse des patients, Mathieu conseille de faire preuve d'empathie tout en conservant une attitude professionnelle. «C'est difficile, mais je ne peux me permettre de m'attrister. Même si je les traite comme je le ferais pour ma propre mère ou mon propre père, je dois conserver un certain recul afin d'agir adéquatement», relate Mathieu.

De plus, la guérison du patient ne dépend pas que des soins du technologue, mais d'une équipe multidisciplinaire composée de médecins, d'infirmières, de préposés aux bénéficiaires. «C'est un travail d'équipe. Il faut savoir collaborer avec nos collègues», ajoute Mathieu. 05/03

mon parcours

Après l'obtention d'un diplôme d'études collégiales (DEC) en technologie de radio-oncologie au Cégep de Sainte-Foy, Mathieu a immédiatement décroché son emploi à l'Hôtel-Dieu de Québec, emploi qu'il occupe encore actuellement.

Les mots en caractères **gras** sont définis à la page 153.

Thérapeute en réadaptation physique
❯ en clinique privée

mon travail

Arthrose lombaire, **tendinite**, **bursite** : voilà quelques exemples de cas que traite Julie Couture au Centre de physiatrie de Québec. En collaboration avec l'équipe de **physiatres**, de **physiothérapeutes** et d'autres thérapeutes en réadaptation physique, elle prodigue des soins qui concourent à améliorer ou à rétablir le bien-être physique des patients tout en soulageant leurs douleurs.

«C'est un travail très physique, explique Julie. Je suis à peu près toujours debout et en mouvement. J'effectue beaucoup de manipulations sur les patients, je les aide à se déplacer, je leur indique des exercices à faire et j'utilise des appareils (pour l'**électrothérapie** et l'application d'**ultrasons**, entre autres). Je dois aussi remplir les dossiers, inscrire les notes destinées au médecin, changer les lits et faire le lavage quand je travaille en soirée.»

ma motivation

C'est à la suite d'un match de volley-ball, au cours duquel elle a subi une **luxation** de l'épaule, que Julie a choisi sa carrière. «J'ai suivi des traitements de physiothérapie; j'étais passionnée de voir que les personnes qui me soignaient savaient exactement quoi faire pour me soulager et me rétablir. Je voulais comprendre le fonctionnement du corps et apprendre comment le traiter.»

Aujourd'hui, elle apprécie la variété des responsabilités qu'on lui confie à la clinique, bien consciente que la tâche peut différer considérablement d'un employeur à un autre. «Je fais bien plus qu'appliquer des ultrasons toute la journée», affirme Julie en expliquant que, si elle doit observer l'opinion clinique du physiothérapeute ou du physiatre, elle a beaucoup de latitude quant au choix du traitement et aux ajustements à y apporter en fonction de la progression du patient.

Julie est heureuse lorsqu'elle réussit à soulager la douleur des patients. «J'aime le contact avec les gens. Quand ils arrivent ici, ils ont mal. Ma satisfaction, c'est de les voir repartir avec moins ou pas de douleur.»

mon conseil

«Auparavant, je croyais que tout le monde faisait religieusement ses exercices!» se rappelle Julie. L'expérience lui a appris que la réalité est tout autre et qu'il est important d'encourager les patients à être assidus. La patience et la capacité d'écoute sont des qualités essentielles chez les thérapeutes, ajoute-t-elle. De plus, le métier demande de l'endurance et de la force physiques puisque les manipulations peuvent se révéler exigeantes. Enfin, il faut se sentir à l'aise avec la proximité physique des patients puisque le toucher fait partie du quotidien. 06/03

mon parcours

Julie a d'abord terminé des études collégiales en sciences humaines avant de bifurquer vers le programme d'études collégiales en techniques de réadaptation physique, qu'elle a effectué au Cégep Marie-Victorin, puis au Cégep François-Xavier-Garneau. Une fois diplômée, elle a immédiatement été embauchée par le Centre de physiatrie de Québec. Julie souhaite maintenant suivre un cours de thérapie manuelle, qui l'autorisera à effectuer des manipulations de la colonne vertébrale.

Des milieux de travail potentiels

❯ Centres de réadaptation

❯ Centres d'hébergement et de soins de longue durée

❯ Centres hospitaliers

❯ Centres locaux de services communautaires (CLSC)

❯ Cliniques privées

Audiologiste

> en milieu scolaire

mon travail

Un enfant sourd et un enseignant qui ne comprend pas son handicap : voilà de bien pauvres conditions d'apprentissage. Heureusement, l'audiologiste en milieu scolaire peut remédier à la situation. «Mon travail est de favoriser par divers moyens la réussite des élèves aux prises avec une déficience auditive», explique Pascale Héon. Officiellement employée de la Commission scolaire des Chênes, à Drummondville, cette audiologiste exerce en fait dans cinq commissions scolaires de la région Mauricie-Centre-du-Québec.

Quand Pascale intervient auprès d'un élève, il a déjà été diagnostiqué par un confrère audiologiste et s'est vu prescrire un appareil auditif. «Je veille à ce que l'appareil du jeune fonctionne correctement. J'évalue aussi ses besoins, par exemple s'il ne faudrait pas recourir au **système MF**, placer l'élève à l'avant de la classe ou encore instaurer des mesures de soutien spéciales lors des examens (allouer plus de temps, faire intervenir un éducateur spécialisé, etc.).» Pascale a également pour rôle de sensibiliser l'enseignant aux problèmes de l'enfant et de solliciter son appui. «Comme le jeune utilise la lecture labiale (sur les lèvres), l'enseignant doit notamment penser à faire face à l'élève lorsqu'il parle.»

Des milieux de travail potentiels

- > Centres de réadaptation
- > Centres d'hébergement et de soins de longue durée
- > Centres hospitaliers
- > Centres locaux de services communautaires (CLSC)

ma motivation

«J'aime travailler avec les enfants», confie l'audiologiste, qui a toujours voulu travailler auprès des jeunes. «Dans le milieu scolaire, ça bouge beaucoup! poursuit-elle. Les élèves sont constamment en apprentissage et leurs besoins évoluent à l'intérieur d'une année. Comme nous entretenons avec eux une relation à long terme, nous pouvons développer de belles complicités.»

L'audiologiste se dit également stimulée par les échanges avec les spécialistes des domaines apparentés au sien : éducateurs spécialisés, orthopédagogues, orthophonistes, psychologues et interprètes en langage des sourds. «Certains intervenants me font part de trucs qui ont fonctionné et je puise dans ce bagage d'idées.»

mon conseil

La plupart des audiologistes exercent en milieu hospitalier et en centres de réadaptation. Pour percer dans le monde scolaire, selon Pascale, il faut savoir se vendre. «Le poste que j'occupe n'était pas offert à un audiologiste. Pour l'obtenir, j'ai dû démontrer à l'employeur en quoi je pouvais être utile concrètement.» Ainsi, Pascale a pris soin de faire valoir que, contrairement à d'autres professionnels, elle avait une compréhension poussée des déficiences auditives et de leurs conséquences pour les élèves, en plus de maîtriser les solutions d'appoint comme le système MF.
05/03

mon parcours

Pascale a fait un baccalauréat en orthophonie et audiologie* ainsi qu'une maîtrise en audiologie à l'Université de Montréal. Elle a ensuite rempli la fonction d'audiologiste clinique au Centre hospitalier Rouyn-Noranda, où elle effectuait des examens audiométriques pour diagnostiquer les déficiences auditives et ensuite élaborer des programmes de réadaptation. Elle a aussi exercé en cabinet privé avant d'obtenir son poste actuel.

* Jusqu'en 1999, l'Université de Montréal offrait un bac qui couvrait les deux disciplines. À présent, l'audiologie et l'orthophonie font l'objet de deux bacs distincts.

| Les mots en caractères **gras** sont définis à la page 153.

Biochimiste clinique
❯ en milieu hospitalier

mon travail

Par définition, la biochimie est la science qui étudie la constitution chimique des êtres vivants et les réactions chimiques qui s'opèrent en eux. Lorsqu'on parle de biochimie clinique, on fait référence à la conduite des différents tests (analyses sanguines, analyses d'urine, etc.) qui permettent d'évaluer l'état de santé d'un patient. Ainsi, quand votre médecin veut connaître votre taux de cholestérol par exemple, il vous prescrit une prise de sang. Entre le moment où l'échantillon est prélevé et celui où vous apprenez le résultat intervient quelqu'un comme Marie-Josée Champagne.

Biochimiste clinique au Centre hospitalier Santa Cabrini, à Montréal, Marie-Josée supervise dix techniciens qui exécutent différents tests biochimiques en mélangeant des prélèvements avec des **réactifs**, à l'aide de robots. Son rôle? Assurer la bonne marche du laboratoire afin que les résultats soient rapidement communiqués aux bons médecins. «Si on obtient un résultat bizarre, c'est à moi de faire enquête pour découvrir que le patient a peut-être pris un médicament qui a interféré avec la technique d'analyse», précise-t-elle. Il lui revient également de déterminer les différents tests qui seront utilisés au laboratoire.

Des milieux de travail potentiels

❯ Centres hospitaliers

ma motivation

Curieuse, Marie-Josée aime la biochimie parce qu'elle lui permet d'approfondir sa connaissance du vivant sans avoir à donner de consultations dans un bureau. «J'adore poser des diagnostics en collaboration avec les médecins ou encore dénicher de nouveaux tests», dit-elle. Chaque jour, elle travaille à offrir un excellent service au moindre coût possible. «Si un médecin me demande un test qui est très cher, je l'interroge pour savoir ce qu'il veut analyser exactement; je peux parfois proposer un équivalent moins coûteux.» Gérer diverses tâches en même temps la stimule, bien que cela apporte son lot de stress. «Si je rédige un rapport d'analyse compliqué, qu'un technicien m'annonce la défaillance d'un robot et qu'un médecin attend mon appel, je dois d'abord m'occuper du robot, dit-elle. Parce que le laboratoire, c'est comme une usine : on sort jusqu'à 500 résultats par jour! Et quand la demande vient de l'urgence, il faut l'exécuter en moins d'une heure.»

mon conseil

«Le fait que je m'intéresse à tous les secteurs de la biochimie m'a aidée à obtenir mon emploi ici», affirme Marie-Josée. En effet, dans un centre hospitalier relativement petit comme Santa Cabrini, le biochimiste clinique doit pouvoir chapeauter seul plusieurs aspects : **endocrinologie**, analyses d'urine, etc. Dans les centres hospitaliers universitaires toutefois, les biochimistes, plus nombreux, sont davantage spécialisés. 06/03

mon parcours

Marie-Josée a obtenu un diplôme d'études collégiales (DEC) en sciences de la santé au Collège de l'Assomption avant de poursuivre ses études à l'Université de Montréal : baccalauréat et maîtrise en biochimie, puis doctorat en sciences biomédicales, le tout ponctué de stages à la Cité de la santé de Laval et à l'Hôpital Saint-Luc. Pour porter le titre de biochimiste clinique, il lui a fallu réussir, en plus, une formation de deux ans sanctionnée par l'Ordre des chimistes du Québec (OCQ). Ce long parcours lui a permis d'obtenir son poste actuel, à Santa Cabrini.

Les mots en caractères **gras** sont définis à la page 153.

Bio-informaticien
❯ en milieu universitaire

mon travail

«Un bio-informaticien, c'est un informaticien spécialisé dans le domaine de la biologie», résume François Major, qui enseigne et mène des recherches dans cette discipline à l'Université de Montréal. «Par exemple, en ce moment, j'observe électroniquement le fonctionnement de la molécule **ARN**», explique-t-il.

Comme le biologiste qui travaille en laboratoire, François cherche à mieux comprendre le fonctionnement de la vie. Mais il s'y prend en utilisant l'informatique, qui permet plus de rapidité et de précision. «L'apport des systèmes informatiques est un catalyseur de la découverte», soutient le scientifique. Un avantage de taille puisque, quand une découverte survient, elle peut déboucher sur de nouveaux moyens de diagnostiquer des maladies, ou encore, sur la connaissance de maladies dont on ignorait jusqu'alors l'existence.

Les bio-informaticiens peuvent aussi produire des diagnostics en employant, par exemple, des cartes à puce d'**ADN**, qui permettent de tester les composantes de l'organisme, comme les protéines. Mais le domaine est très vaste, tient à préciser François. «On peut tout aussi bien parler d'installation d'infrastructure informatique pour l'industrie pharmaceutique ou médicale.»

ma motivation

«Ce qui me motive dans mon travail de professeur, c'est de perpétuer l'intérêt pour cette discipline et de viser à maîtriser encore plus de connaissances», confie François. Le désir de mettre le doigt sur un élément nouveau le tient en haleine. «C'est un défi, parce qu'il faut être patient et ne jamais se décourager. Généralement, quand on découvre la réponse à une question, des dizaines d'autres questions surgissent. En recherche, on a souvent l'impression de n'avoir jamais fini.»

En outre, comme le domaine bio-informatique évolue très vite, il faut toujours se tenir à la fine pointe du progrès. Il y a aussi beaucoup de concurrence internationale. «Autant il y a de l'entraide, autant chaque pays veut être le premier à faire une découverte et à la faire breveter. Ça joue parfois du coude, mais c'est ce qui rend la profession intéressante.»

mon conseil

«Ce que je retiens de mon expérience jusqu'à maintenant, c'est la confrontation avec la nature qui ne se laisse pas facilement découvrir, résume François. On réalise que même l'informatique a ses limites.» Le chercheur souligne qu'il est néanmoins important de croire en soi et de persévérer dans la recherche de nouvelles pistes. «Il ne faut pas avoir peur des échecs. C'est avec les échecs qu'on construit.» 09/03

mon parcours

François a obtenu un baccalauréat, une maîtrise et un doctorat en informatique à l'Université de Montréal. Il a ensuite effectué un postdoctorat en bio-informatique au National Institute of Health, au Maryland, aux États-Unis. À la suite de ses études, qui se sont déroulées sans inter-ruption, il a décroché le poste qu'il occupe présentement en recherche et en enseignement à l'Université de Montréal.

Des milieux de travail potentiels

❯ Compagnies pharmaceutiques
❯ Établissements d'enseignement
❯ Laboratoires de recherche

Les mots en caractères **gras** sont définis à la page 153.

Chipropraticien
> en clinique privée

mon travail

Que vous souffriez d'une hernie discale, de migraines, d'insomnie ou encore d'asthme, François Auger peut vous aider. Il travaille à la Clinique chiropratique Saint-Martin à Laval, en compagnie de trois autres chiropraticiens, d'un massothérapeute et d'un acupuncteur. La chiropratique consiste à manipuler les différentes articulations du corps, notamment la colonne vertébrale, afin de stimuler le système nerveux et de favoriser ainsi la guérison.

Des milieux de travail potentiels

> Cliniques privées

«Lorsque je rencontre le patient pour la première fois, je fais une évaluation complète de son état physique, mais aussi de sa condition psychologique à propos de son travail, de sa vie personnelle, etc. Je lui fais également passer certains examens comme des radiographies, des tests sanguins ou des scanographies. À partir des renseignements obtenus, je décide alors du traitement approprié», explique François.

Pendant le traitement, le patient est allongé sur une table. François effectue des manipulations des articulations, des étirements et applique des points de pression sur les muscles tendus. Le cas échéant, il appliquera sur le corps du chaud ou du froid, selon les besoins.

ma motivation

François retire une grande valorisation de son métier, notamment parce qu'il lui permet d'améliorer la qualité de vie de ses patients. «Les gens sont désemparés face à leur douleur et ils se questionnent sur la cause de leur problème. Un homme qui boîte depuis 20 ans et qui n'a trouvé aucune solution pour alléger sa souffrance, je sais que je suis en mesure de l'aider. Je peux découvrir l'origine de son mal, j'ai des solutions à lui offrir. C'est aussi très motivant de suivre la progression d'un patient.»

En tant que travailleur autonome, François a toute la latitude voulue pour planifier son temps. «J'ai une belle qualité de vie, car j'ai la possibilité de choisir mon horaire et ainsi d'accorder le temps nécessaire à ma famille et à mes projets.»

mon conseil

«Il faut avoir la vocation!» lance François. Outre les 5 000 heures de cours nécessaires pour obtenir le diplôme universitaire en chiropratique, on doit aussi lutter contre les préjugés qui persistent. «Nous sommes encore considérés comme des "ramancheurs" par certains. Le jeune devra se battre tout au long de sa carrière pour s'affirmer en tant que professionnel de la santé. La détermination est aussi de mise, car il faut environ cinq ans pour développer et fidéliser sa clientèle.»
05/03

mon parcours

Diplômé en techniques ambulancières du Collège Ahuntsic, François a longtemps travaillé pour Urgences Santé. Il est diplômé de la première promotion du doctorat en chiropratique de l'Université du Québec à Trois-Rivières (UQTR). En plus de son travail à la Clinique chiropratique Saint-Martin, il possède une clinique privée de chiropratique à domicile. Il est également chargé de cours en chiropratique à l'UQTR et secrétaire de l'Association des chiropraticiens du Québec. Il termine une maîtrise en kinanthropologie (étude de la motricité humaine) à l'Université du Québec à Montréal.

Les mots en caractères **gras** sont définis à la page 153.

Dentiste

❯ en clinique privée

mon travail

La profession de dentiste est loin d'être mal connue. Presque tout le monde va chez le dentiste et comprend que son rôle est de veiller à la santé dentaire de ses patients. Mis à part l'exécution de traitements, comme les chirurgies ou les **obturations** («plombages»), un dentiste tel que Joël Desnoyers doit veiller à la bonne marche de ses affaires lorsqu'il est propriétaire d'une clinique dentaire.

Ainsi, le praticien supervise des employés, comme la secrétaire, qui fixe les rendez-vous et reçoit les paiements des patients; l'assistant dentaire, qui le seconde pendant les traitements; et l'hygiéniste, qui travaille de façon plus indépendante et qui peut prodiguer certains traitements, notamment les nettoyages.

Le dentiste a aussi une obligation importante concernant le respect des normes d'hygiène fixées par Santé Canada. «Je dois m'assurer que les déchets biomédicaux sont bien traités. Entre autres, les aiguilles, les cotons tachés et les dents extraites doivent être jetés dans des contenants conçus pour la stérilisation, jusqu'à ce qu'une entreprise spécialisée vienne récupérer le tout.»

Des milieux de travail potentiels

- ❯ Cabinets privés de chirurgiens
- ❯ Cabinets privés de dentistes
- ❯ Cabinets privés de médecins
- ❯ Centres hospitaliers.

ma motivation

C'est d'abord la possibilité de travailler de façon autonome qui a attiré Joël en médecine dentaire. Puisqu'il dirige sa propre clinique, il peut établir son horaire, fixer le coût des traitements et gérer l'établissement comme il l'entend. «Être entrepreneur est aussi un beau défi. Je dois m'assurer de la viabilité de l'entreprise. Pour ça, les patients doivent être satisfaits du service à la clientèle (accueil, efficacité, ambiance), de la qualité de mes soins et des prix.»

En outre, depuis son enfance, il adore réparer toutes sortes de choses. Comme dentiste, que ce soit lorsqu'il restaure des dents ou des prothèses dentaires, il prend un grand plaisir à imaginer des façons de rendre la réparation solide et efficace. Il sait qu'il a réussi quand un client est satisfait du service reçu.

mon conseil

Patience, minutie et dextérité vont de pair avec la profession de dentiste, puisque certains travaux, comme les chirurgies, doivent être exécutés avec beaucoup de précision. «Être à son compte demande surtout de grandes qualités générales, poursuit Joël. En plus d'être un bon dentiste, je dois bien gérer les finances de la clinique, me montrer conciliant avec mes employés et, par moments, agir comme un psychologue avec des patients trop nerveux ou imprévisibles à la vue d'une aiguille ou du sang.»

06/03

mon parcours

Joël est titulaire d'un doctorat en médecine dentaire de l'Université de Montréal (diplôme de premier cycle d'une durée de quatre ans). Immédiatement après l'obtention de son diplôme, il a acheté d'un dentiste désireux de prendre sa retraite la clinique qui porte aujourd'hui son nom.

Les mots en caractères **gras** sont définis à la page 153.

Ergothérapeute

❯ en centre de réadaptation

mon travail

Dans un décor où se côtoient ballons, crayons de couleurs et jeux de toutes sortes, Karine Caissy aide à améliorer l'autonomie d'enfants atteints de dysphasie (trouble du langage), de retard de développement ou de trisomie 21. À l'aide de tests d'évaluation (dessins, bricolage), d'observation du patient et d'entrevues avec les parents, Karine cible les incapacités de l'enfant, décide des traitements et de leur fréquence.

À quatre pattes sur le tapis de la salle de traitement du Centre de réadaptation de la Gaspésie, situé à Maria, Karine joue avec les enfants, leur montre comment tenir un crayon, dessiner ou encore attacher les lacets de leurs souliers. Ces petits gestes simples augmenteront leur motricité et leur permettront d'améliorer qualité de vie et estime de soi.

Si les trois quarts de sa clientèle sont composés d'enfants, Karine s'occupe également d'adultes qui souffrent d'incapacités physiques, comme les accidentés de la route. Elle les aide à réapprendre des gestes de tous les jours comme s'habiller, se laver ou conduire une voiture.

Des milieux de travail potentiels

- ❯ Cabinets privés
- ❯ Centres de réadaptation
- ❯ Centres d'hébergement et de soins de longue durée
- ❯ Centres hospitaliers
- ❯ Centres locaux de services communautaires (CLSC)
- ❯ Établissements d'enseignement
- ❯ Industries
- ❯ Organismes communautaires

ma motivation

«L'ergothérapie est à la fois une science et un art, car j'utilise des activités artisanales comme le bricolage et le dessin pour faire progresser mes patients. J'aime cet aspect du métier qui me permet de faire une place à ma créativité et d'adapter, même de fabriquer, des objets. Par exemple, je peux modifier le bureau de travail d'un patient en fauteuil roulant afin qu'il puisse s'y installer aisément et avoir facilement accès aux objets se trouvant sur le bureau», précise Karine.

Pouvoir collaborer au bien-être des individus est pour elle une grande source de motivation. «Même si c'est le patient qui fait la majeure partie du travail, j'ai le sentiment de contribuer à son cheminement. Lorsqu'un enfant, jusque-là incapable de dessiner, griffonne son premier bonhomme grâce au traitement, c'est formidable!» Au Centre de réadaptation, Karine travaille avec une équipe composée d'une physiothérapeute, d'une orthophoniste, d'une travailleuse sociale et d'une éducatrice spécialisée. «Il arrive qu'un enfant doive aussi consulter ces professionnelles. Le traitement se fait alors en complémentarité. Ensemble, nous échangeons, fixons un objectif commun et établissons des stratégies. C'est une dynamique intéressante et stimulante.»

mon conseil

Le métier d'ergothérapeute exige empathie et patience. «Il faut être très dynamique et savoir stimuler l'enfant et lui montrer qu'il est sur la bonne voie. On peut, par exemple, prendre un ton de voix enjoué ou faire des gestes d'encouragement. De plus, il arrive que certains parents coopèrent peu, soit par manque d'intérêt ou de compréhension des difficultés de leur enfant. On doit apprendre à se mettre dans leur peau et ne pas les juger», conseille Karine. 05/03

mon parcours

Dès l'obtention de son baccalauréat en ergothérapie à l'Université Laval, Karine a décroché son emploi au Centre de réadaptation de la Gaspésie. Elle y travaille depuis quatre ans.

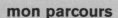
Les mots en caractères **gras** sont définis à la page 153.

Infirmier

> **en milieu hospitalier**

mon travail

Au sixième étage de l'Hôtel-Dieu de Saint-Jérôme se trouve le département de chirurgie où sont emmenés les patients venant de subir une intervention. Du réveil après l'anesthésie jusqu'à la fin de leur convalescence, Martin Lévesque leur prodigue les soins nécessaires. Il veille à la stabilité de leur état en surveillant leurs signes vitaux et leur niveau de conscience. Il administre les médicaments prescrits par le médecin ou pose les pansements. «Je détecte aussi les complications possibles, comme un infarctus, le saignement des plaies chirurgicales ou encore l'apparition de douleurs», ajoute Martin.

L'enseignement et la relation d'aide font aussi partie intrinsèque de son travail. «Je dois faire de la prévention, par exemple en informant un diabétique sur l'importance du contrôle régulier de son taux de sucre et d'un régime alimentaire spécifique. Mais je peux aussi être le confident des patients qui traversent des moments difficiles.»

Des milieux de travail potentiels

> Centres d'hébergement et de soins de longue durée
> Centres hospitaliers
> Centres locaux de services communautaires (CLSC)
> Cliniques privées
> Entreprises privées
> Établissements d'enseignement

ma motivation

Si Martin a choisi ce métier, c'est avant tout pour aider les gens. «Cela demande beaucoup d'efforts, mais on reçoit tellement en retour. Mon vrai salaire, c'est la reconnaissance des patients. Pouvoir améliorer leur qualité de vie est extrêmement valorisant», raconte-t-il.

Il apprécie aussi de travailler dans le milieu hospitalier. «C'est un défi de chaque instant, ça bouge énormément. C'est un métier qui demande toutefois de la force de caractère, car c'est tout un "feeling" d'avoir la vie des patients entre ses mains. Il faut savoir leur administrer la bonne dose de médicaments, détecter un infarctus à temps, etc. On doit être très vigilant.»

Outre les hôpitaux, les infirmiers peuvent œuvrer dans des domaines variés. «Il y en a pour tous les goûts et toutes les personnalités. Je pourrais choisir d'aller travailler en Afrique, ou dans un CLSC, ou auprès des enfants ou des personnes âgées par exemple. C'est un domaine diversifié et stimulant.»

mon conseil

Au sujet du métier d'infirmier, Martin souhaite faire tomber certains préjugés. «C'est une profession qui a longtemps été considérée comme de second ordre, tant sur le plan des responsabilités que des conditions de travail. Avec la pénurie qui sévit actuellement, la situation a bien changé. L'infirmier qui travaillait auparavant sur appel a accès aujourd'hui à un poste à temps plein, sans compter les différentes primes possibles, comme les primes de déménagement. Les possibilités d'avancement se sont également améliorées. Par exemple, un infirmier peut devenir assistant de l'infirmier en chef ou même infirmier en chef.» 05/03

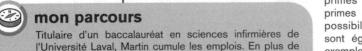

mon parcours

Titulaire d'un baccalauréat en sciences infirmières de l'Université Laval, Martin cumule les emplois. En plus de son poste à l'Hôtel-Dieu de Saint-Jérôme, il est chargé de cours au Département de soins infirmiers du Cégep de Saint-Jérôme et président du comité jeunesse de l'Ordre régional des infirmières et infirmiers de la région Laurentides-Lanaudière.

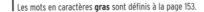

Les mots en caractères **gras** sont définis à la page 153.

Ingénieure biomédicale
› en milieu hospitalier

mon travail

«L'ingénieur biomédical gère l'acquisition et l'implantation du matériel médical dans les centres hospitaliers, comme les **microscopes ophtalmologiques**, les lampes des salles d'opération, les équipements d'endoscopie, les **appareils d'électrochirurgie**, etc.», explique Aurèle Larrivé, ingénieure biomédicale au département de génie biomédical de l'Hôpital général juif – Sir Mortimer B. Davis à Montréal.

Des milieux de travail potentiels

› Centres hospitaliers
› Entreprises privées

«J'ai un rôle de conseillère auprès des administrateurs et des cliniciens en ce qui concerne la planification d'achat, l'acquisition, l'utilisation et l'entretien des appareils médicaux, sans oublier le soutien à la formation du personnel clinique et des techniciens biomédicaux. Les choix que je propose répondent à plusieurs critères comme la sécurité des patients et du personnel de l'hôpital, le respect de l'environnement, les limites budgétaires, etc.

«Je veille à maintenir le parc d'appareils médicaux à la fine pointe de la technologie afin d'assurer le mieux-être des malades et d'améliorer leur traitement.»

ma motivation

«À l'école, ce sont les matières scientifiques qui m'intéressaient le plus. Les mathématiques, la chimie, la mécanique, l'électronique, la physiologie me passionnaient. Apprendre comment fonctionnent les choses et résoudre des problèmes techniques ont toujours été d'immenses plaisirs pour moi. Aussi, la carrière d'ingénieure s'est rapidement imposée, explique Aurèle.

«Je terminais ma maîtrise en sciences de l'activité physique, option biomécanique, sans parvenir à envisager une carrière dans ce domaine. Puis, j'ai accepté d'accompagner une amie inscrite en maîtrise de génie biomédical en stage d'une demi-journée dans un hôpital. Je m'y suis tout de suite sentie à ma place. Ce lieu est en constante mouvance, riche en ressources humaines et technologiques. Il y importe aussi d'approfondir ses connaissances et ses compétences. Ça me convenait parfaitement», confie Aurèle.

mon conseil

«Cette profession requiert des personnes friandes de technologies, curieuses et prêtes à se perfectionner continuellement pour faire face aux progrès technologiques rapides. Il est également essentiel de développer un champ d'expertise, une spécialité. De plus, pour travailler en milieu hospitalier, discrétion et confidentialité, par respect pour les patients, sont des qualités à posséder», souligne Aurèle. 09/03

mon parcours

Aurèle a d'abord obtenu un diplôme d'études collégiales (DEC) en sciences pures au Collège Montmorency à Laval. Elle a ensuite décroché un baccalauréat en génie mécanique à l'Université McGill avant d'entamer une maîtrise en sciences de l'activité physique, option biomécanique, à l'Université de Montréal. Dès la fin de ses études, elle a été embauchée à l'Hôpital général juif où elle exerce depuis. Par intérêt personnel, elle s'est inscrite, à titre d'étudiante libre, aux cours menant à la maîtrise en génie biomédical à l'École Polytechnique.

Les mots en caractères **gras** sont définis à la page 153.

Inspectrice en hygiène des produits primaires

> dans un organisme public

mon travail

«Les produits primaires destinés à la consommation, comme la viande, les œufs, les fruits et légumes, sont soumis à une réglementation très stricte», explique Lyne Drouin, inspectrice en hygiène des produits primaires pour l'Agence canadienne d'inspection des aliments (ACIA), qui relève du ministère de l'Agriculture.

Des milieux de travail potentiels

> Agence canadienne d'inspection des aliments

> Entreprises privées

Lyne est actuellement en poste à l'usine de volaille Exceldor à Saint-Anselme. Sous la gouverne d'un chef vétérinaire, elle surveille le traitement des poulets, de leur arrivée à l'abattoir jusqu'à leur livraison aux supermarchés. Quand l'établissement reçoit une cargaison de poulets vivants, elle s'assure qu'ils ont l'air sains et qu'ils ont été transportés dans de bonnes conditions, c'est-à-dire à une température ni trop chaude ni trop froide, sans stress ni souffrance inutiles. Elle vérifie également que les camions sont nettoyés et désinfectés et envoie les animaux suspects ou morts au vétérinaire.

Lyne voit aussi à la propreté de l'usine et au respect, par les employés, des règles de base, comme le port d'un filet sur les cheveux et la barbe, le port de gants, le nettoyage des tables et des couteaux, etc.

ma motivation

Cuisinière à ses heures, Lyne n'a aucun mal à se mettre à la place des consommateurs qui bénéficient de sa vigilance. «Ce que je ne veux pas retrouver dans mon assiette, je ne le laisse pas passer!» lance-t-elle. C'est un peu par hasard qu'elle a fait son entrée dans l'univers de la réglementation alimentaire, il y a 22 ans. «À cette époque, on pouvait être formé sur place.»

Bien qu'elle exerce «dans le poulet» depuis deux ans, Lyne peut prendre en charge toutes les tâches d'inspection, pour tous les produits primaires. Elle apprécie particulièrement se retrouver dans le domaine du bœuf, parce que les morceaux de viande, comme les défis de vérification, y sont plus grands. Par exemple, une carcasse peut avoir belle apparence, mais cela ne signifie pas qu'elle est propre à la consommation humaine pour autant.

mon conseil

«Je travaille pour une agence gouvernementale dans une usine privée, explique Lyne. C'est une position stratégique et délicate, car je représente la partie neutre entre le producteur et le consommateur. Quand je m'adresse aux employés de l'usine, je dois communiquer avec tact et être capable d'expliquer pourquoi tel ou tel détail est si important. Je dois aussi rester constamment sur le qui-vive, pour ne rien laisser passer.» 07/03

mon parcours

Titulaire d'un diplôme d'études secondaires, Lyne a été embauchée, à l'âge de 20 ans, par le ministère de l'Agriculture à titre de classificatrice dans le domaine du porc. «Je suis plus tard devenue inspectrice des produits primaires après une formation théorique et pratique d'environ trois semaines sur mon lieu de travail.» Elle a également suivi d'autres cours d'appoint dont, récemment, une formation qui l'habilite à superviser l'application du système **HACCP**.

Les mots en caractères **gras** sont définis à la page 153.

Inspectrice en santé animale

> **dans un organisme public**

mon travail

Pauline Talbot est inspectrice en santé animale au bureau de l'Agence canadienne d'inspection des aliments (ACIA) à Lévis. Elle doit déceler tout risque sanitaire lié à l'introduction et à la propagation de maladies animales sur le territoire canadien, comme la **tuberculose**, la **fièvre aphteuse**, la **salmonellose**. «Je travaille beaucoup sur le plan de l'importation et de l'exportation d'animaux d'élevage. Nous faisons également le suivi dans les fermes, les encans. Je fais des tests sanguins sur des vaches, des cochons, des poulets, mais aussi des espèces exotiques importées, comme des perroquets.»

Parfois sollicitée par les douaniers, Pauline doit vérifier la conformité de produits animaux importés au Canada, la viande bien sûr, mais aussi le fromage, la charcuterie, voire une peau de chèvre achetée par un touriste en Amérique centrale! «Je dois vérifier que la peau a été bien tannée et qu'elle ne présente aucun risque de transmission de maladie.»

Des milieux de travail potentiels

> Agence canadienne d'inspection des aliments
> Entreprises privées

---

ma motivation

«Je voulais travailler avec les animaux, mais aussi avec les gens», explique Pauline. Ce qu'elle apprécie tout particulièrement dans son métier, ce sont les visites dans les fermes, et sa mission d'information auprès des éleveurs, même si elle doit parfois sévir. «Dans les abattoirs, il arrive que les inspecteurs détectent des résidus d'antibiotiques sur les animaux abattus. Je dois alors me rendre sur la ferme pour mener une enquête, et donner une amende au propriétaire s'il y a lieu.»

Pauline applique également un programme de tests sur les ongulés sauvages du pays capturés par des éleveurs, comme les cerfs de Virginie, les bisons, les wapitis, qui pourraient transmettre la tuberculose ou la **brucellose** au cheptel bovin du Canada. Elle se retrouve ainsi régulièrement confrontée à de vrais défis, professionnels et personnels, face à des animaux de très grande taille. «Mais que je sois face à un taureau ou un bison, je dois faire mon travail!»

mon conseil

«Il faut vraiment étudier le comportement de chaque espèce, acquérir son expérience sur le terrain et écouter les conseils des personnes plus qualifiées», précise Pauline, qui avoue avoir été la cible de quelques taureaux qui souhaitaient l'encorner... Elle précise en outre qu'une bonne condition physique est souhaitable. «Quand on teste une vache, il y a des efforts à fournir pour l'immobiliser, même si l'éleveur est là pour nous aider. Et l'hiver, les conditions sont plus difficiles. Quand on fait des injections à -30°, on a les doigts gelés.»

07/03

mon parcours

Pauline a obtenu son diplôme d'études collégiales en santé animale au Cégep de La Pocatière en 1982. Pendant six ans, elle a travaillé à la Société protectrice des animaux à Québec, tout en assistant à temps partiel un vétérinaire dans une clinique privée. En 1988, elle est devenue inspectrice en hygiène des viandes; durant 14 ans, elle a visité une grande partie des abattoirs du Québec. Ayant réussi le concours d'inspectrice en santé animale de l'Agence canadienne d'inspection des aliments, elle occupe ce poste depuis 2001.

Les mots en caractères **gras** sont définis à la page 153.

Intervenante en psychomotricité
> **en milieu scolaire**

mon travail

«Les enfants qui viennent de milieux pauvres manquent souvent d'intérêt pour l'activité physique, simplement parce qu'on ne leur a pas montré comment s'amuser en bougeant. Il faut juste leur ouvrir la porte», explique Julie Verrette, intervenante en **psychomotricité** pour le projet Québec en forme, qui favorise l'accès aux activités physiques pour les jeunes d'âge scolaire des communautés défavorisées.

Parcourant la région de Trois-Rivières, Julie visite plusieurs écoles pour rencontrer des groupes d'enfants de quatre à cinq ans, à raison d'une heure par semaine. Au cours d'une séance type, elle propose aux enfants des jeux éducatifs visant à développer leurs habiletés motrices, par exemple lancer une balle par-dessus un filet ou encore sauter dans un cerceau placé au sol. Bien qu'elle prépare ces exercices à l'avance, en suivant un plan de cours établi par Québec en forme, Julie utilise beaucoup sa créativité. Ainsi, elle peut inventer des histoires autour des exercices à réaliser et adapter son intervention selon le matériel dont dispose chaque école.

Des milieux de travail potentiels

> Centres de conditionnement physique
> Centres d'hébergement et de soins de longue durée
> Centres communautaires

ma motivation

«J'ai toujours aimé l'activité physique et je suis une sportive de nature, raconte Julie. J'ai joué au soccer, j'ai fait de la natation, de la danse, du vélo, de l'escalade, de la course à pied, du ski de fond, etc.» Elle n'a donc pas hésité à choisir une carrière qui lui permettrait de rester dans le feu de l'action.

Dans le cadre du projet Québec en forme, la possibilité d'aider les autres l'anime particulièrement. «Je trouvais ça triste que des enfants soient privés de sport ou simplement du goût de bouger... Quand on habite en ville dans un petit logement, la télévision représente la principale distraction, et on valorise le fait que les enfants restent sagement assis. Il est donc important de les éveiller à l'activité physique le plus tôt possible, car on a plus de chances de les y intéresser pour longtemps. Surtout que le manque d'exercice entraîne bien souvent des problèmes, comme l'obésité.»

mon conseil

Si Julie mène aujourd'hui une carrière qui la passionne, c'est qu'elle y a mis du sien. Pendant ses études, elle lisait tout ce qu'elle pouvait sur son futur métier et travaillait déjà dans le domaine. «Pour trouver un emploi, il est important de chercher toutes les occasions de parfaire ses connaissances et de se faire connaître», soutient-elle. 08/03

mon parcours

Julie a obtenu un diplôme d'études collégiales (DEC) en sciences de la santé au Cégep de Trois-Rivières, puis un baccalauréat et une maîtrise en sciences de l'activité physique à l'Université du Québec à Trois-Rivières (UQTR). Parallèlement, elle a travaillé au Centre sportif de l'UQTR, à préparer des programmes d'entraînement individualisés. Un bagage qui lui a permis de se joindre au projet Québec en forme.

Les mots en caractères **gras** sont définis à la page 153.

Kinésiologue
❯ en centre d'activité physique et sportive

mon travail

Virginie Dupuis est kinésiologue au Centre d'activité physique et sportive du Collège de la région de L'Amiante, à Thetford Mines. La kinésiologie est une discipline qui vise la sécurité et le bien-être des individus par la pratique d'exercices physiques. «On procède à l'évaluation de la condition physique de la personne, c'est-à-dire ses habiletés motrices et sa capacité cardiorespiratoire, son pourcentage de graisse, sa souplesse, etc. Ensuite, on lui prescrit des exercices qui peuvent l'aider à améliorer sa qualité de vie.»

Virginie travaille avec une clientèle très variée. «Je traite notamment des diabétiques, des femmes enceintes, des personnes en réhabilitation après un accident de travail. On intervient également dans les entreprises. Dans ce cas, on peut par exemple réaménager un poste de travail pour la sécurité et le confort de l'employé, ou instaurer des pauses d'exercices pour diminuer le stress.»

Des milieux de travail potentiels

- ❯ Centres communautaires
- ❯ Centres de conditionnement physique
- ❯ Centres de loisirs
- ❯ Centres locaux de services communautaires (CLSC)
- ❯ Cliniques privées
- ❯ Entreprises
- ❯ Fédérations sportives
- ❯ Municipalités

ma motivation

«J'ai choisi cette profession parce que c'était nouveau et peu connu, explique Virginie. C'était un défi dès le départ de faire connaître mon métier! De plus, il n'y a pas de routine dans mon travail : ce matin, j'étais en évaluation avec des diabétiques; cet après-midi, j'anime un club de marche; et, ce soir, j'enseigne la danse aérobique.»

Virginie apprécie de pouvoir contribuer, à sa façon, au bien-être de la population. «On est davantage des professionnels de la santé que des professionnels du sport. Ce métier permet d'aider les individus à avoir une meilleure qualité de vie. Même si on pense que marcher est une activité facile, pour certaines personnes, c'est déjà beaucoup.»

Avec une clientèle si variée, Virginie doit résoudre chaque jour des problèmes différents. «Il faut répondre aux besoins spécifiques de chacun et trouver des solutions simples, efficaces et accessibles.»

mon conseil

«Il n'y a pas d'emploi assuré en sortant de l'université, estime Virginie. Encore très peu de postes sont créés dans ce domaine, et la majorité des diplômés cumulent les petits contrats dans des salles de gym, dans les écoles ou dans les entreprises. Il faut donc avoir du leadership et un esprit d'entreprise.» Virginie conseille en outre de participer aux formations connexes au sport et à la santé, comme elle l'a fait elle-même. 06/03

mon parcours

Virginie a obtenu son baccalauréat en kinésiologie à l'Université de Sherbrooke. Cette formation comprend trois stages coopératifs de quatre mois chacun. Virginie les a effectués au Collège de la région de l'Amiante, et, de fil en aiguille, elle a fini par se créer un poste à temps plein dans cet établissement. Elle s'est aussi perfectionnée en suivant diverses formations : brevet de Sauveteur national, formations en aérobie et Programme national de certification des entraîneurs (PNCE).

Les mots en caractères **gras** sont définis à la page 153.

Médecin vétérinaire
> dans un organisme public

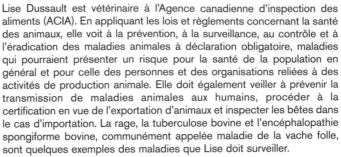

mon travail

Lise Dussault est vétérinaire à l'Agence canadienne d'inspection des aliments (ACIA). En appliquant les lois et règlements concernant la santé des animaux, elle voit à la prévention, à la surveillance, au contrôle et à l'éradication des maladies animales à déclaration obligatoire, maladies qui pourraient présenter un risque pour la santé de la population en général et pour celle des personnes et des organisations reliées à des activités de production animale. Elle doit également veiller à prévenir la transmission de maladies animales aux humains, procéder à la certification en vue de l'exportation d'animaux et inspecter les bêtes dans le cas d'importation. La rage, la tuberculose bovine et l'encéphalopathie spongiforme bovine, communément appelée maladie de la vache folle, sont quelques exemples des maladies que Lise doit surveiller.

«Je reçois des demandes d'enquête de la part de régies régionales de la santé, d'éleveurs, de propriétaires d'animaux et de vétérinaires lorsqu'ils suspectent un cas probable de maladie grave chez un animal. Je me rends sur les lieux pour enquêter sur la bête en question et faire des prélèvements de sang ou de tissus pour fins d'analyse et de diagnostic. À la réception des résultats, j'évalue et je recommande l'application des mesures de contrôle et d'éradication des maladies.» Les espèces principalement visées sont des animaux d'élevage, comme les bovins, les cervidés et les chevaux. Il peut aussi s'agir de chats ou de chiens, car ils sont également susceptibles de contracter des maladies à déclaration obligatoire.

Des milieux de travail potentiels

> Cliniques vétérinaires
> Établissements d'enseignement
> Industries alimentaires
> Industries pharmaceutiques
> Jardins zoologiques
> Laboratoires de recherche
> Organismes gouvernementaux (inspection des aliments)

ma motivation

En préservant la santé des animaux, Lise protège par le fait même la santé des humains qui sont en contact avec eux. Elle s'estime donc titulaire d'une fonction très importante.

Enfin, elle apprécie le fait de ne pas connaître la routine. Chaque journée lui apporte des demandes d'inspection différentes. «Il y a des cas urgents, d'autres moins. Parfois, un cas qui ne semblait pas grave peut se détériorer subitement. Tout évolue très vite.»

mon conseil

Comme l'apparition d'une maladie animale peut faire des ravages sur la santé des animaux et des humains, il faut être assez rigoureux de nature pour ne rien laisser au hasard lors d'une vérification, soutient Lise.

mon parcours

Lise a trouvé son emploi actuel immédiatement après avoir terminé son doctorat en médecine vétérinaire à l'Université de Montréal. Quelques années plus tard, elle a voulu se perfectionner. Toujours à la même université, elle a fait une maîtrise en pathologie et microbiologie vétérinaire. Sans être absolument nécessaires, ces nouveaux apprentissages représentent des qualifications supplémentaires.

«Il faut aimer tous les animaux pour être vétérinaire», ajoute-t-elle. Ceci dit, il est important d'être émotionnellement solide, par exemple lorsqu'il faut abattre un troupeau entier de bêtes malades. En bout de ligne, l'amour des animaux ne doit pas dépasser le sens des responsabilités envers les éleveurs et la population en général.
06/03

Les mots en caractères **gras** sont définis à la page 153.

Microbiologiste
❯ pour une compagnie pharmaceutique

mon travail

Microbiologiste chez Sherings Canada, Carl Vachon s'occupe princi-palement du contrôle de la qualité d'une grande variété de produits médicamenteux, comme des remèdes contre le rhume des foins, des crèmes pour l'eczéma ou même des onguents pour les otites chez les chiens. «Nous devons nous assurer que les médicaments mis sur le marché sont propres à la consommation», explique-t-il. En gros, cela signifie que le nombre de micro-organismes détectés sur un médicament ne doit pas dépasser un certain seuil.

«Afin de ne pas contaminer nous-mêmes les produits que nous analysons, il faut travailler de façon **aseptique**, poursuit-il. Les micro-organismes, tels que les bactéries, la moisissure ou les virus, sont des organismes vivants qu'on ne peut voir à l'œil nu.» Carl travaille donc sous des hottes dites à flux laminaire, dont l'action purifie l'air. «Les micro-organismes ne sont pas toujours nuisibles», précise-t-il. Certains entrent même dans la fabrication d'antibiotiques. Il faut tout de même analyser ces produits pour s'assurer que la quantité de micro-organismes y est adéquate.

Carl est également chef d'un groupe de microbiologistes et de techni-ciens en chimie et en biologie, ce qui l'amène à vérifier les documents produits à la suite des analyses de tout un chacun.

Des milieux de travail potentiels

❯ Centres hospitaliers
❯ Entreprises privées
❯ Laboratoires de recherche privés, publics ou universitaires

ma motivation

Carl avait d'abord songé à devenir chimiste, mais des cours en microbiologie au cégep lui ont donné la passion de l'étude du vivant, un domaine plus complexe, croit-il.

Doté d'un esprit analytique, Carl avoue qu'il aime découvrir des choses qui échappent d'abord à l'évidence. «J'aime travailler avec les éléments qu'on ne voit pas à l'œil nu», dit-il. Mais cela n'en représente pas moins un défi de taille. «Il faut de l'instinct pour s'en aller dans la bonne direction. Il y a des investigations qui peuvent prendre des mois avant d'aboutir à des résultats.» Par exemple, lorsqu'une contamination est détectée, il faut en trouver la source pour arriver à la maîtriser. Une démarche qui peut aller jusqu'à l'analyse de l'air et des surfaces de l'usine d'où proviennent les produits.

mon conseil

Pour réussir en microbiologie, il faut être passionné, selon Carl. «La passion mène à se dépasser, et c'est ce qu'il faut faire pour être un bon microbiologiste.» Il est également primordial de pouvoir travailler dans des délais serrés. «Pour que les compagnies pharma-ceutiques soient rentables, il leur faut mettre rapidement leurs produits sur le marché. Et elles ne peuvent le faire tant que les analyses en microbiologie ne sont pas terminées. On a donc de la pression.» 09/03

mon parcours

Après avoir obtenu un diplôme d'études collégiales (DEC) en sciences de la nature au Cégep Lionel-Groulx, Carl a effectué un baccalauréat en microbiologie et immunologie à l'Université McGill. Il a commencé sa carrière dans une entreprise qui offre des services d'analyse à des compagnies pharmaceutiques avant d'entrer chez Sherings Canada.

Les mots en caractères **gras** sont définis à la page 153.

Nutritionniste
> **en milieu hospitalier**

mon travail

Certains patients, comme les diabétiques, ne peuvent pas manger n'importe quoi. Ils doivent apprendre à adapter leur alimentation à leur état de santé tout en conservant le plaisir de manger. Marilyne Desrochers est là pour eux. Nutritionniste au Centre hospitalier universitaire de Sherbrooke (CHUS), elle évalue leurs comportements alimentaires et analyse leur **état nutritionnel** en se basant notamment sur leur poids et leurs analyses sanguines. Si une patiente aime le sel au point d'en abuser, par exemple, la nutritionniste peut demander à la technicienne en diététique, qui prépare les repas, de saler un peu chacun des plats destinés à la dame, sans toutefois ajouter de sachet de sel sur le plateau.

On pourrait croire que son rôle en est un de contrôle, mais il s'agit plutôt d'enseignement, soutient-elle. «Le défi, c'est de persuader les gens que leur alimentation joue un rôle important dans leur santé.» Pour y arriver, elle doit parfois demander la collaboration de l'entourage. «Si on a des doutes (sur ce qu'une personne boulimique prétend manger, par exemple), on appelle sa famille ou les infirmiers qui lui servent ses repas.» En milieu privé, toutefois, ce défi est moindre, car, comme le patient paie ses soins, il est généralement plus motivé.

Des milieux de travail potentiels

> Bureaux-conseils
> Centres communautaires
> Centres d'hébergement et de soins de longue durée
> Centres hospitaliers
> Centres locaux de services communautaires (CLSC)
> Cliniques privées
> Compagnies pharmaceutiques

ma motivation

Marilyne a choisi cette profession parce qu'elle lui permet d'être en contact avec des gens : médecin traitant, physiothérapeute, ergothérapeute, pharmacien, voire famille du patient. Mais c'est avec le médecin qu'elle collabore le plus. «À la suite de l'évaluation de l'alimentation de la personne, nous faisons différentes suggestions au médecin. Pour quelqu'un qui fait de l'insuffisance rénale, je peux suggérer une restriction en liquides ou en autres aliments. Si une personne ne mange pas assez, je dis qu'un **gavage** serait peut-être requis.» Elle aime particulièrement aider des gens qui s'alimentent de façon insuffisante ou qui ont carrément cessé de manger. «J'aime voir que j'ai contribué à leur mieux-être.»

mon conseil

«N'ayez pas peur d'essayer différents milieux de travail pendant vos stages ou en début de carrière», conseille Marilyne aux futurs nutritionnistes. En effet, la profession présente de nombreux débouchés qui valent la peine d'être explorés, tels que chroniqueur en nutrition dans les médias, consultant dans un centre sportif, dans un centre d'hébergement pour aînés ou encore dans l'industrie pharmaceutique ou alimentaire. 07/03

mon parcours

Après un diplôme d'études collégiales (DEC) en sciences de la nature au Cégep de Victoriaville, Marilyne a fait un baccalauréat en nutrition à l'Université Laval qui comprenait quatre stages : un dans le milieu communautaire, un autre en recherche, un en gestion de cafétéria dans un hôpital, puis un stage en nutrition clinique, également dans un centre hospitalier. Elle a occupé un premier emploi comme nutritionniste au Regroupement de la santé et des services sociaux (RSSS) de la municipalité régionale de comté de Maskinongé avant de faire son entrée au CHUS.

Les mots en caractères **gras** sont définis à la page 153.

Optométriste

> en centre de réadaptation visuelle (réseau public)

mon travail

Cataracte, **rétinopathie**, **rétinite pigmentaire** : pour Julie-Andrée Marinier, ces maladies oculaires n'ont plus de secret ou presque. Travaillant à l'Institut Nazareth et Louis-Braille, elle fait partie des 25 optométristes du Québec à se spécialiser en réadaptation visuelle. «Je travaille auprès des personnes âgées, précise-t-elle. Mon rôle est de diminuer l'impact de leur handicap visuel dans leur vie quotidienne. Je les aide à rester autonomes plus longtemps.» Son intervention commence par un examen visuel complet, qui lui permettra de déceler s'il y a présence de maladie oculaire. Elle mesure alors la pression intraoculaire; utilise un biomicroscope pour inspecter la paupière, la **cornée**, l'**iris** et le **cristallin**, et un **ophtalmoscope** pour examiner le fond de l'œil, le **vitré**, la **rétine** et le nerf optique.

L'examen terminé, Julie-Andrée prescrit une aide visuelle : des lunettes, des lentilles cornéennes, une loupe ou même un télescope, dans certains cas indispensables pour voir au loin le numéro d'un autobus, par exemple. Si le patient présente une maladie oculaire, elle en contrôlera chaque année la progression.

Des milieux de travail potentiels

> Cabinets d'autres professionnels de la santé

> Centres de réadaptation offrant des services en basse vision

> Cliniques privées

> Lunetteries

ma motivation

Pendant ses études secondaires, cette passionnée de physique et de biologie faisait du bénévolat auprès des aînés, des enfants handicapés et des personnes vivant avec le VIH. Habituée à aider les autres, elle se trouve ici dans son élément. Mais au quotidien, répondre aux questions des patients – et des proches qui les accompagnent – représente un défi. «Pour cela, il faut garder ses connaissances à jour en lisant des revues scientifiques d'optométrie et d'ophtalmologie (en anglais) et être à l'écoute du patient.» Par ailleurs, chaque pathologie apporte son lot de mystères, qu'elle tente de percer en consacrant plusieurs heures par semaine à la recherche clinique. Un facteur vasculaire est-il impliqué dans la **dégénérescence maculaire**, une maladie responsable des pertes visuelles en Amérique du Nord? Voilà l'une des questions qui la tiennent en haleine.

mon conseil

«Il est important d'établir un bon diagnostic, et ce, le plus vite possible, parce que le temps peut jouer dans l'évolution des maladies», soutient Julie-Andrée. Pour être optométriste, il faut donc posséder une bonne vision doublée d'un excellent sens de l'observation et d'une grande minutie, pour bien relever les données indiquées par les appareils de mesure. En outre, les longues études en optométrie nécessitent de la détermination, mais surtout d'excellents résultats scolaires, de la curiosité et une passion pour les sciences. 07/03

mon parcours

Julie-Andrée a obtenu un diplôme d'études collégiales (DEC) en sciences de la santé au Cégep de Bois-de-Boulogne, puis a suivi un doctorat professionnel (de premier cycle) en optométrie d'une durée de cinq ans, à l'Université de Montréal. De plus, elle a obtenu dans le même établissement une maîtrise en sciences de la vision pour pouvoir mener des activités de recherche et d'enseignement en plus de ses consultations.

Les mots en caractères **gras** sont définis à la page 153.

Organisateur communautaire
❯ en centre de santé

mon travail

Vous avez une bonne idée pour améliorer le bien-être de vos concitoyens? Il vous faut rencontrer quelqu'un comme Richard Caron. «Mon but, c'est de développer des réseaux d'entraide et d'être au courant des ressources qui peuvent aider une personne à réaliser son projet», explique l'organisateur communautaire du Centre de santé Memphrémagog.

Des milieux de travail potentiels

❯ Centres locaux de services communautaires (CLSC)

❯ Organismes communautaires

Richard passe la majeure partie de son temps dans des organismes communautaires (comité de lutte à la pauvreté, cuisines collectives, etc.). Il aide les citoyens à s'organiser, anime leurs réunions et leur fournit des pistes pour faire avancer leurs démarches. Une halte-garderie va ouvrir pour dépanner les parents du quartier? Richard ne travaillera pas directement à l'ouverture de l'établissement, mais il apportera un sacré coup de main, entre autres dans la recherche de subventions. «Je mets en commun les forces de tout le monde», ajoute-t-il.

ma motivation

C'est en assurant la coordination d'une coopérative jeunesse que Richard a vraiment décidé de son choix de carrière. «Cela regroupait tout ce que j'aimais : travailler avec la population, rassembler des acteurs sociaux et économiques, apprendre aux jeunes à travailler et, de ce fait, contribuer à l'amélioration de la société en prévenant le chômage.» Bref, changer le monde à l'échelle locale, comme il dit.

Il travaille aujourd'hui à prévenir et non à guérir les problèmes de santé : il préfère aider des personnes pauvres à mettre sur pied une cuisine collective plutôt que d'avoir à soigner leurs troubles de malnutrition. Richard apprécie également le travail en groupe, notamment avec d'autres intervenants du domaine de la santé (médecins, infirmières, auxiliaires familiales). «Ensemble, on peut, par exemple, étudier le cas d'une mère pauvre qui, après une séparation, se retrouve à la rue seule avec ses deux enfants.»

mon conseil

Richard a appris à croire au potentiel de chacun. «Pour cela, il faut avoir une grande ouverture d'esprit, dit-il. Une personne est pauvre parce qu'elle a vécu des épreuves, pas nécessairement parce qu'elle est fainéante.» Aux gens qui veulent s'initier au métier, il conseille de s'engager socialement, auprès des jeunes, des aînés, des enfants ou encore des toxicomanes, par exemple. Et de voyager, voire de faire un stage à l'étranger. Tout cela permet de mieux se connaître, selon lui. 06/03

mon parcours

Au cégep, Richard s'est d'abord inscrit en administration, avant de bifurquer vers le diplôme d'études collégiales (DEC) en sciences humaines, pour ensuite effectuer un baccalauréat en psychosociologie de la communication, à l'Université du Québec à Montréal. Parallèlement à ses études, il a fait un stage en travail de rue ainsi que du bénévolat. Avant d'occuper son poste actuel, il a travaillé au Centre local de services communautaires (CLSC) Pointe-aux-Trembles/Montréal-Est ainsi que dans des coopératives jeunesse de services à Villeray-Petite Patrie et à Saint-Henri.

Les mots en caractères **gras** sont définis à la page 153.

Orthophoniste
❯ en centre de réadaptation

mon travail

Les orthophonistes évaluent et diagnostiquent les troubles de la parole, du langage et de la déglutition au moyen de tests et d'observations. Par la suite, ils élaborent un programme approprié de traitement et d'intervention spécifique à chaque patient. Programme qu'ils réalisent en collaboration avec les proches et les autres intervenants. C'est en résumé le travail de Natalie Vertefeuille, orthophoniste au Centre régional de réadaptation (CRR) La RessourSe à Hull.

Les patients de Natalie sont des victimes de graves accidents dans lesquels ils ont subi un traumatisme crânien. Souvent, ils sortent à peine du coma quand elle les prend en charge.

«Je vérifie si le patient est capable de me comprendre et s'il peut répondre à mes questions. Je regarde comment il exprime ses besoins, ses idées. Par la suite, j'entreprends une évaluation complète du langage (expression et compréhension) oral et écrit, dans le but qu'il puisse un jour reprendre son travail ou retourner aux études. Selon les problèmes éprouvés, Natalie établit un programme d'exercices dans lequel l'aspect ludique occupe une part importante.

Des milieux de travail potentiels

❯ Cabinets privés

❯ Centres de réadaptation

❯ Centres d'hébergement et de soins de longue durée

❯ Centres hospitaliers

❯ Centres locaux de services communautaires (CLSC)

❯ Établissements d'enseignement

ma motivation

«La communication est la base de notre vie, c'est ce qui nous permet d'être en relation avec les autres. Sans communication, on est isolé, coupé du reste du monde.» C'est ce constat qui a poussé Natalie à choisir cette profession.

Sa plus belle récompense : les progrès qu'accomplissent ses patients, jour après jour. «Une personne bègue qui va voir un orthophoniste pour obtenir de l'aide le fait volontairement. Mais ce n'est pas le cas de mes patients, qui ont subi un accident et ont de graves troubles **cognitifs**. Ils ne savent pas toujours qui nous sommes ni pourquoi ils sont là. Certains ne veulent pas recevoir d'aide. Il faut donc trouver des moyens détournés pour parvenir à nos fins et le travail en équipe devient donc essentiel.»

mon conseil

«Il n'existe pas de recette miracle pour corriger les problèmes diagnostiqués en orthophonie. Chaque cas est différent, et il arrive que l'on prépare un programme de traitement qui ne fonctionne pas.» Il faut donc une bonne dose d'analyse, de jugement et de créativité dans cette profession. Natalie estime pour sa part que c'est sur le terrain que l'on se forme concrètement. «En stage, on apprend à développer des façons de faire et d'agir qui ne s'apprennent pas dans les livres.» 05/03

mon parcours

Avant d'intégrer le programme en orthophonie de l'Université de Montréal, Natalie a fait une majeure en linguistique et a suivi des cours en psychologie dans cette même université. Après son baccalauréat, elle a poursuivi en maîtrise et effectué son stage au CRR La RessourSe à Hull, où elle pratique depuis sept ans. En outre, elle est la représentante du Québec au sein de l'Association canadienne des orthophonistes et audiologistes.

Les mots en caractères **gras** sont définis à la page 153.

Perfusionniste
❯ en milieu hospitalier

mon travail

Qu'on se le dise, le perfusionniste, vaut mieux l'avoir à son côté lorsqu'on subit une chirurgie à cœur ouvert. «Quand j'explique mon métier aux patients, ils me disent à la blague de ne pas être trop endormie pendant l'opération», évoque Julie Gagnon, perfusionniste à l'Hôpital général juif de Montréal.

Des milieux de travail potentiels

❯ Centres hospitaliers

«Environ 95 % de mon travail concerne la **machine cœur-poumon**. Lors d'une **chirurgie valvulaire**, cardiaque ou thoracique, on arrête le cœur et les poumons du patient. Avec mon appareil, je maintiens la personne en vie artificiellement pendant l'intervention.»

C'est un véritable travail d'équipe, constate Julie. «On doit informer le chirurgien de problèmes qui surviennent pendant l'opération (comme l'afflux de sang insuffisant vers la machine cœur-poumon), en plus de collaborer avec l'anesthésiste, l'**inhalothérapeute** et les infirmières.»

Julie s'occupe aussi de l'auto-transfuseur, qui sert à récupérer le sang du patient. Une fois récupéré, le sang est nettoyé et retransmis au patient, ce qui permet d'éviter le recours à un donneur.

ma motivation

C'est en regardant une série télévisée américaine qui montrait des médecins en pleine action que Julie a été conquise par cet univers. Puis une autre émission où elle a vu un perfusionniste à l'œuvre avec sa machine cœur-poumon l'a captivée.

«Je voulais être dans un métier où on a "les deux mains dedans", se souvient-elle. La salle d'opération m'a toujours intéressée. C'est impressionnant de voir ce qu'un chirurgien peut faire avec deux ou trois bouts de fil pour sauver des gens ou améliorer leur qualité de vie.» De plus, Julie sait qu'elle peut faire la différence entre la vie et la mort. «Quand ça va mal, l'adrénaline se met de la partie. Il faut réagir et penser rapidement. Lors d'un dénouement heureux, j'ai une grande satisfaction.»

mon conseil

Les étudiants refusés en médecine sont le plus souvent pris au dépourvu. Julie a vécu cette situation. Heureusement, la perfusion s'est révélée pour elle une profession tout aussi passionnante. «Ceux qui aiment la médecine devraient considérer cette voie», soutient-elle.

Pour exercer ce métier, il faut toutefois s'assurer d'avoir du sang-froid pour ne pas paniquer en situation d'urgence, avertit Julie. «Il faut être capable de réfléchir rapidement, de vivre dans le stress d'avoir la vie du patient entre les mains.» 05/03

mon parcours

Julie a effectué un baccalauréat en sciences de la santé, à la Nova Southeastern University, à Fort Lauderdale, en Floride. Par la suite, elle a obtenu un certificat en perfusion extra-corporelle à l'Université de Montréal, ce qui lui a permis d'obtenir son poste actuel. Julie a également une maîtrise en pharmacologie de l'Université de Montréal.

Les mots en caractères **gras** sont définis à la page 153.

Pharmacien

> en milieu hospitalier

mon travail

La profession de pharmacien évoque généralement les comptoirs chez Jean Coutu ou Pharmaprix. Ces pharmaciens «d'officine» font principalement de la préparation et de la distribution de médicaments. La profession de pharmacien d'hôpital est différente.

«La majeure partie de mon travail consiste à donner des soins pharmaceutiques, par conséquent à faire partie des unités de soins en compagnie des médecins, physiothérapeutes, ergothérapeutes, infirmières, afin de m'assurer que l'utilisation des médicaments est maximisée», explique Patrick Boudreault, pharmacien à l'Hôpital Saint-François-d'Assise du Centre hospitalier universitaire de Québec (CHUQ). «Par exemple, un médecin fait un diagnostic. En discutant avec lui, je vais suggérer le meilleur choix de médicaments possible. Je devrai ajuster ce choix, ainsi que la dose et la posologie du médicament, selon la situation précise du patient. Je suis totalement impliqué dans le processus décisionnel.

«La plupart du temps, je suis en contact direct avec les malades, insiste Patrick. Mais une demi-journée par semaine environ, je suis affecté à la gestion de la distribution des médicaments à la pharmacie de l'hôpital. En rotation, chaque pharmacien a sa période de distribution.» Cette tâche de comptoir consiste à préparer les médicaments destinés aux malades et à fournir à l'infirmière une feuille d'administration des médicaments pour chaque patient.

Des milieux de travail potentiels

> Centres d'hébergement et de soins de longue durée

> Centres hospitaliers

> Centres locaux de services communautaires (CLSC)

> Compagnies pharmaceutiques

> Établissements scolaires

> Pharmacies communautaires

> Pharmacies d'établissements de santé

ma motivation

Patrick apprécie tout particulièrement le travail d'équipe. «Par la force des choses, les problèmes de santé que l'on voit dans les hôpitaux sont plus complexes. Par conséquent, avoir une équipe médicale et paramédicale sous la main, tout le matériel nécessaire, l'accès aux laboratoires et à l'information sur le patient, permettent de faire des choix mieux éclairés. «De plus, le patient est sur place et il a le temps, ajoute Patrick. À l'hôpital, on peut discuter avec lui, aller au fond des choses.»

Les médicaments sont de plus en plus chers, poursuit Patrick. «Le grand défi, c'est donc d'en faire une utilisation la plus appropriée et la plus judicieuse possible.»

mon conseil

Patrick Boudreault suggère aux jeunes intéressés par cette profession de planifier leurs études en fonction du milieu de travail visé. «On commence avec le baccalauréat en pharmacie. Ensuite, il y a trois choix possibles. La majorité des étudiants vont opter pour la pharmacie d'officine. Une petite partie d'entre eux feront une maîtrise en pharmacie d'hôpital, obligatoire pour pouvoir travailler dans les grands centres hospitaliers. La troisième voie, c'est le travail dans l'industrie pharmaceutique.» 05/03

mon parcours

Patrick a étudié à l'Université Laval, où il a obtenu son baccalauréat en pharmacie et sa maîtrise en pharmacie d'hôpital. À la fin de ses études en 2000, il a été embauché par l'Hôpital Saint-François-d'Assise du CHUQ.

Les mots en caractères **gras** sont définis à la page 153.

Pharmacologue
❯ **en milieu universitaire**

 mon travail

«Tiens, c'est bizarre ce résultat-là...» Voilà le genre d'étincelle qui attise la curiosité de Pedro D'Orléans-Juste. Pharmacologue et biologiste, il consacre ses énergies à comprendre la biologie humaine, les substances médicamenteuses, leur influence sur le corps et les moyens qu'utilise celui-ci pour s'en protéger (l'élimination, par exemple).

Pedro dirige le Département de **pharmacologie** de la faculté de médecine de l'Université de Sherbrooke. Il partage son temps entre l'administration du Département, l'enseignement aux étudiants, la recherche en laboratoire et la rédaction d'articles scientifiques dans son domaine de prédilection, soit les médicaments développés et éventuellement employés dans le traitement des maladies cardiovasculaires. Ses écrits font force de référence dans le monde entier. En 2002, il figurait parmi les 6 pharmacologues les plus cités au Canada et parmi les 108 premiers au monde, d'après la prestigieuse liste alphabétique de l'Institute for Scientific Information.

Des milieux de travail potentiels

❯ Compagnies pharmaceutiques

❯ Laboratoires de recherche privés, publics ou universitaires

 ma motivation

Très jeune, Pedro était déjà dévoré par une immense curiosité scientifique. Il en a passé du temps, enfermé au sous-sol de la maison familiale avec son microscope et son jeu de chimie, à faire expérience sur expérience. «Je savais que je ferais de la recherche, confie-t-il. Quand est venu le temps de choisir, ce qui m'a fait opter pour la pharmacologie, c'est l'immensité du potentiel de ce domaine. L'amélioration des soins de santé passe par l'amélioration des médicaments. Si les hospitalisations durent moins longtemps aujourd'hui qu'il y a 20 ans, c'est en partie grâce aux nouveaux médicaments, qui ont des actions mieux ciblées sur les maladies et qui présentent moins d'effets secondaires», explique Pedro, en précisant que le problème des **interactions médicamenteuses** représente toutefois un défi à relever pour les scientifiques.

 mon conseil

«La première qualité que doit posséder un pharmacologue est, à mon avis, la curiosité», affirme Pedro. Repousser les limites des connaissances actuelles demande aussi de la ténacité et de l'audace, ajoute-t-il. Pour ceux que l'aventure intéresse, l'Université de Sherbrooke a lancé en 2002 un baccalauréat en pharmacologie. Un programme qui répond aux besoins du marché, selon Pedro. «Il y a beaucoup de place en développement et mise en marché de produits pharmaceutiques, en représentation auprès des professionnels de la santé, en recherche et en enseignement.»
07/03

 mon parcours

Pedro est titulaire d'un baccalauréat en sciences (biologie) de l'Université Bishop's ainsi que d'une maîtrise et d'un doctorat en pharmacologie de l'Université de Sherbrooke. Il a également poursuivi des études postdoctorales au William Harvey Research Institute de Londres. Professeur à l'Université de Sherbrooke depuis 1989, il occupe notamment, outre les fonctions de directeur du Département de pharmacologie, celles de conseiller scientifique au Fonds de la recherche en santé du Québec (FRSQ) et de directeur du Réseau en santé cardiovasculaire du Québec.

Les mots en caractères **gras** sont définis à la page 153.

Physicienne médicale
> en milieu hospitalier

mon travail

Dans un département de radio-oncologie, où l'on traite les cancers, le physicien médical agit en tant qu'expert en radiation. «Il faut maîtriser cette radiation que l'on ne voit pas», explique Sylviane Aubin, physicienne médicale à l'Hôtel-Dieu de Québec du Centre hospitalier universitaire de Québec (CHUQ). En effet, si une juste dose guérit le patient, une trop faible dose peut faire échouer le traitement tandis qu'un excès peut entraîner des effets secondaires à long terme.

«Notre but est que le traitement soit précis et bien administré, poursuit Sylviane. Nous devons installer et calibrer les appareils qui vont traiter les patients, pour faire en sorte qu'ils fournissent correctement la radiation. Par ailleurs, s'il y a des problèmes pendant le traitement, les physiciens sont appelés en renfort.» Il arrive en effet qu'il faille apporter des ajustements au traitement prévu quand, par exemple, un patient subit une trop grande perte de poids. Les physiciens médicaux doivent aussi inspecter et entretenir scrupuleusement les appareils. Ils font également de la recherche-développement et de la formation dans leur domaine, en plus de s'occuper de radioprotection, c'est-à-dire les mesures à prendre contre les radiations, comme l'entreposage des sources radioactives et la gestion des déchets radioactifs.

Des milieux de travail potentiels

> Centres hospitaliers

ma motivation

«Nous affrontons continuellement de nouveaux problèmes. Par exemple, il arrive qu'un patient ait déjà été traité pour un cancer. Or, suivant la région du corps affectée, le patient ne peut recevoir plus qu'une certaine dose de radiation. On évalue alors s'il est possible de faire le traitement prescrit par le médecin ou s'il n'y a pas lieu de traiter autrement pour réduire les effets secondaires à long terme.» Et il y a des moments très gratifiants où son bonheur... irradie : «Récemment, c'est moi qui ai planifié de A à Z le traitement d'un patient en attente d'une greffe de moelle osseuse.» Ce traitement impliquait l'irradiation complète du corps du patient dans le but d'éliminer son système immunitaire et ainsi empêcher le rejet de sa nouvelle moelle... en provenance d'Allemagne.

mon conseil

«La physique médicale est un domaine complexe et mal connu, même des physiciens, affirme Sylviane. Pendant mes études, au baccalauréat et à la maîtrise, j'ai fait deux stages en physique médicale pour mieux connaître le métier. Je suggère d'en faire autant à tout étudiant qui se destine à cette spécialité.» 05/03

mon parcours

Sylviane a décroché un baccalauréat en physique à l'Université Laval. De son propre chef, elle a effectué un stage rémunéré en physique médicale au Groupe de recherche en physique médicale, du département de radio-oncologie de l'Hôtel-Dieu de Québec. Ayant obtenu une bourse du ministère de la Santé et des Services sociaux, elle a ensuite fait une maîtrise en physique médicale à l'Université Laval. Sylviane a par la suite été embauchée par l'Hôtel-Dieu de Québec.

Les mots en caractères **gras** sont définis à la page 153.

Physiothérapeute
❭ en clinique privée

mon travail

Tendinite, entorse, **hernie discale**, migraine et **subluxation** : voici quelques-uns des problèmes de santé que traite Mathieu Côté. Il travaille à la clinique privée Physiothérapie Biokin située à Sainte-Foy, avec trois autres physiothérapeutes. Mathieu s'assure d'amener ses patients à un niveau fonctionnel optimal grâce à une réadaptation des articulations et des muscles blessés. Lors de sa première rencontre avec le client, il fait une évaluation de son état physique, détermine quelle est la source de la douleur et établit un plan de traitement.

Mathieu a recours à différentes techniques : il peut, par exemple, mettre en mouvement muscles et articulations pour en rétablir la souplesse, renforcer les muscles à l'aide de poids et haltères ou les masser pour les détendre, ou encore faire des manipulations sur des articulations. Il utilise également l'**électrothérapie** et l'**hydrothérapie** pour diminuer la douleur et l'inflammation et accroître les bienfaits du traitement. Finalement, le patient retournera chez lui avec des exercices de musculation, d'assouplissement ou de renforcement à accomplir.

Des milieux de travail potentiels

- ❭ Cabinets d'autres professionnels de la santé
- ❭ Centres de réadaptation
- ❭ Centres d'hébergement et de soins de longue durée
- ❭ Centres hospitaliers
- ❭ Centres locaux de services communautaires (CLSC)
- ❭ Cliniques privées
- ❭ Établissements d'enseignement spécialisés

ma motivation

La physiothérapie comprend trois champs de pratique : l'orthopédie (c'est celle qu'a choisie Mathieu), la neurologie et le cardiorespiratoire, ce qui implique des clientèles différentes. «Le physiothérapeute peut choisir de traiter des quadraplégiques, des grands brûlés ou des personnes atteintes de sclérose en plaques. C'est un domaine diversifié où l'on peut sans cesse se renouveler.» Mais le principal défi de Mathieu est de mener chacun de ses patients vers une réadaptation complète. «J'aime aider les gens à retrouver leur qualité de vie, c'est valorisant. Du sportif blessé qui peut reprendre ses activités à la mère de famille soulagée de ses migraines, j'ai contribué à leur cheminement. Il est également stimulant de se creuser la tête pour bien cerner la problématique du patient, surtout lorsque les causes sont multiples, et donc pas toujours faciles à trouver», explique-t-il.

Il aime également pouvoir établir des relations privilégiées avec sa clientèle. «Le traitement permet de créer un lien de confiance avec les patients. Au fil des rencontres, j'apprends à les connaître et à les apprécier.»

mon conseil

Selon Mathieu, pour exercer le métier de physiothérapeute, il faut aimer aider les gens et savoir les accompagner dans leur cheminement. «Il est important de développer un lien de confiance avec eux et de réaliser que chaque patient a son propre objectif de guérison à atteindre. Le physiothérapeute doit l'encourager et le motiver, par exemple en l'incitant à faire ses exercices à la maison.» 05/03

mon parcours

Titulaire d'un baccalauréat en physiothérapie de l'Université Laval, Mathieu est actionnaire associé à la clinique Physiothérapie Biokin. Il est également chargé de cours en physiothérapie à l'Université Laval et physiothérapeute pour une équipe de hockey senior semi-professionnelle à Pont-Rouge.

Les mots en caractères **gras** sont définis à la page 153.

Hôpital Général de Hawkesbury & District General Hospital Inc.

Venez faire carrière chez nous:

- **PHYSIOTHÉRAPEUTES**
- **ERGOTHÉRAPEUTES**
- **ORTHOPHONISTES**
- **TECHNICIEN(NE)S DE LABORATOIRE**
- **TECHNICIEN(NE)S EN IMAGERIE DIAGNOSTIQUE**
- **INFIRMIER(ÈRE)S**

Hôpital Général de Hawkesbury & District General Hospital
1111 rue Ghislain, Hawkesbury, Ontario K6A 3G5
Téléphone : 1-613-632-1111, poste 377 (Madame Louise Charbonneau)
Télécopieur : 1-613-632-5126, courriel: lcharbonneau@rnsb.org
Site web:www.hgh.ca

ᔪᓇᕕᒃ ᔪᓇᒋᒋᓕᒃ ᑲᑎᒪᔨᖏᑦ ᐃᓗᓯᓕᕆᓂᕐᒥ ᐱᔨᑦᑎᕋᕐᓂᓕᕆᓂᕐᒥᓗ

NUNAVIK REGIONAL BOARD OF HEALTH AND SOCIAL SERVICES
RÉGIE RÉGIONALE DE LA SANTÉ ET DES SERVICES SOCIAUX NUNAVIK

Vivre une expérience professionnelle passionnante et tout à fait différente, vivre le Grand-Nord... le Nunavik

Des possibilités d'emplois permanents à temps plein et des remplacements s'offrent régulièrement à différents titres d'emplois dans la région du Nunavik tant dans nos centres de santé qu'à la Régie Régionale :

- **Infirmière**
- **Infirmière bachelière**
- **Agent de relations humaines**
- **Éducateur spécialisé**
- **Hygiéniste dentaire**
- **Travailleur social**
- **Nutritionniste**
- **Technicien en laboratoire**
- **Agent d'information**
- **etc**

Également, au Module du Nord Québécois, centre d'hébergement situé à Montréal pour la population Inuite dans l'attente ou en cours de services médicaux dans la région métropolitaine, plusieurs emplois sont offerts :

- **Responsable en milieu de vie**
- **Préposé aux bénéficiaires**
- **Conducteur-escorte**
- **Infirmière – infirmière bachelière**
- **etc**

Finalement, les « Services administratifs régionaux du Nunavik » dont les bureaux sont situés à Anjou, gèrent une partie des services administratifs de la Régie Régionale du Nunavik et du Centre de Santé Inuulitsivik. Des emplois administratifs sont régulièrement offerts à titre de :

- **Technicien en administration – ressources humaines**
- **Technicien en administration – paie**
- **Technicien en administration – finances**

Les exigences varient en fonction des postes disponibles.

Les conditions salariales varient également en fonction du poste et sont conformes aux normes actuellement en vigueur dans le réseau de la santé et des services sociaux.

Au salaire sont ajoutées les primes prévues par les différentes conventions collectives pour les régions éloignées. Frais de déménagement, d'entreposage et sorties annuelles sont défrayés par l'employeur.

Pour plus de détail concernant les postes disponibles, visitez notre site web à l'adresse suivante : www.rrsss17.gouv.qc.ca

Si l'un de ces postes vous intéresse, veuillez nous faire parvenir votre curriculum vitæ, à

Régie régionale de la santé et services sociaux Nunavik
Services administratifs régionaux,
7750, rue Bombardier,
Anjou (Québec) H1J 2G3

Podiatre

> **en clinique privée**

mon travail

Problèmes de pieds? François Giroux, docteur en médecine podiatrique, les connaît tous. Ses cas les plus fréquents sont les verrues plantaires, les ongles incarnés, les cors, ainsi que les problèmes de malformation (pieds plats, pieds creux, orteils marteaux, etc.). Mais il traite aussi les fractures, les tumeurs, les ulcères, les maladies de la peau et des ongles de même que les problèmes d'articulations et de structure osseuse.

«Trouver le problème, poser le diagnostic, c'est l'essentiel de mon travail, résume-t-il. Par la suite, il ne me reste qu'à effectuer le traitement pour améliorer la situation de mon patient.» L'observation, la manipulation, les radiographies et les tests de laboratoire font partie des méthodes à sa disposition pour mettre le doigt sur ce qui ne va pas.

Une fois que le problème est cerné, François explique au patient de quoi il s'agit et prodigue le traitement approprié. Son intervention peut comporter, par exemple, une chirurgie mineure, une pose de plâtre, une thérapie de rééducation du pied ou encore la fabrication de supports orthopédiques.

Le podiatre émet également des recommandations pour éviter les rechutes. À chaque consultation, il collige minutieusement toutes les informations recueillies dans ses dossiers médicaux, qu'il doit conserver plusieurs années.

Des milieux de travail potentiels

> Cabinets privés
> Cabinets d'autres professionnels de la santé
> Centres hospitaliers

ma motivation

L'engagement social est une valeur importante pour François. Il a choisi de faire carrière dans le domaine de la santé pour être en contact avec ses semblables et améliorer leur qualité de vie. En ce sens, sa pratique le satisfait particulièrement. «Ce que je trouve le plus stimulant dans mon travail, c'est que les gens qui viennent me voir arrivent en ayant mal et repartent soulagés. Si leur bobo n'est pas guéri, ils savent au moins à quoi s'attendre parce que je leur ai bien expliqué les étapes du traitement. Pour moi, c'est très gratifiant.»

Autre aspect qui lui est cher : être son propre patron. Depuis qu'il a ouvert sa clinique, François exerce la pleine maîtrise sur ses heures de pratique, sur ses vacances et sur son environnement.

mon conseil

«Pour devenir podiatre, il faut s'expatrier, car, jusqu'à présent, la formation n'est pas offerte au Québec», explique François, qui a étudié aux États-Unis. Par conséquent, il est nécessaire de maîtriser l'anglais. 06/03

mon parcours

À 24 ans, François est devenu le plus jeune docteur en médecine podiatrique du Québec en rentrant de Philadelphie avec son diplôme universitaire du réputé Pennsylvania College of Podiatric Medecine. C'est après avoir travaillé quelques mois en clinique privée qu'il a inauguré son propre cabinet, à Charlesbourg.

Les mots en caractères **gras** sont définis à la page 153.

Psychoéducateur
❯ en milieu hospitalier

mon travail

Michel Laroche est psychoéducateur au centre de jour de pédopsychiatrie de l'Hôpital du Sacré-Cœur de Montréal. Il reçoit en thérapie de groupe des enfants de deux à six ans qui présentent des troubles envahissants du développement (TED) : **autisme**, **troubles du comportement** ou **de l'attention**, **hyperactivité**, **anxiété**, etc.

«Je peux faire des interventions visant la motricité globale, avec un ballon, ou la motricité fine, à l'aide de petits objets. Pour les enfants atteints très sévèrement, l'éveil à la relation passe par du crayonnage, des casse-têtes, des petites constructions. Je stimule leur communication avec des images, de la musique, des contes, etc.»

Michel travaille aussi avec les parents en plus de collaborer avec les autres établissements du réseau d'aide de ces enfants, comme les garderies, les centres locaux de services communautaires (CLSC), les centres de réadaptation et les écoles. «Environ 50 % de mon temps est consacré à l'intervention directe. L'autre moitié va à la gestion», résume-t-il.

Des milieux de travail potentiels

- ❯ Cabinets privés
- ❯ Centres de réadaptation
- ❯ Centres hospitaliers
- ❯ Centres jeunesse
- ❯ Centres locaux de services communautaires (CLSC)
- ❯ Établissements d'enseignement
- ❯ Garderies
- ❯ Milieu carcéral

ma motivation

«Les préjugés entourant les maladies psychiatriques m'ont toujours révolté, confie-t-il. J'avais le goût de m'engager socialement, de me porter à la défense des malades et de les aider à progresser.

«Je travaille en troisième ligne d'intervention, là où les médecins de famille et les cliniques ne suffisent pas à la tâche. Mon intervention est ultra-spécialisée et intensive», précise Michel, qui rencontre généralement ses jeunes patients deux fois par semaine, souvent pendant plus d'un an.

Michel se plaît bien dans son équipe multidisciplinaire, qui comprend une douzaine de praticiens de la santé, dont des psychiatres, des orthophonistes et des ergothérapeutes. «Une des spécialités du psychoéducateur est de mettre à contribution toutes les ressources du milieu pour en tirer le plein potentiel.» Cela implique la coordination de l'équipe, la disposition des meubles, l'utilisation des locaux et les horaires.

mon conseil

Le premier outil de travail du psychoéducateur, c'est sa personnalité, déclare Michel. «Pour bien aider, il faut se connaître, savoir ce que contient notre "coffre à outils". Il faut aussi faire preuve de respect pour la souffrance des autres, avoir de la rigueur pour ne pas se perdre de vue dans l'aide qu'on apporte et savoir fixer des objectifs clairs dans la progression des patients.» 06/03

mon parcours

Michel a obtenu un diplôme d'études collégiales (DEC) en sciences de la santé au Cégep du Vieux Montréal, puis un baccalauréat en psychoéducation à l'Université de Montréal. Il a commencé à pratiquer dans son domaine sitôt ses études terminées. Il continue toutefois à suivre des sessions de formation, par exemple en évaluation de cas ou en supervision de groupes de parents. Ayant contribué à la restructuration du programme de maîtrise en psychoéducation, il est bien placé pour expliquer que l'exercice de la profession nécessite maintenant un diplôme de deuxième cycle.

Les mots en caractères **gras** sont définis à la page 153.

Psychologue
> en centre de réadaptation

mon travail

On a souvent tendance à croire que les psychologues aident surtout les gens souffrant de troubles de santé mentale. Toutefois, leur rôle peut varier d'un milieu de travail à un autre. Ivan Syvrais, psychologue au Centre de réadaptation Lucie-Bruneau, pratique dans le cadre d'un programme de réadaptation au travail.

Des douleurs causées par des blessures subies lors d'un accident ou par une maladie neurologique, comme la sclérose en plaques, peuvent miner le moral d'une personne au point de compromettre son rendement au travail. «Je tente de voir comment la douleur d'un client peut affecter sa vie professionnelle et je lui propose des stratégies de réinsertion au travail, explique Ivan. Par exemple, si après avoir été victime d'un accident, une personne éprouve un stress qui l'empêche de se concentrer, je peux commencer par lui faire essayer des exercices de relaxation.»

Des milieux de travail potentiels

> Cabinets privés
> Centres locaux de services communautaires (CLSC)
> Cliniques médicales
> Établissements d'enseignement
> Organismes communautaires

ma motivation

Ivan a choisi d'œuvrer en psychologie médicale de la santé, car il était particulièrement intéressé par le lien entre la douleur physique et les aspects psychologiques. Pour lui, il est clair qu'une personne souffrant physiquement risque aussi de souffrir psychologiquement, à cause entre autres du haut niveau de stress ou de frustration que peut engendrer une maladie ou une blessure. «J'aime donner une qualité de vie aux gens, les aider à se reprendre en main et les voir progresser», explique-t-il. Créatif, il se plaît à trouver de nouvelles stratégies de réinsertion au travail. Il peut s'agir, par exemple, d'une technique de visualisation positive adaptée aux besoins spécifiques d'un client.

Ivan apprécie également l'interaction avec les autres intervenants du Centre. En partageant des renseignements avec l'ergothérapeute, le médecin, le physiothérapeute, le conseiller d'orientation ou encore avec l'éducateur physique, il acquiert une compréhension globale de l'état de chaque patient.

mon conseil

Puisque, dans un tel milieu, le psychologue collabore avec beaucoup d'autres intervenants, la sociabilité se révèle essentielle au quotidien. L'empathie, la capacité d'écoute, la diplomatie et l'ouverture d'esprit sont également à cultiver afin de venir en aide aux clients.

mon parcours

Le diplôme de troisième cycle n'était pas obligatoire pour exercer comme psychologue au moment où Ivan a terminé ses études. C'est donc grâce à son baccalauréat en psychologie de l'Université du Québec à Trois-Rivières et à sa maîtrise en psychologie de l'Université de Montréal qu'il a pu obtenir son premier emploi, au Centre Lucie-Bruneau. Toutefois, désireux d'augmenter son expertise, Ivan termine actuellement un doctorat en psychologie à l'Université de Montréal. Il a également suivi une formation de deux ans sur les états de stress post-traumatique offerte par un organisme privé.

«Il faut être persévérant pour accéder à cette profession puisque cela demande de longues études, ajoute Ivan. Maintenant, les étudiants en psychologie doivent faire un doctorat pour pouvoir pratiquer.» 06/03

Les mots en caractères **gras** sont définis à la page 153.

Représentant pharmaceutique
❯ dans une compagnie pharmaceutique

mon travail

Francis Veilletto est représentant pharmaceutique. Presque toujours sur la route, il rencontre les médecins pour leur présenter les produits de la compagnie pharmaceutique Pfizer Canada.

Des milieux de travail potentiels

❯ Compagnies pharmaceutiques

«Nous discutons des médicaments qui viennent d'être mis sur le marché ou des nouveautés concernant les produits déjà existants. Je leur parle aussi des dernières recherches réalisées sur des produits qu'ils connaissent déjà.»

Francis ne se rend aux bureaux de Pfizer à Montréal que deux fois par an. Le reste de l'année, il fonctionne de façon autonome et gère son emploi du temps. Il est responsable des régions de la Mauricie, de Lanaudière et d'une partie de la Montérégie et il s'assure de bien quadriller son territoire. «C'est moi qui cible les médecins et qui prends rendez-vous avec eux. Je contacte ceux qui sont spécialisés dans des champs de pratique reliés au médicament que je présente. L'accès aux généralistes est moins aisé, mais plus ils connaissent le représentant, plus le contact est facilité.»

ma motivation

Francis a deux passions : la science et le contact humain. Son métier lui permet d'allier les deux. «C'est pour cette raison que j'ai choisi cette branche. J'ai déjà travaillé en laboratoire, mais ce n'était pas la même chose, il me manquait le contact avec les gens.»

Les relations avec les médecins sont généralement très cordiales, dit-il. «Nous discutons de science, des récentes études, des interactions entre les médicaments. C'est très stimulant.»

Francis doit constamment se tenir informé. Parmi ses lectures de chevet figurent, par exemple, le *New England Journal of Medicine*, *Nature*, etc. «J'aime sentir que je maîtrise mon sujet à fond. Je suis un peu comme une PME : je suis responsable du succès de mon travail.»

mon conseil

L'autonomie et la discipline sont les principales qualités du représentant pharmaceutique. «Nous sommes laissés à nous-mêmes. Par exemple, je dois veiller à ma propre formation en ce qui concerne les nouveaux médicaments. Il faut savoir s'organiser, et accepter d'avoir parfois à travailler le soir.» Francis souligne aussi l'importance de l'ouverture d'esprit et de la soif de connaissances scientifiques. «Si on ne se tient pas à jour, on perd sa crédibilité», dit-il. Être un bon communicateur est également primordial. «C'est difficile pour les malades d'avoir accès à un médecin. Imaginez ce qu'il en est pour un représentant pharmaceutique!» 05/03

mon parcours

Francis est diplômé en biologie médicale. Il a obtenu son baccalauréat à l'Université du Québec à Trois-Rivières il y a cinq ans. Il a ensuite effectué un stage de quatre mois en recherche fondamentale à l'Université de l'Alberta. De retour au Québec, il a été embauché par la société pharmaceutique Parke-Davis, qui est plus tard devenue la propriété de Pfizer.

Les mots en caractères **gras** sont définis à la page 153.

Sage-femme
❯ en maison de naissance

mon travail

Une femme enceinte peut choisir de vivre tout le processus de la grossesse et de l'accouchement accompagnée d'une sage-femme.

Christiane Léonard, sage-femme à la maison de naissance du Centre local de services communautaires (CLSC) Lac-Saint-Louis de Pointe-Claire, assure la continuité des soins avant, pendant et après la naissance de l'enfant.

«Je rencontre les femmes pendant leur grossesse, je les assiste à l'accouchement et je fais le suivi postnatal à domicile. Et si malheureusement un problème survient pendant l'accouchement, je les accompagne également à l'hôpital.»

Des milieux de travail potentiels

❯ Centres hospitaliers
❯ Maisons de naissance

ma motivation

Pendant son adolescence, Christiane a été fascinée par un reportage sur l'obstétricien français Frédérick Leboyer, ardent défenseur de l'accouchement sans violence.

«J'ai réalisé qu'il existait des approches plus douces dans la mise au monde d'un enfant et ça m'a plu. Quelques années plus tard, à la naissance de mon premier bébé, j'ai choisi d'être accompagnée par une sage-femme et cela s'est très bien déroulé. J'ai alors décidé de devenir sage-femme moi-même.»

Christiane aime l'approche globale de la pratique de sage-femme, qui tient compte des dimensions physique, psychologique et sociale de cet événement unique qu'est la naissance d'un enfant. «On touche à toutes les dimensions de la personne. Et les tâches sont variées : on fait des consultations, des visites à domicile, on s'occupe du nouveau-né, de l'allaitement, etc. Il n'y a pas de monotonie.»

mon conseil

Christiane affirme qu'il faut, d'abord et avant tout, adhérer à la philosophie selon laquelle la grossesse, le travail et l'accouchement sont des événements de la vie sains et naturels.

La profession de sage-femme nécessite une grande disponibilité et il faut être prêt à vivre des conditions de travail très irrégulières. «Je suis de garde 24 heures sur 24, 10 jours sur 14. J'ai ensuite quatre jours de congé durant lesquels une autre sage-femme prend le relais.» 05/03

mon parcours

«Auparavant, on apprenait sur le tas. J'ai moi-même commencé en observant des accouchements, puis en assistant graduellement une autre sage-femme.» Depuis maintenant quatre ans, il faut obtenir un baccalauréat en pratique sage-femme à l'Université du Québec à Trois-Rivières. Après un an de théorie, on effectue trois ans de stages dans des maisons de naissance et des hôpitaux. Enfin, les sages-femmes doivent réussir un examen régi par l'Ordre des sages-femmes du Québec pour pouvoir exercer légalement la profession dans la province, où elles sont désormais reconnues comme des professionnelles de la santé.

Les mots en caractères **gras** sont définis à la page 153.

Travailleur de rue

> **en organisme communautaire**

mon travail

À Rimouski, il y a un travailleur de rue qui accueille des jeunes de 12 à 29 ans dans un autobus scolaire réaménagé à cette fin. Il s'appelle Serge Dumont et travaille pour le Mouvement d'aide et d'information SIDA du Bas-Saint-Laurent. Toutefois, à la demande des jeunes, le mandat de Serge englobe plus que la prévention du sida.

Avec eux, il aborde des thèmes reliés à toutes sortes de sujets qui leur tiennent à cœur, comme les peines d'amour, les effets des drogues, le divorce, etc. Parfois, Serge invite des spécialistes, comme des sexologues, pour approfondir tel ou tel sujet. Il offre aussi des consultations privées dans une petite salle située à l'arrière de l'autobus. Quand un jeune a des problèmes sérieux, comme des tendances suicidaires, il l'envoie à un autre spécialiste, un psychiatre par exemple.

«Ici, les jeunes vivent beaucoup d'isolement et ont besoin de communiquer», explique Serge pour souligner la particularité du travail de rue en région. Dans de grandes villes comme Québec ou Montréal, les interventions sont différentes, car l'itinérance, la délinquance, les problèmes de drogue et la criminalité sont plus fréquents.

Des milieux de travail potentiels

> Centres locaux de services communautaires (CLSC)
> Organismes communautaires

ma motivation

Curieusement, Serge ne se destinait pas au métier de travailleur de rue. Ce n'est qu'après qu'il eut été embauché comme intervenant psychosocial par le Mouvement d'aide et d'information SIDA du Bas-Saint-Laurent qu'on lui a proposé de prendre les commandes de l'autobus. «Comme je n'avais jamais travaillé de ma vie avec les jeunes, j'ai trouvé ça intéressant.» Et il ne regrette rien. Dans le véhicule où il travaille seul, il apprécie la liberté d'intervenir à sa façon. De plus, il aime les jeunes et croit en eux. «Si je peux permettre à un seul jeune de réaliser un de ses rêves en l'encourageant, j'aurai accompli quelque chose d'important.»

En plus de briser l'isolement des jeunes, un de ses grands défis est d'aller chercher des subventions gouvernementales, municipales et autres pour payer les coûts de son service. Car, il faut le dire, l'organisme qui l'emploie ne bénéficie que de peu d'argent.

mon conseil

Pour être apprécié des jeunes et bien réussir son travail, Serge obéit à quatre règles d'or à bord de son autobus. Il fait preuve d'une grande discrétion, ne juge jamais les opinions des autres, se considère comme l'égal de la clientèle et essaie d'être assez souple pour s'adapter à tous les genres d'individus. «Les jeunes sont différents les uns des autres et je dois accepter leurs propres valeurs sans les juger ou prendre parti pour l'un plutôt que l'autre.»
06/03

mon parcours

Avant de faire son baccalauréat en psychosociologie à l'Université du Québec à Rimouski, Serge a d'abord suivi des cours en psychothérapie dans une école privée montréalaise. Pendant ses études universitaires, il a travaillé comme intervenant psychosocial à l'Association canadienne pour la santé mentale et auprès des Grands Frères de Rimouski comme agent de communication. Puis, après quelques années de pratique comme psycho-thérapeute à son compte, il a obtenu son emploi actuel.

Les mots en caractères **gras** sont définis à la page 153.

Travailleuse sociale
> en CLSC

mon travail

Le métier de travailleur social est vaste. D'un milieu de travail à l'autre et d'une clientèle à l'autre, la nature des tâches varie considérablement. Selon qu'on exerce dans une école secondaire, dans un hôpital ou dans un centre local de services communautaires (CLSC), le quotidien n'est pas le même, comme on peut l'imaginer.

Geneviève Croisetière, elle, travaille pour le CLSC Arthur-Buies, à Saint-Jérôme. Elle s'occupe du soutien à domicile d'adultes de tous âges dont l'autonomie est compromise par leur état de santé. «Je leur apprends à vivre au quotidien selon leur problème. Il peut s'agir de maladies dégénératives, comme le cancer, ou encore de **paraplégie**. En leur donnant un soutien psychologique, je les aide à accepter leur réalité et je leur fixe des objectifs réalisables, par exemple faire trois minutes supplémentaires d'exercices par semaine.»

Chaque jour, elle se rend au domicile des patients et voit comment ils évoluent. Si, par exemple, l'un d'eux a besoin qu'un auxiliaire familial prépare ses repas, Geneviève demande à la personne-ressource en question de lui rendre visite. Après chaque rencontre, elle rédige un bilan de santé de la personne, qui sera accessible aux autres intervenants.

Des milieux de travail potentiels

> Centres hospitaliers
> Centres jeunesse
> Centres locaux de services communautaires (CLSC)

ma motivation

«J'ai toujours aimé aider les autres, confie Geneviève. J'avais vraiment envie d'occuper un emploi qui me le permettrait et qui favoriserait les contacts humains. C'est très valorisant de se savoir utile.»

Par ailleurs, Geneviève apprécie le fait d'exercer un travail non routinier. Chaque jour apporte son lot de surprises et de rebondissements, comme la détérioration subite de l'état de santé d'un patient. Elle doit donc être en mesure de suivre attentivement le dossier de chaque individu et de s'adapter aux changements.

Le travail d'équipe lui plaît également beaucoup. Au CLSC, elle côtoie constamment des ergothérapeutes, des infirmiers, des auxiliaires familiaux, etc. Elle trouve intéressant d'apprendre en partageant leur expérience.

mon conseil

Selon Geneviève, si le futur travailleur social est suffisamment empathique pour comprendre le vécu d'une personne sans porter de jugement et qu'il a assez de vivacité d'esprit pour réagir vite aux situations changeantes, il ne devrait pas avoir de difficulté à faire carrière dans ce milieu. Elle insiste aussi sur le fait qu'on ne peut jamais changer la vie d'un patient. «On a beau vouloir sauver le monde, si la personne ne veut pas s'aider elle-même, il faut savoir s'en distancer et ne pas se culpabiliser.» 06/03

mon parcours

Après l'obtention de son diplôme d'études collégiales (DEC) en sciences humaines au Cégep Lionel-Groulx, Geneviève a fait un baccalauréat en travail social à l'Université McGill. Durant ses années d'université, elle a fait du bénévolat auprès de personnes âgées en plus d'effectuer deux stages dans le réseau des CLSC, qui l'ont amenée à s'occuper de la coordination des bénévoles, puis du soutien à domicile. Ce n'est qu'après ces expériences qu'elle a pu obtenir son poste actuel.

Les mots en caractères **gras** sont définis à la page 153.

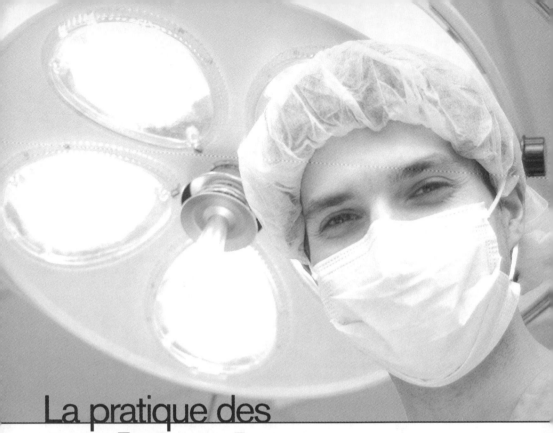

La pratique des
médecins
omnipraticiens
et **spécialistes**

La population québécoise peut compter sur près de 18 000 médecins, soit un peu plus de 9 000 spécialistes et environ 8 800 omnipraticiens[1]. Pierre angulaire du réseau de la santé et des services sociaux, ils œuvrent partout dans la province. C'est cependant à Montréal, en Montérégie et dans la région de Québec que l'on en compte le plus grand nombre.

Par Guylaine Boucher

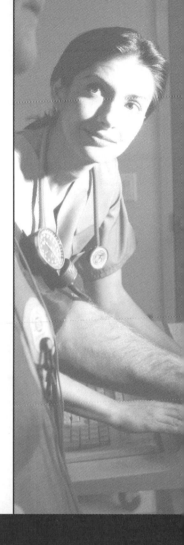

Tout comme les autres employés du réseau de la santé et des services sociaux, les médecins sont rémunérés par le gouvernement. Leur salaire et leurs conditions de travail sont négociés entre le gouvernement et les fédérations médicales qui les représentent. Certains sont salariés, notamment dans les centres locaux de services communautaires (CLSC), mais la majorité d'entre eux sont rémunérés à l'acte, c'est-à-dire en fonction de chacune de leurs interventions auprès d'un malade. Ce mode de rémunération leur confère un statut se rapprochant de celui du travailleur autonome.

En médecine générale, une majorité d'entre eux partagent leur temps entre la pratique en cabinet privé et les divers établissements publics existants. Ils sont très présents en CLSC et dans les centres hospitaliers. Il est fréquent qu'un médecin généraliste soit en lien avec plusieurs établissements. La raison en est simple : les omnipraticiens ayant moins de dix ans de pratique doivent accepter d'effectuer certaines activités professionnelles particulières s'ils désirent avoir leur plein salaire. Par exemple, le fait de travailler en centre d'hébergement et de soins de longue durée (CHSLD), à l'urgence d'un centre hospitalier, auprès des clientèles ayant des problèmes de santé mentale ou encore d'alcoolisme et de toxicomanie est considéré comme une activité médicale particulière. Un médecin peut donc travailler trois jours en clinique privée, être de garde une fin de semaine sur deux dans un CHSLD et effectuer des consultations ponctuelles dans un centre de réadaptation.

La situation est différente pour les médecins spécialistes. Ces derniers concentrent en effet la majorité de leurs activités en centre hospitalier. Un certain nombre d'entre eux ont aussi leur bureau de consultation privé.

Ce portrait général vaut tant pour les médecins spécialistes et omnipraticiens qui pratiquent en région que pour ceux installés en milieu urbain. Seule la rémunération diffère. Les médecins qui exercent à l'extérieur des grands centres voient en effet leur salaire bonifié en raison de l'éloignement et de l'isolement relatif dans lesquels ils doivent accomplir leur travail. ■

1. Collège des médecins du Québec, *Profil statistique*, 2002.

VOUS AVEZ LA PIQÛRE?

Au Québec, quatre établissements universitaires offrent le doctorat en médecine générale et la résidence dans les différentes spécialités. Ce sont l'Université Laval, l'Université McGill, l'Université de Montréal et l'Université de Sherbrooke. On peut obtenir tous les détails sur les études médicales dans le site du Collège des médecins à l'adresse Internet suivante : http://www.cmq.org

Médecin spécialiste en allergie et en immunologie clinique*

mon travail

L'allergologue-immunologue est un médecin spécialisé dans le dépistage, le diagnostic et le contrôle des troubles physiologiques (difficultés respiratoires, éruptions cutanées, démangeaisons, **œdème**, larmoiement, écoulement nasal, etc.) occasionnés par les allergies.

Il interroge les patients sur leurs symptômes et sur leur environnement (à la maison, au travail, etc.). Il les examine et procède à des tests complémentaires comme les **tests cutanés** (*prick tests*) et les **Patch tests**. En cas d'**asthme**, il procède à une **exploration fonctionnelle du système respiratoire**. Il peut aussi prescrire des analyses sanguines pour vérifier la présence d'**immunoglobulines** spécifiques à l'allergène suspecté dans le sang.

Ensuite, il pose son diagnostic et commence le traitement qui peut prendre différentes formes (modification de l'environnement, du comportement, des habitudes alimentaires, médicaments, vaccins, désensibilisation, etc.).

Des milieux de travail potentiels

> Centres d'hébergement et de soins de longue durée

> Centres hospitaliers

> Centres locaux de services communautaires (CLSC)

> Cliniques privées

ma motivation

L'allergologue-immunologue s'intéresse à la personne dans sa globalité en relation avec son environnement. De plus, la réaction allergique peut être causée par une foule d'allergènes comme les acariens, les moisissures, certains aliments, les poils d'animaux, les piqûres de guêpes, etc. La réaction peut aussi toucher différents organes et générer de nombreux problèmes comme la conjonctivite, la rhinite, le rhume des foins, l'asthme, l'eczéma, l'urticaire, etc. Le champ d'action de ce spécialiste est donc vaste et varié, ce qui en fait une discipline à la fois exigeante et pleine de défis.

L'allergologue-immunologue couvre plusieurs aspects de la médecine parce qu'il gère les difficultés qu'éprouve le patient dans son rapport avec ce qui l'entoure et se modifie, comme la nourriture, la nature, l'habitat, etc. Il doit donc pouvoir se faire rapidement une vue d'ensemble pour bien évaluer la situation générale du patient. C'est également une discipline très stimulante, car en constante évolution, où l'on doit suivre de près les modifications des allergènes, l'apparition de nouveaux allergènes et les allergies croisées.

* Exceptionnellement, en l'absence d'un médecin disponible pour un témoignage, nous publions ici une monographie de cette profession.

mon conseil

Dans l'exercice de cette profession, on doit faire preuve de patience et de détermination pour chercher et trouver les causes des symptômes du patient, ce qui n'est pas toujours chose aisée. Tel le détective qui mène une enquête pour trouver le coupable, il faut avoir une vraie passion pour la recherche. Un excellent sens de l'observation et une bonne mémoire sont également essentiels pour parvenir à relier tous les indices et créer une vision d'ensemble qui permettra de poser un diagnostic. 09/03

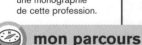

mon parcours

Pour devenir allergologue-immunologue, la voie la plus directe est un diplôme d'études collégiales (DEC) en science de la santé ou en sciences pures, suivi du doctorat en médecine et de la **résidence** en allergologie-immunologie.

Les mots en caractères **gras** sont définis à la page 153.

Médecin spécialiste en anatomopathologie

❯ en milieu hospitalier

mon travail

Quand votre médecin traitant fait des prélèvements sur vous et qu'il les envoie «au laboratoire», il les envoie à un médecin spécialiste en anatomopathologie, communément appelé pathologiste. «Sans la pathologie, il lui serait beaucoup plus difficile d'établir le bon diagnostic», explique Marie-Laure Brisson, médecin spécialiste, pathologiste et directrice du Département de pathologie de l'Hôpital général juif de Montréal.

«Le pathologiste examine des prélèvements de tissus humains, d'abord à l'œil nu, puis à l'aide d'un microscope optique. Par la suite, différentes modalités diagnostiques peuvent venir compléter ses observations, comme l'**immunofluorescence**, la **microscopie électronique**, la **biologie moléculaire** ou la **génétique**.» Une démarche grâce à laquelle il est possible de déterminer la nature d'une maladie, son étendue, sa gravité et son évolution probable. «J'explique les résultats aux médecins traitants. Je suis une consultante pour eux, précise la spécialiste. Dans certains cas, je dois examiner le prélèvement pendant l'intervention chirurgicale afin de poser un diagnostic immédiat et ainsi permettre au chirurgien de pratiquer l'intervention la plus appropriée.»

Des milieux de travail potentiels

❯ Centres d'hébergement et de soins de longue durée

❯ Centres hospitaliers

❯ Centres locaux de services communautaires (CLSC)

❯ Cliniques privées

ma motivation

«Ce qui m'a attirée en médecine, c'est la vie : la sauver, lui redonner une qualité, la prolonger. En posant un diagnostic exact, le pathologiste contribue à l'atteinte de ces objectifs», souligne Marie-Laure, en ajoutant que même la pratique d'une autopsie peut faire avancer les connaissances sur la vie.

«C'est aussi pour la diversité des rôles que le pathologiste peut assumer que j'ai choisi cette spécialité. On intervient dans toutes sortes de cas, allant du **test Pap** à l'étude des malformations fœtales. En centre universitaire, le pathologiste est aussi appelé à enseigner et à faire de la recherche clinique ou fondamentale. De plus, les horaires du pathologiste peuvent être un peu plus souples que ceux d'autres médecins spécialistes, parce qu'il n'a pas de patients à suivre directement.» Cela dit, Marie-Laure affirme tout de même travailler entre 10 et 12 heures par jour.

mon conseil

Un bon pathologiste doit être curieux, rigoureux, perspicace et tenace, et aimer travailler en équipe pour mener à bien les différents tests. Marie-Laure fait aussi remarquer qu'à l'Institut médico-légal du Québec, ce sont des pathologistes qui réalisent les autopsies liées aux morts violentes ou encore aux identités douteuses. «Il ne faut pas craindre cet aspect de la pratique. Il y a beaucoup à apprendre du décès d'une personne. En comprendre la cause est souvent utile pour sauver d'autres vies.» 09/03

mon parcours

«J'ai fait mon doctorat en médecine à l'Université de Montréal, raconte Marie-Laure. Puis, j'ai fait cinq ans de **résidence** en pathologie à l'Hôtel-Dieu de Montréal et à l'Université de Georgetown à Washington DC. Par la suite, j'ai fait ma surspécialité en pathologie des maladies du rein à l'Université de Georgetown et à l'Université McGill de Montréal.» Marie-Laure travaille à l'Hôpital général juif de Montréal depuis la fin de ses études.

Les mots en caractères **gras** sont définis à la page 153.

Médecin spécialiste (résidente) en anesthésiologie

> **en milieu hospitalier**

mon travail

Souffrir le moins possible, voilà ce que l'on espère quand on doit subir une chirurgie. Sophie Collins est là pour y voir. D'abord médecin, Sophie se spécialise actuellement en anesthésiologie. Elle pratique surtout en salle d'opération, sous la supervision d'anesthésiologistes reçus.

Sophie peut rencontrer le patient quelques jours à l'avance en clinique d'évaluation préopératoire ou encore juste avant la chirurgie. Elle évalue alors sa condition physique et, s'il y a lieu, l'envoie passer des tests complémentaires, comme des prises de sang ou des radiographies. Elle détermine ainsi avec le principal intéressé si l'intervention nécessite qu'il soit insensibilisé localement ou «endormi».

Avant et pendant la chirurgie, Sophie administre des médicaments au patient afin de diminuer le plus possible la conscience ou la douleur. En cours de route, elle maintient et surveille ses fonctions vitales, comme son pouls et sa respiration, à l'aide de divers appareils, tel le respirateur artificiel. Une fois l'intervention terminée, elle va voir le patient en salle de réveil pour s'assurer qu'il va bien et lui faire prendre des médicaments contre la douleur au besoin.

Des milieux de travail potentiels

> Centres d'hébergement et de soins de longue durée
> Centres hospitaliers
> Centres locaux de services communautaires (CLSC)
> Cliniques privées

ma motivation

Pour Sophie, l'anesthésiologie est une spécialité stimulante, car elle permet de voir toutes sortes de situations. «Je travaille autant avec des enfants, des adultes, des femmes enceintes que des personnes âgées. J'interviens dans une grande diversité de cas : ablation d'amygdales ou de kystes, chirurgies cardiaques, naissances, amputations, etc. En plus, je vois immédiatement l'effet de mes actions sur les patients et leur douleur. C'est très valorisant de faire du bien à quelqu'un qui a mal.

«Pour une personne qui ne veut pas avoir à faire de suivi de patient, c'est vraiment idéal, poursuit-elle. Une fois que le patient est bien, qu'il n'a plus de nausées ou de vomissements, qu'il respire bien, que sa douleur est contrôlée, qu'il a une bonne pression et un bon pouls, je peux l'envoyer à sa chambre pour sa convalescence. Mon intervention est terminée.»

mon conseil

«En salle d'opération, il se passe de longues périodes où tout va bien, mais je dois quand même rester vigilante. Lorsque survient une situation d'urgence, comme un saignement non maîtrisé, c'est à moi d'agir et de ramener le patient à un état normal. Mon calme agit alors sur toute l'équipe du bloc opératoire.» 06/03

mon parcours

Sophie a obtenu son diplôme d'études collégiales (DEC) en sciences de la santé au Collège Jean-de-Brébeuf, puis son doctorat en médecine à l'Université Laval. En tant que **résidente** en anesthésiologie, elle travaille actuellement à raison de 50 à 80 heures par semaine dans différents hôpitaux liés à l'Université de Montréal, comme l'Hôpital Maisonneuve-Rosemont et l'Hôpital Sacré-Cœur de Montréal.

Les mots en caractères **gras** sont définis à la page 153.

Médecin spécialiste en biochimie médicale

❯ en milieu hospitalier

mon travail

Le médecin biochimiste, c'est le spécialiste de la chimie de la matière vivante. «Nous étudions et analysons différents prélèvements humains (sang, urine, salive, larmes, etc.) pour y déceler des anomalies pouvant être associées à une maladie, explique Jean Dubé, médecin biochimiste à l'Hôpital Fleurimont du Centre hospitalier de l'Université de Sherbrooke (CHUS). Ces analyses déterminent, par exemple, le taux de sucre ou encore de cholestérol dans le sang. Les résultats aident les **médecins traitants** à établir le diagnostic et à ajuster le traitement des patients.»

Jean fait partie d'une équipe de six médecins biochimistes qui se partagent la supervision de plusieurs techniciens de laboratoire, lesquels exécutent les différents tests. Quand un résultat semble anormal, c'est à lui de vérifier, par exemple, si les instruments d'analyse fonctionnent bien et si le prélèvement a été fait dans les bonnes conditions. Jean enseigne également aux étudiants en médecine de l'Université de Sherbrooke.

Des milieux de travail potentiels

- ❯ Centres d'hébergement et de soins de longue durée
- ❯ Centres hospitaliers
- ❯ Centres locaux de services communautaires (CLSC)
- ❯ Cliniques privées

ma motivation

«J'ai toujours été passionné par la science médicale, la recherche et les personnes, raconte Jean. J'ai donc choisi la médecine tout simplement.» Il s'est ensuite dirigé vers la biochimie médicale pour des raisons de qualité de vie. «Je ne me voyais pas en médecin d'urgence. La biochimie me permet une carrière médicale de laboratoire, avec la possibilité de suivre des patients en clinique externe et d'être de garde à partir de mon domicile. Je peux ainsi vivre ma passion tout en me réservant du temps.» Seul sortant en biochimie médicale de son année, Jean a eu l'embarras du choix pour se trouver un emploi. «J'ai choisi ce poste à Sherbrooke parce qu'il se doublait d'un poste de professeur adjoint à la faculté de médecine de l'Université. Pour moi, c'était très important de pouvoir partager mes connaissances et de poursuivre des recherches. L'Université me donne accès à des locaux, à du matériel et à du personnel pour mes travaux.»

mon conseil

Pour devenir biochimiste médical, il faut être curieux de nature en plus d'aimer les sciences et le travail de laboratoire, qui implique beaucoup d'observation et d'analyse. «Il faut aussi être autonome dans ses études. Le programme de biochimie médicale est moins fréquenté, alors il y a moins de supervision et d'encadrement que dans d'autres programmes plus populaires. Il ne faut pas s'attendre à se faire tenir la main!» 08/03

mon parcours

Jean a fait un baccalauréat en biologie médicale à l'Université du Québec à Trois-Rivières (UQTR), suivi d'une maîtrise en sciences expérimentales à l'Institut national de la recherche scientifique (INRS). Ensuite, pendant cinq ans, il a mené de front un doctorat en médecine expérimentale (Ph. D.) et un doctorat en médecine (M.D.) à l'Université Laval. Après un an et demi de **résidence** en médecine interne, il a bifurqué vers une résidence en biochimie médicale (d'une durée de cinq ans), qu'il vient de terminer.

Les mots en caractères **gras** sont définis à la page 153.

Médecin spécialiste en cardiologie

> **en milieu hospitalier**

mon travail

«Je m'occupe du dépistage, du diagnostic, du traitement et de la prévention des maladies du cœur et des problèmes de circulation sanguine dans les vaisseaux. Les principales maladies que je traite sont les infarctus du myocarde, les artères sclérosées et rétrécies, l'**arythmie**, la **péricardite**, le **souffle au cœur**, etc.», explique Simon Kouz, spécialiste en cardiologie et chef de l'unité de cardiologie au Centre hospitalier régional de Lanaudière (CHRDL) à Joliette.

«Dans ma lutte contre les maladies du cœur, le bon vieux stéthoscope est mon principal outil de travail. Je fais aussi passer différents tests à mes patients, comme des examens biologiques (pour vérifier le **dosage des enzymes du muscle du cœur** par exemple), des **électrocardiogrammes**, une **coronographie**, etc., pour obtenir des renseignements sur leur état de santé. Puis j'analyse les résultats et pose un diagnostic. Je prescris des changements dans le mode de vie et les médicaments appropriés.»

Des milieux de travail potentiels

> Centres d'hébergement et de soins de longue durée
> Centres hospitaliers
> Centres locaux de services communautaires (CLSC)
> Cliniques privées

ma motivation

«J'ai choisi la médecine parce que j'aime les gens et que je veux les aider à mieux vivre. Je voulais une profession où les relations interpersonnelles occupent une bonne place. De plus, j'étais passionné par le corps humain et la biologie. Je voulais comprendre comment ça fonctionnait, relate Simon.

«J'ai choisi cette spécialité parce que j'aime les concepts clairs, la logique. Le principe de base de la cardiologie, ce n'est pas plus compliqué qu'une pompe et des tuyaux! J'ai toujours trouvé fascinant qu'une machine aussi complexe que le corps humain soit régie par quelque chose d'aussi simple.

«Dans cette discipline, il y a toujours de nouvelles découvertes, et il se fait d'ailleurs aujourd'hui beaucoup plus de prévention que d'opérations. Toute cette évolution fait en sorte que je suis perpétuellement en formation. Internet me permet d'apprendre beaucoup plus vite qu'auparavant, de voir des photos et de comprendre les nouveautés au fur et à mesure. J'ai le privilège de pouvoir aider mes patients grâce à mes connaissances, et en retour j'ai le devoir de tenir mes connaissances à jour pour pouvoir mieux les aider encore», confie Simon.

mon conseil

Un cardiologue se doit d'être en bonne santé : le travail est en effet si exigeant qu'on n'a pas le temps d'être malade! On doit donc avoir une excellente hygiène de vie pour aspirer à cette profession. De plus, il faut être capable de prendre des décisions rapidement, de garder son sang-froid et de bien réagir au stress. On doit également avoir des aptitudes pour le travail en équipe, car on travaille de concert avec d'autres professionnels de la santé. 09/03

mon parcours

Pour devenir médecin spécialiste en cardiologie, on doit d'abord obtenir un doctorat en médecine, puis effectuer sa **résidence** dans cette discipline. Il est possible ensuite de faire une surspécialité en cardiologie d'intervention, en cardiopathie congénitale, en recherche clinique, etc.

Les mots en caractères **gras** sont définis à la page 153.

Médecin spécialiste en chirurgie cardiovasculaire et thoracique
> en milieu hospitalier

mon travail

Un patient qui se présente à l'Institut de cardiologie de Montréal (ICM) n'a pas le cœur à rire. Louis Perrault, chirurgien cardiovasculaire et thoracique, le sait. «Le patient est déjà envoyé par un cardiologue. Le diagnostic est tombé, la chirurgie est souhaitable dans 95 % des cas. Je discute alors avec le patient des options, du déroulement de l'intervention, des bénéfices et des risques.»

Des milieux de travail potentiels

> Centres d'hébergement et de soins de longue durée

> Centres hospitaliers

> Centres locaux de services communautaires (CLSC)

> Cliniques privées

Louis figure parmi la quarantaine de chirurgiens cardiovasculaires et thoraciques québécois. Des chirurgies, il en fait 270 par année. Trois jours par semaine, il effectue des **pontages coronariens**, des **chirurgies valvulaires**, des greffes cardiaques et des interventions chirurgicales cardiaques pour corriger des problèmes congénitaux.

La chirurgie cardiovasculaire, dit-il, est parmi les disciplines les plus exigeantes sur le plan technique. «C'est une chirurgie microvasculaire. On utilise des loupes pour opérer des vaisseaux qui font aussi peu que 1 mm de diamètre interne. De plus, la clientèle est à haut risque (parce que gravement malade). Nous sommes comme des funambules...» En plus de la recherche fondamentale et appliquée qu'il effectue à l'ICM, Louis prend sous sa houlette les résidents en chirurgie cardiaque et les étudiants de maîtrise et de doctorat en pharmacologie de l'Université de Montréal.

ma motivation

«J'ai choisi la médecine par défi, confie Louis. C'était le parcours qui me semblait le plus difficile.» Puis, ç'a été un coup de cœur pour l'univers de la chirurgie. «Les chirurgiens sont des gens d'action, pragmatiques, qui aiment les résultats immédiats. Cela correspondait à mon tempérament.»

Un patient en attente d'une greffe cardiaque peut avoir moins d'un an à vivre, illustre le chirurgien. Or, quelques jours après la greffe, il peut faire de la bicyclette stationnaire, alors qu'avant, le moindre geste l'épuisait. «C'est spectaculaire! Les résultats sont instantanés, la gratification aussi.» Louis aime particulièrement la décharge d'adrénaline qui accompagne le geste chirurgical.

mon conseil

Bien connaître les implications du métier avant d'y plonger tête première est indispensable, selon Louis. «C'est une spécialité qui demande beaucoup psychologiquement et physiquement. On ne peut pas faire son travail en dilettante. Nos patients nous suivent toujours, même en vacances.»

mon parcours

Avant de travailler à l'ICM, Louis a traversé... 16 années d'études universitaires. À l'Université de Montréal, il a fait son doctorat de cinq ans en médecine, un même nombre d'années de **résidence** en chirurgie générale et trois ans de résidence en chirurgie cardiovasculaire et thoracique. Par la suite, il s'est expatrié en France, où il a fait un doctorat de trois ans en pharmacologie cellulaire et moléculaire à l'Université Louis-Pasteur de Strasbourg.

L'investissement en temps est également considérable : les résidents peuvent consacrer 100 heures par semaine au travail. Louis estime donc que pour réussir la formation, il faut nécessairement trouver sa gratification dans le geste opératoire lui-même. 05/03

Les mots en caractères **gras** sont définis à la page 153.

Médecin spécialiste en chirurgie générale

❯ **en milieu hospitalier et en clinique privée**

mon travail

Bistouri, scalpel sont des mots qui en font frémir plusieurs, mais pas Nancy Roy, chirurgienne générale.

Cette branche de la médecine ratisse large, confirme Nancy. Elle comprend la chirurgie de la tête, du cou, des tissus mous (comme la peau, la graisse et les muscles), des seins, des **glandes endocrines** (sauf l'**hypophyse**), du thorax, de l'abdomen et des vaisseaux sanguins. «La vaste majorité des chirurgiens se spécialisent», nuance-t-elle toutefois.

Nancy exerce en cabinet privé ainsi qu'au Centre hospitalier des Vallées de l'Outaouais, à Gatineau. «Je pratique les interventions chirurgicales du système digestif et du sein. Il s'agit autant de chirurgies majeures en bloc opératoire (pour des cas de cancer, par exemple), que mineures (comme l'ablation d'un kyste ou encore d'une tumeur bénigne).»

Ses autres tâches englobent les consultations, notamment auprès des patients de l'urgence, les **endoscopies** et les **colonoscopies** ainsi que les rencontres périodiques avec les patients qu'elle a opérés. Professeure à ses heures, elle enseigne également aux chirurgiens en herbe qui viennent faire leur stage à l'hôpital.

Des milieux de travail potentiels

❯ Centres d'hébergement et de soins de longue durée

❯ Centres hospitaliers

❯ Centres locaux de services communautaires (CLSC)

❯ Cliniques privées

ma motivation

Nancy a clairement le sentiment de jouer un rôle crucial. «Dernièrement, j'ai sauvé la vie d'une jeune femme de 28 ans aux prises avec la bactérie mangeuse de chair à l'abdomen. Alors qu'en théorie, ses chances de survie étaient presque nulles, l'opération chirurgicale lui a permis de s'en sortir et de repartir chez elle.»

La chirurgienne se dit également stimulée intellectuellement par sa profession, qu'elle qualifie de non routinière. «C'est toujours une surprise! Lorsqu'on est de garde, on peut être appelé d'urgence pour aller opérer un patient, donner un avis médical, assister un collègue, etc. Contrairement à d'autres disciplines très spécialisées, les cas sont plus complexes et plus variés.»

Présentement, un projet l'enthousiasme particulièrement : elle souhaite implanter dans sa région une clinique des maladies du sein.

mon conseil

Avant de choisir ce métier, il faut se demander si l'on est prêt à être dérangé en tout temps, concède Nancy. Week-ends, nuits, anniversaires, réveillons de Noël : rien n'est exclu. «Pour fonder une famille avec une carrière pareille, ça prend beaucoup d'organisation.»

mon parcours

Nancy a d'abord effectué un doctorat en médecine (un programme de cinq ans) à l'Université Laval. Son titre de médecin en poche, elle a fait ses cinq ans de **résidence** en chirurgie générale à la même université, avant d'être engagée comme chirurgienne générale au Centre hospitalier des Vallées de l'Outaouais.

Dans le feu de l'action, il faut aussi oser, souligne-t-elle. «Le mode d'emploi n'est pas toujours dans les manuels. On doit parfois inventer une nouvelle approche ou utiliser une technologie en émergence, comme la **laparoscopie**, qui n'existait pas encore quand j'étais aux études.» 05/03

Les mots en caractères **gras** sont définis à la page 153.

Médecin spécialiste en chirurgie orthopédique
> en milieu hospitalier

mon travail

Hugo Viens est chirurgien orthopédique au Centre hospitalier du Haut-Richelieu, à Saint-Jean-sur-Richelieu. Sa spécialité l'amène à diagnostiquer et à traiter les blessures et les atteintes du système musculo-squelettique dans son ensemble, c'est-à-dire les maladies, les traumatismes et les malformations des os – notamment la colonne vertébrale – des articulations, des ligaments, des muscles et des tendons.

«Les traumatismes musculo-squelettiques, comme les fractures, les entorses et les luxations, concernent le chirurgien orthopédique, explique Hugo. Je m'occupe donc du traitement médical de ces atteintes, et s'il y a lieu, du traitement chirurgical. Le deuxième grand domaine d'activité des orthopédistes concerne toutes les pathologies dégénératives, comme l'arthrose ou le vieillissement des articulations, ainsi que toutes les maladies infectieuses qui touchent les os et les articulations.»

Des milieux de travail potentiels

> Centres d'hébergement et de soins de longue durée
> Centres hospitaliers
> Centres locaux de services communautaires (CLSC)
> Cliniques privées

ma motivation

Après avoir obtenu son doctorat en médecine générale, Hugo a choisi de devenir chirurgien orthopédique par intérêt pour la **biomécanique**, et l'aspect manuel et concret de cette spécialité. «Quand on travaille en orthopédie, on a parfois l'impression d'être dans un garage automobile! On travaille avec des outils pneumatiques, des marteaux, des perceuses, des scies, mais aussi avec des microscopes et différents instruments de précision pour les techniques microchirurgicales.»

Hugo estime également que c'est un domaine où l'on peut avoir une relation très gratifiante avec ses patients. «L'impact sur la qualité de vie des gens est très important en orthopédie, explique-t-il. L'intervention articulaire de la hanche, qui est une chirurgie orthopédique, est l'intervention chirurgicale qui améliore le plus la santé des gens. Des personnes qui ne pouvaient plus marcher reviennent me voir pour me remercier de leur avoir donné une nouvelle vie. C'est très valorisant.»

mon conseil

«Je crois qu'il y a un ingénieur mécanique qui sommeille en chaque chirurgien orthopédique. La biomécanique requiert un intérêt pour le génie mécanique de façon générale, afin de bien comprendre le fonctionnement du corps humain», précise Hugo.

Il ajoute toutefois que cette spécialité implique un nombre d'heures de présence à l'hôpital qui est l'un des plus élevés de l'ensemble des spécialités médicales et chirurgicales. «Durant les gardes, on s'occupe des polytraumatisés et de toutes les pathologies de l'appareil musculo-squelettique. Ce sont des types de cas qui entrent continuellement aux urgences.» 07/03

mon parcours

Hugo a étudié trois ans en biologie à l'Université de Montréal. Son baccalauréat en poche, il s'est inscrit au doctorat en médecine générale à la même université, et a ensuite entamé sa **résidence** en orthopédie. Diplômé en mai 2003, il pratique depuis au Centre hospitalier du Haut-Richelieu.

Les mots en caractères **gras** sont définis à la page 153.

Médecin spécialiste en chirurgie plastique
› **en clinique privée**

mon travail

Ezat Hashim se dit d'abord médecin. «Mon rôle est d'améliorer la santé et la qualité de vie des personnes», dit-il. Mais au quotidien, ses interventions concernent surtout l'apparence des patients. «Je suis un sculpteur de corps. Mes principaux outils de travail sont mon sens artistique, mes connaissances médicales et ma minutie.»

Les patients qui le consultent à la Clinique de chirurgie plastique de Montréal le font principalement pour deux raisons. «Les uns veulent rétablir leur apparence à la suite d'un traumatisme, comme des brûlures ou encore l'ablation d'un sein.» Ces gens ont besoin d'une intervention en chirurgie plastique. «Les autres viennent plutôt par désir de modifier leur apparence, par exemple, pour refaire leurs seins, leur visage, leur nez, leurs mains, faire enlever une tache de naissance, des poches sous les yeux, etc.» On parle alors de chirurgie esthétique. Dans tous les cas, le médecin écoute, prend des photos, examine et détermine de quelle manière il peut aider la personne.

Des milieux de travail potentiels

› Centres d'hébergement et de soins de longue durée
› Centres hospitaliers
› Centres locaux de services communautaires (CLSC)
› Cliniques privées

ma motivation

«Jeune, j'aimais le dessin et les sciences, se souvient Dr Hashim. J'ai donc choisi la médecine pour le côté scientifique, et la chirurgie plastique pour le travail sur la beauté.» En plus de combiner ses deux passions, sa pratique lui permet aujourd'hui un contact privilégié avec les personnes.

«C'est un grand plaisir d'opérer un patient, de rétablir les proportions de son visage ou de son corps et de constater, après la guérison, la beauté retrouvée. Mes interventions changent la vie des gens. Elles les aident à s'accepter et à s'aimer davantage en leur procurant un corps qui correspond mieux à l'idée qu'ils s'en font.» Mais il lui arrive aussi de refuser de pratiquer certaines interventions. «Je ne veux pas créer des clowns. L'éthique que j'observe est celle de la beauté naturelle», souligne-t-il.

mon conseil

«Pour pratiquer la chirurgie plastique, il faut aimer les sciences parce qu'il faut d'abord devenir médecin, prévient-il. De plus, il faut aimer travailler minutieusement et délicatement, être patient et avoir un bon jugement.» Mais, puisque la discipline requiert aussi un bon sens artistique, le chirurgien insiste sur l'importance de développer ses connaissances en art, «par exemple en allant voir des expositions, en se tenant au courant des tendances, en fouillant l'histoire». 09/03

mon parcours

Ezat Hashim a effectué un baccalauréat en chimie/biochimie à l'Université McGill avant d'y faire son doctorat en médecine, puis une maîtrise en chirurgie expérimentale. Il a fait sa **résidence** en chirurgie plastique à l'Hôpital général de Montréal, à l'Hôpital Royal Victoria et à l'Hôpital de Montréal pour enfants avant d'entreprendre deux surspécialités en chirurgie esthétique en Ontario, l'une au Cosmetic Surgery Hospital à Woodbridge et l'autre au General Hospital à Scarborough. Il pratique à la Clinique de chirurgie plastique de Montréal depuis 2000.

Les mots en caractères **gras** sont définis à la page 153.

Médecin spécialiste en dermatologie
> en clinique privée et en milieu hospitalier

mon travail

Si, en revenant d'une escapade romantique en forêt, vous avez des cloches d'eau sur la peau accompagnées d'intenses démangeaisons, vous faites probablement une réaction allergique à l'herbe à puce. Comme ce jeune couple infortuné qui a consulté le dermatologue Pierre Ricard, vous devrez subir un traitement à la calamine ou à la cortisone pour guérir cette «dermite par contact vénéneuse». Pierre soigne des personnes de tout âge qui ont des maladies de peau, reliées ou non à l'esthétique : acné, rosacée, eczéma ou perte de cheveux, par exemple. Il précise que les dermatologues (ou dermatologistes) peuvent également soigner des maladies transmises sexuellement, comme la syphilis ou l'herpès, ainsi que les manifestations externes de maladies internes, comme les éruptions cutanées chez les personnes leucémiques. Ces médecins spécialistes sont aussi habilités à enlever les verrues, les poils, la couperose, les rides et les taches de vin à l'aide du laser, «un bistouri sans saignement qui pourra peut-être un jour traiter l'acné». Président de l'Association des dermatologistes du Québec depuis 1976, Pierre souligne également le rôle que jouent les membres de sa profession dans la prévention du cancer de la peau. C'est grâce à eux si, aujourd'hui, la population est sensibilisée aux effets néfastes de l'exposition au soleil.

ma motivation

L'aspect psychologique occupe une place importante dans le travail du dermatologue, souligne le spécialiste. «Souvent, les gens ont une perception négative d'eux-mêmes», observe-t-il. Réconforter, rassurer et faire preuve d'entregent vont donc de pair avec la pratique. Une dame de 87 ans a un très léger cancer sur la joue? Il vaut sans doute mieux ne pas prononcer devant elle le mot tant redouté si elle semble inquiète de nature. En plus du contact humain, il apprécie de pouvoir déterminer ce dont souffre une personne. «C'est constructif. Par exemple, si vous voyez un **mélanome** chez quelqu'un, vous venez peut-être de lui sauver la vie.» Quand le diagnostic ne vient pas tout de suite, il consulte des livres spécialisés ou demande conseil à l'un des deux confrères avec qui il partage son cabinet.

mon conseil

Pierre déplore avoir souvent vu des gens atterrir en douleur dans son bureau parce qu'on leur avait prescrit ailleurs un médicament inefficace. D'où l'importance de bien écouter les patients. Si un adolescent fait de l'acné, par exemple, son dermatologue doit savoir si d'autres membres de sa famille en font aussi. «Écouter permet d'établir l'histoire personnelle du patient et de sa maladie, afin de lui proposer un traitement approprié.» 07/03

mon parcours

Après sa formation classique, Pierre a entrepris un doctorat en médecine suivi d'une **résidence** de cinq ans en dermatologie, à l'Université de Montréal. Lui qui aspirait initialement à devenir gynécologue (comme son père) s'est aperçu en cours d'études que très peu de médecins savaient traiter les maladies de peau. C'était en 1965, et il n'y avait que 60 dermatologues au Québec. Intrigué par cette spécialité, il a décidé d'y plonger. Une décision qui ne semble pas lui avoir donné d'urticaire!

Les mots en caractères **gras** sont définis à la page 153.

Médecin spécialiste en endocrinologie
> en milieu hospitalier

mon travail

«L'endocrinologie est la science médicale qui étudie les glandes endocrines. Ces glandes fabriquent les hormones qui se déversent dans le sang avant d'atteindre leurs tissus cibles. Parmi les glandes les plus connues, notons la thyroïde, les parathyroïdes, le pancréas, les testicules, les ovaires, les surrénales et l'hypophyse», explique Fernand Labrie, médecin spécialiste en endocrinologie, directeur du Centre de recherche du Centre hospitalier de l'Université Laval.

Des milieux de travail potentiels

> Centres d'hébergement et de soins de longue durée
> Centres hospitaliers
> Centres locaux de services communautaires (CLSC)
> Cliniques privées

«Les glandes endocrines produisent des hormones comme l'hormone de croissance, la testostérone et l'**estradiol**, pour parler des plus connues. Il arrive que ces glandes se dérèglent, amenant ainsi une déficience ou une augmentation de la fabrication des hormones. L'endocrinologue étudie ces dérèglements en procédant à des analyses sanguines afin de connaître les paramètres biologiques du patient et d'établir le traitement hormonal approprié. Les maladies les plus connues reliées au dérèglement hormonal sont le diabète, l'hypothyroïdie, l'ostéoporose, l'infertilité, etc.

«Mon travail de chercheur me permet de concentrer ma pratique professionnelle sur la recherche en laboratoire, alors que mon travail de directeur m'astreint à diverses tâches administratives incontournables pour assurer le succès de la recherche», ajoute Fernand.

ma motivation

«J'ai toujours été intéressé par les sciences. La chimie, la biochimie et les mathématiques étaient mes matières favorites. La médecine m'apparaissait être la meilleure avenue pour travailler dans un milieu scientifique tout en apportant une contribution au soulagement de la souffrance humaine, spécialement le cancer qui est le plus grand fléau», explique le médecin.

mon conseil

«L'endocrinologie est une discipline scientifique qui requiert plusieurs qualités. Ainsi, une bonne dose de curiosité est nécessaire; il faut également se montrer tenace pour se reposer sans cesse les mêmes questions et refaire les mêmes analyses pour s'assurer que tout est aussi parfait que possible; on doit également avoir le goût d'apprendre et remettre les choses en question pour aller au-delà des connaissances actuelles», déclare Fernand. 09/03

mon parcours

Fernand a obtenu son doctorat en médecine à l'Université Laval, puis a poursuivi ses études de spécialisation en endocrinologie. Il a ensuite effectué des études postdoctorales au Département de biochimie de l'Université de Cambridge, puis à l'Université du Sussex et enfin au Laboratoire de biologie moléculaire de Cambridge, en Grande-Bretagne. Il a fondé le Laboratoire d'endocrinologie moléculaire qui est devenu le Centre de recherche en endocrinologie moléculaire et oncologique (CREMO) de l'Université Laval. Ses recherches ont, entre autres, permis la découverte de la castration chimique et du traitement hormonal combiné, utilisés dans le monde entier comme traitements standards du cancer de la prostate.

Les mots en caractères **gras** sont définis à la page 153.

Médecin spécialiste
en gastro-entérologie
> **en milieu hospitalier**

mon travail

Un médecin spécialiste en gastro-entérologie se consacre aux problèmes du tube digestif et de ses glandes annexes, c'est-à-dire le foie, la vésicule biliaire et le pancréas. Chef du service de gastro-entérologie au Centre hospitalier de l'Université de Laval (CHUL) à Québec, Pierre Gagnon explique la particularité de sa pratique.

«En gastro-entérologie, l'un des outils de diagnostic est l'endoscope. C'est un appareil vidéo qu'on introduit par la bouche ou le rectum, et qui permet d'aller voir l'intérieur du tube digestif. Lors de la réalisation de l'endoscopie, on peut également, avec des instruments adaptés à cette technique guidée par vidéo, poser des gestes thérapeutiques, comme enlever des polypes intestinaux. Ceci évite une chirurgie au patient.»

Pierre est responsable de l'admission des patients au service de gastro-entérologie du CHUL, mais il est également sollicité pour son expertise dans les autres services, notamment aux urgences.

ma motivation

C'est après avoir effectué un stage en gastro-entérologie lors de sa formation en médecine générale que Pierre a décidé de choisir cette spécialité. «La gastro-entérologie n'est pas une pratique routinière. Il y a le côté analytique quand on est en consultation avec les patients, et il y a le côté technique lorsqu'on fait des endoscopies.»

Pierre a un intérêt tout particulier pour les problématiques causant des symptômes – douleurs abdominales, diarrhées, constipations, mauvaise digestion, par exemple – qui ne sont pas reliés à une maladie organique, mais aux émotions et au stress.

«Cela concerne de 50 à 60 % des patients reçus en clinique externe, précise-t-il. Il faut être capable de les prendre en charge et de les aider à bien canaliser leur énergie, non pas vers la douleur, mais vers ce qui génère la douleur, c'est-à-dire la sphère psychologique ou émotionnelle.»

mon conseil

«À mon avis, la chose la plus importante est d'aimer le contact avec les patients et d'être à l'aise avec les malades, affirme Pierre. J'ai compris récemment que pour être un bon gastro-entérologue, il faut savoir apprivoiser sa propre souffrance. Si on la connaît, si on la comprend et qu'on l'accepte, cela crée une ouverture qui nous permet d'être réceptif à la souffrance du patient, une souffrance psychique qui se somatise dans le tube digestif.» 05/03

mon parcours

Pierre a obtenu son doctorat en médecine à l'Université Laval. Il a ensuite effectué sa **résidence** en gastro-entérologie à l'Université McGill. Diplômé en 1988, il pratiquera un an au Centre hospitalier de l'Université Laval à Québec, avant de se perfectionner un an en France en endoscopie thérapeutique à l'hôpital Édouard-Hériot, à Lyon. Pierre est gastro-entérologue au CHUL depuis 1990.

Les mots en caractères **gras** sont définis à la page 153.

Médecin spécialiste en génétique clinique
> en milieu hospitalier

mon travail

«Je suis responsable de la recherche et du dépistage des maladies des nouveau-nés pour tout le Québec. J'effectue des recherches sur l'hérédité – le bagage génétique qui nous vient de nos parents – et sur la **composition génétique**», explique Claude Laberge, médecin spécialiste en pédiatrie et génétique médicale, chef du laboratoire de génétique au Centre hospitalier de l'Université Laval (CHUL) et professeur de médecine pédiatrique à l'Université Laval.

«Je reçois des prélèvements sanguins de tous les bébés qui naissent au Québec, soit autour de 75 000 par année. Le laboratoire est entièrement automatisé. Je surveille les tests, les analyses et je commande de nouveaux prélèvements si besoin est. Finalement, j'envoie les résultats d'analyse aux médecins traitants et je leur explique les cas problèmes quand il y en a. Je peux également faire des tests sur des fœtus. Cela permet de savoir si l'enfant à naître sera en bonne santé ou s'il risque de développer une maladie héréditaire.»

Des milieux de travail potentiels

> Centres d'hébergement et de soins de longue durée
> Centres hospitaliers
> Centres locaux de services communautaires (CLSC)
> Cliniques privées

ma motivation

Issu d'une longue tradition familiale (son père, son grand-père et l'un de ses oncles étaient médecins), Claude a grandi au milieu de discussions à caractère médical. «Quand j'ai choisi la pédiatrie, la **génétique** en était encore à ses premiers balbutiements. J'avais un vif intérêt pour ces nouvelles applications de la science au service des populations. J'avais envie de contribuer à cet essor. Les deux spécialités combinées me permettaient d'aider à la fois les enfants et les parents.

«Pour moi, il était primordial de rendre accessibles les nouvelles connaissances par l'entremise des soins médicaux à l'ensemble de la population québécoise. En ce sens, le laboratoire du Centre de recherche du CHUL joue un rôle essentiel, car il permet d'avoir une vue d'ensemble. C'est très gratifiant de pouvoir aider des gens frappés par la maladie et de trouver des pistes d'explication et de solutions là où il n'y en avait pas auparavant», précise Claude.

mon conseil

«Pour devenir généticien, il faut être passionné de biologie, s'intéresser à l'humain et à la santé des populations. On doit aimer se poser des questions et chercher des réponses, effectuer des tests, des expérimentations et même des investigations. Il faut être prêt à apprendre toute sa vie, ne pas avoir peur du changement, ni de remettre en question des vérités établies. Même s'il faut savoir respecter l'autorité, il faut aussi avoir une tête de cochon!» s'exclame Claude en riant. Car ce scientifique visionnaire, qui n'a pas souvent été premier de classe, dit devoir sa réussite à sa persévérance. 09/03

mon parcours

Claude a obtenu son doctorat en médecine à l'Université Laval. Il a fait sa **résidence** en pédiatrie à l'Université de Toronto et sa résidence au Hospital for Sick Children. C'est au Sir Johns Hopkins Medical Institutions de Baltimore au Maryland qu'il a terminé sa surspécialité en génétique. Il a fait sa résidence au Johns Hopkins Hospital. Après ses études, il a participé à la création du laboratoire du Centre de recherche du CHUL qu'il dirige actuellement.

| Les mots en caractères **gras** sont définis à la page 153.

Médecin spécialiste (résidente) en gériatrie

> ❯ en milieu hospitalier

mon travail

Au Département de gériatrie du Centre hospitalier de l'Université Laval (CHUL), on retrouve des personnes âgées souffrant de problèmes de santé multiples (fractures, pneumonie, troubles cognitifs, insuffisance rénale, etc.) et dont l'autonomie est diminuée. «Mon but est de traiter physiquement les patients, mais aussi d'améliorer leur qualité de vie lors de leur retour à la maison», explique Mélanie Hains, médecin **résidente** en gériatrie.

Pour chaque cas, Mélanie évalue, outre les problèmes de santé, les antécédents médicaux, la prise de médicaments et le milieu de vie. Par exemple, le patient vit-il seul ou en couple? Dans son propre logement ou en centre d'hébergement? Elle pose ensuite son diagnostic, duquel découle un plan de traitement. Puis, avec l'aide de la famille et d'une équipe multidisciplinaire, composée notamment d'une **ergothérapeute**, d'une nutritionniste et d'une travailleuse sociale, Mélanie évalue les moyens d'assurer la sécurité et la stabilité du patient une fois qu'il aura quitté l'hôpital. Aide à domicile ou séjour dans une résidence pour personnes âgées font partie des solutions envisageables.

ma motivation

«J'aime traiter les personnes âgées, car elles sont attachantes, confie Mélanie. Elles possèdent une grande expérience de vie, et c'est toujours enrichissant d'échanger avec elles.»

Encore récente, la gériatrie compte peu de praticiens. Mais avec le vieillissement de la population, les besoins augmentent, et les recherches vont bon train. «C'est une spécialisation où les découvertes futures sont prometteuses, et c'est très stimulant», souligne Mélanie, en évoquant notamment les percées dans le domaine des troubles cognitifs.

Sa résidence terminée, Mélanie souhaite demeurer dans le milieu hospitalier, où le travail d'équipe fait partie du quotidien. «Je ne pourrais pas travailler en solitaire, j'ai besoin du contact avec les gens. À l'hôpital, je suis en constante interaction avec les malades et leur famille, mais aussi avec mon équipe. L'expertise de chacun permet de mieux traiter les patients.»

mon conseil

Selon Mélanie, un jeune qui se destine à la gériatrie doit avoir la vocation. «Les études sont longues et difficiles. Il faut s'investir au maximum. L'amour du métier permet de passer au travers plus facilement.»

Cette spécialité demande aussi un intérêt pour le contact humain. «Il est important d'être à l'écoute des malades et de leur famille. Cela permet de faire une évaluation pertinente de l'état du patient et de mieux orienter le plan de traitement.» 08/03

mon parcours

Diplômée d'un doctorat en médecine de l'Université Laval, Mélanie effectue présentement sa cinquième et avant-dernière année de **résidence** en gériatrie, sous la supervision du même établissement.

Les mots en caractères **gras** sont définis à la page 153.

Médecin spécialiste (résident) en hématologie

> **en milieu hospitalier**

mon travail

Jean-Sébastien Delisle est un spécialiste des maladies du sang, qu'elles soient bénignes comme l'**anémie**, ou malignes comme la **leucémie**.

L'hématologue voit au diagnostic, au traitement et à la prévention des maladies du sang et des organes où se forment les **globules sanguins**. Il examine les patients, fait passer des tests et des analyses, interprète les résultats et prescrit les traitements appropriés.

«Mais un hématologue ne fait pas que voir des patients, nuance Jean-Sébastien. Au Québec, nous sommes aussi des médecins de laboratoire. Les hématologues sont donc responsables des banques de sang dans les centres hospitaliers, et de la qualité et de l'interprétation des analyses effectuées au laboratoire d'hématologie de l'hôpital.»

En tant que résident, Jean-Sébastien a un statut d'apprenti. «J'exerce mon métier sous supervision, précise-t-il. Je peux rencontrer seul des patients, mais tous les cas sont ensuite discutés avec les professionnels.»

Des milieux de travail potentiels

> Centres d'hébergement et de soins de longue durée
> Centres hospitaliers
> Centres locaux de services communautaires (CLSC)
> Cliniques privées

ma motivation

Jean-Sébastien a opté pour la médecine, car elle lui permet de combiner une foule de matières qui le passionnent : les sciences fondamentales comme la biologie, et les sciences humaines comme la psychologie et la sociologie.

«Nous avons un contact humain très intense avec les patients puisque plusieurs subissent des traitements de chimiothérapie. C'est un lien difficile parfois, mais très enrichissant sur le plan humain. On aide les gens même lorsque les situations paraissent désespérées et ils nous en sont très reconnaissants», ajoute-t-il.

mon conseil

«Dans cette spécialité, il faut s'attendre à rencontrer des personnes qui souffrent de cancer, avec toute la charge émotive que cela implique. Certains médecins sont capables d'y faire face, d'autres trouvent ça difficile.» Jean-Sébastien estime qu'il faut avoir une bonne dose d'empathie et de compassion.

De plus, il conseille de s'impliquer dans le travail au laboratoire le plus tôt possible. «Je suggère de faire des stages de recherche en hématologie ou en oncologie, ou encore du travail de laboratoire pour voir rapidement si on aime le labo, car cela fait aussi partie de nos tâches.» 05/03

mon parcours

Jean-Sébastien a obtenu son doctorat en médecine à l'Université McGill, puis il a entrepris sa **résidence** en hématologie. Beaucoup d'hématologues se spécialisent ensuite en oncologie en prolongeant leur formation d'une autre année dans ce domaine, mais Jean-Sébastien envisage plutôt d'opter pour la recherche sur le cancer du sang.

Les mots en caractères **gras** sont définis à la page 153.

Médecin spécialiste en médecine d'urgence
> **en milieu hospitalier**

mon travail

À l'urgence spécialisée de l'Institut de cardiologie de Montréal s'affaire une équipe composée d'infirmières, de préposés aux bénéficiaires, de brancardiers et de techniciens en électrocardiogramme. Leur rôle? Recevoir les patients souffrant de problèmes cardiaques, par exemple d'arythmie, d'insuffisance cardiaque ou encore ayant fait un infarctus.

À la tête de cette équipe, Alain Vadeboncœur s'assure de poser le bon diagnostic et de prescrire les traitements appropriés. «En fait, je prends le patient en charge pour un court segment de son histoire. Tout d'abord, j'évalue son état et, s'il y a lieu, on le réanime à l'aide de médicaments, en utilisant des défibrillateurs ou des solutés. Ensuite, je l'examine, je lui pose des questions et je livre mon diagnostic. Je prescris alors des examens afin de confirmer ou d'infirmer le diagnostic. Finalement, je demande l'hospitalisation du patient ou je lui donne son congé. Si le cas est trop complexe, je fais appel à l'expertise d'autres spécialistes, comme des cardiologues. Ensemble, nous allons discuter de l'état du patient et trouver une marche à suivre», expose Alain.

Des milieux de travail potentiels

> Centres d'hébergement et de soins de longue durée
> Centres hospitaliers
> Centres locaux de services communautaires (CLSC)
> Cliniques privées

ma motivation

Alain adore l'atmosphère de l'urgence. «C'est très intense. On touche aux choses de base : la vie, la mort, la douleur. On ne connaît pas la routine et on ne sait jamais ce qui peut arriver dans les prochaines minutes. J'apprécie aussi la relation de camaraderie qui s'installe entre les membres du personnel», raconte Alain.

Pouvoir aider les patients est également une grande motivation. «Je me sens privilégié d'être présent pour eux à un moment aussi crucial. Il est alors facile d'établir un contact qui est bref, certes, mais très fort parce que les gens sont vulnérables.»

mon conseil

Selon Alain, la médecine d'urgence demande des qualités spécifiques. «Il faut aimer être mis en situation de déséquilibre, avoir la capacité de réagir rapidement et de façon cohérente dans des moments de stress important. On doit posséder une certaine force de caractère et beaucoup d'aplomb, afin d'être stimulé par l'urgence plutôt que de paniquer. C'est une profession particulière qu'on peut aimer ou non. Je conseille donc à l'étudiant qui songe à choisir cette spécialisation de passer une journée avec un médecin d'urgence. Il saura alors si cette voie lui convient.»
05/03

mon parcours

Titulaire d'un doctorat en médecine de l'Université de Montréal, Alain a fait sa **résidence** en médecine d'urgence. Il a ensuite œuvré à Urgences Santé, puis au Centre hospitalier Pierre-Boucher où il a occupé également le poste de chef du département de médecine d'urgence. Aujourd'hui, il travaille pour l'Institut de cardiologie de Montréal où il est à la fois spécialiste de médecine d'urgence, coordonnateur de l'urgence et chercheur en médecine préhospitalière et de cardiologie. Il est aussi chargé de formation clinique à l'Université de Montréal.

Les mots en caractères **gras** sont définis à la page 153.

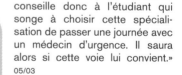

Médecin spécialiste (résident) en médecine interne

❯ en milieu hospitalier

mon travail

«L'interniste, ou le spécialiste de la **médecine interne**, traite uniquement une clientèle adulte», affirme d'emblée Stéphane P. Ahern, **résident** en médecine interne à l'Hôpital Maisonneuve-Rosemont de Montréal.

Il ajoute que la médecine interne s'intéresse aux maladies débordant du champ d'action restreint des autres spécialités. Par exemple, lorsqu'une pneumonie s'aggrave, le patient peut voir sa tension artérielle diminuer, et développer des complications cardiaques, rénales, cérébrales ou hépatiques (au foie). L'interniste, qui connaît bien les différents systèmes et leur interaction, est alors appelé en renfort. On fait également appel à lui en cas de maladies rares ou inusitées.

Les internistes sont des spécialistes polyvalents, soutient Stéphane. «Toutefois, dans les grandes villes, on les voit se spécialiser. Par exemple, certains pratiquent uniquement aux soins intensifs.» Pour l'instant, puisqu'il est toujours résident, Stéphane touche à tout. Selon son horaire, il fait des consultations à l'urgence, auprès des patients hospitalisés, à la clinique externe ou encore aux soins intensifs.

Des milieux de travail potentiels

❯ Centres d'hébergement et de soins de longue durée

❯ Centres hospitaliers

❯ Centres locaux de services communautaires (CLSC)

❯ Cliniques privées

ma motivation

Dans sa profession, Stéphane estime qu'il a le privilège d'entrer en relation avec l'autre d'une façon toute particulière. «Vous ne connaissez pas quelqu'un et vous avez une mauvaise nouvelle à lui annoncer. Vous pénétrez dans sa vie privée aux endroits les plus intimes.» Les relations humaines, dans ce contexte, sont très intenses, dit-il.

Stéphane envisage de se spécialiser en soins intensifs, car il aime travailler avec les patients très malades et gérer les situations critiques. «Ce qui me passionne en médecine interne, et particulièrement en soins intensifs, c'est cette obligation du diagnostic précis, complet, bien structuré, mais rapide. Nous sommes comme Sherlock Holmes. On cherche ce que tout le monde a oublié : un détail, un signe clinique, une erreur... C'est un travail très intellectuel.»

mon conseil

Pour Stéphane, seuls les étudiants qui sentent vibrer en eux une passion pour l'être humain devraient cheminer en médecine. «Il faut être à l'affût de la personne qui est devant nous et profiter de ce moment singulier qui nous est offert.»

Comme interniste, ajoute-t-il, il faut vouloir travailler avec une clientèle adulte, aimer les cas complexes, avoir le souci du détail et une bonne dose de curiosité scientifique. 06/03

mon parcours

Titulaire d'un baccalauréat ès arts multidisciplinaire et d'une maîtrise ès arts en philosophie, Stéphane a été reçu en médecine à l'Université de Sherbrooke. En plus de son doctorat en médecine (M.D.), il possède un doctorat (Ph. D.) en sciences cliniques. Il en est présentement à sa troisième année de **résidence** dans le programme conjoint de médecine interne et de soins intensifs de l'Université de Montréal, dont la durée est de cinq ans. Jusqu'à présent, l'Hôpital Saint-Luc du Centre hospitalier de l'Université de Montréal (CHUM) et l'Hôpital Maisonneuve-Rosemont l'ont pris sous leur aile.

Les mots en caractères **gras** sont définis à la page 153.

Médecin spécialiste en médecine nucléaire

> **en milieu hospitalier**

mon travail

Au département d'imagerie médicale du Centre hospitalier régional de Lanaudière, l'équipe d'Hélène Bernier, composée de technologues et de médecins spécialisés en médecine nucléaire, s'occupe de recevoir les patients devant passer une **scintigraphie**. Permettant de détecter une embolie pulmonaire, un infarctus, ou encore une fracture, l'examen consiste à injecter au malade un produit radioactif par voie buccale ou intraveineuse afin d'observer le fonctionnement de l'organe atteint.

Une fois que le technologue a fait passer la scintigraphie au patient, Hélène reçoit les résultats de l'examen et pose son diagnostic. Pour les cas particuliers qui demandent, par exemple, l'injection d'un médicament afin d'exercer une stimulation cardiaque ou contracter la vésicule biliaire, Hélène procède elle-même à l'examen.

De plus, elle traite par la médecine nucléaire les personnes dont la glande thyroïde est atteinte (traitement par **radio-isotopes**). Pour ce faire, Hélène leur fait passer différents tests, détermine la dose nécessaire de radio-isotopes que le patient prendra ensuite sous forme de médicament.

Des milieux de travail potentiels

> Centres d'hébergement et de soins de longue durée
> Centres hospitaliers
> Centres locaux de services communautaires (CLSC)
> Cliniques privées

ma motivation

Hélène adore le contact avec les patients. «C'est valorisant de pouvoir les aider. Souvent, ce sont des personnes qui traînent un problème depuis longtemps, et la médecine nucléaire permet de poser un diagnostic précis. Par la même occasion, j'aide aussi leur médecin à mieux orienter son traitement.» Le travail en équipe est également une source de motivation. «Il est agréable de pouvoir échanger avec les autres médecins et les technologues, et de mettre en commun nos connaissances et nos compétences respectives pour parvenir à un résultat.»

Encore toute récente, la médecine nucléaire a fait son apparition dans les années 1970. «C'est une spécialisation où les percées technologiques sont constantes. Je ne procède pas aujourd'hui de la même façon qu'il y a cinq ans, et cela sera encore différent dans cinq autres années. C'est passionnant d'assister à cette évolution et de maintenir ses connaissances à jour.»

mon conseil

«Pour exercer cette profession, il faut avoir la vocation et faire preuve d'une grande détermination, souligne Hélène. N'entre pas qui veut dans les facultés de médecine, et la formation est longue et ardue. À titre d'exemple, un résident va passer en moyenne 75 heures par semaine dans les hôpitaux. Il faut de plus posséder d'excellentes aptitudes scientifiques et avoir un esprit logique sans faille pour réussir aux examens. Et les études ne sont jamais terminées! Un médecin est en constant apprentissage et se doit d'être à l'affût des dernières nouveautés médicales.» 06/03

mon parcours

Titulaire d'un doctorat en médecine de l'Université de Montréal, Hélène a fait sa **résidence** en médecine nucléaire dans le même établissement. Elle a ensuite décroché son emploi au Centre hospitalier régional de Lanaudière où elle occupe également le poste de chef de service en médecine nucléaire.

Les mots en caractères **gras** sont définis à la page 153.

Médecin spécialiste en microbiologie médicale et infectiologie
> en milieu hospitalier

mon travail

«La microbiologie médicale a pour objet d'étude les principales infections humaines et les micro-organismes qui en sont responsables (bactéries, virus, champignons ou parasites). Les grands sujets sont les flores humaines normales, les méthodes de contrôle des micro-organismes, les antibiotiques et les interactions entre l'humain et les micro-organismes», explique Jean Robert, médecin spécialiste en microbiologie-infectiologie et en santé communautaire à l'Hôtel-Dieu de Saint-Jérôme.

«Lorsque je suis responsable du laboratoire, je supervise le travail des techniciens médicaux qui procèdent aux différents tests, par exemple, les **cultures bactériennes** (par lesquelles on peut déterminer la nature d'une infection). Je signe tous les résultats qui sortent du laboratoire, je les explique aux médecins traitants en plus de recommander et de prescrire des antibiotiques et des traitements. Je reçois aussi des patients pour lesquels je fais le suivi médical jusqu'à la guérison ou jusqu'au contrôle de la maladie.»

Des milieux de travail potentiels

> Centres d'hébergement et de soins de longue durée
> Centres hospitaliers
> Centres locaux de services communautaires (CLSC)
> Cliniques privées

ma motivation

Alors qu'il était résident en pneumologie à l'Hôpital Saint-Luc de Montréal, Jean a côtoyé un jeune médecin microbiologiste dont la passion était communicative. «Ça m'a incité à faire six mois de spécialité en microbiologie, juste pour voir, et j'ai finalement décidé de poursuivre dans cette voie. Ce qui a motivé chacune des décisions que j'ai eu à prendre, ce sont les gens que j'ai rencontrés, poursuit-il. Je me suis laissé guider par mon ouverture d'esprit et ma curiosité. J'ai voulu contribuer à quelque chose de plus grand qu'une carrière, je crois. Ma passion, c'est la vie, celle des gens qui m'entourent, celle de mes patients, celles que je peux sauver, améliorer, aider... Ce sont ces vies qui donnent un sens à la mienne.»

mon conseil

«Il faut une grande ouverture aux autres pour devenir médecin dans toute la noblesse du terme, ce qui exige dévouement, écoute et besoin de donner, affirme Jean. Pour devenir médecin microbiologiste, il importe aussi d'être curieux de la vie et de la science. Il faut sortir de son milieu, s'ouvrir sur le monde et ne pas juger : les maladies que je vois tous les jours portent des noms comme vaginite, herpès, sida. Les patients qui en sont atteints sont d'abord des personnes et ont besoin de réconfort et de traitement.» 09/03

mon parcours

Jean a obtenu son doctorat en médecine à l'Université de Montréal. Puis, il a voyagé, entre autres en Amazonie, pour se familiariser avec la médecine tropicale, et il a fréquenté les instituts Pasteur et Armand-Frappier à titre d'étudiant-chercheur. Il a ensuite fait sa **résidence** en microbiologie après un bref séjour en pneumologie. Il est devenu chef du Département de santé communautaire de l'Hôpital Saint-Luc de Montréal, avant de se joindre à l'Hôtel-Dieu de Saint-Jérôme pour y ouvrir le Service de microbiologie.

Les mots en caractères **gras** sont définis à la page 153.

Médecin spécialiste (résident) en néphrologie
❯ en milieu hospitalier

mon travail

Paul Ayoub a opté pour la néphrologie. Cette spécialité de la médecine s'intéresse aux maladies rénales. «Le rein est l'organe du corps qui a pour fonction de maintenir l'**homéostasie sanguine**. Il agit en fait comme un filtre qui nettoie le sang, c'est-à-dire qu'il le purifie des déchets accumulés par le corps. Il agit aussi comme gestionnaire de l'eau et des **électrolytes corporels** (sodium, potassium...), ainsi que comme producteur d'hormones qui régulent la composition sanguine», explique-t-il.

Le rôle du néphrologue, précise Paul, est d'une part de comprendre et de traiter les maladies qui affectent le rein, et d'autre part «d'aider» le rein lorsque celui-ci ne fonctionne plus, par la médication, la **dialyse** ou la transplantation.

Des milieux de travail potentiels

❯ Centres d'hébergement et de soins de longue durée
❯ Centres hospitaliers
❯ Centres locaux de services communautaires (CLSC)
❯ Cliniques privées

ma motivation

«La néphrologie est une spécialité passionnante, mais également très rigoureuse et exigeante. Elle demande des connaissances médicales approfondies et est souvent jugée par nos confrères comme l'une des spécialités les plus complexes du monde médical», note Paul.

Selon lui, l'intérêt de la néphrologie réside dans sa pratique diversifiée et dynamique. En effet, on trouve ce spécialiste dans tout un éventail de cas : urgences médicales, soins intensifs, intoxications sévères (aux médicaments, aux drogues, etc.), **hémodialyses**, **dialyses péritonéales**, greffes rénales, **recherche fondamentale**, éthique médicale, néphrologie pédiatrique, etc.

«Les cas sont souvent complexes, car les patients ont généralement beaucoup d'antécédents médicaux et sont très malades. Par conséquent, c'est stimulant intellectuellement, mais cela peut être aussi fort exigeant.»

mon conseil

Selon Paul, plusieurs qualités sont essentielles pour apprécier pleinement la pratique en néphrologie. «En particulier, il faut savoir adopter une approche humaine avec les patients, tout en sachant gérer les situations d'urgence.

«Être à l'aise dans le travail d'équipe et avoir une approche multidisciplinaire sont également indispensables. En effet, le néphrologue doit travailler de pair avec les autres spécialistes, car la plupart des maladies affectent également les reins. Enfin, on doit être passionné de matières fondamentales comme la pharmacologie, la **biologie moléculaire** et la chimie.» 07/03

mon parcours

Après avoir obtenu son diplôme d'études collégiales (DEC) en sciences pures au Collège François-Xavier-Garneau à Québec, Paul a décroché son doctorat en médecine générale à l'Université Laval en 1999. Il termine actuellement sa **résidence** en néphrologie au Centre hospitalier universitaire de Montréal (CHUM), affilié à l'Université de Montréal.

Les mots en caractères **gras** sont définis à la page 153.

Médecin spécialiste en neurochirurgie
❯ en milieu hospitalier

mon travail

Le neurochirurgien Alain Roux est spécialiste du système nerveux. À l'Hôpital Charles-LeMoyne de Longueuil (arrondissement de Greenfield Park), il pratique des opérations au cerveau et à la colonne vertébrale. «J'interviens notamment dans les cas de tumeurs au cerveau, de **ruptures d'anévrisme**, de hernies discales ou d'autres pathologies de la colonne.»

Quand Alain reçoit un patient, il l'examine et décide s'il est préférable d'opter pour un traitement médical sous **pharmacopée** ou pour un traitement chirurgical. Quand une opération se révèle nécessaire, il la pratique et procède au suivi postopératoire pendant quelques mois.

ma motivation

«J'aime traiter les cas lourds! confie le spécialiste. Mon degré de motivation augmente avec la complexité du problème. Parfois, je dois opérer une tumeur dont le diamètre n'est que de quelques millimètres, c'est extrêmement délicat.

«La science regorge d'enseignements, souligne-t-il, mais encore faut-il savoir les mettre en pratique. C'est là toute la difficulté : décider s'il est plus indiqué d'opérer ou non. On a beau avoir appris la théorie par cœur, si l'on n'a pas de jugement clinique, cela ne sert à rien. Je m'efforce de toujours agir dans le meilleur intérêt du patient, c'est un défi perpétuel.»

Pour Alain, avoir le sentiment qu'il vient en aide aux patients est le plus puissant des moteurs. «Je sens vraiment que je rends service. Quand je constate qu'un patient que j'ai opéré évolue bien, j'en suis très fier.»

mon conseil

La neurochirurgie est un travail minutieux et délicat. Cela exige une dextérité manuelle absolument hors pair, insiste Alain. La plupart des opérations s'effectuent au microscope ou au moyen – mais rarement au Québec – d'un neuronavigateur, un ordinateur qui permet au médecin de visualiser l'intérieur du cerveau. «Il faut aussi avoir le sens de l'orientation spatiale, car tout en regardant au microscope, on doit savoir exactement où l'on est.» Un bon jugement et une aptitude pour le travail clinique sont aussi des qualités essentielles pour déterminer quel type d'intervention pratiquer sur le patient. «Ça prend du pif!» s'exclame Alain.

Le neurochirurgien a aussi... les nerfs solides! Il doit résister au stress, car il travaille souvent sous pression et dans des conditions extrêmes. Ainsi, une intervention au cerveau dure généralement entre six et huit heures, et le moindre faux mouvement peut avoir des conséquences désastreuses pour le patient. 06/03

mon parcours

Alain a obtenu son doctorat de médecine à l'Université de Montréal, puis il a effectué sa **résidence** en médecine générale en 1979. Il a pratiqué sept ans comme médecin généraliste avant de s'inscrire en neurochirurgie. «Je sentais que j'avais fait le tour du jardin. J'avais besoin d'autres défis.» Médecin spécialisé en neurochirurgie depuis 1991, il a fait récemment une formation continue en **médecine d'expertise**, ce qui lui permet de témoigner comme médecin expert devant les tribunaux.

Les mots en caractères **gras** sont définis à la page 153.

Médecin spécialiste en neurologie
> en milieu hospitalier

mon travail

Le neurologue est un médecin spécialiste des troubles du système nerveux dus à un accident (choc au cerveau ou à la moelle épinière) ou à une maladie (épilepsie, Alzheimer, Parkinson, etc.). Le neurologue ne fait pas de chirurgie, ce travail étant réservé au neurochirurgien. Éric Lalumière, neurologue, travaille depuis huit ans à la Cité de la santé, un hôpital d'environ 450 lits qui dessert Laval et sa couronne nord, soit plus de 300 000 personnes.

«Je fais de la clinique externe : je rencontre de nouveaux patients ou des gens que j'ai déjà vus, explique Éric. Je les interroge, les examine, j'établis un diagnostic, puis j'élabore un plan de traitement. Je peux aussi être de garde, c'est-à-dire faire des consultations à l'étage où séjournent les patients ou à l'urgence de l'hôpital, pour des personnes qui ont besoin de recevoir des soins rapidement.»

Des milieux de travail potentiels

> Centres d'hébergement et de soins de longue durée
> Centres hospitaliers
> Centres locaux de services communautaires (CLSC)
> Cliniques privées

ma motivation

Outre la satisfaction de soigner ses patients, Éric est fasciné par l'aspect scientifique de sa spécialité médicale, en constante évolution. «On peut toujours en apprendre davantage sur le système nerveux et son fonctionnement, c'est un domaine très vaste. Pour le moment, on n'en connaît qu'une infime partie. Les découvertes scientifiques n'ont pas nécessairement d'impact sur le plan thérapeutique, mais elles nous permettent de progresser dans la compréhension de différentes maladies. Ce sont souvent les premières pistes pour développer de nouveaux traitements.»

Tout un appareillage permet d'explorer le système nerveux. «À l'hôpital, je fais de l'électromyographie, avec un appareil de la dimension d'un lave-vaisselle. Des fils sont branchés sur le patient, un stimulateur envoie de petits chocs électriques et des électrodes enregistrent le passage du courant, ce qui nous donne une idée de la vitesse de conduction des nerfs, donc des problèmes neurologiques qui peuvent affecter le patient.»

mon conseil

«Pour devenir neurologue, on doit être conscient qu'il faudra étudier pendant de nombreuses années, au moins cinq ans à l'université, signale Éric. Il faut avoir un vif intérêt pour les sciences et on doit constamment mettre ses connaissances à jour. Il y a une grande part de formation continue dans toutes les spécialités médicales, qui se fait de différentes façons : lectures personnelles, colloques, congrès, présentations, etc. Tous les cinq ou six ans, il peut y avoir des changements scientifiques assez importants dans le domaine de la neurologie, on doit suivre de près l'évolution.» 05/03

mon parcours

Éric a obtenu son doctorat en médecine à l'Université de Montréal, puis il a effectué sa **résidence** en neurologie. En tout, il a consacré dix années de sa vie à l'étude de la médecine. Son seul employeur à ce jour : la Cité de la santé.

Les mots en caractères **gras** sont définis à la page 153.

Médecin spécialiste (résidente) en obstétrique-gynécologie

> **en milieu hospitalier**

mon travail

Évelyne Caron rêve du jour où elle aura ses propres patientes. Médecin **résidente** en obstétrique-gynécologie, elle étudie actuellement sa future spécialité en effectuant des stages dans différents hôpitaux rattachés à l'Université McGill. «Le rôle de ce médecin spécialiste est d'accompagner médicalement les femmes tout au long de leur vie, explique-t-elle. Je vais m'occuper bien sûr des grossesses, des accouchements et des différentes pathologies affectant les organes génitaux, comme le cancer du col de l'utérus ou du vagin, mais aussi de la santé des femmes en général.» Ainsi, lorsqu'elle sera autorisée à pratiquer, Évelyne deviendra une personne-ressource de premier ordre, notamment pour ce qui concerne la contraception, la planification familiale, la ménopause, l'autoexamen des seins et les problèmes menstruels.

L'obstétricien-gynécologue suit sa clientèle en cabinet privé ou en clinique externe. Il procède lui-même aux accouchements, en milieu hospitalier, mais envoie à d'autres spécialistes les patientes nécessitant des traitements particuliers, comme la chimiothérapie ou la radiothérapie dans les cas de cancer.

Des milieux de travail potentiels

> Centres d'hébergement et de soins de longue durée
> Centres hospitaliers
> Centres locaux de services communautaires (CLSC)
> Cliniques privées

ma motivation

Pour Évelyne, la santé des femmes représente plus qu'une simple question médicale. «Sur le plan humain, c'est très enrichissant. Les rapports médecin-patientes sont étroits. On parle de sujets intimes comme les relations sexuelles, la contraception ou l'autoexamen des seins. Les femmes me font confiance. Je deviens une confidente.

«Sur le plan médical, c'est très diversifié, ajoute-t-elle. Chaque femme est unique et réagit différemment selon sa biologie, mais aussi selon sa culture. De plus, un médecin qui choisit cette spécialité peut voir une clientèle de tous âges : des jeunes femmes pour leurs premiers examens, des couples pendant la grossesse ou en clinique de fertilité, etc. Et les naissances, c'est toujours magique!»

mon conseil

«La personne qui se destine à la pratique de l'obstétrique-gynécologie doit être ouverte d'esprit et tolérante, soutient Évelyne. Quand on parle de sexualité, on parle d'une grande variété de pratiques. Par exemple, on voit de jeunes adolescentes qui viennent consulter pour se faire prescrire des contraceptifs alors qu'elles ne sont pas prêtes à avoir des relations sexuelles. D'autres viennent demander si l'attirance qu'elles ont pour une autre femme est normale. On voit des cas d'abus sexuels, de prostitution, etc. Il faut retenir nos propres valeurs et savoir écouter les patientes.» 06/03

mon parcours

«Quand j'étais au secondaire, j'hésitais entre le journalisme, le droit et la médecine. J'ai pris soin de me garder toutes les portes ouvertes en suivant autant de cours de sciences que je pouvais», raconte Évelyne, qui a obtenu un diplôme d'études collégiales (DEC) en sciences de la santé au Séminaire de Sherbrooke. Elle a ensuite été acceptée à l'Université McGill, où elle a effectué un programme préparatoire d'un an en médecine avant de traverser les quatre années du doctorat en médecine. Elle en est aujourd'hui à la troisième de ses cinq années de **résidence** en obstétrique-gynécologie.

Les mots en caractères **gras** sont définis à la page 153.

Médecin spécialiste en oncologie médicale

> **en milieu hospitalier**

mon travail

Jean Latreille est médecin spécialiste en oncologie médicale et en hématologie à l'Hôpital Charles-LeMoyne de Longueuil (arrondissement de Greenfield Park), sur la Rive-Sud. Il diagnostique, traite et soulage le cancer par des procédés comme la chimiothérapie, l'hormonothérapie et l'immunothérapie.

«Je rencontre des patients atteints de cancer. Ils me sont envoyés par d'autres médecins. Ils viennent pour se faire préciser un diagnostic et pour se faire traiter, explique le Jean. Je suis responsable d'établir le diagnostic. Pour cela, j'analyse les résultats des examens qu'ils ont déjà passés et j'en commande des complémentaires au besoin. Une fois le diagnostic posé, j'explique clairement la situation au patient : le type de cancer, son importance, les implications et effets des traitements possibles et je lui demande de choisir.»

ma motivation

«L'un de mes oncles est médecin. Quand j'étais petit, il m'impressionnait beaucoup. J'aimais ce qui se dégageait de lui, sa façon d'être, sa philosophie de vie. J'ai donc décidé très tôt de suivre ses traces, poursuit Jean.

«L'oncologie m'a séduit pendant mon stage de chirurgie. J'ai vu un jeune homme aux prises avec un cancer des intestins. La chimiothérapie n'existait pas encore. Il n'y avait rien à faire pour lui, rien que de le regarder mourir et d'apprendre. J'ai éprouvé tellement d'empathie pour cette personne, pour sa souffrance, pour sa mort inutile, pour sa vie trop brève, que j'ai voulu faire quelque chose. J'ai voulu m'impliquer et chercher des pistes de solutions. J'ai donc étudié l'hématologie puis l'oncologie, mais toujours dans l'optique de soigner, de soulager, de guérir les patients atteints de cancer.»

mon conseil

«Pour devenir oncologue, on doit être tenace. Aujourd'hui, on souligne mes succès, mais j'ai aussi connu des revers. J'ai dû m'accrocher à ma quête, à mes recherches et avancer souvent à contre-courant. Il faut savoir écouter les patients et leur parler, car ils sont plus vulnérables que les personnes en bonne santé. On doit leur expliquer leur maladie, les comprendre et les rassurer malgré la situation, mais aussi leur montrer les pistes d'espoir.» 09/03

mon parcours

Jean a obtenu son doctorat en médecine générale à l'Université McGill, puis a effectué sa **résidence** en **médecine interne** à l'Hôpital général de Montréal, et sa résidence en hémato-oncologie à l'Hôpital du Sacré-Cœur. «J'ai ensuite complété avec une formation au M.D. Anderson Hospital and Tumor Institute à Houston au Texas. J'ai aussi effectué des études de troisième cycle en psychothérapie à l'Institut de formation humaine intégrale de Montréal. «J'œuvre au service d'hématologie et d'oncologie médicale de l'Hôpital Charles-LeMoyne depuis 1999. Je suis également directeur du Centre intégré de lutte contre le cancer de la Montérégie et du Réseau Cancer Montérégie. Enfin, je suis professeur associé au Service d'hématologie de l'Université de Sherbrooke depuis 2002.»

Des milieux de travail potentiels

> Centres d'hébergement et de soins de longue durée
> Centres hospitaliers
> Centres locaux de services communautaires (CLSC)
> Cliniques privées

Les mots en caractères **gras** sont définis à la page 153.

Médecin spécialiste en ophtalmologie
> en milieu hospitalier

mon travail

Ophtalmologiste, Patrick Boulos se définit comme un médecin spécialiste de l'œil. «Un ophtalmologiste diagnostique et traite toutes les maladies oculaires, explique-t-il. Il pratique également la chirurgie des yeux, que ce soit à l'extérieur de l'œil, par exemple les paupières, ou à l'intérieur, comme une chirurgie du cristallin ou de la rétine.»

Les ophtalmologistes utilisent des appareils extrêmement précis, comme le laser. «On a souvent recours au laser pour les traitements médicaux, dans le cadre d'une vitrectomie par exemple, qui est une chirurgie pour les patients diabétiques qui ont du sang dans les yeux. Après avoir aspiré le sang, on utilise le laser pour détruire les vaisseaux extrêmement fragiles qui auraient tendance à saigner de nouveau si on ne les ôtait pas. Ce sont des chirurgies qui se faisaient autrefois avec des bistouris.»

Récemment diplômé en ophtalmologie, Patrick se spécialise actuellement en oculoplastie. «C'est une formation qui touche la chirurgie esthétique des paupières et les reconstructions après un traumatisme ou une tumeur.»

Des milieux de travail potentiels

> Centres d'hébergement et de soins de longue durée
> Centres hospitaliers
> Centres locaux de services communautaires (CLSC)
> Cliniques privées

ma motivation

«Ce qu'il y a de bien en ophtalmologie, c'est que le diagnostic se voit, explique Patrick. On utilise un microscope vertical qui envoie une lumière dans l'œil, qu'on appelle la lampe à fente. Si les structures semblent normales à l'intérieur de l'œil, tout va bien, mais s'il y a une pathologie, les changements sont apparents. C'est drôle à dire, mais c'est très visuel comme spécialité!»

Les sciences physiques ont également attiré Patrick vers cette spécialité. «En ophtalmologie, on joue avec des formules, des diagrammes, des rayons, des appareils très techniques. Je passe ma journée avec toutes sortes d'appareils : des lasers, des appareils d'imagerie numérique, des microscopes. Les technologies évoluent sans cesse. Il faut apprendre à les connaître, à les utiliser, et comprendre leur fonctionnement du point de vue physique-optique.»

mon conseil

«La plupart des gens pensent que l'œil est un petit organe dont on a vite fait le tour, mais quand on commence sa spécialité en ophtalmologie, c'est comme si on partait à la découverte d'un nouveau monde. Même avec un doctorat en médecine, on a l'impression de recommencer à zéro! D'autant plus que les connaissances acquises durant le doctorat en médecine générale sont moins utilisées en ophtalmologie que dans d'autres spécialités.» 07/03

mon parcours

Après une formation préuniversitaire de niveau collégial orientée vers les sciences de la santé, Patrick a été admis à la faculté de médecine de l'Université de Montréal. Diplômé de médecine générale en 1997, il a poursuivi par une **résidence** en ophtalmologie. Ophtalmologue diplômé depuis 2002, il est actuellement en première année de surspécialisation en oculoplastie à l'Université de Montréal. Il effectuera sa deuxième année à l'étranger.

Les mots en caractères **gras** sont définis à la page 153.

Médecin spécialiste en oto-rhino-laryngologie

❯ en clinique privée et en milieu hospitalier

mon travail

ORL. En plus d'abréger un titre interminable, ces trois lettres désignent une spécialité des plus étendues. L'oto-rhino-laryngologiste, c'est le médecin qui voit au diagnostic, au traitement et à la prévention des problèmes qui affectent les oreilles, le nez ou la gorge, comme les otites, les amygdalites ou les affections de la **glande thyroïde**. Outre sa pratique en clinique privée, Marie-Claude Lanoie, ORL, travaille deux jours par semaine à l'Hôpital Hôtel-Dieu de Saint-Jérôme. Elle en consacre un à voir les patients en clinique externe, et l'autre, à effectuer des chirurgies en salle d'opération.

Lorsqu'elle reçoit un patient en clinique, Marie-Claude l'accueille et lui demande ce qui ne va pas. Ensuite, elle l'examine, évalue son cas, pose un diagnostic et prescrit un traitement, des médicaments ou une intervention chirurgicale.

Les journées de chirurgie, elle pratique des interventions de toute nature, par exemple l'enlèvement d'un kyste à la lèvre ou encore l'insertion d'implants dans les oreilles. Entre deux opérations, pendant le nettoyage de la salle, Marie-Claude ne dispose que de 10 à 15 minutes pour s'entretenir avec le patient suivant, préparer le dossier et les ordonnances postopératoires, voir le patient précédent en salle de réveil... et, à l'heure du dîner, prendre son repas.

Des milieux de travail potentiels

- ❯ Centres d'hébergement et de soins de longue durée
- ❯ Centres hospitaliers
- ❯ Centres locaux de services communautaires (CLSC)
- ❯ Cliniques privées

ma motivation

Alors qu'elle étudiait la médecine, Marie-Claude a particulièrement apprécié le cours d'anatomie ORL. Pour préciser son choix de spécialité, elle a donc fait un stage dans ce domaine. «Chaque jour pendant un mois, j'allais observer le travail d'un ORL. Les aspects médical et chirurgical m'ont fascinée. J'ai choisi cette pratique parce qu'elle me permettait d'être proche de la clientèle. Pouvoir voir le patient en clinique, diagnostiquer son problème et le résoudre en chirurgie, ça m'attirait beaucoup. C'est l'une des rares pratiques médicales à permettre cela.»

La variété des cas à traiter représente une grande source de stimulation pour Marie-Claude. «Le fait que la pratique s'étende aux patients de tous âges, des enfants aux aînés, me plaît énormément.» La rapidité des résultats qu'elle obtient a aussi de quoi nourrir son enthousiasme.

mon conseil

«Pour devenir ORL, il faut être décidé, tenace et acharné!» lance Marie-Claude, en évoquant les dix années d'études nécessaires pour accéder à la profession. Il faut aussi avoir un goût certain pour le travail en équipe, une bonne dextérité et une grande empathie envers les patients.

«Comme la clientèle est très variée, les aspects psychologiques le sont aussi.» Elle ajoute que l'évolution des techniques et des médicaments suppose une mise à jour constante. Lectures, conférences et congrès vont donc de pair avec la pratique. 06/03

mon parcours

Marie-Claude a consacré cinq ans à son doctorat en médecine, à l'Université de Montréal. Elle a ensuite fait ses cinq années de **résidence** en oto-rhino-laryngologie à l'Hôpital Hôtel-Dieu de Saint-Jérôme, où elle pratique toujours.

Les mots en caractères **gras** sont définis à la page 153.

Médecin spécialiste (résident) en pédiatrie générale

> **en milieu hospitalier**

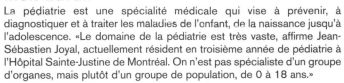

mon travail

La pédiatrie est une spécialité médicale qui vise à prévenir, à diagnostiquer et à traiter les maladies de l'enfant, de la naissance jusqu'à l'adolescence. «Le domaine de la pédiatrie est très vaste, affirme Jean-Sébastien Joyal, actuellement résident en troisième année de pédiatrie à l'Hôpital Sainte-Justine de Montréal. On n'est pas spécialiste d'un groupe d'organes, mais plutôt d'un groupe de population, de 0 à 18 ans.»

La pédiatrie reconnaît plusieurs périodes dans la vie de l'enfant, chacune correspondant à une étape différente du développement physiologique. «On fait beaucoup de **néonatologie** au début de notre résidence : on prend en charge les nouveau-nés, certains prématurés. C'est une tout autre médecine! Actuellement je fais un stage d'un mois à l'étage des adolescents. Je suis responsable de 25 patients qui ont entre 12 et 18 ans.»

Des milieux de travail potentiels

> Centres d'hébergement et de soins de longue durée
> Centres hospitaliers
> Centres locaux de services communautaires (CLSC)
> Cliniques privées

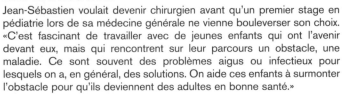

ma motivation

Jean-Sébastien voulait devenir chirurgien avant qu'un premier stage en pédiatrie lors de sa médecine générale ne vienne bouleverser son choix. «C'est fascinant de travailler avec de jeunes enfants qui ont l'avenir devant eux, mais qui rencontrent sur leur parcours un obstacle, une maladie. Ce sont souvent des problèmes aigus ou infectieux pour lesquels on a, en général, des solutions. On aide ces enfants à surmonter l'obstacle pour qu'ils deviennent des adultes en bonne santé.»

Cependant, il arrive aussi que des enfants souffrent de maladies plus pernicieuses, comme le cancer. «Voir un enfant malade, qui parfois va mourir, nous confronte aux grands questionnements de l'existence. C'est vrai dans toutes les professions médicales, mais, en pédiatrie, c'est plus difficile, car on a affaire à des enfants.»

mon conseil

«On a toujours envie de faire et de donner le maximum à nos patients. Les parents sont également très exigeants envers les médecins, les pédiatres, car ils veulent aussi ce qu'il y a de mieux pour leur enfant. Il faut savoir poser des limites franches, mais raisonnables : on doit faire sentir aux patients que l'on est accessible, tout en sachant préserver du temps pour sa propre vie personnelle.» 07/03

mon parcours

Après son secondaire, Jean-Sébastien a décroché une bourse pour aller étudier deux ans au Collège Lester B. Pearson en Colombie-Britannique. Il y a obtenu un baccalauréat international avec option en physique-chimie. À son retour au Québec en 1995, il est entré à la faculté de médecine de l'Université McGill où il a terminé son doctorat en médecine générale en l'an 2000. Il a ensuite entamé sa résidence en pédiatrie à l'Université de Montréal. Jean-Sébastien a mis ses études entre parenthèses durant six mois en 2002, pour participer en tant que pédiatre à un projet de Médecins du Monde dans la région du Chiapas au Mexique. Il est actuellement en troisième année de **résidence**.

Les mots en caractères **gras** sont définis à la page 153.

Médecin spécialiste en physiatrie
> **en milieu hospitalier**

mon travail

Le médecin spécialiste en physiatrie s'occupe du diagnostic, du traitement et de la prévention des douleurs et des troubles fonctionnels de l'appareil locomoteur causés par un accident, une maladie, une malformation congénitale ou une lésion d'origine sportive ou professionnelle.

Gaétan Filion œuvre auprès de la clientèle juvénile du Centre de réadaptation Marie-Enfant à Montréal, au Centre montérégien de réadaptation à Saint-Hubert et à l'Hôpital juif de réadaptation de Laval. Il évalue chaque cas et fait des recommandations aux divers intervenants comme les physiothérapeutes et les ergothérapeutes, pour fournir au patient les soins adaptés à ses besoins. «Si on prend l'exemple d'un enfant qui a subi un traumatisme au cerveau, mon objectif dans son cas est de minimiser au maximum les impacts sur son développement, sa croissance et son apprentissage. Je peux faire des recommandations au physiothérapeute sur des exercices à pratiquer. Pour un enfant atteint de paralysie cérébrale, je prescris des médicaments par injection, afin de détendre certains muscles et d'ainsi faciliter ses mouvements.» Puisqu'il doit aussi parfois apprendre de mauvaises nouvelles aux parents au sujet de l'état de leur enfant, Gaétan a également un rôle de soutien moral aux familles à jouer.

ma motivation

Bien que sa profession soit parfois exigeante, Gaétan adore son travail. «Je m'amuse avec les enfants et aussi avec les parents. Bien sûr, il n'est pas toujours facile d'annoncer à des parents que leur bébé, qu'ils croyaient parfait, est handicapé pour le reste de ses jours... Mais j'essaie aussi d'apporter un sourire pour qu'à travers les pleurs, il y ait aussi un peu de réconfort.

«Au départ, je voulais devenir cardiologue, mais j'ai réalisé que c'était peut-être une branche trop stressante pour moi, avec des horaires très exigeants. En outre, plus jeune, j'avais eu l'occasion de travailler au camp Papillon avec des enfants handicapés. En physiatrie, j'ai retrouvé le plaisir d'évoluer avec eux et de les voir grandir.»

mon conseil

Gaétan a retenu une grande leçon de sa pratique de la physiatrie : «Plus on pense en savoir, plus on réalise qu'on ne sait rien!» Malgré ses 13 ans d'expérience dans la profession, il demeure conscient qu'il continue à en apprendre tous les jours, et c'est ce qui le stimule.

«J'ajouterai qu'il ne faut pas opter pour cette profession pour l'argent. Un peu comme pour toutes les spécialités en médecine, la physiatrie est une vocation. Il faut la pratiquer avec passion.» 09/03

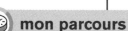

Des milieux de travail potentiels

> Centres d'hébergement et de soins de longue durée
> Centres hospitaliers
> Centres locaux de services communautaires (CLSC)
> Cliniques privées

mon parcours

Après avoir fait son doctorat en médecine générale puis sa **résidence** en physiatrie à l'Université de Montréal, Gaétan a également suivi une formation postdoctorale en neurobiologie à l'Université Pierre et Marie Curie à Paris, et à l'Université Laval à Québec. «Par la suite, j'ai commencé à exercer en physiatrie. Nous sommes peu nombreux au Québec, et les besoins dans ce domaine sont grands. Par conséquent, on ne cherche pas très longtemps un emploi...»

Les mots en caractères **gras** sont définis à la page 153.

Médecin spécialiste en pneumologie*

mon travail

Le pneumologue est le médecin spécialiste qui se consacre à la prévention, au diagnostic et au traitement de l'adulte et de l'enfant souffrant de problèmes de santé aigus et chroniques du système respiratoire. Il traite les maladies comme la pneumonie, l'**apnée du sommeil**, le cancer du poumon, la **bronchite chronique**, l'**emphysème**, l'**asthme**, les **maladies respiratoires environnementales**, etc.

Le pneumologue peut recevoir sa clientèle en consultations externes ou à son bureau privé pour les premières visites et les suivis médicaux. À l'hôpital, il procède à différents examens comme l'**examen direct de l'expectoration**, à des contrôles de la respiration au repos, à l'effort ou en sommeil, à des **tubages gastriques**, des **endoscopies**, etc. Il commande aussi des analyses à d'autres professionnels de la santé comme des analyses sanguines, des radiographies, des examens bactériologiques, etc., afin de pouvoir finalement poser son diagnostic.

Des milieux de travail potentiels

- ❯ Centres d'hébergement et de soins de longue durée
- ❯ Centres hospitaliers
- ❯ Centres locaux de services communautaires (CLSC)
- ❯ Cliniques privées

ma motivation

Sans la respiration, il n'y a pas de vie possible. Le pneumologue essaie d'améliorer la qualité de vie de ses patients en soignant leurs poumons et leur système respiratoire.

Le pneumologue travaille avec des instruments et des techniques variés. Ainsi, il a recours au stéthoscope, à l'**endoscopie**, à la **polygraphie** ou à la **polysomnographie**, etc. Le pneumologue travaille aussi en équipe avec des infirmiers, des **inhalothérapeutes**, des techniciens de laboratoire, etc.

Le cancer du poumon est l'une des premières causes de mortalité en Amérique du Nord. Cette forme de cancer frappe plus souvent les fumeurs. Le pneumologue est en première ligne pour lutter contre ce fléau. Il s'implique dans la prévention du tabagisme et dans la lutte contre le cancer du poumon par l'éducation, le dépistage et les examens préventifs.

mon conseil

Les jeunes qui désirent devenir spécialistes en pneumologie doivent avoir un goût certain pour l'investigation. En effet, les maladies pouvant affecter les poumons sont nombreuses et souvent difficiles à identifier clairement. Il faut donc de la ténacité et de la détermination pour chercher et découvrir les causes des symptômes du malade.

De plus, il faut faire preuve d'entregent, de tact et de diplomatie afin de créer rapidement un climat de confiance avec les patients. On doit également être en mesure de vulgariser ses connaissances pour bien se faire comprendre d'eux. Enfin, on doit s'attendre à apprendre toute sa vie professionnelle durant pour mettre au service de sa clientèle les plus récentes découvertes dans le domaine. 09/03

* Exceptionnellement, en l'absence d'un médecin disponible pour un témoignage, nous publions ici une monographie de cette profession.

mon parcours

Pour devenir médecin spécialiste en pneumologie, la voie la plus directe est un diplôme d'études collégiales (DEC) en sciences de la santé ou en sciences pures, suivi du doctorat en médecine et de la **résidence** en pneumologie.

Les mots en caractères **gras** sont définis à la page 153.

Médecin spécialiste (résident) en psychiatrie
> **en milieu hospitalier**

mon travail

Prométhéas Constantinides est résident en quatrième année de psychiatrie et travaille actuellement à l'Hôpital du Sacré-Cœur de Montréal. «Le rôle du psychiatre est de donner des soins aux patients à la demande de leur médecin de famille ou des cliniques, ou encore, par les urgences pour un problème de santé mentale nécessitant l'intervention d'un spécialiste. Ce sont généralement des personnes dépressives, maniaco-dépressives, qui souffrent de psychoses, qui ont des idées suicidaires, etc., explique-t-il.

«De plus, on s'occupe des patients hospitalisés, on leur apporte les soins médicamenteux et psychothérapeutiques, et on se charge des interventions sociales adéquates. On s'assure, par exemple, qu'un patient a un logement en sortant de l'hôpital. Le psychiatre gère une équipe multidisciplinaire comprenant notamment des intervenants sociaux, des psychologues et des ergothérapeutes pour la réadaptation physique et psychique si nécessaire.»

Des milieux de travail potentiels

> Centres d'hébergement et de soins de longue durée
> Centres hospitaliers
> Centres locaux de services communautaires (CLSC)
> Cliniques privées

ma motivation

«En psychiatrie, davantage que dans d'autres spécialités médicales, explique Prométhéas, on prend le temps de discuter pour apprendre à connaître ses patients. Les cas sont très variés : on peut voir une personne déprimée parce qu'elle a perdu un être cher, ou recevoir un patient qui se prend pour Bonaparte ou pour Dieu... Dans ce cas, il faut l'hospitaliser et établir un traitement par les médicaments. On peut ainsi vraiment l'aider : il rentre complètement désorienté et quelques semaines plus tard il reprend contact avec la réalité.

«La psychiatrie est un domaine en pleine expansion, poursuit-il. De 1990 à 2000, c'était "la décennie du cerveau". Aux États-Unis, il y a eu des recherches très poussées pour comprendre le fonctionnement de l'esprit humain, du cerveau, de la conscience, et on commence à peine à profiter des résultats de ces recherches. C'est fascinant! Un siècle après les premières découvertes de Freud, cette spécialité en est encore à ses débuts.»

mon conseil

«La psychiatrie requiert une grande ouverture d'esprit, une curiosité, une expérience de vie aussi. Il faut avoir voyagé, avoir vu autre chose, être capable de se mettre à la place de l'autre et, surtout, il faut avoir envie de le faire! C'est un travail très relationnel et exigeant psychologiquement parlant. En médecine, on perd les gens par la mort, par l'évolution de la maladie. En psychiatrie, on peut aussi les perdre, entre autres par le suicide. Cela crée parfois un sentiment d'impuissance difficile à gérer, d'où l'importance de s'entourer d'une bonne équipe de travail.» 07/03

mon parcours

Prométhéas a obtenu son doctorat en médecine générale à l'Université de Montréal et y a poursuivi sa **résidence** en psychiatrie. Actuellement en quatrième année de résidence, il est stagiaire à l'Hôpital du Sacré-Cœur au Pavillon Albert-Prévost.

Les mots en caractères **gras** sont définis à la page 153.

Médecin spécialiste (résidente) en radiologie diagnostique

> en milieu hospitalier

mon travail

Visal Pen entame sa quatrième année de résidence en vue de devenir, au terme de dix années d'études, médecin spécialiste en radiologie diagnostique. «En tant que médecins résidents en radiologie, nous sommes en formation, mais nous faisons nos journées de travail comme les radiologues, qui sont en quelque sorte nos patrons.»

Les tâches d'un radiologue consistent à traiter les images, comme les scanners, les IRMN (imagerie par résonance magnétique nucléaire) ou les radiographies, pour pouvoir poser un diagnostic. «On est consultant pour les médecins de première ligne, les omnipraticiens, ou pour les spécialistes comme les chirurgiens, les pneumologues, les neurologues. Le technologue en radiologie prend les images, et c'est le radiologue qui en fait la lecture, les analyse et détermine ce qui doit être fait en fonction du diagnostic.»

Des milieux de travail potentiels

> Centres d'hébergement et de soins de longue durée
> Centres hospitaliers
> Centres locaux de services communautaires (CLSC)
> Cliniques privées

ma motivation

«Je suis entrée en médecine parce que j'avais de bons résultats scolaires, avoue Visal. Ce n'était pas au départ une vocation. Puis, peu à peu, le corps humain m'a dévoilé ses mystères et j'ai trouvé cela fascinant. J'ai ensuite décidé de me spécialiser en radiologie parce que je trouve incroyable qu'on puisse voir des choses dans une personne vivante sans même la toucher.»

En effet, grâce aux progrès techniques, c'est le radiologue qui, le premier, peut détecter un petit nodule cancéreux de trois millimètres seulement, dans un sein par exemple. «On peut donc guérir la patiente plus facilement, car le cancer n'aura pas eu le temps de faire de ravages. C'est extraordinaire!»

Visal considère son choix de carrière comme très stimulant intellectuellement, mais très exigeant personnellement. «Pour arriver au terme de dix ans d'études, il faut de la persévérance, de la discipline, parce qu'à un moment donné, la passion s'épuise et on doit faire beaucoup de sacrifices dans sa vie personnelle.»

mon conseil

«C'est un milieu qui demande toujours le meilleur de soi, conclut Visal, car tous les patients désirent avoir le meilleur médecin, le meilleur chirurgien, le meilleur radiologue. La médecine est vaste, elle se développe, elle évolue. Il y a de nouveaux appareils, de nouveaux médicaments, ça ne finit jamais. C'est impossible de tout savoir, mais il faut en apprendre le plus possible : pour être un bon médecin, on doit avoir une curiosité scientifique inépuisable.» 05/03

mon parcours

Visal a obtenu son doctorat en médecine à l'Université de Montréal en 1993. Elle a ensuite entamé sa **résidence** en radiologie diagnostique. Actuellement en quatrième année de résidence, elle est appelée à effectuer des stages au Centre hospitalier de l'Université de Montréal, à l'Hôpital Sainte-Justine, au Centre de traumatologie de l'Hôpital Sacré-Cœur, à l'Hôpital Maisonneuve-Rosemont et à l'Institut de cardiologie de Montréal.

Les mots en caractères **gras** sont définis à la page 153.

Médecin spécialiste en radio-oncologie

❯ en milieu hospitalier

mon travail

«Je traite des patients atteints de cancer en leur administrant des **radiations ionisantes**, selon le principe de la radiothérapie», explique Carole Lambert, médecin spécialiste en radio-oncologie aux hôpitaux Notre-Dame et Hôtel-Dieu du Centre hospitalier universitaire de Montréal (CHUM).

Un tel traitement demande une grande préparation. Ainsi, la spécialiste rencontre chaque patient à plusieurs reprises avant de procéder. Lorsqu'un patient lui arrive pour la première fois, elle l'écoute et évalue son cas à partir de résultats d'examens. «La seconde visite a pour but de planifier le traitement. Par **tomodensitométrie**, je détermine la zone à traiter, les organes sains à éviter, la dose de radiations à libérer, les angles de traitement, le type de rayonnement, etc. Toutes ces données sont inscrites dans un logiciel spécialisé.»

La troisième visite est une sorte de répétition générale avant l'intervention. Par la suite, le nombre de séances varie selon la quantité de radiations nécessaire pour éliminer toutes les cellules cancéreuses. Carole suit chaque individu jusqu'à ce que tout rentre dans l'ordre. «J'ai sous ma responsabilité de 25 à 40 patients simultanément», précise-t-elle.

Des milieux de travail potentiels

- ❯ Centres d'hébergement et de soins de longue durée
- ❯ Centres hospitaliers
- ❯ Centres locaux de services communautaires (CLSC)
- ❯ Cliniques privées

ma motivation

La spécialité qu'elle exerce aujourd'hui n'a pas toujours été son objectif. «Initialement, je voulais devenir chiropraticienne ou naturopathe. C'est la santé qui m'intéressait avant tout. Je voulais aider, soulager la souffrance, mais surtout favoriser la santé. J'ai finalement choisi la médecine pour contribuer au mieux-être des personnes.

«L'idée de devenir radio-oncologue m'est venue d'un seul coup, poursuit-elle. J'étais en stage, en première année de médecine. Quand je suis arrivée au centre d'oncologie pour suivre le médecin qui m'était attitré, celui-ci m'a tellement impressionnée par son érudition, son expertise, son empathie et sa générosité que je suis repartie, à la fin de ma journée, avec le sentiment d'avoir trouvé ma voie.»

mon conseil

«Pour devenir radio-oncologue, il faut avoir des aptitudes pour les sciences, mais ce n'est pas tout, souligne Carole. Il faut aussi faire preuve d'empathie, de respect et d'une grande ouverture d'esprit. Les patients que je vois m'arrivent tous avec un diagnostic de cancer. Souvent, je dois répondre à des questions graves concernant leur pronostic de vie. Comme chaque être humain a une façon unique de faire face à sa peur de la souffrance et de la mort, je dois faire preuve de beaucoup d'écoute et de discernement.» 09/03

mon parcours

Après son doctorat en médecine à l'Université de Sherbrooke, Carole a fait des études spécialisées en radio-oncologie à l'Université de Montréal, suivies d'une **résidence** dans les hôpitaux affiliés à cet établissement. Depuis un an, elle travaille au Département de radio-oncologie du Centre hospitalier de l'Université de Montréal (CHUM), aux hôpitaux Notre-Dame et Hôtel-Dieu. Elle effectue simultanément une maîtrise en pédagogie des sciences médicales à l'Université de Montréal.

Les mots en caractères **gras** sont définis à la page 153.

Médecin spécialiste en rhumatologie
> en milieu hospitalier

mon travail

«Les rhumatismes touchent autant les enfants que les adultes ou les personnes âgées, explique Dominique Bourrelle, rhumatologue à l'Hôpital Notre-Dame de Montréal. Ils regroupent plusieurs maladies, comme l'**arthrite**, l'**arthrose**, l'**ostéoporose** et les **collagénoses**.»

Dominique reçoit ses patients en clinique externe. À l'affût de ce qui cause leur problème, elle les questionne, les examine de haut en bas (scrutant la peau, la bouche, le cœur, les ongles, le ventre, les ganglions, les articulations, etc.) et les envoie passer des examens complémentaires, comme des prises de sang ou des rayons X. Après avoir posé son diagnostic, elle leur prescrit des médicaments ou procède à des **infiltrations** pour les soulager.

Une semaine sur trois, Dominique est de garde à l'hôpital. Elle voit alors des malades admis à l'urgence qui nécessitent des soins en rhumatologie. Elle répond aussi aux demandes de collègues dont les patients hospitalisés ont besoin de son expertise. «Quand on pratique dans un centre hospitalier universitaire comme l'Hôpital Notre-Dame, on est considéré comme une référence.»

Des milieux de travail potentiels

> Centres d'hébergement et de soins de longue durée
> Centres hospitaliers
> Centres locaux de services communautaires (CLSC)
> Cliniques privées

ma motivation

«Ce qui m'a attirée dans cette spécialité, c'est qu'on peut découvrir beaucoup de choses uniquement en examinant le patient, à la manière d'un détective sur la piste des indices qui mènent au coupable, raconte Dominique. Il faut questionner le patient sur ses symptômes, ses douleurs, ses habitudes. Avec mes connaissances et de la pratique, je peux ainsi avoir une bonne idée de ce dont souffre une personne. Et les tests sanguins ou les rayons X viennent souvent confirmer le diagnostic que j'avais en tête.

«Si une personne a de la difficulté à bouger, à se lever ou à marcher, je peux faire en sorte que sa douleur soit moins grande et qu'elle puisse fonctionner dans son quotidien. Quand un patient revient me voir et que je constate que ça va mieux, c'est très valorisant.»

mon conseil

Au secondaire, Dominique avait déjà décidé qu'elle deviendrait médecin. «Je ne sais pas si c'était par vocation ou si j'ignorais simplement dans quoi je m'embarquais. Je ne me suis jamais posé de questions; c'est peut-être ça le meilleur truc... Et travailler fort, aborder une journée après l'autre, une année après l'autre, foncer tête baissée. Quand j'ai eu fini mes études, je me suis dit : mon Dieu, j'ai fait tout ça!» raconte-t-elle en riant. 06/03

mon parcours

Dominique a entrepris ses études collégiales en sciences de la santé au Collège de Bois-de-Boulogne. Puis, elle a fait son doctorat en médecine générale à l'Université de Montréal, avant d'opter pour une spécialisation en rhumatologie et de faire sa **résidence** à l'Hôpital Notre-Dame. L'institution a par la suite exigé que Dominique aille se surspécialiser ailleurs, comme le veut la pratique dans les centres hospitaliers universitaires. «Je suis donc partie étudier les maladies osseuses en France pendant un an avant de revenir pratiquer à Notre-Dame», conclut-elle.

Les mots en caractères **gras** sont définis à la page 153.

Médecin spécialiste
en santé communautaire
❯ dans un organisme public

mon travail

Le médecin spécialiste en santé communautaire traite des aspects «populationnels» de la santé, c'est-à-dire que sa préoccupation première n'est pas tant le traitement des problèmes de santé que la prévention de leur propagation dans la population. «Mon patient, c'est la population», explique Faisca Richer, médecin en santé communautaire à la Direction de la santé publique de la Montérégie.

Son travail peut ainsi l'amener à tenter de prévenir la propagation de maladies infectieuses comme le SIDA, la gastro-entérite ou le SRAS, ou encore à s'occuper de la prévention relative au cancer, aux maladies chroniques ou reliées au tabac, etc. Elle peut également être appelée à conseiller des professionnels de la santé aux prises avec un cas de méningite invasive dans une école secondaire et qui veulent savoir s'ils doivent vacciner tous les élèves. Son avis est aussi requis dans le cas d'une catastrophe environnementale – par exemple un déversement de produits toxiques – pouvant porter atteinte à la santé de la population qu'elle dessert.

Des milieux de travail potentiels

- ❯ Centres d'hébergement et de soins de longue durée
- ❯ Centres hospitaliers
- ❯ Centres locaux de services communautaires (CLSC)
- ❯ Cliniques privées

ma motivation

Faisca avait initialement opté pour une autre spécialité médicale. Mais elle a vite été déçue de constater que la médecine guérit très peu. «Une fois que le problème est là, il est très rarement guérissable», explique-t-elle. Le fait de voir continuellement revenir en consultation des personnes à qui elle n'avait jamais eu l'occasion d'expliquer comment prévenir leurs problèmes de santé lui donnait «l'impression de ramasser des pots cassés, de travailler beaucoup à des choses qui ne se règlent jamais».

Elle apprécie tout particulièrement la perspective que lui donne son travail en santé communautaire. Il lui permet en effet de s'attaquer aux problèmes non seulement sous l'angle des facteurs médicaux, mais aussi en tenant compte des facteurs sociaux et culturels qui les causent. Elle peut ainsi agir avant que les choses ne deviennent irréversibles.

mon conseil

«Dans la pratique, le médecin en santé communautaire a beaucoup de lectures à faire, de rapports à écrire. Il faut être un peu "rat de bibliothèque" pour apprécier. Et il faut aussi avoir le goût de réfléchir à des problèmes.»

Faisca conseille également de laisser tomber ses préjugés si on veut réussir dans ce domaine. «Il faut acquérir une vision large d'une population : ce n'est pas toujours de la mauvaise volonté qui est en cause; il y a des raisons pour lesquelles certaines personnes vont développer des problèmes spécifiques.» 05/03

mon parcours

Faisca a obtenu son doctorat en médecine à l'Université d'Ottawa, puis a effectué sa **résidence** en santé communautaire à l'Université McGill. «Ce n'était pas une spécialisation très populaire au moment où je l'ai choisie», souligne-t-elle.

Les mots en caractères **gras** sont définis à la page 153.

Médecin spécialiste (résident) en urologie

> en milieu hospitalier

mon travail

Résident à l'Hôpital Sainte-Justine, Alain Duclos doit s'occuper des patients qui vont bientôt subir ou qui viennent de subir une opération en urologie. Cette branche de la médecine traite les affections de l'appareil urinaire (pierres aux reins ou à la vessie, cancers, incontinence, etc.) et celles de l'appareil génital masculin. **Pyéloplastie**, correction de l'**hypospadias** et **orchidopexie** sont des interventions régulièrement pratiquées dans le domaine.

«Avant la chirurgie, je dois vérifier que le patient est prêt pour la salle d'opération et que les tests d'usage avant l'opération ont été passés avec succès. Quand, par exemple, on découvre qu'un patient a un **électrocardiogramme** anormal, il faut décider si c'est dangereux pour lui de se retrouver en chirurgie. Après la chirurgie, je dois m'assurer que le patient récupère bien et que ses plaies ne saignent pas. Si elles saignent, il faut intervenir (on enlève les points, on examine où ça saigne et on referme la plaie). Il peut aussi arriver que quelqu'un fasse un infarctus après une chirurgie. À ce moment-là, il faut réagir très rapidement et demander l'aide des collègues cardiologues et chirurgiens cardiaques», explique Alain.

Des milieux de travail potentiels

> Centres d'hébergement et de soins de longue durée
> Centres hospitaliers
> Centres locaux de services communautaires (CLSC)
> Cliniques privées

ma motivation

«La première gratification que je tire de mon métier, c'est d'aider les gens», poursuit Alain. Une gratification qu'il aurait pu retrouver dans bien d'autres spécialités médicales. «Mon choix de me spécialiser en urologie a été influencé par les gens que j'ai côtoyés au cours de ma formation en médecine. En fait, un urologue et un chirurgien général font presque le même travail au niveau de l'abdomen...»

La communication avec les patients fait aussi partie des bons côtés du travail, selon Alain. «Pour moi, il est très important de prendre le temps d'expliquer à un patient quel est son état et quelles sont les mesures à prendre pour améliorer sa condition physique. Quand un patient comprend bien, il est plus enclin à suivre les directives, comme arrêter de fumer, faire de l'exercice, mieux s'alimenter, etc.», précise-t-il.

mon conseil

Avant de s'embarquer dans une telle aventure, il faut bien y songer, prévient Alain. «Il y a des sacrifices à faire et il faut en être conscient. Une telle spécialisation représente en tout 10 ans sur les bancs de l'école. Pendant les deux premières années de résidence, il faut calculer environ 80 heures par semaine de présence en milieu hospitalier.» Par contre, la démarche comporte des avantages. «Par exemple, au terme des études, on est assuré d'avoir un emploi. Ce n'est pas à négliger!» 09/03

mon parcours

Alain a fait un doctorat en recherche en immunologie à l'Université McGill avant d'entreprendre son doctorat en médecine à l'Université de Montréal. Il effectue présentement sa quatrième et avant-dernière année de **résidence** en urologie, sous la direction du même établissement. Par la suite, il prévoit aller étudier un an en Californie afin d'apprendre des techniques de transplantation des reins et du pancréas.

Les mots en caractères **gras** sont définis à la page 153.

Omnipraticienne
> en centre de réadaptation

mon travail

Marianne Harvey, omnipraticienne, pratique au Centre de réadaptation Lucie-Bruneau à Montréal. Elle se consacre aux lésions musculo-squelettiques graves, et participe à un programme de traumatismes crâniens et cérébraux où, explique-t-elle, elle a d'abord un rôle de médecin-conseil.

«Je reçois des patients qui ont été blessés et j'évalue leur situation : quels sont leurs besoins en matière de gestion de la douleur; s'ils peuvent entreprendre un programme en réadaptation, etc.

«J'assure également la liaison entre le Centre de réadaptation et le médecin traitant des patients, poursuit-elle. Je tiens aussi le rôle de consultante auprès de l'équipe soignante du Centre, car on travaille de pair avec des psychologues, des ergothérapeutes, des physiothérapeutes et des éducateurs physiques.»

ma motivation

Marianne a exercé durant huit ans le métier de sexologue dans un CLSC avant de se réorienter. «Je voulais une profession où l'on travaille avec des patients, qui comporte une part d'écoute, une part de psychothérapie. Je cherchais aussi un métier où l'on doit faire un travail de prise en charge, de prévention, de santé globale. Je me suis donc orientée vers la médecine.»

Elle avoue apprécier énormément le fait d'être membre d'une équipe au Centre de réadaptation. «C'est très important pour moi, confie-t-elle. Avant, j'œuvrais souvent seule sur des cas parfois très lourds à gérer. Ici, j'appartiens à un groupe interdisciplinaire. Chacun amène sa vision, ses connaissances en fonction de sa propre spécialité. Il y a un échange, c'est comme de la formation continue, ce qui est fort stimulant.»

mon conseil

«Quand on pratique la médecine, je crois qu'il faut avoir des convictions, et des doutes aussi. On doit avoir confiance en ce que l'on a appris, mais il faut garder des interrogations, car c'est ça qui permet de continuer à évoluer et qui donne envie d'apprendre.

mon parcours

Diplômée d'un baccalauréat en sexologie obtenu à l'Université du Québec à Montréal en 1980, Marianne a œuvré huit ans au CLSC de Pohénégamook comme sexologue. En 1988, elle a été admise à la faculté de médecine de l'Université de Montréal, où elle a par la suite obtenu son doctorat. Elle a effectué sa **résidence** en médecine familiale avant de s'établir en Gaspésie où elle a exercé durant 10 ans au CLSC Baie-des-Chaleurs à Paspébiac, puis au CLSC Pabok, et à l'Hôpital de Chandler. Elle travaille au Centre de réadaptation Lucie-Bruneau à Montréal depuis février 2003.

Il est également important de réussir à trouver un équilibre entre sa vie professionnelle et personnelle, c'est-à-dire de se sentir responsable de ses patients, sans négliger le fait que l'on est également responsable de sa propre vie.» 07/03

Les mots en caractères **gras** sont définis à la page 153.

La gestion
du système de santé

Derrière les professionnels de la santé qui s'activent pour soigner nos petits et gros bobos, travaillent aussi près de 10 000 personnes[1] chargées de voir au bon fonctionnement des établissements du réseau. Ce sont les directeurs généraux, les cadres supérieurs et les cadres intermédiaires.

Par Guylaine Boucher

D'ici à 2010, plus de 5 000 gestionnaires du réseau prendront leur retraite et devront être remplacés.

En 2003, le Centre de référence des directeurs généraux et des cadres estimait à 400 le nombre de **directeurs généraux** actifs au Québec[2]. À la tête des établissements, ils voient à ce que tout se passe sans encombre, que ce soit sur le plan financier, humain ou clinique. Le développement de nouveaux services, l'attribution des ressources humaines et financières, la signature d'ententes de partenariat entre établissements pour assurer, par exemple, le suivi de la clientèle, doivent entre autres être autorisés par eux.

Présents uniquement dans les grands établissements – comme les centres hospitaliers universitaires –, les **cadres supérieurs** ont quant à eux pour fonctions de planifier les ressources nécessaires, de coordonner le travail des équipes de cadres intermédiaires et de voir à l'organisation des services. On estime qu'ils représentent environ 1 300 personnes[3].

Enfin, les **cadres intermédiaires** sont responsables des activités, c'est-à-dire qu'ils coordonnent directement les équipes qui livrent les services à la population. On les retrouve dans tous les types d'établissements. Ils sont coordonnateurs des soins infirmiers, responsables du maintien à domicile, etc. Dans les plus petits établissements, ils peuvent aussi être responsables des ressources financières et matérielles. Beaucoup d'entre eux occupaient au préalable des fonctions cliniques, c'est-à-dire qu'ils étaient travailleurs sociaux, psychologues, infirmières, etc. Représentant plus de 7 500 travailleurs[4], ce sont les gestionnaires les plus nombreux du réseau.

La formation requise

La plupart des gestionnaires du réseau de la santé et des services sociaux sont titulaires d'un baccalauréat ou d'une maîtrise en administration publique, en plus d'une formation clinique de base. Ils ont souvent accédé à leurs fonctions en gravissant progressivement les échelons. D'ici à 2010, plus de 5 000 d'entre eux[5] prendront leur retraite et devront être remplacés. Devant le manque de relève disponible, le ministère de la Santé et des Services sociaux a mis sur pied un programme de relève des cadres. Pour y avoir accès, il faut cependant déjà travailler au sein du réseau. ∎

1. et 5. Ministère de la Santé et des Services sociaux, *Planification de la main-d'œuvre personnel cadre et hors-cadre du réseau de la santé et des services sociaux*, 2001.
2., 3. et 4. Entrevue avec Nicole Brodeur, présidente-directrice générale, Centre de référence des directeurs généraux et des cadres, mai 2003.

Pour avoir un aperçu des besoins de main-d'œuvre en ce qui a trait aux cadres et du programme de relève, consultez le site du Centre de référence des directeurs généraux et des cadres : http://www.crdgc.gouv.qc.ca/

Cadre intermédiaire
> dans un organisme public

mon travail

Manon Desrochers est coordonnatrice des services de réadaptation en déficience intellectuelle dans une institution publique : Les services de réadaptation L'Intégrale, à Montréal. À ce titre, elle est responsable de l'ensemble des chefs de service.

«Je fais le bilan de la situation de nos quelque 1 000 clients, qui sont, en général, des autistes, des adolescents en état de crise et des adultes aux prises avec des troubles graves de comportement. Je tente de maintenir l'équilibre entre le soutien à leur apporter et les moyens dont on dispose pour le faire.

«En tant que cadre intermédiaire, je joue un rôle important, car je suis à la fois proche du terrain et de la direction. Je peux donc influencer les décisions et les actions.» Manon participe d'ailleurs à toutes les rencontres entre patrons et syndicat, et fait aussi partie du comité de direction.

ma motivation

Passionnée par les relations humaines, Manon se dit très heureuse dans le milieu dans lequel elle évolue. Ce qu'elle aime par-dessus tout, c'est le défi des cas particuliers.

«On peut rencontrer des clients qui cassent tout, qui mangent tout, etc. On doit alors travailler en équipe pour parvenir à les contrôler.»

Manon doit aussi superviser le travail du personnel qui est sous ses ordres, et composer avec la personnalité de chacun pour en tirer le meilleur.

mon conseil

Manon estime que son métier lui en a appris beaucoup, notamment sur les relations humaines.

«Je crois également en avoir beaucoup appris sur moi-même, autant sur mes qualités que sur mes défauts. Le contact permanent avec les autres permet de faire le point sur ses forces et ses faiblesses.»

Selon elle, pour réussir dans le domaine de la réadaptation en déficience intellectuelle, il faut se faire confiance et être déterminé.
06/03

mon parcours

À la fin des années 1960, Manon a suivi un cours en éducation spécialisée à l'École normale Jacques-Cartier, à Montréal. Plus tard, elle a suivi les cours de formation générale au Cégep Marie-Victorin, et a ainsi obtenu un diplôme d'études collégiales (DEC) en éducation spécialisée. Elle a également poursuivi trois certificats à l'Université de Montréal, l'un en créativité, l'autre en communication et le dernier en intervention auprès de la clientèle déficiente intellectuelle. «Mon certificat en créativité m'aide à trouver des solutions novatrices pour résoudre les différents problèmes que nous connaissons avec notre clientèle.» Avant d'obtenir son poste actuel, qu'elle occupe depuis 20 ans, Manon a aussi été chef de service dans un centre de services adaptés.

Les mots en caractères **gras** sont définis à la page 153.

Cadre supérieure
❯ dans un organisme public

mon travail

Le Centre de réadaptation et déficience intellectuelle Gabrielle-Major à Montréal offre des services d'adaptation et de réadaptation à quelque 1 300 personnes déficientes intellectuelles. Directrice à la recherche et à la qualité des services, Mireille Tremblay travaille, avec son équipe, à offrir aux personnes déficientes des services permettant une meilleure intégration sociale, professionnelle et communautaire. «On évalue les besoins des clients et leurs performances. On regarde le niveau d'autonomie qu'ils peuvent atteindre et on met en place des services pour leur permettre d'évoluer, si cela est nécessaire en collaboration avec les CLSC, les commissions scolaires, la famille et certains organismes communautaires.»

Dans ses tâches, Mireille doit également évaluer la qualité des interventions cliniques et professionnelles offertes au Centre.

Des milieux de travail potentiels

- ❯ Centres d'hébergement et de soins de longue durée
- ❯ Centres de réadaptation
- ❯ Centres hospitaliers
- ❯ Centres jeunesse
- ❯ Centres locaux de services communautaires (CLSC)

ma motivation

La carrière de Mireille a été inspirée par une noble cause. «J'ai une passion, celle du respect des droits de la personne. J'œuvre pour que les relations interpersonnelles soient égalitaires, d'adulte à adulte, quel que soit le handicap ou la déficience, ce qui passe par le développement de l'autonomie. L'aspect recherche et développement est tout récent en centre de réadaptation, poursuit-elle. On explore, on innove, c'est très stimulant.»

Aider les personnes déficientes à s'intégrer dans la communauté demeure la motivation première de Mireille. «À partir du moment où elles vivent dans la communauté, qu'elles soient en institution ou non, les personnes déficientes ont droit à une vie personnelle, affective, sexuelle. Et c'est à nous de les aider dans ce sens.»

Mireille a aussi le désir d'améliorer la qualité des services offerts et des expertises que possèdent les personnes œuvrant au Centre.

mon conseil

Mireille attribue sa réussite à sa passion pour les droits de la personne et pour l'équité. «Il faut avoir confiance en soi et aller jusqu'au bout de ses objectifs. En santé mentale, il faut penser à ce qu'il est possible d'accomplir pour aider les personnes les plus vulnérables à s'intégrer dans la communauté.»
05/03

mon parcours

Mireille a décroché sa maîtrise en psychologie à l'Université du Québec à Montréal en 1977, puis a travaillé en hôpital psychiatrique avant d'intégrer la Régie régionale de la santé de la Montérégie en 1983, à la planification et la coordination de services en santé mentale. En 1992, elle devient secrétaire générale, puis directrice générale de la Fédération québécoise des centres de réadaptation en déficience intellectuelle, poste qu'elle occupe jusqu'en 2000, année où elle obtient son doctorat en sciences humaines appliquées, à l'Université de Montréal. Elle œuvre au Centre de réadaptation et déficience intellectuelle Gabrielle-Major depuis l'automne 2001.

Les mots en caractères **gras** sont définis à la page 153.

Directrice générale

> **dans un organisme public**

mon travail

Faire travailler harmonieusement plus de 350 personnes, voilà le défi que relève Madeleine Roy, directrice du Centre Dollard-Cormier, le plus important établissement public de traitement de la toxicomanie, de l'alcoolisme et du jeu compulsif et excessif au Québec. Personne clé dans le fonctionnement du Centre, Madeleine préside les réunions du conseil d'administration, signe tous les chèques et voit aux suivis budgétaires, requis par le ministère de la Santé et des Services sociaux aux 28 jours. «Tous les contrats qui sortent de l'établissement doivent être signés par moi, ajoute-t-elle. Je dois les lire et les comprendre pour les présenter au conseil d'administration afin d'obtenir l'autorisation de les signer.»

Ses journées commencent dès 7 h 15. En arrivant au bureau, elle prend ses messages pour ensuite réexpédier à ses collègues les courriels qui les concernent. Puis, elle se penche sur l'administration courante. Quand son adjointe arrive, elles regardent ensemble la planification de la journée. Vers 9 h, l'enfilade des réunions commence. Conseil d'administration, syndicat, employés... elle passe ainsi d'un groupe à l'autre jusqu'à la fin de l'après-midi. Il lui arrive aussi de donner de la formation, d'en suivre elle-même et de représenter le Centre lors d'événements publics.

Des milieux de travail potentiels

> Centres d'hébergement et de soins de longue durée

> Centres de réadaptation

> Centres hospitaliers

> Centres jeunesse

> Centres locaux de services communautaires (CLSC)

ma motivation

«Comme éducatrice, intervenante et présidente de syndicat, on me disait souvent que j'étais un leader naturel. C'est ce qui m'a amenée en gestion. Je suis bonne en animation de groupe, en présidence de groupe, j'ai fait beaucoup de médiation et je prône toujours la recherche de solutions», explique-t-elle. Femme de tête et de cœur, Madeleine apprécie grandement la possibilité qu'elle a de pouvoir gérer à sa manière un tel établissement. «Je favorise la médiation, l'approche gagnant-gagnant avec le personnel et les syndicats, même si ce n'est pas toujours facile. Je crois au partage de l'information et à la transparence des communications. Ici, tout circule, les procès-verbaux et le reste. Je crois aussi à l'écoute, et ma porte est toujours ouverte.»

mon conseil

Même si son caractère de meneuse la prédisposait à occuper un poste de direction, Madeleine estime que sa formation en gestion a été déterminante. «Ma maîtrise à l'École nationale d'administration publique (ENAP) m'a donné des outils pour mieux diriger», explique-t-elle, en citant comme exemple les connaissances en droit administratif et en organisation du travail qu'elle a pu acquérir. 06/03

mon parcours

Madeleine a obtenu un diplôme d'études collégiales (DEC) en éducation spécialisée au Collège Marie-Victorin, puis un baccalauréat en orthopédagogie à l'Université de Montréal, une formation qui l'a amenée à travailler plusieurs années comme intervenante en éducation spécialisée. Puis, elle s'est vu confier des fonctions de direction, qu'elle a occupées tout en poursuivant une maîtrise en administration publique à l'ENAP. Elle a dirigé plusieurs établissements spécialisés (en déficience visuelle et intellectuelle, notamment), avant de prendre la barre du Centre Dollard-Cormier.

Les mots en caractères **gras** sont définis à la page 153.

Glossaire

A **Aide auditive (ou prothèse auditive)**
Appareil acoustique de type électronique, électro-acoustique ou mécanique destiné à corriger une déficience du système auditif ou à suppléer aux incapacités qui en découlent.

ADN
Abréviation pour *acide désoxyribonucléique*, le constituant essentiel des chromosomes, porteurs des facteurs déterminants de l'hérédité.

Anémie
Trouble hématologique qui provoque la diminution de la concentration d'hémoglobine dans le sang en deçà des valeurs normales.

Anxiété
Sentiment d'un danger imminent et indéterminé s'accompagnant d'un état de malaise, d'agitation, de désarroi et d'anéantissement.

Apnée du sommeil
Interruption des efforts respiratoires survenant pendant le sommeil lorsque les centres respiratoires cessent de commander la contraction des muscles respiratoires.

Appareil d'électrochirurgie
Appareil de chirurgie qui utilise les diverses propriétés des courants de haute fréquence pour coaguler ou sectionner.

ARN
Abréviation pour *acide ribonucléique*, une molécule présente dans la cellule qui sert d'intermédiaire à la synthèse des protéines.

Arthrite
Inflammation d'une ou de plusieurs articulations.

Arthrose
Lésion chronique, dégénérative et non inflammatoire d'une articulation caractérisée entre autres par l'altération du cartilage et causant des douleurs, des déformations et des craquements.

Arthrose lombaire
Lésion chronique, dégénérative et non inflammatoire d'une articulation dans le bas du dos.

Arythmie
Irrégularité du rythme cardiaque.

Aseptique
Exempt de tout microbe.

Asthme
Affection pulmonaire chronique qui se caractérise par une difficulté à respirer. Les voies aériennes des personnes asthmatiques sont hypersensibles ou hyperréactives. Elles réagissent en se rétrécissant ou en s'obstruant lorsqu'elles sont irritées, ce qui entrave la circulation de l'air.

Audiogramme
Graphique représentant la valeur de l'audition de chaque oreille.

Audiologiste
Personne qui évalue les problèmes de l'ouïe et qui les traite avec des aides auditives ou un programme de réadaptation.

Autisme
Détachement de la réalité et repli sur soi avec prédominance de la vie intérieure.

B **Bioéthique**
Champ d'étude et de recherche portant sur les enjeux éthiques posés par les progrès scientifiques et technologiques de la médecine et de l'ensemble des sciences de la vie.

Biologie moléculaire
Discipline qui étudie les mécanismes biologiques en fonction des structures et des interactions des constituants moléculaires de la cellule.

Biomécanique
Discipline qui étudie les structures et les fonctions physiologiques des organismes en relation avec les lois de la mécanique.

Bronchite chronique
Syndrome caractérisé par une toux, permanente ou intermittente, liée à une augmentation de la sécrétion bronchique (et non obligatoirement de l'expectoration), survenant durant un minimum de trois mois, non forcément consécutifs dans l'année et pendant un minimum de deux années consécutives.

Brucellose
Maladie infectieuse, contagieuse, chronique, due à la multiplication d'une bactérie du genre *Brucella* et affectant l'homme et divers animaux (bovins, ovins, caprins, porcins, équidés, carnivores, oiseaux).

Bursite
Inflammation aiguë ou chronique d'une bourse séreuse. Les bourses séreuses ont pour rôle de faciliter les mouvements des organes auxquels elles sont annexées (principalement les articulations).

C **Cataracte**
Opacité du cristallin entraînant une insuffisance de la vue pouvant aller jusqu'à la cécité.

Centrifugeuse
Appareil pour la séparation de matériaux, dont l'élément constitutif essentiel est un réservoir tournant, dans lequel se trouve le mélange à séparer. Appareil à rotation rapide utilisée pour séparer les matières de densités différentes.

Chirurgie valvulaire
Chirurgie visant à réparer ou à remplacer par une prothèse une valvule cardiaque abîmée. Les valvules sont les groupes de valves qui permettent le passage unidirectionnel du sang dans les cavités du cœur.

Glossaire (suite)

Cognitif
Qualifie les processus cognitifs par lesquels un organisme acquiert des informations sur l'environnement et les élabore pour régler son comportement : perception, formation de concepts, raisonnement, langage, décision, pensée.

Collagénoses
Maladies qui ont pour caractéristique commune la dégénérescence du collagène, la substance qui donne au corps sa forme et son élasticité.

Colonoscopie (ou coloscopie)
Technique qui permet d'explorer le côlon et la muqueuse qui le tapisse, dans le but de poser des diagnostics ou de traiter des pathologies.

Composition génétique
Tous les gènes des êtres vivants sont constitués de quatre éléments de base : A, T, C et G. La diversité des organismes vivants de la planète provient des innombrables combinaisons différentes de ces quatre éléments, soit la composition génétique.

Cornée
Membrane fibreuse et transparente, véritable «hublot» qui constitue la face avant de l'œil.

Coronographie
Examen radiologique dont le principe est d'injecter directement dans les artères du cœur un produit réactif faisant apparaître un contraste visible sur une radiographie.

Cristallin
Organe en forme de petite lentille biconvexe, transparent et mou, situé à l'intérieur du globe oculaire, en arrière de l'iris et en avant du corps vitré.

Culture bactérienne
Technique permettant d'obtenir la multiplication des bactéries *in vitro*.

D Dégénérescence maculaire
Altération de la macula (zone centrale de la rétine permettant la vision fine et précise) qui entraîne une perte progressive et importante de la vision.

Désordre électrolytique
Déséquilibre des ions sanguins comme le potassium, le sodium, le calcium.

Dialyse
Technique d'épuration extrarénale faisant appel à des appareils de dialyse fonctionnant sur circulation extracorporelle et appelés hémodialyseurs.

Dialyse péritonéale
Mode d'épuration extrarénale utilisant la membrane péritonéale comme membrane de dialyse des déchets azotés retenus dans le sang urémique, et consistant à introduire dans la cavité péritonéale un liquide de dialyse qu'on évacue et qu'on renouvelle régulièrement pendant un temps déterminé.

Dosage des enzymes du muscle du cœur
Examen qui consiste à mesurer le taux d'enzymes dans le cœur. Par exemple la troponine est une enzyme qui s'élève rapidement au cours de l'infarctus du myocarde.

E Électrocardiogramme
Représentation graphique des signaux électriques émis par le cœur en fonction du temps.

Électrolyte corporel
Corps qui, à l'état soluble, peut se dissocier en anions et cations sous l'action d'un courant électrique.

Électromyographie
Enregistrement graphique des courants électriques qui accompagnent l'activité musculaire ou l'inactivité en vue d'étudier un problème moteur.

Électrothérapie
Emploi des courants électriques continus ou alternatifs comme moyen thérapeutique.

Emphysème
Distension entraînée par la présence d'air dans les interstices du tissu conjonctif ou dans le tissu alvéolaire des poumons.

Endocrinologie
Science qui a pour objet l'étude de l'anatomie, de la physiologie et de la pathologie des glandes endocrines et de leurs hormones.

Endoscopie
Technique qui permet d'explorer l'intérieur des cavités naturelles du corps – appareils digestif, respiratoire et génital – au moyen d'un endoscope (instrument muni d'un tube optique et d'un système d'éclairage), dans le but de poser des diagnostics ou de traiter des pathologies.

Équipe volante
Équipe dont les salariés polyvalents sont affectés individuellement ou collectivement à différents postes pour combler les besoins particuliers de l'entreprise au fur et à mesure qu'ils se présentent.

Ergothérapeute
Professionnel de la santé qui aide les personnes souffrant d'incapacité physique ou mentale à réaliser leurs activités quotidiennes. Au besoin, l'ergothérapeute propose des aides techniques et un aménagement de l'environnement du patient.

Estradiol
Principale hormone œstrogène sécrétée chez l'humain.

État nutritionnel
État de l'organisme résultant de l'ingestion, de l'absorption et de l'utilisation des aliments, ainsi que des facteurs de nature pathologique.

Examen direct de l'expectoration
Examen qui consiste à analyser un échantillon de crachat pour en déterminer son contenu.

Glossaire (suite)

Exploration fonctionnelle du système respiratoire
Examen qui consiste à faire souffler le patient de différentes façons dans l'embout d'un capteur relié à un écran informatique. Les résultats obtenus sont comparés avec des moyennes correspondant au profil du patient, (sexe, âge, poids, etc.).

F Fibrillation (cardiaque)
Contraction rapide et désordonnée des fibres du muscle cardiaque. Ce phénomène peut toucher les cavités supérieures du cœur (fibrillation auriculaire) ou les cavités inférieures (fibrillation ventriculaire). Lorsque le cœur est en fibrillation, il palpite et est incapable de pomper le sang.

Fièvre aphteuse
Zoonose virale de forme aiguë causée par le virus du genre *Aphthovirus* fortement contagieux, exceptionnellement transmissible à l'homme mais affectant sous forme d'épizooties les biongulés domestiques (porcs, etc.) et certains ruminants sauvages, qui est caractérisée par de la fièvre, des aphtes et des érosions au niveau des muqueuses buccales et nasales, de même que sur le bourrelet coronaire du pied et les espaces interdigités.

Flore humaine (ou microflore)
Ensemble des micro-organismes végétaux qui vivent sur les tissus ou dans les cavités naturelles de l'organisme.

Fluoroscopie
Méthode d'imagerie fonctionnelle qui consiste à observer l'image lumineuse des organes internes produite sur un écran fluorescent par l'interposition du corps entre cet écran et un faisceau de rayons X.

G Gavage
Introduction d'aliments dans l'estomac au moyen d'un tube qui passe habituellement par les narines, le pharynx et l'œsophage.

Génétique
Branche de la biologie qui étudie les caractères héréditaires et les variations accidentelles.

Glandes endocrines
Glandes à sécrétion interne, dont les produits (hormones) sont déversés directement dans le sang et la lymphe.

Glande thyroïde
Glande endocrine située dans la partie antérieure et inférieure du cou, responsable de la synthèse, du stockage et de la sécrétion d'hormones ayant une action activatrice sur le métabolisme en général.

Globule sanguin
Cellule arrondie semi-fluide que l'on trouve dans le sang.

Groupe sanguin
Classification des individus selon les caractéristiques de leur sang permettant de déterminer la compatibilité entre le donneur et le receveur lors d'une transfusion sanguine. Le système ABO, qui comprend les groupes sanguins A, B, O et AB, englobe la plupart des individus.

H HACCP (pour *Hazard Analysis Critical Control Point*)
Système qui vise à assurer la salubrité des aliments grâce à l'application de rigoureux mécanismes de contrôle d'un bout à l'autre de la chaîne de production. Les usines d'abattage canadiennes sont tenues d'appliquer le système HACCP pour exporter aux États-Unis.

Hémodialyse
Voir dialyse.

Hernie discale
Saillie anormale du disque intervertébral dans le canal rachidien, due à l'expulsion, en arrière, à la suite d'un traumatisme, du *Nucleus pulposus*.

Homéostasie
Tendance de l'organisme à maintenir ses différentes constantes à des valeurs ne s'écartant pas de la normale (l'homéostasie assure, par exemple, le maintien de la température, du débit sanguin, de la tension artérielle, du pH, des volumes liquidiens de l'organisme, de la composition du milieu intérieur, etc.).

Hydrothérapie
Traitement basé sur une utilisation externe de l'eau, sous toutes ses formes et à des températures variables : bains, douches, enveloppements, compresses humides, sacs à glace ou à eau chaude, etc.

Hyperactivité
Instabilité du comportement de certains enfants, toujours actifs, qui ont des difficultés à se concentrer sur une seule activité.

Hypophyse
Glande endocrine qui sécrète des hormones agissant sur le fonctionnement d'autres glandes endocrines.

Hypospadias
Malformation congénitale de l'urètre de l'homme caractérisée par la situation anormale de son orifice sur la face ventrale du pénis.

I Immunofluorescence
Technique qui consiste à rendre fluorescent un antigène déterminé à l'intérieur d'une cellule (un antigène est une substance capable de déclencher une réponse immunitaire). Cette méthode permet de détecter et de localiser les antigènes viraux dans la cellule infectée.

Immunoglobuline
Terme générique désignant l'ensemble des globulines sériques constituant les anticorps.

Infiltration
Injection, généralement dans une articulation, d'un médicament qui permet de diminuer la douleur.

Glossaire (suite)

Inhalothérapeute
Professionnel paramédical spécialisé dans les soins du système cardiorespiratoire, par exemple, l'humidification des voies respiratoires, la réanimation cardiorespiratoire ou encore la ventilation artificielle prolongée. On le retrouve souvent en salle d'opération, où il assiste l'anesthésiologiste dans la surveillance des fonctions vitales du patient.

Interaction médicamenteuse
Phénomène qui survient lorsque deux ou plusieurs médicaments ayant été administrés simultanément ou successivement, les effets de l'un sont modifiés par la présence du ou des autres.

Iris
Structure pigmentée donnant sa couleur à l'œil et percée d'un trou, la pupille.

L Laparoscopie
Endoscopie de la cavité abdominale, qui se pratique à l'aide d'un endoscope rigide, soit un laparoscope, introduit au travers d'une courte incision. La laparoscopie diagnostique permet de visualiser les organes. La laparoscopie opératoire permet de pratiquer, dans un but thérapeutique, des interventions chirurgicales à l'aide d'instruments miniaturisés.

Leucémie
Terme générique recouvrant un groupe d'affections caractérisées par la présence en excès dans la moelle osseuse et parfois dans le sang de leucocytes ou de leurs précurseurs.

Luxation
Déplacement anormal de l'un des os d'une articulation.

**M Machine cœur-poumon
(ou cœur-poumon artificiel)**
Machine qui permet d'arrêter le cœur et les poumons du patient durant une chirurgie cardiaque. Le sang qui arrive au cœur est collecté par une canule (petit tuyau) puis dirigé vers un oxygénateur, qui remplit le rôle des poumons en oxygénant le sang et en le débarrassant du gaz carbonique. Le sang est ensuite réinjecté dans l'organisme par l'action d'une pompe.

Maladies respiratoires environnementales
Aussi pneumoconioses. Ensemble des désordres broncho-pulmonaires liés à l'accumulation de particules minérales dans les poumons et à la réaction des tissus à la présence de ces particules. Sont souvent reliées au milieu de travail.

Maniaco-dépression
Affection mentale caractérisée par des accès d'excitation psychique qui alternent avec des périodes de dépression.

Médecine d'expertise
Expertise médicale qui permet de fournir au juge saisi d'une affaire un avis scientifique qualifié sous la forme d'un rapport.

Médecine interne
Branche de la médecine qui se consacre au diagnostic et au traitement des maladies générales affectant un ou plusieurs organes, ou des problèmes de santé difficiles à évaluer par une approche conventionnelle.

Médecin traitant
Médecin généraliste qui a la responsabilité du suivi de ses patients et qui les dirige, au besoin, vers un spécialiste ou un hôpital.

Mélanome
Tumeur maligne caractérisée par sa couleur brune et noire.

Méridien
Canal ou vaisseau dans lequel circule l'énergie vitale, véritable ligne de flux énergétique continu, comportant une source, une ligne d'écoulement, des champs d'élargissement et de rétrécissement, de passage et de chute, et sur le trajet duquel se trouvent situés les points cutanés, lieux privilégiés permettant d'en régulariser le débit.

Mésadapté socio-affectif
Personne qui manifeste des problèmes de comportement affectif et social incompatibles avec la qualité et la quantité des situations et des actes éducatifs de l'enseignement régulier.

Microscope ophtalmologique
Microscope spécialisé servant à examiner les yeux.

Microscopie électronique
Technique d'observation qui fait appel à une variété de microscopes à très fort pouvoir grossissant, utilisant un faisceau d'électrons et des lentilles magnétiques au lieu d'un faisceau lumineux et de lentilles optiques.

N Néonatalogie
Branche de la médecine qui a pour objet la surveillance et les soins spécialisés du nouveau-né à risques ou de celui dont l'état s'est dégradé après la naissance.

O Obturation
Opération consistant à insérer un matériau dans la cavité préparée d'une dent.

Œdème
Infiltration séreuse excessive, indolore et sans rougeur des tissus conjonctifs sous-cutanés et sous-muqueux.

Ophtalmoscope
Instrument destiné à la fois à éclairer et à examiner le fond de l'œil.

Orchidopexie
Intervention chirurgicale qui a pour but d'abaisser un testicule, qui n'est pas descendu naturellement dans les bourses.

Glossaire (suite)

Orthèse
Aide technique destinée à suppléer ou à corriger une fonction déficiente, à compenser les limitations ou même à accroître le rendement physiologique d'un organe ou d'un membre qui a perdu sa fonction, qui ne s'est jamais pleinement développé ou est atteint d'anomalies congénitales.

Ostéoporose
Diminution de la masse osseuse.

Oto-rhino-laryngologiste (ORL)
Médecin spécialisé dans le traitement des affections des oreilles, du nez et de la gorge.

P **Paranoïa**
Perturbation mentale caractérisée par de la méfiance et une interprétation exagérée des événements.

Paraplégie
Paralysie des membres inférieurs et de la partie basse du tronc.

Patch test
Test qui consiste à poser dans le dos du patient des pastilles collantes enduites de réactif et à vérifier, au bout de 48 heures, si certaines d'entre elles ont provoqué une inflammation sur la peau.

Péricardite
Inflammation aiguë ou chronique du péricarde sous l'influence d'une infection.

Pharmacologie
Science qui étudie les médicaments, notamment leur source, leur préparation, leur action, leurs propriétés thérapeutiques et leur emploi.

Pharmacopée
Ensemble de matières premières (végétales, minérales et animales) ayant des propriétés médicales et thérapeutiques.

Physiatre
Médecin dont la spécialité concerne le diagnostic, le traitement et la prévention des affections de l'appareil locomoteur (ensemble des fonctions osseuses, musculaires et articulatoires qui permettent le déplacement).

Physiothérapeute
Personne qui pose un acte thérapeutique ayant pour objet d'obtenir le rendement fonctionnel maximal des diverses capacités d'un individu par l'utilisation de thérapies manuelles, d'exercices physiques ou par d'autres agents physiques comme la chaleur, le froid, l'eau et l'ultrason.

Polygraphie ou polysomnographie
Ensemble des techniques permettant l'observation et l'enregistrement de diverses activités physiologiques survenant pendant le sommeil. Permet notamment de détecter l'apnée du sommeil.

Pontage coronarien
Lorsqu'un segment d'artère coronaire est rétréci ou bouché, la circulation du sang vers le cœur se trouve compromise. Pour y remédier, le chirurgien crée un canal contournant la région obstruée au moyen d'une greffe de vaisseau sanguin.

Prothèse
Aide technique destiné à remplacer en tout ou en partie un organe ou un membre et à lui restituer sa fonction ou son aspect original.

Prothèse dentaire
Appareil fixe ou mobile porteur de plusieurs dents (prothèse partielle) ou remplaçant la totalité des dents (prothèse totale).

Psychomotricité
Intégration des fonctions mentales et motrices résultant de l'éducation et de la maturation du système nerveux.

Pyéloplastie
Reconstruction chirurgicale du rein visant à en corriger une occlusion.

R **Radiation ionisante**
(ou rayonnement ionisant)
Radiation utilisée dans le traitement du cancer. On la dit «ionisante» parce qu'elle forme des ions en passant à travers les tissus, ce qui a pour effet de détruire ou d'affaiblir les cellules cancéreuses.

Radio-isotope
Isotope radioactif d'un élément chimique.

Radiothérapie
Emploi thérapeutique des rayons X.

Réactif
Substance qui permet d'en identifier une autre lors d'une réaction chimique.

Recherche fondamentale
Travaux entrepris essentiellement dans la perspective de reculer les limites des connaissances scientifiques sans avoir en vue aucune application pratique spécifique. Ils peuvent aboutir à la découverte de lois et d'éléments nouveaux.

Résidence
Voir résident.

Résident
Étudiant diplômé en médecine qui poursuit en milieu hospitalier un programme de deux ans en médecine familiale ou un programme de spécialisation de quatre ou cinq ans dans une discipline approuvée.

Rétine
Membrane du fond de l'œil sensible au stimulus lumineux.

Glossaire (suite)

Rétinite pigmentaire
Affection d'origine héréditaire consistant en une dégénérescence progressive de la rétine qui aboutit à une cécité totale.

Rétinopathie
Toute affection de la rétine et, en particulier, une affection non inflammatoire (bien qu'il y ait des exceptions à cette règle).

Rupture d'anévrisme
Éclatement des parois d'un anévrisme, qui provoque une hémorragie dans les tissus environnants.

S Salmonellose
Infection due à des germes appartenant au genre *Salmonella*.

Scanographie
Radiographie obtenue par un scanner.

Schizophrénie
Affection mentale caractérisée par un repli sur soi et une perte de contact avec la réalité.

Scintigraphie
Procédé permettant de repérer dans l'organisme un isotope radioactif qui y a été introduit.

Soins de longue durée
Soins personnels et infirmiers, de légers à moyens, qui sont prodigués à des personnes âgées ou atteintes d'une maladie chronique ou d'une incapacité, dans une maison de soins infirmiers ou à domicile, pendant une longue période de temps.

Souffle au cœur
Souffle perçu à l'auscultation du cœur et qui a son origine dans cet organe.

Subluxation
Luxation incomplète d'une articulation. Luxation ou entorse partielle.

Système MF
Système de transmission du son par ondes radio composé d'un émetteur et d'un récepteur. L'enseignant porte l'émetteur, dont le microphone est épinglé sur son vêtement, vis-à-vis du menton. L'élève sourd, quant à lui, porte le récepteur, qui se branche dans ses appareils auditifs. Ce système permet à l'élève de mieux entendre dans les situations où l'enseignant se tient à plus de deux mètres de lui, se déplace constamment dans la classe ou parle parmi un bruit de fond.

T Tendinite
Inflammation d'un tendon, soit la structure fibreuse par laquelle un muscle se fixe à un os.

Test cutané (*prick test*)
Test qui consiste à injecter dans le bras du patient de très petites doses de différents réactifs et à vérifier au bout d'une vingtaine de minutes si certaines injections ont provoqué une inflammation sur la peau.

Test Pap (ou colpocytologie)
Examen microscopique des cellules prélevées sur le col de l'utérus permettant le dépistage précoce du cancer.

Tomodensitométrie (aussi appelée «tomographie axiale assistée par ordinateur» ou, plus familièrement, «scan»)
Technique d'imagerie qui permet de visualiser par coupes n'importe quelle partie de l'anatomie en plus de révéler les différences de densité des divers tissus.

Traumatologie
Branche de la médecine qui se consacre à l'étude des traumatismes physiques et au traitement des patients ayant subi de graves blessures, généralement au cours d'un accident.

Troubles de l'attention
Toute maladie mentale s'accompagnant de troubles de l'attention passagers (délires, hallucinations) ou permanents (débilité mentale, schizophrénie, par exemple).

Troubles du comportement
Difficultés d'adaptation, voire inadaptations qui peuvent être transitoires ou permanentes.

Tubage gastrique
Procédure qui consiste à glisser une sonde gastrique par le nez ou par la bouche jusqu'à l'estomac, afin d'alimenter le patient artificiellement lorsque ce dernier a trop de difficulté à respirer, dans les cas de tuberculose infantile notamment.

Tuberculose
Maladie contagieuse et inoculable, commune à l'homme et aux animaux, due à une bactérie (le *Mycobacterium tuberculosis* ou bacille de Koch).

U Ultrasons
Sons de très grande fréquence ondulatoire (non perceptibles par l'oreille humaine) utilisés comme traitement.

V Vitré
Masse visqueuse transparente occupant l'espace entre la face postérieure du cristallin et la rétine.

Note de l'éditeur :
Ces définitions sont principalement tirées du Grand Dictionnaire terminologique de l'Office québécois de la langue française (www.granddictionnaire.com). Au besoin, certaines définitions ont été complétées par des sources spécialisées.

Répertoire des principales formations
> liées à la santé et aux services sociaux

Attention : Ce répertoire était à jour en septembre 2003.
Des programmes ont pu être retirés ou ajoutés depuis.

La formation professionnelle

Voici les principaux programmes d'études professionnelles pouvant mener à une carrière dans le domaine de la santé et des services sociaux. Ils visent l'obtention d'un diplôme d'études professionnelles (DEP) ou d'une attestation de spécialisation professionnelle (ASP).

- Assistance aux bénéficiaires en établissement de santé (DEP)
- Assistance dentaire (DEP)
- Assistance familiale et sociale aux personnes à domicile (DEP)
- Assistance technique en pharmacie (DEP)
- Santé, assistance et soins infirmiers (DEP)
- Secrétariat médical (ASP)

La formation collégiale

Voici les principaux programmes d'études collégiales pouvant mener à une carrière dans le domaine de la santé et des services sociaux. La majorité visent l'obtention d'un diplôme d'études collégiales en formation technique (DEC). Nous avons aussi ajouté deux programmes permettant d'obtenir une attestation d'études collégiales (AEC) lorsque ce diplôme constitue la principale voie d'accès à la pratique de professions traitées dans ce livre.

- Acupuncture (DEC)
- Archives médicales (DEC)
- Audioprothèse (DEC)
- Cytotechnologie (AEC)
- Soins infirmiers (DEC)
- Techniques ambulancières (AEC)
- Techniques d'éducation spécialisée (DEC)
- Techniques d'électrophysiologie médicale (DEC)
- Techniques d'hygiène dentaire (DEC)
- Techniques d'inhalothérapie (DEC)
- Techniques d'intervention en loisir (DEC)
- Techniques d'orthèses et de prothèses orthopédiques (DEC)
- Techniques d'orthèses visuelles (DEC)
- Techniques de denturologie (DEC)
- Techniques de diététique (DEC)
- Techniques de réadaptation physique (DEC)
- Techniques de santé animale (DEC)
- Techniques de thanatologie (DEC)
- Techniques de travail social (DEC)

Répertoire des principales formations
> liées à la santé et aux services sociaux (suite)

- Technologie de laboratoire médical (DEC)
- Technologie de l'électronique (DEC) – voir aussi le certificat universitaire Technologies biomédicales : instrumentation électronique.
- Technologie de médecine nucléaire (DEC)
- Technologie de radiodiagnostic (DEC)
- Technologie de radio-oncologie (DEC)
- Technologies d'analyses biomédicales (DEC)
- Technologie des systèmes ordinés (DEC) – voir aussi le certificat universitaire Technologies biomédicales : instrumentation électronique.

La formation universitaire

Voici les principaux programmes d'études universitaires pouvant mener à une carrière dans le domaine de la santé et des services sociaux. La majorité mènent à l'obtention d'un diplôme de baccalauréat. Nous avons aussi ajouté des programmes permettant d'obtenir un certificat ou un diplôme de deuxième cycle universitaire lorsque ceux-ci constituent la principale voie d'accès à la pratique de professions traitées dans ce livre. Les titres des programmes sont généraux et peuvent différer d'une université à une autre.

- Audiologie (Bac)
- Biochimie clinique (Bac)
- Bio-informatique (Bac)
- Biologie (Bac)
- Biologie médicale (Bac)
- Biophysique (Bac)
- Chiropratique (Bac)
- Diététique/Nutrition (Bac)
- Ergothérapie (Bac)
- Génie biomédical (Maîtrise ou doctorat)
- Kinésiologie (Bac)
- Médecine dentaire (Bac)
- Médecine familiale (Doctorat en médecine)
- Médecine spécialisée (Diplôme d'études spécialisées en médecine)
- Médecine vétérinaire (Bac)
- Microbiologie (Bac)
- Optométrie (Bac)
- Orthophonie (Bac)
- Perfusion extra-corporelle (Certificat)
- Pharmacie (Bac)
- Pharmacologie (Bac)
- Physiothérapie (Bac)
- Physique médicale (Bac)

- Podiatrie (Bac)
- Pratique sage-femme (Bac)
- Psychoéducation (Bac)
- Psychologie (Bac)
- Sciences de l'activité physique (Bac)
- Sciences infirmières (et nursing) (Bac)
- Sexologie (Bac)
- Technologies biomédicales : instrumentation électronique (Certificat)
- Travail social (Bac)

Les principales formations universitaires liées à l'administration

- Baccalauréat en administration des affaires
  (finance, marketing, gestiondes ressources humaines, etc.)
- Baccalauréat en comptabilité ou sciences comptables
- Baccalauréat en économie
- Maîtrise en administration des affaires (MBA)
- Maîtrise ou doctorat en administration publique

Plusieurs universités offrent également divers programmes d'études liés à l'administration publique et à la gestion des services de santé (microprogrammes, programmes courts, certificats, diplômes d'études supérieures spécialisées (DESS), diplômes de deuxième et de troisième cycle (maîtrises et doctorats). Certains baccalauréats peuvent aussi offrir une spécialisation en administration publique.

Renseignez-vous auprès des établissements d'enseignement qui vous intéressent. ■

> ## Comment savoir où est offert un programme d'études?

La formation professionnelle et technique

Vous pouvez consulter le **Réseau télématique de la formation professionnelle et technique du ministère de l'Éducation du Québec** à l'adresse suivante : http://inforoutefpt.org

Dans ce site, vous pouvez orienter vos recherches à partir d'un secteur de formation ou encore directement à partir du nom du programme désiré. Vous aurez ainsi accès à des informations sur le programme sélectionné : les établissements d'enseignement offrant la formation, les conditions d'admission, la durée, les objectifs et le contenu du programme.

La formation universitaire

Pour connaître les universités qui offrent un programme spécifique, vous pouvez consulter le **Répertoire des universités canadiennes** à l'adresse suivante : http://oraweb.auce.ca/showdcu_f.html Effectuez une recherche par province, par discipline, par diplôme et par programme.

Pour obtenir une information juste et à jour, consultez les sites Internet des universités qui vous intéressent. Vous y trouverez des renseignements sur les programmes d'études, les modalités d'inscription, les cours offerts et la vie étudiante.

Répertoire des principales associations et des ordres professionnels

A **Acupuncture**
Ordre professionnel des acupuncteurs
du Québec
Tél. : (514) 523-2882

Archives médicales
Association québécoise des
archivistes médicales
Tél. : (819) 823-6670 • www.aqam.ca

Assistance dentaire
Association des assistant(e)s dentaires
du Québec
Tél. : (514) 722-9900
www.cdaa.ca/en/prov/quebec.asp

Assistance familiale et sociale
Association canadienne de soins palliatifs
Tél. : (613) 241-3663 ou 1 800 668-2785
www.acsp.net

Association des auxiliaires familiales et
sociales du Québec
www2.globetrotter.net/benevole/aafs

Assistance technique en pharmacie
Association québécoise des assistant(e)s
techniques en pharmacie • www.aqatp.ca

Audiologie
Association canadienne des
orthophonistes et des audiologistes
Tél. : (613) 567-9968 • www.caslpa.ca

Ordre des orthophonistes et
audiologistes du Québec
Tél. : (514) 282-9123 • www.ooaq.qc.ca

Audioprothèse
Association professionnelle des
audioprothésistes du Québec
Tél. : (514) 498-0077 ou 1 877 698-0077

Ordre des audioprothésistes du Québec
Tél. : (514) 640-5117
www.ordreaudio.qc.ca

B **Biochimie clinique**
Association des médecins biochimistes
du Québec • Tél. : (514) 350-5105
www.ambq.med.usherb.ca

Ordre des chimistes du Québec
Volet biochimie clinique
Tél. : (514) 844-3644 • www.ocq.qc.ca

Biologie médicale
Société québécoise de biologie clinique
www.sqbc.qc.ca

C **Chiropratique**
Ordre des chiropraticiens du Québec
Tél. : (514) 355-8540
www.chiropratique.com/ordre

Cytologie
Association professionnelle des
technologistes médicaux du Québec
Tél. : (514) 524-3734 ou 1 800 361-4306
www.aptmq.qc.ca

Ordre professionnel des technologistes
médicaux du Québec
Tél. : (514) 527-9811 • www.optmq.org

D **Denturologie**
Ordre des denturologistes du Québec
Tél. : (450) 646-7922 ou 1 800 567-2251
www.odq.com

Diététique / Nutrition
Association des diététistes au Québec
Tél. : (514) 954-0047
www.adaqnet.org/accueils/Accueil.html

Ordre professionnel des diététistes
du Québec
Tél. : (514) 393-3733 ou 1 888 393-8528
www.opdq.org

Société des technologues en nutrition
Tél. : (418) 990-0309 • www.stnq.ca

E **Ergothérapie**
Association québécoise des
ergothérapeutes en pratique privée
Tél. : (514) 940-6541

Ordre des ergothérapeutes du Québec
Tél. : (514) 844-5778
www.oeq.org/default.asp

G **Génie biomédical**
Association des physiciens et ingénieurs
biomédicaux du Québec
Tél. : (514) 952-0184
www.apibq.org/index.php3

Association des technicien(ne)s en génie
biomédical • www.atgbm.org

Ordre des ingénieurs du Québec
Tél. : (514) 845-6141 ou 1 800 461-6141
www.oiq.qc.ca

**Gestion du réseau de la santé
et des services sociaux**
Association des cadres supérieurs de la
santé et des services sociaux
Tél. : (450) 465-0360 • www.acssss.qc.ca

Association des directeurs généraux
des services de santé et des services
sociaux du Québec
Tél. : (514) 281-1896 • www.adgsssq.qc.ca

Association des gestionnaires des
établissements de santé et de
services sociaux
Tél. : (450) 651-6000 • www.agesss.qc.ca

Répertoire des principales associations et des ordres professionnels (suite)

H Hygiène dentaire

Association canadienne des hygiénistes dentaires • www.cdha.ca

Ordre des hygiénistes dentaires du Québec
Tél. : (514) 284-7639 ou 1 800 361-2996
www.ohdq.com

I Inhalothérapie

Ordre professionnel des inhalothérapeutes du Québec
Tél. : (514) 931-2900 ou1 800 561-0029
www.opiq.qc.ca

K Kinésiologie

Fédération des kinésiologues du Québec
Tél. : (514) 343-2471
www.kinesiologue.com

M Médecine

Association des allergologues et immunologues du Québec
Tél. : (514) 350-5101
www.allerg.qc.ca/indexf.htm

Association des anesthésiologistes du Québec
Tél. : (514) 843-7671 ou 1 877 843-7691
www.fmsq.org/aaq

Association des cardiologues du Québec
Tél. : (514) 350-5106

Association des chirurgiens cardio-vasculaires et thoraciques du Québec
Tél. : (418) 656-4717

Association des chirurgiens généraux du Québec
Tél. : (514) 350-5107 • www.acgq.qc.ca

Association des conseils des médecins, dentistes et pharmaciens du Québec
www.acmdp.qc.ca

Association des dermatologistes du Québec
Tél. : (514) 350-5111 • www.adq.org

Association des gastro-entérologues du Québec
Tél. : (514) 350-5112 • www.ageq.qc.ca

Association des médecins biochimistes du Québec • Tél. : (514) 350-5105
www.ambq.med.usherb.ca

Association des médecins endocrinologues du Québec
Tél. : (514) 350-5135 • www.ameq.qc.ca

Association des médecins généticiens du Québec • Tél. : (514) 350-5141

Association des médecins gériatres du Québec
Tél. : (514) 350-5145 • www.fmsq.org/amgq

Association des médecins hématologues et oncologues du Québec
Tél. : (514) 350-5121 • www.geoq.com

Association des médecins microbiologistes infectiologues du Québec
Tél. : (514) 350-5104

Association des médecins ophtalmologistes du Québec
Tél. : (514) 350-5124 • www.amoq.org

Association des médecins psychiatres du Québec
Tél. : (514) 350-5128 • www.ampq.org

Association des médecins rhumatologues du Québec • Tél. : (514) 350-5136
www.cra-scr.ca

Association des médecins spécialistes en médecine nucléaire du Québec
Tél. : (514) 350-5133
www.medecinenucleaire.com

Association des médecins spécialistes en santé communautaire du Québec
Tél. : (514) 350-5138 • www.amsscq.org

Association des néphrologues du Québec
Tél. : (514) 350-5134 • www.sqn.qc.ca

Association des neurochirurgiens du Québec • Tél. : (514) 350-5120
www.fmsq.org/neurochirurgie

Association des neurologues du Québec
Tél. : (514) 350-5122 • www.anq.qc.ca

Association des obstétriciens et gynéco-logues du Québec • Tél. : (514) 849-4969
www.gynecoquebec.com

Association des pathologistes du Québec
Tél. : (514) 350-5102 • www.apq.qc.ca

Association des pédiatres du Québec
Tél. : (514) 350-5127 • www.pediatres.ca

Association des pneumologues de la province de Québec • Tél. : (514) 350-5117
www.pneumologue.ca

Association des physiatres du Québec
Tél. : (514) 350-5119

Association des radiologistes du Québec
Tél. : (514) 350-5129 • www.arq.qc.ca

Association des radio-oncologues du Québec
Tél. : (514) 350-5130

Association des spécialistes en chirurgie plastique et esthétique du Québec
Tél. : (514) 350-5109 • www.ascpeq.org

Répertoire des principales associations et des ordres professionnels (suite)

Association des spécialistes en médecine d'urgence du Québec • Tél. : (514) 350-5115

Association des spécialistes en médecine interne du Québec • Tél. : (514) 350-5118
www.asmiq.qc.ca

Association des urologues du Québec
Tél. : (514) 350-5131 • www.auq.org

Association d'orthopédie du Québec
Tél. : (514) 844-0803 • www.orthoquebec.ca

Association d'oto-rhino-laryngologie et de chirurgie cervico-faciale du Québec
Tél. : (514) 350-5125 • www.fmsq.org/orl

Collège des médecins du Québec
Tél. : (514) 933-4441 ou 1 888 MÉDECIN
www.cmq.org

Fédération des médecins omnipraticiens du Québec
Tél. : (514) 878-1911 ou 1 800 361-8499
www.fmoq.org

Fédération des médecins résidents du Québec
Tél. : (514) 282-0256 • www.fmrq.qc.ca

Fédération des médecins spécialistes du Québec
Tél. : (514) 350-5000 ou 1 800 561-0703
www.fmsq.org

Médecine dentaire
Association des chirurgiens dentistes du Québec
Tél. : (514) 282-1425 ou 1 800 361-3794

Association des conseils des médecins, dentistes et pharmaciens du Québec
Tél. : (514) 858-5885 • www.acmdp.qc.ca

Association des spécialistes en chirurgie buccale et maxillo-faciale du Québec
Tél. : (514) 389-3890

Ordre des dentistes du Québec
Tél. : (514) 875-8511 ou 1 800 361-4887
www.odq.qc.ca

Médecine vétérinaire
Ordre des médecins vétérinaires du Québec
Tél. : (450) 774-1427 ou 1 800 267-1427
www.omvq.qc.ca

Microbiologie
Association des microbiologistes du Québec
Tél. : (514) 987-3643 • www.cam.org/~amq/

Optique
Ordre des opticiens d'ordonnance du Québec
Tél. : (514) 288-7542 ou 1 800 563-6345

Optométrie
Association des optométristes du Québec
Tél. : (514) 288-6272 • www.aoqnet.qc.ca

Ordre des optométristes du Québec
Tél. : (514) 499-0524 • www.ooq.org

Organisation communautaire
Regroupement québécois des intervenants intervenantes en action communautaire
www.rqiiac.qc.ca

Orthophonie
Association canadienne des orthophonistes et des audiologistes
Tél. : (613) 567-9968
www.caslpa.ca

Ordre des orthophonistes et audiologistes du Québec
Tél. : (514) 282-9123
www.ooaq.qc.ca

Perfusion
Association des perfusionnistes du Québec
www.cscp.ca/apqi.html

Société canadienne de perfusion clinique
Tél. : 1 888 496-2727
www.cscp.ca/french/home.html

Pharmacie
Association des conseils des médecins, dentistes et pharmaciens du Québec
Tél. : (514) 858-5885
www.acmdp.qc.ca

Association des pharmaciens des établissements de santé du Québec
Tél. : (514) 286-0776
www.apesquebec.org/index.asp

Association québécoise des pharmaciens propriétaires
Tél. : (514) 254-0676 ou 1 800 361-7765
www.aqpp.qc.ca/site/index.php

Ordre des pharmaciens du Québec
Tél. : (514) 284-9588 ou 1 800 363-0324
www.opq.org

Physicien médical
Association des physiciens et ingénieurs biomédicaux du Québec
Tél. : (514) 952-0184
www.apibq.org/index.php3

Physiothérapie
Ordre professionnel de la physiothérapie du Québec
Tél. : (514) 351-2770 ou 1 800 361-2001
www.oppq.qc.ca

Fédération des physiothérapeutes du Québec
Tél. : (514) 287-1011 ou 1 877 666-1011

Podiatrie
Ordre des podiatres du Québec
Tél. : (514) 288-0019
www.ordredespodiatres.qc.ca

Répertoire des principales associations et des ordres professionnels (suite)

Pratique sage-femme
Ordre professionnel des sages-femmes
du Québec • Tél. : (514) 286-1313
www.osfq.org

Psychoéducation
Ordre des conseillers et conseillères
d'orientation et des psychoéducateurs et
psychoéducatices du Québec
Tél. : (514) 737-4717 ou 1 800 363-2643
www.occoppq.qc.ca

Psychologie
Ordre des psychologues du Québec
Tél. : (514) 738-1881 ou 1 800 363-2644
www.ordrepsy.qc.ca

S Soins infirmiers
Fédération des infirmières et
des infirmiers du Québec
Tél. : (514) 987-1141 ou 1 800 363-6541
www.fiiq.qc.ca

Ordre des infirmières et infirmiers
auxiliaires du Québec
Tél. : (514) 282-9511 ou 1 800 283-9511
www.oiiaq.org

Ordre des infirmières et infirmiers
du Québec
Tél. : (514) 935-2501 ou 1 800 363-6048
www.oiiq.org

T Techniques ambulancières
Rassemblement des employés techniciens
ambulanciers du Québec
Tél. : (514) 728-6565 • www.retaq.org

Techniques de laboratoire médical
Association professionnelle des
technologistes médicaux du Québec
Tél. : (514) 524-3734 ou 1 800 361-4300
www.aptmq.qc.ca

Ordre professionnel des technologistes
médicaux du Québec
Tél. : (514) 527-9811
www.optmq.org

Techniques dentaires
Ordre des techniciennes et
des techniciens dentaires du Québec
Tél. : (514) 282-3837
www.ottdq.com

Technologie de médecine nucléaire/radiodiagnostic/radio-oncologie
Ordre des technologues en radiologie
du Québec
Tél. : (514) 351-0052 ou 1 800 361-8759
www.otrq.qc.ca

Thanatologie
Corporation des thanatologues
du Québec
Tél. : (450) 826-3838

Travail social
Ordre professionnel des travailleurs
sociaux du Québec
Tél. : (514) 731-3925 ou 1 888 731-9420
www.optsq.org

❯ Quelques organismes clés accessibles dans Internet

Association des centres jeunesse du Québec • www.acjq.qc.ca

Association des CLSC et des CHSLD du Québec • www.clsc-chsld.qc.ca/default.htm

Association des établissements de réadaptation en déficience physique du Québec • www.aerdpq.org

Association des hôpitaux du Québec
www.ahq.org/accueil/accueil.asp

Association des résidences et CHSLD privés du Québec
www.arcpq.org/index.htm

Association pour la santé publique du Québec • www.aspq.org

Croix-Rouge (divison Québec)
www.ifrance.com/croixrougequebec/

Fédération de la santé et des services sociaux • www.pqm.net/fsss/accueil.html

Héma-Québec • www.hema-quebec.qc.ca

Institut national de santé publique
www.inspq.qc.ca

Laboratoire de santé publique du Québec
www.inspq.qc.ca/lspq/default.asp?A=1

Ministère de la Santé et Services sociaux du Québec • www.msss.gouv.qc.ca

Organisation mondiale de la santé
www.who.int/fr

Portail du Gouvernement du Québec – La santé
www.gouv.qc.ca/Vision/Sante/Sante_fr.html

Régie de l'assurance maladie du Québec • www.ramq.gouv.qc.ca/crc

Regroupement des CHSLD de la région de Montréal • www.rchsldm.qc.ca

Réseau des soins palliatifs du Québec
www.aqsp.org

Santé Canada • www.hc-sc.gc.ca/francais/index.html

Urgences-santé • www.urgences-sante.qc.ca

Index

Des professions et des témoignages
> Par ordre alphabétique

Voici la liste par ordre alphabétique des professions traitées sous forme de témoignages et figurant de la page 42 à la page 152.

Index

Des professions et des témoignages (suite)
> ❯ Par ordre alphabétique

Index

Des professions et des témoignages (suite)
❯ Par ordre alphabétique

Remerciements à nos annonceurs

Éducation
Québec

100 carrières de la santé et des services sociaux

Rédaction

Directrice de la publication
Annick Poitras

Rédactrices en chef
Emmanuelle Gril, Christine Lanthier

Collaborateurs
Hélène Belzile • Guylaine Boucher •
Suzanne Bouilly • Brigit-Alexandre Bussières •
Louise Casavant • Séverine Galus •
Claudia Larochelle • Jean-Sébastien Marsan •
Kareen Quesada • Sylvie L. Rivard • Martine
Roux • Anne-Marie Trudel • Valérie Vézina

Recherchiste
Mariève Desjardins

Secrétaire à la rédaction
Stéphane Plante

Réviseures
Christine Dumazet • Johanne Girard •
Sylviane Hesry

Production

Coordonnatrice de la production
Nathalie Renauld

Conception de la grille graphique
Amélie Beaulieu

Illustration de la couverture
Katy Lemay

Infographie
Gestion d'impression Gagné inc.

Distribution
Mélanie Larivée

Ventes publicitaires

Représentants
Jean-Philippe Doucet • Christophe Verhelst

Date de publication
Novembre 2003

Dépôt légal
Bibliothèque nationale du Québec
ISBN : 2-89582-046-5
Bibliothèque nationale du Canada
ISSN : 1708-5705

100 carrières de la santé et des services sociaux
est publié par les Éditions Jobboom, une division
de Jobboom, membre du groupe Netgraphe inc.

Jobboom

Président
Bruno Leclaire

Vice-président Éditeur
François Cartier

Vice-président Production & Diffusion
Marcel Sanscartier

Vice-présidente Produits Web
Élisabeth Fortin

Vice-présidente Ventes
Julie Phaneuf

**Directrice – Le groupe de recherche
Ma Carrière**
Patricia Richard

300, rue Viger Est, 7ᵉ étage
Montréal (QC) H2X 3W4
Téléphone : (514) 871-0222
Télécopieur : (514) 890-1456
www.jobboom.com

De la même collection
100 carrières de la culture • 100 carrières de l'administration • 500 diplômes express